THE LADY IN BLACK;

OR,

THE WIDOW AND THE WIFE.

A Romance.

BY THE AUTHOR OF "VARNEY THE VAMPYRE," "FAMILY SECRETS," ETC.

What is that dark form, so mark'd with sadness,
Whose measur'd footsteps, slow and painful, sound,
To the gay world, like echoes of tho past?
We'll lift the veil, and see.—*The Tombsearcher.*

LONDON:
PUBLISHED BY E. LLOYD, AT THE OFFICE OF "LLOYD'S WEEKLY NEWSPAPER,'
12, SALISBURY-SQUARE, FLEET-STREET.

THE

LADY IN BLACK.

A Romance.

" Tread gently o'er her hallow'd dust,
She sleeps, and grief is past;
But with the lov'd one, even she
Will happy be at last."

LONDON:

PUBLISHED BY E. LLOYD, AT THE OFFICE OF THE ILLUSTRATED EDITIONS
OF STANDARD WORKS, 12, SALISBURY SQUARE, FLEET STREET.

1847,

THE LADY IN BLACK;

OR,

THE WIDOW AND THE WIFE.

A Romance.

CHAPTER I.

DESCRIBES AND INTRODUCES THE BLACK LADY.

WE need not call upon the oldest of the inhabitants of London to go with us in our recollection of the being whose singular and most eventful story these pages record, because she has been familiar to the eyes of most, even of the young. No one who has formed an item of the individuality in the vast population of this metropolis, can have failed to have noticed the Black Lady.

Young and old knew her well—that is to say, by sight—for she spoke to no one, held communion with no one, but, wrapped in her sombre garb of woe, she glided about among the busiest haunts of man, not like an inhabitant of the earth, although on it.

Her thoughts were far away from the busy, bustling crowd among which she moved, like some automaton that had been made to walk wonderfully well; she traversed the great thoroughfares of the great city; she saw not the churches, the public buildings, the marts of trade and commerce; she heard not the roar and the rattle of the carriages; wrapt up in herself, and the stagnation-like despair of her heart, she moved, spectre-like, among the busy herd, as if to point some startling moral or adorn some wondrous tale.

Clad in sombre vestments from top to toe, all our readers must recognise the portrait that we draw. Her only head-dress was a veil of crape confined singularly in the centre of the forehead by some old-fashioned ornaments of woe, which might have been the rage when George the Third was young. Her cheeks were rouged, alas! not from vanity, but from the custom of her time. Her whole attire was that of the first deep mourning of one who had lost some object so very precious, that no extremity of exterior mourning habiliments could sufficiently bespeak the woe that had taken up its abode in the heart.

Her walk was around the old Royal Exchange, before fire had laid its glories level with the dust, and about the Bank and Cornhill, and Change-alley, and Lombard-street. The inhabitants of all these places knew her well. The children had, from their earliest infancy, learned to look and wonder at the Black Lady.

Many looked upon her with curiosity, some with indifference, and many more with pity. A certain number of nursery-maids and old women elected her into a bugbear for children, and she held a startling position along with Old Bogie, the Old Man, and divers other imaginary personages, who are supposed to come up into any nursery or any number of nurseries, at any required moment that the fastidiousness of Master Tommy or Miss Mary may sanction.

And yet how positively harmless was this poor wandering creature. If she had in her heart deep and agonising affliction, no one knew it—if she mourned, no one heard it—if she shed tears, no one saw them. She asked not the poorest boon one human being can ask of another—human sympathy—but like some isolated being whose heart has been completely stranded upon the rock of affliction, she barely might be said to live, and certainly ought not to have been calculated among the inhabitants of London, so different was she from all others, and so little connected with any by that community of hopes, fears, wishes, and interests that binds society together.

Summer and winter, spring or autumn, all were alike to her ; the season's difference appeared to affect her not. The sun shone without bringing to her gladness ; the sky loured, but it could not deepen the gloom that dwelt eternally within her breast.

In rain, wind, hail, sleet, or snow—in the summer's heat and the winter's cold, she still wandered, like some perturbed spirit, a sad epitome of woe !

        *   *   *   *   *   *

It was late one afternoon in the gloomy month of November, when there had been such an incessant fog in the city that the Lord Mayor's show, which happened on that day, looked like some ghostly train of tottering spectres, and the men in armour were the men in a fog likewise, that Miles Atherton, a wealthy and respectable dealer in pickled pork and real York hams, turned on the gas in his shop window, as he said—

"Well, here's a day to be sure ! a regular Lord Mayor's day of the old school ; here's a fog, such as never was known ; it would take a man with a hatchet nose to get through it."

"Ah, but," said his wife, "what I look at is the dresses, and that love of a stage coach which goes so nice and swiggy swaggy along. I think I see the old gentleman with the fur cap and the state sword a winking and coughing like nothing as never was known with the fog in his mouth."

"Well, it can't be helped," said Miles Atherton, "if they will have Lord Mayor's day in November, of course there must be a fog. It's getting worse every minute, and I really don't see much good in keeping the shop open. Ten minutes ago I could just see old Crumble the tallow chandler's bald head opposite, and now I can't see nothing at all."

"Perhaps he's took it in," said Mrs. Atherton.

"No, he hasn't. Don't tell me he has took it in ; I know better. I mean to say it's no use keeping the shop open, that's my opinion."

"And my opinion," said Mrs. Miles Atherton, in a shrill voice, "is that you want to go to the Bull and Perriwinkle round the corner, to meet some of your drunken, low, swilling, and guzzling set, when you have got a lawful wife at home, and a fire-side wasting away."

Mr. Atherton cast a glance at the rotund figure of his decidedly better half, but discretion was the better part of valour, and so he made no reply, but, setting his back against the counter, he tried to look at the fog as if it would become any clearer by his so doing, or as if one glance at such an atmosphere of yellow-looking mist was not more than sufficient to give any one as great an insight into it as it was possible to have. And, in truth, that fog was a desperate one,—quite a pattern of a London fog was it, as thick and yellow as possible. There was none of the moving, swimming about appearance that ordinary fogs present ; on the contrary, it looked like an immense mass of batter pudding wedged around every object.

"Nobody can see nothing," was the remark of the errand-boy, who was in the service of Mr. Atherton, and wonderfully expressive did those words sound, putting out of the question all ideas of grammar.

"Well, well," said Atherton, after a long pause, so long indeed as to preclude the possibility of his wife supposing that what he was about to say was in any way intended as a reply to her last observation respecting the Bull and Perriwinkle— "Well, this is a fog ! I've seen a goodish many Lord Mayors' days, and consequently I've seen a goodish many fogs, but this one I think beats 'em all.—Jem ?"

"Yes, sir," said the before-mentioned errand-boy.

"Don't you think you could cut it with a knife ?"

"Sure I could, sir. Wouldn't it be a good joke, sir, to get a bottle or two full of it, and serve it to the people in the middle of summer ?"

"So it would. You are a genius Jem   Mr. Miller says you are a genius."

"Oh, I seed Mr. Miller, sir, pass the door a little while ago—leastways, I knew it was him, though I couldn't see him; for he says, says he, 'hilloa,' says he, 'I'm a going,' says he, 'to the Bull and Perriwinkle,' and then on he goes."

"Oh," said Miles Atherton, with a deep sigh, and he took a sidelong glance at his wife, to see how she took this allusion to the public-house round the corner, which she had so recently denounced.

All was stern virtue on the part of the lady; she had not the least relenting look in the world; at least, so far as he could see by the aid of the gas-light, which struggled wonderfully well, considering all things, with the fog.

"And so, Jem," added Mr. Atherton, "he was going round the counter was he?"

"Yes, sir; he was. I heard him a going. A nice man, sir, Mr. Miller is. I dare say, sir, he's shut up his shop, and gived everybody a holiday."

"Do you dare say he has, you idle, good-for-nothing scamp," said Mrs. Atherton. "How dare you say anything of the sort, I should like to know, you parish-brought-up, poor-law looking scrub."

Mr. Atherton whistled, but said nothing, and the errand-boy was equally prudent, for well he knew that a wordy warfare with his mistress was likely to be a very protracted conflict indeed; besides, one in which he or any one else was tolerably sure to get the worst.

"A holiday, indeed!" added Mrs. Atherton, with sundry interjectional sounds, strongly resembling the dying agonies of some great fish. "A holiday, indeed! what next, I wonder; I supposes you is what they call one of the rising generation."

"If you please, ma'am," Jim now ventured to say, in a very submissive tone.

But the lady had no scruple of thumping anybody well who was down, and so, although morally and metaphorically speaking, Jim had not a leg to stand on, she continued abusing in good set terms.

"You'd like the shop shut up, and so would your master. Every idle, discontented fellow does like a shop shut up; indeed you would never like it to open. Perhaps you would like to lodge at the Bull and Perriwinkle, and then you could both of you—for it's like master like man—go on sotting from morning till night. It's all very well, but I won't have the shop shut up, and so I tell you; I won't have anything of the sort done, and so there's an end of that. Oh, don't tell me that nobody will come; don't tell me that it's of no use flaring away the gas for nothing; don't tell me that it's a lost day. Don't ——"

"My dear," said Miles Atherton, striving to make some reply, "I never told you, or dreamt of telling you anything of the sort."

"Perhaps, Mr. Atherton, after that you had better call your lawful wife, who has kept house and home over your head for the last fifteen years, when otherwise you would have been in the workhouse, a liar."

"No, my dear, I only ——"

"Oh, dear, yes, you only. That's the only excuse. You men fancy you can play as long as you like with a woman's feelings, and when you find that you have cut her to the bone, and she has worked night and day for you, and expects some gratitude, you only—that's it—oh, you only. You are a vile, insignificant man, Mr. Atherton."

"My dear."

"Indeed you are no man, or else you would have got me a ticket for the ball at Guildhall to-night."

"Well, but you know I did ask the alderman of the ward, and he said he was so tormented that he would quite as soon be transported as go through so much persecution for tickets to the dinner and ball again."

"Mr. Atherton," screamed Mrs. Atherton, "don't tell me. Mrs. Prentwheezle is going. Think of that. Oh, I would cut my throat if I was you."

"Thank you, my dear, I'd rather not. It isn't every man who has such a fine woman for a wife."

"I saw you, sir."

"Saw me!"

"Yes, I saw you wink at Jem, as much as to say, 'What a joke.' I saw you, sir, holding me out to ridicule. Oh, it's well worthy of you. But what could I expect—what could I expect, eh—ch?"

To whom this question was addressed appeared to be a profound mystery. To all appearance it seemed directed at some sides of bacon that were packed on a high shelf with some straw between them. At all events, Mr. Miles Atherton did not feel himself compelled to answer the interrogatory, but after some few minutes he said, with an extraordinary degree of courage for him,—

"It's all nonsense keeping open on such a day as this. Not a soul will come out to buy anything. Jem, get out the shutters."

"Yes, sir."

Jem had scarcely moved one step to carry into effect this daring act of rebellion on the part of Mr. Atherton, when, as if fate would have it that Mrs. Atherton should be in the right, a man made his appearance at the shop-door, which was flanked by several huge York hams hanging on hooks.

A look of triumph sat upon Mrs. Atherton's countenance, but she forbore to say anything until the stranger should have made some purchase, which would have given her a most decided advantage over her husband.

The fog was so dense that it was quite impossible to see what sort of person the stranger was, as he came no nearer than the threshold of the door; he looked like some yellow old musty apparition.

His voice was loud and jolly as he took down one of the large hams and said,

"Hilloa, Mr. What's-your-name, you see this ham?"

"Yes, yes," said Atherton, coming round the counter.

"Very good," said the customer. "Then you will never see it again;" and away he darted into the fog, and was out of sight in a moment.

The idea of running after anybody in such a state of the atmosphere, when it was impossible to say whether the delinquent had gone to the right or to the left, was ridiculous indeed. The daring manner in which the robbery had been committed, sufficiently proclaimed the knowledge, on the part of the thief, of his perfect immunity from any consequences; and so the ham vanished, and the first piece of business that had been done that day in Miles Atherton's shop was consummated.

Here was a dreadful defeat to the lady. But when Atherton turned and said,

"There, you see, we are doing a wonderful trade in the fog," he found that his better half had retired to the back parlour, thus virtually leaving him master of the field.

"Jem," he said,

"Ye—ye—yes," gasped Jem, who had opened his eyes and mouth so wide at the cool way in which the ham had been abstracted, that it seemed doubtful if he could ever shut them again.

"Put up the shutters, Jem."

"Yes, I should think so; it's time now, master. Did you ever see a robbery ekal, sir, to that in all your life?"

"It was just what I might expect. Up with the shutters, Jem."

The boy was no less anxious than his master to take advantage of the state of the weather to have a holiday, and he obeyed with alacrity the order to close the shop, humming as he went,

> "Of all the gals as is so sweet, there's none like pretty Sally,
> She is the darling of this heart, and she resides in our alley."

The last shutter but one was put up when a rapid sound of carriage wheels, as if some vehicle had just turned round the corner from the direction of the Bull and Perriwinkle, came upon their ears simultaneously; then arose a loud and piercing shriek, so terrific and sudden, that Jem let fall the last shutter with such a smash upon the pavement, that it sounded as if the house had fallen, or some great piece of ordnance had gone off.

"God bless me!" cried Atherton, coming out into the street and falling over the shutter. "What's that? what's that?"

"Help! help! help!" cried a voice, in tones of agony. "Help! help! oh, God! to die at last such a death as this!"

The noise of the wheels of the vehicle, whatever it was ceased, and several voices began muttering sundry exclamations.

"It's--it's somebody run over in the fog, sir," said Jem.

"D—n you! what made you lay down one of the shutters here?" said Atherton, as he managed to scramble to his feet.

"It laid down of itself, sir."

"Hilloa," said a voice. "Help here! help! There's a woman been run over. Is anybody near? Help, help!"

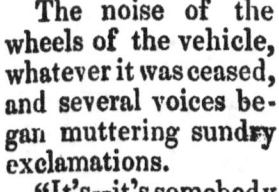

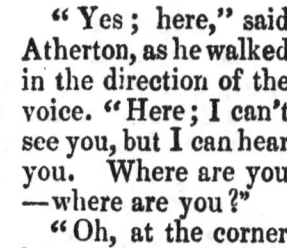

"Yes; here," said Atherton, as he walked in the direction of the voice. "Here; I can't see you, but I can hear you. Where are you—where are you?"

"Oh, at the corner here. It's a woman. I don't know, but I rather fancy that she must be killed. However, it was no fault of anybody, the fog is so thick you can hardly see a yard before you."

Miles Atherton was guided by the voice, and he made his way by feeling the houses as he went to the corner of the street wher-

the catastrophe had occurred, and where, when he fairly reached it, he could see some dim, dusky-looking figures moving about in the dense vapour.

"What is it?" he said. "Where is she?"

"On this step," said one.

"It ain't a step," cried another; "we are close to the curb; and, i anything comes by, she will be run over again."

"Well, I'll be hanged if I know where I am," said the first speaker.

"I don't hear the woman," said Atherton. "Is she killed, poor thing?"

"God knows—she lies here, all of a lump. She was crossing, it seemed, and, as the coachman could not even see his own horses' heads, it was not very likely he could see her."

"That's about it," said a gruff voice. "I was taking the cattle to the stable ; for, as for driving in such a fog as this, it's quite out of the question. You'll easily find me if I'm wanted ; I'm Sir Shovel Broomwig's coachman."

"Lift the poor creature up," said Miles Atherton, "and follow me. I'll guide you to my house with her. It's just there where you see the stream of gas light."

This proposition was at once acceded to, and the female was raised from the pavement, and carried by two men to the cheesemonger's house, preceded by himself, as he kept on saying,—

"Straight on, straight on—keep close to the houses, or you will be sure to stray into the roadway. Look at the light and you will be all right. This way, this way. Was there ever such a fog as this ? I'll be hanged if it don't seem to me to be getting worse every minute—I never did in all my life see its equal."

CHAPTER II.

THE LADY IN BLACK.—THE RECOVERY AND THE GRATITUDE OF THE STRANGE BEING.

THE men walked with extreme deliberation, and being guided as well by the flare of light from the unextinguished gas from the shop which made a difference in the colour of the fog, as well as by the voice of Atherton, they managed to get on very well, and, without any accident, they reached the door.

"Bring her in—bring her in," said Atherton. "Poor creature, I hope she ain't killed. This is a bad evening for any man to be out, and women should certainly keep at home. This way. Ah, that will do—that will do."

The female was perfectly insensible ; and, whether she was dead or alive, they had no means of immediately knowing ; but when she was brought fairly into the shop where the gas lights overpowered the fog in a great measure, and seemed to consume it, every one started in surprise, and Atherton exclaimed,—

"Why, it's the Black Lady."

"It's the Black Lady," said every one, and Jem added,—

"So it is, sure enough. It's she as walks round the Bank, and there's her black veil, and her odd-looking head dress. Well, here's a go. The idea of the Black Lady being killed and brought in here."

"She ain't killed," said Atherton. "I saw her move. Fetch a doctor, one of you."

"And pray," shouted Mrs. Atherton, emerging from the back parlour, "and pray what may be the meaning of all this, I should like to know ?"

"A poor creature has been run over, ma'am."

"Good gracious ! it's the Black Lady."

"You know this person by sight well enough," said Miles Atherton. "Let us be as kind to her as circumstances will permit, wife. Poor thing, I believe she is not right in her senses."

"Oh, she is as mad as a March hare," said one of the men. "I never saw her speak to anybody but once in all my life, and that was once in Cheapside. There was a man coming along, dressed like a sailor—a better sort of sailor, he seemed— perhaps, captain of some trading vessel, and, the moment she saw him, she clung to him, and shouted, 'Vengeance ! vengeance !' and would not be shaken off by him."

"What did he do ?"

"Oh, he turned as pale as death, and shook like a leaf. It took two men to make her undo her hold of him ; and then she was held while he made off, and all the time she kept screaming, 'Vengeance on Neville !—vengeance on Neville !'"

The moment this name, Neville, was pronounced, the apparently insensible woman, as if there had been some potent spell in it, sufficient to call her again to existence, sprang to her feet, shouting,—

"Who named him ?—who named him ? Is he here ? Neville ! Neville ! Vengeance ! the vengeance of God upon Neville !"

She looked so wild and frantic, that no wonder Miles Atherton ran round his counter, and the men who had carried her to the shop made towards the door.

But they need not to have alarmed themselves, for the poor creature's strength was gone again on the instant, and she sank, with a deep groan, into the chair where she had been first placed.

" I don't think," said one " as any bones is broke."

" I should think not," remarked the other. " She couldn't have stood up in that sort of way, if there had been much the matter, you may depend."

" Give—give me a draught of water," she gasped, " and then I will go. I shall some day meet with him again. I cannot die till I meet with him again."

" Who do you mean?" said Atherton.

" The villain Neville—Neville, the murderer! the man of blood!"

" You had better rest for some hours where you are," remarked Atherton. " The fog is as thick as ever, and you will never be able to make your way through it."

" I suppose," she said, " I am in some hospital?"

" No, you are in my shop. Come into the back-room; there is a fire there, and you will be more comfortable. A glass of my wife's home-made wine won't do you any harm. I've sent my boy for a doctor."

" And you won't see him back again till the fog's over," said one of the men. " If he can find his way to a doctor, no doctor will ever think of finding his way here."

" I want no medical aid," said the Black Lady; " I am not much hurt. I am bruised a little by the horses' feet, and I am terrified."

" Then you shall accept of my offer," added Atherton, " and stay here some time till the fog clears. Wife, can you find a glass of your ginger cordial?"

Now Mrs. Atherton was rather a tartar, but she was not a bad sort of woman, take her for all in all. Moreover, she had that very rare feeling among the ladies, of curiosity, so she readily assented to the invitation which was given to the Black Lady to walk in, or be assisted into the parlour; " for who knows," thought Mrs. Atherton, " but she may tell us something about herself, and how she came to go about in the odd way she does."

Mrs. Atherton, therefore, expressed her willingness to find the ginger cordial, and to assist the mysterious Black Lady into the parlour, and a very few moments more saw her seated there.

Miles Atherton then went out, and after again tumbling over the shutter which Jem had let fall in his fright, and duly consigning Jem to a very warm place for so doing, he picked it up and completed the shutting up of his shop.

Then he made his way into the parlour again, where he found the mysterious female had been supplied with the ginger cordial, and had placed her black veil a little on one side, so that her countenance, which still bore the impress of much early beauty, was visible.

There was a strange, wild, searching look about the eyes, which sufficiently proclaimed that the poor creature's wits were tangled, and along with that there was an expression of deep suffering upon her countenance.

Perhaps it was merciful of Heaven to disturb the reason of that poor creature, in order to soften the pangs of memory; for certainly no one could look for many moments upon that face without feeling certain that grief of no ordinary character had made her what she was.

Miles Atherton and his wife did not very well know what to say to her, and they looked at each other rather puzzled to know what style of conversation would suit her best.

Suddenly she herself broke the awkward silence by saying,—

" Who mentioned Neville?"

" Oh, it was one of the men who picked you up when you were run over," said Atherton. " He said that he saw you once speak to a man whom you called Neville."

" He is right. Twice in twenty-eight years only have I encountered that man. That dreadful ——"

" Twice?"

" Yes; once as that kind stranger who assisted to bring me here has related to you, and once to-night."

"To-night? What—in the fog do you mean?"

"I do. 'Twas he who coward-like struck me down, and tried to kill me. Yes, 'twas he—Neville—the fiend Neville. When we meet again it will be fatal to one or to both of us."

"Did he strike you?"

"He wanted to take my life. It was only the sudden coming up of the coach that saved me from him."

"Indeed! well, that is singular," said Mrs. Atherton; "and pray who is Neville, and what does he want to do you any harm for?"

The Black Lady appeared so little to expect being questioned concerning her eventful history, that she remained for some moments looking at Mrs. Atherton in silent amazement; then she rose, and drawing her veil over her face, she said,—

"Farewell, farewell! I might have expected this. It was because I dreaded this that I would fain have gone at once. God of Heaven! why should I be asked now to tell the tale of horror—the tale which has shrivelled up my own heart till it has scarce a human feeling left—those horrible particulars that have settled in my brain in such frightful companionship as to drive from it all pleasanter earlier reminiscences. Oh, no—no—no."

She wanted strength to persevere in her intention of leaving, and she sank back upon the chair again, and for a moment or two seemed as if she would have fainted.

"Never mind," said Atherton, "never mind. If it displeases you, we won't ask you any more. As far as I am concerned now, if I have got any trouble, I like to tell somebody of it, and so make it seem not half so great."

"Had you ever a trouble that seared your very brain?" said the Black Lady, vehemently. "Had you ever a trouble so gigantic that a thousand deaths had been nothing in comparison? Had you ever a trouble that drove you mad?"

"No, no. I——"

"Then do not talk to me of finding any consolation in my affliction by making a confidant of any human being."

"Well, I did not intend to press you; I was only saying what I did myself. You are quite as welcome to all the good we can do you without your telling us your story, as you would be if you were."

"Indeed!"

"I assure you of it, so don't say any more about it."

"Who mentioned Neville?"

"I told you before, don't you recollect? It was one of the men who brought you here."

She pressed her hand upon her brow for a moment, as she said,—

"Oh, yes, yes; I remember now. I am strangely confused to-night, and memory holds not her accustomed place. Yes; yes; I remember now. He mentioned Neville. What month and what date is this?"

"This is the month of November, 1830."

The Black Lady shuddered, and rose from her chair, and as she did so, there came a heavy blow, as if made by a stick, at the shop-door.

She stretched out her arms imploringly, as she said,—

"Oh, save me, save me. Have compassion on me, and save me from that dreadful man of crimes and blood."

"What man?"

"'Tis he, 'tis he; my heart tells it is he. 'Tis Neville."

"Oh, dear, no; I dare say it's Jem come back. Make yourself easy."

Bang came the knock again at the door, and then she trembled excessively, as she clung to Miles Atherton, saying, in a half-choked whisper,—

"Oh, God, save me from him to-night. He seeks my life to-night. It is the anniversary of a dreadful deed, and I have no power to resist him. Save me from the villain Neville, I implore you."

"No harm can come to you here."

Again came the dull heavy knock against the outer door, and the agitation of the

Black Lady became so extreme, that Atherton could not disengage herself from her grasp to go and see who the person was who demanded admission.

"You will protect me," she said. "Oh, have you no place in which to hide me? Save me from him to-night—only for to-night. I am weak and fearful to-night. Save me—save me."

"Let me go to the door," said Atherton; "you may depend no harm will come to you. Sit down and make yourself comfortable. There, whoever it is is getting impatient and knocking louder. Let me go and open the door, or I shall have it knocked in."

"Mercy—mercy! Have some mercy upon me! Oh! do not let him see me! It is my life he wants. He has deprived me of all besides, and now my very existence is to him a horror. Save me from him, or let me die by some other means, not by his hands. It would be too terrible. I plead to you as the only one from whom I have received a word of sympathy, for a longer time than I can tell. You will protect me?"

"Most certainly I will. You need be under no apprehension, be it whom it may. Besides, I tell you, I think it is my boy Jem."

With difficulty Atherton released himself from her grasp, and then he proceeded to the door of his shop, where the knocking now was continuing louder than before. There was an iron bar placed over the door, and this, upon being moved, allowed it to open.

"Who are you?" said Atherton, as he saw a man, enveloped in a very large shaggy-looking great coat, on the threshold.

"There has been a poor woman run over," said the man.

"Well."

"Do you know where she was taken to?"

"What if I do, and what if I don't?"

"Well, that's an odd way of answering a question. But, if you must know all about it, she is my sister, and not being quite right in her mind, I want to take her home."

"Your sister?"

"Yes, to be sure. You seem to doubt it, as if you knew something to the contrary. I am rather inclined to think she's here; indeed, I've been as good as told she is."

"And if she is?"

"Oh! then, I am very much obliged to you for the attention you have shown her, and I will take her home with me at once."

"Now, my friend, if you must know, she is here; but mind me, she don't go hence with you, are anybody else, without her own consent."

"What! the consent of an insane person?"

"Insane or not, I won't have her forced from my house."

"Oh! we shall see that, Mr. Cheesemonger. Get out of my way, will you, or else you shall have some reason to repent it."

"Come, come," said the cheesemonger, in a determined tone—"no nonsense. Do you see this—eh?"

He took up an immense cheese-knife as he spoke, and its large, flat, curved blade certainly had rather a formidable appearance.

"D—n you!" said the man, "do you offer violence?"

"Nay, my friend, it's you who are offering violence. You must recollect that I am in my own house, and have a right to defend it in any way I like against whom I like. There's the law open to you as well as to me, and I've no objection to meet you before the lord mayor to-morrow."

"The lord mayor may hang himself, and you too," said the fellow, as he made a sudden movement to pass Atherton.

He did not succeed, however, but the cheese-knife came so close to him, that, had he not shrunk back again, he might have received a very ugly wound.

In this brief struggle his hat fell off, and it was astonishing then to see how much older a man he looked than he had done when he had it on. He was completely bald, and his overhanging brows and retreating forehead gave his whole face a baboon-like and repulsive appearance.

"Come—come," said Atherton; "now, be off with you; it's of no use your making yourself ridiculous here. I won't have it."

"I will not be debarred from seeing my sister."

"If she is your sister, and is willing to go with you, she may, of course, but not otherwise. I'll ask her. Hilloa! my dear Mrs. Atherton, just ask the Lady in Black to look at this not very civil fellow, and say if she knows anything of him."

The parlour door was flung open, and the Lady in Black appeared in the entrance with her veil drawn over her face, and in all respects as she usually appeared in the public streets.

"There she is—there she is," cried the man. "I knew d——d well she was here. There she is, my mad sister."

"Villain!" said the Black Lady, in a deep sepulchral voice. "Your own heart knows well the lie your lips now utter. Neville—Neville! Murderer—false witness—accuser of innocence—trafficker with the dead—I denounce you."

"Come, come, all that is nonsense," said the man, shifting his eyes about uneasily, as if he dared not look for long upon that form before him in that solemn garb of woe. "Are you coming—that's what I want to know?"

"Sooner to the grave than with you."

"Then I will make you."

A shriek burst from the lips of the Black Lady, and she rushed to the further end of the little parlour, crying,—

"No—no. I will die where I am. He wants to get me out into the fog, and then he would kill me with a certainty of escape. Now look at him well, so that you may at another time be able to recognise, when you see them, the features of as dreadful a villain as ever breathed the breath of life. Look at him well—oh, look at him well."

So close an amount of scrutiny seemed anything but pleasing to the man, for with an imprecation he snatched up his hat and pressed it down far above his brows.

"What infernal madness is all this!" he said. "You know well enough that I am your brother, and that I have a comfortable home for you. Come, now, Mr. Cheesemonger, don't you make family differences worse then they otherwise would be. No nonsense."

"If you don't get out of my shop pretty quick," said Atherton, "you will find that its no nonsense. I am not going to stand here letting my house get full of fog, while you go on making a fool of yourself."

"Do you dare to talk of insolence to me?"

"Oh, don't bluster. An Englishman's house is his castle, and he ought to defend it, and send everybody away from it with his head in his hand who he don't like to have in it. Now just be off with you at once before I make you."

"While you make me? D—n you, it would take half a hundred such as you to make me do anything I didn't choose. Are you going to get out of my way?"

"Not a bit of it."

"Then take the consequences of your own folly."

As the ruffian spoke he drew from his pocket one of those short but tremendously powerful and mischievous weapons called life-protectors, and aimed so heavy a blow at Atherton, that had he not quickly held up the cheese-knife, and so warded it off, it must have felled him to the floor; as it was, the cheese knife was dashed from his hand, and he was defenceless. Without, however, waiting to commit any further assault upon Atherton, Neville rushed past him into the parlour, no doubt intent upon the murder of the Black Lady,—a deed which, if he could have done, he would most likely have escaped the consequences of, on account of the fog favouring his escape. Scarcely, however, had he set foot in the parlour when a most unexpected obstacle presented itself to him. The poker happened, at the time of the affray, to be in the fire, and to be quite of a white heat. At the impulse of the moment, Mrs. Atherton snatched the glowing iron from among the coals, and the first notice Neville had of it was in feeling it laid across his face. The howl of pain he gave was perfectly demoniac, and he recoiled from so fiery a reception with far greater precipitation than he had advanced. Mrs. Atherton, however, was not satisfied with simply repulsing the enemy, but she followed him up, and before he reached the shop door she had singed his back desperately.

Here a new obstacle presented itself, for just as he was about to dash out into the street, Jem, who had been so long gone for a doctor, made his appearance, and seeing, with the ready tact of a shop boy, that he must be run over by the man who was running out of his master's shop in such a hurry, he immediately stooped down and made a back, over which the discomfited ruffian tumbled as readily as if he had quite projected doing so all along, and had well practised the feat.

"There you goes," said Jem; "what is the use o' being in sich a hurry."

Half stunned by the thump with which he came upon the door-step, for he had made a complete summerset over Jem's back, Neville lay for about half a minute without moving. But Mrs. Atherton was at hand with the powerful restorative, and placing the red hot poker against the side of his head, she began sawing away as if she meant to get his head off, while there arose such a smother of smoke from his burning clothes as, combined with the fog, was quite suffocating.

This was a state of things not likely to last, and the fellow sprung to his feet again as if he had been galvanised, and then, with a yell that was heard for some distance, and alarmed a number of people, he darted off and was lost in the fog.

"I think you got it then," said Jem. "Lor, missus! you've gived him a reg'lar singe, and no sort o' mistake. What a go to be sure! I can't find a doctor; I've been, I don't know where, and quite lost myself; I knocked my head agin Aldgate pump at last, and here I is. Missis, what a out and out brilin' you have gived that fellow!"

"Yes," said Mrs. Atherton, flourishing the poker, for that lady was in a warlike mood, "and I'll lay it across you if you don't shut the door this moment."

Jem shut the door with an activity that showed he considered the threat as no idle one, or one to be neglected, for the poker yet retained a dull crimson colour about the end of it.

"Yes, missus," he said; "anything else, missus, as I can do?"

"No. Stay where you are."

"Yes, missus."

"Mr. Atherton, you are a goose, and no man."

"No man, my dear?"

"No; or else you would never have let that fellow pass you. Oh! if I was a man, not twenty fellows should have passed me."

"My dear, you have certainly gained the battle, and gained it unassisted too; I am extremely glad the poker was in the fire; but where's our poor frightened guest? she must be dreadfully alarmed at all that has taken place."

CHAPTER III.

THE PROMISE OF THE BLACK LADY.—THE CURIOUS OATH.—THE PACKET.

WHEN Miles Atherton and his wife went into the parlour, they found the Lady in Black kneeling by a chair on which her head was resting, apparently in prayer. The cheesemonger approached her gently, saying—

"There's no danger now. He's gone; he's gone."

She looked up, and then burst into tears.

"Come—come," said Mrs. Atherton, "there's nothing to cry about now. The wagabone is gone; I soon settled him. I think I see such impudence—he'll do this, and he'll do t'other. Marry come up, I'll soon let him and any such know what I can do."

"My life—my life!" said the Black Lady, "I owe to you my life; I am certain his inclination was to murder me. You have saved a worthless life, but yet it is a life, and one that I would not have had wasted at his hands."

"We have done no more than we ought to do," said Atherton.

"We!" exclaimed his wife. "It's like your confounded assurance, Mr. Atherton, to say we; yu did nothing."

"Well—well, my dear, I——"

"But it is not well, well, sir. For all you helped it, Heaven only knows what might have happened. Don't say we again if you please while I'm here; among your low set at the 'Bull and Perriwinkle,' I have no doubt you will go and make a fine boast—Mr. Atherton, but it won't do here, sir, I can tell you that it won't do here."

"Well, don't be angry."

"Angry! goodness gracious! I would appeal to a stick, or a stone, or a lump of coal, that has no feeling, whether it is not enough to make a perfect saint angry to be incessantly aggravated by such a man as you are, Mr. Atherton."

"Ah!" said Atherton, "ah!" and down he sat; for well he knew that his wife had got now upon a vein of oratory which she was not likely very soon to abandon, and that, by answering, he should only be adding fuel to the flame of her indignation.

"Oh, let not me, I pray you," said the Black Lady,—"let not me be any ground of contention. I will leave at once if I am to involve those to whom I owe so much in quarrels."

"Oh, you needn't go," said Mr. Atherton. "It makes no difference, I assure you. Use is a second nature; so never mind, never mind."

"Now, Mr. Atherton, for another half pin," exclaimed the lady, "I would have a separate maintenance to-morrow, and then I should like to know what would become of you, sir?'

"My dear, I could not do without you."

"That's no news, I know that well enough. You'd go to the dogs."

"Yes, and the cats too, I have no doubt."

"Now, don't be laughing, Mr. Atherton. I insist upon your saying no more. You know I have saved all our lives to-night, and you don't like to admit it; so say no more upon that subject—I know what I have done."

Mr. Atherton nodded.

"Oh," said the Black Lady, "if now you could point out to me any way by which I could show to you that I have a grateful feeling for the kindness that has been exercised towards me this evening, how gladly I would do it."

Mrs Atherton smiled, and figeted about a little before she replied,—

"Why, why, I must confess ——"

"Is there anything I can do?"

"There certainly is, but I am certainly afraid I should offend you by asking."

"Nay, do not think so. I cannot take offence at you. It would be as ungenerous as it would be ungrateful."

"Well, then, I must confess that, if you wouldn't mind ——"

"Mind what?"

"Just telling us how you come to go about as you do all in black, with a veil, and speak to nobody, and why it is that you are so much afraid of Neville, and call him a murderer, and how it is he wants to take your life, and why you don't mind him on any other day than the ninth of November, and what you mean to do, and all that you have done, and all about it, and who you are, and anything else about yourself, or about any one else."

The Black Lady clasped her hands and sighed deeply.

"If so be," added Mrs. Atherton, "you wouldn't mind all that, you know, I must confess I should very much like to hear something about it."

She was silent for some moments, and then, in a voice of much emotion, she said,—

"You have touched upon the chords in my heart which vibrate painfully, but yet I know not how to refuse the request you made to me."

"That's a good soul."

"You shall hear from me to-morrow; but will you consent to one condition?"

"What is it?"

"It is that for some time you will keep what I shall communicate to you a profound secret. It is that you will swear to me that until fifteen years are past you will allow no one to share with you in your knowledge of my painful and most eventful history."

"Fifteen years! bless us."

See page 21.

"Fifteen years!" said Mr. Atherton; "why that will not be, then, till the year 1845."

"Not till then," said the black lady, "not till then, let me implore you, not till then, to allow the world to know of those circumstances which I shall communicate to you. Under no other circumstances can I tamper with the vow I had made to tell my dreadful story to no one,—to allow no one to know it until I and some others are in the grave. The period of time I mention will accomplish that, for certain I have not long to live."

"Well," said Mrs. Atherton, with a half groan, "I should certainly have liked to tell Mrs. Pyne, the grocer's wife; but if I must not, why I must not, so that is settled."

"If," continued the Black Lady, "you will both swear to me in the name of Heaven, that you will keep my secret till the time I mention, you shall know all."

"Oh, I don't want to tell anybody," said Atherton.

"Nor I," said his wife, "I won't even mention it to Mrs. Pyne, you may depend."

"The fog's all gone," said Jem, popping his head into the parlour. "There's such a change. It's a mizzling with rain, and the fog's all used up, somehow."

"Be off, you rascal."

"Well, I only ——"

"Will you go?"

Jem pulled his head out of the parlour, thinking himself very scurvily treated, considering that he had brought such gratifying intelligence as he had concerning the dispersion of the fog, which had enveloped everything in such uncomfortable and alarming obscurity.

The Black Lady, however, seemed pleased with the announcement, and she at once rose, saying,—

"I need trespass now upon you no longer. When you think of me, do not think of me as one mad, but as one who, having suffered much, may, to a certain extent, have quarrelled with the usages of the world, and adopted fashions and styles of my own. I have no interest now in life, and, therefore, I walk about like one rather belonging to the grave. I feel myself like a spectre of the past, and that as I traverse the thoroughfares of this mighty city, I have no business among mankind."

The cheesemonger was not a very sentimental or a very educated man, but he had a fund of good feeling about him, although he did not always give utterance to it in the most elegant manner, or in the best language in the world.

"You should not," he said, "fancy you and the world have done with each other because you have not been happy in it. Time enough yet, you know, for a good deal of comfort."

"No, no, no! A sad delusion—too manifest a delusion for me to cherish."

"It's a long lane, you know, that hasn't a turning," said Mrs. Atherton.

"Ah," said Atherton, "better luck another time, is always my motto, and it generally comes; so keep up a good heart."

"I have striven—Heaven knows how I have striven. But will you swear?"

"Swear!"

"Yes—not to reveal my history till 1845?"

"Oh, yes, to be sure; but we don't know it yet," said Mrs. Atherton. "You have not told us one word of it yet, you know."

"To-morrow you will receive from me a packet, which will contain all that you wish to know. Retain it in your possession until the period I have named, and then you have my full and free permission to do with it what you please. I shall have gone to my last home as others have gone,—even he, Neville, who would, I feel assured, have taken my life to-night, will not by then be among the living. Swear to me now, and then I will depart from your roof in peace."

"I can't say as I like taking oaths," said Mrs. Atherton; "but if so be as we must, why, then, in that case, I ——"

"There is no occasion whatever," said the Lady in Black. "If you can, now that you know the only condition under which you can be gratified, forego knowing who and what I am, let me implore you to do so, and then you will escape the necessity of taking any oath upon the subject."

"No, I should like to hear it."

"Then swear."

"I swear, then, by Heaven, that no one shall know what you confide to us until the year 1845."

"And I, too," said Atherton, "I swear to the same; so now you can have no scruples, I suppose?"

"I have none—I have none; you shall know all. That the melancholy story of my sufferings will make you any the happier is not to be supposed; you will, however, be wiser and sadder."

"But you do not mean to venture out alone?"

"Yes. The mist has dispersed, and I am now safe. Neville is a coward—it is because he is a coward that he would fain take my life; but even that he dared not attempt with light sufficient for me to see who was my assailant, unless he succeeded in waylaying me in some retired spot where I could get no help."

" But I will accompany you to your home, and see you safe," said the cheese-monger. "After doing as much as we have already managed to do to save you from the evil consequences of Neville's attack, it would be hard to subject you to a renewal of it."

" No, no, no," she said, " I am safe."

" You cannot tell that."

" You would shrink from walking the streets with me now. Your good nature prompts you to make me the offer, but you would not like to be pointed at as the companion of the Lady in Black. Nay, make no remonstrances ; the feeling is a natural one, and I can as easily forgive it as I can comprehend it, so say nothing of it, I beg of you. I can go alone."

She walked through the shop, and before the half bewildered cheesemonger and his wife could recover from the state of surprise her appearance and all the odd circumstances connected with the night's adventure had produced, she was far away from the shop.

" She's off," said Jem. " Well, who would a thought of the Black Lady ever coming here ? Wonders won't never cease, that's quite clear."

" Jem," said Atherton.

" Yes, master."

" Which way did she go ?"

" Down the street. What's her name, master ?"

" I don't know, Jem."

" And if your master did know, you scrub," exclaimed Mrs. Atherton, who, like a well up bottle of ginger-beer, was always ready to go off at a moment's notice, " what is that to you ?"

" Nothing, missus. I only thought that—that ——"

" That what ?" said Atherton.

" She might tell fortunes, and then I should perhaps find out from her whether I should ever be made into one with the divinity of infections."

" And how dare you talk to me, or before me, in such language ?" added Mrs. Atherton. " You are an ungrateful wretch. I now know well how it was you were not killed when you fell into the streets when you were cleaning the windows."

" Do you, missus ?"

" Yes. You were born to be hanged, and so couldn't get your neck broke any other way, so now go about your business, and if you dare to make a remark about anything in my absence, you shall repent it the longest day you have to live !"

" I suppose," said Jem, " that would be the 24th of June." But he took care to make that facetious remark in an under tone, so that Mrs. Atherton, although she heard that he had growled out something, could not very well make out what it was.

" Be off with you down stairs, Jem," said the cheesemonger. " My dear, I don't think I shall go out to-night, so let us have something nice and tasty for supper."

" Ah !" said Jem, " that will be the dodge. Suppose we has three penny faggots. How prime and fat they is round the corner, along the alley, and down the court. Lor, when I think of 'em my mouth goes all *slickery slockery*."

" All what ?"

" Oh, it's a way I have of describing anythink as ——"

" Take that," said Mrs. Atherton, as she threw the hearth broom at Jem, and as that was indeed commencing hostilities in earnest, he looked upon it as a very good signal to be off, and was off accordingly, singing as he went—

" And when my seven long *ears* is done,
    Oh, then I'll marry Sally ;
    For she's a rum-un, and no mistake,
    And lives in our alley."

"Oh, that boy," ejaculated Mrs. Atherton, "you must get rid of him, Miles; he will be the death of me."

"My dear, he is honest."

"But so dreadfully vulgar."

"My dear, he is honest."

"Yes; but, Mr. Atherton, you know I had a genteel *edication* myself, and that anything in the shape of vulgarity sticks right in my throat."

"I can't discharge him. He's the only honest lad I ever had, and as such I prize him. Come now, my dear, you see I have given up the Bull and Perriwinkle to-night for your sake, so what can we have for supper?"

"I really don't know, Mr. Atherton. As for giving up the Bull and Perriwinkle, I don't know anything about that, but you may have your own reasons, Mr. Atherton, and as for supper, I think beef steaks and onions would not be amiss."

"The very thing. Oh! how I do long to learn all about the Black Lady."

"And do you really think, Mr. Atherton, that she will keep her word?"

"Why, you don't doubt it?"

"Yes, I do though."

"What a pity—what a thousand pities."

"Pho—pho. After all she may be so mad as to fancy what isn't, and forget what is. Don't you recollect my poor uncle Tobias, poor man? Before he went to everlasting glory he got foolish."

"He had not much to get."

"Mr. Atherton!"

"My dear?"

"I say, my uncle Tobias went foolish."

"Then, my dear, he had not far to go."

"Oh, gracious! was there ever a woman so tormented by a man. My uncle Tobias used to put the flat chamber candlestick on his head instead of a night-cap, and keep on blowing at his own nightcap to put it out."

Mr. Atherton knew that when his good lady began once about her late uncle Tobias, who had gone to glory, that it was a theme which lasted a considerable time usually, and one likewise upon which she could not and would not bear any contradiction, so, like a prudent husband, he forbore attempting any.

The rump steaks and the onions consequently in due time made their appearance; and so, in defiance of the charms and allurements of the Bull and Perriwinkle, round the corner, where some of the substantial tradesmen of the neighbourhood were wont to congregate, the cheesemonger spent that evening at his own fireside.

The fog, as Jem had announced, had completely vanished, and the night become one of those clear damp ones which we are occasionally visited with, when the air is so full of small particles of moisture that we can, although no rain may be falling, feel at every inspiration of breath as if we were inhaling some curious phenomena in the shape of cold steam.

How the Black Lady got home, or where was her home, the cheesemonger and his wife had no means of hearing; but they had no more disturbance that night, with the trifling exception of some bacchanals from the Lord Mayor's dinner and ball, who came down Cheapside declaring in a very loud voice their intention of not going home till morning, a fact which they might just as well have kept to themselves.

CHAPTER IV.

THE MYSTERIOUS COMMUNICATION OF THE BLACK LADY TO THE ATHERTONS. —THE DREADFUL TREACHERY OF JEM.

IT was very wrong and spiteful of the weather, but the tenth of November was quite a pattern sort of day, and a wonder and an endless theme for admiration.

It was warm, and genial, and pleasant as one of those spring mornings which induce everybody to observe to everybody that the summer is really coming. And the day before had been the Lord Mayor's day ! The state coach had been dragged out of the warehouse it is left to repose in for the year. The men in armour were procured. The mace-bearer and the sword-bearer each looked, if any one could have seen them through the fog, important. The city barge had been uncovered ; and all the pride, pomp, and circumstance of civic dignity had been marshalled in those streets, the atmosphere of which so strongly resembled unusually thick pea soup, while on the following day all was so fine and beautiful.

It was a decided conspiracy of the weather. There could be no mistake about that. Everybody said so ; and that of course settled the matter. The Lord Mayor himself was heard to to say that the desperate fog might just as well have been on the tenth instead of the ninth ; but it could not be helped, and as many of the corporation, in consequence of the arduous duties they had performed on the day previous (it was not the wine), could not conveniently get up, it mattered very little to them indeed.

" Well," said Atherton to his wife, " here's a day. Did you ever see the like on the tenth of November, my dear ?"

" Often," said his wife, who was not in a to-be-surprised mood by any means.

" Ah, well, I never did. Didn't all about the Black Lady last night seem to you like a dream, my dear ?"

" No, Mr. Atherton."

" Well, it does to me. I don't think now we shall see her any more, upon my word. Really now, do you know, it strikes me ——"

" I say, master, she's a-coming," said Jem, who was scraping some bacon to make it look fresh, on the board outside.

" Who ? who ?"

" The Black Lady."

" The Black Lady ! God bless me ! where ?"

" There ; there. Don't you see her, sir ? she's crossing the road. Here she comes. Look how slow and steady she moves along."

The cheesemonger and his wife both hurried to the door of the shop ; and upon looking in the direction indicated by Jem, they sure enough saw the Black Lady moving slowly towards the shop, with her veil down after its accustomed manner, while the stray passengers she passed paused to cast upon her the usual glance of curiosity and speculation she always excited.

" Yes, it's she," said Atherton.

" And coming here," added his wife.

" Well, let her come. Let her come. She don't seem looking this way though."

Whether or not the Black Lady was looking that way, she certainly came that way, and in a few moments more she paused before the cheesemonger's door.

Without even removing the veil from before her face, she took a small parcel from somewhere where she had had it concealed about her, and handing it to Atherton, said—

" I have kept my promise."

" Your—your promise ?"

" Yes ; I said that you should be acquainted with my history. You will find it there recorded ; remember, I have kept my word. Do you be as particular about your oath. Farewell, farewell !"

" But—but won't you walk in ?"

She shook her head, and sighed deeply.

" Perhaps you have come a good way," remarked Mrs. Atherton. " You can always take a rest here, you know, whenever you like ; you will always find the shop open, and you must be tired sometimes."

" No—no—no, I thank you, but I cannot again mingle so much with my fellow creatures as to accept of continued acts of courtesy from them. I am alone ; let me continue so. My heart is the shrine of buried hopes. Do not, oh ! do not seek again to exhume them, and make them see the light of day. Farewell ! farewell !"

She turned, and, with a quicker step than usual, left the shop; while the cheesemonger held the small packet in his hand, and looked after her in amazement, for the last few words she had uttered had been spoken with more vehemence by far than she usually allowed herself to use.

We say, usually, because the Athertons had passed some hours in her company, and were consequently tolerably well able to judge of her ordinary mode of address.

Mrs. Atherton, however, soon put an end to his reveries by snatching the packet out of his hand and exclaiming,—

" What is the man staring at?   Why, Atherton, you look like a stuck pig."

" Ha! ha!" laughed Jem; but a ringing box on the ear from the not over small hand of his mistress convinced him how ill-timed was his mirth, and like the imprudent courtier in " The Sleeping Beauty," he had laughed in the wrong place.

" Take that," she said.

Jem shook his head, for he felt as if all the bells of all the general postmen, and all the dustmen, and all the muffin men were ringing in his ears.

" And now, Mr. Atherton," added his wife, " if you have done gaping there like an idiot, you will come into the parlour and see what's in this parcel."

The cheesemonger offered no consolation to Jem, who, on the whole, he thought, was all the better for a box on the ears from his wife, but he followed the lady into the parlour, and then and there they both set about unfastening the mysterious-looking packet which had been handed to him by the Black Lady.

It was carefully sealed in several places with black wax, and when these obstructions to the opening of the parcel were removed, there were found several wrappers before the contents of the parcel could be got at.

" It reminds me for all the world of a gipsy mummy," remarked Mrs. Atherton, " it is so difficult to get at."

" It is, indeed; but patience you know does wonders, so here goes."

The last wrapper was a piece of fine linen, and when that was removed there appeared a compact packet of written paper, and beneath it a coiled up piece of rope, and a large, singular-looking, old-fashioned key.   To the rope was attached a ticket, on which was the following words :—

" This is the rope which took his life at the Old Bailey, Anno Domini, 1802."

On the key hung a label, likewise on which was written,—

" This is the key which let him into St. Paul's by the small door with the three crosses, which is near to Paul's Chain.'"

" Lor!" said Mrs. Atherton, with a shudder, as she dropped the rope, " what a horrid idea; a man has been hung'd by this rope—oh! good gracious!"

" Well, but you know, there is no harm in the rope, my love."

" No harm in the rope a man has been hanged by!   I can tell you, Mr. Atherton, that there is harm in it, and that if it remains in the house, I shall expect his ghost to call, and the ghost of the hangman that hanged him, and of the reverend ordinary which preached to him, and of everybody else as ever had anything to do with him."

" Oh, stuff, stuff."

" You may say, oh, stuff, stuff, as long as you like, Mr. Atherton; you will allow me to remark, that every fool can say, oh, stuff, stuff."

" Yes, but my dear——"

" Don't my dear me, Mr. Atherton, I won't have it, sir.   If I hate any one thing more than another, it's the hypocrisy of a man calling his wife my dear."

" Look here; how rusty the key is."

" Ah, it is, indeed; I do wonder now what little door in St. Paul's that is where this key will let anybody in."

" So do I; but here's a bit of parchment; what does it say on it, I wonder."

There was a bit of parchment at the top of the written packet, and on it were these words :—

" George the Third was applied to for a respite for the prisoner, as there were circumstances which went to prove his innocence; but it was refused, and Sir Robert Knowleys, who saw the king upon the matter, reports that he said,—

"'What, what, what?—not hang him, not hang him?—must hang him,—you know. Take away somebody elses money! What, what, what?—eh, eh, eh? Hang him, hang him!—must hang him, Knowleys, you know. Eh, eh? what, what, what?'"

*   *   *   *   *   *   *

Just beneath this was another slip of parchment, on which was written,

"He suffered innocently. God receive his soul, and grant to him a glorious recompense in another world for his unmerited suffering in this. Such is the prayer of her who yet lingers for a brief space ere she rejoins all she loved beyond the stars. Amen."

Then these various little pieces of parchment being removed, there appeared to be something in the form of a regular narrative, the first portion of which had the one ominous word "EXECUTION" at the head of it.

"Lor," said Mrs. Atherton, "let's read that."

"Well, I don't mind," said the cheesemonger; "but it's very odd for anything to begin with an execution, ain't it."

"And why so?"

"Because that's generally the end."

"Well, never mind that. You don't understand these matters, I dare say, so well as the Lady in Black, so let's have it. What does it say, Mr. Atherton?"

"It seems very dreadful."

"All the better, I like anything very dreadful; I do enjoy anything horrid and full of shivers. It makes me ill, but I like it."

"Humph! well, there's no disputing about tastes, but this is no doubt real, and so you may shiver away at it as much as you like, you know."

"Are you going on, Mr. Atherton?"

"Yes, yes; but now recollect you really must not tell any of it to any of your gossiping cronies, my dear."

"My gossiping cronies! well that is too bad; oh, if I was not a woman among ten thousand, I don't know what I wouldn't say. My gossiping cronies! Oh, men, men, you accuse women of gossiping, and you go to Bulls and Perriwinkles, and Sir Somebody's Heads, and the What-d'ye-call-'ems Arms, and there you gossip and gossip away till it's enough to make a cat cut her throat to hear you."

"Well, there is something in that," said the cheesemonger; "I only, however, cautioned you; and now here goes."

"Now what are you looking at, Mr. Atherton?"

"I was only casting an eye to the shop, to see if Jem was attending to it. I don't see him at all anywhere."

"Oh, of course, he's outside, as he ought to be."

"Ah, I dare say he is. Very good. Now, Mrs. Atherton, it says 'Execution,' and this is the commencement of the beginning."

*   *   *   *   *   *   *

It is a smiling summer's day. Even London is full of life, and animation, and beauty. Field birds, seduced by the balmy air and the sweet sunshine, have come into the huge city. There is nothing but what looks bright and beautiful but—Newgate.

Yes, Newgate. That is black, dismal, and frightful, and within its walls lies a doomed man, one who is slowly counting the many hours that interpose between him and eternity—those hours which will soon dwindle to minutes, and minutes to moments. God have mercy upon him, and upon those who love him, for man will have none.

It is seven o'clock. The crowd thickens; ballads are sung under the gallows, and itinerant venders of all kinds of food and drink are swearing against each other their various wares. It is a gala of death. Crowds of people are each moment pouring in from the suburbs. The windows have each their occupants, for the dreadful show is about to commence.

It is a quarter after seven, and the multitude has increased by thousands. Their voices make a loud roar like the sea, and as they are looked down upon from the windows of the houses, they seem to rock to and fro in huge masses, like waves suddenly stirred by a tempest.

And among that mighty throng of human beings there are women! Some, too, clasp sucking babes to their breasts. Rather than not see the execution, they have brought with them those young things who, in demanding their care at home, would have kept them from seeing the sight of a fellow creature's life taken away coldly and deliberately on a scaffold.

Oh! horrible profanation of all that is bright, and beautiful, and gentle, in woman!

Now 'tis half-past seven, and then are heard loud ear-piercing shrieks from the more dense places among the crowd. Some have fallen, and are getting trampled to death by their fellows, and it is all to see an execution. One woman is carried away dead, and her infant is a shapeless hideous mass among the feet of the people. It has been kicked hither and thither by many who knew not what it was. It looked like a ball of bloody meat snatched from some butcher's stall, to make fun for the expectant populace who had come to see the execution.

But this deters not others. It is not their child, and what care they? Who ought to look for common feelings of common humanity from a woman who would go to see an execution?

It is beyond the half hour. Ah, what a scene of terror does the crowd exhibit! Many would now be glad to leave it, but they cannot. The work of retribution has begun! They are suffering now for coming so far to make holiday, and to seek amusement in the death pangs of the poor doomed man. There are shrieks and cries, but who can pity them from whom such arise? Who would pity them? They have come to see the execution!

Near to an old inn in the Old Bailey, was a low ancient house. Its windows are full of expectant people, who are congratulating themselves upon the good position they have secured to see the sight.

On the roof of this there is a man—a man of dark and sinister aspect. He lies in the gutter behind the coping-stone, upon which his head only rests, so that any one who from below might chance to look up, would see nothing but a human face.

But what a face was that! It looked dreadful. It was distorted by evil passions struggling with surely some feeling of horror and remorse. Surely, oh, surely nothing human can be wholly destitute of such sensations.

There he remained fixed, as if he had been a statue. He moved not hand nor foot. He looked not at the crowd, he looked not at the prison, but his eyes were rivetted upon the scaffold. He heard not the roar and the noise of the multitude below; he heard not the shrieks of despair that came from those who were knocked down, and, in the last gasping agonies of a worse death than that they had come to see inflicted upon another, were crying for mercy. He heard nothing but the chimes of St. Sepulchre's clock, as it indicated each quarter of an hour that the doom of the prisoner would soon be accomplished.

That man has committed the crime for which he who is in the condemned cell is to perish. He has procured the condemnation of the innocent, and he has come there, as if dragged by the chain of some invisible destiny, to see the consummation of his own dreadful iniquity and wickedness.

It is a quarter to eight. There is a terrific rush on the parts of some people who have newly arrived at the spot to get good places from which to view the dreadful spectacle, and, consequently, those who are nearest to the scaffold are forced forwards.

In vain the officers try to keep them back. They might as well attempt to stem the advancing tide of the ocean. Then they strike the most forward down with their staves, and then commences a short but terrific conflict. One officer has a knife forced up to the hilt in his back. There is nothing but riot and confusion.

A troop of horse comes at a sharp trot up Ludgate-hill. Some of the mob fly. There is a general panic, and, trampling on every one in their way, the military, who had been sent for by the alarmed sheriffs, range themselves round the scaffold. Comparative tranquillity is restored. Several prisoners have been taken, and some lives have already been lost at the execution.

Hark! hark! The prison bell is tolling—sad signal that the dreadful pro-

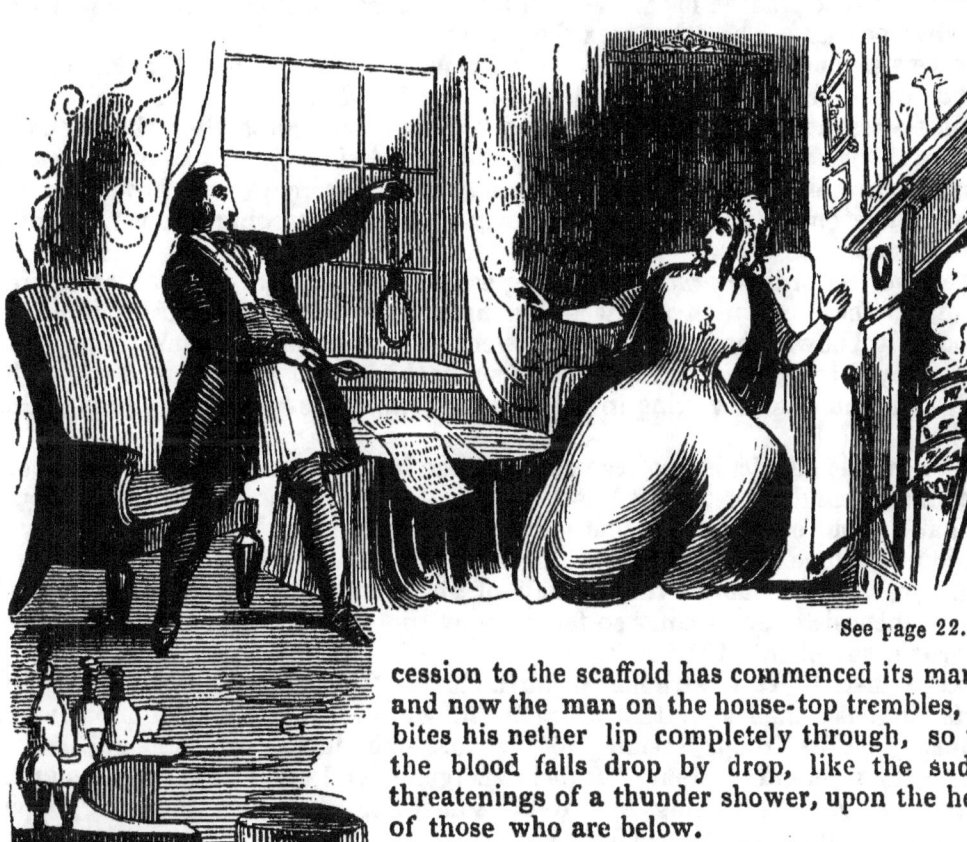

See page 22.

cession to the scaffold has commenced its march; and now the man on the house-top trembles, and bites his nether lip completely through, so that the blood falls drop by drop, like the sudden threatenings of a thunder shower, upon the heads of those who are below.

"It's raining blood," said a boy, and he ran home so terrified, that his reason became seriously affected by the shock.

And now a door is flung open. It is the too well known debtors' door of the Old Bailey, through which so many unfortunates have passed to that dreadful death without, which is one of the worst, and the most cruel and horrifying to which criminals can be put.

And, oh, what a strange noise arose from the crowd when they saw the door flung open. It was not a shout—it was not a scream; but it seemed as if every one present had uttered some terrible exclamation, and that all combining together produced such a shout as by no other means could have been at all effected.

The first who came out was a man with a white wand, and he evidently trembled and looked appalled upon the vast multitude which was before him. Moreover, he had come from the dimly lighted narrow passages of the prison at once into the full broad glare of an uncommonly light day, and he appeared to shrink like some owl which suddenly merges from a leafy covert, and finds the sun has risen.

Then another with a white wand came, and then one of the sheriffs of London with his gown of office, and looking not at all well pleased with the task which the duties of his office compelled him to perform. A strange silence now had crept over the multitude. Not a soul spoke, or shifted his or her position in the least. Nay, so profound was the stillness, that it seemed as if for some moments every one had agreed not to breathe.

The low wail of some young child, who had been dragged by its wretched mother to the dreadful scene, now came plainly upon every ear, and then at the door there appeared two persons. One of these was the clergyman—the ordinary of Newgate, as he is called—and his black robes sufficiently denoted who and what he was. The other was the prisoner.

He was a young man, tall, and well formed. He was ghastly pale, and he wore a suit of black, the coat of which was buttoned close up to his chin. He had on no cravat, and his head and neck, take them altogether, had a most superb and classical look about them. This expression, joined to his excessive paleness, gave him a strange, statue-like appearance, which would have attracted all eyes, independently of the painful position of all-absorbing interest in which he was placed.

The reverend ordinary was conversing earnestly with him, or rather talking to him, for the young man who was thus brought out to die heeded him not.

God only knows where his thoughts were at that awful moment. They probably strayed to a sweet cottage home, where had dwelt a young girl whom he loved, and who was now lying in the stupor of madness. God help her!—God help her!

And now the convict is upon the scaffold, and he stands at his full height, looking calmly around him. The ordinary touches his arm, but he shakes his head.

What a shout of execration that is from the multitude. Ten thousand throats have joined in one roar of derision. The hangman had appeared.

And yet where would be the holiday of an execution without the hangman? Strange inconsistency to come so far to enjoy the show, and then to execrate, and groan, and shout at the showman.

Hark! hark! It is striking eight o'clock. The doomed man hears the solemn sounds; the last of that character he will ever hear. For a moment he is shaken, and he droops, seeming to have lost some inches of his height.

Then the reverend ordinary becomes energetic, and takes him by the hands, and appears to be imploring him to do something, to which the other, apparently, has some insuperable objection.

And now let us take a glance at the man on the house-top. He is suffering; yes, yes, he is suffering, surely. There is some satisfaction in that, at all events. He has clutched at the stone parapet unconsciously with such force, that he has broken every one of his nails, and his fingers are bleeding. His face looks of a dull ashy bluish colour; and now, then, there is a quivering through his limbs, as if he were about to die.

Oh, what a hell must be raging in that man's breast. Does he who is doomed to death by the hands of the common hangman endure one-half that that man suffers? No, no, he does not, for he is innocent. The reverend ordinary continues speaking to him. The sheriff has said something, too—the executioner is ready. Now, with a sudden movement, the young man advances to the front of the scaffold, and at once resuming his full height and noble bearing, he elevates his arms above his head, and, standing like one inspired, he cries,—

" By that living God who now hears me, and in whose dread presence I so soon shall stand, I swear I am innocent."

There was not a living soul, old or young, near or remote, in that vast assemblage, but heard him utter these words. Nothing could equal the effect they produced. The multitude seemed paralysed by them. It appeared as if, with the full force of conviction, they had at once sunk deep into every breast. The reverend ordinary shakes his head, and goes back, like one who should say, I have done all that I can, I can do no more.

The fatal noose is about the young man's neck, and he stands upon that drop which was then a new invention ; there seems some angry words between the sheriff and the hangman—perhaps it is about how the culprit came to be so badly pinioned that he could have so much use of his arms. And the fatal moment arrives—the drop falls ; the man on the housetop uttered a loud shriek, and fell over the parapet among the people below.

CHAPTER V.

THE PROJECTED VISIT TO THE LITTLE DOOR IN ST. PAUL's.—THE NIGHT's ADVENTURE IN THE OLD CATHEDRAL.

MILES ATHERTON paused at this juncture in the narrative, and looked up in his wife's face, for that lady had said nothing for many minutes past, although she had been, in the commencement of his reading, rather profuse in her interruptions, with which we have not thought it at all advisable to trouble the reader.

On her countenance now sat wonder and amazement, mingled with no little share of apparent fright. Her eyes were very wide open, and so was her mouth, while every feature of her face indicated the intense interest she had taken in the brief but awfully expressive narrative that had been read.

When Atherton stopped, there was a pause of some moments' duration, and then his wife contrived to gasp out,—

" Well, well ?"

" Well ; what ?" he said.

" Go on. What are you stopping for, Mr. Atherton ?"

" Because that's all of that, my dear."

" All,—all ?"

" Yes ; that's all on this sheet of paper. Don't you think it's quite enough ?"

" Well, but Mr. Atherton, it's very unsatisfactory."

" Unsatisfactory ? Why, good God ! wasn't the young man hanged, and didn't the other tumble off the roof of the house whack into the street below ? You call that unsatisfactory, do you ? Upon my word, women are never satisfied, and if you were to cut off a man's head, they would say, ' Well, what next ?' "

" Of course, Mr. Atherton. You must know as well as I do, that it is not at all satisfactory. I want to know," and here Mrs. Atherton held up her left hand, and spread the fingers out like a fan, while she counted off upon each the items of what she wanted to know, " I want to know, Mr. Atherton, who the young man with the high forehead was ?—who the other man was who fell off the house ?—what the young man with the high forehead and the pale face had done to be hanged, and what he hadn't done ?—what sort of a villain the other man was before he fell off the house, and what sort he wasn't ?—What he did, and what he didn't ——"

" Goodness me !"

" Hold your tongue, Mr. Atherton."

" Well, well."

" I want to know who was the young person who is said to be lying in some cottage quite mad ?—I want to know why she went mad, and whether she got well again ?—and I want to know what became of the woman whose blessed baby got smashed in the crowd ?—and what became of her, and what her husband said to her when she got home ?"

" And so does I," exclaimed Jem, as at that moment he popped his head in at the parlour-door, " and so does I."

" You villain !" said Mrs. Atherton.

" You have been listening," said his master.

" No—no—I—I—ah, that is—you know—wasn't it horrid ?"

" What's to be done, now ?" screamed the lady. " Here we have been taking oaths, and swearing dreadfully that nobody should know anything about it, and it turns out that Jem has been listening all the while. Oh, we are lost, completely, Mr. Atherton, and the ghosts of everybody will haunt us."

" Stuff," said the cheesemonger, " stuff. We can't help anybody listening. Jem, come here, you scoundrel."

"Here you is, sir."

"How long have you been listening?"

"Ever since the very minute, master, as I first begun."

"Don't prevaricate with me; you know it won't do.   What did you hear first?"

"First, oh, first? Ah, at the beginning, you mean.   The very first.   Ah, oh, what did I hear?"

"Now, Jem, I won't have this sort of thing.   Return me a complete answer, or else take your discharge."

"There, master," said Jem, adroitly, "as you have once promised not to discharge me, I just begun to hear clear when the bell of Newgate was a tolling, and the young chap was being brought out to be scragged."

"Oh, you low wretch!" exclaimed Mrs. Atherton.   "Scragged, indeed! You talk of a human being as if he was a scrag of mutton."

"Jem, Jem," said his master, "I am very sorry you have heard any of this, because your mistress and I had taken an oath to keep it a profound secret."

"A oath!"

"Yes, Jem; and the only plan I can now think of is for you to do the same. You must swear, Jem."

"Well, I don't mind.   Remember, you know, master, you told me to swear, so if missus gets in a rage I can't help it, and it ain't my fault."

"Your fault! certainly not.   It was a great fault to listen; and, mind you, Jem, it is an act that I will not again tolerate, but since you have listened, it becomes necessary for our peace of mind that you should swear."

"Well," said Jem, "this is the rummest start ever I heard of in all my life, but if I must I must, so here goes.   D—n all the world; d—n a coach-wheel.   D—n everybody to eternal sticks.   D—n ——"

"Hold your tongue, you villain," exclaimed Mrs. Atherton.   "How dare you swear in that dreadful way before me?"

"Swear! why, master told me I must, so here goes again ——"

"Take that," said Mrs. Atherton, flinging the key, which was in the mysterious packet, at Jem's head, where it made a tolerable bump, for it was by no means a remarkably small key, but old-fashioned, and, as Jem himself said, with a great number of crinkly crankly ends, and ins-and-outs and corners about it.

"There's no pleasing nobody," said Jem.   "Here, master asks me to swear, and when I begins swearing away like an old tom cat, and is just a getting into the spirit of the thing, whack comes a key at my head."

"Now, Jem," said Mr. Atherton, gravely, "my impression is that you know better, and that you are more rogue than fool."

"Oh, don't say that, master.   Consider my feelings."

"Bother your feelings," exclaimed Mrs. Atherton; "I should like to know what business you have with feelings."

"I haven't got no business with 'em, missus," said Jem.   "Ever since I was left a horphin, they has been a melancholy pleasure."

"Left a what?"

"He means an orphan," said Atherton; "and it's true."

"You took me from the workus, master," added Jem; "and ever since then, I've cultiwated a little in the feeling line now and then."

"Jem, you must swear an oath that you will not reveal to anybody what you have overheard to-day."

"Oh, a davy?"

"Yes, a kind of affidavit."

"Oh—oh, if you had said a davy, I should have know'd what you meant; but, 'stead o' that, you only says ' swear,' and then, in course, I say, d—n all ——"

"Silence."

"Oh! werry good.   Here goes, then, for the davy.   So help me everything and everybody, I won't tell nothing to nobody."

"I suppose," said the cheesemonger, looking at his wife with a perplexed look, "I suppose, my dear, that must do."

"Well, well; I suppose it must."

"There's only one thing," said Jem, with a sigh, "that goes agin my conscience. You know Sally Smith?"

"Sally Smith? Who is she?"

"Her father keeps the pusseys' meat shop in the court, at the back of the Bull and Perriwinkle."

"And what of her?"

"What of her? what of her? I pays my devours to her.

> "'Of all the gals as is so smart,
>   There's none like pretty Sally;
> She is the darling of my heart,
>   She lives here in Bull Alley.

Now, I tell you what it is, Missus Sally has a taste for gore."

"For what?"

"Gore, gore. The sanguinhairy, you know. She likes to feel all her inside of a crawl, and to be pictrified. She likes it to be all hot cockles with her mussels. Now, do just let me tell her of this baby as was kicked to death in the crowd, and made into a bundle o' bad-looking meat. I ask no more but the baby; that'll last Sally never so long."

"I cannot consent that any portion of the narrative should be communicated to any one," said Atherton. "You must not tell her."

"Well, but you know, master, it may be supposed to be a ficteratious baby, you know, and it would please her above a bit."

"I must not allow you."

"Well, then, in course, if I mustn't, I mustn't. Sally's father has been a warying the way in which he gets grub lately. He's a shoemaker by trade, and likewise he's took to selling fish when it's in season."

"Indeed!"

"Yes, master; but he isn't a man as will listen to reason. Of course, I meant to marry Sally, so I spoke to her father about it."

"What did you say?"

"'Why,' says I, 'old brick,'—you see, I thought I'd smoothen him down a bit,— 'old brick,' says I, 'what a help I should be to you.' 'How?' says he. 'Why,' says I, 'you could attend to the shoe-making,' says I, 'and I could attend to the fish,' says I. 'I'm quite conwinced,' says I.

> '——— some want of help you feels;
> And while you drive nails in folk's toes,
>   Why, I can skin their eels.'

And what do you think he did?"

"I cannot say, Jem."

"Why, he pretended to think as I was making game of him, and he throws a jolly great last at my head; so, in course, I began to think as it was prudent to take myself off."

"And that's just what you can do now," said the cheesemonger. "Take yourself off and attend to the shop, or else somebody will be taking off some of the things."

This was a hint which Jem thought it prudent to take, since he now considered that he had succeeded in restoring his master to good humour with him after his feelings had so far taken him astray as to induce him to expose the manner in which he had been listening to the reading of one of the manuscript papers belonging to the Black Lady.

When he had gone, Atherton said,—

"There, you see, my dear. That's the way secrets get told from one to the another; Jem will never be able to keep what he has heard to himself."

"Do you really think not?"

"Certainly. My firm belief is, that he will tell the cats'-meat-man's daughter all about it at the very earliest opportunity."

"Well, Mr. Atherton, if I find that he does so, of course it won't be considered a secret any longer, and there would not be much harm in me just mentioning it to Mrs. Finnikin, the mercer's wife."

"No, no, no! Remember, you have sworn to keep the secret till 1845, my dear, and that another person, and that person, too, an ignorant errand-boy, should break his word, can be no excuse for a woman of sense and refinement doing the same."

Alas! There is most decidedly a weak side to human nature, and that is a very weak one indeed, and consists of the love of flattery.

Mrs. Atherton smiled benignly upon her husband, and said,—

"Very well, my dear, I won't mention it to Mrs. Finnikin. As you say, it would be wrong in me. We ought always to set an example to the lower classes. But go on, Mr. Atherton, go on."

"Go on, how?"

"Reading, to be sure."

"Lord bless you," said the cheesemonger, lifting up the manuscript, "it would take a long while, and I've got my business to attend to. I tell you what I'll do. To-night, after the shop is shut up, we will have a read at it. There's something in the next, but that I've only taken a glance at; but it gave me a sort of shiver."

"A shiver! Then it's dreadful!"

"I—I think it is. But wait till to-night; and besides, you know, then Jem will be more out of the way, and cannot so well interfere with us or listen. What he knows now, is not much; but when we get a little further on, and begin to find out the names of the different people, there's no knowing what mischief might come of his hearing any of it."

"Well, well, perhaps you are right. Let it be, then, till to-night."

"I will lock up the papers and the key. As for this rope, I really don't like to have it in the house."

"And so the young man with the pale face and the high forehead was hung with this?" said Mr. Atherton, as he looked at the cord. "It's a curiosity, you know, Mrs. Atherton, to say the least of it; so I couldn't throw it away. I'd put it somewhere out of sight, where we know it will be safe."

"Then I'll lock it up in the small closet on the second floor landing, and if the Black Lady ever comes here again, I will beg of her to take it away with her, for we don't want it, whatever curiosity it may be."—"Very good. Let it be so."

This arrangement, then, was completed, and the papers of the Black Lady, along with the mysterious-looking key, with the label to it, that announced that it would open the small door in St. Paul's Cathedral, near to Paul's Chain, were again locked up.

No doubt both Mr. and Mrs. Atherton were extremely anxious for night to come, that they might continue the perusal of these papers, which had so whetted the already sufficiently keen edge of their curiosity. Atherton strove to attend to his business as usual, but he found that the dreadful details of that execution had taken so firm a hold of his imagination, that he could not shake them off.

To a customer who came for half a side of bacon, he said, in answer to a question, if it would eat mild,

"Oh, certainly. Were you at the execution? Wasn't the crowd tremendous?"

Then, again, to a lady who wanted some Bath chaps, which he happened not to have in stock, he said,—

"Would a kicked-to-death baby do, ma'am, looking like a bundle of bad cold meat, or a cap that the young man was hanged with?"

These evidences of absence of mind were very much against the transactions of business in a business-like way, and although Miles Atherton, as soon as he uttered any of these odd speeches, checked himself, the people, nevertheless, went away with a firm impression that he was a little mad or so, and that it was highly expedient to get out of the shop as quickly as consistent with not making him furious by showing any haste.

As for Jem, he was enormously delighted whenever his master made one of these blunders, and laughed outrageously, although the cheesemonger looked anything but pleased. But then it was of no mortal use in the world to be angry with Jem, so the best thing was, just to let him laugh away as long as he liked, and as loud as he liked, taking no notice whatever of it."

As the day, however, advanced, the cheesemonger recovered his wonted energy and look in his business, and began to make rational answers to people, and Jem seemed to have something on his mind, for he was more grave than usual by many degrees, and uncommonly silent.

At length, just as dusk was coming on, Jem came up to Atherton, and said,—

"I say, master."

"Well, what do you say, Jem?"

"Why, about that key."

"What key?"

"The key as missus flung at my head, you know. It opens, you understand, a door in St. Paul's."

"Yes, it does, certainly; and your knowledge of that circumstance, Jem, convinces me that you listened to what was passing in the parlour much earlier than you owned to, when I questioned you."

"No, no; I did hear the little bit about the key, and then I was forced to go away to serve an old woman with two ounces of cheese, and she would taste every one in the shop before she would make up her mind, and so when I came back, you had got as far as where the bell of Newgate was tolling."

"I don't know, Jem, whether to believe you or not," said the cheesemonger; "but, however, let it be so. What were you going to say about that key?"

"Why, master, if I was you, mind you I only say if I was you, I wouldn't rest easy in my bed till I'd tried that key."

"Tried it?"

"Yes, I'd go and find out the little door it fitted, and then I'd be satisfied as the rest wasn't all gammon."

Miles Atherton looked at Jem for some moments in silence, and then he said,—

"Jem, that is not a bad thought."

"I knows as it isn't, master."

"It would, indeed, be a confirmation, or otherwise, according as it turned out, of the truth of what is recorded in the papers that the Black Lady has left with me."

"In course, sir, in course."

"I think I will try, Jem; but I should not like to be seen. Who knows what the consequences might be of being detected in an attempt to enter the cathedral in such a way; and I am placed in the awkward predicament of not being able to explain the circumstances, if I were apprehended, in consequence of the oath I have taken not to do so."

"There's no reason to be apprehended. The nights are now as dark as pitch, and what's so easy as to get over the rails into the burying ground opposite the corner of Paul's Chain, without anybody being a bit the wiser."

"That's very true. Jem?"

"Yes, master."

"I'll do it."

"Very good. Spoke like a trump; and, I tell you what, I'll go with you."

"You, Jem?"

"Yes; why not? Do you think I'm afeard? No. Do you think as I'd let you go alone, master? No. I'll go with you, and there will be an adventure, and no sort of mistake whatsomdever. I shouldn't wonder if it was to lead into the blessed vaults where there's all sorts of odd things—regular blood-curdlers. Lor, what a treat it would be to get shut in."

"Would it?"

"Yes, into one of the vaults, and you have to eat a stone coffin, while I feasted on a leaden one, to support nature. There would be a go! Why, they'd make us into a story, sir, as sure as fate they would. Oh, I'm confident they would, and we should be great and celebrated characters."

"Hush! Jem; here's your mistress. Remember, we will go to-night. Don't say a word."

CHAPTER VI.

THE DISMAL VAULT IN ST. PAUL'S.—THE PREDICAMENT, AND ITS CONSEQUENCES.

THE suggestion of Jem to test the accuracy of the statements contained in the papers of the Black Lady—an attempted visit to St. Paul's, with the old key, the label attached to which declared that it would open a low door opposite to Paul's Chain, grew upon the mind of Miles Atherton each mement stronger and stronger. As the evening advanced he thought of it over and over again, and the more he did so the more feasible the scheme appeared, and the more easily to be executed.

"There can be no trouble," he told himself; "there can be difficulty, as Jem says. Here it is dark before four o'clock, and pitch daik, too; so the matter can be easily enough managed. A child might get over the rails."

It was quite clear that the cheesemonger intended to go; for, in truth, although at first the idea of entering St. Paul's Cathedral surreptitiously lent to his mind an odd sort of feeling, familiarity with the idea soon got him rid of that; and by the time it became necessary to light the gas in his shop, he was quite familiarised to it, and looked upon it as nothing.

"Besides," he said, "I needn't go in."

This was an argument which decided the business. There was certainly no sort of necessity for going into the sacred building; he need only see if there was a door in the spot mentioned, and then see if the old key he had would turn the lock of it. When he had got that far, then he might pause, and come away again, without so much as setting a foot within the cathedral.

But there was one difficulty connected with the enterprise, and that was to find some excuse to get away from Mrs. Atherton, and to avoid the promise he had made to resume at night-fall, after the shop was closed, the reading of the manuscripts of the mysterious Black Lady. In such a predicament there was no person so likely to give him good advice as Jem, who had a very fertile genius indeed, and was quite well accustomed to make the most artful suggestions in the world to get over difficulties.

"Jem," he called.

"Here you is, sir," said Jem.

"I shall take the key, Jem, and see if it will open the door, if there is a door at the place mentioned on the label attached to it."

"You couldn't do better."

"But then, you know, Jem, I can't go till the shop is shut up, and, unfortunately, I have promised then to remain at home and read to Mrs. Atherton the Black Lady's papers."

"Oh!"

"Such is the case, Jem. How—how am I to get over that, Jem?"

"Easy enough. I'll come to you and say, loud enough for her to hear, that you must call on a Mr. Smith, or a Mr. Jones, it don't, you know, matter which, at nine o'clock at night, and then you must go."

"That will do, then. You do so. And then, Jem, before that time, I will manage to have the key in my pocket, and we can proceed at once."

Thus, then, was this difficulty surmounted; and when nine o'clock came, which was the hour at which the cheesemonger closed his shop, the shutters were put up by himself and Jem with as much despatch as was possible, and then Miles Atherton betook himself to the back parlour, where he said, with all the duplicity of a married man, to his wife,—

"Well, my dear, I think we will begin upon the Black Lady's papers."

"Of course," said Mrs. Atherton.

"Don't you forget, please, sir," said Jem, popping his head into the parlour.

"Forget what?"

"Why, Mr. Horatio Snoggersmouthminden."

"Gracious, what a name!" said Mrs. Atherton. "Who may he be?"

"Really, I had quite forgotten," ejaculated Atherton; "I must call upon him."

"Yes, you must, master; you know you said you would call upon him at a quarter past nine, to hear what he would give for a side of bacon once a fortnight, and some Chedder cheese, which was to be sent to him regularly, and he was to pay always six months in advance for the same. I think you'll find him a good customer, sir."

" No doubt, no doubt."

See page 40.

" How very provoking," said Mrs. Atherton.

" Well, but, my dear, business, you know ———"

" Oh, I know all that, and I suppose it can't be helped ; so be off at once. The sooner you go, Mr. Atherton, the sooner you will be back."

" Certainly, certainly."

In five minutes more Miles Atherton and Jem met at the corner of St. Paul's churchyard, to go on their expedition.

It was a very dark night, indeed. There was no fog, as on the preceding evening, but it was a night on which not a star showed its twinkling face, but the whole sky was like a mass of black velvet.

" This is just the kind of night, Jem," said Atherton, " to go and make such a trial as we wish. No one can possibly see us now, so come on at once."

" You have got the key, master ?"

" Yes, yes."

" What a go. Well, I do like this. I hope it won't all go off smooth and even. Something dreadful ought to happen, don't you think now, master ?"

" I hope not."

" Lor ! How can you hope not ? Why, the great fun of the thing would be for something out-of-the-way to happen."

" Nothing can ; for I don't mean to go into the cathedral, even if we find that the key I have will open the door."

" What !"

" I say I don't mean to go into the cathedral."

" Oh, nonsense ; not go in, indeed. Lor ! what's the harm? You can't see nothing, master, outside. Ah, you'll alter your mind, I know ; when you see the door open, you'll go in, I'll be bound ; but it's no use talking about it yet, till we know as we can get in."

" No ; and, after all, there may not be such a door as is mentioned. I don't at all recollect one ; many and many a time I have passed the old cathedral and never noticed one."

" There is such a door," said Jem.

" There is ?"

" Yes ; I looked for it and seed it. Don't you know I had to take a ham, cut in two, to Doctors' Commons ? Well, as I went, of course I looked, and there I saw the door. It's a little one ; and it don't look as if it had been opened for a hundred years. It's as black as ink, and there's a little grating, about as big as your hand, near the top of it."

" Then," said Atherton, " I have no longer any doubt about the key fitting it. I feel certain, in my own mind, Jem, that it will."

" I hope so, sir."

" You hope so, do you say ? Why, what manner of difference on earth can it make to you whether it does or not ?"

" Why, sir, I like things to turn out correct. Besides, it would be worth while having a key to the cathedral. If we ever wanted to do a little of the gloomy, we could go, you know, and sit on some old coffin in one of the vaults for an hour or two. But here we is, master ; shall I climb over ?"

" Yes, certainly. There seems nobody near."

" Not a soul, sir. Nobody thinks of walking on this side, and it's a deal too dark for anybody to see us from the other, so we are quite safe."

It was not by any means difficult to get over that bit of low old worn stone wall, with the iron rails surmounting it, and so into the burying ground of St. Paul's, where so few interments now seem ever to take place.

Mr. Atherton accomplished it safely, with the exception of tearing the skirt of his coat, and as Jem wore a jacket, he escaped even that casualty, and got nimbly over without doing himself or his garments any damage whatever.

They dared not, of course, have a light, so that they were compelled to feel their way as best they might among the rank grass and the old grave-stones which were about. More than once Miles Atherton nearly fell over some of these latter obstructions, for Jem kept telling him to come straight on, which piece of advice brought him against several of the grave-stones ; but the distance, after all, was very short, and a few minutes sufficed, let them go as slowly or as cautiously as they would, to place them close to the walls of the cathedral itself.

" We shall never be able to see what we are about, or where we are going," whispered Atherton. " I do think I was never out in such a pitchy dark night before. I cannot see my own hand held before my face."

" In course you can't."

" And as for a door, I have not the least idea of where one is to be found."

" We must do as everybody does in the dark, master ; what we can't see we must feel. I warrant we shall soon find the door."

In a few moments Miles Atherton found that the darkness was by no means so intense as it had at first appeared to be. His eyes were getting accustomed to it, and he could see tolerably well, and began to be able to distinguish the different features of the huge building before his eyes.

" Here," said Jem, " here's the door."

The cheesemonger looked hard before him, and he saw a difference of colour in the apparent wall, which, for all he knew, might be a door.

When, however, he used his hands, he felt convinced that he was correct, for he not only felt the little grating at the top which had been described by Jem, but lower down he felt the lock likewise.

" Yes," he said ; " here is a door, sure enough."

" You see," said Jem, " all's right."

" Yes, yes."

" Now for the key, master."

" I have it here ; I have it here."

Miles Atherton felt some degree of agitation, as he took the curious old key from his pocket, and fumbled about with it to try if it would fit the lock.

" It's rather a joke in the dark," he said.

" Oh, go on trying," said Jem, " you'll soon find out if it will do or not."

Atherton did go on trying, and by the assistance of both hands, he at last got the key fairly into the lock. Then he exerted all the power he was capable of, and there was a low, strange, grating sound, as the lock moved back.

The rust of ages appeared to be upon it ; but it did yield to the key. There could be no mistake on that head.

" It's unlocked," he said.

" Is it ?" said Jem, eagerly.

" Yes—yes,"

" What a good joke."

" Well, well ; I am satisfied now. I am satisfied, and now I shall come away. All is right, now. I am completely satisfied. Come away—come away "

" What ! now that you have unlocked it ? Oh, bother coming away. Won't it open, master, now ? Won't it open ?"

" I have not tried it. I cannot lock it again, the key is so rusty."

" It wants a little grease upon it. I've got ever so many bits of candle in my pocket."

" Bits of candle ?"

" Yes."

" Why, what do you want with them ?"

" I thought it would be dark inside, you know, so I brought a tinder-box with me, and a whole pocket full of candle ends."

" Then you seem quite to have calculated upon entering the building."

" Of course I did."

" No, Jem, no. It wouldn't be proper."

" Proper be blowed, master. Everything is proper if you don't mean no harm, and it doesn't do any. We don't hurt anybody by going into St. Paul's. The only difference is, that we get a look at some of it without paying, which we ought to do at any rate."

" There's something in that, Jem."

" There's a good deal in it, sir. The people in this here land o' liberty, pay for building up something as fine as possible, and then they give so much a piece for going to look at it. That's how it's managed."

" What you say is too true, Jem."

"Very good.　Then what need we care about going into St. Paul's?　Whose is St. Paul's?　Bother everybody.　What need we care?"

As he spoke, Jem gave the door a kick, and it creaked back upon its old rusty hinges, showing, thereby, that there was now no obstruction to a free ingress, at least to some portion of the cathedral.

"But we don't know," said Atherton, "where this door may lead to, Jem."

"That's the very reason I should like to find out," said Jem, "so come inside, and we shall soon find out, master."

Miles Atherton, to tell the truth, was still a little reluctant; but his curiosity was greatly stimulated by the actual opening of the door, and he found himself fishing up arguments to induce himself to go in.

"Where's the harm? as Jem says," he thought now.　"Where's the danger?— none.　Ah! I'll go in.　Yes, I'll go in.　I don't see why I shouldn't.　I'll go in, Jem."

"That's right, sir."

The cheesemonger advanced a step within the doorway, and then he suddenly disappeared, with a loud cry of terror.

"Murder!" cried Jem.　"Here's a pretty go."

There was a death-like stillness, and where Miles Atherton had gone to was a profound mystery, for the darkness within the doorway it was impossible to pierce. The hair almost stood on end on Jem's head, as in an attitude of bewilderment and horror, he stood at the open door.

Then, as if by a sudden impulse, he sat down upon the ground, and producing the tinder-box he had spoken of, he began striking a light with a vehemence that soon ignited the tinder.

"Master's gone," he said to himself, as with a hand that shook so, that he could hardly accomplish the feat, he held a match to the smouldering tinder.

"Master's gone, and I persuaded him.　There's some deep well, or a out-and-out deep staircase, just through this door, and down he's gone.　Here's a pretty sitivation I'm in.　Oh, dear! oh, dear! what will become of me now? and I persuaded him.　What shall I say to Mrs. Atherton?　It's all up with me, that's quite clear. Hang the match.　Oh, dear! oh, dear!　I don't hear him now.　He's done for, that's as clear as mud in a wine-glass.　I shall be hung."

Jem uttered this opinion in a tone of voice which was quite conclusive of the fact that he had no manner of doubt but that such would be his fate. He firmly believed that his master was no more, and he had an opinion, which is very prevalent with many people, that he, as the last person seen in his company, must, as a matter of course, be hanged in the absence of any testimony to save him.

"It's all up," he muttered.　"I'm a dead mutton, or as good as one.　This is my first and last adventure at St. Paul's.　There's no mistake about that.　If he wasn't dead, he'd be sure to say something, and, as he didn't say nothing, why dead he is.　That's settled, and I should like to find anybody who could dispute that?"

By the time Jem had finished this intricate piece of reasoning he had got a light, and such was now his state of agitation, that he quite forgot that somebody was almost certain to see him, for he was outside the door.　He lit one of the bits of candle he had brought with him, and having secured that in the end of a cleft-stick, he turned the light towards the narrow door-way.　As he did so, he very nearly fell back with fright, for about on a level with his chest was the face of his master.

Yes; there was Miles Atherton, so frightened that he could not speak, and yet he had only fallen down one step, for there were no more; but the suddenness of the shock, and the full belief that he was going some tremendous distance, had paralysed all his faculties for a time.　He had assumed a sitting posture, and there he was glaring at Jem all the while he was getting a light, and unable to say one word to assure him of his safety.　It would have been quite a picture to see them both now looking at each other, the one without and the other within that doorway.

Jem was shading the candle with his hand, and his eyes were opened a tremendous width, while the cheesemonger was looking as pale as death, and only just beginning to have a faint suspicion that he was a great deal more frightened than hurt.

"Master!" ejaculated Jem.

"Jem!" said Atherton.

"Ain't you killed?"

"Not that I know of."

"Then I sha'n't be hung this time. Here's a reprieve! Well, I never. Here's a go—here's a go! We shall be found out."

The idea of the light discovering them flashed across Jem's mind just as the rays of his candle flashed into the eyes of an old lady who lived opposite, and he at once withdrew the ancient key from the outside of the lock and passed through the doorway, pulling it close shut after him. The door closed with a latch-lock, so that when pulled shut it was fast, except by the use of a key on the outside.

"Get up, master," cried Jem. "Here we are all safe after all. Don't be sitting down on them cold stones."

"Lor, what a fright I have had to be sure," said Atherton, as he slowly rose to his feet. "I—I thought I was going to fall half a mile at least."

"But, why didn't you speak arter you found as the half a mile had turned into about eight inches, instead o' frightening me out of my wits? If anybody had a come up to me, and said, 'Jem, will you sell your life for half a farden?' I should have said, 'Yes, and it's dear, too.' I gived myself up for lost."

"But you didn't fall down, Jem?"

"No; but I should have been hung, you know, accordin' to law, cos o' being the last person as was seed in your company, safe as bricks."

"Oh, dear no. Oh, no. But never mind that, Jem. Come away now."

"Come away? What, come away, and get no satisfaction arter being frightened to death almost? Oh, dear, no. I want to see something now I have come."

"No, no."

"Oh, I says yes. Yes, governor. Come on. Here we is in a old looking vaulted passage. You know it must lead to somewhere. The door's locked, you know, and nobody can come behind us, so all's safe, and here's lots o' bits o' candles. Come on, master. Come on, and don't be afeard."

"Gracious heavens! what's that?"

There came a loud solemn booming noise, which seemed to shake the whole of the large building to its foundations. It continued for about as long a time as a person might deliberately have counted one, two, three, four, and then, with a loud sonorous clang, the great clock of St. Paul's, for it was that made the strange noise, began to strike ten.

"It's the clock—it's the clock," said Miles Atherton, with a tone of relief. "It's only the clock, Jem."

"Well, didn't I tell you so?"

"No; you didn't, indeed. You never mentioned it, but you shook so that you nearly dropped the candle."

"Oh, no. Not me, not me. That's a mistake—quite a mistake. I didn't shake. Come on, who's afeard, eh? Not me. Come on, master. Lor! Here's a flight o' stairs. Now, master, if so be as how you had fell down these, it would have been a go."

There was a steep, and apparently a very deep flight of stone steps, after they had reached about eight or ten paces along the vaulted passage to which the door had led; and, although Jem held his candle, which was burning with a steady enough flame, as low down as he could, they could neither of them see to the termination of these stairs. It seemed perfectly adventurous to descend them, and even Jem, with all his love for the romantic and the terrible, hesitated, and glanced in the face of his master, as if to gather from its expression what he thought of it.

The cheesemonger shook his head.

"Shall we go?" said Jem.

"I—I don't know. I wonder where it leads to, now? I suppose the vaults. I don't know what to think; I don't, do you know, much mind going up stairs, but I on't like the idea of coming down, especially when you don't exactly know what's at the bottom of 'em.   Yet, I should like ——"

"Come on, then," said Jem.   "Who's afeard?   We should be sorry arterwards if we didn't see all as was to be seen.   Come on, master, it costs no more, you know.   Come on."

CHAPTER VII.

THE VERY UNEXPECTED MEETING IN THE VAULT. — THE IRON DOOR IN THE NORTHERN AISLE, AND THE ASTONISHMENT OF THE DOOR-KEEPER.

THUS encouraged by Jem, whose curiosity appeared to be fully sufficient to overcome any sensation of fear, Miles Atherton, after hesitating a moment, followed him very cautiously and slowly down the long steep staircase that had so unexpectedly presented itself.

From the strange earthy smell which came upon them, they could not doubt but that this staircase led directly to some of the vaults beneath the old cathedral, and after they had gone down nearly thirty steps, Jem, who was in advance, could see to the bottom of the flight.

"Governor," he said, "we haven't far to go now; there ain't above a dozen more steps now to go down."

"I am glad enough of that, Jem," said Atherton, "for we are going underground, and that is always an uncomfortable idea, you know."

"Well, so it is, when you come to think of it.   It does look as if you was a-going to be smothered, and no mistake; I don't like an underground kitchen on that very account."

"Nor I, Jem.   But here we are at the bottom at last, thank God, and now I certainly will not go down any more steps, on any account."

"Well, I don't suppose there will be any more, master, to go down, but just look about.   Ain't this rather a rummy place?"

The cheesemonger, when he did look about him, agreeably to Jem's request, was to the full inclined to agree with him in his opinion of the place they were now in.   It was a wide, vaulted passage, with a flooring composed of very small red tiles, which seemed, indeed, to have been put in edgeways, by the narrow top they presented each to the eye.   On the walls were ample evidences of dampness, and here and there was a rudely sculptured coat-of-arms, and underneath each of these heraldic embellishments was the appearance of a doorway, but which was built up or fastened by some sort of cement.

"These are some of the vaults, Jem," said Atherton.

"I shouldn't wonder, master.   But they seem wonderfully careful about 'em, for there don't seem any way of getting in."

"No; they are all fast; and now, Jem, I think we have seen enough, and may as well return."

"Seen enough, governor? why, we haven't seen nothing at all yet.   Lord bless us, what have we seen?"

"Why—why, a great staircase, you know, Jem, and this stone passage.   We can't, you see, get into the vaults, if we would, for they are all fast."

"Come on, though.   Who knows, master, but we may find something curious, if we go on; I don't at all expect everything is shut up, and if we can but find one vault open, it will be enough for us.   Ain't there a romantic, earthy sort of smell here, eh?"

"There is, indeed."

"And the candle looks rather blue, master, don't it? wouldn't it be a lark to lose our way in these vaults, now, and not be able to get out at all? and be found two mouldering skeletons a hundred years arter this; what a sensation we should make, shouldn't we?"

"I'd rather not, Jem, make any sensation.   It gives me already a very uncomfortable one to think of such a thing; and now I come to recollect, what a rage Mrs. Atherton will be in!   I really think we had better go."

"What! give up an adventure like this, because a woman may be in a rage! No, never—not by any manner of means, governor. Come on. Hilloa! did you hear anything?"

They both listened attentively, for both thought they had heard something like a deep, hollow, moaning sound, proceeding from the direction towards which they were walking.

"It was something," said Jem.

"Only the wind blowing along this vaulted passage," said Atherton. "I thought I heard something very similar as I came down the steep staircase."

"Well, I don't know, governor; it may be. I only hope as it isn't; that's all I have to say about it."

"You hope it is not?"

"To be sure I do. I have a great hope as it's some dreadful-looking ghost of some one as has been buried here a long time ago. There would be a adventure now, governor."

"Such an adventure as we should, perhaps, never get the better of, Jem."

"Oh, lor, yes. Do you believe in ghosts, master?"

"Jem, Jem—this is not exactly the place nor the time to talk upon such a subject, let me tell you."

"Well, I think it is, now. Lor! there's another flight of steps!"

"I positively will go no lower."

"Nobody wants you, governor. Don't you see they go up, and not down."

"Yes—yes. I see now; I was a pace behind you, and, as you held the light, you cast so great a shadow before you, that I could see nothing."

At this moment the strange moaning sound which had already twice given some uneasiness to Atherton, notwithstanding he had said he thought it was but the wind careering along the old passages, came upon their ears, and they both paused and looked at each other, as much as to say,—" There can be no mistake about it now."

"You—you heard that, Jem?"

"Rather."

"And—and what do you think?"

"I don't like to think."

"Then it's high time to come away. Come along—come along. Three times, now, we may be said to have had a warning not to intrude here any longer; and who knows but if we stay any longer we may see something as well as hear something? so the best thing we can do, Jem, is to come along and get home as quick as we can. I begin rather not to like it."

"It's a thickening," said Jem. "There it is again."

There could be now no mistake. Some sound from human lips came upon their ears. It was not exactly a groan, but it rather seemed like some word being attempted to be pronounced by some one who was by far too much absorbed in grief to be able to give it a just and a clear accentuation, and so it dwindled down to a moan of agony, instead of presenting itself to the ear as an articulate and understandable sound.

Jem's interest and Miles Atherton's terror seemed to go together hand in hand, and in proportion as the cheesemonger appeared anxious to leave the precincts of the cathedral, Jem's wish to push on, and make what discoveries he could, became the greater.

"There's something a-coming now, governor," he said. "I do think, and no mistake, we shall find out that we haven't come here for nothink."

"I won't stay—I won't stay."

"Oh, do,—nonsense! What have we to be afeard of? We have not murdered anybody, you know. None o' the ghosts ought to have anything to say to us except quite social. Come on, governor; all's right."

All, however, was wrong in a few moments, for such a sudden and unequivocal groan came upon their ears, that even Jem, who had been so much congratulating himself upon the thickening of the adventure, began to think it was thickening too fast, and gave a start of alarm. In doing so, he fell against a portion of what appeared to be the wall, but which really was a door, and as it gave way with him immediately, he fell backwards, candle and all, extinguishing it as he went, and leaving the place in total darkness.

This, to the cheesemonger, was anything but an agreeable state of things, and he called out rather lustily,—

"A light, a light—murder—Good Mr. Ghost, we are going now ; we are, indeed, as soon as we get another light. The Lord have mercy upon us ! we don't mean any harm, give me leave to assure you."

"Don't make that riot," said Jem. "I can easy get a light ; don't you see how red the snuff of the candle is ?"

Even as he spoke he produced a match, which instantly ignited upon being applied to the red snuff of the candle, and the moment, by this means, a light again illumined the vaulted passage, a strange voice said, clearly and distinctly,—

"What want you here? Are you men of rapine or of blood?"

Miles Atherton cast one terrified glance in the direction whence these words had proceeded, and, to his intense surprise, he saw the Black Lady standing a few paces from him.

The most unexpected appearance of her in such a place gave him so sudden a shock of surprise that he staggered into the small vault where Jem had fallen, and then the Black Lady walked slowly on, as if, although she had asked the question of the intruders, of what they were, she yet felt not sufficiently interested in the answer to press for it.

It was evident she either did not or would not recognise the cheesemonger. The probability was that she did not, for to keep up the delusion to his wife, that he was going to call upon a gentleman, he had put on his best coat, and looked a very different man to what he did when he was in his shop and attending to his business.

Jem seemed transfixed with surprise, and they both continued to stare after the Black Lady in speechless amazement, as she walked slowly in the direction from whence they had come, and then disappeared in the gloom which lay beyond the limited sphere of the candle's influence.

"I—I had a suspicion from the first," gasped Miles Atherton.

"A suspicion o' what, governor ?"

"That that woman was not mortal."

"Lor! you don't mean that !"

"I do, Jem—I do. Did you notice how she walked? she seemed to move along, without lifting up her feet at all. Jem, there's something curious about all this, or else we should not have found her here."

"She wants us to follow her, master."

"You may do as you like, Jem, if you leave me the candle ; but I wouldn't follow her for a thousand pounds."

"That's a deuce of a lot of money, master, ain't it ?"

"D—n it ! she's coming back."

Miles Atherton just caught sight of the returning figure of the Black Lady, and he had worked his mind up to such a pitch of alarm concerning her, that he at once snatched the candle from Jem's hand at the great risk of putting it out again, and ran up the staircase which they had just both noticed before the appearance of the Black Lady.

Impulsively, although he would rather upon the whole have remained where he was, Jem followed him, and they both, after ascending about as many steps as they had previously descended, found themselves in a small stone apartment, in the centre of which was a strong stone slab, supported by four stout short columns of brick-work, each about five feet in height.

They now paused to take breath, and Miles Atherton, who most devoutly wished himself at home, even if he were receiving a curtain lecture from his wife, leant against the slab, or rather against one of its upright supports, and with a deep sigh said—

"Jem, what's to be done now?"

"I don't know," said Jem, "except it's to run down the stairs again as hard as we have run up them, governor."

"But the—the Black Lady."

"What of her?"

"She was coming back, Jem; and when you come to consider, it really might not have been her at all."

"Not her?"

"Certainly not," said Atherton, whose fears had enabled him to get hold of a

new crotchet; "who knows but it is some ghost who has taken her form on purpose to make us suspect nothing, and then lead us into some horrid place?"

"Gammon," said Jem.

"You are fool-hardy; I shall leave the cathedral now as quickly as I can, you may depend, Jem; but it must be by some other way than that at which we came in. I cannot make up my mind to go down those stairs again. We shall surely find some other way of getting out."

"Well, if you won't stay, you won't, governor. If I only had a saveloy or two, or a pot of half-and-half, I wouldn't mind staying all night, just for the fun of the thing—that I wouldn't."

"I don't see any fun in it," said Atherton. "I shall always tremble whenever I look at the Black Lady now. The idea of finding her, or something so exactly like her, in this place, never entered my head. It seems almost like some odd dream. What, if it be her, can she want here?"

"Who knows?—she may lodge here."

"Impossible!"

"Not at all. I don't see why it's impossible, master. She may, you know. She gave you a key to get in here, and she may have another to let herself in, for all we know. She is a little maddish or so, and may fancy living in one of the vaults of the cathedral. Suppose now we come down and ask her?"

"No—no—no. I will not descend these stairs again."

"But how are we to get out?"

"I have been looking about. Here is a door, don't you see? It's fastened in some way, but I dare say between us we shall manage to get it open."

"Well, we can try. And first of all I'd see if the old key would fit it, governor."

"A good thought, Jem."

Miles Atherton produced the key which had been before handed to him by Jem, who had taken it from the door through which they had at first found an entrance to the building, and he soon found that there was every chance of opening this other door with it; and by the manner in which it fitted into the lock he felt convinced that nothing but disuse prevented it from turning easily.

"It's all right," he said, as he placed two hands to the task, and turned the lock with a grating sound. "The door is open."

"Good," said Jem; "we may have some other adventure better still than the one we have had, after all, for what we know."

"Heaven forbid!" ejaculated Atherton. "The only adventure I want now is one that will enable me to get home; and here's some more stairs."

The door opened into the room in which they were, and immediately on the outside of it were some steps to ascend.

"I'll tell you, Jem, what this place is," said Atherton. "This is one of the entrances from the body of the church to the vaults, you know, and that slab of stone, so strongly supported by the brick pillars, is to set the coffins on before they are taken down the steep staircase."

"It's like enough, governor,—it's like enough, for all I know."

"I am certain of it. Come on, Jem; we shall soon see."

With better spirits, now, Miles Atherton went on up the stairs which presented themselves, and which only consisted of twelve. The fact was, they were, before ascending these last stairs, on the level of St. Paul's Churchyard, and they were just sufficient to bring our friends on the same level as the floor of the church itself.

There was now a long straight passage, and at the end of that again a door, the upper half of which was composed of gilt iron work, and which, although only to be opened on the outside by a key, was like a street door, easily opened from within by the hand.

The most casual observation was sufficient to show Jem and his master that this was the case; and, to their mutual surprise, when they passed through this door, they found themselves in the northern aisle of the cathedral.

"There now," said Atherton, and he spoke in a tone of great relief. "It's just as I said, you see. Here we are, fairly in St. Paul's, and far from all those dark places which nobody will ever persuade me to go into again."

Jem gave a short cough, as he said,—

"Don't it strike you, master, that they don't have the door of St. Paul's open of a night?"

"The door open?"

"No. How are we to get out unless we go the way we came, and out at the little door opposite to Paul's Chain? That's the question, governor. Here we are, shut up, you see, and, unless we tarry here till the doors are opened in the morning, we must go back the way we came."

This was a state of things which Atherton did not seem to have at all taken into his consideration, and he looked very rueful when it was pointed out to him. He was silent for some minutes, and then he said,—

"No, no, Jem, I would rather stay here two nights than go back again by all those gloomy passages, and will get into some corner, and try to get some sleep here, till morning comes."

"You will?"

"I will, indeed."

"Well, that is a nice go, but I don't care. Oh, what will missus say? Won't all the fat be in the fire, master, when you do go home, above a bit, rather, I should think?"

"I'll tell her exactly how it happened."

"Oh, but will she believe you? You may tell a female woman anything you like, you know, but unless it's just what she wants to believe, she won't believe it. Come, now, you had better come back, governor."

"I will not come back, and that's flat."

"Very good. I haven't any wife, so I can stay, comfortably enough."

They did stay, and they did get some sleep, and it was nine o'clock in the morning before the doors were opened. When that was the case, they walked out, to the amazement of the man, who stood to receive the threepence charged for admission, and who felt quite confident he had taken nobody's money yet, and looked after them as they walked away with much suspicion and bewilderment.

"'Pon my soul," he said, "now that's too bad. They must have slipped in while my back was turned. How infernal shabby, there's sixpence gone, to begin with. Hang me if this won't be an unlucky day, and no mistake. Sixpence! what a take in. There's the value of two pots of porter. Well, if I let anybody else in, without paying, my name ain't Jones, that's all. I could punch my own head, out of spite, I'm in such a thundering passion, I am. D—n everybody!"

CHAPTER VIII.

MRS. ATHERTON IS SO INDIGNANT AT THE BASE CONDUCT OF MR. ATHERTON, THAT SHE BOLTS AND BARS HIM OUT, AND READS THE BLACK LADY'S MANUSCRIPT ALL TO HERSELF.

AFTER Mr. Atherton had left his house, in order to keep the pretended appointment with the fictitious gentleman, who was asserted to want so much bacon, Mrs. Atherton all at once began to have what she called her suspicions.

There certainly was something hasty and flurried about the manner of Miles Atherton; he had been rather too polite, always a bad sign in a husband, and one which prudent wives invariably regard as a piece of duplicity. He had talked with such an air of suavity; he had found fault with nothing; really, no wonder Mrs. Atherton had her suspicions; and when ten o'clock came and no Mrs. Atherton, no wonder that she shook her head, and said,

"That man has gone to the Bull and Perriwinkle; it's all an excuse, a wretched excuse. That man has gone to the Bull and Perriwinkle. Oh, I ought to have seen it in his looks; I ought to have seen that there was the Bull in one of his eyes, and the Perriwinkle in the other; but I am a foolish, confiding woman, and too mild and good-tempered to deal with such a brute upon two legs, that I am. But only let me get hold of him, and I'll let him know what it is to deceive me; I'll make him remember it, the blessedest, longest day he's got to live, the ungrateful wretch,—and such a wife as I've been to that man, too!"

Half past ten came, and no Mr. Atherton. Eleven o'clock came, and no Mr. Atherton. Then, the boiler of Mrs. Atherton's wrath became very hot indeed, and the steam of her passion was decidedly of a high pressure.

"Good gracious! he don't come home," she exclaimed. "Eleven o'clock, and he don't come home. Oh, was there ever such an injured woman as I am? will there ever be such another? no, never. There he is, boozing and drinking along with the wretched low set at the Bull and Perriwinkle, while I, his lawful, legal, married wife, am left here alone; but I'll Bull and Perriwinkle him,—I'll let him know what I can do. And the wretch was to go on reading the Black Lady's papers to me; but I don't care, not a bit."

Mrs. Atherton was getting too indignant to care much. Half-past eleven came, and she sprang from her seat for all the world, as the maid of all work afterwards declared, like a bomb-shell. Then she proceeded, with that amount of determination which disdains to express itself in words, to lock, and bar, and bolt all the doors, so that no means of ingress to the house should be left. When she had completed this defensive proceeding, she turned upon the before-mentioned maid of all work, and said,—

"Sarah !"

"Ye—ye—yes, ma'am," said the trembling girl, for she saw that "missus" was out of sorts above a bit.

"If you presume to open the door when your master comes home, I'll have your life."

"Me, mum, open the door? lor, mum! I wouldn't presume on no account, mum ; oh, lor, no."

"Be careful, then, and go to bed directly.   Do you hear?"

"Yes, ma'am, I'm a going."

"Be off, then, and don't stand staring at me like a stuck pig."

Thus admonished, Sarah went off ; but no sooner had she gone than a new thought struck Mrs. Atherton, and she stood for some moments in an attitude of profound meditation, while she arranged in her own mind all its possibilities and probabilities.

"Yes," she said.   "Yes; I'll go—I'll go."

Then she proceeded to the foot of the staircase, and called down Sarah, who came, not without serious apprehensions.

"Sarah," she said, and her voice was indicative of the suppressed volcano of rage that was in her breast,—"Sarah, you will please to stand in the passage behind the private door."

"Yes, ma'am."

"While I am gone out—I sha'n't be long—don't let anybody in.   When you hear a knock, you can call out, 'Who's there?' and unless you hear a voice say, 'It's me,' you must not open the door.   If you do you'll wish you had never been born in this world."

"Oh, I won't, ma'am, you may depend."

"I'll do it—I'll do it," exclaimed Mrs. Atherton ; "I'll do it ;" and she put on a shawl and bonnet.   "I'll do it.   I'll go to the Bull and Perriwinkle, I will.   I'll go there at once, for the first time, and I'll let them all know a piece of my mind—that's what I'll do.   Oh, dear! yes.   I fancy I see Mr. Atherton with his glass and his pipe, grinning and smiling like an old violin ; but I'll be down upon him.   It's a lucky thought.   I'll go to the Bull and Perriwinkle."

It was quite a mercy of Providence that Atherton was not that night at the Bull and Perriwinkle.   It was far better for him that he should be where he then was, among the gloomy passages leading to the vaults of St. Paul's, for Mrs. Atherton was just in that state of mind, when the piece of her mind which she intended to bestow upon him would have been a very large piece, indeed, and a piece anything but pleasant or satisfactory for him to know.

The Bull and Perriwinkle was not above three minutes' walk from the house of the cheesemonger, so that it was very easily accessible ; and although Mrs. Atherton had never been within the doors of that house of entertainment, she had frequently passed them.

The night was cold as well as dark, but the excitement of the lady's spirit prevented her from feeling the former state of things and from noticing the latter ; and as she walked with a quick step, she was at the door of the Bull and Perriwinkle in so short a time, that the distance from her own house to it appeared to be nothing at all.

"Now I have him," she muttered, as she lingered a moment on the threshold. "Now, I rather think I shall astonish you, Mr. Miles Atherton, and let you know that even a weak woman is not always like a worm, to be trampled on by a wretch."

With this sentiment she pushed open the swinging door of the tavern, and walked in.   It was just at that time of the evening when people who want anything from the public-house before it shuts up, feel the propriety of at once sending for it, or else they must go without ; so there were a number of persons at the bar with jugs and bottles, of all sorts and sizes.

This happened fortunately for Mrs. Atherton, for it prevented her from being

asked any troublesome questions as to who or what she might happen to want.
She looked about her till she saw upon a piece of ground glass, of an oval shape,
let into the upper panel of the door, the word "parlour." This was conclusive.
Behind that door was, no doubt, Miles Atherton, and a glow of satisfaction came
over the mind of his wife as she said to herself,—

"Now for it. I rather think I shall astonish you, Mr. Atherton."

She had an eye to effect, for she made one rush from where she stood right
into the parlour, exclaiming,—

"Now, you odious monster, what have you got to say for yourself?"

It so happened that there was an extremely little old man, who used to frequent the parlour of the Bull and Perriwinkle every night, and always occupy
the same seat, which was exactly opposite to the door; so that when Mrs.
Atherton bounced in so suddenly, she could not stop herself till she came within

an inch of the little old man's nose; and as he was about to say something,
he was so shocked at the sudden interruption, and the violent interrogatory that
accompanied it, that he went fairly over backwards, chair and all, with his pipe
in one hand, and a glass of brandy-and-water in the other, with as great a smash
as so small a personage could be expected to make.

Mrs. Atherton took as rapid a survey of the room as she could, considering the
amount of tobacco smoke that was in it; and not seeing her liege lord, she added,
in a loud tone,—

"Where is he?"

Some one thought she meant the little old man, and said,—

"Why, ma'am, you've knocked him over into the corner, grog and all. Don't
you see him, ma'am?"

"Murder!" said the little old man, in a faint voice. "This is my death!"

"She's mad," said one.

"Or drunk," said another.

He who made this ungracious remark happened to be sufficiently near to Mrs.
Atherton to feel the effects of her vengeance, for she lifted up a pint pot that was
within reach, and gave him such a topper on the head with it, that instead of the
two gas burners that were in the room, he saw a hundred at least, and felt confused for an hour afterwards.

"Pray, ma'am, what do you want?" said one, who was in a corner, and well protected by having a wide table before him.

"What do I want?   Miles Atherton, to be sure."

"Oh, he's not here."

"Not here?"

"No, he's not been here to-night, ma'am, I assure you."

"Don't deceive me.   It will be the worse for anybody who deceives me.   I'm his lawful wife, and if he deceives me by hiding anywhere, I'll have vengeance!"

"There's nowhere to hide here, ma'am, I can assure you.   He has not been here to-night, as you will find, if you ask at the bar.   They will tell you at once."

"Then where can he be?"

"Ah, that he knows himself; I am sure nobody here does, for it was proposed to send for him, as he was not here last night either, and we all thought something must be the matter with him."

Mrs. Atherton was a little staggered at the coolness of this speaker, and a strong impression that he was uttering neither more nor less than the exact truth came over her.   She was silent, and she looked about her for some moments rather discouraged, and a little ashamed of being where she was.

"Will you take a drop of anything, ma'am?" said one.

This produced a laugh, and as Mrs. Atherton felt convinced she could not combat with the whole room-full, and was sure that Miles Atherton was not there, she rather, on the whole, gave the matter up as a bad job, and she had the prudence at once to leave the room.

Before leaving the house, though, she took the advice which had been given her, and pausing a moment at the bar she said—

"Has Mr. Atherton been here to-night?"

"No," was the reply.

"Then he's gone to some other public-house, the villain!" exclaimed Mrs. Atherton, "on purpose that I should not find him out.   He knows I have often threatened to come to the Bull and Perriwinkle, and has gone, no doubt, now to the Sir Somebody's Head; but I'll be even with him,—I'll sit up all night, and when he does come home, I shall have the pleasure of telling him he shall not come in, and of throwing a jug of cold water over him."

With this hostile resolution Mrs. Atherton went home and knocked at her own door.

"Who's there?" said the servant.

"It's me."

Then the door opened, and Mrs. Atherton having ascertained that no one had been during her absence, retired to the back parlour, and having had the fire replenished, she dismissed Sarah for the second time to bed, and determined herself to sit up, on purpose, as she said, to have the pleasure of letting that wretch Atherton see that she was not going to let him in at all times of the night.

Whether, if the cheesemonger had come home, his better half would have persevered in her resolution of keeping him out of his own house or not, it is hard to say.   The probability is, that the lady would have relented, as ladies generally do in such cases, and have compromised the matter with a curtain lecture.

But the reader is aware that Miles Atherton did not come; and after waiting another half hour, Mrs. Atherton suddenly said—

"What's to hinder me reading the Black Lady's papers myself?   Nothing in the world.   Nothing in the world, that I know of.   Of course, nothing in the world, and I will too, and what is more I will put them away, and Miles shall not see them at all yet, for being such a wretch as to behave in the manner he has."

Armed with this resolution, she proceeded to where the packet had been placed, and taking it from the drawer, she lit another candle and resolving to dismiss all thoughts of the rebellious Miles Atherton, she opened what appeared to be the first part of the regular narrative, after the episode of so exciting a character which had been named "The Execution," and which had produced so much anxiety in her mind to know to what it referred.

It struck twelve precisely as Mrs. Atherton commenced the narrative of the Black Lady, which contained so much that was eminently qualified to produce a great amount of interest that we must not feel surprised that even the rebellious Mr. Miles Atherton was forgotten as she proceeded.

THE NARRATIVE OF THE BLACK LADY.—TIME, 1801.

In a small cottage house in the immediate neighbourhood of Epping Forest dwelt a mother and daughter. They were in reduced circumstances; but still, from the wreck of what ought to have been a handsome competence, there was enough left them for the necessaries of life. Its chiefest luxury they found in each other's love, for a more tenderly attached parent could not exist, and a daughter who so fully reciprocated a mother's affections could scarcely have been found.

The time is evening. It is in early spring; and the sweet crocus, with its varied hues, and the snowdrop were the only floral ornaments of the little garden in which they both took so much delight. The mother and daughter were sitting together by the cottage porch, around which the woodbine and clematis sweetly twined, and it would seem as if they had been talking of the past, for a tear was in the widow's eye, and the daughter had one of her mother's hands clasped in both her own, while the expression of her countenance betokened the tenderest sympathy.

The daughter was called The Rose of the Forest; she was esteemed beautiful— God of Heaven! what is she now?

"And so, my darling," said the mother, "it has become altered times with us, you see, since your poor father died. I can hear nothing, know nothing of the Indian speculation about which he was so sanguine that he allowed all he possessed to be converted into money to carry it on. He would often smile at my fears, and assure me that every pound would soon be doubled, and that we should have the pleasing perplexity of not knowing what to do with our money."

"Oh, mother," said the daughter, "this a subject which always makes you unhappy; say no more of it; we will be content where we are."

"But, my dear, it is for your sake that I am troubled. You know Mr. Simon Godfrey, your poor father's partner?"

Marian, for such was the name of the young girl, shuddered at the mention of this name, and her mother, regarding her with a look of anxiety, said—

"My dear child, why is it that the mention of Mr. Godfrey's name always appears to fill you with dismay?"

"Mother—mother, you know I do not like him."

"To be sure he is not the handsomest man in the world certainly, but then he appears to be blunt and honest."

"No—no—no."

"My dear, what can you know of business arrangements? He assures me— that is to say, he did assure me after your poor father's death—that he considered the Indian speculation a mere chimera of the imagination, and that it could not succeed. He declared he had urgently argued with your father about it, and that he, although his partner in other respects, held a deed of idemnity from any losses in that one adventure. He promised, though, that he would attend to it, and if anything came of it, he would make my interests his own."

"No doubt, mother. Perhaps he means by appropriating them to himself."

"Now, my dear, you are, I think, really severe. We have no reason, as you well know, to believe that Mr. Godfrey is other than a real friend, and——dear, who can that be? Was there ever such a ring?"

There had been so violent a pull at the bell handle, which was outside the garden gate, that it seemed as if the little cracked bell would never have done its monotonous tinkle, tinkle; and even when it seemed inclined to cease, whoever had given such an impetus, showed his or her impatience by ringing it again with such violence that put the wire to a severer test, probably, than it ever had since it was first placed in its situation.

The mother and daughter looked at each other in alarm, and yet they had not much to be alarmed about, while they could so look at each other at all, for they were alone almost in the world. What distant family connexions they had were far away in the country; but yet so violent an appeal to the bell was enough to frighten any one."

"I'll go, mother," said Marian, rising. "I'll go."

"No, my dear, let me, let me."

They both rose together to answer the loud summons for admission, and walked hastily along the circuitous gravelled path just as a third ring at the bell showed that whoever it was, was determined to persevere in the effort to obtain admission to the place.

There was yet light enough left to distinguish objects with tolerable distinctness, and through the lattice-work which composed the upper half of the door, the mother and daughter could perceive the figure of a man. The moment he espied them he rang again, and the mother, trembling with agitation, approached close to the lattice-work, and before she would open the door, she said,—

"What do you want? We do not know you."

"You—you are Mrs. Whitehead—I—I—believe," said the stranger, panting as he spoke, as if he had so completely lost breath, that it was the greatest effort in the world for him to speak.

"Yes," was the reply. "Yes."

"I—I—have—something to say. I am exhausted! Open—the—gate. Godfrey will be here."

"Good heavens, what has happened?"

Marian stepped forward, and opened the gate, saying,—

"Mother, this is a gentleman. He comes. perhaps, on some errand of great importance to us."

The stranger staggered through the entrance, and as the lattice-work was no longer between them and him, they were enabled to obtain a better view of him. He was a young and handsome man, his figure was tall, and finely proportioned, and the most remarkable feature in his face consisted of a pair of dark, large hazel eyes, which gave a great brilliancy and animation to his whole countenance. He was attired plainly, but there was a certain air of elegance about his apparel which at once bespoke the gentleman, let his pecuniary resources and present position in life be what they might.

As he came into the garden he exhibited the most unequivocal signs of extreme weakness and exhaustion. He was evidently fatigued to a great extent, and scarcely able to walk at all. His face was pale, and the perspiration stood upon his brow, as he looked from one to the other of the ladies, and said, in a faint voice,—

"Am I—am I in time?"

"In time! What's the matter? In time for what?"

The young man sank into a garden-chair with a deep sigh. It was quite evident that, somehow or another, he had over exerted himself dreadfully, and was now suffering the penalty of so doing in an unexampled amount of fatigue, which had completely prostrated all his faculties. He was unable to speak or to move for some minutes.

"He is dying," exclaimed Marian. "Oh! he is dying, mother."

The young stranger made a faint gesture of dissent as he contrived to gasp out the words, —

"Water—water."

Marian ran to the house, and fetched him a glass of cool, clear, filtered water, which she held to his lips. He drank off the refreshing liquid, and then with more strength he said,—

"God bless you—God bless you! I do not now regret that I have come so far, and at so desperate a speed. Oh! what agony would have been mine, had I

fallen ere I reached this spot. It is the last mile that has nearly killed me. But am I in time?—only tell me that!"

"He must be a little mad, my dear," whispered Mrs. Whitehead to her daughter. "Keep away from him; he must be a little mad."

"No, mother, no—oh! no."

"You do me no more than justice, Miss Whitehead," said the stranger, who had, to the mortification of Mrs. Whitehead, overheard her remark. "You do me no more than justice, miss. I am not mad: but exhaustion, and the anxiety of my feelings, have made me talk, I fear, incoherently. I wish to know if Mr. Godfrey has been here."

"Mr. Godfrey—Mr. Simon Godfrey?"

"Yes, yes—the same."

"We have not seen him for months."

"Then you will see him soon. Thank God! I am in time. He is even now on his road hither, and will be here now very shortly indeed. I am better now, and shall be able to tell you the purport of my visit. Will you permit me to walk into the house?"

"Yes, yes; most certainly," said Marian.

"But we do not know you, sir," suggested Mrs. Whitehead, with an appearance of hesitation.

"No, no—you do not. My name is Charles Ormond. I am a clerk to Mr. Godfrey. Do not, oh! do not despise or think lightly of the warning I now come to give you. It comes from my heart. In all ordinary matters I feel bound to do Mr. Godfrey such service as he may choose to demand of me; but this is not an ordinary matter, and the tie which binds me to him is at once broken, when he seeks to perpetrate an act of the greatest dishonesty and injustice."

"Mother, you hear this gentleman," said Marian. "He comes to do us an act of kindness; he comes to warn us of something which otherwise we should have known not of. Pray come in, sir. Nay, lean on my arm; I am strong enough to afford you some support."

"No, no," said the young stranger, "rather take my arm. Fatigue had for the moment overcome me, but I am much better now. I know not how to excuse myself for giving you so much alarm."

With much grace he offered his arm to Marian Whitehead, who, with a slightly heightened colour and a flutter at her heart which did not then, but which ought to have told her that the young, handsome stranger was far from being indifferent to her, accompanied him to the house.

The shades of evening were now coming on very rapidly indeed. It was just at that period of twilight when the last few rays of splendid sunshine appear to collect for the purpose of shining with as much brilliancy as possible, before they disappear for the night, and so sudden a darkness fell upon the face of nature now, that it had all the effect of some thick veil having been hung across the before partially light sky.

"How dark it has become," said Marian.

"And yet to me how light and beautiful," whispered the young man. "The heart makes its own sunshine."

Marian scarcely understood whether to take these words as complimentary or not, but yet they were uttered in a tone of so much tenderness, and accompanied by so soft and slight a pressure of the arm that was within his, that she could not doubt but Charles Ormond fully intended them to have some reference to the effect which her beauty had had upon him. She made no reply, but Mrs. Whitehead, who took care to keep close to them, and appeared rather fidgetty concerning the sudden way in which Marian and the young stranger had struck up an acquaintance, said,—

"Of course, sir, we are much indebted to you, if you come to give us any information of a serviceable nature; but, otherwise, we prefer the seclusion of our home to many visitors."

Marian thought this a most ungracious speech of her mother's, but she said nothing, for she could not very well take part with the stranger under such circumstances. He, without any anger, replied,—

"My appearance here, without some good and substantial errand, would be one of the most unjustifiable things in the world. I hope, by what I shall be able to tell you, thoroughly to acquit myself of such an imputation. I have scarcely relaxed speed all the way from London here. I could get no conveyance that was not far beyond my means, and, as I had an earnest desire to see you before the arrival of Mr. Godfrey, I ——"

At this moment, a loud, but not an impatient kind of ring at the bell of the garden gate caused the whole party to give a start of alarm. They were just within the porch of the house. It might be Mr. Godfrey, and whatever Charles Ormond had to say concerning him, in the shape of warning and advice, must now be said quickly, to be of any effect.

"If that is Mr. Godfrey, as doubtless it is, hear me for one moment before you admit him. He comes to offer you an annuity in addition to what you have of one hundred pounds per annum, upon condition that you assign over to him all right and title whatever to any expectations, near or remote, as regards the speculations of the late Mr. Whitehead. Do not do it. I implore you not to do it."

Another ring at the garden bell now warned them that whatever decision was come to, must be come to promptly, and while Mrs. Whitehead looked all amazement, Marian cried,—

"Mother, mother, there is truth in what this gentleman says. Refuse the offer of Simon Godfrey, if that be him at the gate."

"He must not see me," added Charles. "That would be to involve me in ruin, and to do no good to any one."

"But I am bewildered," said Mrs. Whitehead. "I am bewildered."

"Mother, mother, do not be so undecided! Take this gentleman somewhere where he can remain concealed till Mr. Godfrey is gone, while I open the gate. Do you not understand, mother?—he comes to do us a service, and it would be his ruin to be seen here."

Mrs. Whitehead seemed now suddenly to awaken from the kind of lethargy into which she had fallen by this sudden interruption to the even tenor of the life she and her daughter led in that quiet cottage home, and she exclaimed,—

"Heaven forbid that any one should come to injury by an attempt to do us service. Marian, my dear, take the gentleman into the house, and I will go to the gate."

There was no time to say anything for or against this arrangement, for a third ring at the bell, and this time a decidedly impatient one, warned them that it must be acted upon immediately. Marian at once led Charles Ormond into the house, while Mrs. Whitehead went to the gate to admit Mr. Godfrey, if indeed it should be that personage, who desired admittance.

The interior of the cottage was very dark indeed, but Marian was so well acquainted with every nook and corner of the little abode that she was able, with great celerity, to procure a light, and then, as she glanced round the room in which they were, she said,—

"I know not, unless you take this light and go to one of the rooms above, where to place you."

"Let me get behind that screen," said Charles Ormond, as he pointed to a large screen which filled up a corner of the little room. "I shall be better able when Mr. Godfrey has gone to give you good advice, if I am permitted to overhear what he shall say to you."

"Quick, quick, then," said Marian. "There is not another moment to be lost. I hear approaching footsteps on the garden path. Be quick, be quick!"

Charles Ormond heard the footsteps likewise, and in another moment he got behind the screen, where he certainly was completely hidden from all observation. Marian was much agitated, and as she sat down to the table and took up a piece of unfinished work, her hands trembled to that degree, that any one could have seen that something of the most anxious nature was upon her mind.

The footsteps now upon the gravel path just outside the door of the cottage could be heard quite plainly, and Charles Ormond said, in a whisper,—

"Dear Miss Whitehead, do not, I implore you, permit your mother to sign any paper which Godfrey may bring."

"No, no, no!" said Marian. "Hush, for Heaven's sake! Hush!"

In the meantime Mrs. Whitehead had gone to the gate, which, however, she did not reach until a fourth ring at the bell showed that whoever the visitor was, he was persevering, and not inclined to be put off by not being immediately answered by the inmates of the cottage. It was manifestly too dark for Mrs. Whitehead to see through the lattice of the upper part of the door who was there, so she said, when she reached it,—

"Pray what do you want?"

"My dear madam," said a rough voice, which was evidently endeavoured to be modified to soft and courteous tones, "my dear madam, you will, perhaps, recognise me by my voice, although you may fail to do so by seeing me, in consequence of the small portion of light that is left."

"Mr. Godfrey, I believe."

"At your service, Mrs. Whitehead. I am Mr. Godfrey. It is pleasant to find that even one's voice is known to those whom we esteem. My dear madam, may I solicit the favour of a few moments' conversation with you and your amiable and charming daughter. Oh, Mrs. Whitehead, I have always said that one of the most remarkable likenesses between any two persons that could be, was between you and Miss Marian. My dear madam, you seem to have a great difficulty with the lock of this gate."

"Yes, sir," said Mrs. Whitehead, who was purposely delaying time in order that Marian might be enabled to place Charles Ormond somewhere where he could not be seen by Godfrey. "Yes, sir; it is a troublesome lock."

"Indeed, it seems so;" then turning from the gate a moment, Godfrey addressed some one who was with him, saying,—"John Dorey, you need not go away. You can keep the horses here; I shall not be long."

"Sha'n't you," growled a voice in reply. "You'll find me at the public-house we passed at the end of the lane. I'm not going to stay here in the cold."

"A very faithful servant that," remarked Mr. Godfrey, as he passed through the now open door way, "but somewhat rough and rude in speech. It would be in vain to teach John Dorey politeness. It is contrary to his nature."

"Indeed, sir."

"Yes, madam; and now may I indulge in the flattering hope that you and your charming daughter are both well?"

"We are very well, I thank you, Mr. Godfrey. Pray stoop, sir, or you will knock your head against the branches of this tree."

"D——n!" said Godfrey, as at that moment he did give his head a hard blow against one of the branches; but he recovered his equanimity in a moment, as he said, in the same affected bland tones he had before used, "My dear madam, I beg to suggest that you should allow these trees to be lopped of their lower branches. This cottage and garden I know is quite a little paradise, but still it has its inconveniences if people have their heads nearly knocked off at its entrance. I thought, madam, you had some visitor, as I heard voices when I first reached the gate."

"I was talking to Marian," said Mrs. Whitehead.

"Oh, I believe you have already assured me she is well. Really, what a pleasant place this is, and what a wonderful relief it is to come here, after being shut up in the close, murky atmosphere of London. It's quite a delight. The very air, although the spring is yet so young, is fragrant and refreshing. I often think, madam, that the country is favourable to virtue, for we behold around us the sweet serenity of nature, where no jarring elements are found. Who could, in such a sweet little spot as this, contemplate doing anything wrong?"

"I hope nobody will," said Mrs. Whitehead.

"Amen, madam. Most emphatically do I say amen to that aspiration," replied Mr. Godfrey. "I hope and trust nobody ever will."

They had now reached the cottage porch, and, in another moment, Godfrey made his appearance in the little parlour, where Marian sat with the light.

Marian rose, and curtseyed distantly to Godfrey, and now that he has come into the light, we may as well state what sort of person he was.

Simon Godfrey was of unusual height, but dreadfully ungainly with it. He looked as if he had been composed of odds and ends culled from a crowded churchyard. His countenance was harsh and repulsive in the extreme. Although a man not above forty years of age, he was quite bald on the top of his head, and there was a remarkable peculiarity about two of his front teeth, which, when he closed his mouth, rested over his under lip, and gave him a most strange and inhuman aspect.

Such was the man who, with a hideous smile, which, no doubt, he intended to be quite fascinating, advanced to Miss Whitehead, and insisted upon shaking her warmly by the hand, and complimenting her upon her looks, while she trembled, and turned pale, and flushed by turns, as she thought of the possible consequences of some awkward accident discovering the young stranger behind the screen.

"Pray be seated, sir," said Mrs. Whitehead, as she handed Mr. Godfrey a chair. "Pray, sir, sit down, if you please."

"Thank you, madam—thank you. I dare say that you are somewhat anxious to know the object of this visit, and as I dislike suspense as much as any one can, and think it the cruellest state of mind in which any human being can be left, I shall proceed at once to state why it is that I have intruded upon your privacy."

Mr. Godfrey paused, and looked from one to the other, as if he expected some reply, so Mrs. Whitehead said,—

"As my late husband's partner, sir, we are quite sure, whatever you come upon, it is for our benefit."

"Madam, you do me honour; at the same time you do me no more than justice. What I have to propose is for your benefit, and for the benefit of your accomplished and, permit me to say, lovely daughter. When I come to consider how great must be the change in your circumstances, induced by the death of the lamented Mr. Whitehead, my heart is much grieved. It is a melancholy fact, that he had nearly withdrawn the whole of his capital from the concern before his death, in order to embark in some wild speculations of his own, which no one can regret more than I do. Taking, however, all this into consideration, and upon what a small income you have retired, and likewise that you are the innocent sufferers from Mr. Whitehead's imprudent speculations, I have determined upon settling upon you, out of the profits of the business, the additional sum of one hundred pounds per annum."

Mr. Godfrey glanced from one to the other of the ladies, as if he wished to see what effect this statement had upon them, and no doubt he was a little disappointed when Marian said,—

"Sir, we have learned to be content with what we have. It is certainly little, but we have now got used to a change of life, which at first had its pangs, but which now we find has its pleasures."

"That is true," said Mrs. Whitehead, "and well spoken, my dear."

"But, really," said Mr. Godfrey, with an incredulous smile, as he spread out his hands;—"really, ladies, you will permit me to say, that an additional hundred pounds per annum is seldom considered to detract from any one's comforts or means of contentment."

"And yet we can do very well without it," said Marian.

"Very well, my dear young lady," added Godfrey; "but still you may do better with it, you know. I am sure you and your excellent mother are sufficiently well versed in the secrets of the human heart to know that nothing can be much more grievous to any one than the having a generous intention frustrated."

"But we feel that we ought not, at your cost, increase our income," said Mrs. Whitehead; "while, at the same time, we feel how very generous it is of you to offer it."

"Certainly," added Marian; "we thank you, and respectfully decline."

"Come, come," said Mr. Godfrey, as he, laughingly, and with a great swinging of his ugly head to and fro, took from his pocket a prepared legal instrument; "come, come, this is coquetting with fortune and despising her gifts. You will sign this paper, which will secure to you the annuity I have mentioned in a legal way. Some of your honest neighbours can be called in to witness it. It will be a great satisfaction to me to have paid such a mark of respect to the memory of my late most esteemed, but a little imprudent, partner, Mr. Whitehead. Pens and ink, my dear madam, and we shall soon settle this little piece of business, which will make you a hundred a-year the richer and me none the poorer, for I shall not miss the amount. Miss Marian, will you oblige me by calling in two neighbours to witness this deed, and then all will be well?"

Neither the mother or daughter stirred, although Godfrey had acted his part well, and no doubt, if they had not been forewarned, would have carried his point. As it was, however, the more anxiety he displayed for the signing of the deed he had now spread out upon the table, the more they felt inclined to believe that what Charles Ormond, little as they knew of him, had said was the truth, and the less did they relish the idea of signing to anything produced by Mr. Godfrey.

Still it was rather an ungracious position to be placed in to refuse such a seeming act of generosity. But Marian was quite resolved that her mother should sign nothing that night, so she said firmly,—

" Mr. Godfrey, you must be content with our thanks for your intentions, but we cannot accept your offer."

" Cannot accept !" he repeated, with surprise.

" No," said Mrs. Whitehead; " we have habituated ourselves to be content with what we have, sir, and we beg to decline."

" Decline !"

" Yes," they both said together, " yes, we decline."

" Well, of all the extraordinary romances in a man's life that was ever heard of, this transcends them," said Godfrey. " Here are two people, with an income of about eighty pounds a year, refusing to add, merely by signing their names, another hundred to it."

" Yes, we decline."

" Come, come. I can appreciate the delicacy which induces you to decline. I can appreciate the pride of independence which induces you to fancy that, by accepting this from me, you are my debtor to a certain extent; but I pray you to dismiss from your minds all such fancies."

" We beg to decline."

" Can you do nothing," said Godfrey, " but reiterate these words? Have you no reason whatever to urge?"

" Surely, sir," said Marian, as she saw that her mother hesitated, and knew not what reply to make to him, " surely, sir, we need scarcely, after refusing such an offer as this, be compelled to go at length into our reasons. If we suffer in your mind the penalty of being thought foolish, we are content to do so."

" Do you mean to tell me," said Godfrey, and a dark shade passed over his face as he spoke, " that you will not?"

" If, sir," said Marian, " you will not be satisfied with a determination expressed otherwise than in these ungracious words, we shall be compelled to use them, and to say at once, and most explicitly, that we will not."

There was now a dead silence of some moments' duration, and then Godfrey turned to Mrs. Whitehead, and said,—

" You are silent, madam."

" I can but affirm what Marian says," she replied; " I consult her wishes in all things, Mr. Godfrey."

He doubled up the deed hastily, as he cast a withering glance at Marian. Then, rising to his full height, he said, in so different a voice to that in which he had been speaking, that no one could for a moment have supposed it came from the same lips,—

" D——n! I see it all now. You have been tampered with by some infernal scoundrel—I am certain of it. You don't convince me that people will refuse a hundred a-year without some special reason."

" Perhaps," said Marian, calmly, " we do not believe that people will offer others a hundred a-year without some special reason."

Godfrey turned a petrifying glance at her, as he said,—

" Indeed ! Now you have convinced me that some one has been and raised in your minds expectations which you shall find futile—I thought as much from the first. Beggars you now are, and beggars you will remain, because you foolishly refuse to sign a simple document to produce you a large addition to your income."

" But, Mr. Godfrey," said Marian, " cannot you carry out your generous intentions of bestowing upon us one hundred pounds per annum, by just giving so much money to us at what period you please, without there being any necessity for legal documents on the occasion?"

" Oh, indeed !" said Godfrey, furiously; " you don't object to the hundred a-year, but you are afraid you may be committing yourselves by signing this paper. Now, hark ye, some one has been here: he must be one of a very few, and I shall find no difficulty whatever in discovering who it is. Let him dread my vengeance

I am not a man whose promise in such matters is to be despised, I can tell you, and I have promised him, be he whom he may, a fate at which he may well shudder when it shall, in all its horrors, come upon him. I swear it, I will have a most ample revenge."

"Revenge for what?" said Marian. "Good God! Mr. Godfrey, what revenge can you require because we refuse to take from you one hundred pounds per annum? If you are angry with any one on that score, let it be with us, for we are the parties who have refused you."

"I am terrified," exclaimed Mrs. Whitehead. "Oh! Mr. Godfrey, recall your words."

"And you will sign the paper?" said Godfrey, dropping his voice suddenly from a high angry tone to one of great softness.

"No, mother, no," cried Marian; "make no such disgraceful compromise. You will sign no paper."

"And you are the prime mover in all this," said Godfrey, turning abruptly to her. "So young, too, and so sharp. D—n me if I think you will live long."

"Do you threaten me?"

"Yes, I do."

"Oh! have mercy upon us," cried Mrs. Whitehead.

"Hush, mother, hush!" said Marian. "This man dare threaten females, but he dare not attempt to put his threats into execution. The same cowardice which dictates the threat will stay its execution. Let him say what he will, I am not afraid."

"Are you not?"

"As Heaven is my judge, I am not."

Although Marian spoke so confidently, yet she trembled very much while she did so, but it was not for herself. The terrible threats of vengeance against whoever had told her and her mother not to sign the deed conveying to them the annuity, rung in her ears; and as she knew against whom they were likely to be carried into effect, it was for his sake that she trembled and felt pangs of alarm, which she would not for worlds have confessed to Godfrey. To say that Marian Whitehead loved Charles Ormond already, would be, perhaps, to go too far, notwithstanding love is indeed a flower of rapid growth; but that he had succeeded in establishing an interest in her heart which time nor circumstances could not ever efface, we can state.

Godfrey, for some moments, was now silent. He seemed to be revolving in his own mind what it was possible for him to say or do next. Then he subdued his tone as he said—

"Once again I ask you to sign this deed, Mrs. Whitehead, and I will forget and forgive the little angry scene which has passed."

"No, no—I dare not now; I cannot—I cannot."

"You will not. Well, and now Marian Whitehead, if it were not that I could do so with so much ease that it is not worth my while, I would knock that d——d namby-pamby looking head of yours off."

As he spoke, he advanced a step towards her, as if he really meant to carry this threat into execution; and she, in the moment of alarm which such a movement gave her, screamed aloud.

It might be that Charles Ormond intended to confront Godfrey before he left; but it is more probable that the scream of Marian deprived him of all prudence and caution as regarded himself, for, at the instant, he closed up one of the leaves of the screen behind which he was concealed, and, with one stride, placed himself between Godfrey and the terrified girl.

So sudden and utterly unexpected to Godfrey was this movement, that he started back as if an apparition had confronted him, nor stopped until he was compelled to do so by coming into contact with the wall of the apartment. A scream of dismay came from the lips of Mrs. Whitehead, and Marian grasped one of the hands of Charles Ormond, for she had been thoroughly convinced that Godfrey really intended some violence towards her.

Charles did not speak first, but he fixed his sparkling eyes upon the countenance of Godfrey so sternly, that, after a vain attempt to return the steady, unflinching glance, the villain cowered before him, and said, in a low, growling tone,—

"So, sir—so, sir, it is you, is it, who have played me this scurvy trick. It is you, my confidential clerk, who have acted the character of traitor so well. It is you, Charles Ormond."

"Traitor in your teeth!" said Charles, in a tone of indignation that rung through the cottage; "traitor in your teeth! Dare such a man as you, who came here to betray, under the guise of generosity, those who, but for me, would have trusted you, use such a word to me? Godfrey, I have unmasked your villany and defeated you. You know it, and you feel it. Do your best and your worst—I glory in what I have done, and now, if you so much as lift a finger menacingly against this young girl, look to yourself, for I will strike you to the ground."

"Oh, of course," said Godfrey; "oh, of course. The bully could not be far off, or this pert, forward girl would not have been so bold. I expected some one was near at hand, but I will confess I did not expect you, Charles Ormond. 'Tis well—'tis well. Very well—look to it."

"I despise your threats as much as I do yourself," said Charles. "I always thought you a trickster, but I never thought you the villain you have shown yourself to-night."

"Indeed!"

"Indeed, no. Mrs. Whitehead, the Indian speculations of your deceased husband have realised twenty thousand pounds. The object of Simon Godfrey was to get you to sign a deed, making it all over to him, on consideration of an annuity of one hundred pounds per annum. He is defeated, and now you see how the shallow trickster grinds his teeth with impotent rage."

"Yes," said Godfrey, "I am defeated. Enjoy yourselves while you may. I give you joy of exchanging one trickster for another. Mrs Whitehead, this young man saw in this occurrence a good chance of making a famous match. He will now do the tender to your daughter, and, perhaps, before you encourage him too far, it will be as well to tell you that he is a penniless, nameless bastard. Ha! ha! Charles certainly he was christened, and Ormond he was named, because he was picked up when an infant in Ormond-street. I give you joy of him. Some footman's bastard, scoured by the kitchen wench, his mother, and so set out upon a door-step to take his fate. Ha! ha! I wish you all joy—a great deal of joy; and, in the meantime, Simon Godfrey may turn over in his mind some means by which he may have the laugh on his side."

There can be no doubt but that Charles Ormond would have made a rush upon Godfrey, and there would have been a personal conflict between them, but for Marian, who, dreading the consequences, threw her arms around Charles, and held him with a firmer grasp than a giant could have done, because it was one he could not shake off for fear of hurting her.

"You owe your safety," he said, "to this lady, Godfrey."

"Charles Ormond, heed not what he says," said Marian, "heed not what he says. He speaks savagely from disappointed malice. You are far above his reproaches. Heed them not, oh, heed them not."

"Very good," said Godfrey, as he clapped his hands applaudingly; "very good—very good. You had better hold him very tight."

"Leave this house, sir," said Mrs. Whitehead; "leave us, sir; we desire never to see your face again."

"Dear me, don't you, indeed? Well, well, I am inclined to believe that you will on some other occasion, although, perhaps, on not so interesting an one as this. My dear Miss Whitehead, you may make much of the adventurer you are so ready to take to your arms—the bastard. Ha! ha! Oh, you will have a most decided offer from him soon. The cause of the offer is all as plain now as a child's primer, and I must say he has played his cards well, always considering that he is a young hand."

"Marian Whitehead," said Charles, while a flush of shame pervaded his

bravo! and now, good folks, I will leave you to yourselves, and you can arrange all your little affairs comfortably, no doubt. But remember—always, I say, remember that there is such a person in the world as Simon Godfrey, because all landscapes require a shadow, and you will see the shadow to yours. Mark me, I threaten nothing—mind, nothing; I only wish you joy, that's all, and I wish you may get it."

He snatched up his hat that was upon a side table, and dashed out of the cottage. They heard his hasty footsteps as he proceeded down the gravelled path, and then they heard a loud crash—he had with one kick demolished the garden-gate, and striding over its ruins he sought the public-house where 'John Dorey had so graciously promised to wait for him with the horses.

cheeks, " need I say that this man wrongs me? God and my own conscience will acquit me of the design he imputes to me. I—I ——"

" Go on—go on," said Godfrey.

" I am what he says—a foundling. I will see you rid of him from this house, and then take my leave of you for ever."

" No," said Marian, " you will not—you shall not. For us you have sacrificed the position you held—let it be the pride and the pleasure of my mother and myself to place you in a far higher one."

" No—no—no."

" Ha, ha! How coy he is. What a pretty paraphrase of Venus and Adonis," exclaimed Godfrey. " Bravo!

When he was fairly gone, Maria released her hold of Charles Ormond, and dropping her head upon her hands, she burst into tears, while her mother looked like some one newly awakened from a dream, so confounded was she by all that had occurred.

Charles Ormond was perplexed. He evidently knew not what to do or say for some minutes, but then a sudden impulse seized him, and taking up his hat, which had fallen on the floor close to the screen, he said,—

" Farewell. God bless you, and may you be happy in the new position in life to which your extended means will now call you. Any respectable solicitor will place you in the way of recovering possession of the late Mr. Whitehead's Indian property. God bless you—farewell."

He had reached the door of the cottage, when Maria sprung after him, and held him by the arm, saying,—

" No, no. Can you think us such monsters of ingratitude that we would let you go thus ? Mother—mother, why don't you speak ? It is your silence which induces our preserver to think us so cold-hearted and ungrateful. Mother, why do not you speak to this gentleman ?"

Thus urged, Mrs. Whitehead immediately responded to the call.

" You must not leave us, sir," she said. " What would have become of us but for you ? Heaven knows what that dreadful Mr. Godfrey might not now attempt if he thought we were alone. Send some messenger to your friends, and remain here, let me beg of you."

" Friends !" ejaculated Charles, mournfully ; " alas ! I have none. You heard from the unfriendly lips of Godfrey what I was."

" Then as you have been a friend to us," said Maria, " when we had no other, we will be friends to you. Years of acquaintance could not have made us more known to each other than have the events of this night."

" No, no, no—I cannot."

" I implore you to stay."

" What ! and lie under the imputation which Godfrey has thrown out against me of being a scheming adventurer—a calculator upon the amount I can gain from having done you this service ?—no, no."

" Then leave us if you will to the machinations of a man who will scruple at nothing to be revenged. Mr. Ormond, I did not think that, because your enemy has said that which was untrue of you, you would desert your friends, who put no faith in the scandalous imputation. Desert us, sir, at once, if you please."

" No," cried Charles Ormond ; " no, may Heaven desert me if I do. I am your slave for ever. Direct me how you will, command me how you please. I will live but to stand between you and all harm."

CHAPTER IX.

MRS. ATHERTON'S VISITOR AND THE TEMPTING OFFER.—THE RICHES OF THE
DEEP AND THE TREASURE IN THE STRAITS OF MOSAMBIQUE.

MRS. ATHERTON had got thus far into the perusal of the interesting documents which had come under her observation, and had nearly forgotten the very existence of her husband in the excitement and interest that the narrative had afforded her, when the tingle of the shop-bell struck upon her ears.

" Atherton," she exclaimed, " as I am a sinner, and a pretty hour of the night, or rather in the morning, I should say, to come home to his lawful wife. Oh, I'll let him know that I am not a worm to be continually trampled upon. I am not his slave, nor his horse, nor his—ahem ! nor anything that is his. There, he's ringing again. I thought I had got him over all that sort of thing ever since I had set my face against free-and-easies."

The ring now ensued for the third time, and a little more loud than on the previous occasions, which seemed to imply that whoever was demanding admittance had some eventual limit to his patience.

"Oh, you may ring," exclaimed Mrs. Atherton ; " I am not going to be what some wives are, a miserable wretch without a will of my own. I'll let you know, Mr. Miles Atherton, that I am a female, and intend behaving as such. Ah ! you may ring—you may ring till you are black in the face, Mr. Atherton, but you don't hurry me."

How ringing at a bell could produce the singular physiological phenomenon of blackness in the face, Mrs. Atherton did not stop to inquire, but, taking in her hand a small saucepan which had been placed in the fender for the purpose of warming beer, or any other strong compound which might at that inclement season of the year be required for the purpose of aiding, abetting, or comforting the physical energies, she, with as stately a movement as she could well command, took her way towards the door, which she reached just as the visitor, whoever he was, had made up his mind to keep on perpetually ringing so long as the door presented one even surface to his face.

"Oh, indeed," said Mrs. Atherton, " now you are beginning to show your vile temper, are you ? I knew you would, Mr. Atherton. I am not a witch, but still I knew you would ; but I'll let you know a suffering woman, and a lawful married woman, who can produce her certificate to the eyes of the whole world, is not to be trampled upon like a Russian or gallus slave. Ring away."

This last injunction was a work of supererogation, for the bell had never ceased for the last two or three minutes ; and now Mrs. Atherton, with that increased flush upon her face, which indicated mischief, laid her hand upon the lock, flung the door wide open, and with one vigorous blow of the saucepan, nearly knocked down the intruder.

Now it had never occurred to Mrs. Atherton, that by some remote possibility this might not be Mr. Miles Atherton at all, but a perfectly legal and constitutional visit from some one else who ought not by any means to have been saluted by the black bottom of a saucepan being placed forcibly against the bridge of his nose.

"Oh, gracious !" exclaimed Mrs. Atherton, when she saw the individual was not her husband.

With the exclamation, Mrs. Atherton started back a pace or two. This movement gave the stranger free liberty of ingress, a liberty of which he was by no means slow of availing himself, for he stepped at once into the shop, and with considerable dexterity bolted the door, and placed a bar across it as if he had been in the habit of doing so for years.

"Murder !" exclaimed Mrs. Atherton, for in the person of the stranger she recognized him whom she had so vehemently made acquainted with the merits of the red-hot poker on a foggy night on lord mayor's day. She would have given her life for one half of the smallest pin, she afterwards declared. She felt that she was a lone woman, with the exception of Maria, the servant girl, who had gone to bed long ago.

"Do not be alarmed," said the man, as he showed her from his breast-pocket the blade of a long glittering knife ; " do not be alarmed ; I am not what I seem, but if it be necessary for my own safety, or if my humour jump that way, I will make this knife acquainted with your inside, madam."

Mrs. Atherton staggered back amongst some Dutch cheeses, and very nearly fell as she gasping said,—

" Is it my virtue, my money, or my life you come after ?"

" Neither," said the man. " What is your life to me? Money I have, and as for your virtue—ah ! ah ! you'll find few bidders for that commodity."

" I can tell you," exclaimed Mrs. Atherton, " you insulting vagabond, that for all you say ——"

" Psha," said the man ; " this is idle, and my time's precious. I have come here to speak seriously to you, madam—very seriously. You think me a rough fellow, and I am, sometimes ; but I have a heart, notwithstanding ; I can feel for those who have a claim upon my sympathy—and, first of all, do I feel for my poor deranged sister, the Black Lady."

"But she says she's not your sister at all."

"Ah, but she is, though."

"But she called you Neville, and her own name is Whitehead; so, my good man, as I don't want any argifying with you, just go away. I wonder at your impudence, I do."

"You have not heard me out. Have you a light in the back parlour?" said the stranger.

"And pray, sir, what's that to you? If you think I am alone here, sir, you are very much mistaken; my husband's in the house, and there's Jim, our boy, besides two strong men in the first-floor, so you'd better be off."

"Your husband's not at home," said Neville; "Jim is with him, the first-floor is vacant and to let, and your servant girl has gone out unknown to you to meet the baker's man, her sweetheart."

"The hussey!" shrieked Mrs. Atherton, "if I didn't suspect it, for ever so long; I always thought she went out after we went to bed."

"Then you thought right; and now, Mrs. Atherton, as you and I are here alone, I think we must strike a bargain; and I can produce reasons which may induce you to consent to my taking my sister from beneath your roof the next time she comes here. She's mad, I tell you, but I don't want to make any fuss about it; I want some day to pop her quietly into a coach, and take her away where she will be well provided for, poor thing, and not suffered in all weathers to go about the streets, as she does, subject to the stare of vulgar curiosity, and sometimes practical insults of the ignorant. You are a woman, a fine woman, and a feeling woman. You can appreciate my feelings, and I only wish you had married some man who would have placed you in the situation of lady mayoress, which you so eminently deserve."

"That is neither here nor there," said Mrs. Atherton. "Being a fine woman is nature; people aint blind; but, as to being lord mayor, Miles Atherton hasn't the ambition, the sneaking wretch."

"Ah," said Neville, as he produced a small square box from his pocket, "how well these gems would become you—this necklace, of orient pearls, these bracelets, studded with the finest gems of Golconda, and these earrings, each of which is worth the dowry of a princess."

As he spoke he exhibited to the dazzled eyes of Mrs. Atherton the contents of the box, which, to all appearance, consisted of the articles he had mentioned. Closing it then abruptly, he replaced it in his pocket, exclaiming,—

"What is wealth to me? What to me are these costly jewels? Literally nothing. But, in your possession, Mrs. Atherton, they would find some legitimate use; aid me to gain possession of my sister, either with or without your husband's knowledge, as your own discretion may see fit, and this box, with its precious contents, is yours."

"No, no," said Mrs. Atherton; "I can't—I can't do that; besides, who knows——"

"Psha, you are wonderfully scrupulous, madam. Why, there is not a lady of the court who would not envy you the possession of these gems, and all I ask of you as the price of them, is your assistance in placing my poor mad sister in my power; I believe this is the only threshold in London she will now cross. The next time you see her, make some appointment with her, on any pretence you like—let it be after dark. You can apprise me of it, and all can be managed satisfactorily. In which case the jewels shall be yours."

Mrs. Atherton hesitated.

"If I were quite sure," she said, "that she was your sister, I wouldn't so much mind."

"That she is, you may be assured. There was a time when wealth for me had many allurements, but now it has none, and I am content with just sufficient to keep me above the pressure of want. You would hardly believe this possible, Mrs. Atherton, from a man who knows, as I do, where two millions and a half of money lie hidden."

"What !" exclaimed the lady.

"I repeat it, deliberately, that two million and a half are in the straits of Mosambique."

"The straits of Moses's beak. Somewhere in the Minories, I suppose."

"No, madam; I allude to the coast of Africa. I have not the slightest objection to give you the particulars after my sister is in my hands, and you can then charter a vessel to fetch it away. Only consider, then, Mrs. Atherton, what a position in life you would be in. Reflect, for a moment, upon the gorgeous equipages."

"Yes, yes," said Mrs. Atherton; " and the cream-coloured horses !"

"And the out-riders !"

"And the dresses !"

"Ay, the liveries, the wines, the feasts, and the dances !"

"Yes, and the beds of down, with the satin coverlets !"

"The drawing-rooms at the palace, the royal assemblies ——"

"Yes, and the mansion."

"Ah, to be sure, the mansion !"

"Oh, dear me, what a wista—what a wista opens to my eyes—I see it all. Two million-and-a-half! We'll part with the cheese business, and we'll discharge every servant who so much as mentions backan. We'll take a grand tower on the continent, and get put into the fashionable arrivals everywhere. I'll have a box at the Opera, and Mrs. Atherton's carriage shall continually stop the way. My house slippers shall be white satin."

"Right," said Neville. " Now, indeed, madam, do I perceive that in you I have met with a congenial spirit. Now do I perceive, well and truly, that wealth will not be ill bestowed. Mrs. Atherton, we understand each other."

"Yes, yes, yes."

"And you will assist me in the manner which I have mentioned to you."

"Yes, certainly."

"I will call again when no one is in the house but yourself, and we will talk it over; in the meantime, take this precious emerald as an earnest of what is to come. Dream of the future, and let your dreams depict grandeur. You can have a house built, the flooring of which can be of cedar."

"Yes, yes, yes, I can; and the people who can look at me, will say, they never seed her equal."

"Precisely."

"Oh, I feels all over in quite a flustration. How little the shop looks. Oh, the city! Oh, who can live in the odious city? the west end and the court for me. My dresses shall not be trimmed with lace, they shall be lace itself; and the newspapers shall be continually describing how I looked, and how I moved, and when I took an airing. We don't know what we are born to, or what we may come to. What a world it is—I may be a countess yet."

"A duchess !" exclaimed Neville.

"A duchess ! I think I shall faint."

"Farewell ; I will leave you to reflect. Think over these matters at [your own convenience."

He now left the place abruptly; and there stood poor Mrs. Atherton in such a state of amazement and exultation, as would have afforded a most ludicrous picture to behold. In her outstretched hand reposed the bright green stone which had been given her by Neville, and as she gazed upon it, it seemed to be a confirmation of all the glory and magnificence which had been depicted to her by her mysterious visitor.

"A duchess !" she whispered to herself; " I, a duchess ! with a coronet resting upon my brow, continually basking, as the newspapers say, in the smiles of royalty, and wallowing in gold dust. A duchess ! What will the noodles round the corner say, and that odious family of the Tuckses, that think themselves so fine. I think

I see them when the duchess's carriage dashes mud in their eye. My best plan will be to give Miles Atherton a small pension, and let him go to New South Zealand, or what's the place—Van Somebody's Land, when I'm a duchess. Oh, I'll let them see what I was born to. Make way for the duchess!"

Bang came a heavy knock upon the private door. It seemed to recall Mrs. Atherton back to the world she had forgotten. She sat down upon the butter-tub with a deep sigh, as she said, despondingly,—

" But it's all to come yet, and till it does I am but Mrs. Atherton, the cheese-monger's wife."

It was, indeed, a delightful train of reflection into which Mrs. Atherton had now fallen. The strange man who had held out to her such golden promises, had for the time completely got possession of her imagination, and it was a good thing for the poor Black Lady, that Mrs. Atherton had not an immediate opportunity of surrendering herself to him who chose to call himself her brother.

" I should think it was all a dream," said Mrs. Atherton to herself; " if it wasn't for this emerald he has left me. I really should think it was nothing but a dream; but here's the emerald, and there's no getting over that any way. What shall I do? I wish Mr. Atherton was at home—no I don't—he'd be making half-a-dozen silly objections about the matter, I have no doubt. Let me think—perhaps if I go on reading the Black Lady's papers, who knows but I may really find out that this man Neville is her brother, and so I shall have nothing in the world to reproach myself with on that account. I mean as to giving her up to him, which I dare say, after all, would be the best possible thing that could happen to her. I wonder where that wretch Atherton can be. Here's a pretty hour of the night; but never mind,—never mind ; I will go on reading the papers, and there's one thing I'll do ; whatever of them I read while he is not here, I'll place on one side, so that he shall not be able to see them or find them, and he will have the satisfaction of losing completely the thread of the story, while I know all about it."

Mrs. Atherton having come to this determination, resumed the perusal of the papers.

———

CHAPTER X.

THE FIRE AT THE COTTAGE.—THE HEROIC CONDUCT OF THE YOUNG CLERK.

Although the young clerk had made some natural hesitation about accepting the invitation of his new friends to remain at the cottage, there can be no doubt in the world that it was one of the most delightful things that could, by any possibility, have happened to him.

The strong sense of rectitude which had brought him to the cottage of the White-heads, was a feeling totally apart from the new and delightful one which had, since his visit to that place, taken possession of his heart; at almost the first sound of Marian Whitehead's voice, at almost the first glance of her eyes, he could have said, " it is my fate to love you," and he felt in the inmost recesses of his heart, let time bring about what revolutions it might of circumstance or fortune, she would ever continue the loved object of his fondest solicitude.

And yet he had hesitated to accept of the invitation to remain, until it had assumed to his mind the irresistible shape of a command. But having once consented, and with a feeling of which we might call an utter abandonment of care, he gave himself up to the delight of the society of her who had so suddenly, as it were, become a portion of his very existence.

Never until that time had he felt the exuberant flow of spirits which imparted eloquence to every word he uttered ; his eyes sparkled with joy, and his countenance became so animated, that as he caught a glimpse of it himself in a little mirror that hung in the cottage parlour, he was surprised at the alteration in his own appearance, and could scarcely refrain from an exclamation concerning it.

" Have you been long in the service of Mr. Godfrey?" said Mrs. Whitehead.

" I have not, madam," said young Ormond, " and from the character of the man, for I had heard something of him, I from the first had entertained a strong dislike to entering into his employment at all; but necessity compelled me to be doing something, and although, while in the service of such a man, I might unconsciously aid in the perpetration of injustice, I could not accuse myself of a wish to do so, and it might happen, as it has in your case, that some opportunity might arise of thwarting the evil which he meditated."

"You have said you were friendless nearly," remarked Marian.

"I am indeed."

"You will not again repeat that assertion," she added, in a lower tone of great feeling, "for you who have befriended us shall be our friend, as we will be yours, and whilst we will know no care which we will hesitate to appeal to your friendship to assist us in removing, we will know no joys in which we will not wish you to be a participator."

"Then, indeed," said Ormond, "the remark will be a superfluous one, and will never again pass my lips; but to turn from so pleasant a topic to one of a more business-like character, let me strongly advise and urge you, Mrs. Whitehead, to collect together at once, to-morrow morning, whatever papers you may possess concerning the partnership of your late husband with Godfrey, and place them in the hands of some respectable solicitor, who will quickly enforce him to come to an account."

"That I can easily do," said Mrs. Whitehead. "They are all, you know, my dear Marian, in the little leathern portmanteau upstairs, and I have never had the heart to touch them since your poor father's death."

"You will have no difficulty," said Ormond, "in forcing Godfrey to an exact account; indeed, I dare say he will not require forcing now, for he will be too much alarmed at the idea of the proceedings of this evening being detailed, which would tell so immensely to his prejudice. I am induced to think that the Indian property of the late Mr. Whitehead will turn out to be very large."

"Alas!" said Mrs. Whitehead, "and he died of a broken heart at the supposed failure of those very speculations the proceeds of which will enrich us."

Marian burst into tears, as she exclaimed,——

"Oh, that we had remained in our poverty, as we were; better that Godfrey had taken all, and that we had never known of this circumstance."

Mrs. Whitehead was about to second this sentiment of Marian's, but Charles Ormond interposed.

"Pardon me," he said, "but since you have called me friend, let me use a friend's privilege and speak freely, which I do, when I tell you that you are taking a more impulsive than a reasonable view of this matter. You do not reflect, Mrs. Whitehead, how noble a monument it is in your power to rear to the memory of your husband, by the good you may do with this amount of wealth which is thrown into your hands. Will it not be to you one of the most exquisite of pleasures to dispense among the deserving the means of comfort; you'll be able to relieve where you can do now nothing but pity."

"That is true," exclaimed Marian. "Mother, that is strictly true, and, therefore, we will rejoice at these means of usefulness which fortune has placed at our disposal."

"What is that?" said Charles Ormond; "I thought I heard a footstep without. And as this cottage is completely enclosed by its own garden, the step must surely be that of an intruder."

He rose as he spoke, but Marian laid a hand upon his arm, and in accents which betrayed her interest in him, she said,—

"Nay, nay; do not go. Do not think of going. There may be danger."

"Yes," said Charles, "to you; and therefore 'tis that I wish to meet it. Do not fear; I will be very careful. But, there again! I feel convinced I hear a footstep."

Disengaging himself as gently as he could from the delicate grasp of Marian, he darted from the cottage into the garden, but when there, he felt how utterly futile was any attempt at observation, for the darkness was excessive, and to him, of that absolutely pitchy character which a sudden transition from the lighted apartment was sure to produce.

Yet he fancied he heard the rustling of leaves in a particular direction, and with more courage than prudence, for he was ignorant of the locality, he darted forward in the direction of the sound; as he did so, he felt something whistle past his head, and by the sound of its fall upon the gravel path, he fancied it must have been a stone hurled at him by some one.

At this moment Marian appeared with a light, but that shed a very inefficient ray around it in the open air, and Charles, in his fear that some injury might be done to her, hastily entreated her to retire, and as she would not do so without him, they both returned to the cottage, where they found Mrs. Whitehead in a considerable state of alarm, as the falling of the stone upon the gravel path had sounded to her as if some scuffle was taking place.

"What is it? what is it?" she exclaimed. "I know we are surrounded by dangers now. One's lives are not safe. Ah, what would have become of us to-night if you had not stayed, Mr. Ormond?"

"I rejoice now," he said, "that I did; but banish your fears; the days are gone by now when any daring act of iniquity could be committed; people do now what they can by finesse and the chicanery of the law."

"I do not know," said Mrs. Whitehead, "my fears may be groundless, but I once heard my husband say that Godfrey was a man who, when he had an object to carry out, stopped at no deed or act, however iniquitous, that promised greatly to advance it."

"Yes," said Ormond, "but like most villains, he is a coward."

"I remember," added Mrs. Whitehead, "being once or twice at his house, and it seemed to me to be ever infested with spies. Mr. Whitehead and I had a private room; a newly furnished chamber in the place, because then the house, you understand, was the joint property of the partners, and the lower part of it was entirely devoted to business purposes. Of course we used to converse freely in this chamber, which we considered our own, but one day a circumstance occurred which induced me to believe that every word we uttered was overheard by some creature of Godfrey's."

"The treacherous villain," said Ormond.

"Yes," added Mrs. Whitehead, "my husband had left me, and I was sitting alone in the room I mentioned. A large looking-glass was opposite to me, upon which my eyes happened to fall, and reflected in it I saw the door of the apartment gently opened, and a most villanous-looking fellow peer into the room."

"You made an alarm?"

"I did; but inquiry was stifled by Godfrey, and in such a manner as convinced me that he was privy to the fact of such a person being in the house. I told my husband, and since then, we became cautious in what we said while there."

"Such a circumstance," said Ormond, "is of a piece with his general conduct. There is a half lad, half boy, and yet I scarcely think I ought to call him either, for some say he is more advanced in years than he appears, who is always skulking about the place. He is supported by Godfrey; and many do not scruple to assert that there is an extremely close relationship between them; be this, however, as it may, I have seen enough to convince me that that person is employed frequently as a confidential spy by Godfrey."

"What is his name?" said Marian.

"They call him Neville," said Ormond, and as he uttered the words, Marian shuddered and turned pale.

"You are unwell," said Charles.

"My dear Marian," said her mother, "what ails you?"

"Nothing, nothing," said Marian. "I know not how it was; but at the mere mentioning of that name, a kind of shuddering horror crept over me. A presentiment of evil which stopped the healthy current of the blood, and makes me tremble even while I condemn the folly of my fears. I shall never forget that name. As you uttered it, it seem stamped upon my mind indelibly. Is he still with Godfrey?"

"He is; and if there be villany afloat, let it bear what complexion it may, be assured that Neville is an agent in it."

A kind of mental depression came over Marian, from which she strove in vain to rally herself. Surely in the human heart there are some strange and hidden sympathies. It was the mere pronunciation by Ormond of Neville which had so affected her. It could be nothing else, and soon finding that she could not readily recover her lost spirits, she rose, and bade the young clerk good night, and left the room.

"I will not keep you," said Charles Ormond, "beyond your usual time of retiring to rest, but will remain here to guard the house."

"No, I cannot consent to that," said Mrs. Whitehead, "much as it is at your disposal."

"Excuse me," said Charles; "but I feel so uneasy at the certainty that some persons have been in the garden unknown to you, that I would rather remain here on the lower part of the premises, as watchful as I can. If I were to go to bed, I am certain I should not sleep, and my anxieties would be much greater than they will be here when I have reason to suppose I shall be the first to become aware of any cause of alarm ; and here is a couch, too, if I wish to lie down, so that I shall have all the comforts I shall require, or wish for."

" But," remarked Mrs. Whitehead, " you can scarcely sit up ; you will be fatigued."

" And then I can sleep," said Ormond.

" The fire will go out, and you will be so chilly and cold."

" Never mind, that ; I will undertake to keep it alight, or else I shall deserve to be cold ; in short, Mrs. Whitehead, if you please to permit me to say so, I have made up my mind to pass the night here. It will be of the greatest utility to us all, and myself included, if selfish thought must prevail, for I shall be ready, and less at a disadvantage if anything happens."

" If you really desire it," said Mrs. Whitehead, " I will not oppose your wishes, but set about making the place as comfortable for you as I can ; but I would rather you had chosen a more comfortable place of rest."

" I can choose no better than that in which I may be of use," said Charles Ormond ; " and I will remove the couch up by the fire, where I wi l be as comfortable as I can be, when I believe some mischief or other is meditated against you."

" I hope there may be no occasion for your being disturbed at all," said Mrs. Whitehead. " However it may be, our thanks are not the less due to you."

" I am much concerned and interested," said Ormond, " in this affair, and I shall feel more real pleasure in serving you than you can possibly feel in being served."

" Here are some books, if you feel disposed to read."

" Thank you ; they will serve to pass away the hours, should I feel so disposed."

Mrs. Whitehead placed the table within his reach, and laid on it the books and such things she considered would be of service to him during the night, should he not feel inclined to sleep. Having trimmed the lamp, she turned to Charles Ormond, and said,—

" Since I must leave you here, let me wish you a good night, and an undisturbed one."

" Thank you, thank you," returned Charles. " Good night, and may you rest easy. Be assured, if I know anything that will give you any alarm, I shall be the first to let you hear of it ; therefore, do not disturb yourself with thoughts that may only be harassing you with fears that have no real foundation."

" I shall rest much more easy now I have such a protector as yourself in the house."

" Good night ; and may we laugh at our fears at breakfast in the morning."

" I hope so. Good night."

Mrs. Whitehead now left the room, and retired to rest much more easy in her mind, now that Charles Ormond was keeping watch below.

" We shall," she thought, " at least have a protector, and the knowledge of that may be essential to our comfort and repose this night, while the presence of such a one may be an effectual bar to any attempt, for it is seldom that these men will attack openly those who are in any way prepared to meet their aggressions by resistance."

" My being here," thought Charles, " may disconcert some scheme, or some plot or plan, that has been concocted to the injury of the Whiteheads by the man Godfrey."

Comforting himself with this reflection, he sat himself down before the fire, and drawing a book towards him, he began to read to pass the time away, for the hours would be dull and heavy even with thinking upon those whom he so much respected —he could say loved—as the Whiteheads.

The tale he was reading was scarcely finished, when he thought he again heard some one moving in the garden.

" Hark !" he whispered to himself ; " surely there must be some one prowling about in the garden. It is strange that they are not driven away by the disturbance which they have already received. Any ordinary robber it would have had the effect of not only disturbing, but of causing him to fly altogether from the spot, and to give over the attempt. This, however, seems not to be the case, and whoever it is, he is a determined villain, and not easily scared from his prey; perhaps he knows exactly the strength that may be brought to oppose him, and hence his boldness. But he shall not have much to boast of if he encounters me; but never mind, come what will, my arm will be strengthened by the cause I have at heart."

"Yes, yes," he muttered, after a pause, spent in listening, "Marian Whitehead would nerve a weaker arm than mine in her defence. She will add the strength of two men to mine, if I have occasion to exert myself in her defence."

Again he paused, for he thought he heard the sounds of footsteps outside, as if some one was cautiously reconnoitring the outside; but the sounds were very indistinct, and he remained listening attentively for some minutes; but he heard no sounds that at all indicated the presence of intruders.

"Well, well," he said; "it may be fancy, but I thought I heard footsteps; however, I will have all in readiness for a sudden rush out upon them, in case I hear the sounds again, and I'll have a weighty argument for them if they choose not to quit the place the moment I show myself."

He now arose, and taking the poker, which was a somewhat formidable weapon, for it was not too big nor too heavy to use with rapidity and effect, Charles Ormond, quietly opened the door of the room he was in, and then going to the outer door, he undid some of the fastenings.

He posted himself by the door, and awaited in silence a recurrence of the sounds he had before heard; but it seemed that now he was in readiness for anything that might happen, nothing would occur.

He waited there for nearly half an hour, and feeling tired, he returned to the parlour, and sat himself down on the sofa, and felt a sensation of drowsiness come over him that it was difficult to resist.

Suddenly he heard the sounds of footsteps quite plain; he had fallen into a half doze, but he was perfectly conscious of all that was passing around him, and could hear well; but he heard the sound of footsteps several seconds before he started up to rush into the garden to search for the cause of this noise.

He started, and seizing the poker, quietly, yet swiftly, made towards the door, and then he as quickly and silently as possible opened it, and stepped out into the garden.

For some moments he stood upon the threshold of the door, but could see nothing; and when the darkness that reigned without had become familiar to his eyes, he could see objects that were at no great distance from him, though none far off.

Nothing, however, was there that could in the least disturb the silence that seemed to reign around. The night air scarce wafted the leaves of the trees, and even the rustle of a leaflet was not heard at that moment; and no sound whatever was there, though he listened for some time with eagerness and attention.

"It is strange," he thought, "that though there have been so many alarms, yet when I am listening like this, I cannot hear a sound. I will just draw the chair outside, and shoot a bolt, and then I can not come to any harm. I will take a walk round the garden. They cannot attempt to enter the house without my perceiving them."

He did even as he said, and then took a quick turn through the garden. The cool air of the night played round his temples, and dispelled the fears that his heated imagination had engendered, and he walked all over the garden, and, as far as he could discover, into every nook and corner of it.

Having neither seen nor heard anything that in the smallest extent justified any of his fears or anticipations, he returned to the house.

"There can be no doubt," he thought, "but what some one has been here, and I have disturbed them, and may be, disconcerted their intended attack on the house; and yet it must have been connected with that Godfrey, for who else could be capable of doing such a deed? The professed plunderer generally takes some place where a booty may be collected that would at once pay him for his trouble; money or plate is his object; but this seems scarcely the place to come for it; it must be some vile plot of that yet viler man Godfrey. However, as there is nothing to be done or seen here, I may as well go in again, and sit the night out, or sleep, which seems to be coming over me."

He reached the door, and once more turned round to listen attentively, but he could hear nothing, though he waited a long time.

Entering the cottage, he once more secured the fastenings, and taking his seat on the couch, stirred up the fire, and once more composed himself to rest, being assured that there could be nothing or no one in the garden, and that if any one had been there, they had no doubt been deterred from their attempt, and had gone away. Scarcely had he seated himself, and begun to read, when the same sounds again attracted his attention.

He started, and listened, but they had died away in the distance.

"Surely," he muttered to himself, "these are not fancy's freaks. My imagination is surely not deceiving me, else the deception is perfect indeed."

However, there was no return of the sound, and he again turned to his book, and endeavoured to beguile the time by reading, which occupied his attention for a time.

The tale he had scarcely concluded before he felt he was likely to become overpowered by sleep. He therefore shut the book up, and then turning to the fire, which was burning low, he made it up; and then taking his seat on the couch, he began then to lose himself in wild reveries of thought.

He watched the dancing flames as they were projected into the open grate by the little jets of gas that were thrown out by the coal, and which flared up with a loud noise.

The fire burned brightly, and Charles Ormond's gaze became steadfast, and his thoughts presented themselves unto himself, and yet he could scarce take cognizance of them; he had scarce will or volition, but thought was busy.

By degrees he fell into a slumber. He leaned against the back and arm of the couch, and then became happily unconscious of all things.

How long he remained in this state, or what complexion his thoughts took, he knew not: he could not remember whether he was dreaming, and the dream awoke him, or whether any noise had been uttered; but when he did awake, there was a strange confusion in his ideas—there were lights about. At last he thought there was a strange and brilliant glare about him; the cause of it he could not tell, nor, in that moment of dreamy wakefulness, did he think about, but by degrees his partially awakened senses became cognizant of the fact that there was a greater and stranger light about him than there had been some short time before he went to sleep.

A curious noise then awoke him to a state of consciousness, and he opened his eyes to become aware that there was a strange glaring, red light, and much smoke.

"Good God!" he exclaimed, starting up; "the place is on fire!"

He had scarcely uttered these words, and got on his feet, before he became aware that there was somebody present, who immediately grappled with him and seized him.

Charles Ormond was by no means an unequal antagonist to most men, and now as he was urged by every consideration that could urge a man to exertion, he struggled fiercely with his opponent, who was resolute and strong.

For a few moments neither of them moved, but stood holding one another by whatever grasp they could seize by, and thus they stood for nearly two minutes, the efforts of each being paralyzed or counteracted by the other.

However, a sudden twist of the man gave Ormond the advantage, for he instantly turned him over and shifted his own position; but the villain held so securely that he could not shake him off.

"Villain!" he exclaimed, "you shall not go; you shall suffer condign punishment for this."

The man made no answer, but still maintained his struggle, which seemed rather for the purpose of detaining him there, than to enable himself to get away.

Charles Ormond was thoroughly awake to the necessity of immediately getting to the assistance of Marian and Mrs. Whitehead, and now endeavoured to release himself, but without being able to do so, or to shake off his opponent.

The struggle continued for several minutes, and, in the end, they both rolled into the passage, and then it was that Charles Ormond became aware, thoroughly aware, that there was indeed a fire.

The cottage was on fire. He had suspected, nay, believed it; but now he saw it, but could not release himself. He heard the cries of Mrs. Whitehead and of Marian, but he was unable to go to their assistance.

"Oh, Heavens! the house is on fire," he could distinctly hear Mrs. Whitehead say. "Help—help! Marian has fainted."

With herculean strength he raised himself, and the man he was struggling with, and dashed him against the door-post. The door stood open, and they both rolled together on the hard gravel path.

Finding the case desperate, he shifted his hold, and seized the ruffian by the throat, and contriving by some exertion to get the fellow underneath, he then seized him with one hand by the hair of the head, and then placing his knees upon his chest, he began lifting the head up and down, and beating it as hard as he could upon the bare stones.

This in a very short time produced the desired result, for the man relaxed his hold and groaned. Charles seized a stone that came to his hand, and struck him over the head. Of course this stony application to the head of the stranger rendered him perfectly insensible, he straightened himself out and then lay quiet.

In an instant Charles Ormond was on his feet, and dashed into the house and then up stairs.

"Marian! Mrs. Whitehead!" he shouted, "the house is on fire."

"Oh, Mr. Ormond!" exclaimed Mrs. Whitehead, "the house is on fire! What has happened—tell me what has happened? Are you hurt? I thought I heard ——"

"Yes, yes, you did, but there is no time for explanations now; for God's sake come down, or you will be burned alive."

He seized Mrs. Whitehead round the waist, and hurried, and half lifted her down stairs into the garden.

"Stay here," he said; "stay here."

"Marian! oh, where is my my daughter Marian? See, see, the fire increases! she will be killed. Oh, Marian, Marian!"

"Stay here," repeated Charles. "I will save Marian, or perish with her."

"Oh, my dear child. Where is she? Look, look! how the fire increases."

"It does," said Ormond, and on the next instant he dashed through the open door, and rushed up stairs.

"Marian, Marian! where are you? For Heaven's sake, speak, or we shall all perish. Speak, oh, Marian, speak!"

He entered one room, but there was no one there. With frantic eagerness he rushed into a second—the smoke was fast filling the place, and it rendered breathing difficult, and he feared, lest she had begun attempting to escape, and had failed in finding her way out, and thus lost herself.

"Marian, Marian!" exclaimed Charles, "where are you—speak, for mercy sake?" He came to a door, and heard a stifled scream, and instantly dashing himself against it, he burst it open, and in the next instant he stood by Marian's bedside, but she was in a half stupor from the effect of fright and smoke.

Charles Ormond snatched her off the bed, at the same moment he seized a blanket, and wrapping it entirely over her, he carried her in his arms to the head of the stairs.

But here an appalling sight presented itself to him, and he had a danger to encounter that at first he shrank from meeting. It was not one of strength against strength, but of a mighty power he could not hope to overcome.

The fire was now raging furiously, and the hot volumes of white smoke that ascended from below, and the roaring, and crackling of the flames told him the fire was now in good earnest raging, and had commenced below where he must pass.

But for the precious burthen he bore, he would have flung himself out of window, and have chanced all; but his frame thrilled at the touch of her whom he carried, and, determined to save her or perish, he rushed headlong down the stairs,

How he got down he could scarcely tell; the lower stairs on which he trod were on fire, and but for the headlong haste he made, he must have been suffocated, and have fallen and perished miserably.

As it was, however, he came down four or five steps at a time, without being able to stay himself; he could not tell where, or on what he stepped, and the last stairs he felt crumble beneath his feet; but he fell not—his downward impetus was superior to any new force, and projected him forwards into the garden, before he was at all aware that he was safe.

Grateful, indeed, was that delicious draught of fresh air; his lungs had almost been inflamed with hot smoke, and his senses began to reel; but the impetus he had acquired in going down stairs saved him.

He could not stop himself, and hence both were saved. Oh, the gasping agony he felt, as with the almost last attempt at respiration he drew in the cold night air. Then, again, he heaved his breast, and drew in another long breath, and then he felt his consciousness returning; but he felt as if his chest and lungs had been seared.

He now became conscious that there were other persons in the garden besides themselves. In fact, the screams of Mrs. Whitehead had alarmed some of her neighbours, who now arrived at the cottage to proffer assistance.

They brought ladders and ropes, but this was by far too late, and they came in time to witness the miraculous escape of Charles and Marian. He heard them say,—

" Bravo, bravo! Well—well done! They are saved—they are saved!"

Various sounds of commendation and applause were uttered, and he was held up by some persons who surrounded him, saying,—

" All right, sir—you are safe. You have saved her nobly!"

" Oh, my child, my child! my dear Marian!" exclaimed Mrs. Whitehead, as she flung herself upon Marian.

Then turning to Charles Ormond, after the first flood of emotion was over, she exclaimed, in accents that showed her feelings,—

" You are my more than preserver—my deliverer—but you are the saviour of my daughter. This night has indeed made us deeply indebted to you. We never can be grateful enough; we never can repay you."

" To save this dear girl and yourself," said Charles Ormond, " is, indeed, a happiness of which I cannot say how deeply I feel, how much indebted to your misfortunes, for my greatest happiness. Say no more about it; you are both saved, and what more can I desire?"

" Is there any one else in the cottage?" inquired one of the neighbours.

" No—no one."

" Because we have ladders, and the flames will, in a few moments more, be in the upper rooms, if they be not there already."

" Ah, the papers!" exclaimed Mrs. Whitehead.

" What papers?" inquired Ormond.

" Those relating to the partnership affair of my late husband and Godfrey."

" They must not be lost," said Ormond, " else that base man will have gained his object, for I believe this was the work of his agents. I have no doubt of it."

" They are in a small portmanteau."

" Where was it?"

" On the drawers in my bed-room."

" Which is it?"

" That room there; that is the window of it, and the drawers are a little to the right of that."

" A ladder—a ladder!"

" No—no—no, Ormond, you must not risk your life in such an attempt; it is too valuable and too loved by us, to permit you to encounter such a risk."

" The papers must be had."

" But consider ——"

" I will—I will take great care; be assured I will be very careful."

"No—no; care will not do; see—see, the flames are rapidly increasing in power and fury; do not attempt it, Mr. Ormond."

But Charles had quitted the side of Mrs. Whitehead, and had approached the cottage.

"A ladder—a ladder!" he cried.

A ladder was instantly brought him, and, pointing to the window, he hurriedly exclaimed.

"There, there, place it there, and break the window in with the end of it."

This was done, and scarcely had the ladder been placed, when Charles Ormond ran up it with surprising ease and agility. When he had reached the top he dashed in the remaining part of the frame, and disappeared amid a shout from the crowd.

For a few seconds there was an intense and painful excitement in the breasts of those below, which each second of time increased.

Several men now approached the foot of the ladder, and several shouted to him to return, for the fire had burst through the lower rooms, and appeared in a body of flame immediately below that at which he had entered; this was announced by a loud shout.

"He will be lost—he will be lost!" exclaimed Mrs. Whitehead. "Oh, save him, some of you; do not let him perish such a miserable death—so young, so noble, and so courageous."

"Come back—come back," shouted the bystanders, and several men began to ascend the ladder, calling as they went, "Here he comes—he's safe."

"Thank God for that!" exclaimed Mrs. Whitehead, fervently, as she clasped her hands.

Charles Ormond was now seen at the window; but they could all see from the glare of the light below that he was very weak and could scarcely stand.

"Be quick—be quick," shouted the crowd.

With a sudden effort he got outside of the window, and the heat from below was so great, the smoke so thick, and the flames were now almost seizing upon the rounds of the ladder, that he stood in the utmost danger.

"Be quick," again shouted the mob.

"Slip down the ladder," exclaimed the men at the bottom; "slip down, we will save you at the bottom."

From choice or necessity, Charles Ormond chose to adopt the advice; indeed, it might fairly be questioned if it were done voluntarily, for he could not help it, and but for the ladder he would have dropped through exhaustion, and it also served to lengthen the descent and to break the fall.

The men at the bottom caught him as he came down, and he was once more saved.

"Saved—saved—saved!" cried Mrs. Whitehead, in joyful accents; "thank God, he's saved!"

Some cold water was instantly dashed into his face, and some given him to drink, which aided much to restore him. He kept the portmanteau firmly in his grasp, and lift or carry him where they would, still he held that safe. Now, however, the whole cottage was one mass of flames; there was not a room or a window that was not now illuminated most fearfully by flames. In a few moments more the roof fell in with a tremendous crash, and the place was a burning ruin.

"Oh, Mr. Ormond," exclaimed Mrs. Whitehead, "to what an extent are we not your debtors; but yet to no one else could I feel so much pleasure in being indebted."

"You pay me the greatest compliment I could receive; but had you not better have some shelter?—surely there will be some one who will afford you a night's shelter."

"Yes," said a gentleman, stepping forward towards them, "to such accommodation as my place affords on such a sudden emergency, Mrs. Whitehead, her daughter, and yourself, sir, are welcome to."

"Thank you, sir," said Mrs. Whitehead ; "your offer is seasonable and kind, and I am now without shelter, and therefore I accept it with thanks."

"You shall be most welcome. Will you please to follow me ; there can be nothing saved from the ruins now, and your remaining here will but injure you all."

"It will, it will, sir—we thank you for your kindness."

"Yes," said Ormond, "there is nothing now to be done there ; the house will be a complete ruin, a mass of rubbish, in less than another quarter of an hour, and the fall may occasion some danger to those who are near it."

"My name is Winter," said the gentleman turning to Mrs. Whitehead, "and my house is close at hand. I do not know if you recollect my name."

"Yes, yes, very well, sir, and your house also—I am much obliged."

"Say nothing about that ; this is a calamity that might happen to any one."

"It might," said Charles.

"The night is very dark," remarked Mr. Winter, "but there is light enough."

"Marian, Marian, dear Marian !" exclaimed Ormond, almost involuntarily, as he supported her along, "are you any better now—have you been hurt by the fire ?"

"No, no, Mr. Ormond, you have taken too much care of that ; you are my preserver ; to you I owe not only my own life, but that of my mother. I never can thank you, or do enough to evince my gratitude and sense of the obligation that you have laid us under."

"Do you not think, Marian, that I have not reaped a high reward in saving you alone ? It amply repays me all ; I am happier than ever I was in being an instrument of your safety ; if you are safe, then indeed I am well and amply paid and satisfied."

"But it can never release us from our obligation, our debt of gratitude ; nor can we wish it should, for while we are ourselves, we cannot for one hour forget who has done so much for us."

They now arrived at Mr. Winter's door, and were at once shown into some private apartments, for neither Marian nor Mrs. Whitehead were dressed ; a few things had been huddled on in the bustle of the moment, and now, when they came into a lighted room, they discovered their deficiency, and were at once supplied by the kindness of the family amongst whom they had found so seasonable a refuge.

When these changes had been effected, they all again assembled in the parlour, where a large fire had been made. It was warm and comfortable, and it was, moreover, what they most desired and wanted, for to sleep then would have been impossible, and they fell into conversation.

"How were you alarmed about the fire, sir ?" inquired Charles Ormond of Mr. Winter.

"My bedroom, you see, directly faces the garden and cottage of Mrs. White-head."

"You saw the flames ?"

"Yes, I did ; but I was awakened by loud screams, and then, jumping out, I came to my window and saw the flames."

"It was while you had gone back for Marian," remarked Mrs. Whitehead.

"It was a sight that made me feel somewhat alarmed, because I understood that Mrs. Whitehead had no male protector in the house."

"On this night I had a very efficient one," said Mrs. Whitehead.

"You had indeed, madam. However, I soon got up and alarmed the household, and I alarmed several others as I came along ; however, there were others there when I reached the cottage."

"Yes," said Mrs. Whitehead, "there were several who had probably been up and saw the fire."

"While you were in the house I certainly thought you were lost, and it seems to me a perfect miracle how you got away. I saw you passing through a body of flame and smoke that would have killed, I should have thought, at least ten men ; however, I was glad to see you come out with your burthen."

"Yes," said Marian, "I have given much trouble and great danger to Mr. Ormond."

"Say no more about it."

"And the portmanteau?"

"I have it safe," said Charles, pointing to it. "I don't know how it was, but I thought that several persons were desirous of getting it away from me, and that made me hold it much tighter than I should otherwise have done."

"Well," said Mrs. Whitehead, "I thought you held it with singular pertinacity, and knew not what it could contain that could induce you to hold it so carefully, and refuse all aid or assistance."

"That was the reason, and I was very glad that I preserved my senses sufficiently to enable me to do that."

"How did you become acquainted with the fire, Mrs. Whitehead?"

"I can hardly tell you; but I heard a great noise, or something of the sort. I could not see what it was, and then a sudden smell of fire aroused me from my lethargy.

"I awoke entirely, and got out of bed, and at that moment I heard a struggling below, and then the light of fire came strong upon me; I screamed out, and called to Marian to arise. The struggling continued, and went in the garden, where it continued till Mr. Ormond ran up stairs and brought me down, for I was so terrified that I knew not what to do, and feared to move."

"How were you awakened, Mr. Ormond?" inquired Mrs. Whitehead. "There was more done and happened at that time than I can tell of."

"There was, indeed," said Charles; "I heard, on several occasions, the sound of footsteps pass the window. At first I did not go out; but at length I did, and searched the garden."

"You ventured out, did you?" said Marian. "It was very wrong."

"Oh, no harm resulted from it at all; I found no one. All was as still as you could imagine, though I stood for some time; but it was all to no purpose. I came in and sat down, and again the footsteps passed the window."

"Did you go out again?"

" I did not ; it seemed to me that it was merely a freak of fancy ; or else it was some one who was too well aware of what he was to do to allow me to come near him ; however, I sat for some time before the fire, and fell off into a sleep. The exact cause of my waking I cannot at this moment say ; but I thought something strange was going on. There was an odd noise, a light, and a strong smell of smoke. All at once, aroused to the consciousness of fire, I started up, and found myself grappled by a man who endeavoured to fling me down ?"

" A man !"

" Yes."

" How could he get there ?"

" I cannot tell. I have no knowledge, even in the remotest degree. All I know is, I was met by a powerful man, who struggled most desperately with me for some time. I could not throw him, nor he me."

" Good heavens ! Mrs. Whitehead, then, that was the voice that woke me."

" Very likely ; but in our struggles we could not maintain any superiority over each other for some time, until we both rolled into the passage, and then I I saw, for the first time, that the cottage really was on fire. This increased my desperation, and I, now, instead of trying to secure the man, endeavoured to shake him off, but could not."

" What did he want with you ? I should have imagined he wanted to get away."

" He seemed to aim at compelling me to remain in the burning house ; but we rolled out into the garden, and there I contrived to knock him on the head with a stone, and he became senseless and unable to move, and for the rest, you know all I can tell you."

" What became of that man," inquired Marian, " with whom you had so desperate a struggle, and who was he ?"

" He was in the house when first I saw him or felt him, and as to what became of him I don't know ; but I suppose he made his escape while I was in the house."

" How very singular," remarked Mr. Winter ; " the fire was not an accident then ?"

" No."

" It was the work of an incendiary, then ?' said Mr. Winter.

" I have no doubt of it ?" said Mrs. Whitehead."

" Nor I," said Marian.

" By-the-by, Mr. Ormond," said Mrs. Whitehead, " did you notice the features of the villain who made such a diabolical attempt at murder ?"

" I did."

" Had you ever seen him before ?"

" I think I have ; by the light of the fire which glared into the passage I had a view of his features, which he seemed to have a great disinclination to exhibit. He reminded me of some one whom I believe I may have seen about Godfrey's."

" Then he was the author of this calamity."

" No doubt, no doubt, he is at the bottom of it all. His object was, without doubt, to destroy the claimants and the papers. Were it the case, he has failed, signally failed, for they are all safe, and he has committed one crime more, but it matters little to him."

They all sat up some time longer and some refreshments, were served them, and then, by the advice of Mr. Winter, they retired to sleep for a few hours to refresh themselves. It was just about daybreak.

CHAPTER XI.

GODFREY AND HIS ASSOCIATE.—THE CELLAR AND ITS INHABITANTS.

THE places of which we are about to speak, have for the most part disappeared from the locality in which they once stood rampant and flourishing, but though suppressed, or otherwise got rid of, places of a similar character and spirit may exist, but most probably they have assumed a different shape.

In the far-famed Seven Dials, were once a number of old rambling houses, built in places that enabled them to have more than one mode of ingress and egress. They were strange old places, such as no mortal would now think of constructing for any purpose whatever; they would be unwholesome, inconvenient, and useless; but they had their use once, and were no doubt thought models of domestic architecture.

Of these old houses it would often happen that several of them would be built together, or rather they had been left standing beyond the remaining tenements. They were large rambling places; nobody could tell from the outside what one room was, or for what another was designed—they all differed much from each other.

Cupboards there were, and plenty, and some of them sufficiently capacious to hide a man, while others were in such strange out-of-the-way places that nobody would have believed in their existence.

These houses were once inhabited by wealthy people, but their last inhabitants were either the most wretched or the most guilty wretches that could be found among the refuse population of London. The rooms were now uneven, and the boarding rotted, the skirting in many places had been torn off, windows broken, and wooden panes put in permanently, while brown paper and rags stopped up others for the nonce.

The houses were dirty and dingy, and had a most miserable appearance, and were known to be the resort of the most worthless and degraded beings that the neighbourhood could produce; and though this was known to the police of that day, yet they could do nothing—the villanous lot were at home, and who could touch them? besides, they were always sure to escape.

In an upper room, in one of these houses, lay a man, extended on a kind of mattress asleep. He was a powerful-looking ruffian, with a hang-dog looking countenance. He was, in fact, the personification of all that was low, degraded, and villanous in man.

The room was of moderate dimensions, seemingly destitute of every description of furniture, except a solitary stool, that had once been a chair, but which was now denuded of its back, and converted into an almost bottomless stool, of uncertain capability for sustaining any weight that might be placed upon it.

In one corner was placed the mattress of which we have spoken, and on it lay the man. He was in a profound sleep, and his breathing, deep and hoarse, induced the suspicion of an excessive indulgence in spiritous liquors.

He lay still—he was stout built—squat, and square, with a countenance it would be difficult to describe, save it was very pale, with deep and strong lines in it. His hair was strong, and straggling, and with his wide mouth, and low forehead, served to increase, if possible, the hideousness of his features, upon which it was impossible to look without a feeling of terror and disgust.

The room we have said was destitute of furniture, and its bare walls locked dirty and broken; for here and there the wainscoting was torn away, the paper had long since disappeared, and the plaster was broken away in many places, and the laths appeared.

A candle burned on the mantlepiece, and lighted the room; it had burned some time, for there was a very long snuff to it, and its light was dim and obscured.

There appeared no means of ingress or egress but a hole in the roof, which was made seemingly on purpose. This trap, or hole, seemed constructed on purpose to admit visitors; it was uncovered, and anyone could get in.

There now appeared the visage of a man, who peeped into the room from above for some minutes, and noted well everything that was there to be seen, and then after having satisfied himself that there was nothing to be apprehended, he shifted his position, and then his legs appeared, and then his body, till he hung down to the full length of his person, holding on by his hands.

In this position he swung for a moment or two, and then dropped. The fall was but a short distance, but yet he came with a heavy crash upon the floor.

However lightly this might have been intended to be, yet the want of agility on the part of the visitor and his Wellington boots, together, came with more noise than was intended to have been.

The sleeper started up as if awakened by an electric shock.

" Hilloa !" he growled out ; " who's in the ken, now, eh ?"

" It is I," said the visitor, who was no other than Godfrey.

" You. Oh, what do you want ?"

" That's what I have come to tell you," said Godfrey ; " did you think I didn't ?"

" I haven't thought yet at all ; and, therefore, it doesn't signify what ; but I was asleep, and you woke me up."

" Yes, it was coming into this blessed infernal den backwards, like a bear. What can induce you to have only an opening at top, like a butter churn, as if, when you had an enemy at the top, you shut off all kinds of retreat ?"

" Never mind, I know very well what I'm about ; you keep your house as you like, and I'll keep mine."

" That's but reasonable and proper."

" And Bill Hunt will have what's right, whether or no ; but tell me what brought you here to me ; you didn't come here out of mere love, I know d—d well."

" Why, Bill Hunt, you seem to think I have no natural affection towards old friends ; now, that's wrong of you."

" Oh, none of your curst nonsense ; because, arter that, you know there is sure to be a little extra rascality going on."

" How very censorious—that is not right of you ; and yet people must live."

" If it is by cutting throats."

" Exactly—precisely my meaning. How very odd we should both think alike upon the same subject, isn't it ?"

" Not at all, we are both upon the same ladder, you know, Godfrey, but only on different rounds."

" Well, it matters not ; you know, Hunt, that we can't both stand on the same spot, eh ?" said Godfrey.

" True enough, I daresay ; but what have we to do together ?"

" You shall hear. Have you got a seat ?"

" Yes, there's one ; sit down," said Bill Hunt, kicking the stool towards him.

" A truly dubious affair this. I hope it may not fail me."

Hunt only passed a ribald jest by way of a reply, and Godfrey continued,—

" The conveniences of this place are not greater than need be."

" That may be," said Hunt ; " but they are mine, and you may as well say no more about them, unless you intend to replace them by better. Curse your old stingy carcass, you want to have luxuries without paying for them."

" That is an erroneous impression of your own, Master Hunt. I come here with the intention of doing a little business, and if we can agree we shall prosper, and that will, of course, put money into your pocket."

" Very well, I'm your man, if it is anything that is worth while."

" It may be "

" Is it ?"

" I should think so, if you will undertake it. I will make it worth your while. You know I do what's right."

" If you'll say that much, and mean it, I know you can, and then there can be no difficulty. What's the dodge?"

" I have been strangely thwarted and crossed by a young scamp of a fellow, who goes by the name of Ormond—Charles Ormond."

" Ay, go on."

" Well, he was in my office ; but he must go and blow upon a plan of mine that I had, and should have completed, but for him."

" The devil."

" D—n him, say I," said Godfrey, stamping his foot, and scowling most diabolically, with all the concentrated fury of an enraged tiger. I could tear him limb from limb."

" Very like, this 'll be a good job."

" Pretty well. Are you able to go about now ?"

" I am well enough."

" Ay, but I mean, can you be seen in public yet?" inquired Godfrey, with a meaning look. " You are not out of town ?"

" Why, I'd rather not be seen more than I can help."

" I see you have attentive friends?"

" Rather, but nothing that I care about. You know that I take something like care of myself," said the man, with a grin.

" Why, truly, you have reason to take care of yourself."

" Exactly so. I am ready to wait upon you at any time ; but yet I must be secret, and keep dark."

" That is what I wish. Now, this Ormond has spoiled me of a very handsome sum, and I hate him, and will never rest until I have been his utter ruin and destruction."

" Bravo !"

" Now, I want you to attend to this ; watch and follow him, bring him to ruin, disgrace, and to an ignominious death."

" In fact you wish him hanged ?"

" Most unequivocally."

" Then I'll undertake the job."

" Here's an earnest."

At the same time Godfrey drew from his pocket a piece of paper in which was wrapped some money, which he threw towards Bill Hunt, who caught it and proceeded without ceremony to open and examine the contents.

Apparently he was satisfied with this, and at once assumed a less ferocious aspect, though equally repulsive.

" That will do ?" said Godfrey.

" To begin with," returned Hunt.

" What a conscience you have got."

" I ain't got any. I'm no hypocrite, Mister Godfrey ; I ain't got more conscience than you, so don't compliment me."

" I didn't mean to do so."

" But when you talk in that way you do," said Hunt ; " but is this to be a cut throat job, or what are we to make of it ?"

" I cannot precisely yet say," said Godfrey ; " but at present take whatever advantage opportunity offers, and any papers you may find ; and at the least hang upon him and let me know whatever he does, where he goes to, who are his friends, and in short everything about him."

" An extensive and roving commission truly ; to do any one of these things a man ought to be paid—well paid too ; but to do all he ought to make a fortune."

" And if you had a fortune you would spend it," said Godfrey.

" To be sure I would, like a brick ; and why not ? What do I care for those who come after me ? What are they to me, or I to them ? I don't run any danger for them ; they'd run little for me. No, no, a short life and a merry one say I, though it end by a halter. I never could think of what use all your money could be to you ;—why, man, you'll die."

" Well, well, there's time enough—time enough for that, you know."

" But then it's worth while considering," said the ruffian, grinning as he saw the other not over anxious to enter upon it; "it is worth consideration, because if you are likely to live long, it is well to provide for such a case ; but if you are likely to go off in a hurry, why, enjoy yourself."

" So I do.'

" Very well, that's right then ; I wouldn't try after no more money, because it will only serve to gild your rope."

" My rope !"

" Yes, your rope ; you'll come to be hanged as well as I—eh ?"

" Come, this is enough ; each understands his own business better than the other ; so if you have some leisure, we will talk over the affair I have spoken to you of."

" Well, then, come below ; we shall want a pal or two."

" As few as possible."

" Oh, I know on whom I can depend, and upon whom I cannot."

" Ay, but even then I would never trust to any one more than you are obliged ; it's a plain maxim and a good one never to trust anybody, and it is one to be followed as closely as it is possible, but you can't do without help sometimes, and confidence becomes absolutely necessary ; and as necessity knows no laws, you see I am compelled to trust you thus far, my dear Hunt. Do you see that ?"

" Yes, I do ; but if you only let me know what you are obliged, what a precious rascal you must be in your own mind."

" Exactly."

" Well, then, we'll go down stairs and see what's going on there. I have had a sleep—I've been up some hours."

" Got too much drink."

" No, I thought I might ; it isn't often I get too much of any good thing."

" I see ; well, well, I'll go with you. We shall be perfectly safe, eh ?"

" Yes quite, else I wouldn't go."

Then the man got up, and stretched and yawned fearfully. Now his great strength became apparent, while his hideous aspect was by no means diminished.

" There, get up again, I'll follow."

" Yes, but I can't jump."

" Then take the stool."

" Ay, the stool, and an infernal affair it is too ; why it goes sea-saw when I sit upon it, and it will break if I stand upon it."

" Oh, will it," said the other ; "then you must stop here in the dark, for look, the candle's going out."

" D—n the candle ; what an infernal den this is," said Godfrey, much enraged ; but he took the stool, while the man stood laughing at his awkwardness.

" Well," said the man, " be a plucked 'un, and do it well ; show some confidence in the stool if in nobody else."

" The stool is as rotten as humanity," said Godfrey bitterly.

" There he goes again."

However, as Godfrey saw there was no help, he stood upon the opposite edges of the stool, and reached upwards till he got hold of the sides of the trap, and then he slowly pulled himself up.

" You've done it !" exclaimed the man, and at the same moment Godfrey made a slip, which was very like to have precipitated him into the room below, had he not retained his hold by one hand, and quickly recovered the hold of the other.

" Ha ! ha ! did you do that on purpose, Godfrey ? You couldn't have done it better."

Godfrey muttered something which could not be heard, though, no doubt, it was a malediction of unusual heartiness.

Hunt put the candle out, kicked away the stool, and then making a spring at the trap, succeeded in catching the edges with his fingers, and quickly drew himself up and got out.

"It's easy enough," he said, as he got up; "it's only a little use."

"A life time wouldn't make me used to it; but here we are now; where are we going? that's the question."

"And if you'll follow me it will be answered to your satisfaction; for there will be a tolerably good lot of rum 'uns, regular bricks, who don't care a d——n for nobody—them's the coves I like."

"Push on; but mind, if this chap, Ormond, can be hanged publicly, so much the better. I have set my mind upon that point; I have, indeed."

"We'll see what's to be done bye-and-bye; but walk straight after me, because there are several holes which you may fall through and break your neck."

"Did I come this way?"

"You did."

"D——n."

"Very true; but had you indulged in any unnecessary curiosity you would have paid dear for it. I shouldn't have told you, only I thought I couldn't spare you yet."

"I am obliged."

"Don't say anything on that subject, because our obligations are mutual."

They now passed through several rooms and passages, and then came to the wall, where, on one side of a large beam, which seemed to prop something up, was a concealed door, which Hunt opened, and then they both went through, and the door was closed upon both.

This door opened into a small narrow passage, at either end of which was a staircase, one of which seemed to lead upwards, and the other downwards.

It was down the latter they both proceeded for several flights, till they came to a kind of ground floor, and then entering a small back room, he pulled up a trap-door, saying, as he did so,—

"Here we are. Go down."

"After you," said Godfrey.

"As you please; only take care how you shut the trap, because it may fracture your skull. It's intended to serve those who are not used to it thus, to prevent intruders."

"Oh! never mind," said Godfrey, "I'd sooner trust to you to shut it."

"Very well, then, be quick."

"Is it deep?"

"Not very."

"Where are the steps?"

"There are none—jump in."

He accompanied this intimation by a gentle push, that soon put Mr. Godfrey at the bottom, and then he came down after him, when bang went the trap-door. Godfrey started at the sound, but he soon recovered himself, and they proceeded to the end of the passage, and then, opening a door, he entered into a night cellar.

Here was a scene that it was difficult to describe. In all parts of the place were men and women, crammed and packed together until there was scarce space to move. Hunt was welcomed by several in a quiet way, but his companion seemed to excite only a passing look.

There was much laughing and jesting going on, till the place rang again.

The smell of tobacco and liquors was very great; besides the impurities of the place, the heated atmosphere was filled with reeking perfumes of one kind or another.

The noises, too, were very great. It was difficult to hear any one speak in such a Babel of sounds.

"Well," said Hunt, "what do you think of the place? Don't you think there are some rum 'uns here?"

"Indeed I do."

"You may well say that, but you must have something to drink, and a smoke, or you'll not be able to stay here."

"I don't want," whispered Godfrey.

"But you must send for some."

"Very well, let it be what you will."

Hunt whispered to a girl, and she arose, and, going out, returned with some liquors, and tobacco, and pipes, which she gave Hunt. Godfrey gave some money, out of which he received no change.

He stayed here some time a silent spectator of the scene, which seemed uncongenial to the soul, though to the personal appearance of the man, it was scarce in place; not but the dark hard features of Godfrey were at all misplaced here, he was at home.

There was a strange collection of human beings in this fearful den of iniquity. Some of all kinds were present. Men and women, and they were apparently in the various stages of intoxication, produced by the liquors they were drinking, and the heat and smoke of the place.

Godfrey, after he had been there an hour, whispered to him that he desired to leave, and it was not without difficulty that he found himself once more in the fresh air, and walking side by side with his iniquitous companion, Bill Hunt.

CHAPTER

THE EXTREME CLEVERNESS OF MILES ATHERTON.—JIM'S EXCUSES FOR HIS MASTER.—AND MRS. ATHERTON'S SUPPOSED LUNACY.

It is a trite proverb, but one most especially true, that man never is, but always to be blessed. Physiologists tell us that two pains at the same time cannot be felt, for that the greater will always overpower the lesser. Possibly, as regards mental anxieties, this may be to a considerable extent true; and the troubles of this life appear comparatively insignificant in proportion as they are thrown completely into the shadow by some leviathan of their number, which for a time engrosses all consideration.

To descend from great things to small, we may apply these highly philosophical opinions practically to our friend, Miles Atherton, cheesemonger and dealer in hams, and Jim, errand boy to the aforesaid, and general utility lad to the establishment.

It was rather fearful to get shut up and lost among the vaults of St. Paul's, and to reach the vast area of the upper portion of this cathedral seemed at the moment a relief from all trouble and anxiety.

But so, however, was it, although the greatest trouble of getting out of these vaults was knocked down, the lesser one of how to get out of the cathedral without going back again the way they came, promptly supplied its place.

We have already recorded how, with snatches of repose at intervals, Jim and his master contrived to pass the night, and when, to the chagrin of the gentleman who was in the habit of taking the threepence, they emerged into St. Paul's churchyard, both Jim and his master looked at each other with faces of deep congratulation, that at length their somewhat exciting and troublesome adventures were over.

This was, however, but a fleeting thought, for too soon there rose up before Miles Atherton the vision of the insulted and neglected Mrs. Atherton.

He paused, and looked ruefully at Jim, who was not slow in translating the feelings which were beginning to agitate his master.

"Ah," said Jim, "I knows what you are thinking on, sir. It's what missus will say; but never mind, sir."

"It's all very well," said Miles Atherton, "to say never mind; but I know there never was a blessed row at home that'll come near this one; but all night, for the first time since Mrs. A. has been Mrs. A.—I begin to wish, Jem, we had stayed in the vaults."

"Do you?" said Jem. "I ain't married; but I tells you what, master, it seems to me, now, as missus always makes as jolly a row as never she can, whatever it's about."

"Well, I don't know, Jem, really; she is certainly a violent woman at times; I think I see her eye."

"Lor!" said Jem, in a great fright; "where—where?"

"I mean fancy's eye, you know, Jem. I think I see her now."

"Well, master," said Jem, "what's the use of giving in? who knows what may happen. Suppose, now, she was to get into such a rage as to be smothered or to *bust*, and fly all about the shop in small pieces, there'd be a go. You'd be able to sell that ere key then, master, to lots o' married men, on account of its wirtue. Lor! what a load of people we should have in the vaults, to be sure, underneath St. Paul's, if staying a night would make a regular *bust* of their missuses as is at home."

"Ah! ah! I dare say that's all very well, Jem, but the question happens to be not exactly what other people might do, but what we are to do. I don't mind telling you, because you have seen a little of what takes place at home; but the fact is, I don't half like the idea of crossing my own threshold."

"We must come the cunning, sir," said Jem—"some out-and-out—famous plan we must think of, and no mistake. Now, what, suppose, sir, I was to go home, and say you was dead, and then, after harrying up Mother Atherton's feelings a little, ask of her what she'll stand if it was quite the other way?"

"Dead! You know that wouldn't do; she'd just cut out like bricks, and buy a widow's cap; so there'd be an end of that; and perhaps she'd be so aggravated at finding me alive, that there'd be more row than ever."

"Well, then," said Jem, "I'll go and say you was took ill in the street, and that I've been a-waiting on you all those hours, and afeared to move. I'll tell her as you had a sort o' conwulsion in the spine o' your back, and that you did nothing all the while but pronounce the name of Mary Anne, which is hers, you know; and arter that what can she say?"

"Well, Jem, some such scheme must be resorted to. It may be a very bad thing for a man to do, after staying out all night, to walk into his house with a bounce, and ask for his breakfast; but it's a touch above me; I couldn't do it. So I tell you what you do, Jem; I'll wait at the Bull and Perriwinkle while you just hop home and see what sort of humour Mrs. Atherton's in."

"Very good, sir," said Jem; "I'll do it. In course the first piece of tenderness I expects is something shied at my head; but howsomedever, let her do it; Jem's not one that stands upon trifles between old acquaintances, and if so be as she shies a ham at me, why, the only thing for me to do is to carry on the blessed war with a side of bacon."

"No, no, let me have no violence, Jem. You must be specially careful. You know Mrs. Atherton's a remarkably sensitive woman, though she's a little violent."

"A little violent," said Jim. "You said a little. I never seed such fellows as some husbands is; they never likes nobody to think anything's wrong at home but themselves; but howsomedever, master, here goes. I'll go in, and ascertain the state of affairs, while you stay at the Bull and Perriwinkle."

This course, then, which, really considering all the circumstances, was not a very injudicious one, was finally adopted, and with no small degree of satisfaction Mr. Miles Atherton made his way to the Bull and Perriwinkle, while Jem proceeded, with all the audacity in the world, to make his observations with regard to the temper and disposition of Mrs Atherton.

There was no shrinking from the task he had asigned to himself; he set about it to all appearance quite *con amore*, and when he arrived at the shop, the air and manner with which he walked into it were anything but those of a person who came to make excuses for himself, or for any one else.

Mrs. Atherton had got a man, who happened to be passing, to pull down the shutters, and when that necessary commencement of the business of the day was accomplished, she stood at the back parlour-door, the whole of which she obscured by her portly person, while such a whirlwind of feelings rushed through her mind, that as Jem had vaguely anticipated, she seemed quite inclined to burst upon the smallest possible amount of additional aggravation.

"So, so," she was saying to herself, "this is very fine, indeed; not home all night, Mr. Miles Atherton. Of course wives know very well what to think when that is the case; but I won't think—he's not worth a thought, the wretch. I hope something dreadful's happened to him, and that when I do see him, he'll be brought home in a truck, all in pieces. Oh, the villanies of men! But whether he comes home or not, I'll leave him. If old what's-his-name, the brother of the Black Lady, performs only a half of his promises, I shall be superior to such a scrub. I am glad he's gone; I should only just like to see him come in at this moment; I haven't got two Dutch cheeses on the parlour table for nothing, and if they don't go deliberately at his head, I'm not a woman. I think I see me putting up with everything and nothing, continually, for all the world as if I was a fish. I'll let him know, when he does come home, who's who, and what's what, and that females are not created to be continually trampled on by men with iron heels. A skein of silk will lead us, but we won't be driven, and that I'll let Mr. Atherton know, always providing he ain't dead, which is most to be wished, for if I really was a widow, with any advantages, I really don't know what might happen. I'd marry somebody, and let the world see what could be done by people with a spirit. Oh, gracious thingamy, there's that rascal, Jem!"

With the effrontery of ten persons rolled into one, Jem walked into the shop.

"Good morning, missus," he said; "took anything, eh? Miles and me's been out on the spree! Couple of devilish fine girls!—the Eagle—lots of cigars and brandy-and-water for the million. Oh, you should have seen us, mum, pitching it strong! I don't wish to hurt your feelings, mum, but they was divinities! Sich eyes! sich lips! sich ankles! and they was so out-and-out good-natured!"

This was very treacherous of Jem, and it certainly was not doing what he promised Miles Atherton he would do. We do not question his motives, however, for there can be no doubt but he considered it a piece of generalship, and that possibly by treating the affair so boldly, he might get Atherton better through the scrape than by pursuing a more modified and peace-making course of action.

First appearances, too, seemed greatly to favour this supposition, for Mrs. Atherton certainly looked staggered, and retreated step by step into the parlour, as Jem advanced into the shop.

"It'll do," said Jem, to himself. "That's the way to tackle 'em; there's nothing in the world like putting a bold face on the matter."

Scarcely had he uttered these words when he began to find out the fallacy of them, for Mrs. Atherton, like a skilful general, was only falling back upon her ammunition.

She might have been a little staggered at the imperturbable coolness of Jem, but it was not sufficient to smother all hopes of vengeance. Accordingly, when she reached the table, upon which she had deposited the two missiles, in the shape of Dutch cheeses, she suddenly seized one, and sent it whirling at Jem's head, like a cannon shot.

But if Mrs. Atherton was a good general, Jem was an able tactician, and when he saw this round shot coming, he just stooped low enough for it to touch slightly the nape of his neck, and then it bowled with fearful velocity along his back, and having thus a more definite direction given to it, it shot out of the door, and hit an old gentleman who happened to be passing in the stomach, doubling him up completely, and rolling him in the kennel, as if he had done so on purpose.

"There, now, missus," said Jem. "Now you have done it."

"Murder!" cried the old gentleman; "murder!" and then out came the other cheese, and fell on his head.

"Here's a go," said Jem. "There goes the stock in trade. Why, mum, them Dutchmen was worth sevenpence a pound, if they was worth a bit; I'm sure they was."

"I'll have somebody's life!" exclaimed Mrs. Atherton, as she went into the shop, where Jem avoided her by vaulting over the counter. "I'll have somebody's life, I will. I'll let them see what it is to insult a respectable married woman with a certificate up stairs!"

Several people had now stopped to assist the old gentleman out of the kennel. He happened to be one of those fiery old bucks whom anything in the shape of a personal injury drives to an absolute frenzy. He had never relinquished the grasp of his umbrella, and when again he did gain possession of his feet, he flourished it wildly above his head, and made a rush at the shop, where, in about another minute, he demolished every pane of glass he could see; then he rushed in, and began hammering away at the butter, smashing eggs, and, altogether, creating such a scene of confusion, that it was quite terrific to see it.

"Go it!" cried Jem; "go it. While you are about it, have a bellyfull. It'll all go down in the bill, my old Grecian."

"You are the villain!" cried the old man, and he made a frantic attempt to get over the counter to Jem. "I'll have your life, you infernal scoundrel. You threw two d—d skittle balls at me just now."

"What a mistake," said Jim; "them was two Dutchmen."

"I don't care," cried the old man; "I'll sacrifice somebody."

"You will, will you, you old wretch?" said Mrs. Atherton, arming herself with a ham, and laying it over the old man's back with a velocity which one would have believed it impossible anything short of a steam-engine could have executed.

"Very good," said Jem; "I think now I may as well go and tell master what the blessed row is. I think I've seed the best of it; and, in course, he'll naturally be a little anxious."

The topography of the shop was well known to Jem, and by making a detour round a lot of butter firkins, he passed the combatants, and reaching the street, ran round the corner to the Bull and Perriwinkle as fast as he could.

Miles Atherton was anxious, but he was not so anxious as he had been, for he had fortified his inward man not a little by some of the strong compounds vended at that house of entertainment.

Still he looked rather nervously for Jem's arrival, and when he, at length, came into the room, Atherton said to him, in something almost above a whisper, although there were other parties present,—

"Well, Jem—well, Jem, what is it? What does she say?"

"Oh, nothing particular," said Jem; "nothing to speak of. How precious dry I am, to be sure."

"Well, well, that's more than I expected," said Atherton, "much more."

"Much less, master, I should say. Oh, I have managed it nicely for you. She's as mild as the best fresh; but, the fact is, half a night acts differently upon her to what a whole night would."

"Ah!" said Atherton, "what can be the reason, eh? I am glad of it."

"Oh, I don't know; but I suppose it's constitootional. She says eighteen-pence has been took in the shop."

"It's open then, Jem?" said Mr. Atherton. "Well, I am amazed at that, too. So the shop is open, eh?"

"Very open," said Jem; "and more nor that, missus has been crying. She says as how men will be men, and she can't help it; so you see I've done the business for you. What shall I have, eh, master?"

"Why, what you like, Jem. What you like, only be quick. I'll go directly."

"Bring me a glass of rum and milk," said Jem to the waiter. "I'll take it out-side at the bar. She said, sir, she hoped you'd come at once. Don't keep her in suspense any longer. Nothing shall be said about it."

It is difficult to say which most took possession of Miles Atherton's faculties. Amazement at his wife's extraordinary forgiveness, or satisfaction at the sudden change in her behaviour, as reported by Jem. He arose and left the room, having paid for Jem's treat of rum and milk at the bar, and then turned out of the house.

"There," said Jem, as he swallowed the last drop of the contents of the glass, "it's uncommon good, quite a treat; I don't have that every day. I wonder what's going on now; what particular part of the entertainment. It's a tragedy there; and a mellerdram here."

Jem now followed on the heels of his master, who, quite felicitating himself upon the most unexpected turn affairs had taken, and really accusing himself of behaving ill to so excellent a woman as Mrs. Atherton, soon reached his own shop-door.

Then, and not till then, a dim suspicion shot across his mind that all was not as it should be. The stock in trade presented rather the appearance of a wreck, and he was rather surprised to see a large dog crouch down with all the effrontery in the world almost upon his very door-step, and making considerable way into a Dutch cheese.

He walked in with considerable misgivings, and a faint idea that Jem must have played the traitor. To his surprise he heard a terrible confusion of female tongues, which evidently proceeded from the parlour behind the shop. With anything but a comfortable feeling he passed on, and looking through the half-glazed door, to his surprise he saw a vast number of females there collected, while all their heads seemed inclined in one direction, and shaking ominously; as, no doubt, with the laudable desire of saving time, they all gave their opinions at once upon something which had occurred, apparently in connection with the domestic economy of his household.

After a time he succeeded in catching a stray sentence or two, which enabled him to learn something of the subject matter under discussion, and then the suspicion that Jem had played him false became a matter of undeniable convic-tion, of which there could be no possible doubt.

"Oh, it's the way with them all," exclaimed one lady; "there's my husband, Wilkins, you'll travel far on a long summer's day before you'll find a man like him in the aggravating way."

"Oh, to be sure," said another, "no doubt. Never mind, Mrs. Atherton; look up, there's a dear, and don't mind the wretch. I mean to say this, ladies such as we ought to have ——"

"No, to be sure," exclaimed a third; "and if I had knowed what I know now, I'd sooner have been a toad under a harrow than Mrs. Jenkins."

Then all at once they said, as if it were one of those subjects upon which conviction reached every mind at once,—

"But Mr. Atherton's worse than nobody."

"Yes, yes," gasped Mrs. Atherton. "Two gals at the Eagle. I think I see 'em. I wish I had,—ladies, I'd brought home their whole six eyes, and shown 'em to you."

"And serve them right too, the hussies; a married man too; it puts one out of all patience to think of such disgraces to female society."

"I tell you what it is, my dear friends," suddenly added Mrs. Atherton; "if it were not really that something has happened to give me other prospectuses in life, I couldn't and wouldn't stand any of Miles Atherton's nonsense. A more unfeeling monster, ladies, never drew the blessed breath of life; but I needn't speak to you; the man who, after having been married a matter of seventeen year, could stay out all night, and go to the Eagle with two dreadful females, must be worse than nothink; but as I say, ladies, I have got other prospectuses. Something has happened which he knows nothing of, the wretch, nor shall he."

"What is it, Mrs. Atherton?" cried all the ladies in chorus. "What is it? What is it?"

"Why, as I must say, and it's just as well to be hung for a sheep as a lamb, while I was here, quite lonely and promiscuous, there came a ring ——"

"Yes, yes."

"And a gentleman, that I found he was when we came to an explanation, quite a jewel of a man, and perhaps after all everything is providential. If Atherton had been at home, with his vulgar cheesemongering ways, there's no saying what might have occurred, instead of a emerald."

"Instead of a what?" said everybody.

"A emeral, ladies; a green emeral."

"Well, I never," thought Miles Atherton; "she's gone a little maddish or so, that's quite clear. It's the first time I ever stayed out all night since I have been married, and it has turned her wits, poor thing. She can't stand it. Bless my heart, what does she say now?"

"What's a sheriff?" exclaimed Mrs. Atherton. "Nothink. What's a lord mayor? Nothink; when you can roll about in your own diamonds. There'll be a sensation in the city: and on the next blessed ninth of November, as will be, if I don't have a show of my own, in opposition to the lord mayor, I am not at this present speaking, a living and a breathing female."

"That's a settler," thought Miles Atherton; "she'll find herself in Bedlam, that's quite clear; the idea, now, of her going on in such a way. Perhaps I was blaming poor Jem wrongfully after all, and this has only come upon her since he left her. Well, I never—who would have thought it; I did expect, of course, a blessed row, but I had no idea of her going maddish, not in the least. It's took me all of a heap that has. No wonder I find the cheeses laying all out in the road, and all the eggs broke; and what a pretty smash of windows, too, there's been; bless my heart and life, what downs and ups there is in the world; we are here to-day and nowheres else to-morrow."

So unequivocal to Miles Atherton did his wife's mental aberration appear that he began to feel the criminality of his staying out all night from home in a much more serious light than he had originally, and to blame himself much for producing a result certainly which he never intended, and beyond the bounds of reasonable calculation, but still one which he could not but believe himself the indirect cause of.

"Dear me," he said, "it is all her violence that's come to this. I always did consider that if ever Mrs. Atherton went cracked, it would be on the subject of a sheriff's carriage; for the last five years she has been doing nothing but dinging into my ears how, if I had been a persevering man, I might live to be lord mayor; but, Lord bless me, I ain't ambitious, I don't want to be an emperor, let alone being a lord mayor.   I suppose I had better go in and say something.   Perhaps she won't know me."

With quite a sympathetic sort of face, Miles Atherton made his way into his own parlour, where he was speedily convinced that, whatever might be the amount of Mrs. Atherton's insanity as regarded diamonds and lord mayors' shows, it by no means involved any forgetfulness concerning him.

Mrs. Atherton sprang to her feet, crying out, " Oh, vengeance !" and before the cheesemonger knew where he was, or what sort of warlike demonstration was intended, a handful of hair was plucked from his head, and parallel scratches, commencing at his eye and terminating at his chin, demonstrated sufficiently Mrs. Atherton's full capacity to fight her own battles.

" Murder ! police !" cried Atherton.   " What do you mean by that ?"

" Oh, I'll make you remember the Eagle, as long as you live," cried Mrs. Atherton.   " So you must have three women at once, must you ?"

" Three women !" said Atherton, as he dodged behind a chair.   " I should say the one I have got is more than a dose and a half ; and what do you mean by the Eagle ?"

" Oh, you wretch !" continued the indignant lady ; " do you think I am as blind as a beadle ?   Out all night, are you ? and then think you can walk in in the morning as if nothing was the matter !   How can you look me in the face, you monster in the form of a cheesemonger ?"

" Easy enough," said Atherton ; " I wasn't very well, and I didn't want to shock you with the news, and here's all the reward I get for my consideration."

" You didn't want to shock me," said Mrs. Atherton, with such an elaborate sneer that it was enough to annihilate anybody.   " You didn't want to shock me, indeed !   Oh, you demon in disguise !"

" Ah, indeed !" exclaimed all the ladies present,—" very considerate ; a man stays out all night out of consideration for his wife."

" Ladies," said Atherton, " I dare say you have all heard that it's rather a thankless affair to interfere with man and wife.   Perhaps, ladies, you'll take the hint ; that's the way to the street."

There was such a general turning up of noses, and tossing of heads now, and a swinging of skirts, that it was quite edifying to see it.

" Oh ! I'm sure," cried one, "you are a nice article.   We don't want to stay ; and if it wasn't for your poor wife, sir, we should never have crossed your dirty threshold—no, never.   My dear Mrs. Atherton, do you think you can manage the brute ?"

" I know I can," said Mrs. Atherton, " so don't let me detain you."

Miles Atherton, when he saw the phalanx of spectators moving out, began almost to think it would have been better policy on his part to have allowed them to remain, than chance a pitch battle with so furious an antagonist as Mrs. Atherton was likely to become.   However, he said nothing, but took care to intrench himself as well as he could behind various pieces of furniture, in case any very formidable demonstration should be made by the lady.

A very prudent thought then occurred to him, and one for which we commend him highly ; that was, that it would be the best policy in the world to tell his wife exactly what had occurred, and when once such a notion was started in his brain, he only wondered that he had been so foolish as to invent any excuse upon the subject, which, in all probability, would not have been believed, while the correct statement of the case admitted of the easiest demonstration.

He was revolving in his own mind how he should commence, when Mrs. Atherton herself broke the rather ominous silence, by saying,—

" Mr. Atherton, I have made up my mind, sir.   You can go where you please, and do just what you please."

" Oh, thank you," said Atherton, " I don't want to go anywhere, or to do anything."

" Don't contradict me, Mr. Atherton.   I say you shall, sir ; and when I say a thing shall be, you ought to know pretty well, sir, that it is."

" Well, my dear, what is it ?" said Atherton, rather mildly, for he felt rather astonished at the address.

" What is it, indeed? Was there ever such effrontery—he asks me what it is ? He actually asks me what is it ?"   And Mrs. Atherton looked around her as if she were actually calling upon some mysterious persón to bear witness to Mr. Atherton's amazing effrontery.

" Well, my dear," said Atherton, calmly, " it is quite impossible I can know what it is, unless you are kind enough to tell me.   I shall be much obliged, of course, if you will do so, but if you won't, you won't."

" You abominable wretch without bowels," said Mrs. Atherton.

" Without what ?"

" Bowels, sir, without bowels.   It says bowels, sir, in Scripture, and I believe I may take upon myself to repeat it.   So I say again, without bowels."

" Oh, very good," said Atherton. " I don't want to make any row about whether I have got any bowels or not ; but what is it you say you are going to do, Mrs. Atherton ?"

" Have a separation, sir, and allow you so much a week."

" Allow me ?"

" Yes, sir, allow you."

" Well, I am a little astonished at that."

" Henceforward, Mr. Atherton, I am going to move about continually in the polite circles, and become one of the what-do-you-call 'ems of fashion.   I mean to cut low society, and begin with you."

" Well, that's civil, at any rate."

" And when you see me with a stomacher of diamonds, I'll trouble you not to know me."

" Oh," said Miles Atherton, " that's a stomacher, at any rate."

" You can go to a Negal with your vile associates.   Your two wretched females, Mr. Atherton.   I wish you joy of them ; but I have done with you, sir."

" Go to a where, did you say?"

" A Negal, sir—a Negal in the City-road."

" Oh ! the Eagle.   I never was in the Eagle in my life."

" What, not last night ?"

" Certainly not.   I was in St. Paul's."

" St. Paul's !—Peter, come down and judge us."

" Yes, Mrs. Atherton ; and if you'll only have the patience to listen, I'll just tell you how it happened, and then you may go and move in whatever circles you like."

Mrs. Atherton thought out of curiosity she would hear the wretch ; and then with a simplicity and precision, which convinced her almost against her will that he was speaking nothing but the truth, he detailed to her the circumstances under which he had been induced to remain out the whole of the night.   Concluding by saying,—

" And now you see, Mrs. Atherton, you've put yourself in a passion for nothing, for, after all, what does it amount to ?"

" Mr. Atherton, I don't see anything of the sort ; if you had chosen to tell me what you were about, none of this mischief would have occurred.   But it's always the way with you men, you are so particularly anxious to keep everything from your wives, and you see what you get by it, you wretches.   What harm could there be in telling me you were going to try the old key, and see if it fitted St. Paul's Cathedral.   It's a very strange thing, Mr. Miles Atherton, why you were so very anxious to keep me in the dark upon that subject, but you've got your reason, sir ; and what's more, I have been reading away at the manuscript of the Black Lady like one o'clock, and I know a great deal more than you do, I can tell you. I have found out who's who, by this time, and what's what, Mr. Atherton, while you were making a fool of yourself ; but, after all, I can't tell, for all I know, you may have expected, whatever you may say to the contrary, to find some woman in the vaults of St. Paul's."

"A dead woman, perhaps," said Miles Atherton. "Somebody's wife, perhaps, who's been so kind as to walk off."

"What do you say, Mr. Atherton?"

"I say somebody's wife, who has been kind enough to walk off, and leave a jolly widower behind her."

"Hurrah!" said Jem, popping his head in at the door. "That's the way to do it, master. Merry and free are a bachelor's revelries. How do you feel, mum, by this time? Lor bless you, it was only my fun about the Eagle and two gals. I didn't think you was so green, missus, as for to go for to believe sich a thing. Why, master and me, missus, when we goes out, is wirtue itself."

Mrs. Atherton was in such a rage, that she completely rivalled the colour of a huge copper fish-kettle, that formed one of the principal ornaments of the back parlour, and was always kept preternaturally bright. She evidently preferred action to language, and had not Jem withdrawn his head, after uttering this bold and defying speech, he might have had cause for a considerable time to repent his facetiousness.

He was accustomed to carrying on this guerilla warfare with his mistress. He was content to strike a blow, and then beat a speedy retreat, and Mrs. Atherton on these occasions always found herself, like the French in Algiers, in a terrible fume, and in full possession of just the ground she trod upon, while the enemy was Heaven knows where.

"Mr. Atherton!" she rather screamed than said, "I now insist upon the immediate discharge of that wretch!"

"My dear, my dear," said Mr. Atherton, "calm yourself; Jem is an eccentric, odd sort of lad; but then, you know, Mrs. Atherton, there is no denying that he is ——"

"I know very well what you are going to say, Mr. Atherton—honest, you are going to say. I know your mind as well as if I were in your inside; but you know very well there was that good looking young fellow we had of the name of Orgustus Plantagenet."

"Yes, I do know," said Atherton; "his real name turned out to be John James, and he robbed the till."

"Ah, but how polite he was! he was never made for a shopman—he had a soul, Mr. Atherton, above cheese and bacon. Let you say of him what you will, some of these days you'll hear of him shining in a proper spear."

"I have heard of that already," said Atherton; "he's been six weeks at the treadmill, and that is, I think, his proper sphere. Now I have done with such ungracious subjects, Mrs. Atherton, I repeat that Jem's honest, and I mean to keep him, and now pray drop all further contentions. I had no particular reason for not telling you I was about to visit St. Paul's Cathedral, and I don't know now well how I came to do so."

"We'll wave all that," said Mrs. Atherton, with a wave of her arm, as if she were actually waving something; "we'll wave that, sir, if you please. Circumstances are altered; if you think you can be a little more genteel than you are, so as not to bring disgrace upon me, I have no particular objection to continuing with you; but otherwise, Mr. Miles Atherton, as I am very likely to have an unlimited command of rubies, and emeralds, and other precious stones, you may go as soon as you like."

"There she goes again," said Miles Atherton; "she is mad. What do you mean, Mrs. Atherton, by all this talk about rubies, and diamonds, and emeralds?"

"What do I mean!" said Mrs. Atherton, as she made an amazing rattling in an immense pocket, and at last succeeded in catching the large emerald which Neville had given her. "That's what I mean, Mr. Atherton, what should you say that was, now?"

"Well, I really," said Atherton, "can't take upon myself to say—it's certainly green."

"I believe it is green, Mr. Atherton; any fool can see that. I can tell you, sir, it is an emerald."

Atherton shook his head as he said,—

"Our neighbour Smith, the jeweller, showed me one once that wasn't half as big as that, and it, he said, was worth three hundred pounds."

Mrs. Atherton gasped again; for her estimate of the value of the costly gem, which she supposed to have been given to her, reached nothing like that amount.

"Gracious Providence!" she said; "then this may be worth six!"

The parlour door opened, and Jem, as if he were master of the ceremonies, announced Mr. Smith.

"The very man," said Atherton, "to tell you what it is worth; now, Mrs. Atherton, we'll see."

"And we shall see," said Mrs. Atherton. "I believe I may have a dozen of them for the asking for; and they, I believe, will be amply sufficient to enable me to live like a princess."

"Very good," said Atherton. "Come in, Mr. Smith, we are glad to see you."

"Good morning," said Mr. Smith, the jeweller; "I am glad to see you so comfortable. Somebody told me there was no end of a row here."

"Ah, but there is though," said Atherton; "all's right; and now, Mr. Smith, as you are a jeweller, what should you say was the value of that?"

"Ah," said Mrs. Atherton, with a self-satisfied look, "be candid, and tell us what you think of that."

Smith very demurely took up the glittering gem and held it between him and the light, and he then held it in his hand for a few moments, as if calculating its weight, and not a muscle of his countenance moved.

"Well, well," said Atherton, "at a rough guess—what's it worth?"

"You needn't be nice to a shade, Smith," cried Mrs. Atherton; "tell us near about."

"It's very good," said Smith; "I've seldom seen a better; and I should say, roughly speaking, that you wouldn't get them under seven shillings a dozen."

"Seven what?" screamed Mrs. Atherton.

"Shillings," said Smith; "which makes it worth, you see, about sevenpence."

"Providence look down upon us!" said Mrs. Atherton; "what do you take it to be?"

"A green drop, off some fancy chandelier."

"Bravo!" said Atherton. "I'll be hanged if I didn't think as much. Why, my dear, a dozen of those wouldn't enable you to go far in the princess line; nor do I think they'll pay the expences of a show that will break the Lord Mayor's heart on the next ninth of November."

Poor Mrs. Atherton looked petrified for a few moments; anybody might have abused her. Jem, if he had chosen, might have walked in and pulled her nose, and gone out again, quite alive and well, if he had so chosen; but not for long did this state of mind continue. Like a flash of lightning a sudden thought came across Mrs. Atherton's brain; and flying at Smith like a tigress, she wrested the assumed jewel from his hand, crying out as she did so,—

"Oh, I understand your villany, Mr. Smith; I can see quite as far through a mill-stone as anybody else. You want to get this emerald for nothing, Mr. Smith, and then go and sell it to the Great Mogul. I can see your vile intentions in your face, you squinting vagabond! Go home, you swindler—go home! I dare say you thought you'd make a nice day's work of this, but you are deceived. I only hope that my carriage, with eight gray horses and twelve postilions, will ride over you some of these days, and then you'll see what the emerald has done. I am an injured woman! Don't look at me, Mr. Atherton! None of your grinning at each other, you two monsters!"

Here Mrs. Atherton gave some unequivocal symptoms of hysterics, upon which Atherton whispered to Smith,—

"I say, I shall just pop round the corner to the Bull and ——"

"Perriwinkle!" said Smith; "I'll go with you—come along."

And then they both shot out of the parlour, upon which Mrs. Atherton, somehow or other, miraculously recovered, and did not go into hysterics at all.

CHAPTER XIII.

THE NARRATIVE OF THE BLACK LADY CONTINUED, WHICH SHOWS A GREAT CHANGE IN THE FORTUNES OF THE WHITEHEADS.

"What?" exclaimed Mrs. Atherton, when she was left alone, "is my emerald not only to be declared glass, but am I to be insulted into the bargain? Well, I never! This is an improvement upon old times with a vengeance! A nice riot I used to make about Mr. Atherton going to the Bull and Perriwinkle in the evenings, but now he's begun upon it in the morning. I don't know what I sha'n't say about it. But is the emerald really an emerald, or a bit of a fancy chandelier? My heart fails me, and I feel all of a heap! I don't know what to think or what to do. I don't half like that Smith. Of course it's a great temptation to a man like him. Sevenpence, indeed, for an emerald. I think I see it. Stop a bit—a lucky thought. There's Mr. Big, the pawnbroker, round the corner, he'll tell me. I can rely upon an uncle; I won't tell him I want to sell it, so he shall have no interest in saying it is what it isn't. I warrant now I shall have the truth from him; and if he says it is an emerald, just let that Smith look to it, that's all—he'd better not have been born than come near me. I'll go at once—yes, directly; and then I shall have that off my mind, and be satisfied of Mr. Smith's falsehood."

Having come to this determination, Mrs. Atherton at once proceeded to arrange a very elaborately trimmed bonnet on her head, which, however, was a work of some time, seeing she was in great haste, and contrived to catch some wires of the flowers in her hair, which produced a kind of irritable action of the hands, and much pulling and scratching was the consequence.

"Bless me, everything happens on purpose to vex me. I am sure it's all through that Smith. But never mind; I'll let him know who's who."

By dint of great perseverance, she did get the bonnet on, and then, flinging her shawl on her shoulders, and at the same time knocking a case of artificial flowers off the mantelpiece, she left the house for the dubious relation, her uncle, Big, the pawnbroker.

The more Mrs. Atherton thought of the wickedness of human nature, and the desire for gain which is supposed to inhabit the hearts of jewellers, the more she became convinced that she really possessed an emerald, and that the expedition which Smith and Miles Atherton had gone upon was to consult upon some means of getting it out of her possession, and dividing the plunder.

"Oh, of course, they don't want me to have it—it's not likely they would. The avariciousness of men is beyond everything. I saw them wink at each other as they went out, as much as to say they'd get the better of me easily; but they'll find themselves mistaken."

Casting a withering look upon Jem, as she went out, Mrs. Atherton proceeded to the universal relative of all mankind, to demand his unbiassed opinion on the important question of emerald *versus* glass.

At that time in the morning no one was in the shop, and Mrs. Atherton, when she walked in, thought she had better take the initiative of the business, so she at once said,—

"Mr. Big, what is the value of that emerald?"

"Emerald, ma'am," said Mr. Big, as he took it up and looked at it. "Stuff, ma'am; who put that rubbish into your head? Somebody has been making a precious fool of you; they should have waited till the first of April."

"And what—what is it?" said Mrs. Atherton.

"Glass, to be sure."

Here was a horrible confirmation of a horrible truth. She could now no longer doubt Smith was right, and all her dreams of splendour were at once dissipated. She had not courage to speak to Mr. Big, but with the luckless mock jewel in her hand, she almost staggered from the shop, feeling herself quite a different person to what she had been during the continuance of her visions of wealth and renown. The drop was certainly a terrific one. To be reduced from a princely fortune to seven-pennyworth of glass was certainly a cruel blow of destiny.

With what different feelings she now entered the shop, and how amiably she looked upon the cheese and bacon, from the vending of which she was to derive comforts, in comparison to the glances of scorn she had cast upon those humble commodities, when she considered that all the luxuries of life were within her grasp.

Jem could not fail to see the change which was in her countenance, and much surprised was he thereat; and when she spoke to him, his astonishment knew no bounds.

"Jem," she said, "mind you are diligent in the shop, and do all the business you can. When Mr. Atherton comes in, tell him I want to see him directly."

"Yes, ma'am," said Jem. "Ain't you well, missus?"

"Quite well," said Mrs. Atherton, as she walked into the back parlour, and sat herself down, with a deep sigh, to brood over ruined hopes.

"Well, I never!" said Jem. "She's going to do something desperate now, I know. Won't I keep a bright look-out — that's all. No, no, missus, you don't take me by surprise ; I know yer."

Jem's precautions, however, were thrown away, for Mrs. Atherton had no intention in the world of taking anybody by surprise, and the only effort of indignation that she could at all muster was when she suddenly exclaimed, with something of her old spirit,—

" If ever I meet that villain Neville, I'll let him know what it is to have deceived me. He may come here again—let him, that's all ; and here comes Atherton, I declare."

The fact was, that Atherton and Smith had been extremely moderate at the Bull and Perriwinkle, for neither of them contemplated remaining long away from business at such an hour in the morning, so that their absence altogether had not exceeded more than half an hour.

" Jem," said Atherton, " I suppose your missus is in ?"

" Yes, sir," said Jem; " she's a laying some sort of mine."

" A mine !"

" Yes, to be sure, master ; she's so uncommon quiet."

" Well, Jem," said Atherton, " I really can't lead this sort of life. I don't see why, if I choose, I shouldn't stay out all night ; and, when I come to take a thought of things, I don't see why, because a man's married, he should be kept in a constant state of fear about this thing and the tother thing, just as if he were a slave."

" Nor me either," said Jem. " If ever I get married, master, I'll make another affair of it, I can tell you."

" Well, I must go in and speak to her—there's no help for that."

Arming himself for the worst, Atherton made his way into the back parlour, but what was his astonishment when his wife said,—

" Miles, my dear, sit down. Smith's right, after all. The emerald is but a bit of glass, so we need not have any words about it."

" Come, now," said Atherton, " no nonsense ; if you are going to make a row, or throw something at me, do it at once, and don't be treacherous."

" You have no cause to fear any violence from me," said Mrs. Atherton. " I assure you all I ask of you is to forget what has occurred this morning, and to find some opportunity, if you can, during the day, to read the Black Lady's papers up to the point where I shall show you I left off, and then, to-night, when the shop is shut up, we can resume reading them together."

" Very good," said Atherton ; " be it so ; and I can only say, my dear, that I am very much rejoiced to find you in such a pleasant frame of mind."

" Let bygones be bygones, Mr. Atherton."

" Very good, my dear ; it's a long lane that has no turning."

There had not been so good an understanding between Mr. and Mrs. Atherton for years past ; and when at night the shop was shut, and all was still and quiet, they resumed, with more satisfaction and more appearance of domestic comfort than they had yet enjoyed, the narrative of the Black Lady.

* * * * * * *

The weakest enemy that any human being can have is not to be despised : if it be that the malevolence of his disposition knows no touch of honour—if it be the will of any one individual, regardless of all conscientious scruples and all consequences, to do injury to another, to a certain extent he must succeed.

It is not the justice of a man's cause, or the irreproachable character of his position, which shall preserve him from the shafts of calumny, or the effects of that more deliberate villany which shall succeed in doing him some serious amount of damage. Innocent blood, ere this, has been shed ; and although a retribution, sooner or later, is sure to come upon the false accuser and the false witness, yet it is but a retribution, not a recompense. The evil that has already been accomplished is none the less, from the fact that the evil-doer suffers a penalty for transgressing those laws, human and divine, of which he could not be ignorant.

Hence, then, the reader sympathises with the position of that young clerk, whose innate perception of right made him revolt, in the remotest manner, from aiding, even by his silence, the villany of Godfrey.

We do imagine that much evil way come to him from the implacable resentment of that individual. Heaven send that innocence, and not injustice, may prevail. At all events, there is one feeling now lighted up in the breast of Charles Ormond, which to him appears a compensation for every evil that cruel fortune might attempt to cast upon him. That is his love for Marian Whitehead—a love which the events of the last four-and-twenty hours had fully matured, and made so strong a part of his very nature, that to attempt to tear her image from his heart, would be to destroy all its best and dearest energies, and to leave him so situated that henceforward the world and he could hold no pleasant companionship.

We do not mean to say but that he had loved her even before that night on which he came with such breathless haste to her cottage home ; but it was a love without a hope. He had viewed her, as it were, from a distance, and he loved her as he might have loved

"Some bright particular star"

in the blue firmament of Heaven, whose beauties dazzled him, but a nearer approach to which was quite out of the question.

He knew his own dependent and friendless situation ; he knew almost at a moment's notice he might be destitute, and his affection was not of that selfish character which could have induced him for a moment to yolk one whom he loved to the meagre chances of his fortune.

Although he had loved Marian, he had kept the secret of his honest passion to himself, and having never allowed it to mingle much with his dreams of the future, it had never acquired that extreme supremacy over him which now it had obtained. Oh ! what a world of change had taken place in his feelings within four-and-twenty hours. He had saved her whom he loved, first from destitution ; for, probably, Godfrey would have formed some excuse for evading the annuity ; and then, in all likelihood, he had saved her from a dreadful death, amid the burning timbers of that cottage which chance or malevolence had set in flames.

Now, indeed, he felt that fortune had favoured him with opportunities of showing her, far beyond what it was in the power of language to express, how truly he loved her.

And she, too, had spoken to him such gentle words of friendly and affectionate encouragement, that he could not doubt that he had succeeded in lighting up in her bosom the flame of an affection which, while life itself should last, could never be extinguished.

Mrs. Whitehead, too, could not but feel how great a claim Charles Ormond had upon her gratitude and her daughter's affections, and it was clear to him that she silently acquiesced in the furthering of an affection which had certainly begun under such suspicious circumstances.

They sat together at breakfast the morning after the fearful conflagration. Their wants were amply provided for by the liberal kindness of the family that had afforded them a shelter, and, at all events, to two out of the three composing that small party never had a morning meal passed off so pleasantly and so happily.

Marian and Charles said nothing of their love, but their eyes, those intelligent interpreters of the intelligence of the soul, expressed far more than any language would have enabled them to utter.

There needed between them no formal declarations of affection ; the heaven-born feeling showed itself in every look, in every action ; that secret sympathy, which binds together human hearts in such sweet bondage, showeth itself even in the most trivial circumstances. The hours flew like minutes, the minutes with the fleeting rapidity of moments, and the sun was creeping on to its meridian, ere Charles Ormond could withdraw himself from that delicious interview, and, with a sigh, he urged the necessity of some immediate course of action contingent upon the proceedings of the preceding night.

"It is highly necessary, Mrs. Whitehead," he said, "that legal steps should be taken on the instant regarding the property of which you will now, no doubt, obtain a complete and full restitution of."

"Mr. Ormond," said Mrs. Whitehead, "you will allow us to consider you as our friend and adviser. I am sure we both feel it necessary to have some one with us who will protect us from many of the evils which, in our friendless condition, would ye almost certain to fall upon us. Let it be quite understood, Mr. Ormond, that hou remain with us—that where we go, you go—and that our home shall be your ome."

Marian said nothing, but she gave to Charles Ormond an imploring look, a look which he could well translate, a look which told him how much she wished that he should accept, fully and frankly, the invitation of her mother.

And nothing loth was he to do so, situated as he was, indeed, and deprived of the means of subsistence he had had, as a consequence of the step he had taken to preserve Marian and her mother from the iniquity of Godfrey; he had nowhere else to go, and there was scarcely a shelter for him where he could with confidence say he could lay down his head.

Under these circumstances he could not but with the greatest pleasure accede to the proposition which had been made to him, especially feeling that it was made in all sincerity of purpose, or it would not have been made at all.

"Mrs. Whitehead," said Charles Ormond, "your offer, dictated by so much kindness and generosity, is too agreeable, and too important to myself, to decline it."

"Remember," continued Mrs. Whitehead, "that we are in all things your debtor, and should you say any more upon that subject, you will oblige me to repeat my obligations to you, for we cannot express the full sense of them; however, it is not so much from what has passed, as to what may happen to the future, that will make us much more your debtor."

"Nothing can give me greater satisfaction than to know I have been of service to you, and to learn that I may yet be so."

"You may be so, I assure you; and first and foremost you may do so, by taking those steps you think best calculated to secure the end we so much desire."

"And that would be the taking of legal steps for the recovery of your late husband's property, and preventing the meditated plunder of this Godfrey."

"Yes," said Mrs. Whitehead; "but at present we have not the means of bringing this bad man to account. Money is requisite for the commencement of a suit at law, and now we have no means, as the breach with Godfrey has dried up the only source we had, and now he will not furnish us with weapons against himself."

"No; I agree with you, Mrs. Whitehead," said Charles Ormond, "that nothing is to be expected from him, save, indeed, such evil deeds as his malevolence may dictate, and chance offer him the means of perpetrating."

"And that shows us the necessity for your protection," said Mrs. Whitehead. "We are, I hope, free from harm, while we are under the roof of these kind neighbours."

"At all events," said Marian, "he cannot think of following up one attack so closely by another; he would be tempting his fate, for he, or the instruments of his villany, would be secured, and both crimes brought home to them."

"Godfrey is capable of anything, however bad, and the only bar that there may be to a second attempt, would be the impracticability of it, or the fear his myrmidons may be imbued with; they no doubt will relax for a time, fearful lest they should run a double chance of detection."

"No doubt," said Mrs. Whitehead, "we are better situated for avoiding the attempts of this man, but we cannot remain here much longer."

"And about the legal advice, mother," said Marian; "what can be done?"

"We must take Mr. Ormond's advice, my dear. The chief thing that I see as a difficulty, is the want of acquaintance with any one in the legal profession, and the want of money to carry on a suit at law."

"I think I can get over that evil," said Charles Ormond.

"In that case," returned Mrs. Whitehead, "you will be our good genius, and make difficulties disappear that seem as insurmountable as the mountains."

"I only think so; not, I will say, without some prospect. The law is a liberal profession, and the members are mostly honourable men, and to some one of these I will go and lay a statement of your case, accompanied with all the documents, which are ample, and there will be no fear but some one will undertake the cause without paying him a sum of money to secure him from loss, which is the usual course of business, when the parties are strangers to each other."

"That is what I imagined we should be expected to do."

"And so you would; but your case is a peculiar one, and one that is so clear, and so easily proved, that any attorney can readily ascertain the truth of the main statements, that I expect to be able to enlist some one in the cause."

"Should any one undertake the cause, it will be a fortune to us all," said Mrs. Whitehead. "I shall be anxious to know the result of your application to some of the profession. Do you know any one to whom you can apply?"

"I should not hesitate about making the attempt, or even despair of success, if I did not; but I am so far known to one gentleman, that I think I can obtain a patient hearing from him."

"I am sure, Mr. Ormond," said Marian, "that your presence with us has been of the most essential service. Life and fortune we shall owe to your efforts. What could we refuse you, for what have we not to thank you?"

"I thought we were to have truce," said Charles Ormond, "smiling, for you seem to forget I cannot but be deeply interested in the success of all these efforts which are for our common good, if I may be allowed so to say."

"You may—you have the right," said Mrs. Whitehead, fervently. "How happy we are to have met with you."

"And I am not less happy," said Charles Ormond, as he glanced at Marian, whose eyes were fixed upon his countenance, but she quickly withdrew them in some confusion.

"And now," said Charles, "I think I had better lose no time, but go at once to London, and ascertain the exact situation of affairs, by making the attempt to interest some respectable solicitor in this affair, and for that purpose I must take the papers with me, and then I can at once reply to any question, and hand in the proof of my assertions. Such a course will at once command the attention of a man of business."

"Have you the papers?" inquired Mrs. Whitehead of Charles.

"No, they were in the portmanteau; but I believe that is somewhere in the house, for I brought it in."

There was an anxious search for a few moments, during which Charles Ormond felt the greatest inquietude lest the papers should have been either lost or fallen into the hands of Godfrey—however they were found.

"Well," said Charles, "I am glad they have not escaped us; I can hardly form any idea of the extent of the calamity that would have befallen us."

"It would have been an irreparable misfortune to us all," said Mrs. Whitehead.

The young clerk now selected all the documents that in any way related to the affair of the partnership and to the Indian speculation.

Having taken all that he deemed useful to his purpose, he bade the mother and daughter good bye, and, accompanied by their kindest and most fervent wishes for his success, Charles Ormond left the house where he had been so hospitably entertained by the Whiteheads.

What different feelings animated his breast when he found himself alone to what he had hitherto felt. What a change had come o'er the spirit of his dream within a very short period; but he indulged as little as he could in these thoughts and feelings; and as little as he could did he gloat over the prospects of his love for Marian Whitehead, for he knew he had a mission that would require all his care and skill to bring to a successful issue.

This he knew was of the utmost importance to them all, and he felt a weight of responsibility attach to himself, and an anxiety upon his mind that he had scarce ever felt before.

When he arrived at the part of the town he intended visiting, he paused for a few moments to collect his ideas and to consider well the best mode of introducing the subject. He might, however, just as well have saved the time, for he could not succeed, and he at once sought the chambers of Mr. Blake, a respectable solicitor in Lincoln's Inn. He knocked at the door, which was soon answered; and in answer to his inquiry, he was informed that Mr. Blake was at home but at present engaged.

"He will not be long, I dare say, sir," said the clerk, "and if you will sit down you can see him."

Ormond said he would do so, and sat down to wait patiently the leisure of Mr. Blake. This was not lost time to Ormond, because he had more leisure to arrange and re-arrange, in his own mind, the leading facts of the case, and the minor details which were upon it.

However, the individual departed, and he was shown into the apartment where Mr. Blake sat, surrounded with papers and documents of a variety of causes. Ormond introduced himself by saying he had trespassed upon his time relative to an affair of some importance, and in which a large sum of money was at stake.

"You wish me to become attorney in this case, then," said Mr. Blake; "I think that is what you mean."

"Precisely."

"Who are the parties?" inquired Mr. Blake, who was desirous of coming at the points of the case seriatim, so that he might the better and more speedily comprehend the case.

"The widow and daughter of the late Mr. Whitehead, against Mr. Godfrey, merchant and partner of her late husband, who is endeavouring to exclude her from the benefits of the partnership, and also of the benefits of her husband's single-handed enterprise."

"Indeed; then there are some partnership accounts withheld?"

"There have been, sir; the widow has been debarred the benefit of all share of the profits by the existing partner, because he affirms that his late partner, in effect, dissolved the partnership by breaking some of the clauses of the deed."

"I see."

"He then induces the widow to sign a deed to receive a small annuity, declaring in the deed that she will not trouble him respecting any accounts which might have ever existed between him and the late Mr. Whitehead, he having ceased to be a partner some time before his death."

"Well, sir?"

"Now——"

"But stop; you desire he should render these accounts, I presume?"

"No, that is not our object."

"Indeed; what then?"

"That deed may stand as he originally intended it should; he, however, fearing a loss, wished to bar the widow from receiving any benefit from her husband's connection with him."

"Well, sir?"

"Affairs, however, were not so bad as imagined, and a large return is likely to be the result of these exertions and speculations repudiated by Godfrey; and this he has ascertained to be the case, for he now endeavours to claim a share."

"Of what he repudiated?"

"Exactly. He endeavoured to induce the widow to sign another deed, by which she would for a certain sum of money barter away her whole benefits arising out of the transaction, but it was baffled by one who saw the whole affair, and who knew what the widow would lose, though she did not, and the deed was never executed."

"Upon my word this appears a very black affair, Mr. Ormond; and if you have documents in support of what you have advanced, the case is clear, and can be easily carried through a court of law."

"I have them here, sir," said Charles Ormond, as he produced a bundle of papers, being those he had selected in the morning for the purpose. "Here you will find the original deed of partnership; some correspondence, and other papers relative to the Indian affairs, with many other documents and vouchers."

The solicitor looked over the papers, and selecting the principal, gave a hasty glance at them, and when he had done, he said,—

"This affair to me appears very clear. You say that the widow has [signed a deed, by which she admits this Godfrey's [assertion, that the partnership was dissolved by her husband's own act?"

"Yes."

"That deed bars him from any participation of benefit arising subsequent to that date," said Mr. Blake.

"It does so. And now, sir, let me tell you another part of the tale. Though there are large sums coming to the widow of the late Mr. Whitehead and his daughter, yet, in consequence of this Godfrey's conduct, they have not the means of carrying on the suit against him."

" You mean they have not powder and shot to expend in the fight ?"

" They have not ; and last night they were turned out of their home."

"God bless me !"

" Will you, when you have perused these documents, think yourself sufficiently secured by the justice of the case to carry the suit on for her ?—that is the object of my present visit."

" Yes, I will ; and moreover, I will advance her money. I know a few of the names here to be highly respectable. The case is so clear and so well esta-blished, no one link or proof appears to be wanting, that I have not a moment's hesitation in advancing her money for her immediate use. Give me the other documents, and I will undertake that a favourable result shall ensue.   And in the mean time, as she has met with such an accident, if a hundred pounds is of any service to her you can take it."

" It would, I know," said Ormond, "be of essential service, as her small annuity is stopped by this man Godfrey, who hopes that poverty may overtake them and prevent their prosecuting a suit against him."

" Than take it, sir.   I think they had better come to town, as I can easier com-municate with them. They need not hide thems.lves in any obscure part, I will be their banker to any amount within reason, and a short time will, I have no doubt, only elapse before they are possessed of an ample fortune."

Taking the money, and thanking Mr. Blake for his kindness, Charles Ormond left the chambers and pursued his way to the house where they had been so kindly entertained from the preceding night.

CHAPTER XIV.

THE LODGINGS IN TOWN.—THE MEETING AT MR. BLAKE'S CHAMBERS.

WHEN Charles Ormond entered the room in which Mrs. Whitehead and Marian were seated, they both looked up, and they read in his countenance that he had not been altogether unsuccessful.

" I see, Mr. Ormond," said Mrs. Whitehead, " that you have not had a bootless errand on this occasion ; your countenance would not bear such an expression of pleasure without sufficient cause."

" Indeed it would not ; but I have more than expected cause for congratulation on this occasion."

" Indeed !" said Marian.

" The gentleman will no doubt undertake our cause, then ?" said Mrs. White-head.

" He will ; and moreover he will be your banker while the matter is contested ; he will and has advanced you money on account of what you are to receive."

Mrs. Whitehead and Marian looked at each other, and at Charles, and the former replied,—

" I am more than ever obliged to you, Mr. Ormond ; you have indeed placed us in a position we could not hope for."

Marian looked upon Charles with one of those fond endearing looks that say so much, for the whole soul is in the eye ; he saw and appreciated her feelings, and amply was he rewarded for his exertions.

" Mrs. Whitehead," he said, " it will be as well to leave this place for town im-mediately—the sooner we are in London the better. You can procure lodgings upon the instant, especially if you pay money in advance."

" We place ourselves entirely under your guidance, Mr. Ormond," said Mrs. Whitehead ; "and in doing so, do not let us be misunderstood, we are not to part when you have piloted us to our new home, for the same roof that shelters us, shelters you also."

" Madam, how can I thank you ?" said Charles Ormond.

" No more of that, Mr. Ormond.   What are we not indebted to you for ? and for what shall we not have to thank past, present, and to come ?"

Charles Ormond could not, had he the wish to do so, battle against such kind words, and at once acquiesced in so gratifying an arrangement, at the same time, though Marian said nothing, yet he saw well that she was by no means averse to the proposition that placed Charles in the same dwelling with herself.

That hour, with many thanks to the family who had so kindly befriended them during the fire, they left the neighbourhood for the new residence in town that was to procure them so much happiness, and to open such a new scene for them all in fortune and in life.

The young clerk had made one or two inquiries as he quitted Mr. Blake's, with the view of securing lodgings for them if they adopted the attorney's advice. Now he called again, and taking Mrs. Whitehead to them with Marian, to see if they were such as would suit them.

There was but little time for choice, for the day was well nigh spent, and there was but little light; indeed the lamps were fast lighting up, a sure sign that the evening is at hand in London.

However, there was but as little room for doubt as there was time for the lodgings, which were furnished, and were of a very handsome character.

"This will do admirably," said Mrs. Whitehead to Charles Ormond; "what do you say, Marian, my dear?"

"That we could not do better. They are very handsomely furnished, and I am sure that you will be pleased with them when day-light returns."

"Then we are decided upon taking them." And then turning to the landlady who stood by, she said,—

"I suppose as they are empty they can be immediately occupied?"

"Yes, ma'am; but it is usual to give a reference, and time to inquire about respectability, and so on."

"That can be done," said Charles Ormond, "but it must be done afterwards, as the fact is this lady's house was burned down only last night; but instead of references we can pay you money down—rent in advance."

"Well, sir," said the landlady, "under those circumstances we must dispense with the references."

The whole was soon settled and they were installed in their new apartments, and passed one of the pleasantest evenings that for some time any one of the small party had experienced.

That night was spent in blissful repose; no danger and no apprehension disturbed the slumbers of the mother and daughter, or of the young clerk; peaceful slumbers and pleasant waking dreams were their only midnight companions.

At breakfast the next morning the little party met. It was a pleasant scene. Mrs. Whitehead, and Marian, and Charles Ormond, all three sat in a gaily furnished room, filled with all the modern paraphernalia of breakfast, and filled with little ornaments, and vases with flowers, carpets, and looking-glasses, that set the place off to advantage.

"This," said Mrs. Whitehead, "reminds me of our earlier career, and if we should succeed, which I cannot doubt, since the solicitor himself has advanced us money, our fortune will be more ample than ever it was before, and not subject to any fluctuations or uncertainties."

"That is most true," said Ormond; "your fortune and your income will be fixed, and you will know what you can do, and that, unless I am mistaken, will be much more than you can at all imagine."

"Indeed!"

"Yes; and as to the success, I have no doubt of it myself, and a respectable, clear headed man of business, like Mr. Blake, would not voluntarily have advanced money, had he not been well assured of the goodness of the cause, and the certainty of the issue."

"I am glad to hear it, though there will no doubt be every fraudulent attempt on Godfrey's part, to meet the affair by every possible shift and art that can be resorted to."

"There can be no doubt about it," said Ormond, "and yet in a plain case they will have but little chance of even causing more than ordinary delay, which in all cases they can."

"He will avail himself of that ; but, however, we shall not be the less happy, because we are here more secure from any danger that may, or might have sur-rounded us, before we came here.'"

" Yes, you are much better off in that respect, at all events."

" And all others."

The days passed by pleasantly enough in their new lodgings, and many happy hours were spent, until at length a note came from Mr. Blake, saying he had begun the suit, and had received a communication from a Mr. Norris, Godfrey's attorney, who would be there the next day, at eleven o'clock, and that he would be glad if he, Charles Ormond, were present.

" You will go, Charles, will you not?" said Marian, as she read the letter which her mother gave her.

" Yes, certainly."

" Most probably," said Mrs. Whitehead, " Mr. Godfrey is now desirous of pro-posing terms of some kind of accommodation."

" Which cannot be accepted, unless Mr. Blake presses it, which is very im-probable."

" Yes, it would scarce be equitable to take a portion, where so clear a right is established to the whole."

*   *   *   *   *   *   *

The next morning at eleven o'clock, Charles Ormond was at Mr. Blake's offices in Lincoln's-inn.   That gentleman had scarce time to welcome him, and say a few words, when Mr. Norris was announced.

" Let him wait half a moment," said Mr. Blake, and then turning to Charles, he said, " I have commenced proceedings, and have filed a bill in Chancery for the production of the deed in which the partnership was dissolved at his own instance, and the promise of the annuity was given by him as an equivalant to the widow; and I have also written legal notices not to pay any money to Godfrey, upon the account of the late Mr. Whitehead, or Godfrey and Whitehead, but to retain all monies until the action pending should be settled."

" That will prevent any waste of the money, and further litigation," said Charles.

" Exactly ; and now we will have Mr. Norris in," said the attorney.

Accordingly ringing for his clerk, he then ordered the attendance of Mr. Norris, who was accordingly shown into the office.

" Well, sir," said Mr. Blake, " you have come respecting this affair of White-head and Godfrey, I presume ?"

" I have, sir."

" Be seated."

" But have we not a stranger here ?" said Mr. Norris, looking at Ormond.

" No, sir; this gentleman has an interest in the affair, I believe.   Mr. Charles Ormond, Mr. Norris."

" You are a friend of the widow, I presume ?   I have heard the name."

" I am, sir."

" Yes, Mr. Ormond introduced the affair to my notice, Mr. Norris, and is, I believe, conversant with the whole affair."

" Well, sir, I come to ascertain what it is you require, and the cause of the suit ?"

" You are aware of the whole history of the perfectly events that have taken place?"

" I believe I am," said Mr. Norris. "The late Mr. Whitehead was, while living, and to the time of his death, the partner of the present Mr. Godfrey."

" Not until the time of his death," said Charles Ormond.

" I am instructed otherwise."

" That is one of the points then, upon which we are at issue," remarked Mr. Blake.

" The affair is compressed in a small space," said Charles Ormond, " and perhaps I may as well relate them, and then you can see where you differ, and the legal points that may be raised."

"Very good," said Mr. Blake; "the papers I have perused, render the matter so plain a tale, so straightforward, that there can be no mischief done in re-stating it."

"Of course not, if the papers are not confidential," said Mr. Blake, "and merely for the purpose of ascertaining correctly our point of difference. That well known, we may come either to a compromise, or to some definite arrangement. Of course I do not make any offer, and what I have said, is equally without prejudice with what may fall from yourself."

"Well," said Ormond, "then the affair of the widow stands thus :—Mr. Whitehead and Mr. Godfrey were partners, as export merchants, both having a certain amount of capital in the firm. Mr. Whitehead engaged in some Indian speculations, which took a large sum out of the firm. News was brought that these speculations had failed, and Mr. Godfrey fearing that a large loss was the consequence, turned round, and said,—

"'You are no longer a partner. You have dissolved the partnership, by withdrawing your capital, and have broken, in so doing, one of the clauses of the deed of partnership.'

"Mr. Whitehead died of a broken heart, in consequence of his unfortunate condition, being deprived of all benefits of the business of which Mr. Godfrey was now the sole partner.

"A small annuity was offered the widow upon her repudiating all right to anything from the firm, or title to anything flowing from the partnership that had been dissolved by infraction of the deed of partnership, and which Godfrey declared no longer existed.

"After this was accomplished, news was brought that the speculation, instead of being a failure, had increased to admiration, and a large sum was realized by it. Now, Mr. Godfrey wishes to reap the benefit of this, and endeavours to set up a claim to a moiety, and insists, now there is a profit, that the partnership yet exists. He wants, indeed, to undo what he had done, by the deed the widow signed."

"Of course," said Mr. Blake, "he cannot reap a benefit he has repudiated."

"There again we join issue," said Mr. Norris; "we say that he has not done so at all."

"But there is the deed."

"Where?"

"In Mr. Godfrey's possession; it was given for his security, and of course he is the party who of right should hold it."

"Ay," said Mr. Norris, "there is the question. Where is the deed?"

"I have answered the question."

"Mr. Godfrey says there is no such deed in existence."

"But," said Charles Ormond, "affidavits of its existence can be had. I have seen it, the widow has seen it, and others too."

"I am instructed to the reverse of all this," remarked Norris.

"I have seen correspondence and other papers relative to this affair, that go far towards corroboration in this matter, that I cannot doubt it," said Mr. Blake.

"Well, it seems," said Norris, "that we are both placed in different positions, and it will be difficult to come to any definite conclusion."

"Entirely so. Your ignorance of the existence of the deed, and our certainty of its being, makes any cordial understanding impossible, for you must be aware that it entirely alters the complexion of the case."

"Of course," said Norris; "the affair must go to legal arbitration."

"We shall proceed with all reasonable despatch," said Blake, "for my client of course will be anxious for a settlement, as her situation requires it."

After a little more conversation the meeting broke up, and Mr. Norris retired, leaving Mr. Blake and Charles Ormond alone.

CHAPTER XV.

GODFREY'S NEW ALLY.—THE FORGED CHEQUE, AND THE DANGER OF CHARLES
ORMOND.

IT was about a fortnight after legal proceedings had been put in proper train,
that Godfrey was seated at his breakfast, ruminating upon the past and present,
and scheming for the future, when a visitor was announced. He was in no humour
to see any one, for the circumstances as they were, were to him peculiarly aggravating; for a cunning, scrupulous man to be caught in his own toils, is vexing in
the extreme; and the vexation in this case was by no means lessened, when he
considered the sum that he was likely to lose.

Godfrey requested the visitor's name, when he was informed he had given none,
that he merely said he wished to see him.

"Then go and inquire his name," said Godfrey, "I am too busy to see anybody."

The servant departed, and in a few moments more returned with the information
that the visitor's name was Neville.

"Neville," repeated Godfrey.

"Yes," said that person, presenting himself. "Here I am, Godfrey—I've just
come from sea. How are you, eh?"

"Ah!" said Godfrey, "so you are in England again, are you, Neville? What
do you do here?"

"Why, I haven't been long from sea, you know, but I thought you would be
anxious to see me."

"Indeed! I am not at all anxious about you."

"Oh, but between relatives, you know. You recollect I have been all my life
at sea, and therefore I have some claim upon your sympathies."

"Oh, yes; my sympathies are by no means extensive, and they are not at all
likely to be excited, because you have had a sea voyage, with a doubtful object.
Pray, did you go on your own account, or merely to oblige the authorities?"

"I went because I went," said Neville, "and that's enough; but, come, you
will do something for me now I am here, won't you?"

"Nothing."

"You don't mean to say that, I am sure. You know, Godfrey, you were always
tender towards relatives."

"Come, I have no time to spend in this foolery—begone."

"Indeed! but you must do something for me."

"I will not, and unless you go instantly, I'll turn you out. I tell you what it is,
I have no right to support every hulking fellow who won't support himself, so
be off."

"No, no, Godfrey. Come, I shall not be a heavy burden, and you can support
a small call upon your purse."

Godfrey rose in a great rage, with the intention of putting the intruder Neville
out by force, but before he reached sufficiently close to his unwelcome visitor to
be enabled to carry out such an intention, he saw, or fancied he saw, a determined
aspect about Neville, which might possibly make such a proceeding dangerous, and
as reckless courage is by no means an attribute of villany, Godfrey stopped short,
taking wisdom in his anger, before he had proceeded a little too far for personal
safety.

"What do you mean," he said, in an altered tone, "by coming here as if you
had any possible claim or demand upon me?"

"Oh!" said Neville, sneeringly, "you have taken a better thought of that, have
you? It's just as well you have, and I'll tell you why, cousin Godfrey."

"Cousin," exclaimed Godfrey, "what do you mean by that—you are no cousin
of mine?"

"Why, the fact is," said Neville, "it's the only name one can give to distant
and undefined relationship like ours, so cousin it must be. You may make a friend
or an enemy of me as you please, Godfrey. I am an useful fellow enough in my

way, to those who know how to make me so. I have something to gain from your friendship if you choose to tender it, but I have nothing to lose from your enmity. The fact is, fortune has already done her worst, and if you dare to lay a hand upon me, the prison to which you might succeed in consigning me for resisting you—for, of course, being such a respectable man, you would have it all your own way—would be a better place of shelter for me at present, than any other I am likely to procure."

"I'll have nothing to do with you," said Godfrey. "Go in peace. It matters not to me whether your claim of relationship be near or remote, a reality or a delusion, I will have nothing to do with you, and now you have your answer. You can do yourself no good by remaining here."

"Well," said Neville, "I don't mean to assert that I can force you to do anything; but you are a fool for all that, Godfrey. You are well to do. The small sum that would keep me above starvation point, you would never miss, and it is probable that I might be able to do you a service for it that would repay you a hundred fold. It is not possible but that such a man as you must have occasionally work of a troublesome, and, perhaps, of a hazardous nature; some piece of villany to execute, which you dare not do yourself, not from disinclination, but you would be personally known, and so mar the plot, which might by a stranger be satisfactorily conducted. Now you know enough of me, Godfrey, to be aware that I am not a man to stand upon trifles. Society and I have quarrelled, and as the weakest goes to the wall, why of course I got the worst of it, so I am just in the humour to do anything by way of retaliation."

At the conclusion of this speech there was a silence of some moments' duration; Neville was rather anxiously watching Godfrey, while he, Godfrey, seemed, by the expression of his face, to think that after all there was something in it which merited his consideration.

It was a very home truth indeed that which had been uttered to him; he was just the sort of man always to have some villany afloat, in the conducting of which he required some skilful and daring confederate; and probably never did such a truth come so strongly upon him, as at the present moment, when the affair of the Whiteheads appeared more than likely to turn out of vast importance to him.

He knew enough of the character of Neville to feel convinced in that quarter there would be no qualms of conscience at any act which promised in its results a satisfactory consideration.

Like most rogues who have fallen under the law's penalties in any way, Neville, no doubt, really considered himself an ill-used personage, and that feeling that he had expressed to the effect that society had got the better of him through their power, was, probably enough, his real opinion.

"If I thought I could depend upon you," said Godfrey, "I might perhaps feel inclined to endeavour to put something in your way."

"Ah!" exclaimed the other, "we shall understand each other yet. Come, Godfrey, what's in thy mind now? I am not only one that will and can advise you, but unlike most advisers, I am willing to carry out what I suggest. Be explicit."

"You understand that, of course," said Godfrey, as he handed him a five pound note.

"Good," said Neville; "I rather think I do. I take it as a retaining fee, and now wait for instructions."

Godfrey's mind was not quite made up; he still paused a little ere he could resolve upon placing himself by any trusty confidence in the power of such a man.

"Take your time," said Neville; "there is no hurry. It will be all the same in the end. You will trust me because you know you may. Self interest, that most powerful of all human bonds, will hold me faithfully to you, and if I were to go from here, and make an attempt to betray you, who do you suppose would believe the uncorroborated testimony of such a man as I? or what reward could I hope for by tendering it?"

"None, none," said Godfrey. "I think you are perfectly right. Listen to me. I have at present an affair in progress of great magnitude. It is one which, although it may not harm me, be the result what it may, yet if I could so conquer circumstances as to force that result the way I wish it, I should unquestionably benefit largely, and I should be able to reward you in a commensurate manner."

"Go on," said Neville, as he flung himself into a seat; "go on."

Godfrey did go on, and he related to Neville precisely how the circumstances stood between the Whiteheads, and enlarged upon the necessity of doing something to alter the aspect of affairs in that quarter.

"Not knowing," he added, at the termination of his statement, "or thinking if you were alive or dead, I have sought assistance in another quarter; but it is probable enough that you have something more satisfactory to propose than what has emanated from them, and I have not gone so far in that quarter but that I can retreat with ease and safety."

"Well," said Neville, "retreat then. You don't care, I presume, what amount of mischief you do so that you accomplish your purpose?"

"Not a whit."

"And the law you state is clearly against you?"

"It is. That is a proposition I feel myself compelled most reluctantly to admit."

"Then I tell you what, Godfrey; the only way to manage such an affair as this, will be to do something which shall induce these Whiteheads to jump at a compromise, and the only way to effect that will be to place that young spark, who is now such a great man with both mother and daughter, in an awkward position."

"But how?"

"Do you owe him any money?"

"Yes, his last quarter's salary, which I presume now he is too haughty to demand."

"Then you have him. I will tell you of a plan by which, if he don't swing at the Old Bailey, he'll be a most marvellous lucky fellow. Are you sure we are out of ear shot?"

"Quite. This private office has witnessed many a conference which it would not exactly have done to make public. There are double doors, as you must have perceived, to the room. You may speak freely."

"I will do so upon that assurance, and as sure as you and I will be of great mutual assistance, shall I be able to convince you how easily I can place your enemy in your grasp."

"Convince me of that, and I shall not regret the circumstances that have brought you here. The two greatest, and indeed, I may say, the only passions that have ever found a place in my heart would be gratified by such a result,—the love of money and the thirst for revenge. I do not mind owning to you that I feel both these impulses most fully and completely."

"I cannot thank you for your confidence," said Neville; "you tell me only that which I know, and which, indeed, I know in common with every one at all acquainted with you. But to business; if I succeed in placing you precisely in the position you wish to obtain, as regards these people you have mentioned to me, what am I to expect as the amount of my reward?"

"You may rely upon my liberality"

"May I, indeed? a slender reliance truly, and one I am not much inclined to trust to. No, Godfrey, I must have something clear and explicit upon that point. You know yourself what the service is worth to you, and consequently you can tolerably estimate the reward you ought to give. Make it ample, and it will be the better for you in the end."

"What say you to twenty pounds?" remarked Godfrey.

"A flat refusal," said the other. "For five times that amount I will undertake that young spark, Charles Ormond, shall be placed in so critical a position that, to buy him off, the Whiteheads will sacrifice anything, and, at all events, no pecuniary considerations will stand in the way of obtaining even his conditional release from a prosecution, which, they must be convinced, if carried on, would prove effectual."

"A hundred pounds is a large sum."

"Psha! I'm not in the habit of casting up money lately, and therefore, probably, it appears of more importance than it really is. I ought to have doubled or trebled my demand; but since I have said a hundred, so be it, and let me have an answer at once, Godfrey—yes, or no."

"Yes," said Godfrey, "I consent; and what is more, Neville, notwithstanding your sneer at my liberality, you shall find, if complete success crown your efforts, that I can and will add something even to the amount you have named; and now tell me, candidly, your plan of operation."

"I will. You know that among my acquaintances for the last few years abroad, it is extremely likely that I have succeeded in gathering a tolerable amount of worldly wisdom as to the management of matters of this sort."

"True, most true."

"I hold it as a maxim that any two or three men conspiring together, and keeping faith one with the other, can, have they any tact at all, accuse, and successfully convict, any ordinarily situated individual of almost any crime."

"I think so too. The mode of administering criminal law in this country, from its very justice and the weight it gives to direct evidence, most peculiarly enables such a thing to be done."

"You're right. Now mark me. You owe to Charles Ormond equitably, his last quarter's salary, as well as salary for whatever amount of notice you ought to have given him previous to his discharge. Now I'm enough of a lawyer to know, Mr. Godfrey, that that notice always has a direct reference to the period of hiring and payment of the stipulated amount of stipend. You pay him quarterly, and therefore he is entitled to a quarter's notice; now I want you to send him a check for six months' salary along with a note, but not together, that you don't intend to pay him a farthing."

"The deuce you do. I must confess that the first part of your plan is rather paradoxical."

"It may seem so. Where's your check-book?"

"Thank you; I generally keep that for my own private use."

"Psha! you need have no delicacy with me."

"But I positively refuse to draw a check in favour of Charles Ormond for any such amount."

"I will, then."

"You?"

"Yes, to be sure; I've no delicacy upon the subject, Godfrey; if this affair is to be managed at all, you must let me do it my own way. Produce your check-book, man, and then your natural sagacity will show you in a few minutes what use I intend to make of it."

"From curiosity," said Godfrey, as he unlocked a desk and took a check-book from it—"from curiosity, rather than other motive, I will gratify you so far. There is the check-book, what do you propose doing with it now you have it."

Neville opened the book considerably in advance of that part whence the last check had been taken, and he tore out two blank checks together.

"These," he said, "will accomplish all that you desire as regards this young man. Fill up one of them to the amount of his six months' salary; and then send the two together in a note, as if the blank one had been torn from the book in consequence of an accidental adhesion between it and the other. But, mark me, disguise your hand somewhat in writing the one you fill in; let it be sufficiently like your ordinary mode of drawing a check to awaken no suspicion in Charles Ormond's breast, but yet sufficiently unlike to induce your bankers to refuse to cash it. You perceive now, Godfrey?"

"By Heavens I do! He will be given into custody at the banker's for presenting a forged check."

"True; and you're sent for and asked if the signature is yours, which you repudiate."

"Yes, and state that some time since I missed two blank checks from my book."

"Decidedly, both of which are identified as those in the prisoner's possession."

"He is ruined; it is as good as accomplished. A more direct case never came before the magistracy. His committal follows as a thing of course, and upon such evidence a conviction must ensue."

"Most decidedly; nothing on earth can save him but your own impeachment of yourself, or the Whiteheads coming to you and making terms with you with regard to the Indian property, which shall induce you so to conduct the prosecution that the prisoner shall escape."

"And that they will do so I feel convinced; this young spark has obtained a firm hold of the affections of Marian Whitehead, and she will induce her mother to take any step for the purpose of saving his neck,—for hanged he will be, to all intents and purposes, if this affair be carried out. I'll about it at once."

Godfrey then drew the check, without a moment's hesitation, in the manner which had been suggested by his rascally companion, and then the following letter was concocted between them.

"To Mr. Charles Ormond.

"SIR,—In answer to your application for six months' salary due to you, I have to state that I consider, by your own conduct, you have forfeited all right thereto; and, if you insist upon such a claim, upon your request I am quite ready to furnish you with the name of my solicitor.

"I am, &c.,
"SIMON GODFREY."

"That will do," said Neville; "of course that note will be found upon him, and be a link in the train of evidence which will hurry him to destruction. It will be clear to any jury in the kingdom that the check must have been drawn by him or you; and that you would draw it after such a communication is absurd, while, at the same time, doubtless, whoever you bring forward with a knowledge of your handwriting will swear that it is not your signature. How he can then clear himself I don't know. His protestations of innocence will be of no avail; indeed they will do him more injury than otherwise."

"Decidedly they will. Would it not be glorious now to get all the concessions I want from the Whiteheads, with regard to the property, and then let this young fellow swing after all."

"Why, that," said Neville, "is a little refinement upon the matter I must leave to you. It really don't matter to me you see in the least, and now I'll trouble you for an instalment of the hundred pounds."

"If you will call to-morrow," said Godfrey.

"Oh! dear no. Between this and then I might be tempted to go to the Whiteheads' attorney, and ask him what he'd give for the history of this little episode."

"For Heaven's sake," said Godfrey, "don't start such a proposition; I would rather give you the whole amount at once, than you should be in such a frame of mind."

"And so would I, and, therefore, we are both of a mind, so hand it over."

Godfrey drew him a check for the amount, and then without another word Neville rose, and left the office.

Godfrey looked after him for a few moments in silence, and then he muttered,—

"A hundred pounds—a hundred straws. The Indian property is five and forty thousand. So, so, Mr. Neville, I think I've bought your services somewhat cheap. You're not so cunning as you might be."

Neville, when he reached the street, turned, and gave a strange kind of laugh as he glanced at the merchant's door.

"Indeed," he said, "so you think I'm paid! Wait a bit—I have you now, Simon Godfrey, and you shall not call two sixpences your own, but one of them shall reach my pocket."

CHAPTER XVI.

THE CHANCE OF SAFETY.—THE ARREST.

THE highly favourable opinion which counsel had given as regarded the claim of the Whiteheads to the whole of the Indian property, sufficed to put Mrs. Whitehead completely at ease upon that subject.

Indeed the manner in which Godfrey had outwitted himself was as clear to legal understandings as anything could possibly be. He had placed himself in such a position in consequence of his own insatiable avarice, in the first instance, that his going to law at all upon the subject, now looked far more like an obstinate wish to protract proceedings than anything reasonable.

The legal opinions he had procured were all against him, but if a man with money at command, be obstinate, and will litigate a plain case, of course he will find some attorney to hand him comfortably into court, and counsel to say what human ingenuity can say in such a case.

Such we say was the outward appearance of things. The private manner in which Godfrey was endeavouring to bend circumstances to his own purposes no one but himself and his confederate knew anything of. Indeed such a scheme would never have entered into the imagination of the Whiteheads, or have seemed possible in the wildest conjectures of such a man as Charles Ormond.

There was, however, something in the plan which made it frightfully likely to succeed. At that period the crime of forgery was considered one of the most heinous character, and never pardoned. It was well known that the king had a particular predilection for hanging every one who committed that offence, so that after conviction an execution came, of course.

If Neville be true to Godfrey, we tremble for the result. But let us now look at the Whiteheads in their altered state.

How well the beautiful Marian graced her new and elegant abode. If she made the humble cottage home, when first we introduced her to the reader, full of elegance and refinement, not the less did she seem to be in all respects well suited to the new position in which fortune had placed her.

Surrounded by the luxuries and refinements, of civilized life which for some years she had been a stranger to, she yet stepped at once gracefully from compara-tive poverty to wealth and luxury. The transition seemed to be so natural and easy, that no one could for one instant have guessed, that she seemed as if only for a brief moment she had stooped to adorn a humble station.

Poor Mrs. Whitehead was in a state of bewilderment for some days, and seemed scarcely to know where she was, or what she was expected to do; but such a feeling gradually wore off, and she dropped contentedly enough into her new position.

Charles Ormond, welcome as he knew and felt he was, perhaps was the least happy of the three. He seemed to be ever thinking how greatly overrated by the Whiteheads was the service he had been able to render to them. To be ever shrinking from their acknowledgments, and notwithstanding the very heaven of delight it was to him to be so frequently in the presence of her whom he loved, yet he looked at times unhappy, as if he felt the dependence of his position to partake something of a degradation.

This was a feeling when once awakened was not likely to decrease. It was just one of those mental crotchets which imagination makes gigantic, and which grows in the human mind from a small beginning to something which at last tinctures every other thought and feeling.

He felt it to be so humiliating to be faring sumptuously from day to day at the cost of two females, towards whom he had certainly acted the part of a friend, although not to have done as he did would have been to place him almost on a par with his formerly rascally employer.

He who knows of an iniquity and makes no effort to prevent it, tacitly acquiesces in its commission, and makes himself an accomplice of the evil doer.

This was not at all a likely state of things for Charles Ormond to fall into, and, therefore, he could not conceive that he was entitled to so much for having done what he termed so little.

It is sad to think that this state of mind, arising as it did from the most generous impulses, and the best of motives, was just the one to further the infamous designs of Godfrey.

The acquisition of such an amount of money as by the check would be placed at his disposal, would enable him to assume a more free and independent position, and, therefore, was he much the more likely, considering that the amount was but his legal due, to avail himself of it to his own utter destruction.

"Oh! that I could indeed," he would exclaim frequently, when he was alone, "be the protector, and not the protected. Can I longer maintain so singular a position as that in which I now am? No; some honourable course of industry shall earn for me, let it be at what amount of toil it may, a subsistence. The Whiteheads are now surrounded by those who, from love of justice, as well as self-interest, will see them righted. They have no need now of the aid and countenance of one so poor as I. All that I could do for their benefit I have done; shall I now stay basking in this kind of indolence, and living upon them? No; I will speak to Marian—I will tell her what I feel upon this subject. I know her pure nobility of soul will feel with me, and that she would be the last to press me longer to occupy a position which deprives me of any portion of my self-esteem."

Full of these thoughts, Charles Ormond sought the earliest opportunity of explaining them with what gentleness he might to Marian. Residing together in the same house, that opportunity soon occurred. Why he particularly chose an occasion when Mrs. Whitehead was not present, we must leave to the tact and judgment of our readers to determine.

It was towards the evening when, as chance or fortune would have it, Mrs. Whitehead had left the house with an intimation that she should not return for an hour, Charles, upon entering the drawing-room for his hat, which he had there left, saw Marian with her head resting upon her hands and leaning upon a table, as if in the deepest meditation. And yet, as Charles Ormond gazed upon her and saw, to his partial fancy, concentrated in her face and form all that was beautiful, he did indeed shrink at the thought of voluntarily placing a barrier between himself and the joy of seeing day by day one whom he loved so well, and for whom he entertained an affection which he felt confident no other human being could awaken.

And yet a high sense of honour urged him forward; he told himself he ought to take the step which conscientious reason had dictated; but the contest between prudence and love was great indeed.

No wonder he hesitated, knowing himself to be unseen, before he commenced appealing to the reason of Marian to assist him to put an end to the dream of happiness in which they had been indulging.

And what could her thoughts be? thoughts which lent a sadness to her brow, and so far abstracted from the present as to make her unconscious of the presence of him towards whom probably her meditations tended.

Could it be possible that she, too, thought as he did, and felt the anomalous position in which he stood? this was an idea which produced a decision in his wavering mind, and he stepped forward, pronouncing her name as he did so sufficiently loud to rouse her from her reverie, and induce her, with a start, to look up to see who was the intruder.

"Charles," she exclaimed; "I—I mean Mr. Ormond, I did not know you were here."

She then observed by the expression of his countenance that he was unhappy, and fearing that something of a new and alarming character had occurred to make him so, she was most eager in her inquiries as to the cause of his disquietude.

"Nothing, nothing, Miss Whitehead, I assure you," he said; "nothing new has transpired, and be assured that whatever can now occur will be to your advantage."

"And yet you look sad, Mr. Ormond; and you address me, likewise, with a strangeness not usual with you; there was a time when you named me Marian."

"And more than once," he replied, "you have named me Charles; but even now you have taught me the distance that is between us, by dropping that more familiar appellation."

" It was in the confusion of the moment ; I scarcely knew to whom I spoke, let me assure you it was so ; but that something has occurred to make you sad I am convinced, your looks proclaim it, and if you will not treat me as a friend, to tell me what it is, I think I may well complain of having lost a confidence I thought I once enjoyed."

" I am sad, Marian, if you will permit me to address you by that name ; I am sad, because I have arrived at what, to me, is a sad conclusion, and yet a necessary one, inasmuch as it presents itself to my mind in such a form that I cannot doubt its correctness,—I must leave you !"

" Leave us ?" exclaimed Marian, and the colour immediately deserted her cheeks, showing but too faithfully how that intelligence affected her. " Leave us, Charles Ormond ? you cannot mean what you say. What has happened ? what have we done that you should deprive us of your society and your protection ?"

" You have done nothing," said Charles ; " nothing but what has been dictated by such kindly and excellent feelings as are rarely met with. It is I who am doing that which I feel I ought not to do, by trespassing longer upon you."

" Trespassing !"

" Yes, Marian ; and in a manner from which I may well shrink from continuing. Listen to me, for I am quite certain that your judgment and your feeling will alike go with me in that which I have to say. When first our acquaintance commenced, on that night when your cottage home was invaded by Godfrey with his insidious propositions, I felt that I had had the happiness of being of service to you. To have left you then, till those affairs which then began first to show themselves were placed in the even train they are now in, would have been selfishness ; it is now selfishness for me to remain."

" Indeed, indeed, Charles, you speak in riddles ; I cannot understand what odd fancy possesses you. Have we shown ourselves ungrateful to you ?"

" No, no ! rich is my reward beyond all deserts ; but I am young, and in all the vigour of health and strength. I have hands with which to work, and I cannot longer dream of passing an idle existence, as the creature of a bounty ever so liberally bestowed or so ungrudgingly heaped upon me."

" Ah ! now I understand," said Marian ; " you have become possessed with a false sense of honour ; you can heap benefits upon us, but you feel that it is a condescension on your part to receive any. You can save us from absolute ruin and destruction, and it hurts your pride to receive at our hands the least practical result of a gratitude which will be eternal."

" No, Marian, you place the matter not in its true light. I am a man ; and is it manly, is it generous or just, that I should lead my present life of idleness dependent upon your bounty ? No, Marian, let me leave this luxurious home, to which I am not entitled ; let me, without thinking me unkind, seek my own fortunes, humble or great as they may chance to be. Although away from you I need not ——"

" What would you say ?"

" I need not love you less."

" Charles ! Charles ! is this kind ?" said Marian, and tears gushed to her eyes as she looked into his face.

A whirl of confused thoughts rushed through his brain ; nothing had been further from his thoughts than at that time to make any passionate avowal of his fond affection.

He had considered for some time past that she must be aware he loved her ; but although a thousand little acts had doubtless proclaimed to her the fact that he viewed her with the eyes of affection, yet never had he yet uttered a sentence so expressive of his feelings as that which had now almost inadvertently fallen from his lips ; now, however, he had broken the spell which had kept him mute upon that subject which lay so near to his heart, and while she paused and listened, with a flushed cheek and downcast eyes, he told her, with all that eloquence so characteristic of such a passion as his and associated with the imagination he possessed, how much he loved her.

He told her how once he had seen her at Godfrey's counting-house, when she had come upon some message from her mother. He told her how then her beauty had dawned upon his soul and awakened what he then considered one of the wildest dreams of his existence, namely, the possibility that he might one day be able to tell her how he loved her.

Then he told her how her very name had been to him a spell to clear away uneasy thoughts, and how he had clung to the recollection of that first glance of her face as some saint would to some glimpse of heaven in his dreams; and so on, he traced the story of his love until, from becoming a very part and parcel of his being, it would seem to him his life itself.

He paused, and there was a silence of some minutes' duration ere Marian could find courage to make any reply to that appeal to the tenderest affection. At length she looked up into his face, and it was with a smile of almost child-like beauty, as she said,—

"And yet, Charles, you came to bid me farewell."

"I did, Marian; and Heaven only knows what impulse of the moment induced me thus to speak. I had no thought of telling you I loved."

"And will you leave me now?"

"Marian! Marian! why tax my resolution thus cruelly? Let me go and win honourable fame and fortune if I can, and let me go with a consciousness that I may hope for the best and dearest reward Heaven can possibly bestow upon me in your love; give me but that hope as a stimulus to exertion, and I may achieve much; believing, too, at this moment that some good angel must have whispered me to tell you how I loved you."

"No, Charles, no, you must not go. Have you not made us what we are? Came you not to us to save us from a ruffian without common sense of justice or of honour, and would you now leave us still to his machinations? Is this a way to love?"

"Oh, judge of me not by ordinary rules of conduct. It may be, dear Marian, that I take too romantic a view of my position; but you understand me."

"I do, Charles, and you will not leave us. Do you understand me?"

She placed her hand in his as she spoke, and looked into his eyes with so much tender confidence, that a far less apt spirit than his would not have hesitated to come to the conclusion that the declaration of affection had been anything but ill received.

In a moment he clasped that hand to his heart and then to his lips.

"My Marian!" he cried; "my Marian! best and dearest—mine for ever—for ever ——"

A startling knock at the street door disturbed the conference, and sent a strange chilling feeling to both their hearts.

CHAPTER XVII.

THE OPPORTUNE ARRIVAL.—THE UNDERSTANDING BETWEEN THE LOVERS.—CHARLES ORMOND'S PROSPECTS OF HAPPINESS.—A PRESENTIMENT OF EVIL.

THERE was nothing so remarkable in that knock at the street door that it should have made both Charles Ormond and Marian Whitehead feel so very uncomfortable; but yet somehow or another it sounded strange to both of them, like the signal for the commencement of some period of misfortune and terror, the results of which, time alone will disclose.

"You tremble," said Charles.

"And you," said Marian; "you seem nervous and alarmed."

"I know not why, but that knock feels as if it had been struck upon my own heart."

"Hush! some one comes."

The door was opened, and a letter was brought to Charles ; his hand shook as he received it from the servant, but his fears were soon dissipated, giving way completely to pleasanter feelings, as he opened the note, and exclaimed,—

"Can this be possible ? Some latent feeling, after all, of ordinary justice has been awakened in the mind of Godfrey, without even a demand upon my part, and indeed, I never intended to make one ; he has sent me here a check for fifty pounds, in lieu of discharging me so suddenly without notice."

"Indeed !"

"Yes. You cannot be more astonished than I am at such a spontaneous act. Knowing the man as I do, I can scarcely believe it real ; and if the question had been put to me, I should most undoubtedly have said that he was the very last person in the world to have dreamed of such an act of justice, not to call it generosity."

"Are you sure it is from him, Charles?"

"There can be no doubt ; look at the check, drawn and signed by himself upon his well known banker."

"And what will you do ?"

"Do, Marian ; take that which is mine own."

"Nay, Charles, let me advise you, have none of his money. Touch not a piece of his gold ; send it back to him with a message that you are free of him, and independent of him, and that you thank him you are so."

"Nay, but Marian, why should I, from any foolish scruple, cast away that to which I am fairly entitled? Part of this money is unquestionably mine own. t has been hardly earned. The remainder I could claim legally, and the circumstances under which I could legally make such a claim are of a nature that Godfrey knows he dare not attempt to resist."

"Yes, yes, Charles but still wherefore take money from that man ?—have we not abundance ?"

"You may, Marian, but not we. Do not attempt, I implore you, to destroy that feeling of independence which even the possession of this small sum will give me. I shall now feel myself more your guest than your pensioner, and with a better spirit I shall be better able to throw what protection it is in my power to afford around you and your mother. I have no scruples in taking this money, because it is my own."

"I will strive to think, Charles, that your better judgment corrects the hasty impulses of my own feelings ; and while I seem to shrink, with an unknown fear, at your retaining that money, I can give no reason why I do so, but the woman's one, at which you will smile—because I do."

"And, having no better reason, Marian, you'll permit me to retain this amount ; but still, utter but one heartfelt regret that I should do so, and in two minutes it shall be speeding its way back to its former owner."

"No, no, Charles."

"Nay, say but the word, and you shall know and feel, love, the power you have over all my actions."

"Charles, I covet not such power. Your own better judgment shall decide not only for yourself but for me ; and I shall feel happy in the thought that, under any circumstances of doubt or difficulty, I may, with a full reliance, seek your aid and counsel, knowing that both are not only freely given, but are dictated by a judgment and a sense of honour which if they err, will err on the side of virtue and of goodness."

"Dear Marian, commendation from your lips sounds so unlike from all ordinary flattery, that you will make me vain indeed if you repeat such words. But I will leave you now with the blessed assurance that you do not look with anger upon the honest avowal of the passion which can know no change."

A glance from those speaking eyes of Marian were amply sufficient to convince him that he might indeed, to the very utmost, feel such an assurance.

There were between them some few whispered words of tenderness, the light of joy beamed from their eyes, and in the full assurance of that dear felicity of being each beloved where most they had treasured up their dearest hopes, they parted—Charles Ormond to proceed at once to Godfrey's banker to realize his unexpected treasure, and Marian to dream of the felicity which time would surely bestow upon her, as the happy wife of him whom she felt she could love so truly and so sincerely.

Strangely soon, however, as Charles proceeded at a rapid pace towards the banker, did his feelings of satisfaction subside, and that same strange presentiment of coming evil which had crept across his breast before he opened Godfrey's letter, again began to flutter his nerves and to give him sensations of uneasiness, such as he was commonly an utter stranger to.

Not even the recollection of Marian's affection, concerning which he could now have no doubt, was sufficient to fill his mind with that serenity which he could have sworn previously to such an assurance could not have failed to produce.

Twice he paused, and thought that, after all, he would take the advice that she had tendered to him, and refuse the acceptance to him of any money whatever from so polluted a source as that from whence the twenty pounds' check had emanated, but as often he chid himself for such a superstitious feeling, and he blushed at what he denominated his own weakness in entertaining such ideas.

"What is this," he said, "that has come over me? Wherefore do I shrink from pursuing an even and correct course, because of this strange and unknown fear that has taken possession of me? I never have been, and will not now be a believer in what are called presentiments of coming evil. If once the mind allows itself to be so preyed upon by the imagination, the individual will know no mode of action whatever or fixity of purpose. It must not be. Hence, vain and foolish fears, I will take that to which I am justly and honourably and fully entitled."

And thus reason beckoned him onward, although imagination and a thousand vague presentiments would have kept him back.

To escape the accumulation of disagreeable thoughts that still kept pressing on him, he made great haste, and as he neared the door of the banking-house, he naturally felt in his pocket for the cheque which he was about to get cashed.

He took it from his pocket and glanced upon it, when, as he was about again to fold it up, he discovered for the first time that there were two, which by some accident had partially stuck together, and had been torn from the check-book at once.

"Godfrey must have been in a great hurry," he thought, "when he drew this check to tear out a blank one along with it."

His first impulse was then to tear up the blank check in the street, but on a second thought, which, alas, in this instance, was not the best, he decided upon preserving it, saying, as he did so,—

"He may miss this check from his book, and may fancy some one has stolen it for a sinister purpose. I know well his suspicious nature. There is not one in his whole establishment who would not be suspected, therefore I will preserve it, and send it back to him with as short an intimation as possible as to how it came into my hands."

Charles Ormond now stood upon the steps of the banking-house. It was a period o the day when much business was being transacted, and numerous persons were passing in and out of the establishment.

Several of them seemed to notice him pause for a moment, and a liveried porter who had a seat behind the door, as if he were on the watch to pounce upon every one who came with any bad intent, eyed him curiously as he walked in.

Possibly this official personage had seen him hesitate a little on the step, through some peep-hole adapted for such espials, and consequently had had his suspicions aroused that all was not quite so correct as it should be.

Alas! poor Charles Ormond, we tremble at the circumstantial ruin that awaits thee. Never was innocence worse betrayed—never was an individual, replete with all the highest attributes of honour and generosity, so surrounded by circumstances calculated to lead to the full presumption of the deepest guilt.

CHAPTER XVIII.

THE DISCOVERY OF THE FORGERY.—THE APPREHENSION OF CHARLES.

If Charles Ormond had been asked, when he was on the threshold of the banker's door, why he paused, and entered not at once with all the confidence of one feeling that he was going about a very ordinary affair in a very ordinary manner, he would have found it extremely difficult to reply.

Probably had the question been put to him by any one to whom he would have been inclined to be perfectly confidential, he would have said, that he felt a presentiment of some evil, which he could not define or shake off, while his reason scouted the notion that any harm could befall him under his present circumstances.

Yes—these presentiments are feelings which at times find a place in the breast of every one, and by no means are they confined to the illiterate, the prejudiced, or the superstitious.

On the contrary, they generally take the firmest hold of highly cultivated imaginations, and present themselves in their strongest colours to those minds which probably never really practically give way to them.

Charles Ormond then, to the full, felt one of those presentiments as he approached the banker's counter. It seemed a kind of relief to him to find that he could not be served for some minutes, and then, as his nervousness increased, he got ashamed of himself for hanging back, and excited the attention of every one present, then, by a marked eagerness to present his check for payment.

At length it was taken from him, and the clerk looked at it with a strange sort of expression on his face, and then at Charles Ormond, and then at the check again. After that, he said, with an unconcerned air,—

" How will you have it ?"

" Gold," said Charles Ormond.

The clerk walked off with the check in his hand, and was absent for some minutes, then some bell rang with a curious kind of sound, which made everybody look round to see from what direction it came, and as Charles Ormond did so likewise, he encountered a gentlemanly looking man, who said to him,—

" Will you be so good as to follow me, sir?"

" Follow you!" said Charles. " Wherefore ?"

" Merely into a private room."

" I am quite willing to transact my business at the public counter."

" I am sorry to trouble you, sir, but I have something to say to you respecting the check you presented, which will be more conveniently said in private than here."

Charles Ormond was still far from suspecting the truth, but he saw that the various persons who happened to be in the banking-house were having their curiosity attracted, and were crowding closer round him with looks of surprise.

It was to escape this infliction that he now said to the man who addressed him,—

" I will follow you, sir, if you please, although I really cannot understand what all this is about."

" Thank you, thank you," said the gentlemanly-looking man. " We shall soon come to an explanation," and then addressing one of the clerks whom he passed, he added, in a low tone, " you can tell Smith he can unbolt the door again, it's all right."

" Yes, sir," said the clerk.

All this passed in a much less space of time than we have been compelled to continue in recording it, and before Charles Ormond could take a thought upon the probable consequences of what was going on, he found himself in a small but neatly got up room, where sat several persons, who immediately rose upon the entrance of the gentleman who had invited him there. There was a silence of a few brief moments' duration, and as Charles looked from face to face, he fancied he saw expressions of regret which he could not for the life of him understand the cause of.

We have said that Charles Ormond's appearance was strikingly interesting. Nature had bestowed upon him in his appearance a letter of recommendation, which every one whom he encountered felt the influence of, and it was probably that circumstance which made the gentlemen who were in that apartment look so regretful, when they reflected upon the course which a stern sense of duty to themselves and the public compelled them to pursue towards him. It was Charles who first broke the silence, by saying,—

" Gentlemen, I have been invited into this apartment. Will any of you, now that I am here, have the goodness to explain to me the reason of so much courtesy?"

" Young man, young man," said the eldest of the gentlemen who was present, as he shook his head at Charles Ormond. " I am very sorry for you. Such a thing has not happened here for many years. I had hoped it would never happen."

" Sir, said Charles, " you speak in riddles to me. If my intrusion into this apartment is what you allude to, I can assure you that if I had not been urgently required to come in here, so far as I am concerned, it would not have happened at all."

" Oh ! dear me, dear me," said the old gentleman ; " hardened, I am afraid."

" Not a doubt of it," said the others.

"Good God," said Charles, "what do you mean, all of you? Pray favour me with some explanation."

"Oh, here he is," they all said at once, as the door opened, and a stout man with a hard-looking set of features, deeply indented with the small-pox, made his appearance. "How do you do, Mr. Bland?"

"Pretty well, thank you, gentleman," said the new comer. "I suppose," he said, looking at Charles, "this is my customer?"

"Yes, Mr. Bland, that's your prisoner."

"Prisoner!" exclaimed Charles.

"Ah! come, come," said the officer, for such he was. "None of that nonsense. It don't go down with us. You're my prisoner, young chap. You seem a cool hand, and yet you are a new 'un, I think, for I never saw you before."

"Of what am I accused?"

"Of forging the check," said the old gentleman, "which you presented for payment."

Before Charles had time to reply, the door was again opened, and some one said, respectfully,—

"Mr. Godfrey, gentlemen."

"Show him in, show him in," said the old man; and in another moment Charles's eyes fell upon the countenance of his former villanous employer.

"Mr. Godfrey!" he exclaimed, "thank God you have come; for the first time in my life the sight of you is pleasant to me. You sent me a check for fifty pounds."

Godfrey opened his eyes very wide, and gave a stare of unmitigated astonishment, as he said,—

"I sent you a check for fifty pounds! Oh, dear!—oh, dear!"

"You know you did!"

"God bless me! what will the world come to? Was that what I was sent for?"

"Mr. Godfrey," said the old gentleman, "step this way. Did you draw this check?"

"That check!—'Pay Mr. Charles Ormond fifty pounds!' Oh, dear no—certainly not. Why, where did it come from? Really, now, this is too bad. Young man, young man, this comes of sabbath-breaking and bad company! Well, to be sure, after all the benefits I have heaped upon your head—but this is human nature."

"As the Lord Mayor is sitting," said the officer, "you had better come to the Mansion-house at once, and he'll be committed or remanded, just according as you think proper. Now, young fellow, if you please. I don't wish to do anything unpleasant, so if you'll trot along pleasantly with me there need be no trouble, but if you have any idea of being a little obstropolous we'll do the best we can."

In the last few moments Charles had been thoroughly bewildered at the turn affairs had taken. He could hardly believe in the evidence of his own senses. The whole circumstance appeared more like the phantasma of some dream than anything real and tangible; and when the officer laid hold of him by the arm he almost expected that at that touch the vision would be dispelled, and he should awaken to a conciousness of real existence, with a deep congratulation that such a vision of slumber had passed away.

"Hear me but for a moment," he said, "before we leave this room. I cannot take upon myself to say how this frightful affair has been arranged, but I do know and feel that I must have been made the victim of some diabolical conspiracy, which seems but too likely to effect my ruin. I am as innocent as any of you can possibly be, of that which I am charged with. I received this check, now declared to be forged, in a note from Mr. Godfrey, it is in payment of two quarters' salary, justly due to me from him. I must confess I little expected such an unsolicited act of justice at his hand; but so it was, and I have my own suspicions, knowing well the character of the man, and what he is capable of, that this is his plan to ruin one who has thwarted him in one of his infamous projects."

"Now really, young fellow," said the officer, "give me leave to say, that you are doing yourself no good—this is very absurd, you know. I shall have to repeat it, as well as I can recollect it—you had better say nothing, but come along quietly, like a lamb."

"I have said all that I can say—I am innocent, do with me what you will. I am not so mad as to resist, and therefore will accompany you as quietly as you could wish."

"Well that's sensible; come along, there's no need of a coach, gentlemen, as the distance is so short."

The officer placed Charles Ormond's arm within his, and they walked along to the Mansion-house without exciting any attention whatever, beyond a passing glance, for no one could have supposed Charles to be a prisoner; and as for Godfrey and the witnesses from the banking-house, they kept at a sufficient distance behind not to appear to have any connection with the officer and his charge.

Less than ten minutes sufficed to bring the whole party into the justice-room in the Mansion-house, where the Lord Mayor was, being as oracular as Lord Mayors usually are.

———

CHAPTER XIX.

MARIAN AT HOME.—BLISSFUL ANTICIPATIONS.

MARIAN WHITEHEAD—beautiful, loveable, and affectionate being, full of all the finest and freshest feelings with which a benignant providence ever gifted one of its wisest creations—could you, but for one moment, have imagined the dreadful danger which was surrounding him whom you loved, how soon, how fatally soon, would the cup of happiness have been dashed from your lips, and how useless, vain, and fruitless, would have seemed all those beauties and luxuries which your change of circumstances had so suddenly surrounded you with.

But as yet you were in that ignorance which, then surely, was bliss indeed. You were enjoying the last hour of conscious happiness in this world, and it was strange that it seemed to you, without having a thought or a suspicion that it was your last, the sweetest you had ever experienced.

There were certainly circumstances which had a tendency to make it so, for the brief cloud which had hovered over the star of her happier destiny, at the thought of Charles Ormond leaving her and her mother on a point of delicate honour, had disappeared.

He had now told her that he loved her, and he could not say that such an announcement from his lips had been received either coldly or with indifference.

With all the trusting fondness of a frank and generous nature, she had not attempted to disguise that he had become dear to her. Without departing from that maiden modesty, which makes love not spoken more delightful even than that which is proclaimed in the most tasteful and glowing language, she had yet let him know sufficient of her heart, that he would have been but a poor connoisseur indeed had he found, or fancied he found, any cause for doubts or for despair.

"Now," she said, "he will remain—he will no longer hesitate. He has told me that he loves me, and the false point of honour on which he would have left us has been explained away. Can I ever hope to be happier than I now am?"

It was thus that in the, to her, most dreary interval of Charles Ormond's absence, Marian Whitehead reasoned with herself, and felt no pang for the future. All to her seemed indeed *couleur de rose*. Fate, weary of persecuting her, seemed now to have resolved to shower down upon her head some of its choicest blessings.

Under any circumstances the love of such a being as Charles Ormond would have been a great solace, and a consolation against all possible evils; but now, as if one blessing was not sufficient, fortune was to be showered upon her, at the same moment that such an extended prospect of being enabled fully to enjoy wealth was opened to her as she could not have found in any other combination of events.

She thought over all this, until the very joy which those reflections, so cloudless as they were, induced, brought with it a sense of nervousness, and she felt the necessity of withdrawing her mind from too close a contemplation of her own happiness;

she hastily turned to a volume which lay upon the table close at hand, and in the following narrative sought a different mental occupation :—

In the good city of Liege there dwelt one Hans Hoffen, a rich citizen in that place, and a man much respected—as who, indeed, is not that has a deep purse that's well filled, and, besides, has no blemish on his name, but who has pursued the track of trade for many years.

It would be a moral phenomenon. He might be neither; but if he be one he must be the other—there's no help for it. He couldn't help it, unless he took any particular pains to be otherwise to his great injury; but that is only an extreme case, and extreme cases we abhor, unless they be extremely good.

Hans Hoffen was a very good citizen, and had had three wives, all of whom were dead, and it would have been difficult to say how many more had acted in that capacity to him; but the number was vast, and he was much likened to Solomon, King of the Jews, on account of his leaning towards the tender passions, as did that celebrated monarch, who was said to be so wise that on several occasions he forgot himself.

However, Hans Hoffen was sometimes called the Solomon of Liege, chiefly in reference to his concubinage, which was extensive. However, he was feeble, for none of his wives lived for more than two years; and the—the—the housekeepers didn't last so long—but they were only discharged.

There was one inhabitant of Hans' house that was much sought after, and that was no other than Hans' own daughter Flora.

Now Flora was a rare blue-eyed golden-haired Flemish maiden, whose beauty was great and her qualifications great also, independent of her father being a very rich man. This was no mean attraction among the wooers of Liege.

Everybody said she was the most beautiful girl in Liege. She was not only beautiful, but she had that which made beauty more beautiful—a scent in this case to the rose—for Flora Hoffen was rich also.

The young men sought her favours—many for the sake of her beauty, many because she was rich, and many more because she was both beautiful and rich.

Notwithstanding, however, that the finest and most adventurous of the Liegers sought her alliance, yet they none of them obtained any particular acknowledgment from the lady that they were at all pleasing to her; that, in fact, they had any chance of being accepted.

No; Flora Hoffen was obliging to all—listened to all with profound respect and attention; but it never produced more than a general smile of approbation, and she would declare how very much obliged she felt for their good opinion.

To the great chagrin of old Hans, the young men gradually began to fall off. This appeared to them to be very much like quizzing; they couldn't quite understand it.

Flora did it, however, with so much simplicity, that it at first surprised them, and then cooled their ardour so much that, from the impassioned warmth with which they began, they degenerated gradually into a whispered compliment.

They were surprised, confounded, and believed she played a most excellent part.

One day, when Hans Hoffen caught his daughter alone, he spoke to her with some asperity concerning her conduct.

"Daughter," he said, "I have watched you for some time past."

"Indeed, father?"

"I have; and am very much dissatisfied at your behaviour."

"I am sorry, father; but I have never willingly done an unworthy deed. Inform me, I pray you, of what I have been guilty, that I may amend."

"I do not accuse you of that, but your behaviour to your suitors. You do not accept one of them."

"No, father; I can't love any of them; but as they are so kind as to make me some little compliment, I, of course, thank them, but cannot accept them. I cannot love them."

"That is of no consequence. I never loved your mother, nor any of my wives;

but what did it matter? We got on very well through life; we didn't feel the want of it. We had no extravagant anticipations when we were married; thus it did not happen that we were disappointed, but jogged on comfortably and easy. Do you see, Flora?"

" Yes, I hear you, father," said Flora; " but I cannot comprehend the doctrine: however, I don't see why I should get married, unless father, you intend to bring home another wife."

" That, my dear," said Hans, " is a matter for my consideration, and not yours. I shall do what I think proper."

" But who would like to trust themselves with you now, father? It is very unlikely that they will do so without some ulterior motive. Who can the adventurous individual be?"

Old Hans turned away very angry, for he had suddenly taken a fancy to the widow of the burgomaster, who had very recently died.

Now Flora had some idea of this from some of her numerous suitors, for they had made use of the knowledge to induce her to wed, seeing the burgomaster's widow had several children, and might have more. This was an event she much dreaded, and feared that the new mother-in-law would make home very uncomfortable indeed.

She was intriguing, and she and her children would occupy the old man's mind, and Flora would lose all, save her mother's jointure.

Now Flora had made greater advances in love than her father gave her credit for. The fact was, her lover was poor, and yet she sought such a man in preference to all the rich merchants' sons in Liege.

He was poor and he was humble; but he possessed an understanding far above any of those who had sought her hand in a higher rank of life.

He was an artist of no mean merit; but he had as yet not freed himself from his master's tutelage. He was, however, of great promise, and had met with Flora at the house of a friend of her father. He fell madly in love with Flora.

She certainly looked favourably upon the manly form and the handsome, ingenuous countenance of the young painter; for he was handsome, and the high, open forehead spoke of the mind within. He was himself a study for a sculptor.

" Well, Flora," he would say, " you have preferred me to the gay, glittering youths who frequent the house of your father to view the beautiful daughter of Hans Hoffen."

" And rich, you should say."

" And rich, since you will have it so. But still there are some who must love you for yourself alone. 'Tis impossible it should be otherwise. I am more than happy in possessing such love as yours, Flora—more than happy; but when —— "

" When what?"

" Shall I claim this hand and heart as my own, so that I may never fear any chance turn or malignancy of fate?"

" That I may not tell you. Hans may not forgive me. I can do much, but I cannot be disobedient."

" Indeed you would not be disobedient by doing such a thing, for he would not have prohibited you; but, in fact, you have many eligible suitors whom you cannot well refuse, without a breach, if your father were to insist upon your accepting one."

" I would not."

" Why not put it out of your power to obey him, and then you could not incur his displeasure—at least, so lastingly."

" Well, well, we will see—we will see soon. But I fear there will be some change take place at home."

" How?"

" My father —— "

" Is he not well."

" Quite well; but I have some very strong suspicions that he, too, is contemplating another marriage very shortly."

" Your father—another marriage ?" said the painter, in surprise.

" Yes."

" Why, he's over seventy now !"

" He is."

" How absurd ; how very unfortunate, too. I wonder what can be done."

" That is what I cannot tell, and what I wished to see you about, that we might talk it over, and see what could be effected."

" Who is the object of his choice ?"' inquired the young painter.

" The burgomaster, who died a few weeks back, has left a young widow of constrained means, but of a designing temperament. She has several children besides."

" Good Heavens ! how uncomfortable it will be to you !"

" So it will ; and, moreover, I think she will drive me from my father's home, or force me to wed some one whom I don't like. My father but this day has been speaking upon that very subject."

" Then why not at once make me happy ? and if you must be ill friends with your parent, have at least the consolation of knowing you exchanged unhappiness for happiness."

" But I may forfeit the money I shall be entitled to when he dies ; for should I offend him, he may will it away."

" Never mind—never mind about that, Flora ; I'll work night and day before you should suffer. But you need not say anything about it at present to your father. We may find some means of terrifying him from his intended marriage."'

Flora was silent.

" Come, dearest Flora, consent—be mine ! and then we can set about defeating the ends of the widow of the burgomaster. We will terrify her, too, and she shall be unwilling to consent to the intended marriage, if one be intended."

" When I spoke of it, my father did not attempt to deny it."

" Then, Flora, let us take the only steps that will ensure our safety and union."

" I own," said Flora, " that but for this one unhappy circumstance, I should scarce listen to it without my father's consent."

" But now, dearest, say had we not better put this one effectual bar to separation ? Should all be discovered, he may insist and attempt to force you to marry some one whom he pleases ; think then, dearest, what would be our misery, our desolation—think of this, and then say you consent—consent to be mine."

" I do consent," said Flora, blushing, and allowing the delighted painter to clasp her hand within his own, and press her lips with soft kisses.

" I have," he said, " interest with the fathers of the neighbouring monastery ; thither will we repair, and be united in bonds that can never be severed, not even in death."

Thus they sealed their compact. They were married that very night, but they separated after the ceremony, after having agreed upon a plan by which they intended to save Hans Hoffen from the machinations of the young widow.

That very night a visitation to Hans took place while he was in bed.

It was midnight when Hans Hoffen was awakened by a low groan in his room. He lay and listened. There was another groan—and then a third.

Hans Hoffen began to feel warm, and then moist, and then he thought his hairs were wonderfully thick and uncomfortable.

Suddenly the curtains of the bed were thrown open by some invisible agency, and then a sight met his astonished gaze.

There was a large illuminated space in the room ; it seemed as if a circle of light enveloped the form of a female in her winding or grave clothes. Hans Hoffen gazed, but the figure was gone ; but illuminated characters danced in fire, which said,—

" Listen to the words of the dead ! The spirit cannot speak ; but he who runs may read."

"Oh!" groaned Hoffen, "what have I done, what have I done, to deserve this?"

The thought had scarce crossed his mind when the same figure, dressed in the grave clothes, again presented itself to him, and looked on him with a threatening aspect. He looked and trembled; for there were the form and features of his best beloved wife of all the three—the mother of Flora. There she stood, with a sad and mournful look; but she moved not.

Hans groaned, and said,—

"Oh! what have I done, what have I done, what have I done, that I have deserved this terrible visitation?"

He groaned, and passed his hands across his eyes, but he could not refrain from again looking up, and then he saw the figure gone, but in its place were the following characters in letters of fire against the wall.

" You have thought of marriage, and you are near your end !   Repent ! oh, repent !"

" Oh !" groaned Hans, " I do repent, I do repent ; God forgive me ! I'll never think any more of the burgomaster's widow."

Even while he spoke, the words suddenly vanished, and some others, after the lapse of a few moments, supplied their place, which ran to the following effect,—

" You who have had three wives have had enough. Beware the fourth ! You have had warning enough. A fourth wife shall be your destruction, for she will not die while you live ; she will live her full allotted space ; ponder, and repent !"

Poor Hans felt in an almost deathlike trance, and an ague seized him ; he shook violently, and was not able to call for aid, but he lay helpless and staring.

The words gradually died away, and others seemed to grow out of them, and then he saw the following,—

" Hans Hoffen, seek your daughter's happiness, and where love endures there see she is bestowed ; her happiness depends upon it. Farewell ! as you observe this, so will you no longer be visited by her whom you have reason to fear."

" No, no ; I will not disobey," said Hans, softly and inarticulately. " I will do all, everything. I repent ; I will do nothing contrary to the behest of Heaven, for such I feel it is."

The words disappeared, and the form of his wife again came before him ; she looked benignantly on him, he thought, and then she slowly disappeared from his sight.

*   *   *   *   *   *   *

The next morning Hans Hoffen was not seen at breakfast ; he had not got up, and Flora, in some alarm, watched for him with much anxiety ; at length she could wait no longer, but rang a bell, and the attendant waited until she was spoken to.

" Has my father got up yet ?"

" No, miss."

" Has anybody seen him ?"

" No, miss ; but he is thought to have slept longer than usual."

" Go and see what is the cause of it, and tell him I sent to know if he be well."

The servant quitted the room without further words, and did not return for some moments, which caused Flora to turn pale as she whispered to herself,—

" Surely, surely, he cannot have been frightened by the scene of last night ; if so, I shall never forgive myself."

She had scarcely uttered the words when the girl re-entered the room in a fright, saying,—

" Oh, miss ! oh, miss Flora !"

" What's the matter ? speak."

" Master ——"

" Well, speak ; speak, I charge you."

" Well, so I am, miss ; but you stop me.   Master is so ill, so very ill."

" Ill ! did you say ?" said Flora, rising.

" Yes, miss ; and, as we judge, wants you, miss—though he can't speak, he can only grunt. We think he's dying, miss ; but don't be afraid, but come at once."

Before the girl had finished this speech Flora had rushed from the room, and entered the apartment of her father, who lay gasping and fearfully convulsed.

He seemed more composed when he observed her, and held out his hand, which shook violently as he did so.

" Father, father !" she said, as she flung herself upon the bed ; " what is all this ? what is all this, I beseech you ?"

" Oh, Flora, I am dying !"

" Dying ! oh, God ! and I—I ——"

" You will be provided for."

"Do not think I am sordid; I cannot part with you, father; I cannot part with you; I shall break my heart, I shall die."

"Nay, nay, my child; live to enjoy life," gasped the old man, "else I shall not rest happy in my grave; I shall deem myself the cause of your death. I have passed a fearful—oh, a fearful night; I have seen a vision."

"Think no more of it, dear father. Oh, God! this is dreadful!"

"No, my child; it is not the vision that affrights me."

"Indeed, father?"

"No, child; 'tis the dreadful thoughts that it gives rise to, things and deeds that have long since been forgotten, but which now sear my brain. Oh, Heaven! I have been a great sinner, a bad man."

"Father, father!"

"Hold, my child; my days, my hours, my very moments are numbered."

"Speak not so, speak not so; I cannot bear to hear you speak thus; you will make me wretched for life."

"My dear child, receive my blessing; all is yours that I have, but beware how you love gold, how you seek it; and be careful, oh, be exceedingly careful, how you choose your partner through life; it will be for good or evil, and your happiness or misery depends upon it."

"I know it, father, I know it."

"I would my soul were free from crime; but—but—oh, God! I am going."

"Father!"

"Below—it is below; get it, and you will see what I moan about—the cause of my horror and my fears."

"Oh, father, of what is it you speak?"

"Oh, save me, save me!"

"Father!"

"Water—water," gasped the old man.

Some liquid was placed in the man's lips, and he drank; but it was useless—the old man was dying, and he knew it; he gasped awfully, and seemed to be fighting against something, or trying to prevent something coming near to him; the rattles came in his throat, and, with a gasping attempt to catch his breath, he expired, fixing his glassy eyes with a frightful expression upon his daughter Flora.

Flora, too, was insensible. She had fainted as she saw her father's last breath depart. The attendants had carried her to her own apartment; they could not allow her to remain in the chamber of death; they laid her gently down.

They retired when they saw she came to, and left her to weep in privacy.

When they were gone a man stepped from out a small closet and fastened the door, and then he approached the bed on which Flora yet lay.

"Flora," he said.

"Oh, Theodore."

"What ails you, love?" said the painter, for it was he; "has anything happened to cause you grief?"

"Oh, we are murderers!"

"Murderers!" exclaimed the painter, starting back aghast.

"Yes, murderers, Theodore; murderers!"

"God of Heaven, what mean you, dearest? you speak enigmatically; I never harboured an evil thought against any one, and very sure am I that I have done no ill deed."

"But we have killed my father."

"Your father?"

"Yes, he is dead."

"Dead! you cannot mean it?"

"I do," she said, "from fright, caused by the trick we played him last night."

"God of Heaven! you cannot mean that, Flora? Surely I have never done so much evil as this? I am not guilty of your father's death."

"You are, and so am I."

"It must be surely some fatal mistake   Did you see him alive?"

"I did."

"And what said he?"

"That he had seen a vision."

"Yes."

"And the remembrance of things past haunted his mind so strongly, that he shook dreadfully, and cried for water."

"Indeed! I——"

"He did. It was a dreadful sight to see him! I shall never get the remembrance of that dreadful scene from my mind!"

"Dearest Flora, do not let grief become too triumphant in your breast. You will have other thoughts and things to occupy your mind. It is true that this unfortunate occurrence—the use of the magic lantern may have caused him some fright, but you must be aware he spoke in bed perfectly sane, and in a tone that, while it showed fear, betrayed no such symptoms as those which followed it. There must have been something else upon your father's mind, the remembrance of which must have given him such a dreadful shock."

"He talked of things unknown to me—things that I don't understand from him."

"Never mind, dearest; it cannot do any good, but it may do harm; bury the secrets of the dead with them. It can do no good now to remember it, but yet if you are calm enough to do so, I should like to hear a relation of what he did say at that moment in the last hour of his life."

"You shall hear, Theodore, though my heart burst in telling you."

Flora then repeated word for word what her father had said to her during the dreadful hour she was with him. The young painter listened with attention, and he could not help feeling surprised at the expressions made use of, which seemed to him so different from what he had anticipated from Hans Hoffen.

"And now, Theodore," said Flora, sorrowfully, while the tears chased each other down her face, "and now do you not see what a dreadful state we have driven ourselves into! It is dreadful to think of it!"

"I admit, Flora, it is singularly unfortunate, and we are the cause of this affair happening at this precise moment, though it is very plain your father was nearer his end than he thought for; but listen, dearest; do you not think his death was caused by remorse?"

"Remorse, Theodore?"

"Yes."

"What for?"

"Heaven alone knows! but the expressions are most certainly those of remorse for some deed done, and for which this affair has for the first time, perhaps, for years, awakened in his mind a feeling of sorrow and repentance."

"Impossible!"

"I should have thought so, too, but the words of a dying man convey too significant a meaning to be doubted or misunderstood."

"Do you think so, Theodore?"

"I do, dearest. We have unfortunately raised up a spectre in his mind, the existence of which no one knew, save himself, and on our parts the act was one of purely an accidental character, which might have been raised up by any other accidental means. But let it not disturb you, be the cause of his repentance or remorse what it will—be it real or imaginary; but now he is dead, let it be buried with him."

"Oh! Heaven!"

"But I must admit that I am amazed about one thing!" said Theodore, musingly.

"And what is that, Theodore?"

"The expressions he made use of respecting something below."

"'It is below.'"

"Yes. What could he have meant by that? It seems very strange! There was something on his mind, depend upon it, and had he lived any longer, he would, doubtless, have disburdened his soul of the weight that oppressed it."

"Well it stills not thinking," said Flora, relapsing into tears; "he is gone, and we shall never know."

Theodore endeavoured to console and soothe her grief, but she was inconsolable, and grief would have its way.

*　　*　　*　　*　　*　　*　　*

The funeral of Hans Hoffen was superb, and the friends of the deceased were invited to the house of the dead, to partake of the funeral feast.

When they had all eaten and drunk of what was prepared for them, Flora arose, and said, to their utter astonishment,—

"Friends and relations, this is a moment of grief and mourning, and, therefore, but ill-suited to a marriage feast. My poor father died suddenly, and I had not the time to break to him intelligence that would, perhaps, have angered him. I had no time to tell him. I had no time to say, father, your blessing—I am married."

The guests looked at each other in amazement, and sat with open mouths in expectation of what was to follow.

"I am married," said Flora, taking the hand of Theodore, "and this is my husband. Honour him, for he is master here."

There was a momentary pause, during which amazement sat on their countenances, and they sat entranced. At length one old man rose and said,—

"Niece, you have done wrong in concealing this from your aged and indulgent parent; and yet may have saved him a pang. Be that as it may, what has been done cannot be undone; I only hope your choice has fallen upon one who is worthy of it. I give you joy, sir. I wish you long life and happiness."

In another minute or two the bride and bridegroom were overwhelmed with caresses.

*　　*　　*　　*　　*　　*　　*

The first twelve months passed over, and the new married pair were happy. It had been a year of bliss to them. The anniversary of the death of old Hans came round, and on the night that completed the year they were horrified at awakening at midnight and seeing the figure of a man, dressed in his grave clothes, appear in the moonlight.

They could not sleep, nor move, nor speak; fear had frozen up their faculties, and they lay gazing at the figure, which stood beckoning them to follow with his hand.

There was an expression of pain and sorrow on the countenance, but yet they were unable to move. Flora knew it was her father, and Theodore knew him too.

Then the figure stood beckoning until the cock crew, and then it suddenly disappeared from their sight.

The morning came, and yet Theodore and Flora had not slept. They were paralyzed with fear, and they arose that morning with saddened faces. They sat in silence at their breakfast—both appeared to have some secret thought that weighed heavily on his or her mind.

At length Flora broke the silence by saying,—

"Theodore, what could the vision we saw last night mean?"

"I cannot tell, Flora; it was very dreadful! and what a time it stood in the moonlight. I thought it would never go."

"And—and how fearfully it beckoned us to follow it! I fear there will be a sudden end to our career! We may be called to our account while young, Theodore."

"We may, but not on account of that dreadful apparition! But why do you regard it as the omen of death?"

"Because it was the spirit of one from the grave, and it beckoned us to follow it. Can anything be plainer?"

"I would that I had not been so spell-bound."

"Why?"

" Because, if I had not, I would have followed the spirit wherever it would led me."

" Theodore !"

" I would, Flora. It is possible—nay, probable, that something remains to be discovered or done to enable the spirit of your father to repose quietly in his grave."

The next night came, and with it came not the spectre. They slept on, but the spectre came not, and they gave up the thought.

*   *   *   *   *   *   *

Twelve months again passed over, and the second anniversary of Hans Hoffen came round, and again the spirit came, and stood in the cold moonlight.

Again the spirit beckoned to them to follow, and Theodore arose, and followed the spectre. It went before him, and he followed it until it came to some vaults. The spectre pointed to a small niche in the wall.

Theodore looked in it, and saw a rusty key; he took it, and followed the spectre ; until they came to a door, before which lay much rubbish. He removed it, and then opened the door ; he entered the vault, and then the spirit pointed to a heap of boards, and to a place in the earth.

Theodore saw that he should require the aid of tools to get at it, and, as the spirit vanished, he quitted the place.

Afterwards he proceeded leisurely to perform the necessary labour of digging up the earth, and then he discovered a lot of bags containing gold and silver, and beside them was the body of a man that had been forced into its recumbent position. It must have been there long, for it was decayed, and fell to pieces.

Up in the other corner, where the rubbish lay, was the body of a young female. Her wearing apparel had been superb, and by her side lay heaps of gold and jewels.

*   *   *   *   *   *   *

The gold and jewels were removed, and the bodies buried, and the cellar walled up, and the matter never spoken of ; but when Flora questioned him as to what he saw, he refused to say, save there was a treasure ; but she suspected much ; but she could not but admire the kindness that dictated this silence on Theodore's part. The spirit never revisited the glimpses of the moon.   *   *   *

The tale was over, and feeling herself much relieved from the state of excitement into which the hurry of her feelings had thrown her, Marian closed the volume.

Scarcely had she done so when a servant entered the apartment and handed to her a note. It was a rough, hurried-looking epistle, and from its outward appearance seemed as if it must have been written by some one who either had been in too much haste, or had not possessed the convenience for more politely conducting a correspondence.

The address to her was perfectly correct ; therefore, she could not doubt but that for her it was intended, and fully expecting to find that it was some appeal to her charity from some needy applicant for such bounty as she might feel disposed to bestow, she at once opened it.

The first glance was sufficient to let her know that something must have happened to Charles Ormond, for there was his name. Her hands trembled so excessively that she could not for some moments read any more ; but sat with the note extended before her, looking the picture of terror and dismay.

After a time she succeeded in quelling, to a certain extent, the tumultuous feelings of her heart, so that, at all events, she was able to peruse the few words which Charles had written to her in the hour of his peril and grievous agony of mind.

They were simply these :—

" Marian, it is better that you should hear from me than from any one else that I am accused of a crime of which I am innocent, and am in the hands of the city police. I will communicate with you more at large on the first opportunity.

" CHARLES ORMOND."

A film seemed to spread itself over Marian's eyes, and for some minutes she made sure that she was about to faint. Under such circumstances, however, a strong determination not to give way to such an impulse frequently conquers the physical prostration which otherwise would induce such an effect, and so it was now. The strong feeling that she ought to do something immediately to bring succour, comfort, and assistance to Charles, conquered the bodily weakness, and she did not lapse into that insensibility which, without such an impulse, would in all likelihood have ensued.

Her mother was from home, but she at once took a step which was the most prudent one she could have adopted had she consumed days in the most profound reflection—that was to proceed at once to the solicitor who had been employed by Charles for her and her mother in their affairs, and seek from him advice and direction how to act.

Briefly, then, we may state, that through him she obtained an order to see Charles, which she availed herself of after he had been conveyed to Newgate.

CHAPTER XX.

THE EXAMINATION OF CHARLES ORMOND, AND HIS COMMITTAL.

AND now, having left Charles Ormond longer than our inclination would have prompted us, it is necessary that we return to him for the purpose of seeing what befel him at the Mansion-house, where we last left him before the Lord Mayor.

Some case of trivial importance was proceeding, which was soon over, and then, as the news got whispered from mouth to mouth that a case of so much magnitude as a forgery was on the tapis, the justice-room became crowded with interested spectators, and a scene of more than usual bustle and interest ensued.

The case which had been proceeding was over, and then a whispered communication was made to the Lord Mayor, who sent a messenger for one of the aldermen who was near at hand, after which silence was procured, and Charles Ormond was placed on the spot appropriated to prisoners.

There was a deathlike stillness in the court, for every one there present was intent upon looking in the face of the young man who stood there charged with an offence which, if proved against him, would as assuredly bring him to the scaffold as that the sun would rise on the following morning.

The youth, the noble bearing, and the intelligent look of Charles Ormond won him abundance of sympathy, and, when the first feelings of curiosity were over, there were many whispered expressions of regret among those present at his situation.

The fact is, that such a crime as forgery makes no call upon general and popular indignation. It is only those who have directly suffered, or been nearly suffering in pocket by the attempt of the criminal, who can feel any sense of aggravation at all upon the subject.

To the multitude there is nothing in the crime which comes home to them or to their feelings, however really great an one it is in a social point of view, and deserving of severe punishment.

The silence was broken by the chief clerk of the Mansion-house, who asked what was the charge against the prisoner, as a matter of form, although he knew very well privately.

"Forgery," was the officer's brief but most fearfully significant reply to this question.

There was a visible sensation in the justice-room as this word was uttered. Perhaps there was something in the utterance of it, as to manner, which brought a kind of conviction to those who heard it of the substantiality of the charge, and a certainty that the fate of the unfortunate prisoner was sealed past all hopes of human redemption.

"I am innocent of any such crime," said Charles.

"You had better," remarked the Lord Mayor, "reserve anything you have to say until you hear the evidence against you. Of course, every opportunity will be given to you to say what you please in answer to the charge."

"The hearing evidence against me," said Charles, "can make no difference as to fact. I hear myself charged with the commission of a particular crime, and I hasten at once to declare solemnly my innocence of it."

"Very well; we will now proceed regularly."

Of course Charles had no desire, if he had had the power, which he had not, to disturb the regular course of proceedings, so he said no more at this juncture, satisfying himself that by his first protest he had deprived any one of the opportunity of saying or of thinking that by his silence he had given any sort of implied consent to the charge.

The first witness examined was the clerk at the counter of the banker who had received from Charles the check which was declared a forgery. This witness said,—

"My attention was drawn to the check by its being hurriedly thrust into my hands by the prisoner. At the first glance I suspected it, and yet not being quite sure, as I had not paid so many of Mr. Godfrey's checks as some other of the clerks in the establishment, I took it to a Mr. Smithson, who was at hand, and asked his opinion."

"What did he say?" demanded the Lord Mayor.

"He at once declared the check a forgery."

"What steps were then taken?"

"It was my duty to communicate at once to Mr. Anderson, one of the partners of the firm, who was on the premises at the time."

"Is that gentleman always there?"

"No; the partners take such duty by turns."

"What ensued then?"

"The prisoner was requested to walk into a private room, where he was detained until an officer was sent for from here."

"Did he make any remark?"

"Nothing in particular; but he seemed very much surprised, and his conduct, to my mind, was quite compatible with innocence, or amazingly well acted."

"Do you wish, prisoner, to ask the witness anything?"

"Nothing whatever. He is quite correct."

The check, which was the subject matter of the prosecution, was handed in to the Lord Mayor, who thereupon said,—

"Is the supposed drawer of this check present—Mr. Godfrey?'

"Yes," said Godfrey, and, avoiding the eyes of Charles Ormond, he at once stepped forward, and was sworn.

"Look at that check, sir."

"I do."

"Is that your handwriting?"

"It is not."

"You distinctly swear that?"

"I do, most distinctly."

"Did you authorise any one else to write it?"

"No; I never authorised any one to write a check under any pretence whatever."

Here there was a pause, and the Lord Mayor was heard by those who were close to him to whisper something to the chief clerk about the case lying in a nutshell. Then he turned to Charles Ormond, and said,—

"You have heard the evidence it has been my painful duty to receive against you, what have you to say? Of course, you may say nothing if you please, reserving any defence which you may have for your trial, and, for your better guidance in that matter, I tell you at once that, after the evidence which has been brought before me, I have no discretion but to commit you at once."

"I will ask some questions of Godfrey," said Charles.

The moment he announced this intention, Godfrey faced round towards him

with such a jerk of his whole body, that it seemed like some act of violent determination, which, to be accomplished at all, must be done quickly, and at once.

"Ask what questions you please," said the lord mayor. "The witness is
upon his oath, and must answer you."

"Do you know me?" said Charles.

"Yes. I—I know you."

"Was I in your service?"

"You were."

"And why did I leave?"

See p. 136.

"Because I had no further occasion for you."

"Then, I presume, I received proper notice to leave, and was paid what salary
was owing to me?"

Godfrey was on the point of saying "Yes" to this; but, doubtless, he suddenly
recollected that the Whiteheads could contradict that much, and he said,—

"I had reason to be dissatisfied with your conduct, and therefore discharged you without notice."

"What reason to be dissatisfied?"

"If that has anything to do with the distinct charge of your having forged a check, I am quite willing to enter into it; but a subject of a more foreign character I cannot well conceive."

"This is certainly," said the lord mayor, "very extraneous. I do not think, prisoner, that such a line of examination can result in anything advantageous to you here."

"My lord," said Charles, "I can well be of your opinion, that any examination of this man Godfrey can produce no good results to me, because he has, no doubt, thoroughly made up his mind what to say. Nevertheless, as I have but one tale to tell, on all and on every occasion connected with this affair, I will tell it now, as it will again and again be told, whether it be believed or not."

"As you please," said the lord mayor. "It is not my province to advise prisoners, but I do earnestly entreat you to take the opinion of some professional gentleman before you make any statements; and, besides, you must be aware that if what you have to say has no tendency to contradict what has been so distinctly sworn against you, it can avail you really nothing."

"I am quite aware of that," said Charles. "I thank you for what I know you mean in kindness and courtesy, but I must speak."

"Very good; as you please."

"I was in the service of that man Godfrey as a clerk, at a salary of a hundred pounds per annum, which, by being paid to me quarterly, entitled me to a quarter's notice to leave my situation, as well as compelling me to give such notice.

"One day some papers were placed in my hands to copy, which enabled me to see that Godfrey meditated a transaction which, although the law might not be able to lay hold of it, and pronounce it a fraud, was of so dishonourable a character that I could not for one moment shrink from warning those innocent persons who were his meditated victims. This was the cause of my sudden discharge from his service. I have foiled him in an act of deep and desperate villany, and hence he has concocted this charge of forgery, in order that he may have against me an ample measure of revenge.

"There was, of course, properly due to me, upon my discharge, fifty pounds. The precise amount for which the check in dispute is drawn. I never expected from Godfrey this sum, and was much surprised when, to-day, there came by post a letter containing this cheque. I have a witness to my reception of that letter. I never for a moment suspected the snare into which I had fallen, but innocently took the check to get it cashed, where my eyes were opened fully to the nature of the dreadful plot which it seems but too probable will for a time be successful in confounding innocence with guilt."

Charles ceased, and then the lord mayor said,—

"Your witness to the reception of the letter and the check will certainly be an important testimony in your favour. If you like, I will remand you till you can procure that witness, as well as any others you may have."

"What so easy," said Godfrey, "as for him to have forged the check, and then posted it in an envelope to himself?"

Several voices in the court said "Shame! shame!" and Godfrey shrank back with a feeling that he had gone rather too far in his partisanship against the prisoner.

"There can be no action, however innocent," said Charles, "which may not, by some possibility, be tortured into an appearance of guilt. I am innocent, and can say no more."

"You do not require a remand?"

"No, no. Do with me as you please."

"Then you are committed for trial. I am very sorry for you, but I never knew a clearer case."

A malignant smile came across the countenance of Godfrey for a moment as the lord mayor uttered these words; but it was too fleeting to be made a subject of re-mark, except by those who were very close to him. Charles Ormond was at once removed by the officers; but, as he neared the door, he called out to the lord mayor,—

"I trust I may have facilities given me for sending to those who would feel in-terested in my fate?"

"Certainly, certainly. Officer, you will provide the prisoner here with the means of writing to whom he pleases, and send one of the messengers with his letters."

"I have to thank you, my lord, for this great courtesy," said Charles; and then, in a small room, upon which a good watch was kept, he was accommodated with writing materials, with which he produced a small note containing but a very few words, and addressed to Marian Whitehead.

There was no one else to whom he cared to communicate what had happened to him, and then, turning to the officers, he said,—

"Now, I am ready."

Two of these useful personages accompanied him from the room, and, when they were nearly in the street, he said,—

"Where are you going to take me?"

"To the jug," said one.

"The what?"

"Oh, he means Newgate," said the other. "You'll be as comfortable there as a gentleman at his hotel, I can tell you. A genteel sort of independence it is to be sent there. It is a large residence, where you will be provided with coals, candles, and perquisites, in the heart of the city."

Both the men laughed; but as may well be supposed, Charles was in no humour to appreciate their gaiety, which, doubtless, was indulged in from mere thoughtless-ness, and not from any desire to exult over his misery.

CHAPTER XXI.

THE PRISON.—THE MORNING VISITORS.—THE MYSTERIOUS PROPOSAL.

AND now another act of this fearful drama was consummated. In spite of an amount of innocence—so complete and perfect, that not even in thought had he contemplated the commission of any crime which ought to have brought punish-ment upon him—was poor Charles Ormond the inmate of a prison and the com-panion of wretches, necessarily persecuted by society for the common weal.

Like some terrific and regular piece of machinery, so artfully and admirably con-structed that when once set in motion it pursues its undeviating course, heedless of what victim it may entangle in its meshes, had the dark, intricate, but well con-structed plot for his destruction, gradually advanced, step by step, without the sha-dow of an interruption.

And there he was, the victim of that scheme, admirable in its very simplicity, which had marked him among the whole herd of men for a victim.

He felt like an individual battling with the ocean, or as a pigmy struggling with some mighty giant who needed to make no effort to crush him, but was sure to ac-complish that result by quietly and evenly pursuing his ordinary path.

And, indeed, there was but one solitary circumstance that now could have saved Charles Ormond, and that was one the least likely of all to occur, namely, the be-trayal of Godfrey by the villain Neville, who, to accomplish such a result, must have damnified himself beyond all redemption.

Moreover, in a financial point of view, it was not likely that Neville would quit the strong hold he now had of Godfrey's coffers. It is unquestionably true that the Whiteheads would have purchased his secret of him at an enormous price; but that price would have been the first and the last payment he would have received at all on account of the transaction.

Moreover, it was not like a secret which could be told and paid for at once, leav-ing him who divulged it to disappear from the pages of society, with the wages of his candour.   It was not a thing of this sort, but it was a thing which, to be valuable at all, required to be substantiated in the face of the most rigid criticisms and the most careful analysis that forensic talent could bring to bear upon the subject.

An accusation of Godfrey by Neville, certainly eventually must have ruined Godfrey, because the tale Neville had to tell was of too clear, plain, and distinct a character to be shaken.

There was no circumlocution about it, no intricacy, nothing to make fit together, nothing to reconcile, no hiatus, no link wanting in the chain of evidence which would have made the plot clear and explicit, and, to such a man as Godfrey, frightfully natural.   There it stood in all its dark iniquity, a deed of terror, and one from which was sure to flow precisely the results which had been achieved.

But then, from the first to the last, Neville must have accused himself, he must have commenced his confession with his own suggestion to Godfrey to do the deed, and he must have concluded it by proclaiming that he was likewise villain enough not to keep faith with the man whom he had whispered into the commission of such a crime.

From all these circumstances and considerations, then, we say that it is most unlikely indeed, that Neville should ever be induced to betray his infamous employer; and, in proportion to the unlikelihood of such a circumstance occurring, is poor Charles Ormond's fate the worse, and the chances of his innocence prevailing the fewer.

Nothing could be clearer than the evidence upon which he had been committed for trial.   Had he been himself sitting in the magisterial chair, he could not have done otherwise than as the magistrate did.   Every remark that was made, probably with the exception of a few trivial ones, would have risen to his own lips as things of course ; and when he came to think of all this, and to feel that just and good men, men of high honour, spotless integrity, and nobility of soul, must and ought to conclude him guilty, while a sneering ruffian looked on, and pointed at him the finger of scorn knowing his innocence, no wonder that his heart sank within him, and he felt inclined to utter an accusation against Providence for abandoning him to such frightful contingencies.

How those fearful words rang in his ears as he left the justice-room, which were uttered by the lord mayor,—

" I'm very sorry, but there never was a clearer case."

That brief sentence seemed to haunt him.   It was little in itself, and the remark was about as trivial a one as could very well be made upon the subject, and yet, somehow or other, the short sentence seemed imprinted in indelible characters upon his very brain, and he repeated to himself over and over again,—

" I'm sorry for it, but there never was a clearer case."

His lips unconsciously moved to the utterance of the sounds, and he was made alive to the fact that he had actually uttered them by one of the officers looking at him with surprise as he said,—

" Well, I'm d——d if you ain't a rum chap.   You think it's a clear case, do you ?   Curse me if I ever saw anybody take anything so cool in all my life.   I say, Bill, he says he's sorry for it, but he never knew a clearer case.   There's a go.   He's only sorry a little.   My eye."

" I did not speak," said Charles.

" Oh! very good.   We ain't no grand quisitors.   It strikes me uncommon forcible, as it's not much matter now what you says, or what you doesn't.   It's all up, and as you says yourself, ' I'm sorry for it, but there never was a clearer case.' "

" Oh! you're always a gammoning," said the other officer.   " Come along, don't keep us here in the street chattering all day."

Charles Ormond said no more.   He began to have a sort of consciousness that he must have uttered the words which had taken so firm a possession of his mind, and even as he proceeded in the custody of the two men, who kept a watchful eye upon him towards Newgate, he still could hardly refrain from repeating the sentence, and more than once he fancied he saw it pictured in the sky like a flaming banner dancing before him in very mockery of his misery.

In those days prisoners were conducted through the streets without any regard to that public decorum and dispatch of needful business, which has brought into existence the prison van.

It was no unusual thing for prisoners remanded to the House of Correction, in Coldbath-fields, and other such places, to be brought up to the police-offices in a procession, two and two, handcuffed, and a rope running down the middle of the cavalcade, to which each couple was attached. An officer would march in front, and another one in the rear, and so this melancholy and degrading spectacle would wind its way through London streets, followed by the rabble rout of squalid men, women, and children, who were akin to the prisoners by the actual ties of relationship, or sympathy of pursuit.

Acting upon this same principle, individual offenders, when committed from the police-courts for trial, were very frequently, especially if the offence were one of any magnitude, conducted at once to Newgate by one or two officers, as the case might be.

This was done as regarded Charles Ormond. Nothing could be clearer or more tangible than the case against him. There was not the slightest necessity for a remand. The evidence adduced was ample, and, if it were not, there was no more to be adduced.

No wonder, then, that the Lord Mayor was very sorry, and had never seen a clearer case in his life. Of course he hadn't, and was never likely. To have hesitated about the committal of such a prisoner would have been to have declared himself incompetent to hold the seat he occupied.

The offence, of course, was a capital one ; and, moreover, at that time, it was one of those capital ones which it was thought great policy in a commercial country like this to visit always with death.

Perhaps this was the reason that Charles Ormond grew into so much importance as to have two officers sent with him to Newgate, along with his warrant of committal.

And soon the gloomy portal of this terrible building was gained. That building upon which might well be inscribed the fabled words which are said to appear upon the gates of hell :—

"Enter, and bid adieu to hope."

Charles Ormond felt a shuddering conviction as he did enter, that he was bidding adieu to hope ; and, as the low, massive door clang to behind him, he felt that never again should he look as he had once looked upon the light of Heaven.

There was a strange sort of desolate quietude about that place, which was enough to strike terror into any soul, be it innocent or guilty. The very atmosphere seemed different to that of any other building ; it seemed heavy with the sighs of imprisoned wretches who had bidden adieu to all joy, and to all the amenities of social existence.

In due form the unhappy prisoner was handed over to the custody of the officials of Newgate. A printed receipt for him was filled in as if he had been a bale of goods ; and then, without a word, the two officers departed, looking as unconcerned as if they had only performed an ordinary routine duty, and had not consigned an innocent man to what was virtually his living tomb.

There was a pause of some moments, during which, one or two official personages came and looked curiously at Charles Ormond. He then spoke, and in as resolute a tone of voice as he could assume, he said,—

"I have but one request to make, which I hope will be granted to me."

A man was standing opposite to him with his hands in his pockets, who now commenced whistling some popular tune, with a variety of flourishes and variations.

"I hope," said Charles, "that I may be at least allowed the solitude of my own thoughts."

"Oh !" said the man.

"I trust that I shall not be forced into an association with characters from whom I should revolt."

"Oh, indeed!" said the man. "Perhaps you'd like a little scented soap and a new set of cheyney—anything else?"

"Surely," said Charles, "such an appeal as this should not be made a jest of."

"Lor! a jest! it's you as is joking. I say, Jack, have you got any lavender-water, with the chill off, for this 'ere cove?"

Charles saw that it was useless to talk to these men, and he resolved to endure in silence whatever might occur to him until he should come in contact with some person in higher authority, and probably with more education and gentlemanly feeling.

In a few moments a man walked up with a piece of paper in his hand,—

"No. 2, north," he said; "that's the ticket."

"Kim up," said the gentleman who had been whistling; "a spangle, if you please."

"I don't understand you," said Charles.

"Don't you? How green we are—a guinea, then."

"A guinea from me!"

"Ay, to be sure; you've found it out, have you? We shall have to turn you out, you know, if you don't pay."

"And, pray, what for?"

"The use of a pitchfork, to pick your teeth with."

"Ho! ho! blowed if that ain't good!" said another; "I haven't heard that since yesterday. It's enough to make a fellow cry till he laughs. What a wit you be, Joe; why don't you set up some sort of shop in that line?"

"You mind your own business, and I'll mind mine. Come, my young spark, you'll find yourself the more comfortable for dubbing up."

Charles recollected that, when he had been searched, his money had been given back to him, and he placed the requested coin in the hand of the man, as he said,—

"It seems strange that an involuntary inhabitant of this place should be forced to pay for any accommodation he receives."

"Yes, don't it?" said the fellow, as he pocketed the coin. "There's a blessed many stranger things in the world than that, though."

This was such an incontrovertible remark that nobody said anything about it, and Charles Ormond followed his conductor along a variety of narrow passages, and through several doorways, until they came to a gloomy looking paved court-yard, into which looked a number of windows strongly grated.

"There you are," said his conductor; "here's comfort—look what we does for you. Lor, bless me, if I wasn't a gaoler I'd be you. These ere's cells; the doors is through here, and along a passage—they're opened at eight o'clock in the morning, and closed at dusk. It's better to get out in the morning when they're opened, 'cause they ain't in no ways very big, and a pail of water's throwed in; howsomdever, you've the use of the yard to walk about in, along with the other covies; and here you may live like an emperor till the sessions comes on. Your place is No. 2, mind."

Without waiting for any reply the man walked away; and after being alone for two or three moments, some strange, ill-looking fellows skulked out of the cells and began pacing the yard with all that restless kind of movement which is so characteristic of some wild animals confined to the narrow dimensions of a den in a menagerie.

CHAPTER XXII.

LIFE IN NEWGATE.—THE PLOT DEVELOPS ITSELF.—THE MISERY OF THE WHITE-
HEADS.

Poor Charles knew not, upon reflection, whether to regret or to feel satisfied that he had availed himself of the permission which had been given him by the authorities at the Mansion-house, to send to his friends.

Alas! he had no friends to send to but those whom he had attached to him by the ties of gratitude and esteem, and upon whom he knew that this sad stroke of destiny would fall with terrific severity.

And yet, could he refrain from letting them know personally from himself, what had happened—would not his silence look like a conscious admission of his guilt? Yes; he was glad he had sent, and he was glad he had sent the sort of message he had to Marian, because that was likely to be the gentlest mode in which she would hear of what had befallen him.

When he should see her he would have time sufficient, at least he hoped so, to explain to her what he really considered to be the kind of plot that had been concocted against him.

And he meant to tell her to be hopeful—although hope was fast leaving his own heart—he meant to try and assure her that all would be well, although he trembled himself at a conviction decidedly the reverse. The question that arose in his own mind was, not how he should be proved guilty, but how he should prove his innocence. He stood in the position of a man called upon to substantiate a negative of the most troublesome character. He had to prove, if it were possible, that he did not do something which it was stated, with the most remarkable perspicuity and clearness, he had done.

And how was he to set about it? Would not the vague accusation against Godfrey, of having plotted and planned to place him in his present position, be scouted by every one? Alas! his position was one which thought did not alleviate, but, on the contrary, only tended to render more cruelly hopeless.

Several of the gloomy-looking ruffians who, with him, shared the immunities and rights of the small court-yard, addressed him, and as it was not in his nature to reply discourteously to any one, he answered them, although in such a manner as to let them see he rather then preferred the company of his own thoughts.

Ruffians as they were, they let him be, and, satisfied that he had treated them civilly, they obliged him by forbearance.

In this state an hour might have elapsed, or perhaps a little more, for Newgate must be a sad place to measure time in, when one of the official personages of the prison entered the court-yard and walked up to him, evidently with the intention of making some communication.

He spoke in a whisper, saying,—

" Mr. Jacobs wishes to know if you'll have him."

" I don't know what you mean," said Charles ; " you talk here in a language of your own, and use allusions which, to a stranger, are inexplicable."

" Oh! Mr. Jacobs is an attorney, and does business for most of the gentlemen here."

" Then, for the present, I must decline his services ; he may, or he may not, be an eligible person, for all I know, to give me advice ; but, until I have seen the only friends I have in the world, I can give no answer."

" Very good—mind, I've mentioned him to you—I'll tell him what you say. By-the-bye, you'll have your rations directly. Humph! ahem!"

" Well ?"

" Well ; ahem!"

The fellow held out his hand, and then Charles comprehended that he expected to be paid.

" Am I to give you money," he asked, " for coming to ask me whether I chose to employ Mr. Jacobs or not?"

" It's usual."

" And how much may your modesty demand?"

" Oh, we leaves that to your generosity."

" Nay, name your amount."

" A dragon."

" Take it," said Charles ; " I'm as wise as ever;" and he handed him his purse.

The fellow grinned, took some coin from it, and handed it back, as he said,—

" I'll tell you what it is, young fellow, you're a d—d deal too free with your money; you don't seem to have much either, if this is all; anybody but me would have taken advantage of you. I asked you for a dragon, which is a dollar; some fellows would have took a spangle, I've only nibbled half a one—there's a warning; here's wirtue—haw!"

The fellow walked away with a sort of mock heroic stride, which did not enable him to see a brother functionary who came into the yard at the moment, and whom he was nearly tumbling over.

This second man walked straight up to Charles and said,—

" There's a visitor to you, with an order to see you. I'll be hanged if I know how or where she got it; they're the kind of things which are not picked up in the streets, I can tell you."

" Who is it? who is it?" said Charles.

" How should I know? Come on."

In two or three minutes Charles was shown into a dingy room; no daylight penetrated to it, but a hastily lighted and untrimmed lamp swung from the ceiling.

In another moment Marian Whitehead was in his arms.

For the first few moments neither of them spoke; their feelings were by far too interested to allow them to utter a word, and probably, in the delirium of joy that accompanied that pure and sinless embrace, Charles Ormond forgot that he was a prisoner, and Marian Whitehead forgot that she was within the walls of the much-dreaded Newgate, and that he who loved her with so much purity and tenderness was all but a convicted felon.

It was Charles who spoke first, and it was the tears of Marian, which he felt upon his cheek, that roused him to the necessity of playing the comforter, as best he might, to her whom he knew would feel so acutely all that might befal him.

" Marian, my Marian," he said, " do not weep; this is a sad trial, dearest, but we will not even now despair. Look up, my Marian; look into my eyes, and there read my innocence; but, ah! you need not read it there, my heart has too long been in your hand like an open book, every page of which was free to you to read and full of love for thee. You see, dear Marian, that I speak cheerfully."

" Not—not cheerfully, Charles," she said, " not cheerfully but nobly. Great God of Heaven, what have we done that we should suffer thus?"

" Hush, hush, my Marian, hush; this, after all, may be but some passing cloud, which mars the beauty of a landscape to make the sunlight look doubly delicious when it is gone."

" Oh! Charles, Charles, could I but believe for one moment that you thought so. But tell me, tell me what it is they say that you have done; what monstrous act do they attribute to you who are all justice, all honour and purity? Oh! let the false accuser dread the offended majesty of Heaven."

" Hush, dearest, you are much excited, be calm, I pray you."

" Its vengeful lightnings will find him, let him cower where he may. But now, Charles, tell me, tell me what it is they say that you have done."

" You were present, Marian, when I received a check for fifty pounds?"

" Yes, from Godfrey."

" The same."

" By post it came. Well, Charles, well?"

" I took that check for payment, and it was declared a forgery."

" By whom?"

" By Godfrey's banker, and afterwards by Godfrey himself, who is my prosecutor."

Marian wrung her hands despairingly.

" I see it all, I see it all," she said. " You have told me enough. This is the scheme which is to revenge him upon you for your noble advocacy of myself and my poor heartstricken mother. Godfrey is your accuser—the villain Godfrey!

He wrote the check—he sent it! It is a deep laid plan! Oh! Charles, do not you see it all as plainly as if it were mirrored before you?"

"I do, Marian, I do. My trust is in Heaven alone, for man, I fear, can avail me little. When the tiger gives up its prey; when the gaunt wolf allows the placid lamb to go in peace to its fold; when the midnight stars shine out in presence of the sun's broad disk; when all that seems impossible on earth, or air, or Heaven, shall come to pass, then may I expect Godfrey to forego his deep revenge, and own that he has wronged me!"

Marian paused, and but for the supporting arm of Charles she would have fallen to the floor of that miserable cell in which she had listened to the recital of him who now supported her.

Charles Ormond stood mute and sorrowful, with his arm clasped round the despairing form of her he loved. Oh! what exquisite pangs of sorrow and grief shot through his heart as he recollected his own sad and helpless situation.

There was she whom his heart adored, and whom his reason told him was well worthy to fill that place in his affections that he had accorded her, almost fainting in his arms, leaning upon him for aid and support.

Had this happened when he had been at liberty, what thrills of pleasure would have circulated through his veins at such a state of things; but now, alas! he had such a melancholy prospect before him, that the thoughts of death were far more bitter than they would have been had he never known the hopes, and felt the love that filled his mind with the purest and most noble thoughts.

Now it was not only to leave life, but to leave one whom he loved more, far more, than life itself.

A deep sob escaped him. It was involuntary; not for himself; the emotion was caused by a mixture of feelings, of hope, and despair.

"Oh! Charles," said Marian, "I would that this check had never been presented! I would it had been returned or burnt!"

"If I had been wise, Marian, and taken your advice, I should have done so, and now have been happy. But it is my fate, I suppose, and I was urged on by some irresistible impulse, and I could not escape my destiny."

"Do not speak of destiny, Charles. Don't you think that something could be done? Surely one so innocent cannot be permitted to fall into so deep laid a snare as this?"

"I fear, Marian, that is the very reason why I should. It has been so deep laid, that there can be no possible escape."

"Oh, God of heaven! surely, surely this cannot be permitted? I am sure Heaven will not look down calmly and see you perish and the unrighteous prosper over the righteous?"

"Heaven may interfere when it sees fit, but until that time shall arrive, I must submit, and bow to its decisions, hoping that hereafter I may reap my reward for suffering in this world."

"Oh! Charles, Charles, and we have been the cause of bringing you to this sad situation. Your nobleness and love of justice have made you the victim of treachery, and deceit, and injustice. I never can forgive myself, for, however involuntarily, being the cause of your being the victim of that villain Godfrey."

"I am his victim, Marian, and I pray Heaven that I may be the only one who may have occasion to feel his villany."

"Something must be done though, Charles; you must not fall without exertions being made to combat this conspiracy against your life. I will see Mr. Blake, the attorney."

"I fear," said Charles Ormond, shaking his head gravely, "that all will be useless—all is so clear against me."

"But legal advice."

"Legal advice may be of service in some cases, in mine I fear not. I do not in a desperate case like mine cling to the advice of a lawyer, who may advise, when the case is doubtful; but mine, alas! is too clear, much too clear to admit of doubt in the mind of a stranger, nor would Godfrey plan, and appear personally in a matter that would be any way doubtful."

"I fear—oh, Heaven! but it cannot be; something must be done, though. Alas! I cannot tell what that should be. Pray Heaven direct me in my endeavours! Charles, you shall not sink without some effort, poor, and ill-directed as that may be; but you must not despair. Despair is death itself!"

"And that may be welcome—ay, welcome, to put an end to the exquisite sorrow I must feel when I come to part with you, Marian. May God then support me!"

"And me, too, Charles; but I cannot—shall not live to see that day! Your death would be more ——"

"Arm yourself for the worst, my dear Marian. You have yet a mother; you have yet to foil the schemes of injustice concocted and devised by Godfrey and his companions in crime. Again, I say, arm yourself for the worst; I am fully prepared to encounter the worst, which I feel must come."

"No, no, Charles, do not give up hope entirely."

"I do."

"Hope yet."

"No, despair alone stares me in the face! I cannot shut my eyes to the danger, it is too immediate, too imminent; it must be endured, Marian."

"No, we will try to doubt it. Surely some incident may happen that may alter the complexion of the affair."

"None can happen, Marian. The whole case is clear; there's a person accused, and witnesses of the fact. What can I say? I presented the check. Every link in the evidence is there clear, and to them satisfactory."

"May Heaven open their eyes to the iniquity of the proceeding, and enable them to see through the deep villany of this man."

"Alas! there can be no hope of that! But, dear Marian, take care of yourself; do not run into the least danger, for Godfrey will not hesitate to do anything that will injure you, provided it will further his own objects."

"I am sorry to trouble you," said the turnkey, stepping in, " but the time is up, sir. You have at least scarce a couple of minutes left. I am sorry to disturb you."

"Marian, we must part, but you will see me again?"

"Yes, yes, I will see you again, Charles; in the meantime I will exert my utmost to do something in this matter."

"Farewell, Marian."

"Adieu, Charles."

These words were spoken hurriedly, and in scarce a whisper. The tears fell fast down her cheeks, and Charles Ormond, as he took the proffered hand, silently pressed her lips to his own. The pressure of his hand was returned, and he turned away in a state of mind better imagined than described.

"If you please, sir," said the turnkey.

"I am ready."

Silently he followed the man, whose duty it was to look after the prisoners. Marian followed too, and the turnkey directed her through a number of passages, and in a few minutes, after traversing several, she came to the wicket gate which led into the Old Bailey.

Here she was let out, and traversed the sad and sombre neighbourhood—for such it is to all who do not look at it, save in a business point of sight, shadowed as it is by the gloomy walls of our principal prison.

She drew her veil closely over her features to prevent the gaze of the curious from perceiving the tears she shed, and that even now bedewed her cheek.

Her step was slow and faltering—for she was almost blinded by her tears, and could scarce distinguish the road she was going, or how to avoid mischief.

She had nearly reached the bottom of Skinner-street, when she thought she observed the same individual step once or twice before her and gaze beneath her bonnet at her countenance with a scrutinizing glance.

Justly offended by such a freedom, or rather piece of insolence, she knew not hardly how to avoid it, save by quickening her pace, or crossing to the other side of the way. Quicken her pace how she would she found the stranger still dogged her footsteps, and appeared desirous of entering into conversation, but Marian took care to avoid either hearing what he said or even turning round and thus prevented him from speaking.

She was becoming somewhat alarmed, and at length crossed the road, and found that the individual did not then follow her; but after she began the ascent of Holborn-hill, he crossed over behind her some few paces.

Marian, more than ever alarmed, turned up Ely-place, hoping to escape the pertinacious stranger, expecting he would believe her ahead, and go on after her, but in this she was mistaken, for he too turned up without hesitation, as though he had been aware of her intentions. When he came up to her—which he did almost immediately, and there being no one at hand, he at once spoke to her, as he gently touched her arm,—

" I am speaking to Miss Whitehead, I believe ?"

" This is an intrusion," said Marian ; " I desire you will desist, and allow me to proceed as I will."

" As you please ; but if I am not mistaken, your name is Whitehead. I can guess it, because you have but just left the prison of Newgate, where you have been to visit the unfortunate Charles Ormond."

" Since you know so much, sir, it is a useless annoyance to come and inform me what you have found out by prying curiosity. Allow me to proceed home, sir."

" That is hardly civil for a civil intention, and a praiseworthy one too. What I have learned I learned involuntarily, and have taken some pains to find you and obtain an opportunity of seeing you. I knew not where you lived."

" I know not what you would have," said Marian ; " I hold no converse with strangers, there are too many snares now in being to allow of its being safe."

" Yes ; but chance has led me to the knowledge of circumstances that make evident to me the plans of Mr. Godfrey, whose name you have so much cause to detest."

" I have indeed ; but I cannot but look upon all whom I don't know as being connected with him in some way or another."

" Which is committing an injustice."

" I know you not."

" Nor I you ; and yet I have endeavoured to serve you."

" You have ?"

" Yes—at least I have learned something that will probably be of some service in the cause of Charles Ormond."

" Charles Ormond !"

" Yes ; I repeat it, something that may be of service to him if it can be done ; and from what I have seen, I should imagine it could be easily done."

" Speak quickly."

" Well, I had occasion to discover that Charles Ormond is quite innocent of the crime with which he stands charged."

" And how know you this ?—can you give evidence of that fact if required ?"

" I am not in a condition to swear to anything that I may tell you, because I know nothing of my own knowledge, only from the chance words of other people, and the moral conviction of my own mind."

" You can be of no avail then."

" Pardon me, I can. I say I have discovered Godfrey's motives, and those can be ruled."

" And what are they "

" Money is the most expressive word I can use. If you desire to save Char Ormond, all you have to do is to make some bargain with Godfrey, and he will ensure the safety of Charles Ormond, or he will assuredly be executed."

" Great God !"

" It is but too true ; but you cannot save him otherwise ; all now rests with God-frey, he may manage it—he will forego revenge for gain."

" No, no," said Marian, " I will not pollute a good cause by means of corruption and bribery—Charles Ormond would not be saved so."

CHAPTER XXIII.

MRS. WHITEHEAD'S WEAKNESS OF INTELLECT.--MARIAN'S GRIEF.--THE INTERVIEW WITH MR. BLAKE.

MARIAN, when she refused to adopt the plan suggested by the stranger, turned away abruptly from the quiet spot in which she had been walking and regained the crowd that were proceeding along Holborn, and soon became mingled with them. She saw no more the man who had given her so much uneasiness.

" No, no," she thought, " Charles Ormond shall not be indebted to such dishonourable and dishonest shifts, or, indeed, would he think life valuable when disgrace would for ever afterwards be his portion; he would not think I had done him any favour; he would never again look any human being in the face; and, less than ever would he aspire to become that to me to which he had once aspired; he would not unite me and an ill name for life, he would not bring such disgrace upon me; we should be for ever as strangers, for he would shun me. No, no, some honourable means must surely exist to disentangle him from such a nest of difficulties and dangers that now beset him."

She came to her mother's lodgings, and there found that Mrs. Whitehead had been unwell.

"Mother, mother, what can be done for poor Charles? That villain Godfrey has been successful in revenging himself upon him whose only crime is his honour and having defended us."

"Oh, my dear, Godfrey is a villain."

"Yes, mother; but what can be done for him?"

"Oh, my dear Marian, nothing that I see, nothing; it is a bad world we live in, a very bad world. I should think that all that can be done is to have patience."

"Patience, mother!" said Marian; "patience!"

"Yes, my child; why not?"

"Good God! and can you recommend such to me or to him at such a moment of sorrow, danger, and disgrace?"

"Well, my dear, you are young and I am old, and that, you know, makes a vast deal of difference."

"In what?"

"The way we take things."

"What do you imagine, mother, that I am speaking about?"

"About, my child, about; oh, why, yes, it was about patience, I think. But you haven't told me how Charles Ormond is, and when he will be home."

"Good Heavens!" exclaimed Marian, and she gazed upon the face of her mother, but she saw nothing but the most placid serenity, touched, indeed, with some melancholy, but she appeared to be utterly incapable of aiding or offering advice in the difficult state that affairs had run into.

It was some time before Marian could be persuaded of the fact her mother was not insane, for her mind seemed almost incapable of thought or any new impressions; but there were now other pressing matters; at another time this would have been a cause of deep grief, but when counter currents come together they in some measure alter the course of each.

"I must send for Mr. Blake," she muttered to herself. "I must send and request he will call. It is no time to hesitate or to grieve; I must act, since my poor mother cannot."

A letter was at once dispatched to Mr. Blake, the purport of which was that she desired to see him immediately at her lodgings.

During the time the letter was going and the return of the answer, Marian bethought herself of several schemes by which she might benefit Charles Ormond, but none of which could she entertain for one moment.

Each plan when rejected produced a sense of disappointment and depression scarcely to be described. Her sorrow broke out afresh, and there was no apparent prospect of doing anything that would benefit the unfortunate and innocent Charles Ormond.

The case was so clear that even the most merciful jury could not do otherwise than decide against him, and bring him in at once guilty of a crime he would have suffered death before he would have put his hand to.

"Mother," she said, "what would you advise me to do in this affair? I am almost incapable of thought."

"And so am I, child."

"Don't you think it is a very horrible thing?"

"Yes, my dear, but we can't help it; I wish, for my part, Charles Ormond was here, child."

" And so do I, mother, God knows."

" He was so pleasant and gentlemanly."

" Yes, yes."

" And the hours used to pass without knowing how."

" Yes, yes. Good God, what misery !"

" Yes, yes, it is. I wish, my dear, you would tell him, when you see him, I miss him very much, and he must come back—I'm sure nobody is more welcome."

Marian turned away, the tears fell fast from her eyes ; she could not bear to hear Charles spoken of in this manner, and anything tended to recall him to her mind.

At that moment a knock at the door tended to divert her thoughts into another channel, and she sat in expectation of seeing Mr. Blake enter the apartment. In this she was not disappointed, for a servant came in to announce Mr. Blake.

" Send him in," said Marian.

In another moment Mr. Blake entered the apartment, and bowing to Marian, he said, looking at Mrs. Whitehead,—

" Mrs. Whitehead, I believe ?"

" Yes, sir ; my mother is so much affected by recent circumstances, that I fear at present she can take no part in the business that I wish to consult you about."

" The letter I received was from you, then ?"

" Yes, it was."

" I came here immediately I received it. Have you done anything with Godfrey, or rather, has he made you any offer or attempt to shake your intentions respecting himself ?"

" No, not exactly that, but he has began to take his revenge—he has plotted against the life of Mr. Ormond, and has, I fear, too nearly succeeded."

" Indeed !"

" Yes ; he swore revenge, and he has been setting about it with suitable means and confederates."

" What has he done ?"

" Why, Mr. Ormond left Mr. Godfrey suddenly, on account of his acting too honourably towards myself and mother, as you are no doubt aware."

" Yes, I have heard of it."

" Well, then, he left Godfrey in his debt, and a quarter's salary was due, as well as a quarter more for want of warning. To our surprise, about three or four days ago a check came to the house, enclosed in an envelope, from Godfrey ; the check was for this money that was due."

" Well, Miss Whitehead, I remember the case in the paper yesterday ; I saw it, I can save you the recital."

" Ah, you saw, then, it was declared a forgery ; and then Charles Ormond was given in custody, and at once committed for trial on the charge."

" Yes, I saw that."

" What can be done ?"

" Nothing."

" Nothing !" repeated Marian.

" No, Miss Whitehead, there is nothing that I can see ; the case is too clear, and however true the defence may be, there will be no means of proving it."

" Indeed !"

" No ; Godfrey swears it is not his handwriting."

" He does."

" And of course he will obtain the aid of others to do the same thing ; and as far as I am concerned, I think it is very likely to be the truth."

" You think so ?"

" I do. It is easy for such a man to get up a forgery in that manner, by getting some one to imitate his handwriting ; but the bankers would be sure to detect it at once, when another person would be sure to take it ; so you see, both he and they can swear it is a forgery."

" Heavens ! what an abominable plan to ruin the unfortunate, but innocent, Charles Ormond."

"I think his condemnation certain."

"Then there is no hope?"

"I can give you none."

"What shall I do—what can I do, to save him?"

"Nothing, that I can see. The case, you see, is so clear. There is a forged check, the forgery is satisfactorily proved, and it is found in Mr. Ormond's possession; and more, he attempted the utterance of the forged check—that is all that will go to a jury, and he will be cast for death."

"Merciful God! and cannot you, as a legal man, aid him; Mr. Blake? Do, for heaven's sake, attempt, sir!"

"I can employ counsel to watch the case; in case any informality should arise, they may take advantage of it."

"And nothing else?"

"And nothing else at all, I assure you, Miss Whitehead."

Marian hung down her head, to hide a tear, but it fell on her hands, and Mr. Blake rose, desirous of escaping from a scene which was likely to become both painful and useless.

It was no pleasure to him to watch the grief of Marian, or listen to what she might say or do, in the height of her sorrow. Mr. Blake was a gentleman, and a man of feeling, and he believed that he had heard all she had got to say, and now she was struggling against the expression of her grief, it was time he took his departure.

"Miss Whitehead," said Mr. Blake, as he stood with his hat in his hand, "I will see that Mr. Ormond is not neglected on his trial. I must, however, tell you candidly that it will be of no avail. You had better make up your mind for the worst, and console yourself, as well as you can, that you have done all in your power to counteract the evil."

"Mr. Blake, I am much obliged to you. Do what you can, and may Heaven be propitious to the unfortunate!"

"Amen! I hope so, with all my heart. Do not hesitate to come, or send for me."

"Thank you, sir."

"Good day to you, and permit me once more to advise that you moderate your sorrow as much as possible. It will be dangerous to all."

With a few more kindly words, Mr. Blake left the house, and then Marian Whitehead gave way to Charles Ormond her grief, for the situation of peril in which he was placed.

She could not but think that so innocent a man ought not to be allowed to suffer, and yet if a jury pronounced him guilty, where was succour to come from?

What was to be done was a thing she could not tell; to know that he was to lay there in prison, awaiting his trial, and that awful moment nearing, was madness, especially when he had so clear a case against him. Reason tottered in the extremity of woe.

CHAPTER XXIV.

MARIAN'S RESOLUTION TO SEE GODFREY.—THE INTERVIEW AND ITS RESULTS.

POOR Marian was much afflicted at the turn affairs were taking. It seemed to her but a dream, to suppose that so bad a man as Godfrey, should succeed in his nefarious designs against so generous and honourable a one as was Charles Ormond. It was against the nature of things that he should, she thought, and, therefore, some special interposition of Providence would take place, and that he, Godfrey, would be most severely punished, and in a most marked and emphatic manner.

But there was no hope, much less probability, that such would be the case, at all events in time enough to save the object of revenge from its effects.

What was to be done, was the theme she harped upon; but she could not tell, even being on the scene where all was going on, would neither retard nor advance, nor aid Charles.

Suddenly, however, she remembered the injunction of the man who followed her all the way from Newgate, and informed her that he knew Godfrey had planned Charles Ormond's destruction, but was by no means inaccessible to money.

"Oh! surely," she thought, "even these means must not be altogether despised, for what is the life of Charles Ormond? or what are the means for its preservation, in comparison with such a life itself?"

Charles would, no doubt, shrink from accepting life upon any dishonourable terms, but then it need not be known by any one; even Charles need not be aware of it, but would merely see that the evidence was short; true, he would find it out afterwards; still she thought to live without honour could not be more objectionable than to die under the same stigma.

In either case he would have the proud consciousness of knowing he did not deserve the calumny of the world, nor its aspersions; but then he would be restored to Marian Whitehead; that would console him for the loss of that outward show of respectability which may cover the blackest heart that ever beat within the breast of a human being.

It was not that Marian judged there was anything dishonourable in buying off a powerful and unscrupulous prosecution, any more than there would be in giving a footpad the purse to purchase her safety from any further violence. It was much the same thing in either case, and so she considered it.

However, she was well aware what construction would be put upon such a course by many; but what was the opinion of the whole world in comparison to the life of Charles? But she had yet to learn what were the terms upon which such a boon as that which she required would be sold, and whether the terms could be agreed to or not.

"What shall I do?" she exclaimed; "shall I wait, or go to Godfrey? There can be neither harm nor danger in doing so. Godfrey dare not harm me! He could gain nothing by doing so, and I shall have that security for my safety, which is the greatest of all."

Marian paused a moment in her train of thought, clasped her hands, and exclaimed,—

"And what would I not risk to save him? Life and all I hope for—all I ever wished for. Has he not done so for me?—Has he not risked all?—And is he not about to lose all? But no, I must endeavour to prevent that. I must sacrifice something for him who would sacrifice everything for me!"

She arose, and putting on her walking garments, arrayed herself for the streets.

"Yes, yes, I will go to Godfrey, and see what he will do, or what he will require to induce him to forego this scheme of revenge that he has concocted."

Then looking at her mother, who sat sleeping, or dozing on a couch before the fire,—

"You, alas! have become incapable of mental exertion. Alas! then, that it should be so at a moment which above all others is fraught with so much danger to our future welfare."

She left the room, and proceeded to the streets, and took her way slowly to Godfrey's house. It was not without some ill-defined feeling of dread that she approached it, and when she saw the door, her heart almost failed her; but then the recollection of Charles Ormond's probable fate recurred to her, and she determined to be guided by the necessity of her position, rather than the demerits of the case. She would not treat Godfrey as he deserved, with scorn, and reproach; indeed she was now about to become suppliant when she ought to command.

She rang and knocked—the door was opened by a man, she did not know.

"Is Godfrey within?" were the only words she could bring herself to utter, and the man looked at her steadily, ere he replied; which he did by saying,—

"Yes; will you walk in?"

Marian did walk in, but she spoke not.

"Will you walk this way," said the man, as he led her towards the private office of Godfrey.

"What name?"

"Whitehead."

The man paused, then opened the door, and half entered, saying, as he stood in the entrance,—

"Miss Whitehead wishes to see you, sir."

"Show Miss Whitehead in," replied Godfrey, in insinuating tones, that grated on her ear more than even his harsher notes, because they were more natural.

Marian entered the room, and the door was closed, but she uttered not a word; she was now face to face with one of the deepest-dyed villains that ever breathed the breath of life.

She paused, and scarce dared to speak; while he, wary and cunning as a fox, waited patiently for a moment or two without saying a word, or permitting his eyes to encounter hers.

At length he said,—

" Will you be seated, Miss Whitehead ?"

Marian felt obliged to occupy the seat that he pointed out to her, else she would not have sat down.

" Will you inform me," he said, " of the cause of this unexpected and favoured visit ?"

" I came, Mr. Godfrey, as I dare say you can well imagine, respecting this prosecution you have commenced against Charles Ormond for this forgery."

" Yes ; I understand."

" Then we shall have but little to say respecting the justice of the case ; it is for your mercy that I come—to solicit you to forego that which is the result of a thing that never happened, the consequences that flow to the accused who has witnesses and circumstances against them."

" And more never is against them," replied Godfrey, looking up into her face for a moment or two.

" No ; but you are well aware he is innocent."

Godfrey shook his head, saying,—

" No, no, that does not follow. I am sorry to be engaged upon a criminal prosecution, but the bank is the prosecutor, I am only a witness ; all will be conducted independently of me, and I am not responsible, and if was I don't see how I could interfere."

" You know Charles Ormond is guiltless."

" What I know is my business."

" You can save him."

" But why should I save him ?"

" For mercy's sake."

" Ay," said Mr. Godfrey, taking snuff, " that is the cry of every criminal who is detected."

" But he is none."

" Wait and see what the law says."

" I wish to avoid that, and am willing to become the sacrifice, if need be."

" Your sacrifice could not benefit him now. I do not, however, deny but I could save him, innocent or guilty."

" You do not ?"

" No ; because it may be that I may choose to say something, or omit to say something, and so get the whole affair quashed.'

" Will you do so ?"

" That depends upon whether I have any motive ; without one, I cannot and will not take the trouble."

" And what motive could induce you better than the knowledge you are doing an act that you ought,—that you are merely or hardly acting to satisfy the ends of justice."

" No, no, not so, Miss Whitehead ; he is guilty."

" He is not."

" The cheque is forged."

" But he did not forge it."

" He is guilty of uttering it, though he be not of the forgery—which is very likely."

" Very likely, Mr. Godfrey ! very unlikely. It is unlikely that Charles Ormond should forge a cheque for what was due to him ; very unlikely indeed ; but you, sir, know he did not, you know it is a deep-laid scheme to entrap him, to ruin him, and cause his destruction ; this you know, and know well."

" If you came here to scold, Miss Whitehead, you might have saved yourself the trouble of coming here, as it will produce no result such as you desire."

You say you can save him."

" I do."

" Then you know him to be innocent ?"

" It by no means follows that I do; but that has nothing to do with my power of saving him."

" What a hard, callous-hearted villain you must be, to attempt the ruin of a young man whose character is too honourable and high-minded for you even to understand."

" I think I could," said Godfrey.

" You cannot, or else you must have known he never meditated injury to you."

" Indeed !"

" Never ! The act upon which you quarrelled was one as highly honourable in him, as the attempt to defraud myself and mother was cruel, iniquitous, and base."

" Ah, well, you see that we look at these matters in a different light; I should have all the trouble and possibilities of failure on my side, whereas you would have a certainty."

" But how disproportioned."

" I don't think so."

" Will you set him free ?"

" I cannot ; why should I ?"

" But what do you require should be done ?"

" I will exert myself so that his acquittal shall be certain—for he must be tried—if you accept the original conditions I once offered you," said Godfrey.

" And what were they ?"

" A deed conveying to me the right to receive all monies, coming from whatsoever source, and going to the late Mr. Whitehead, connected with business, for which I give you in return an increased annuity, settled and determined upon your lives, amply secured."

" Then you desire to receive for doing that which you ought to do voluntarily, the whole of an immense property coming to me and my mother; in fact, you desire to ruin us almost, before you would do a simple act of justice."

" I'm afraid," said Godfrey, " that we shall never come to terms about the release of Charles Ormond. His life is at stake, and so is some property, it seems, and you decline exchanging the one for the other. I believe that is how we stand relatively."

" Monster !"

" You think that I ask more than it is worth. You want the article, and yet think it too dear."

" Wretched man ! what state can you be in to have such thoughts as these ? Heaven must have rendered your heart callous, to show the extent of deformity of which the human heart is capable. All that is base, sordid, and mean, lie heaped in one huge deformity ! Heaven look down upon him, and see the hideousness of the wretch who would murder the innocent ! rob the widow ! despoil the orphan ! and commit every crime which our imperfect nature stands chargeable with !"

During this, Godfrey sat in his chair, his eyes irresistibly attracted towards Marian's, and they appeared of a dead and leaden lustre from beneath his shaggy eyebrows. There was a sallow hue, too, upon his countenance, which wore such an expression of deadly hatred and revenge, that it was impossible to mistake, even for an instant, the workings of the soul within that bad and dangerous man.

But, excited as was Godfrey by this appeal, yet he had great powers of self-command; for he never betrayed any anger, but merely smiled, as he said,—

" Well, since we can't agree, since I won't take less, and you don't think it worth while to give so much, we may as well part, like buyers and sellers who can't agree."

" Oh, God !" exclaimed Marian, in a burst of grief and indignation, " and is it come to this, that man should sell the life of his victim at a price—that the life he cannot give should be taken away in a moment of gratified revenge—the worst passion that disfigures our nature! Man, man! have you no feeling of remorse and sorrow for the misery you have occasioned?"

"If you will have a direct answer, I must say no. I have no feelings of remorse, or sorrow, for I have no cause. Before I leave you to the possession of this apartment, inform me, if you please, whether you accept my offer or no?"

"Your offer?"

"Yes. What come you here for?"

"To beg the life of Charles Ormond."

"You have treated me with a pretty piece of declamation, in which you have not spared insult, and then in the face of all this you expect me to be mollified and complacent."

"If I have erred, do not let him suffer."

"No; he will suffer for his own error, and not for yours. But do you intend to answer me?"

"I can scarce imagine Charles Ormond would thank me for purchasing his life at such a price! But Heaven must guide me in this extremity, for I have no councillor!"

"You have a few days—but a very few—to pass before it will be too late; if you cannot make up your mind now, you can by that time."

"My mind tells me that Charles Ormond must be saved, let it cost what it will."

"Then we are agreed."

"No, no; I will agree to nothing now. I cannot say how I may act. I must see my mother. I cannot do it all by myself, and of myself."

"As you please," said Godfrey, and he rang the bell.

The same man appeared who had let her in, and she followed him out.

CHAPTER XXV.

MARIAN'S RETURN HOME.—A VISITOR.—NEVILLE'S OFFER, AND MARIAN'S
REJECTION.

MARIAN WHITEHEAD hurried homewards, her mind a chaos of confusion, and unable well to imagine any course of conduct that would steer her clear through all the difficulties of her position, and extricate Charles Ormond.

This, however, was by far too difficult a matter, and she regretted that she had not at once accepted of Godfrey's offer, and relinquished the whole of the property, however disproportioned to the small annuity she and her mother were to receive.

Before, however, she could come to any definite conclusion, or adopt any determined course of action, she arrived at her own door, and was soon ushered in.

"If you please, miss, here's a person here as wants to speak to you. He's been a-waiting some time."

"Indeed!"

"Yes, miss."

"What is his name?"

"I don't know, miss. I haven't asked yet, because you were not at home."

"Do so, now, if you please."

"Yes, miss;" and the servant went into the small room appointed for a waiting-room, and soon afterwards returned, saying,—

"It is Mr. Neville, miss, who wants to speak to you concerning Mr. Ormond."

"Show him up here," said Marian, who could not repress a shudder as the name crossed her mind; but the name of Charles Ormond was to her a charm that would gain admission to her, be she where she might.

In a few moments more, Neville entered the apartment. To Marian, his appearance was truly forbidding, and she felt solicitous to know what such a man could have to say concerning Charles Ormond.

Neville bowed, and fixed his eyes unblushingly upon Marian, as if he had been fascinated, and she was obliged to speak first.

"What may your business be with me?" inquired Marian.

This recalled Neville, and he said,—

"You are, no doubt, surprised at receiving a visit from a stranger, Miss Whitehead?"

"I am, rather."

"But the object upon which I come will, I trust, be my justification for my intrusion."

"Go on, if you please."

"My object is to speak with you respecting Charles Ormond, who now lies in Newgate, on a charge of forgery, at the instance of a Mr. Godfrey."

"Yes, yes; that is simply the truth."

"I know this Godfrey."

"I fear that little credit is to be gained by such an acquaintance," said Marian.

"No, no; I am sure of that, from what I know of the man; and it so happens I am well acquainted with the whole of his scheme for ruining Charles Ormond, and securing the property you have coming to you and your mother."

"Can you aid me in unmasking this man, and making his plans futile?" inquired Marian.

"I can."

"And will you?"

"I will."

There was a pause of a few seconds, during which time Neville looked doubtfully into the face of Marian, who scarce knew what to say or think of such sudden promises, and so unconditional. It seemed as if there was too much of hope to be real.

"How can you shake this accusation of Godfrey's against Mr. Ormond? You see the banker has given evidence against him, and of course his evidence must be contradicted."

"Oh, no, that could not be done; and, if done, it would be unsuccessful," said Neville.

"What can you do?"

"Confirm it, and say it is so, but it was sent to Mr. Ormond without his knowing it to be forged."

"Can you do this?"

"I can; and, much more, accuse Godfrey of a conspiracy to procure the death of Charles Ormond, and to defraud you out of certain property."

"All this I know and believe; but the only doubt is, as to who will aid and help me to prove what is so necessary to prove, and whether it can be done upon such terms that will make it possible."

"All that," said Neville, "may be made a matter of bargain. Godfrey's object is to get the property into his hands, and of course he cares not what he do, or whom he injures, so long as he obtains his ends."

"I can easily believe all that."

"I am in a condition not only to save Charles Ormond, and save him with honour and credit to himself, but punish Godfrey, and to secure you from all attempts upon your property."

"Upon what condition?"

Marian could not forbear asking this question. There was something in Neville's countenance, or manner, that compelled her to speak thus. She knew from the man's appearance, or rather she felt it was so, from an unseen impulse.

"That I am in some difficulty about mentioning, because my introduction has not been in character; but the urgency of the case must be my justification. I have seen you, Miss Whitehead, and to see you is to love you."

Marian shuddered.

"Yes, I say I love you, and to prove how sincerely I do love, I will incur hazard and danger in the attempt, and succeed in doing what nobody else can do."

"Such a proposition cannot be entertained for one moment."

"Do you reject my offer?"

" With scorn."

" Nay ; his life goes with your consent."

" He would not accept life on such terms, nor am I called upon to sacrifice my-self in the sight of heaven and man, to condescend to such a state of degradation."

" You misreckon your case entirely, if you talk about degradation," said Neville ; " you may fare worse, after all. With me you would be safe ; for I defy Godfrey to catch me napping in the way he did Ormond. I know too much of him to per-mit him to allow the attempt, and it would be a perpetual safeguard from him or his. Godfrey has no power over me, but I have over him ; he is quiet when I am by. Say at once you will give me your hand, and then I will secure Ormond, whole and in honour, and you shall have no trouble respecting the property."

" Not if all the lives of those I ever knew and my own were dependent upon my own consent. You men, who would barter life, honour, and all that is worthy or noble on earth for the gratification of your favourite passion, you would sell each other's lives, betray each other in guilt ; all, all are worthless and degraded beings. To associate myself with such as you, would be to make myself as guilty and worth-less as you are. Go, and learn that such offers are spurned, as being too degrading and too criminal for any one less guilty and wicked than yourself, to consent to. Go, and say no more ; you cannot alter my resolution, and you cannot make your-self less criminal and worthless."

" You shall live to repent this," said Neville ; and, with a deep scowl upon his brow, too well marked to admit of any doubt of its meaning, he left the apart-ment.

Marian heard his retreating footsteps with a shudder. She could not but feel a dread of the future creep over her insensibly ; and she was scarcely able to reach a seat as the street-door was banged to by Neville.

CHAPTER XXVI.

THE STRUGGLE OF FEELING.—LOVE AND DUTY.—THE PRECARIOUS POSITION OF CHARLES ORMOND.

THE villany was now as apparent as any villany could possibly be ; and no one who could in any way become cognisant of the circumstances had room for a mo-ment's doubt as to the real facts of the case.

And yet, such was the nature of the offence of which Charles Ormond was ac-cused, and such the completeness of the evidence against him, that, even supposing Marian Whitehead was to come forward, and state, with all the aspect and mien of truthfulness which the circumstances warranted her in assuming, what had occurred between her and Godfrey, as well as the agitating interview she had had with the scoundrel Neville, a jury would be called upon by counsel not to believe her on account of the peculiar position in which she stood with regard to the prisoner, who would then be at the bar.

Godfrey had taunted her with this, when she declared her intention of making public the offer of compromise which he had made to her. He had asked her who would believe her when she came forward to say something in favour of one who was known to be her lover.

Neville, too, had taken occasion to make the same remark ; and she, even with her little knowledge of the world, felt that, unjust and cruel as such a course would be, every word that fell from her lips in favour of Charles Ormond would be viewed with suspicion, while, if she said anything against him, she would be considered heroic.

What, then, was she to do ?—whither was she to turn for succour, under these most melancholy and distressful circumstances ? The past seemed like a dream ; the present, a season of dread and anxiety ; and the future, a prospect at which to tremble for the events it might shadow forth.

Poor Mrs. Whitehead seemed in a perfect state of bewilderment ; she knew not what to do or what to think as regarded Charles Ormond. At one moment she seemed as if could have staked almost anything upon his innocence, while at another the facts, as they appeared against him, came across her mind with such overwhelming force that she was completely staggered into a belief of his guilt.

This latter feeling, however, never for a moment was breathed to Marian. Mrs. Whitehead saw that her whole soul was bound up in a consciousness of the innocence of Charles, and that to endeavour to shake such a faith would be an act of the greatest unkindness.

And so events proceeded languidly, as regarded any circumstances favourable to the prisoner, but with a frightful and gigantic rapidity as concerned the approach of the time which must condemn him to a dreadful death, provided nothing intervened to snatch him from the destruction which seemed but too surely awaiting him.

She found a greater facility in procuring orders for admission to him at Newgate than under ordinary circumstances the friends of prisoners usually find; and this very facility arose from a conviction, on the part of the authorities, that the case, as against the prisoner, was so very clear that it was impossible it could be in any way tampered with on the points of evidence upon which it was to rest.

No stroke of human ingenuity could set aside the conclusive evidence, first, of the banker's clerk, to the effect that Charles Ormond was the man who had presented the check, and, secondly, of Godfrey, who had deposed, upon oath, to the fact that it was not in his handwriting.

These two circumstances, although they by no means proved that Charles Ormond was the writer of the check, were quite of themselves sufficient in those good old times capitally to convict him.

And where was his defence?—a simple denial, which would look like the coolest piece of impertinence that ever was perpetrated by a human being; and yet that denial was strictly true.

We tremble, indeed, to think how many persons may have fallen victims to such plots as the one we have recorded against Charles Ormond, at a time when human life was not considered of that account and value that it is at present, but when people were made to suffer an ignominious and a painful death for what, after all, cannot but be considered as venial offences.

This remarkable case shows how clearly and distinctly evidence ought to be weighed. It shows what particularity and caution ought to be exercised before any human being is declared guilty of any offences imputed to him.

And, moreover, it shows how carefully the motives of witnesses should be scanned in cases of this description, and how, when it is shown that it would be perfectly easy for a prosecutor himself to have done all that appears against a prisoner, how very chary of his conviction those who hold his destiny in their hands should be.

But let us look at the state of mind of Charles Ormond, now, a short time before his trial, upon one of the occasions when Marian Whitehead paid him a visit of sympathy in his lonely prison-house—lonely to him, although crowded with the unfortunate and the guilty, because in them he found no society, but shrunk, as it were, into himself, and let his gloomy thoughts prey upon him till they reduced him to the very shadow of what he once was.

He could no longer even summon up a smile with which to meet Marian; the effort was too great; he had not lost courage, but he had lost confidence in the result of his trial—he had lost that confidence which at first an innocent man is sure to feel in that innocence being made apparent; and the more he dwelt upon the calamitous circumstances in which he was environed, the more he seemed to feel that he was within the toils of a deadly fate which could not be avoided.

He was allowed to see Marian in that same little room in which we have already recorded that one of their interviews took place, and this which we now mention was the last that could occur previous to the trial.

She had not seen him either since her interview with Neville, though she had that piece of intelligence to give him if she chose to utter it, of little avail though it was in rescuing him from the perils with which he was surrounded.

At the first sight of Marian a flush of colour visited his pale cheek, and as he held her hand in his for a moment he seemed to forget that there was anything like unhappiness in the world.

Alas! too soon, however—and roughly enough—was he likely to be awakened from any such felicitous dreams; those mournful eyes, yet beautiful, but lacking the lustre of happier times, which were bent upon him, recalled him to the present.

" Once again, my Marian," he said, " once again you visit me ; you still cling to me, dear one, though all the world desert me."

" And will ever cling," said Marian. " Do not, even yet, Charles, desert all hope."

" Nay, my Marian, it is hope has deserted me, not I that have turned my back upon that blissful vision."

" But it will come again, Charles, it will come again."

" Alas ! no, my Marian ; when that last refuge of the unhappy once departs, I think it never comes again."

" You are too desponding."

" Not so, not so. Am I not environed by circumstances which would make the stoutest heart tremble, and turn the expectations of the most sanguine to bitterness and despair."

" Nay, but, Charles, have you not often heard and read of how, when all hope and chance of succour seemed at an end, some wondrous circumstance, little dreamed of, and little expected, would arise to free the innocent from the toils which encumber him ?"

" Yes, my Marian ; I have heard and read of such things ; and you put my case correctly when you place it among those which require some special wonderful circumstance to interpose to benefit it."

" But, Charles, you cannot tell ; I will come forward, you know, upon your trial ; they may believe me. Do not ; oh ! do not, fancy that all men are so callous as is Godfrey, and that equally dreadful associate of his."

" Of whom speak you ?"

" A man named Neville."

" I know him not, Marian—what of him? Has he, too, come into the arena against me ? Godfrey alone surely would have been enough against the unhappy Ormond."

" From both Godfrey and this man Neville, Charles, have I had proposals, pointing towards your release. Godfrey is willing, provided I and my mother sign that deed of settlement which he brought to our happy cottage home, when you were paying to us your first visit, to release you."

" Indeed !" said Charles, with an incredulous look. " Marian, Marian, do not listen to the arch tempter. He cannot, dearest, he cannot, I tell you, release me if he would."

" Nay, I've not yielded, for I doubted his sincerity, even if he could."

" Doubt !—can there be room for doubt with such a man, or rather with such a fiend, in the form of humanity as Godfrey ——"

" But little—but little ; and then came this Neville to me with an offer to betray Godfrey, and so free you much more effectually upon conditions."

A gleam of hope shot across the countenance of Charles, and he said, eagerly,—

" What condition—what—what condition ?—is it a very hard one, my Marian ? What does he expect, or wish me to do, as a reward to him for not being so great a villain as he might be ?"

" Nay, Charles, of you he hopes, expects, and wishes nothing ; it is of me."

" Then reject at once all offers. I would not have you make the slightest sacrifice to these men for my life's sake."

" And the sacrifice he asks is even equal to the sacrifice of life itself—he would make me his, Charles."

" The villain !"

" Nay, another word is thrown away upon him. I need not tell you how I met the offer."

" No, Marian, you need not ; and for your sweet sake I'll assume a hopefulness, if I have it not, without absolutely despairing. I will arm myself with fortitude to meet the will of Heaven ; but whatever my fate may be, let me have the sweet consolation of knowing that you endeavour to bear up against the vicissitudes of cruel fortune, and await that better and happier time, when, in a world above the stars, where a false accuser cannot be, we shall meet to part no more."

See p. 116.

" It shall be so, it shall be so, Charles ; and yet my voice shall be lifted for you when those who would destroy you say that of you which is untrue ; I will denounce them before God and man as false witnesses, and those who would pursue a fellow-creature even unto the death, knowing well his innocence of all they would impute to him. Oh ! can such men lie down to taste of sweet repose, and hope for that serenity of soul which rest bestows upon the virtuous and good ? they cannot—they cannot."

The interview had now lasted almost longer than the regulations of the prison allowed, but Marian's guileless and devoted manner had even won upon the stern officials, and they let her be longer than duty warranted them in doing.

So reluctant was she to tear herself from Charles, with even this latitude, they always had to tell her that it was time to go, and on this occasion she left the prison with a heart and brain so full of agony that she could scarcely see her way into the street.

The bright sunshine that was upon everything seemed a mockery, and, without reflecting, she wondered how the busy, idle crowd could pass that dismal prison-house without seeming to cast a thought upon those who pined within its walls.

CHAPTER XXVII.

THE EVENING BEFORE THE TRIAL.—GODFREY AND HIS ASSOCIATE.—MUTUAL DISTRUSTS.

IT is the evening before the trial of Charles Ormond, and Godfrey, looking as pale as death itself, and with a nervous expression on his countenance, which plainly indicated a mind ill at ease, sat alone in one of the apartments of his house.

Drinking materials were before him, of which he had partaken largely, but, in the state of his feelings, the stimulant had but little or no effect upon him, and he could not screw up his courage, as he wished to do, to look comfortable and happy.

Never did a human being appear to be in such a fidgetty and inconstant state; he could neither sit, nor walk, nor stand, nor lie down, for five minutes together.

At one moment he would seem to assume a position of ease and serenity, then it would hastily be succeeded by another, and then, again, he would start to his feet and pace to and fro through the room with unequal and agitated strides.

" What a strange thing," he muttered, " it is that opiates which would kill a man under ordinary circumstances have not even the power of sending me to sleep. Sleep! when did I sleep? when do I sleep? I think, never; I fancy I shall never sleep again."

He paused a moment, and then he suddenly exclaimed,—

" And what for, and why is it that I am thus agitated and driven almost past the bounds of reason? Is it because I swore I would have revenge against one who thwarted me, and am fully succeeding in accomplishing my purpose? so it would seem—so it would seem. Where can Neville be to-night? It is very strange he makes not his appearance. Does he suspect anything?"

As he uttered these words, Godfrey fixed his eyes upon a suspicious-looking black bottle that was on a table before him. It was a bottle from which himself he had partaken nothing. It looked like any ordinary bottle of port wine, with the usual dash of whiting at the lower part of it; but it was not what it looked like, as we shall presently perceive.

" Why don't he come? he cannot know, he cannot have the least suspicion, of course he cannot. I thought not of the plan myself until to-day, although I have been calculating deeply how to counteract the effect of any projected treachery of his to-morrow."

There came suddenly a knock at the door, and Godfrey started as he cried, in a voice of terror,—

" Who's that? who's that? I'm not at home to anybody; hide me somewhere—hide me somewhere. No, no. How nervous I am to-night; how full of terrors. What would I not give to restore myself to my usual manner! I'm afraid Neville when he comes will suspect something, and that surely must be he, for I've few visitors."

He stepped cautiously to the room door, and listened over the head of the stairs; he heard the street door opened, and Neville's voice asking if he were within.

" Yes, yes," he said, " it's Neville. Now—now to get rid of the tool who has served me so long, but who may now begin to find out its own edge and temper, and turn against its master."

He returned back to the table, and, with trembling eagerness, uncorked the suspicious-looking bottle; that bottle that he had made suspicious by glaring at in so strange a fashion.

But he took none of its contents; he only poured what might have been a wine glass and a half of it among the ashes, and then replaced it on the table; he poured himself a glass of port wine from a decanter, but he placed the bottle close to his hand, so as to convey the impression to any one who might come into the room that most assuredly from that he had helped himself.

These preparations were complete, done as they were with trembling eagerness, before the room door was opened, and a servant said,—

"Mr. Neville, if you please, sir."

"Show him in, show him in," cried Godfrey, with a wild sort of mock hilarity. "Show in Mr. Neville, always."

"How very kind," said Neville, as he strode into the apartment; "that is what I call friendly. I suppose you were enjoying your bottle all by yourself, and didn't expect a visitor?"

"Why, really," said Godfrey, "I scarcely expected you, as it had got late; but, never mind, sit down, you're all the more welcome."

"Thank you," said Neville, and, drawing a chair, he seated himself on the opposite side of the table.

"You drink, of course," cried Godfrey; "I've been overhauling my cellar, and find that I've only port in the house, but it's delicious, as fine a wine as ever I tasted, and as I know it's the only wine you drink I don't mind being reduced to it."

"Oh, you're too good," said Neville.

"Will you allow me to assist you?" said Godfrey. "I've just made a little inroad into this bottle."

"No, thank'ye."

"What! you—you won't?"

"No; I've turned temperate, and mean to drink nothing but water with the chill off for the future, and mean to draw that always myself out of the water-butt."

"Ha! ha!" laughed Godfrey, but it was a most horrible attempt at a laugh; "a good jest; after that we'll have a bumper."

"Well, I don't know," said Neville; "it's tempting; good wine can't do a man any harm."

"Harm! no, a world of good! Come, I knew you were only joking. You may take a glass of wine now and then, and yet be temperate. Come, a bumper, a bumper."

"Well, if I do take it, it shall be a bumper," said Neville, and he laid hold of the bottle, "and so shall you."

With a rapidity of action, then, that prevented any opposition on Godfrey's part, he leant over the table and filled up his glass to the brim.

Godfrey shrunk back and looked positively blue, while Neville drew towards him an empty glass and appeared to be on the point of filling it from the bottle; he paused, then, a moment, and left the glass as it was.

"No," he said, "no, I've made myself a promise, and I'll keep it. I won't drink till after Charles Ormond's trial, come what may of it. You drink yourself, Godfrey, and I'll look at you; there's virtue, I didn't think I'd got so much self-denial in me."

Godfrey was completely staggered; he made two attempts to laugh, which only ended in diabolical contortions of his mouth. He said "Very good," in a tone which was much more significant of "Very bad;" and then, with a sudden movement of his hand, he upset the glass of wine that was before him.

"Bless me!" he cried, "how awkward," as he jumped up.

"Never mind," said Neville, "there's more in the bottle;" and he laid hold of it by the neck, while he leered in the face of Godfrey, as if he would read the secret purposes of his soul in his blanched and terrified-looking visage.

It would have been a study for a painter, those two men at that moment. Godfrey, with all the trembling, cowed look of a detested villain upon his countenance ; while upon the other's sat a triumphant leer, as if he would have said,—

"Godfrey, I know you ; I saw it in your looks ; there's poison in that bottle."

"Won't you drink ?" said Godfrey ; and he said it rather because he'd nothing else to say than from the most distant hope that the other would partake of the drugged wine now, for drugged it was.

"No," replied Neville ; "won't you ?"

"Not just now."

"How singular ; I thought you were going to empty the bottle. If you won't drink it, and I won't drink it, which most assuredly I won't, I don't exactly see the use of it ; so, here goes."

He took up the bottle ; and before Godfrey could be aware of his intention, he flung it against the wall, so exactly over Godfrey's head, that it seemed as if he had thrown it at him.

The smash that it came with was prodigious.

"Good God !" said Godfrey ; "what did you do that for ? Is this decent conduct in a man's house ? I tell you, Neville, this is unsufferable."

"Is it ?" said Neville, rising to his feet ; "then tell me—is it sufferable that a man should keep in his house drugged wine ? but it won't do, I can tell you. I've done you some service, and the labourer's worthy of his hire, especially when he labours in such a vineyard as I have worked in for you. I say I may be insatiable in my demands, and you shall not, cannot help yourself, do what you will."

"I have no desire, Neville ; you do me a great injustice."

"Never mind ; we shall meet again, to-morrow. To-morrow's Friday, you know, Godfrey ; and, on that day, Charles Ormond will be tried for his life ; he will be convicted."

"Hush ! hush ! hush !"

"Nay, I'm glad on't ; I hate the fellow ; he's as great a bore to me, as he is to you. I say I hate him, and would gladly see the rope about his neck, which it will be next Monday morning, as surely as we stand here at present. I have found out an old cause of hatred towards him, as well as having a new one ; so, beware, Charles Ormond, and if you had not fallen into the pits spread for you, I would soon have laid some that would have encompassed your destruction. He will be hanged on Monday morning next, Godfrey."

"I shall go out of town," gasped Godfrey.

"Out of town—psha! I shall go and see the execution. And now good night to you, and take a lesson from these proceedings ; don't play with edge tools, or they may chance to cut you."

———

CHAPTER XXVIII.

THE TRIAL OF CHARLES ORMOND, AND THE ADJOURNMENT.

The morning of the trial came, one that was of the deepest importance to Charles Ormond. A morning of such importance had never yet beamed upon him ; and one which he felt was to decide his fate, or rather one on which he felt he was to be condemned, for he saw no chance of safety, except it was by some of those inexplicable chances, which no human foresight can at all reckon upon, or even perceive ; he, in his state, could see no termination to that day's proceedings, save the one most fatal to himself.

To a criminal a trial, if we may be excused the use of a manifest trueism, is a trial. Even to Charles Ormond, who was no criminal, this was strictly true ; and, perhaps, more strikingly true than it is in many cases, for those who know their guilt, go up with a chance in their favour, while he ran all the risk, and expected no justice ; they go merely to hear their doom, and, at the same time, to have a chance ; he had none—no chance—because, had he been found not guilty, it would have been a simple act of justice, and no more in his favour than he deserved, while a condemnation was a yet greater injury than his accusation.

Charles Ormond could not feel that unruffled calmness which a man may feel, who goes out to meet certain death ; nay, the soldier who mounts the breach, and "seeks the bubble reputation even in the cannon's mouth," does so because he deems he is performing an action worthy of imitation, and brings him fame and glory ; he dares dangers, and faces death under far more favourable and favourably exciting circumstances, than the unfortunate Charles Ormond faced his hour of peril and danger.

The latter, indeed, had no credit—no meed of praise to reward him if he braved it successfully ; and more depressing still was the knowledge that, if he fell, he must do so with dishonour ; and no pitying eye would shed a tear to his memory, that no one would cherish his name, or do him the poor justice of believing that he was innocent, save one ; and to her he regretted to believe he should cause more unhappiness, and leave more than ever unprotected, and exposed to the machinations of a villain, than ever she was before ; that, in fact, his generous attempt to befriend them would, in all probability, now that he was in process of being swept away from among men, draw down a deeper revenge upon them from Godfrey.

He looked upon himself as a sacrifice ; and yet he determined, that, placed as he was, he would meet his fate with the fortitude becoming his nature ; and that, think what the world might, Marian should not see that he shrunk from the sacrifice—his want of nerve should not be an additional pang to her.

That morning was one of bustle and excitement for many in the prison. The authorities were busy, too ; and men were busy who were confined for various crimes who were not to be tried, because they frequently inquired, and were solicitous about the fate of some of their former or present companions.

The case of Charles Ormond had not excited much sympathy among the men who were prisoners with him, for he was no companion to them ; and yet he gave no offence to them ; but he kept himself aloof, because their guilt was of a different class to what it was presumed his was ; but the fact was, they were generally the worst species of mankind, and with them Charles could not associate ; there was a natural repulsion between them.

And yet, when it became generally known that his trial was approaching, there was something of an interest, certainly of a curiosity to know what would be the result of his trial ; the circumstances were pretty well known, and those who spoke of the trial, said,—

"We all know his fate. It will be a black cap affair ; he's booked ; there's no help for it."

Such was the pithy and unceremonious way in which the fate of the unfortunate Charles Ormond was disposed of, or, as they called it, reckoned-up and balanced.

On the morning of the trial, Charles Ormond was filled with many emotions and apprehensions ; real fear he felt not, but it was the trying circumstances of being innocent, and, by the leaguing of unprincipled men, he was made to appear guilty, and, perhaps, even worse than that came the vision of lost happiness, the felicity of life that might have been passed with Marian Whitehead, under almost any other circumstances but those which had turned up.

"Ormond," said the turnkey, beckoning him.

"Yes ; I am ready," he replied.

"You are wanted in the court, or will be, presently."

"I am quite ready."

"I am glad of it. I wish you well over this unpleasant business. You have breakfasted, I believe ?"

"Yes ; I have."

"In another half hour your name will be called, and then you will be carried into the vicinity of the court until the names are called over, and then you must make your bow to a British audience, but that will be no gratification to you."

"None, none," said Charles.

"Well, keep a good heart up on this occasion, and things may go better than we expect."

"I can hardly expect that," replied Charles ; "because you see the case is so clear, and my prosecutor has laid his plans so well, that there can be no doubt but he will follow it up by swearing as clearly as he did before."

"Very likely," said the turnkey; "but here, you are wanted. I wish you safe over it."

Ormond was given into the care of the proper officer, and was conducted across the yard into the old court-house, where the sessions were held.

He had not much time given him. A short conference was held with his attorney, and then he was touched upon the arm by the gaoler, in whose custody he was.

"You are wanted above; his lordship has taken his seat, and proceeds with your case at once."

Charles Ormond was conducted into court by his guide, and he felt, for the first time, a burning blush upon his cheek, as he felt rather than saw that the eyes of other men were fixed upon him; but it was not occasioned by any sensation of guilt—far otherwise, it was because he was surprised in a position that implied guilt.

In another moment he stood in the dock, pale but self-possessed; and he answered to his name in a clear, audible voice, and then some preliminary forms were entered into. The jury were sworn, and the indictment was read by the clerk of the court, who imposed silence upon all present, under certain pains and penalties.

Charles Ormond found that he was indicted with uttering a forged check, with a guilty knowledge, and upon this they rung the changes, by varying the modes of expression three or four times, and then multiplying the manner and nature of the crime by these modes of expression by itself, accused him of being guilty of acts to the amount of what the arithmeticians would call the square root of the original variations.

This is the usual mode of drawing an indictment; and, to a person unaccustomed and wedded from professional taste to this kind of jargon, it appears foolish and absurd; but if, for instance, they set out, accusing a man of murder, they vary the accusation, perhaps, in four different ways; then multiply these four by four more, and you arrive at the number of sixteen, which is the probable amount of repetition in different modes of expression.

When this was over, Charles Ormond was asked the usual question by the clerk.

"Prisoner at the bar, do you plead guilty or not guilty, to the crime of which you now stand charged with?"

"Not guilty," replied Ormond, in a clear voice.

There was a short space allowed for some necessary forms to be gone through. Charles Ormond looked around the court while this was proceeding, and gazed upon the judge who was to try him, and the jury upon whose fiat depended his life.

The judge was a calm, middle-aged man; he had an unruffled, placid-looking countenance, with a broad and high forehead, large eyebrows, which from habit were somewhat contracted; but the whole expression of the face was calm, patient, and piercing, and he was one that seemed capable of going through the merits of the largest and most difficult case, with great precision and accuracy, but who was too calm to allow his judgment to be swayed by his feelings, be they ever so great or acute; he was apparently a man who could, under the most trying circumstances, do his duty with all the appearance and reality of equanimity.

As for the jury, they were composed, as juries usually are, of the most odd and ill-assorted number of men—many of very mean appearance, as far as physiognomical expression goes—and were confined together on the right hand side of the court, while the witness-box was on the left.

The counsel were seated below, and in front of the bench, on which the judge sat.

The counsel for the prosecution was one who had been engaged in that capacity very often before, and had become habituated to look upon prosecuting a criminal as a very praiseworthy deed; and, moreover, he was one who decidedly fought for victory, which is not the usual case among practitioners at the bar, especially on a crown prosecution.

But at this time the punishment for crimes against the mercantile community was much heavier than at present, and were more frequent.

"My lord and gentlemen of the jury," said the counsel for the prosecution, as he commenced his address in slow and measured terms; "the prisoner at the bar is charged with a very grave offence—an offence, gentlemen, against the commercial portion of this large community, and which offence affects the prisoner's life.

"It is, therefore, not only a matter of importance to the prisoner, but one that affects yourselves, as being integral portions of that community so offended against; and, therefore, it demands your especial consideration and attention.

"The crime itself is one that militates so strongly against the interest and well-being of the inhabitants of this great city, that it cannot be too severely punished, nor too carefully sought out by the public, and punished, for its own sake.

"The prisoner at the bar, gentlemen, stands charged with the crime of forgery, and of uttering that forgery. He held a responsible and confidential situation, in the employment of Mr. Godfrey, a merchant, whose multifarious concerns required the aid and assistance of a trustworthy and confidential person, such as he believed the prisoner at the bar to be, gentlemen.

"Think how many merchants and traders who, in this great and enterprising community, are in the same situation, and what a vast amount of confidence must be placed in their keeping, and the enormous power they have of abusing that confidence, and even of irretrievably ruining their employers; for, if they can withdraw the means of carrying on trade—of destroying the capital by which it is supported—then, gentlemen, they not only ruin those who have faith in their honour, honesty, and integrity, but, gentlemen, they utterly destroy the thousands of families who depend upon the prosperity of the merchant or trader for employment—for bread.

"Thus you see, my lord and gentlemen, the great necessity of there existing between the employer and the employed a bond of union, and which, when once broken, demands the keenest inquiry into its cause, and the punishment of the guilty who may have abused that confidence that is of necessity reposed in them; it is a trust for the benefit not only of themselves, but of the community at large, and, therefore, it is the offence is a public one, and punished accordingly by the public.

"The prisoner who now stands charged with this crime, was, as I have stated, in the employment of Mr. Godfrey—in his confidential employment for some short time; from some reason or another, unnecessary to mention, he was discharged, and never entered the office of Mr. Godfrey afterwards.

"Now, gentlemen, mark the premeditation in this case; he had easy access to Mr. Godfrey's check-book, and with the view to the future commission of this crime, he tore two checks out of his book, and kept them by him until the time arrived when he thought he could safely commit the crime with which he now stands charged before you to-day.

"It is strange, gentlemen, by what singular circumstances guilt is often accompanied, circumstances of themselves of little note, save as to manners, that are apt to excite suspicion, and eventually a trifling circumstance causes the whole affair to become known.

"This young man, who has no excuse of ignorance, he being, I am informed, intelligent, and well educated, and fitter to grace a better place than the court of justice in such a capacity, and, therefore, well aware what he was about, forged, no doubt, the check, which he afterwards presented at the bankers. It was filled up for the sum of fifty pounds.

"The check was suspected, and he was given into custody, under peculiar circumstances, which will be related to you in the evidence, and, therefore, I need not occupy your time in repeating them here, but I will say this, he evinced remarkable hesitation, and when searched, there was found upon him a blank check, the fellow to the one he had forged, and which he had only by an over-sight, so strange, yet so common to guilty persons, retained about his person; and had he succeeded in this instance, there can be no doubt he would have pre-sented the other, filled up, in all probability, for a much heavier sum.

"This, gentlemen, is the whole of the case, and which I shall be able to establish upon such testimony that will render your task one of less responsibility, I am happy to say, than usual, for it is an unpleasant duty, but one that I must, for the well being of society, and the safety of thousands, demand at your hands, and they will not demand it in vain."

When the counsel had delivered this very bitter speech against Charles Ormond he sat down, drew his breath, and looked at the witness-box with an air, as much as to say,—

"I have set myself on good terms with them, and I have done all I can for victory, and I think I am sure of it."

He seemed pleased with this notion, and during the few moments' pause that occurred, he wiped his mouth with a white handkerchief that he carried in his hand, and turned over some leaves of the brief that he held in his hand.

"My first witness," he said, "is Edward Jones. Call Edward Jones, if you please."

"Edward Jones," shouted the clerk.

"Edward Jones," sung out the criers, until the sounds died away in the distance, and seemed as if somebody was calling out, as no doubt they did,—

"Now, Ned Bowes, where are you?"

"Edward Jones," shouted a crier, as he came out of the court to a waiting-room.

"Here," exclaimed a gentleman, retreating from the vicinity of the crier a few paces, as if he feared to have his ears split.

"Oh, you are wanted."

"Very well."

"Come this way. His lordship is waiting."

"I am ready."

"This way then," said the crier, who wanted to persuade himself that there was always a great deal to be done in bringing witnesses into court, and they always betrayed a desire to escape, which they would but for the vigilance of the crier.

Mr. Jones was then sworn, and deposed as follows :—

"I am cashier at the bank where Mr. Godfrey keeps his account. I know his handwriting very well. I have often cashed his checks, and when I saw this one I knew it to be forged."

"Do you know the prisoner?"

"I have known him as Mr. Godfrey's clerk."

"Have you cashed checks for him before?"

"I have."

"And all genuine?"

"Yes."

"State what occurred on that occasion when he presented this check, for which he was given into custody?"

"There were many persons present when he first entered, and he had to wait until his turn came, then I noticed that he seemed strangely agitated, or at least nervous and fidgetty, and when he offered the check, it was not done in the usual way. I do not mean that he did anything unusual, but he was, as I have said, nervous, and hesitating?"

"This aroused your suspicion?"

"It may; but I can hardly say so. Until I saw the check I had no notion anything was wrong."

See p. 166.

"And the signature—what was that?"

"It purported to be Mr. Godfrey's, for fifty pounds."

"Is that the check?"

"Yes, it is."

"And is not Mr. Godfrey's?"

"To the best of my knowledge and belief it is not. I thought so at the time, and then I walked back to the managers, and consulted with them, stating my suspicions that the check was a forged one."

"And what was the result of your consultation?"

"That he should be invited backwards into a room, and given into the custody of an officer, who was sent for."

"And he went?"

"After some hesitation."

"That is all you know about it?"

"Yes, yes; all. I have no more to say."

"Prisoner," said the judge, "have you any questions to ask the witness before he goes down?"

"None, my lord," said Charles Ormond.

Charles Ormond knew the main facts of what was stated were true, though somewhat coloured, and yet he remembered he was somewhat agitated, and might have confirmed what was said of him; but, at all events, he could not question the clerk's statement.

"You may stand down," said the judge to Mr. Jones.

Mr. Jones left the witness-box, and he was followed by another person, of the name of Arthur Power, who stepped into the witness-box.

In answer to a question, he said,—

"My name is Arthur Power. I am manager in the banking establishment named. I recollect, on the day in question, the last witness coming to me and saying he had a check of Mr. Godfrey's presented to him, which he thought was not genuine. I looked at it, and saw it was not his signature, but a very good imitation, and might pass very well with less careful people."

"What did you do upon that?"

"Advise his detention."

"Well, sir?"

"I went out and requested him to walk into a private room, which he did, after considerable hesitation. While we were conversing in the private room the officer and Mr. Godfrey entered, both of whom had been sent for."

"What took place then?"

"The prisoner appealed to Mr. Godfrey, who, when asked if he had signed the check, declared it to be as we anticipated he would—that it was a forgery."

"Did he make any remark?"

"He said something about it being a plan to ruin him, and that it had succeeded. He was then given into custody, and was taken away and charged before the lord mayor."

"Do you remember anything more?"

"Nothing."

"Have you any questions to ask this witness, prisoner?" inquired the judge of Charles.

"None," replied Charles, in the same tone as before.

The officer was next called who took Charles Ormond into custody at the banking-house; but as he was an officer, and wanted, he was, as usual with the fraternity, found only in some neighbouring public-house, whence he was dragged as he was just in the act of raising a glass of rum-and-water to his lips.

"You are wanted," exclaimed the messenger.

"Who wants me?"

"His lordship—they are waiting for you."

"In one moment," he said, seizing the glass with the intention of swallowing the cherished mixture.

"Oh, dear, no, not a moment; his lordship will commit you; and you'll smell strong of rum."

"Well, there's no violets smell like it."

"But it may not be so well in a court of justice, you know, and you may be suspended."

Thus urged, and being dragged likewise, he was soon brought over the road, and just entered the court in time to escape very severe censure for the time he had kept them waiting.

The officer had now shaken off the effects of the hot compounds, of which he had taken a surprising quantity; but it is to be recollected that as he was an officer, and that his authority was great, so was his capacity of containing, and he accordingly held much without spilling; and it took more to injure the usefulness of a seasoned vessel than it would have done one less accustomed to it.

"You are an officer, are you?"

" Yes, I am."

" Did you take the prisoner into custody ?"

" I did."

" Just relate under what circumstances."

" I was sent for to the banking-house, and was told that this young man was my prisoner, and I made him my prisoner accordingly."

" Upon what charge ?"

" That of passing a forged check."

" State what occurred."

" Oh, he said Mr. Godfrey gave it him for half a year's salary, and that it was all a planned thing to get him into trouble. I took him to the Mansion-house before the lord mayor."

" What did you find upon him ?"

" Another blank check, which he said was sent to him with the other, which was forged."

" There was no other circumstance that occurred ?"

" No, sir, none."

" Have you any questions to put to this witness ?" inquired the judge, of Charles Ormond.

" None," he replied, as before.

The officer was therefore ordered to stand down, which he very gladly did, being very thirsty, through having talked so much with nothing to drink ; and, now that he was released, he determined to go back, and, if possible, recover the lost rum-and-water. As he went along, he ruminated upon the probability of any of it being left, and that he looked upon as being highly improbable, because he knew that, though it was his turn to pay, yet his friends were too jovial to permit it to be lost because he wasn't there ; but what was more probable, he was pretty sure it would be his turn to pay for another by the time he reached the house of entertainment.

" If it is so," he muttered, " I'll drink it all at once."

And, filled with this laudable determination, he walked rapidly towards the spot whence he had been led.

The next witness that was called was Godfrey.

" Godfrey !" shouted the crier, from one place to another, in all the various passages, and all the rooms, and in the court-yard, but there was no answer.

The name was called out three several times in the body of the court, but still no answer.

" What is the meaning of this ?" inquired the judge.

" I am really at a loss to determine, my lord. Mr. Godfrey ought to be here, we well know; and I do not know of any cause that I can attribute his non-attendance to ; but I submit to your lordship, that there is evidence enough, should he not be present, to convict the prisoner ; and, therefore, however unfortunate this neglect may be, the ends of justice cannot be defeated by it."

" I think his evidence necessary," said the judge.

There was a consultation held between the counsel and the attorney for the prosecution, who had but that moment entered the court, and then the counsel arose, and said,—

" My lord, I have just received a communication from Mr. Godfrey; he has been taken suddenly very ill, and cannot leave his bed without danger."

" Have you a medical certificate ?"

" We have, my lord."

The individual who brought the certificate stepped into the witness-box, and was sworn.

He knew Mr. Godfrey was ill, though he couldn't tell what was his complaint, but he had a doctor attending him, and that was his certificate which he brought with him. Mr. Godfrey wished, if possible, that an adjournment might take place, and that to-morrow would enable him to attend with safety.

The witness was ordered to withdraw.

" I submit, my lord," said the counsel, " that an adjournment under the circum_ stances will be the best means of arriving at public justice, and meet the necessities of the case."

"It must be a matter for consideration," said the judge.

"I must also submit to your lordship," said the counsel for the defence, "that it would be better to permit the trial to proceed at once, and when your lordship comes to consider the shortness of time afterwards, there is a sufficient reason for proceeding with it at once. Moreover, we have the learned counsel's own opinion, that he had a sufficient case to send to a jury."

"But, my lord," rejoined the opposing counsel, "that is no reason why I should peril the case, by omitting the evidence of so respectable and important a witness as Mr. Godfrey."

"It is a difficulty," said the judge. "My brother judge is in the other court, and I will retire, to consult upon what course had better be pursued, though I cannot help expressing my opinion that the trial should be postponed."

The judge then rose, and the gentlemen of the bar rose also, as he left the bench, and then there was a general bustle and hum on all sides, as if the exuberance of conversation, which had hitherto been pent up, now burst forth again for a short time, to discharge itself of its overflow.

Charles Ormond, too, was amazed; he could not imagine the cause of the non-appearance of Godfrey, whose hatred to himself he very well knew. That he was ill, he could hardly doubt, and yet he knew not how to believe. He knew very well, if he were so inclined, he would be able to obtain a medical certificate of ill-health, or almost anything else, so long as he had money or inclination to procure them.

At one moment he thought perhaps something had happened, and some discovery concerning Godfrey had been made, which made it dangerous to him to be present in court.

As this hope flashed across his mind, he felt a momentary gleam of joy; but it was but momentary, for he was convinced it could only happen by some ineffectual attempt on the part of Marian to soften the obdurate heart of Godfrey; but do what she would, he felt convinced that it would be ineffectual, and that, in fact, it would be labour lost, for he was just the man to accept the reward of his villany, and then refuse to perform the stipulated functions to save him.

This was a bitter reflection to Charles Ormond, who felt that his doom was, indeed, sealed.

A bustle was now observable in the court, and this indicated the return of the judge, who took his seat on the bench, and then, after a pause of some minutes, he said,—

"Upon consideration, and after a consultation with my brother judge upon the subject, I am of opinion that the case ought to be adjourned until to-morrow, and then proceeded with."

This was, for the present, a termination of the affair. The jury were discharged from their attendance on that day, with the usual caution, and glad enough were they to escape for the time being from the task of finding a fellow-creature guilty of a crime for which they would take his life.

Charles Ormond was removed in the custody of the gaoler.

CHAPTER XXIX.

MARIAN'S APPEAL TO HER MOTHER.—GODFREY'S PROMISE.—THE SIGNING OF
THE DEED.

WE must now return to the other parties in our narrative, and account for the absence of Godfrey at a moment when it was so entirely unexpected by those in court, and by every one connected with the case.

Marian Whitehead, as the day approached for the trial of Charles Ormond, became more and more distressed in mind, and unable to form any resolution as to what course she should pursue. All was a chaos in her mind, and she could think only of her lover's danger, which was so imminent.

On that dreadful morning on which the trial took place, she went early to Godfrey, and had another interview. It was with the same object that had attracted her there before—the life of Charles Ormond, which she deemed to be in his hands.

Again she reiterated all her prayers, but to no purpose.

"If," said he, "you can procure your mother's signature to the deed, I will take care to give my evidence so hesitatingly that you shall see your friend leave the court a free man."

"Will you do this?"

"I will."

"But how can it be done?" inquired Marian.

"That will be for me to find out. I will agree to do it, and I will do it. I can find the means if I have the motive for so doing, and I'll do that and more."

"I must gain my mother's consent first," said Marian.

"And that had better be done very quickly. The trial will commence about nine, but I will remain here till the last moment; and, if I find you are not here, I must go to the Old Bailey, as my evidence will be wanted."

"Stay to the last moment," said Marian. "I will lose no time;" and, as she spoke, she arose, and, without even casting a second look upon the man who had so much injured them all, she quitted the office, and proceeded with all haste home.

Her mother was seated before the fire, engaged in some trifling task, to amuse her leisure moments.

Marian threw her bonnet on the table, and her shawl. She then, while tears were streaming down her face, gazed wistfully in her mother's countenance.

Mrs. Whitehead was attracted by the deep sobs that her daughter made, and, looking up, saw her grief.

"Marian, my dear," she said, "you really ought not to grieve, and go on in this way; it is quite dreadful to hear it. I grieve and sorrow, too; but it is wicked to do so to excess."

"Mother!" said Marian, throwing herself upon her knees before her mother.

"Well, Marian?"

"Have I ever disobeyed you, or given you a cause for an hour's unhappiness?"

"You have not."

"Would I not sacrifice every hope, every prospect, every wish, if I thought that, by so doing, I could render you happy?"

"Yes, Marian, you would, I believe; but what does all this mean? Why do you ask?"

"You shall see."

"Well, but ——"

"Nay, listen, mother. Would you not do something for my happiness? Would you not sacrifice much for the life of one who must be dear to us both, and who has incurred disgrace and danger to serve us?"

"Oh, I see you are speaking of Charles Ormond, poor fellow; that Godfrey deserves to be placed in his position."

"Yes, mother; but this Godfrey has the means of saving Charles, if you will furnish him with a motive—if, indeed, you will purchase his freedom."

"I, Marian?"

"Yes, you, mother."

"What can I do, child? You know very well how glad I shall be to see poor Charles free from his prison once more; he never ought to have been there."

"No, mother, he ought not; time flies, however."

"Yes, yes, very ——"

"Mother, will you give up this Indian property?"

"What, Marian?"

"Give up the hopes of this Indian property; make an assignment over to Godfrey."

"What, such as he wanted me to sign before, which Charles Ormond himself

"Marian, I fear you are not well; take some rest, my child; tranquillize your mind."

"I will, mother; I feel I require it; I must now exert my strength to wait patiently until the time arrives for his acquittal; then a new but a happier trial awaits me."

"What do you mean, my child?"

"That the transition from such grief as mine to the joy I must and shall feel, will be very great indeed."

"Lie down on the couch, Marian, by the fire; quietness and repose will do much for you. Let me prevail upon you for once; take a glass of wine, it will compose your spirits and quiet your agitation—be persuaded."

"I will," said Marian, and she sank upon the couch wholly exhausted by the exertion she had made, which was wholly beyond her strength.

"What said Godfrey?" inquired Mrs. Whitehead, as she threw a large shawl over the reclining form of Marian.

"He would stop the trial to-day—have it put off until to-morrow, when he would take care that Charles Ormond was a free man again."

"And the deeds?"

"Must be signed to-night."

"I do not like giving Godfrey the deeds without having some security for the performance of his promise," said Mrs. Whitehead, thoughtfully. "It seems to me we are as much at his mercy as ever."

"We are, and yet it is the only chance, and, as the only one, what else can be done?"

"Nothing, my child."

There was a long pause; Mrs. Whitehead not wishing to prevent the sleeping of her daughter, if she would do so; and Marian, on her part, was buried in a thousand different reflections and thoughts upon the probabilities of the morrow.

Tired and exhausted by excitement and exertion, she fell into a deep sleep, from which she awoke only when the darkness of night had set in.

"Mother," she exclaimed, "what is the time?"

"It is past seven, Marian."

"Has Godfrey been?"

"No, Marian; but there is time enough."

Marian did not speak; she arose, and for the first time that day attempted to take some food. A little tea was all she could swallow, and that refreshed her.

It was after ten o'clock, and now they had both began to despair of Godfrey's coming to them that night.

"If not here to-night," observed Mrs. Whitehead, seeing her daughter's anguish of mind, "it is more than likely he will be here early to-morrow morning."

"Why not to-night?"

"I really don't know, my dear, though to-morrow morning will not be too late. Indeed, he may not have the deeds ready this evening, and, only getting them too late, he will not come till early next morning before the court opens."

"It may be so," sighed Marian.

At that moment there came a rap at the street-door, at which they both started, and seemed to have a chill run through them, and yet they could not tell the reason.

"That must be Godfrey," remarked Marian. "I never felt so chilly and sad before. It is surely he!"

In a minute afterwards the servant entered the room, saying, at the same time,—

"Some one of the name of Godfrey wishes to speak to you, ma'am."

"Show him up," said Mrs. Whitehead.

Immediately afterwards the footsteps of Godfrey were heard upon the stairs, and then he entered the room in which they were seated; neither of them rose to greet him, but Godfrey thought nothing of that, he did not expect it, and he was by no means abashed at this circumstance, but coolly shut the door, and carrying a chair to the table, sat down, and placed his hat with his gloves in, on one side of the table, and a bundle of papers on the other.

"Good evening, Mrs. Whitehead; my visit was expected, I believe—I do not come unawares?"

"No—I expected you."

"Then I needn't make an apology for coming."

See page 170.

"I would be needless."

"Very good. I should, however, not have been here so late, but I couldn't get the deeds done before."

"The trial," said Marian, hastily; "what has been done with regard to that?"

"It has been adjourned till to-morrow."

"Indeed! and why?"

"Because I would not go up."

" And will you go?"

" I must, else he'll never get out. I must make some mistake in my evidence, that will vitiate the whole affair, and render the prosecution useless."

" Well, about these deeds?" said Mrs. Whitehead.

" They are ready for your signature. That done, and all is ready. You will see Mr. Ormond here by to-morrow afternoon, Miss Whitehead."

Marian took no notice of this insinuatory speech, but allowed her mother to go on.

" What is the purport of these deeds that I have to sign?" inquired Mrs. White-head, of Godfrey.

" They assign over to me the whole of the Indian property," said Godfrey, coolly.

" The whole?"

" Yes ; no more," said Godfrey, rather jocosely.

" And what am I to have in return?" inquired Mrs. Whitehead, carefully, so much so, that Godfrey almost supposed she was inclined to be ironical.

" You will have," he said, " an annuity of twice the amount you have had of me before, which I propose shall be the final settlement of the question."

" And Charles Ormond?" said Marian.

" He is not mentioned in the deed," said Godfrey, " because it would have vitiated it ; but that I look upon it as the main thing that you sign this deed for."

" Yes, yes, it is," said Mrs. Whitehead.

" Will you sign your name to this, and Miss Whitehead can be a witness?"

Mrs. Whitehead signed her name on the required spot, and then declared the act and deed hers.

" Now, Miss Marian, if you please, sign your name here, just after the word witness."

Marian did as she was desired, and signed her name, and Godfrey, after having carefully examined the signatures, blotted them, and as he folded them up, a smile of malignancy and triumph played across his features, and he said, putting the deed in his pocket,—

" This, then, is at last done."

" Yes, it is, and I trust you are satisfied?" said Marian.

" Pretty well, for this time."

" And to-morrow you will free Charles Ormond?"

" Why," said Godfrey, sneeringly, " you have left it till the eleventh hour is nearly past—too far to do much good for him now ; but I'll be at the Old Bailey to-morrow, depend upon it."

So saying, he opened the door, and walked out, and they could hear him chuckling as he went down, and then he shut the door behind him.

A melancholy consciousness came across the mind of Marian, and her mother, too, that the sacrifice was too late. They had given Godfrey the advantage, and the villain had coolly taken it, and never intended to perform his part of the conditions for which the deed was given.

CHAPTER XXX.

THE RENEWAL OF CHARLES ORMOND'S TRIAL.—THE VERDICT.—THE SCENE IN COURT.

THE morrow was an eventful day, and Charles Ormond, when he was carried back to his cell in Newgate, to await the issue of the adjournment, felt an unwelcome respite from the fate, or rather the knowledge of that fate, for he felt assured that it was but a delay, and that a very temporary one, too, and that there was not the slightest hope.

" They may have been tampering with Godfrey," he thought, " but, alas, they neither know the man they have to deal with, if they imagine he will keep any bargain that may be struck with regard to terms, nor do they understand his position. He has but to swear that signature is not his, because he must know it at once, and hesitation on his part, after the direct manner in which he gave his evidence at the police-office, would only draw down severe censure upon his head, and not benefit me."

He was conducted back to the same cell, and when the turnkey saw him return, he said,—

"I'm sorry to see you come back again."

"My fate is not settled yet," said Ormond. "I am to have another day yet, before they decide."

"That is very unusual.'

"It is very unsatisfactory," said Ormond.

"Could they not agree in their verdict?" inquired the turnkey.

"It hasn't yet come to the jury."

"It is very early to return."

"The absence of the principal witness against me is the cause of this delay," said Charles, "but he must be found to-morrow, and then my fate is certain."

"And yet you have pleaded not guilty."

"I pleaded what I knew to be the truth," returned Charles, "though you may not believe it; but I expect to be convicted, nevertheless, for I know too well the villany of the man, and his hatred towards myself, to doubt for one moment the success of the scheme that has been practised against me."

"We all have our troubles," said the turnkey; "there's none who are entirely exempt, and I know an innocent man has but little chance against a clever rogue, though when it comes to a life affair, there are many things that will turn up in the chapter of accidents, and overturn the best planned schemes that were ever devised; but you know your own case better than any one else."

"Yes, yes. I am well aware of that," said Charles, and he entered the iron gate the turnkey had opened for him.

"Well," said the turnkey, to the one who had brought him, "I am very sorry for the young fellow."

"And so am I," said the other, with a shake of the head, which seemed to mean much.

"How did it go with him in court, to-day?"

"All against him."

"Ay, ay."

"Yes, he'll be turned off as sure as fate. There wasn't one point in his favour."

"Poor fellow; and how came it that the trial did not finish to-day?" inquired the other.

"Because, as he told you, the principal witness was not there, and couldn't give his evidence."

"Why?"

"Oh! ay, I had forgotten, he was too ill—medical certificate, and trial adjourned."

"I see—perhaps all sham."

"Don't know; he seems to think he will be there to-morrow, and therefore there can't be much in it; but if this witness comes forward, and swears as he did before, there can be no doubt as to the result."

"Ah! it will be a black-cap business."

"Yes, safe as the bank."

The two turnkeys parted, and Charles Ormond retired that night as early as the prison regulations would allow, and there, bound in profound reflections, he appeared to sleep to his companions, who knowing what he had to meet, and how ill he appeared calculated to meet the fate that many of them who were hardened in crime would have shrunk from the encountering of, did not attempt to disturb him.

Charles pondered over the events of the day, and endeavoured to extract some food for hope, but in the temporary absence of Godfrey, he saw none. Mr. Blake and his counsel would give him no hope, though each endeavoured to cheer him up, and tell him not to allow his spirits to flag, as they would leave no opportunity untried that would tend to serve him.

To that Charles merely shook his head despondingly, but he said a moment after,—

"I thank you heartily for your kindness that you show me, in my distress and need, but I am too well acquainted with the man I have to deal with, from whom I can expect nothing but the most unrelenting hostility."

"Well, well, we shall see. Perhaps some of your friends have been to intercede with Godfrey."

"Not to my knowledge."

"Because, should they fail, it will have a prejudicial effect upon both judge and jury."

"I am not aware of anything of the kind being done, nor have I wished that it should, because I am convinced of the utter inutility of the attempt."

*   *   *   *   *

The morning came, and Charles Ormond was taken from his cell at an early hour, and his legal adviser saw him, and held a conference with him respecting the line of defence he should adopt.

Charles had no hesitation in entering into the details of the whole case, and how he came possessed of the check which had proved fraught with such fatal circumstances to him.

The barrister informed him he had seen Miss Whitehead, and had heard from her a similar account, and that she would be in court, and give her testimony in case Godfrey came.

It was with a pang, and yet a hope, that he heard this, for he knew not the whole of the transaction that had taken place ; indeed, it was not deemed necessary to let him know all, lest he should build too strong hopes upon it.

"I cannot tell you that you are safe," said the barrister, "but there may be a chance, and that is all."

"And that is more than I have any reason to expect," said Charles Ormond, "but I cannot but feel grateful for your care and solicitude."

*   *   *   *   *   *

The adjournment of the trial had created much sensation among those who had been in court during the proceedings on the preceding day, and it was crowded to excess.

The counsel, too, seemed to consider it rather an interesting affair, for they were more numerous than usual, and at an early hour the whole appeared an animated scene.

But before proceeding with the trial, we will just turn our attention once more to Marian and her mother, for they will be brought forward prominently enough on the trial.

After the departure of Godfrey, Marian and her mother sat many minutes gazing earnestly at each other, with an expression on their countenances not easily to be described.

The feelings of Marian were intense ; she thought she could see the treachery of the man as palpably before her as she had seen him personally but a few moments since. Surprise, agony, and despair, each found an expression upon her beautiful but mournful features.

She could not doubt, and she could not hope. She gazed vacantly into the face of her mother, who was no less painfully surprised and terrified than her daughter.

Mrs. Whitehead was the first to speak.

"Marian," she said, "I fear we have done wrong—very wrong, indeed, in trusting this man."

"It was a chance," murmured Marian ; "it was a chance."

"And that has gone."

"I fear entirely ;" and as she spoke, she heaved so deep a sigh that it seemed as though she had not breathed for some time ; it was something more than a sigh or a sob.

Mrs. Whitehead was terrified.

" For Heaven's sake," she said, " do not give way, Marian ; we know not what may yet happen."

" Yes, yes—I do."

" You do ?"

" Yes ; but I will let the whole world judge of that man's iniquity ; for I myself will proclaim the bartering of his evidence."

" You alarm me, Marian. We have done wrong, I say, in trusting to this man at all, because he is capable of no good deed."

" He is not."

" To give him an opportunity of playing the traitor was to court such treatment."

" It was."

" And Charles Ormond is no way benefitted by it, for he cannot enforce the condition upon which I have signed the deed. Now all is lost—irretrievably so."

" Yes, yes—all is lost !" said Marian, emphatically.

" But," added Mrs. Whitehead, " all would not have been lost had I had my own way. Godfrey, at least, should have been none the better for your father's money ; he should not have succeeded in robbing me or you, and in destroying Charles Ormond, too ; if he succeeded in one thing, he should not in another."

" But, then, mother, who could have foreseen this last, basest act of all ?" said Marian.

" Who !"

" Yes ; who, mother ?"

" We, Marian, ought to have known it better than any other persons whatever. We knew his nature, and we know it now. We knew he was base, villanous, and crafty. Was not the way in which he endeavoured to defraud us in the first instance an example ? Was not his accusation and trap to ruin Charles Ormond another ? What more could we have by way of proof ? What other experience could we have of this man's perfidy ?"

" None were wanting, mother," said Marian, slowly. " None, save this last, basest act of all."

" No, that were not wanting, Marian," said Mrs. Whitehead, " for that ought to have been predicated from his former conduct, as surely as light follows the rising of the sun, and darkness its absence from the earth."

" And yet, mother, should we not have tried the last and only chance that seemed to present any hope ?"

" It gave none to me."

" And yet you did it, mother."

" I did, to save you from distraction, my child."

" And in that, I fear, you will have no prospect of success. I should have known no rest, had it been that, while there was a chance of life for him, we had not made every effort. Success has not crowned our endeavours—that is a misfortune, a heavy misfortune, but not a fault ; if it be, it is one I would with my own free will commit again. But, oh ! mother, do not regret a sacrifice made for his sake— to save his life."

" My dear, he did not intend, or think he was about doing anything of the kind."

" Oh ! mother, mother, you are not naturally unfeeling—do not talk thus. You will have enough, by the terms of this very deed, to keep you ; for more I will work my hands off, while I have health and reason to enable me to do so, to procure you luxuries ; but never regret the sacrifice made to save such a one as Charles."

" I do not, Marian," said Mrs. Whitehead, who seldom could manage to understand more than one idea at one time. " I do not regret it, but it is wretchedly vexing to know that a man like Godfrey has been successful in tricking us, in robbing us, and adding to his own stores, by taking from us."

" But, mother, to return to this subject. You think that this Godfrey will still play the traitor, and give his evidence against Charles Ormond ?"

" I do."

"God help him, then! God help him! but I will be in court, too, and I will relate all that has occurred—all that has taken place this day."

"Marian."

"Ay, mother, I will; and you must come with me, too. I will avow all—everything, however hidden I would wish it to be, shall be made plain to the eye of day—all, all, for Charles—yes, yes— all, all, for Charles!"

These words were uttered with a wild abandonment of manner, that Mrs. Whitehead had never seen the like before; and she was not only surprised, but alarmed, at the excited manner she betrayed, and she feared much for her health, both of body and mind.

"Marian, you must not give way to these wild bursts of passionate grief. You will go distracted, child, and then you will not know what happens."

"I would to Heaven I could not, it would be a favour; but, mother, you will—you must go with me to-morrow."

"Where, child?"

"To the Old Bailey.—to this trial. I will go to Mr. Blake, and we will relate all that has happened before the whole court. Surely this must have some effect."

Mrs. Whitehead shook her head. She was slow to be moved in a belief in almost anything sometimes, and since she had been so palpably deceived by Godfrey, she could not readily give credence to anything.

"I fear, Marian, that there will be but little or no probability of doing Charles any good."

"We must try."

"You see, Godfrey would never have acted so boldly as he has done, had there been any chance left for poor Charles. You may depend upon it, he has left no hole by which he can escape. He has made all so clear against him, that all shall not be able to effect any good in his favour."

"But we must try, mother. Think, dear mother, think what you would have done, had my father's life been in danger. Would you not have tried every means in your power, however poor they might be? Would you have allowed a chance of benefitting him to escape you, merely because you could not calculate with certainty upon its success? Would you not rather have tried to do him service by every little circumstance in your power? Oh! I know you would—you could not have done otherwise. I am sure of it—quite sure of it. You would think as I do, that where no one circumstance can be relied on, at least something may be gathered from a number; besides, you increase the chances. I say, dear mother, you would have thought of all this, and more—you would have acted upon such thoughts."

Mrs. Whitehead was overwhelmed by her daughter's rapid utterance and impressive earnestness, and, while she spoke, the tears flowed fast from her eyes—she was more than moved. Early impressions had been recalled, and Mrs. Whitehead mingled her tears with her daughter's, and they sat some time in mutual silence.

"Mother."

"Marian."

"You will do what I ask of you?"

"Yes, my child, I meant not to do otherwise. If I can do any good, and if you think so, I will go with you to Charles's trial to-morrow."

"I am certain we ought to try, mother, and I feel convinced that we shall not be wholly useless. We shall, at least, have done our duty, and in doing that, we shall derive a holy consolation if what I most fear should happen."

"Be it so, my dear Marian. I have promised you, but be persuaded by me to retire to rest, else you will be far too ill to attend to what you so much desire to-morrow morning at the Old Bailey."

"I will do so, mother, and that, too, now. Good night, may God protect you."

Marian arose, and, throwing herself into her mother's arms, nearly fainted away; but after a time she staggered, rather than walked, from the room to her own apartment.

So agitating a scene as that which had taken place between the mother and daughter, had a serious effect upon the system of Marian. She threw herself upon the bed, and lay for some time in a state almost bordering on a stupor; but a reaction took place, and she became fully conscious of all that had taken place, and all that she most feared should take place.

After a while she fell into a deep sleep, and awoke not until the morning.

Mrs. Whitehead and Marian breakfasted early that morning, or rather they went through the ceremony at an early hour, for scarce any food could they swallow; and then, before eight o'clock, Marian was ready to go out.

"Mother," she said, "are you ready?"

"I will be, Marian; but I didn't expect you would be so early; it's quite an unseasonable hour."

"But not too early, mother. At nine Charles Ormond's trial will be called on again, and he may be sacrificed. We must not let a few short hours or minutes destroy our usefulness."

"Certainly not; I will be with you in one moment, Marian; you should have told me the hour."

Mrs. Whitehead had forgotten the hour; but it mattered not, five minutes more sufficed to attire her for walking; then mother and daughter quitted the house for the offices of Mr. Blake.

Half an hour had barely elapsed before they reached Mr. Blake's office, which was in Furnival's Inn, and fortunately for them he was at home.

Much surprised at the visit he received, he immediately guessed the nature of the affair they came about, and at once opened the business by saying,—

"You are anxious about Mr. Ormond's trial?"

"Most anxious."

"Yes," said Mrs. Whitehead. "What do you think, Mr. Blake, of the whole affair? I am convinced he is innocent, and my daughter knows he is, because she was present when the note containing the check was given to him."

"Her evidence will be most useful and important," said Mr. Blake; "though the amount of benefit it may do him is doubtful, since it goes in direct contradiction of a fact sworn to by several persons who have no interest in the affair."

"Then Godfrey came to us last night."

"Indeed!"

"Yes, for a certain object."

"No doubt."

Mrs. Whitehead then related the manner in which he had acted; the signing of the deed, its object, and his departure with it in his pocket.

"It is a bad affair," said Mr. Blake.

"Do you think there is any possibility of the chance of his coming forward in such a manner as would give Charles any chance of his life?"

"I believe not."

"Good heavens! what can be done?" exclaimed Marian. "I hope such a monstrous iniquity will never be permitted to be perpetrated with impunity."

"As for that," replied Mr. Blake, "you must not be surprised; certain circumstances, you know, follow in the train of others, and we see their consequences, and there is no avoiding them. All I can do is to recommend you to come to the court, and there wait until you are called; it may so happen that there may be occasion to call you up as witnesses, and your testimony may be beneficial; indeed, it must, if it have any effect at all."

"It must, surely it must."

"That remains to be seen," said Blake.

"What time will the trial begin?"

"I dare say in another quarter of an hour; if you please, we will all ride together."

"As you please."

"You did very wrong in allowing Godfrey to persuade you to sign that deed, Mrs. Whitehead."

"Indeed I know it, Mr. Blake," she replied; "but it was done under the express understanding that he, Godfrey, should be instrumental in obtaining the release of Charles."

"It was not in his power to effect it; even if he had the will, he had not the power; his words were taken down, and he has signed the declaration at the Mansion-house, and it would have brought down severe reflections upon him had it happened otherwise, and very possibly punishment also."

"And yet he had led us to believe he could perform such a promise as that we have named."

"It may be so, but he could not; all he desired to know was, whether you would sign over everything to him upon the chance of Charles Ormond's acquittal, and when he found you would, he at once agreed to all kinds of impossible things."

"But we can state this incident."

"Yes, you can; but it being an illegal affair altogether, I know not exactly how far it may benefit you; but still everything must be tried, without reference to improbabilities; at such a time it will not do to calculate to niceties."

"Certainly not."

"And here we are. Now I will place you where you can be within call."

"Will you place us in court?"

"You ought not to go into the court being witnesses in the case, and, if you will take my advice, you will not do so; it may cause some confusion."

"Will you see the counsel?"

"I will, and relate all to him that you have told me, and I will have some consultation as to what is best to be done under the circumstances."

"Do so, and you will place us under the greatest obligations," said Marian.

At this moment the coach pulled up; they got out, and Mr. Blake conducted them to a low-looking room, where there were some seats, and said,—

"Here you will wait until I send for you, when you will be sworn as witnesses."

After this he hurried away, and went in search of the barrister who was engaged, and then the two had an interview with Charles Ormond, which we have before related.

This was scarcely ended when the bustle in the court announced the fact that his lordship was seated on the bench, and Charles was once more placed in the felon's dock.

He was somewhat paler than he was even on the previous day, but that might be accounted for from the fact of the harassing nature of the previous day's proceedings, which gave him no idea as to what might be the probable termination of the struggle.

The names of the jurors were called over, and the proceedings re-stated, when the counsel for the prosecution rose, and said,—

"My lord, and gentlemen of the jury, our proceedings yesterday were brought to a close by the sudden and alarming illness of Mr. Godfrey, the principal witness in this case. A medical certificate was put in of the state of his health. I am happy to say that he is so far recovered from the attack as to be able to attend before your lordship to-day."

"Call Godfrey."

Godfrey was called, and stepped into the witness-box with a staid and steady air.

"Now, Mr. Godfrey," said the counsel, "pray do you know the prisoner at the bar?"

"I do; he was once my clerk."

"And was discharged?"

"Yes."

"Had he access to your check-book?"

"He had."

"Did you ever authorize him to fill up, or sign any check for you?"

"Never. I never authorize any one to do that for me; I invariably do it myself."

"Upon all occasions?"

"Yes, upon all."

"Did you ever give him a check for fifty pounds?"

"Never."

"Look at that, and tell his lordship and the jury if that be your signature or not."

The check was handed to him, and Godfrey put on his spectacles very leisurely, and then took the check in his hands, which he examined carefully, and, folding up his spectacles, he said,—

"No, it is not my hand-writing.'

"You can swear to it?"

"I can swear it is not."

"Have you missed any blank check from your book of late?" inquired the counsel.

"Yes; since this affair I have examined my check-book, and find that some way on a couple of check blanks, were torn out with a view to use them, I suppose. There is my check-book, you can compare them."

Godfrey produced his check-book, which his lordship took up, and after examining the leaves and the check found, they corresponded exactly, the torn edges fitting together.

The book was handed to the jury and the counsel, who naturally returned it to Godfrey.

"There can be no doubt," said the counsel for the defence, "that the check has been torn from the book; but here is neither miracle nor proof that it was done by the prisoner. I protest against this proceeding as very irregular."

The object being gained, the counsel for the prosecution made no reply to this.

"Have you any question to ask the witness?"

"Yes, my lord, I have," said the counsel for the defence. "Now, Mr. Godfrey, I wish to ask you a question or two, and I shall be obliged to you to be as candid as you can."

"Certainly."

"You were ill yesterday—were you not?"

"I was."

"And what might be the nature of the disorder under which you suffered?" inquired the counsel.

"It was a fit ——"

"A fit."

"Yes, a fit, sir."

"Well, it must have been an extraordinary fit, that could have left no trace behind it."

"I have had them before; and they usually lay me up from thirteen to twenty-four hours."

"You will swear you were not engaged in preparing a deed of settlement?"

"I will."

"You had no deed of settlement, then, about the success of which you were more anxious than you were about the proceedings that were occurring?"

"A deed of settlement might have been prepared during the time I was ill—it is very likely—my business don't stand still if I am afflicted with a temporary illness."

"Was not this deed one of consequence to some of the parties connected with these proceedings indirectly?"

"I submit, my lord, that this is extremely irregular."

"My lord, I have evidence to rebut the denials of this witness. I must submit that I am justified in doing as I am."

Some cavilling ensued, and the counsel proceeded,—

"Have you never heard of such a thing as settling your evidence upon this matter?"

"What do you mean?"

"You have not said to any one that you would abstain from giving evidence if a certain deed were signed?"

"No, certainly not."

"Was a deed executed by you and some other parties, last evening, at a late hour?"

"Yes."

"And certain property conveyed over to you?"

"Yes, for a consideration."

"And what was that consideration?"

"An annuity, to be paid by me to them."

"And you had no conversation about the prisoner at the bar, that you remember, sir?"

"I can't remember what never occurred."

"Did not the prisoner, when he left, disoblige you?"

"Yes, he divulged my confidence; and he, therefore, did disoblige me," said Godfrey, who was determined to understand everything his own way, or not at all.

"You are very stolid for a merchant. Pray, sir, did you, or did you not, agree that if that deed were signed, you would be the means of the acquittal of the prisoner?"

"No."

The counsel paused; he saw well that nothing could be made of Godfrey, who was armed at all points, and met him by the most obstinate indifference, sometimes meeting his questions by a total and wilful misconception; but, at the same time, he gave answers that served his own cause.

"You were not well enough to be here yesterday?"

"I was not."

"And yet you could be about at a late hour?"

"I was about in the latter part of the afternoon," said Godfrey, thoughtfully. "I was taken ill about eight in the morning, and at five I was able to walk about—very weak, but no absolute inability. I would not have gone out on any trifling matter."

"This was no trifling matter; it was greatly to your advantage, Mr. Godfrey."

"It may turn out so; but I have no certainty. I have given, I believe, a fair consideration, and would not have given so much, only it was a long, and, perhaps, unsatisfactory partnership series of accounts, which would be very difficult to investigate."

"I have done with the witness, my lord," said the counsel; "but I may want him again, by-and-bye."

"You may go down, Mr. Godfrey."

Mr. Godfrey bowed, and left the witness-box; but never once did he look at the dock, save when he was asked if he knew Charles Ormond, and then he cast an angry look at him; but there was concealed beneath it a look of malicious triumph.

"This, my lord," said the counsel for the prosecution, "is my case, to which I shall add nothing, merely observing, that this deed, to which reference has been made, is merely a composition deed with the widow of his late partner, and has for its object, the adjustment of certain affairs that could not be otherwise settled without possibly years of ruinous litigation, and has no connexion with the present case."

So far the case of Charles Ormond assumed a yet more unhappy phase; and the spectators, in themselves, saw nothing but his condemnation, unless he could bring strong evidence to rebut all that had been said, and no one could think that likely.

After a lapse of about five minutes, the counsel for the defence arose, and commenced his address,—

"My lord and gentlemen of the jury, I rise, fully impressed with the various difficulties which beset a case such as that now brought before you; difficulties of no ordinary character, for they are so numerous and distinct from each other, that, to get over one, is scarcely any aid to the overcoming of another.

"The prisoner, who is now placed on his trial before you, gentlemen, stands charged with a crime that affects his life—a crime, too, so easy of commission, that it behoves every one to stop, for the sake of the community, such acts that might lead to the ruin of many; but while it is easy of commission, it is difficult to successfully execute. But it is yet far easier to place a young man in the precise situation of a guilty person, to raise around him all the little appearances of guilt—nothing in themselves—but when added to one great fact, they bear an alarming evidence against him. Such, gentlemen, is the case of the prisoner, and, to elucidate the truth of what I have stated, I now beg your most serious attention.

"To understand thoroughly his position, you must be made acquainted with a few facts preceding the alleged commission of this crime of forgery.

"Mr. Godfrey, the individual who was last examined, was the partner of a Mr. Whitehead; both had certain sums in the concern, and the withdrawal of this sum by either was considered an act of dissolution of partnership.

"Well, gentlemen, the late Mr. Whitehead engaged in certain speculations in

India, and they were presumed to have failed, and would have involved the firm in a loss, when Mr. Godfrey says,—

"' You have committed an act of dissolution of partnership. You have withdrawn your money from the firm. In consequence you have nothing more to do with it."

"Things were thus, when Mr. Whitehead died, some say, of a broken heart; and Mr. Godfrey allowed the widow a small annuity not to have the books made up, and a balance struck, which must have been inconvenient, and might have been unproductive of anything but expense.

"By-and-bye, news comes over, that the speculations in India, instead of a failure, have proved a ———"

"I cannot see," said the counsel for the prosecution, rising, "what all this has to do with the defence of an act of forgery, by one who has no connexion with Mr. Godfrey, or the partnership."

"I confess I cannot," said the judge.

"I entreat your lordship's patience. It does bear on the case; there is a feeling of revenge against this young man, and because he interferes in the affairs to prevent fraud, he has been accused of forgery; he is, in fact, the victim of a vile conspiracy, which has been got up against him.

"I was about to say, the speculation, instead of a failure, proved very extensively prosperous. This news came to the man Godfrey—he saw the advantage of this, immediately got up a deed, by which he bound himself to give the widow a double annuity, if she would assign to him all the expectancies in the partnership, which, he said, would greatly save trouble, and release him from difficulties, and enable him to enter free into other matters.

"This, my lord, and gentlemen of the jury, happened while the prisoner was in his employment, and the prisoner was the means of foiling the attempt at fraud, by putting Mrs. Whitehead on her guard, and informed her of the true state of her affairs, and she refused to sign the deed.

"That is the breach of confidence for which he was discharged; this, without the accompanying circumstances, sounds as if the person had been discharged for some dereliction of duty; no so, however; he acted nobly and disinterestedly. He was discharged immediately, and upon the spot, without payment of his arrears of salary, and without hearing.

"Now, gentlemen, the prisoner had the sum of fifty pounds, the amount of this check, due to him; and for some time he heard nothing of Godfrey, until one day he received a check for fifty pounds, and, in the presence of another person, he opened it; this person is Miss Marian Whitehead, whom I shall call.

"With this check was a blank one, as if the two had been stuck together, and been so torn out. It was presented, and the check declared to be a forgery.

"You know all the subsequent stages.

"Since the prisoner's incarceration, since this very trial has begun, attempts have been made, without the knowledge of his legal advisers, and I firmly believe without his own knowledge, to buy the evidence of the witness Godfrey off.

"This was not only foolish and injurious to him, but it was altogether injustifiable and improper; it did not succeed: but, gentlemen of the jury, this man Godfrey was not ill yesterday; he was not otherwise engaged than in answering the prisoner's friends, by getting the deed signed, and putting the trial off for a day, promising the release of the prisoner, receiving the bribe, and then defrauding them out of these conditions.

"These, gentlemen, are the simple facts of the case. I well know the value of evidence that goes to prove a case, and, when well got up, it is a most difficult thing to disprove direct evidence; but consider, gentlemen, only assuming my statement true, and I am prepared to prove, I hope, to your satisfaction, that it is true,—I say, only assuming it to be true, what a position is the prisoner placed in !

"Every circumstance is against him, because his real prosecutor only comes forward as a witness. The bank is his prosecutor; a disinterested party so far as this under-current of circumstances is considered.

"I say, gentlemen, the prisoner is placed in a position of considerable peril. The onus of proof is laid upon all save the man Godfrey, and his questionable testimony is, however important it may appear, only subservient to that of others. All that he says has first been said by persons who are entirely guiltless of any unworthy motive, and who speak only of what they saw or know, and they are made to bear false testimony unknowingly, or they are compelled to bear good and true testimony of a thing which, of itself is true, but not true when predicated of the prisoner at the bar.

"Gentlemen, I beseech you to look narrowly into the probability of this case, and see where the motives lay the heaviest. Was it at all likely the prisoner would, when discharged, have forged a cheque, and yet never have been guilty of a dishonourable act in his whole lifetime? Was it likely, above all, he would forge a cheque for a sum that was due and owing to him, and which might have been recovered by ordinary means?

"The tale is too improbable, gentlemen; much too improbable; but, gentlemen, consider this, how easy it was to have a name forged and send it by post, with the accompanying blank cheque, and the unsuspecting nature of an honourable mind, who would have hesitated a moment in securing that sum which was their own, by presenting the check?

"Imagine the catastrophe!"

The council paused, he saw that he had made a considerable sensation, and he saw, also, that he was listened to with great attention.

"My lord and gentlemen, I will not occupy your attention much longer. I have stated to you the simple truth, and this I shall in part be able to prove to your satisfaction. I shall be able to prove to you the receipt of the letter by post, but not the posting of it; because, when deeds of this kind are done, there are generally no witnesses. All that is capable of proof, I am fully prepared to prove.

"And now, gentlemen, let me turn your attention to the nature of the crime and its punishment. The penalty is life! the policy of such severity of punishment may be questionable, but we have to take the case as it stands. If you feel, gentlemen, conscientiously compelled to pronounce my unfortunate client guilty—the penalty is death. It therefore behoves you to receive the testimony and the probabilities on both sides with attention and care, and if you have any doubt upon your minds, it is to the side of mercy you should incline—that divine attribute of Heaven!

"I say, gentlemen, if you have the least doubt on your minds, give it to the prisoner, and do not be responsible for the blood of one who, if innocent, and convicted by you, will cry aloud to Heaven upon all who have had a hand in the commission of, perhaps, the most cruel crime that was ever inflicted by man on man —a judicial murder! because it is unaccompanied by sorrow and remorse; the individuals believing they have done their duty. Once more I appeal to you for that favourable consideration for this case which, as men who have a trying duty to perform, I am sure you will accord to it, and remember, save this one alleged act, no dishonourable thought is even imputed to the prisoner,—he is even unsuspected."

The counsel sat down; there was an impression upon all present that he had done his utmost to place his client in a favourable position, and had enlisted the impression of the jurymen in his favour.

The first witness that was called was Mrs. Whitehead.

Charles Ormond looked around to see the mother of Marian approach. He had scarcely taken his eyes off the council who had been speaking for him, and once or twice a ray of hope had sprung up in his mind.

He did not even know that so strong a case had been got up in his favour; but Charles could not be blind to the fact that the evidence was as yet against him; that was the main point; but the council had done all he could do, and that was to gain a favourable impression, and upon this he proceeded to examine his witnesses.

Mrs. Whitehead ascended the witness-box and was sworn.

" You are the widow of the late Mr. Whitehead ?"

" I am."

" And you know Mr. Godfrey?"

" I do."

" Your husband and Godfrey were in partnership as merchants, I believe?" continued the council.

" Yes, they were ; some years."

" And subsequently dissolved ?"

" Yes, they did."

" Just be good enough to state to the court under what circumstances this took place."

" I appeal to your lordship," said the council for the prosecution, " that this is irrelevant."

" No, my lord, I submit that it is not irrelevant ; it goes to prove the nature of the connection with these parties, of the strong presumption that the principal is, what I may term the grand conspirator of the whole affair, the concocter of the whole plot ; my learned brother would turn round and say to the jury, ' what motive has this man for doing all this ?' I am, my lord, about to prove the motive does exist, and that is a very strong one."

" I submit, my lord, both speech and evidence are irregular and improper."

The judge overruled the objection, and the examination proceeded as before.

" State to the court the cause of the severance between the late Mr. Whitehead and Mr. Godfrey."

" My husband agreed to place a certain sum in the firm, and Godfrey the same, and that whichever took that sum out was to consider as having withdrawn himself from the firm.

" My husband engaged in many speculations, and some succeeded, by which Godfrey benefitted the same as my husband ; then occurred an Indian speculation, which was supposed to be a failure, such news coming over. Godfrey then turned round and said,—

" ' You are no longer my partner ; you have withdrawn money to the amount you paid in, and have no further interest in the concern.'

" Unfortunately, my husband, not suspecting the nature of the man, made no provision against such an emergency, and we were thrown into indigence.

" A small sum annually was all I received from Godfrey, and this was given me because the partnership accounts had not been made up, and were complicated, and it was inconvenient to do so. I was also assured that at the end of a long period, I should have but a very small sum coming to me.

" I heard nothing more until one evening when Mr. Charles Ormond came to me and informed me that Mr. Godfrey intended to double my allowance, upon condition of my signing a deed of settlement by which I should assign everything coming to my husband in the way of business.

" The reason of this was, he said, news had come that the whole of his Indian speculations had turned out most successful, and a large fortune would be mine.

" Godfrey came, in fact, at that moment; and with him he brought the deed which by Mr. Ormond's advice I refused to sign."

" And what said Mr. Godfrey on that occasion ?"

" He was much exasperated, and bitterly vowed to be revenged, especially upon Mr. Ormond, whom he upon that instant discharged, and he, Godfrey, after repeating his threats left the place."

" And do you think he has kept his word ?"

" I am sure of it."

" You think ——"

" The witnesses thoughts are of no consequence," said the judge.

" Why do you say you are sure he has kept his word?" inquired the counsel.

"This prosecution is, no doubt, the result of his malice. I am sure he is capable of it."

"State about what occurred yesterday?"

"My daughter begged I would consent to sign this deed of settlement, as the only means that wou'd induce Godfrey to forego the prosecution of the revenge he had against Charles Ormond."

"The prisoner?"

"Yes, it is so."

"And he brought the deed?"

"He did; and it was signed last night late."

"Upon what condition?"

"That he should so give his evidence as to permit the acquittal of the accused. Upon no other condition would I have signed it, since I have now but a small annuity to depend upon; and Heaven only knows what chicanery may not be used by this man to deprive me of that. I have signed away for this purpose a large—I know not even how large a fortune!"

The counsel for the defence intimated that he had done, and he of the prosecution rose, and said,—

"Now, Mrs. Whitehead, allow me to ask you a few questions, to which I shall be obliged by direct answers. How long have you known this person?"

"Who? Godfrey?"

"No; the prisoner."

"But a short time."

"Oh! but a short time; very well. And he has taken a great interest in your affairs, I believe."

"He has. I believe because he saw we were unprotected, and exposed to manifest injustice of this man, Godfrey."

"Exactly. But you say we."

"Yes, I did."

"What do you mean?"

"Myself and daughter."

"Oh! yourself and daughter!"

"Yes."

"She is, I believe, or would be, in case there was any property left by her father his heiress?"

"She would."

"And in addition to the charms naturally attendant upon the possession of great property, she is a young lady of great beauty."

"It is not for me to say much about that, sir; she is my daughter, and they say there is a family likeness," said Mrs. Whitehead, with much simplicity and some pride.

There was almost a smile upon the lips of many present, and a very slight, but hardly perceptible curl upon the lips of the counsel for the prosecution, who immediately said,—

"Ah! I see, the same charms that captivated the father might well, in the person of the daughter, captivate another. Your daughter, is young, I see, by your own appearance."

"Yes."

"Has the prisoner paid any attention to your daughter?"

"Yes."

"You have seen him often since the night on which you say he was discharged?"

"Yes."

"Oftener since than before?"

"Oh, yes."

"Where did he live?"

"He lived with us."

"Us?"

"Yes; myself and daughter."

" Oh ! I see."

" I could do no less than invite him to take up his residence with us, after he had been discharged without means, for our sakes. He had for us ruined himself."

" In doing good."

" Yes, he had."

" It was kind and considerate of you. Pray, did your daughter object to it?"

" Oh, no, she did not."

" Perhaps felt pleased at an opportunity of evincing her gratitude for such generous devotion on his part towards yourselves?"

" Exactly."

" Pray have these young people,—for I think it but natural they should—formed any tender attachment for each other?"

" I cannot say."

" You cannot say—certainly not, but still you think so?"

" Why, yes, it may be so."

" She would not have sought Mr. Godfrey to obtain his escape, if it had been otherwise, for fear of misconstruction?"

" No, she would not."

" Ah! then this young man has been living with you ever since Godfrey discharged him?"

" Yes, with us."

" With your daughter?"

" No, with us."

" Ah! exactly, with your daughter and you. Did you never think there was any impropriety in such a course of life?"

" What do you mean?"

" Why, permitting a young man to live with your daughter under the same roof."

" He did not."

" He is an admirer of your daughter?"

" He is, I believe."

" You only think so, but are you not sure of it?"

" Yes, he is."

" But you believe that there can be no impropriety in his living in the same lodgings with you all?"

" None."

" And they were much alone?"

" Yes, they were alone sometimes."

" The young lady was fond of him?"

" Yes."

" And he of the young lady?"

" Yes."

" And they were much together, and alone?"

" Yes."

" You never observed any impropriety when they were alone?" then said the counsel, archly.

" Never."

" I can easily credit that assertion, gentlemen," said the counsel to the jury," and it is the only one I can implicitly receive."

Re-examined by the counsel for the defence.

" Mr. Ormond had an apartment to himself, and she looked upon him as a son and he lived there as a brother to Miss Mariam. He was too honourable to commit even an approach to an impropriety on any one occasion."

" What means had the prisoner?" said the counsel for the prosecution, resuming his cross-examination.

" I don't know."

" Had he any at all?"

"I believe he had none."

"And he lived upon you?"

"He lived with us."

"He had no means of obtaining funds elsewhere?"

"None, that I am aware of."

"Did he have any of you?"

"None, that I remember."

"But he used to walk out with your daughter?"

"He did."

"I have done," said the counsel for the prosecution, and then Mrs. Whitehead was informed that she might stand down, and very glad she was, too, for she was completely exhausted by the long examination and cross-examination she had undergone.

The next person that was called was Marian Whitehead; and, oh! how Charles trembled at the thought of what she would have to undergo; and all she could say, he could well see, would do him no good. The artful cross-examination of the counsel was a sufficient proof of that, and, had he at that moment been able, he would have forbidden her to step into the witness-box.

"They may have some regard for her beauty and innocence," he said to himself. "At all events, she means well, and I am sure innocence cannot be made the instrument of guilt."

Marian Whitehead now stood in the witness-box; all eyes were directed towards her. She wore a large white veil, which was down when she stepped into the witness-box.

"Remove your veil, if you please," said the clerk, as he held the book towards her, and tendered the customary oath.

She was very pale, but calm; there was an indescribable air of intense suffering and feeling, which was evidently kept down by a strong effort.

Her beauty too, as well as youth, procured her much sympathy among the audience, and even the bar. Many looked at her with mingled commiseration and admiration.

"Take your own time, Miss Whitehead, and answer my questions calmly. There is no haste. Do you know the prisoner at the bar?" inquired the counsel for the defence.

"I do," she said, in a tone that went to the heart of Charles Ormond, even as he then stood, almost on the brink of the grave.

"Do you recollect any particular circumstance respecting the receipt of a letter which the prisoner received?"

"I do."

"Relate what occurred?"

"A twopenny post letter was delivered at the door, which the servant brought, and gave into Mr. Ormond's hands. It was directed to him."

"What were its contents?"

"Two checks. The one filled up for fifty pounds, and the other was a blank, apparently torn out at the same moment; the two adhering together, so as to appear but one."

"And what occurred?"

"I would have persuaded him to have rejected it, and returned it by post to Godfrey, and refuse to receive anything from such a man, as I felt there must be danger in having anything from him. There was a presentiment on my mind."

"And what said the prisoner?"

"He said it was merely a woman's fear; the money was his lawfully, and he must admit it was an act of justice he would not have asked for, and yet was quite unexpected from such a man as Godfrey."

"Have you seen Godfrey since?"

"I have repeatedly upon this matter. He said he could save Charles Ormond if he chose, and he would do so if my mother was to sign a deed that should give him power over some Indian property. In consequence of this I begged my mother to accede to the condition."

"And did she do so?"

"She did; but the deeds were not ready, and he agreed to obtain an adjournment of the trial until they should be signed, and they were signed late last night."

"Upon condition that he should contrive the acquittal of the prisoner Ormond?"

"Exactly. But when the deeds were signed, and he had secured them about him, he declared that he thought it was now too late to do so, but we should see in the morning."

The counsel for the prosecution now rose to put some few questions to the witness.

"You know the prisoner at the bar?" he said.

"I do."

"Have you known him long?"

" Not very long."

" You feel much interested in his fate, if one may judge from the efforts, illegal as they are, you have made to evade the ordinary course of justice."

" It was for the sake of justice I made those efforts. In a bad cause I would not have made them."

" Nor had it been for another person."

" I cannot undertake to say what I might or might not do in cases that have not yet happened."

" Where was the prisoner living when he received this letter that you alleged contained the checks ?"

" He was living in the same house."

" With yourself ?"

" In the same house."

" Exactly. But you were all looked on as one family ?"

" We were."

" It was he who even took the apartments ?"

" Yes, he did. We had been burned out, and were unable to do so. He took the task on himself."

" But you paid for all ?"

" I have no means."

" But your mother ?"

" Yes, my mother did. She paid for all."

" And you had apartments in common."

" We had."

" Pray, Miss Whitehead, were not you and the young man sweethearts at the time ?"

" I do not precisely understand what you mean by the terms of your question."

" The prisoner was an admirer of yours. He made love to you. I am at a loss how to make the matter plainer to you. But was not that the fact ?"

" Yes," said Marian, faintly.

" And of course you felt interested in his fate ?"

" I did."

" You went about, as you say, endeavouring—to use the common phrase—to stir Heaven and earth in his favour."

" I sought Godfrey, and begged him to forego the revenge he swore he would have on the first night he was baffled by Mr. Ormond making my mother acquainted with his nefarious designs against her property."

" Ever since that night you have lived together ?"

" Yes."

" And your mother was aware of it ?"

" Of course ; she could not be otherwise."

" You considered it to be right and proper to attempt to tamper with the principal witness in this case ?"

" I could not be said to tamper with a man who has perjured himself here to-day, and I call Heaven to witness that I only sought him, not to induce him to say what was not true, but to tell the truth, or at least to render the falsehoods he had uttered nugatory in their effect."

" The prisoner never told you he was guilty, then ?"

" He could not have done so."

" You would not have believed it if he had."

" I could not. But I cannot give any answer to cases which have not happened."

" He always protested his innocence ?"

" Yes."

" It would have grieved you very much if he had not ?"

" It would. But he is too honourable to know aught of guilt."

" I would for your sake it may turn out so," said the counsel. " I have done ; you may go down."

Marian did go down, but, as she turned to leave the witness-box, she could not but cast a glance at the unfortunate Charles Ormond, in whose fate hung her future welfare.

That glance was but a momentary one, but, oh, what volumes did it speak to the heart of Charles! It was one that told him of the great love she bore for him—that he, and he alone, in the whole world, was able to make her happy; and, should fate be unkind, what anguish would he have to suffer on her account as well as his own.

Marian saw but his features—the form and features of him whom she loved so well—she saw that deep admiration and love that shone in him; but there was such an air of sadness and melancholy about him, that spoke to her in the most impressive manner of the hopelessness of the case.

As she did not leave the court, Mr. Blake said,—

"Allow me, Miss Whitehead, to take you from this place. You must not remain here."

"Yes, I will remain here, and know and see the worst."

"You had better be persuaded."

"No, no; I will not."

"If you will not, I cannot gainsay you."

"No, no; do not attempt it. I am determined. But, tell me, have I done right?"

"What, as a witness?"

"Yes."

"Excellent. The counsel for the prosecution made but little out of you on his cross-examination. I would your mother had been as fortunate. But she had not the presence of mind that you had."

"Do you think there is any chance?"

"I am afraid to answer your question."

"Is it so doubtful?"

"Yes; there is no evidence, beside your own, as to the way in which he became possessed of a check. Besides, they look upon you in the light of an interested person."

"God help him!"

"So say I. Do not make any remark here whatever, or you may create much confusion, and do him certainly no good—perhaps harm; therefore, sit quite quiet."

"I will—I will."

There were one or two individuals called, who gave Charles Ormond an excellent character for honour and integrity, and who declared, from what they knew of him, they did not believe one word of the accusation.

This concluded the prisoner's defence.

The counsel for the prosecution now rose, and said,—

" My lord and gentlemen of the jury, I should not have thought it necessary to add one word to the observations I addressed to you in my opening speech, but for the very extraordinary course pursued by the prisoner's advisers, and the nature of the defence set up, as well as the testimony of the witnesses brought forward to substantiate that line of defence.

" My lord and gentlemen, I am sure the prisoner cannot complain that he has not had scope given him for proving almost anything, and asserting everything. The defence has been varied in its character, and the examination of its witnesses, and their cross-examination, have as well been comprehensive enough.

" I cannot conceive—I do not even remember such singular advantages given to any prisoner in all my life. Mark, my lord and gentlemen, I do not complain of this—I rejoice at it, and so will you, gentlemen, when you consider he has been entitled to, and permitted to assert and attempt a proof of anything that was deemed necessary for the full development of his defence, because, gentlemen, it relieves you of a load of responsibility—for, to fail with such advantages in proving his innocence, you must be relieved of many doubts that might influence your conduct,

" I contend, gentlemen, he has failed ; but in my observations now, I shall not endeavour to inculpate him more deeply—that is impossible ; and, moreover, my case stands complete and unshaken ; but I rise to reply to some observations, or rather slanderous insinuations, that have been made against the fair fame and character of an individual, who is not the prosecutor in this case, nor was he instrumental in the prisoner's being brought to the bar of justice.

" Mr. Godfrey, gentlemen, is a merchant, one of a large class. He, among that class, particularly wealthy as they are usually, is one of the wealthy, and far above the temptation of perilling his fair fame, and all he possesses, for the sake of a fifty pound note ; much less would such a man unite with others to form a conspiracy to take the life of the prisoner, because the men with whom he must associate, would be the very men, of all others, who would ruin him with their exactions, knowing, as they would, that his character would be entirely in their power. There is not, I contend, from this very circumstance, the least probability in the mode of defence adopted by the prisoner, and, instead of benefitting his case, I fear that it has, if possible, greatly injured it.

" I am content, now, gentlemen of the jury, to leave the case entirely in your hands, and, from the instructions you will receive at the hands of his lordship, I am convinced you will come to such a decision as will fully answer all the ends of justice."

The counsel resumed his seat, and the attention of all in that crowded court was then turned to the judge, who, with great deliberation, proceeded to read his notes of the case, which he had been glancing through while the counsel was delivering his address.

The whole of the evidence, for and against the prisoner, was summed up by his lordship in a calm and impartial manner, and then, with breathless anxiety, all waited for the decision of the jury—that decision upon which hung the life of an innocent fellow-being—that decision which would be fraught with joy of the most rapturous kind, or agony the most indescribable.

Charles Ormond leaned heavily on the front of the bar, and his whole soul seemed concentrated on that spot where sat she who was to him the whole world ; and if, at that moment, he felt the hopeless agony of despair, it was more upon her account than upon his own.

Marian sat by her mother's side, with her small hands clasped before her, her eyes fixed upon the box containing the twelve men whose words were to bring life or death to him she loved so dearly ; and her pale lips, slightly parted, gave an expression of the most painful anxiety to her death-like countenance.

Ten minutes had scarcely elapsed, when the foreman of the jury, addressing the judge, declared that they had resolved upon their verdict.

" Gentlemen of the jury," asked the clerk, " what do you find the prisoner—guilty, or not guilty ?"

A pause of a few moments ensued, and then the foreman—casting a hasty glance upon Charles, who had turned eagerly towards the box, when he heard the question asked by the clerk—said, in a subdued tone,—

" Guilty."

Marian rose to her feet for a moment—a convulsive spasm crossed her face, and then, with a choking scream, she fell senseless into the arms of Mr. Blake, who instantly had her carried from the court.

Charles heard that cry, and, burying his face in his hands, he seemed at once to give himself up to the despair against which he had been so long contending. It was, however, but for a moment, and then, by a fearful effort, he gained sufficient firmness to listen with a forced calmness to his lordship's address.

As might have been expected, the sentence was death, and then, with a feeling of hopeless despair tugging at his heart, Charles suffered himself to be led to his cell.

CHAPTER XXXI.

AFTER THE TRIAL.—THE PRISONER IN HIS CELL.

AND now that all was over, and the worst was known—now that every sacrifice had been made, and made in vain, and that all attempts to propitiate the man who had worked such an amount of woe to the innocent and the noble-hearted, had utterly and completely failed, our readers may probably imagine, far better than we can describe, the almost helpless wretchedness into which Charles Ormond fell.

It is well enough for those who have never endured such heart's agony as fell to his lot, to talk about the majesty of innocence, and how he, who can tell himself that his prosecution has been a persecution, ought to stand up against any evils that may befall him; but they cannot really know what such a being as Charles Ormond was likely to endure under such distressful circumstances, unless they were to find themselves in parallel ones.

He was all that any one could wish him in point of firmness and self-control, but still he was human, and, being such, it was impossible but that he should feel, and that acutely, too, the fearful injustice that was being done to him.

Not even in the blissful recollection that he was still, in all difficulties and dangers, beloved by her who was the first ever to awaken in his heart kindred emotions, could he find a solace for the cares that beset him.

Love will support many a heart through grievous trials—it will make the weak strong, the undecided and the infirm of purpose full of valorous resolution; but when a man stands upon the threshold of eternity, an eternity, too, which he is to reach through the process of a most ignominious death, he would needs be something less or more than human, were he not to feel such a situation, and acutely.

At that time it was not usual to provide a condemned prisoner with company in his cell.

Alone, all alone, he was left, with the exception of occasional visits from the chaplain, and from those who brought him necessary sustenance, until the dismal hour arrived when, with all the frightful paraphernalia of an execution, he should be brought out to be put to death formally, and in cold blood, by his fellow man.

The fatigue of the trial, too, had been excessive; he had stood, the observed of all observers, for many hours, with both body and mind in the most painful stretch of excitement, the reaction from which was of a terrific character.

When the cell door closed upon him, he felt at that moment as if he could have died, and, with scarce a mental pang, he could have bidden adieu to the world and all that it contained.

After a time, however, when the bodily fatigue wore off, and he had drunk a draught of water, and partaken, rather mechanically than from a wish to do so, of some portion of the food which had been brought to him, much of his fatigue wore off, and the mind was left fearfully active to dream of that which was coming.

And, oh! in what frightful colours did that coming future present itself. In his mind's eye he saw the crowd, he saw the scaffold, and he saw the dismal preparations which were made to usher him into the presence of his Creator—the terrific scene, in all its affecting solemnity, loomed upon his mental vision.

Such thoughts as those were madness, and the idea began to take possession of him, that it would be to him more desirable, and more glorious, to cheat the scaffold of its victim, and to die by his own hand, than to make a holiday for a heartless crowd that would come to look upon his agonies.

But this was a notion which, though it clung to him for hours, during which he in vain sought for some means of accomplishing his deadly purpose, was not likely to last with such a mind as his.

When calmer reflection crept over his soul, he began to ask himself if, by such a self-sacrifice to the horors of his position, he should not be greatly countenancing the presumption of his guilt.

"Yes," he said; "I must endure all, even to the very worst that cruel fortune can inflict upon me. Ay, even to that death which has ever, to my imagination, presented itself in such an awful aspect—even that I must endure, rather than that the finger of scorn should be pointed at Marian Whitehead, and the idle vulgar should be enabled to say to her, 'He whom you loved proved his own guilt, by cowardice that would not suffer him to meet the fate to which he had been condemned.'"

This consideration swayed him much, and for Charles Ormond once to think that it would be in any way cowardly to commit any particular act, was more than sufficient to place the committal of that particular act far beyond all the bounds of probability.

And now, with a dreadful and a gloomy firmness, he made up his mind to meet his fate, fearful as it was, and calculated to unnerve the boldest.

And all was over as regarded what exertions could be made to save him from condemnation—the traducer of innocence and the felon witness had had their way. Providence seemed about to permit one of the best specimens of its handy work to fall a victim to some of its worst.

At such a period, to hope for anything in the shape of pardon, or a commutation of such a sentence, was completely out of the question.

A notion was prevalent, and it continued for years after, among a number of well-meaning enough persons, that because this was a commercial country, the punishment of death should inevitably follow any such breach of trust as it was presumed Charles Ormond had committed.

Hence, any crime, however slight, that could by human ingenuity be tortured into being called that of forgery, was sufficient to bring its unhappy perpetrator to the scaffold.

And it most unhappily occurred, that the monarch, George III., who then filled the throne of these realms, was such an idiotic bigot, that, having once got the idea ingrafted among his small quantity of brains, that it was necessary to hang people who interfered with other persons' property, he discarded all notion of interfering to save any one from such a doom.

Instead of being the fountain of mercy, this man was the fountain of folly; and the nation was suffering all that a nation could suffer, in consequence of the highest authority within it having far below the average of intellect, and that being of a decidedly vicious and vindictive character.

Thus poor Charles Ormond, although those who loved him might make friends among the great and the compassionate, had no chance whatever of success, but was compelled to await his doom with what firmness and resignation he could call to his aid.

We have already recorded, in an earlier portion of this work, the answer of George III. to the application that was made to him for a pardon, and, therefore, we need not repeat the senility that fell from his lips.

But if Charles Ormond suffered, let us not suppose that he was the only one who was terror-stricken at the result of the trial.

Yes, for poor Marian Whitehead can be claimed an amount of sympathy greater even than for him who is about to perish so wrongfully. Alas—alas! worn out almost by anxiety and by exertion before that dreadful day which crushed every hope, the sentence against Charles Ormond seemed likely to be thy death warrant likewise.

She was carried from the court in a state of total insensibility. Mrs. Whitehead, who was nearly bewildered, and scarcely knew what she said or did, had her conveyed home, and there they were, in that splendid abode, which, with all its advantages, they had bartered away in a vain attempt to save the life of him who was yet to be sacrificed, alone and desolate.

They had no friends, no associates; there was not one person to extend to them the hand of sympathy or of kindness. In their former state of humble poverty, they had purposely abstained from making acquaintances, on account of the insufficiency of their means, and prosperity had not sufficiently long dawned upon them to enable them to form new connections.

Hence they found themselves now with just about enough money in their possession, and that was part of what had been advanced by the solicitor, to enable them to pay what debts they had incurred in their new abode, and to shrink back unmolested to their former state of poverty and insignificance.

But could they shrink back to their former state of negative happiness ? Could they bury in oblivion the busy records of the past, and not feel that for them had been sacrificed one of the best and noblest hearts that ever beat in human bosom ?

Oh, no, the remembrance of those few months of agitation, of hopefulness, of joy, and then of despair, would cling to them for ever.

Happy—happy, indeed, would they have been to awaken in their humble little home, and to have been able to say to themselves,—

"This has been nothing after all but a feverish and excited dream—there is no such being as Charles Ormond, and no one has suffered such mortal agony for us."

But that might not be. No—no; never for one moment again was the light of joy to beam from the eyes of Marian Whitehead ; and never had such a succession of circumstances surely occurred to one individual, to scare away for ever all thoughts of well doing or of happiness.

As may be well imagined, the solicitor who had taken up the cause of the White-heads against Godfrey, was extremely angry at the injudicious course that had been pursued by the Whiteheads.

It was not to be supposed that he could enter into all the feelings of Marian—those feelings of self-devotion which had induced her to scatter every other consideration to the winds, but that affecting the welfare of Charles Ormond.

Their claim upon Godfrey had been to the solicitor's eyes so clear, so distinct, and so palpable, that, as we are aware, he had not hesitated to furnish all the requisite funds for carrying on the cause ; but feeling likewise that its termination would be in favour of the Whiteheads, he had provided them with sufficient funds to at once assume the rank of life which the possession of their property, he considered, would so soon entitle them to.

To find, then, that after all, they had actually and voluntarily assigned to Godfrey the whole of their large interests for a paltry annuity, was to him most especially provoking.

He was by no means a bad sort of man, that solicitor ; indeed, as the world goes, he was liberal and just ; but the matter of fact character of his education, and his legal knowledge enabled him to see the transaction in a light such as it was not to be expected Marian Whitehead could ever behold it in.

The utter inutility of the sacrifice that had been made to him, would have been evident from the first, for when the deed of assignment was executed upon Godfrey's premises to rescue Charles Ormond from the fearful situation in which he was placed, he, Godfrey, had no power, if he had had all the inclination in the world, to do so.

The thing had gone too far, and it was quite out of the question, that, in a serious charge of felony, a prosecutor could so tamper with a jury, as to gainsay, in any manner, the evidence upon which a magistrate had thought proper to commit a prisoner.

But women do not reason closely upon these matters as men do. All that was present in the whole transaction to the mind of Marian was, that Godfrey accused Charles Ormond of a crime he was innocent of, and offered to withdraw that accusation upon certain terms.

The terms were acceded to ; and we have seen with what a villanous satisfaction Godfrey still pursued his vicious career, which was to lead poor innocent Charles Ormond to the scaffold.

And now how rapidly do those hours seem to pass, each one of which brought the unhappy victim of falsity and deceit nearer to the unmerited doom which awaited him.

It was this thought which aroused Marian from the lethargy in which she seemed to have fallen, and gave her for the time a strength which was purely the result of excitement, and the re-action from which was likely to be fearful indeed.

Despite the remonstrances of her mother, she now rose on the morning after the conclusion of the trial. It was a Sunday; but still, despite every circumstance, she resolved to make some effort in favour of the condemned criminal.

Her first step was to proceed to the private house of the solicitor. She found him within, and repugnant although he felt to seeing her now, he yet consented to do so, when the servant, who left her in the hall, told him that she looked like one newly risen from the grave.

She was shown into a small private room which he now used as his study. It was strewn with books and papers, and there she was invited to state her errand to him, who certainly had some cause of complaint against her.

Before she came in, he had prepared himself to remonstrate with her upon the folly she had been guilty of in assigning or persuading her mother to assign their whole interest to Godfrey in the Indian property; but when he saw her wan and miserable aspect—when he saw how really wretched she had become, even his heart sank within him, and he could not utter a reproach to one who was evidently already suffering so much.

He forgot in a moment all his reproaches—he forgot that legal education which enabled him to be so much shocked at the foolish conduct of Marian ; and, like a gentleman, as he really was, he only then saw before him the distressed and heart-stricken young girl, whose sufferings he would have gladly assuaged, and for whom he felt the tenderest sympathy.

He was a man of sufficient age to have got rid of the romance of existence ; but there are feelings of a kindly nature which are not dependent upon those early dreams of the imagination, but which, in some dispositions, settle down only into a more reasonable aspect, and preserve all their real beauty.

She was silent for a few moments, for, in fact, her heart was too full to allow her to speak ; she knew, too, that this gentleman had cause of complaint, and she wished, before she uttered a word, that she should hear in what manner he felt inclined to receive her on her errand of mercy.

She was not disappointed ; he did speak first ; nor were her most sanguine expectations destroyed by his tone and manner ; they were both kind in the extreme, and such as might have been addressed to her by an affectionate relative.

"Miss Whitehead," he said, "pray be seated ; I need not ask you how you are, for it is evident you have suffered much, and cannot be well ; believe me, that if I can be of any service to you, you have but to point out the way, and I will take it."

Now, Marian could speak less than probably she would have done had his words been of a harsher complexion. She felt almost suffocated by her emotions, and it was not until tears had come to her relief that she was able to say,—

"Sir, I'm not so unmindful, even in the midst of my own great affliction, of other subjects, not to feel that you have much to complain of. I cannot expect that you should excuse me, because no one, not feeling as I felt, could for a moment sanction the acts which I urged my mother to."

"Let that pass," said the attorney ; "it is a subject which I wish not to revert to ; you must yourself now be fully aware of what a grievous error of judgment you have committed ; but it is done, and, therefore, cannot be undone. I have no doubt but that, with every legal formality, Godfrey has possessed himself of the whole of the Indian property, so that you have no remedy whatever."

"I have no doubt," said Marian, "that it is so. Let that pass, sir, for the present, and let us think of the dreadful circumstances in which the innocent are placed."

"I know to what you allude," said the attorney ; "you fancy that by exertion, by intercession, and by entreaty, something may be done to stay the hand of the law, and save Charles Ormond ; but if you flatter yourself so much, your disappointment will but be the more bitter. Be assured that no intercession whatever from any quarter will have any effect in saving him."

"Oh, do not deprive me of all hope."

"I do not think it is cruel to do so. The case is utterly hopeless, and from the first you had better feel and know that it is so."

"Nay, sir, while there is life there is hope, and I will cling to it. If you will not aid me, I will go alone, and I will besiege them with entreaties who have the power to be just."

"But, my dear young lady, they think they are being just."

"And you, too," said Marian, "can you believe him guilty?"

"What on earth can I say? I would not have been on that jury for a million of money."

"Nay, now, this is unkind, indeed," exclaimed Marian. "I swear to you his innocence—I know it ; I am as certain of it as I am of my own existence."

"My own feelings and my own impressions," said the attorney, "all go that way ; but I feel that in entertaining an opinion of the innocence of Charles Ormond, I am more swayed by my knowledge of all the parties to the transaction than by the evidence."

"The evidence is false."

"Possibly a person may know enough of Godfrey to feel that he is a man who would willingly perjure himself, even to bring a fellow-creature to death rather than leave his own ends unanswered, in order to believe in the innocence of Charles Ormond."

"And Godfrey is such a man; and shall he triumph, and an innocent life be taken because he is a villain? Forbid it, Heaven—forbid it, justice."

"What can be done?"

"An appeal to those quarters where the power exists to save him may surely be made?"

"Which will be useless; but still, Marian Whitehead, to convince you that I take not a cold and unsympathetic view of your position, I will see that such an appeal shall be made; you shall not be without the satisfaction of knowing that all has been done that can be done; and one thing, I think, I can promise you."

"What is that?"

"While there is an affectation of the strictest justice, coexistent with the prede-termination on the part of the authorities to show no real mercy, they will always go out of their way for the purpose of making some sort of a display of impar-tiality."

"To what conclusion would you lead me? Is it a hopeful one?"

"Not at all. From what you have said and sworn to upon the trial, there is enough to warrant, say some two or three respectable parties in making affidavits to the effect, that they believe, if a respite is granted to the prisoner for a certain time, evidence will be forthcoming which will place the crown in a position to save him."

"Oh, a day—an hour's delay is a great boon."

"I think that by setting about it seriously, and by making it almost a personal matter with some parties, who would do me a favour, a week's respite will be pro-cured."

"Then he will be saved—he will be saved!"

"There—there," said the solicitor, "I was afraid you would view it in that light. What hope have you that, during the week, Godfrey, or the man Neville, will confess the villany you impute to them?—Can any inducement be offered to such men?"

"They may repent them of the evil they have done."

"Not they, indeed."

"There may come some moments, when conscience, which makes cowards of us all, may so far terrify them with its secret admonitions, that they may yet save themselves from consummating their villany in the death of their victim."

"A most forlorn hope, indeed."

"But yet a hope."

"Well—well, have it so: a drowning man will cling to a straw."

"You will get the respite."

"Nay, I cannot say I will get it; I will try to get it; but, before even I make the attempt, I will see Charles Ormond, and let him know its real character, so that the chalice of hope may not be presented to his lips but to be dashed away by the stern hand of death."

Although the conversation between Marian and the solicitor continued for some time longer, we have recorded its principal features, which consisted in the renewal of his promise to procure, if it could possibly be procured, the respite for Charles Ormond.

It was not likely that a careful man, such as this gentleman was, could make that promise, unless he believed he had good grounds to think he could perform it.

This was Marian's opinion: and she left his house with a better heart, because she felt that she had half succeeded in, at all events, rescuing Charles from immediate death, if she could not eventually altogether save him from the dreadful doom that awaited him.

The solicitor got from her a promise before she left him, that she would take no steps of her own in the matter, because, as he told her, by so doing, she might mili-tate against anything he might attempt.

But this was a promise he might have spared himself the trouble of getting her to give him; for the temporary excitement, which had enabled her to reach his house, disappeared by the time she was again in her own home, and she sank exhausted into the arms of her mother, totally unable, even had she felt inclined, to busy herself further for the present in Charles Ormond's affairs.

CHAPTER XXXII.

THE RESPITE.—THE ANXIOUS INTERVAL.

This respite for a week, which the attorney had taken upon himself almost to promise Marian, was a matter really more likely to be obtained, under the circumstances, than he or she had first imagined.

Our readers will recollect that the trial had lasted the whole of the Friday, and had been only completed upon the Saturday, so that the period of the execution, counting Sunday as the *dies non*, which in fact it was, would have been Tuesday morning.

Now it was such an extraordinary thing to hang anybody upon Tuesday morning, and so nearly without all precedent, that the authorities quite took the alarm upon the subject, and of themselves would have been quite ready upon that ground alone, however ridiculously insufficient it was, to apply to the Secretary of State to put off the execution till the following Monday morning at eight o'clock, that being the legitimate and acknowledged day and hour for such a scene to be enacted.

Little they thought, and little they cared, what might be the sufferings of the unhappy prisoner condemned to die, while they were stickling for forms and ceremonies; and thus, poor Charles Ormond was not only condemned wrongfully, but it seemed highly probable that their cruel sport would be played with him by persons having no real sympathy with his condition.

He might, or he might not, view the prolongation of his life for six days as a boon; but, whether he did so or not, there was great danger that it would instil into his mind hopes which would only again be frustrated by his being led forth at the conclusion of that short period to execution.

The attorney was as good as his word, for he at once went to one of the sheriffs, and, without difficulty, procured an order to visit Charles in the condemned cell.

The sheriff was an old and intimate friend of the solicitor, and to him he related the interview he had had with Marian, and the promise he had made her.

"Oh," said the sheriff, "certainly. Humanity should be one of the first considerations in this world; and I mean to say that a man hung upon Tuesday will have a right to complain. Now, my dear sir, did you ever hear of anybody being hung on a Tuesday?"

"Well, I don't think I ever did."

"No, nor nobody else. I have taken the trouble, sir, to call upon no less than seventeen past sheriffs, and they never heard of a man being hung upon a Tuesday; and I should say, sir, that my solemn conviction is, that we should not be entitled to the marrow pudding and the breakfast, usually provided out of the city funds, on that occasion, if it wasn't done on Monday."

"Well, well," said the solicitor, "at all events, place it in what light you like, so that I have your assistance in getting the respite, if the prisoner himself does not strongly object to it. Give me an order to see him, and I will talk the matter over with him."

"Certainly—certainly. And, my dear sir, do tell him that for him to be hung upon a Tuesday, is one of the most extraordinary and out-of-the-way things he could think of. Just explain to him that he must have eight-and-forty hours, and that that will place me in the unpleasant situation of hanging him upon a Tuesday. Ask him to feel for the city authorities—play upon his feelings, sir, and his sense of gratitude."

"I'll do all that, and, whatever may be his impression at the first flush of the affair, I doubt not but that the instinctive clinging to life which characterises the human race will induce him to hope for six days more existence, although with the conviction that that six days can bring him no new hopes. Do you know, Mr. Sheriff, that I think he is innocent?"

"Innocent!"

"Yes, I do."

"Oh, now, really, really—why I heard the verdict myself—guilty. Never saw such a fat man as the foreman in all my life—a highly respectable jury. I should say, sir, that jury could have put down ten thousand pounds among them, and never have felt it, and yet you tell me that the man's innocent!"

"But he may be innocent for all that."

"Why, he's in the condemned cell—the condemned sermon's going to be preached to-day; tell me a man's innocent when I saw the judge's black cap with my own eyes!"

"Very good. You know you can have your opinion, and I can have mine, Mr. Sheriff."

"D--n it, if it wasn't Sunday I should swear. Everything's been quite regular up to this point, and if we don't hang him on the Tuesday, but save him up till next Monday, why, things will be regular all together. A man's tried, and is convicted, and condemned, and he's put in a cell, and the Reverend Jonas Snuffleton preaches the sermon, and he's hanged on a Monday, and yet you tell me the man's innocent!"

The solicitor saw that it was no use arguing with the sheriff, so he merely possessed himself of the order which entitled him to see Charles Ormond, and then at once repaired to Newgate.

The discipline and the strict order which is now preserved within that establishment, which a stern necessity has created, were by no means so conspicuous at that period as they are at present.

The management of the prison was too much confided to the practised cleverness of men in a very inferior grade of life, instead of being the result of system, which would make any one with ordinary understanding and integrity to do his duty.

The order of the sheriff, of course, readily admitted the solicitor, and he was conducted through the gloomy passages of the prison to one of those barred, ill-ventilated, and badly lighted cells, which are now only used to keep in awe the refractory, but never for those whom the policy of society has condemned to death.

What are called the condemned cells in Newgate are not above eight or ten in number; they occupy one side of a court-yard, which is an oblongp arallelogram, and into which the small grated windows of these cells look.

It was in one of these that Charles Ormond was placed to await his final doom.

It was, indeed, a needless mental torture to place those unhappy beings, on whom society had determined to wreak its worst vengeance, in such a place. Surely, surely it was enough that, with all the solemnity of legal punishment, ceremonies with all the implied regret of men of religion and humanity, some unhappy human being should be picked out from the great mass of his fellows, and by common consent put to death as a noxious thing, unfit longer to breathe that breath of life which his Creator had given to him, without the pettiness of malice, of putting him in a dark cell, as if that could add in any manner to the stupendous amount of punishment to which he was doomed.

It was, indeed, a mean and a contemptible idea, and the light of knowledge and intelligence which has now penetrated through the iron gratings of our prisons, inducing a system more consonant with humanity, has scattered it, and a hundred such trivialities, to the winds.

At the sound of the grating lock of his dungeon door, Charles Ormond rose, and there was something about the flashing of his eye as it met that of the gaoler, which made that official shrink back a step, as if he feared his victim, or rather the victim of the system of which he was an integral part, would spring upon him, and seek for vengeance.

"A wisitor," said the turnkey; and he gave the solicitor a poke in the back as an intimation that he might go in. "D'ye hear?—a wisitor."

"Who visits me?" said Charles; and then he recognised the solicitor, and added,—" Ah, sir, is it you? This is kind; for you can at least tell me of one who, for her own sake, I hope never to see again."

"Mr. Ormond—Mr. Ormond," said the attorney, "keep up your spirits. I have come to talk to you; but not to give you any hope, mind."

"Is she well?"

"She is—you mean Miss Marian Whitehead?"

"Yes—yes; I—I could not bring myself to utter the name. Implore her not to attempt to see me—beg her to think of me as of one already dead. It would unman me to look upon her face again; and mine, with the borrowed complexion of this hateful place, would haunt her while she lived."

"I hope, Mr. Ormond—I sincerely hope, that I shall be able to induce her not to tamper with her own feelings and yours by visiting this dreadful place."

This was sufficiently feeling and unselfish on the part of Charles Ormond to meet with the full approbation of Mr. Blake, the attorney; and, although not in the habit of giving any full expression to his opinions, he could not help saying,—

"Mr. Ormond, in addition to the whole of the facts, connected with your alleged crime, being of a nature to suggest many doubts, your own personal conduct to my mind speaks volumes in your favour. Now, Marian Whitehead has set her heart on getting a week's respite for you: she fancies that in that time something may be done to save you from your impending fate; and, if this respite be not procured, I can well perceive that, for the remainder of her existence, she will imagine that it, and it alone, has been the bar to your preservation."

Charles looked him in the face as intently as the semi-darkness of the cell would permit him.

"Sir," he said, and his voice trembled a little as he spoke, "I do not think that you would mock me; and I should regret that you should imagine I was so nerveless that I could not hear good news without too much agitation."

"Ah," said the attorney, "this is what I feared. I tell you, Mr. Ormond, upon my word and honour, that not the remotest hope has sprung up of rescuing you; and that if this respite for a week be granted you, you must consider it as merely a personal matter, and as having no sort of connection whatever with the merits of your case. Do you understand me?"

"I do, I do," said Charles; "and I tell you, do with me as you will, and bear in mind, that I have but one wish now in this world, and that is, for the happiness of Marian Whitehead. There is much that I think I could say to her, if I dared to trust myself with the opportunity, but I dread that if I were to see her I should forget all my admonitions in the agony of a consciousness, that I must soon part with her for ever."

"Then do not seek the interview; you'll have ample scope and opportunity here to write whatever you please to her. And besides, if you were to see her, it would not be alone, for I, as your solicitor, would probably be the only person admitted to a private conference with you."

"Then we are alone." said Charles; "unobserved, and not overheard?"

"Certainly; to the best of my belief."

"That has awakened a feeling in my breast again, which I thought that I had smothered."

"What feeling?"

"Is it not dreadful to die upon a scaffold, to endure the gaze of thousands who come, from curiosity, to see how the condemned man will comport himself upon the brink of eternity? Is not this dreadful, and does it not almost justify the use of some means to avoid being so degrading a spectacle?"

"Hush!" said the attorney; "you must not speak in that way. You assert your own innocence, and you best know it; consequently, I consider you in a position which justifies you in using all possible exertion to escape an unjust punishment."

"True—most true!"

"I can understand the feeling of resignation creeping over the mind of a man who knows himself to be guilty, and that his punishment is merited, but such is not your case. Those who have your fate in their hands are not those who are convinced of your guiltlessness, and therefore I consider you in a position to make any attempt to save yourself from the scaffold but the one you have insinuated—and that appears like cowardice—which can suggest itself to you."

"To what do you allude?" said Charles, eagerly.

"Nay, can you not understand me? I feel that I ought not to suggest anything to you; but still I've always had an impression on my own mind, from a knowledge of the condition of these condemned cells, that a determined man might possibly escape from them."

"You think so?"

"I do, certainly. And besides, you should bear in mind that, let you encounter what danger you may in your attempt to escape, to remain here is certain death."

"It is—it is."

"There is a small court-yard, as you know, adjoining these cells; one man, and one man only, guards the door leading from it, and he generally sits on this side and smokes his pipe, while the key is in the lock of the door."

"It is so—it is so."

"As to getting out of the actual cell, as well as getting rid of your irons, I think that might be managed by perseverance and ——"

"What?"

"A file."

Charles Ormond felt something cold touch his hand, and he immediately found that the attorney had brought him some tools and implements, with which he might have a chance of working his way to freedom.

"A thousand, thousand thanks!" he exclaimed.

"Hush, hush; mind I don't know what you mean. When once you get out of this court-yard, there is a narrow passage; pursue it, until you come to a small room, which leads to the governor's house; it is very seldom locked, especially the door of it next to Newgate, although the other one, as a general thing, is kept fast on the other side."

"I attend—I attend!"

"If, now, by chance, you should get into that room, I should advise that you lock the door you enter at on the inside, and then find some means of forcing the other one; half a dozen steps takes you then to the governor's street-door, in a manner of speaking; open it, descend that sharp short flight of steps, and you're in the Old Bailey. But mind you, the passage is intricate; but you must come to it if you keep on your left hand all the way."

"Should I meet no one?"

"Perchance you would."

"Then I must have weapons."

"No, certainly not, I cannot supply you with those; you must do the best you can, I only wish you success. I will do all I can for you, should you succeed in getting clear of the building."

"It shall be done—it shall be done. Now, indeed, I have a new hope; far better to die in an attempt to escape from an unjust imprisonment than to remain here, caged up until the time should arrive at which it shall be deemed politic and necessary to make of me a public spectacle. I will do all, and dare all, to again breathe the free air of heaven."

"Hush! hush! hide what you have. And, now, farewell; for I cannot pay you another visit."

"Farewell, dear friend, you have rescued me from despair; for death, in an attempted escape from here, by no means presents itself to me in half so terrific an aspect as the cold blooded and dreadful preparation for my execution; besides, some whispering spirit seems to tell me I shall succeed."

"Heaven send it may be a true one! I shall say nothing of this to Marian

Whitehead; she has suffered enough already, and the agony of suspense would be too much for her."

"Do keep it from her; and if I can but succeed in freeing myself from my prison-house, the time may come when I may fold her to my breast in some other land, and be happy."

"I sincerely hope it may; and be assured, that when once you gain the street you will not be without a friend to lead and direct your steps to some place of greater safety than you yourself, on such an emergency, would be able to do."

"And that kind friend will be no other than yourself. But do not, I pray you, run any risk on my behalf. Rather would I, a thousand times, run all the chances of my own evil fortune, than involve a kind and generous friend like yourself in mischief, for endeavouring to do me a service."

"I must confess to you," said the solicitor, "that, considering my profession, I am placed in a worse situation, as regards those affairs, than any mere private individual would be; what in any one else would seem but a natural impulse, probably arising more from social than legal feelings, in professional men becomes rank treason, because all the world would say he ought to have known better, and all the world is perfectly right in so saying; but, as I tell you, Mr. Ormond, I have a strong presumption of your innocence, and such being the case, I cannot, without an effort to save him, allow an innocent man to be subjected to a frightful death such as that, unless some effort is made to save you, seems to be in store for you."

"A thousand, thousand thanks, generous and best of friends; believe me, that I no longer look upon my position with that appalling sense of utter helplessness with which, so short a time since, I regarded it."

"Beware," said the solicitor, "of falling into the other extreme. Do not step at once, as persons situated as you are, may be considered as too apt to do, from the depths of despair to the height of a hopefulness, which circumstances are far from warranting them in indulging."

"Believe me, I shall be careful of any such excesses."

"Hush! not another word; do you not hear footsteps approaching?"

"It is the gaoler."

"Yes, to tell me that my time is up, and probably that I have already made too long a stay—farewell!"

"Farewell! and whether I succeed or fail in the attempt which I am about to make, believe me, sir, that your name will be linked in my last prayers, with Marian Whitehead's."

"Hush!" said the solicitor, and he placed his finger on his lips; "be careful, the slightest sound here is enough to provoke suspicion."

The door of the cell was at this moment opened, and one of the turnkeys appeared.

"Please, sir," he said, "you've been here longer than the regulation time; but howsomdever, of course we don't think much of that, as regards a lawyer; but you see, sir, there's the condemned sermon, and it's expected as all malefactors should go and hear it, and look uncommonly blue and pious while it's being preached."

"That may be all very well," said Charles Ormond, "for guilty men; but I, as an innocent one, decline attending to hear the condemned sermon."

"You declines! Oh, stuff, you don't know what you are talking about; I never heard of such a thing."

"Nothing but positive force should compel me to go through that pious farce which is enacted when a condemned sermon is preached."

"Why, everybody goes. 'Twas but t'other day as we had two malefactors as was going to be hung. I wasn't there, but they says it was a most delightful sight to see them at the condemned sermon; and, when they comed out to be scragged, the reverend Mr. Bobbington, as is our chaplain, he says to him, says he, ' Is you going to address the populous?' and one of the fellows says, ' Ask my eye,' and another one wanted him to take something out of his elbow; but, howsumdever, he's not the sort of being to be discouraged; so, when the fellows was steady on the drop,

See p. 202.

and half scragged, he pertends to lean for'ard and listen to something as they said, and then he calls out with a loud voice,—

"'The unhappy prisoners say as it's Sabbath breaking and evil company as is brought 'em to this untimely end,' says he.

"Then, afore as they could as much as say they was damned if it was so, they was launched into 'ternity."

"All that cannot affect me," said Charles Ormond. "I cannot recognise any argument in what you have said which shall induce me to attend the condemned sermon."

"Nor I neither," said the solicitor; "and yet, as it is a custom, perhaps it may be as well to go."

"You can imagine, sir," said Charles, "that I regret differing from you; but, if it be a custom, it is one in my opinion far more honoured in the breach than in the observance. I will not go."

"Wery good," said the turnkey; "blessed if I know whether they'll come and make you. It makes no difference to me, of course, one way or t'other. I tells you, that's all, and there's the blessed bell again."

"I'll leave you, now," said the attorney. "Use your own discretion."

"Oh, there's no occasion," said the turnkey, "for him to do anything of the kind, sir. We perwides 'em with everything. Now, mister, will you go, or won't you?"—"Assuredly not," said Charles.

"Done agin," said the turnkey, and he shut the door of the cell, leaving Ormond alone to reflect upon the probabilities or the possibilities of his escape from that building whence so few had ever succeeded in emerging by their own individual exertions.

In fact, when he came to consider the massive nature of the structure, and the many contrivances for safety which time and observation must have induced in those who had charge of the prison-house, he began to view his projected attempt as about one of the most desperate and hopeless of things that could be set about.

But still it was a chance, and when it came to be set in the scale against certain death, he felt that it was worth the trying, and that, even if it were to be attended with total destruction to him, that destruction would come in a far more agreeable shape than at the hands of the public executioner.

"At least," he said, "I shall have a struggle for my life, and have a battle for that existence which I have a right to cling to. How preferable is death under such circumstances to that which would present itself to me upon being passively led forth to the gaze of an assembled multitude, with every circumstance of official solemnity, to suffer upon a scaffold!"

Scarcely had he concluded some of these reflections, and others of a similar tendency, when his cell door was opened again, and the chaplain of the prison, attired in his ecclesiastical robes, and, apparently, in great haste, made his appearance.

"Young man, young man," he said, "is it not dreadful to think that you should be so carried away by the impulses of the evil one as to refuse to attend the condemned sermon?"

"It's far more dreadful to my mind," said Charles, "to find you so uncharitably disposed."—"Uncharitably!"

"Yes, to be sure. I am innocent, and declare my innocence. Why should you presume upon my guilt?"—"But you have been found guilty."

"And yet am not the less innocent, for human judgment is not infalible."— "But really, you know, it's setting a very bad example for you not to attend the condemned sermon."

"I'm not going to be a hypocrite myself, for the sake of encouraging others to be so likewise."—"Then you won't come?"

"Decidedly not."—"Then I must speak to the sheriffs, sir, and to the authorities, sir, and to the—the—learned recorder, sir, and to everybody else, and we must see what can be done with a refractery man, who will not see his own proper path to glory."

"You may speak to whom you please, sir; and, I must add, that intemperate expressions and passion on the part of a minister of religion, have a great tendency to diminish even respect for religion itself."—"You be—blessed!" said the parson, and he abruptly quitted the cell.

Whatever the reverend gentleman said to the learned recorder and the other authorities, if he said anything at all, it certainly did not induce them to force the attendance of Charles Ormond in the chapel.

The fact is, that a case had occurred some short time previously, in which a condemned man had refused to go, and, upon being asked his reason, had replied that, upon mature conviction, he had turned a Mahometan, and claimed some of the freerights of every one in this country, religious toleration.

This was rather a choker for the parson, so he let the gentleman be hung very quietly, reserving a fling at him until after his decease, when he actually wrote and published his confession of errors, abounding in evangelical expressions, and all the usual nonsensical raving, which is the characteristic of the last moments of those who are said to die in the Lord, as we see occasionally in the obituary of the *Times* newspaper.

It was not until half an hour afterwards that Charles Ormond began to think that he should not be interrupted, and so turned his mind to an attentive consideration of how he should set about his escape.

He turned over and over in his mind the advice that had been given him, and the more he did so the more its possibility appeared to him. He knew perfectly well that there was but one turnkey who had charge of the gate leading from the little court-yard, which was free even to him as a prisoner in the condemned cells during certain hours of the day.

To suddenly rush upon that man, and overpower him, was a thing easy to be done, because, let a man be ever so powerful, let him be taken unawares, his opponent has a decided advantage over him.

But this was the least of the job, and, in his consideration of the chances of success, Charles Ormond felt that he might begin after that point had been concluded, and that all his danger was in threading the various passages, until he reached that little room which had been described to him by the solicitor, through which he had to pass, in order to reach the governor's passage, and an egress from the prison.

Hour after hour he remained alone, and wrapt in contemplation, and at length he could come to no other determination than that he would essay the adventure on the first opportunity which presented itself to him to do so.

"I will not wait," he said, "with any vain hope of bettering my chances, although from what has been said to me by the friendly attorney, I believe I shall have a week before me for consideration as well as for action; but I will not wait, and, let the time come when it will, when I see an opportunity for commencing my undertaking, then at once will I commence it, and stand or fall by its chances."

Some food was now brought to him, of which he was really in need; for, since now a chance had presented itself to his mind of a rescue from an ignominious death, an appetite had sprung up in him which before the state of loneliness and despair into which he had fallen had prevented him from feeling.

By some singular arrangement in the economy of our gaols, a suspected man, and one whom the bar assumes to be innocent until he be found guilty, is fed very badly; but, when he is found guilty, he is allowed to have just what he likes.

Charles Ormond was therefore politely asked what he would choose, and he took care to partake of a hearty meal, which should assist to nerve him for the dangers he had to encounter.

He succeeded likewise in finding out from the man that, for an hour or two before sunset, he would be permitted to walk in the court-yard adjoining to his cell; and, the moment he heard so much, he made up his mind that then he would attempt to make his escape, let the consequences be what they might.

"Freedom," he said, "may be mine, and I may sleep beneath a different roof than this to-night. Oh! if I could but look upon the green fields, hear the song of birds, see the sweet sunshine sparkling through the forest trees, and, more than all, if I could but look upon the face of Marian, what rapture would be mine! and it may be so sooner perchance than I expect."

Absorbed in these pleasant reflections and anticipations, he waited, with what amount of patience he could exert, for the time when it should be announced to him that he might walk in the court-yard, an announcement which, he hoped, would be, to a certain extent, the prelude to his deliverance.

CHAPTER XXXIII.

THE REPRIEVE FOR A WEEK.—MARIAN'S ILLNESS.

THE attorney who had promised Marian that he would procure a reprieve for Charles Ormond, was as good as his word. In fact, had he not known that he possessed the power to accomplish so much, it is very unlikely that he would have made the promise he did; for he was one of those exceptions to the general rule, an honest lawyer, and extremely chary of leading any one astray.

His only fear in the whole transaction was, that, notwithstanding all his explanations, and all he could do or say to induce a proper understanding with regard to the affair, that Marian would consider that there was some hope of total safety for Charles Ormond, in consequence of the reprieve.

This we know he had done his utmost to place correctly before her, and consequently it would be none of his fault if she fell into the error.

He did not like to call upon her again until he had actually obtained the reprieve, so, when he left Charles, he set about it in real earnest, going to a friend whom he had, who was at once likely to be able to do it, by writing a line to the minister.

This friend, upon the attorney telling him that it was hoped evidence in favour of the prisoner could be adduced, if a week's reprieve were granted, wrote the required note, and the business was all done within about a couple of hours.

A government messenger was sent down to Newgate with the reprieve, while the attorney himself hastened to Marian, to tell her of his success so far, and again implore her to put the correct and only construction upon the affair which it ought to bear.

He likewise wished to consult with the Whiteheads upon the propriety of their immediately, or, at all events, as soon as possible, giving up the expensive house in which they lived, and retiring to some other quiet country abode similar to that which they had left upon the great change taking place in their affairs, in consequence of the result of the late Mr. Whitehead's Indian speculations.

He was received by Mrs. Whitehead, who wore an appearance of great distress, and, upon his inquiring if there were any additional cause, beyond those with which he was already acquainted, for her unhappiness, she led him into a small room, and, requesting him to be seated, proceeded to explain to him her fears.

" Sir," she said, " I would not mention it to another person for the world—it's too dreadful almost to think of; but the fact is, I cannot help suspecting that poor Marian's troubles have touched her mind a little—she seems wandering and unhappy; at times, too, she answers me strangely, and evidently scarcely knows what she says, or where she is."

" Oh! madam, you must expect such a result as this; you should consider what great cause for distress she has, and how likely it is to affect her powerfully."

" I do, I do; but yet it's very dreadful."—" It certainly is, I admit; but still you must view it as one of those effects of grief which will wear off."

" I hope to Heaven it may."—" Be assured it will. Time will do for her as much as it always does for those who suffer mentally. No doubt this is the severest shock she has experienced, or ever will experience; but the impression will become less and less, until in a few years it gradually wears away, becoming but the reminiscence of what it now is."

" Well, you've given me new hopes. It is not the loss of fortune that I care about so much, although that grieves me for Marian's sake, because you will understand that the annuity is granted to me, and not to her, and so I understand it ceases with my life; but, if her mind becomes weakened, I think I shall go mad myself."

" Do not look forward to such a catastrophe; it is extremely unlikely to happen; and, if it does, it is one of those calamities which human prudence cannot obviate; therefore is it that I say you should not think of it so as to allow it to disturb your equanimity."

" Well, well, sir, will you see her, and judge for yourself?"—" I've come purposely to see her, and should be much disappointed if I left without doing so."

" Come up stairs, sir; she is sitting all by herself, and with such a thoughtful expression of countenance, it make's one's heart bleed, poor thing, to look upon her. Alas! alas! I never could have thought that in my old age such a string of misfortunes would come upon me. When Mr. Whitehead died, and it was found how poor we were, that was bad enough; but still I had Marian to turn round to, and we were happy in the quietude of our cottage home."

" Well, well, do not despair; time may do something for you yet."

He ascended the staircase, preceded by Mrs. Whitehead, until they reached the room in which she said Marian was. The first glance which the attorney got of her, convinced him that the mother's description of her depressed state was not overcharged in any degree, for she looked the very picture of unutterable woe. The moment she saw the attorney, she rushed forward and caught him by the hands, exclaiming,—

" You have seen him, sir, you have seen him—tell me that you have seen him. They have not murdered him yet?"

" Marian, Marian, compose yourself," he said; " I had hoped to find you actuated by better feelings. Where is now your courage and your confidence?"

" Lost, all lost," she said, mournfully; " how could I maintain it in the face of such dreadful disasters! Have you saved him, sir? but no, your looks proclaim that you have not. All is lost, and I have no friend."

" Now, Marian, is this just to me to make such a remark?"—" No, no, no; but can you expect justice from one who is heartbroken? Bear with me, sir, I know not what I say."

" There needs no apology, Marian, from you to me. Heaven knows how much, and how sincerely I pity you. If by encountering personal risk, or by any personal sacrifice whatever, I could benefit you, it should be done cheerfully; but you should recollect, that to all human miseries there is a certain clear and defined limit—fix your eyes upon that, tell yourself that it can go no further, and then build up the fabric of your better hopes in the world which is to come."

" Your words fall intelligently and clearly upon my heart—I ought to feel their force; but speak to me of Charles, speak to me only of him. What said he—how looked he?"

" He bears up with a noble and a gallant confidence against the frightful blow of fate which has so depressed him."

" I must seek him, and remain with him even until the last."—" Nay, Marian, that would not be permitted; besides, he is saved for a week."

" Saved—a week—what is that I hear?"—" Why, gracious heavens, you understood all that before."

She clasped her head with her hands, as she said, in a low voice,—

" My brain reels, I do not know myself. Memory leaves me when I have most need of it. Heaven help me, I do remember now. There was to be a reprieve, but from it was to be gathered no hopes."—" Exactly."

" No flattering balm to the wounded spirit was to spring from that reprieve. It was but danger put off, yet still as dangerous."

" You rightly understood it; I hoped that you would so. And now, Marian, let me implore you not to attempt to visit Newgate for some days. When you do go, I will attend you there; but do not go without me. I wish to exact this promise from you that you will not."

" I feel," she said, after a moment's pause, " I feel that I ought to promise you, and I will do so. You have been too good a friend to me and mine to ask for any promise that I can give in vain."

" Place it in what light you like, so that you make me the promise; because I know that it is one for your own advantage. If I did not feel so much, I should be the last to ask it of you; and now, Marian, it becomes necessary that your mother and I should make arrangements for your leaving this house—both of you. It is one to which your means are inadequate, and, consequently, one in which you could not feel happy."—"Not until all is over," said Marian. "I implore you, sir, let us remain here until all is passed."

"I advise you to the contrary, but I will not oppose you."—"A thousand thanks. We will go, sir, when the tragedy is concluded."

She shuddered as she spoke, and a strange, wild expression crossed her countenance. The attorney, as he noticed it, could not help glancing at Mrs. Whitehead, as much as to say, "Did you see that?" and she answered him with a nod and a sigh.

He, then, soon rose to go, intimating to Mrs. Whitehead that, as they were not to remove for a week, it would be unnecessary just then to trouble her with any business connected with pecuniary affairs.

"Remember, though," he said, as he was departing, "that I do not yet give up all hope of wresting from Godfrey some of his ill-gotten money. I will take an opinion with regard to the means which he employed to get from you your signature to the agreement which you have last entered into with him; at all events, if we can frighten him out of a larger allowance, we will."

After he was gone, Marian's mind seemed to wander more and more, and, now and then, she almost seemed to forget Charles Ormond's dreadful situation; a dreadful kind of fatuity seemed to be coming over her, which her mother trembled to observe ; and, in the shadow of that new and most frightful of all evils, insanity, Mrs. Whitehead felt as if she could forget every minor calamity completely.

She watched, with the most attentive diligence, every change in Marian's countenance, sometimes gathering materials for hope and sometimes for despair.

This was very dreadful, and the apprehension that Marian's reason would not stand the shock of the execution of Charles Ormond began to haunt poor Mrs. Whitehead like some grim and horrible spectre, which she could never banish from her memory.

Now she began to watch Marian with all that dreadful nervous anxiety that the mere dim likelihood of such a catastrophe taking place was sure to produce.

Mrs. Whitehead was not one of the most imaginative women in the world ; but still she saw, or fancied she saw, enough to convince her that her suspicions were not all in vain, and that poor Marian's reason was already a little shattered by the misery she had gone through.

Terrified beyond all former terror that she had ever in her life experienced, she hastily went to a physician, to whom she stated the case.

He heard her with the profoundest attention, and when she had concluded, he said,—

"It is impossible for me to deny, madam, that what you have said to me is invested with the gravest suspicion ; but still, we must not jump too hastily to a conclusion that the very worst possible consequences are to ensue from this mental depression of your daughter."

"But what am I to do, sir?"

"Reason with her upon the subject, and get, if you can, some judicious friend to do so likewise ; and, above all, if you can persuade her to such a step, take her away from London immediately, so that she may be surrounded with other scenes and other associations than will recall to her the memory of her miseries."

This was judicious advice, there can be no doubt, if it could be followed; but Mrs. Whitehead seriously doubted if anything would induce Marian, just at that juncture, to leave London. The physician, however, promised to call upon her in the course of the day, and so Mrs. Whitehead left him, with that sort of hopefulness which a recital of one's griefs to anybody who listens calmly, sympathisingly, and patiently to them, is likely to produce.

When, however, she reached home, she found that a change very greatly for the worse had taken place in Marian, and that she was seriously ill, and at times a little delirious.

In the greatest agony of apprehension, she awaited the arrival of the physician, who, towards the latter part of the day, made his appearance.

"Oh! sir," exclaimed Mrs. Whitehead, "she is much worse than her condition this morning warranted me in telling you."—"Indeed! Well, well, do not alarm yourself. After all, perhaps, some bodily indisposition may have the effect, as it often does, of withdrawing the mind from too close a contemplation of its griefs. Will you permit me to see her?"

The weeping Mrs. Whitehead led the way up stairs to Marian's chamber, and had she been skilled in the expression of the physician's face, she would have seen that he regarded the condition of Marian with grave apprehensions.

It was not likely, however, that he would make any such remark; but after a time he said,—

"It appears to me, madam, that now will be your time for making an effort to get this young lady away from London."

"What, now, sir; ill as she is?"—"Yes; let me strongly advise you to do so. She is not in a state of mind to offer any opposition, and the probability is, that you will, with very little difficulty indeed, now succeed in removing her from the immediate neighbourhood of scenes and events which are calculated to prey much upon her intellect."

"It shall be done, then, sir. It shall be done."—"Let it be so, and to-morrow, if possible."

"We are differently situated," added Mrs. Whitehead, "to what we were when fortune placed us in this house. Our temporary wealth has gone from us, and a change becomes absolutely necessary. We came to London from a little cottage abode, some distance out of town, and to some such an one must we return."

"It will be the best thing for your daughter's health you can do, madam, whatever your means might be, I assure you. But mark me; it is not anything in the shape of seclusion that she requires; it is quiet and gentle occupation—few and cheerful visitors, so that her mind should be kept in as even a state of serenity as possible."

The physician took his leave, and Mrs. Whitehead, scarcely able to refrain from tears, sat down by the bed-side of Marian to think of the immediate means of effecting the change which the physician recommended. She had not sat long, before Marian spoke to her.

"Mother—mother!" she said, "who has been here?"—"Only a friend, my dear, to inquire how you were. Are you better, Marian, than when you last spoke to me?"

"Yes. Has Charles come home?"—"Come home!"

"Yes; he said he was not going far, and he has not returned yet. What can delay him, mother? I have had a frightful dream."

Mrs. Whitehead wrung her hands, for she considered that this incoherent language of Marian's was a confirmation of her worst fears, and that she had really become quite distracted.

"Shall I tell you, mother, what a dream I have had, or shall I wait until Charles comes home, and tell him at the same time? No—no; he will smile, and call me superstitious, so I will not tell him; but you shall know, mother. I seldom dream at all; I never did dream aught that looked so like a terrible reality as this vision."

"Well, my dear, compose yourself," said Mrs. Whitehead. "Perhaps you had better not tell me."

"Nay, mother; I am not to be scared at a vision, merely. How my head throbs; and yet it does not ache. Let me think. What was my dream? Ay, I remember, now—I remember, now. Listen, mother,—I was walking in a beautiful garden, full of the choicest flowers, and I was waiting for Charles; but hour after hour passed on, and he came not. I began to get anxious, and the more so as dark clouds began to lour over the sky, and what had been a sunny, smiling landscape, was soon obscured by a kind of half darkness, portentous of a coming storm."

"Yes—yes," said Mrs. Whitehead, who was interested in spite of herself, by what Marian was saying. "Yes, my dear; and what then?"

"The sky grew darker and darker still, until I could see nothing; and then I began to look about me with great anxiety for some place of refuge. I saw at a short distance before me, a faint glimmering light, and, upon reaching it, I found that it proceeded from the entrance to a cavernous-looking place, which, however uninviting it otherwise was, at all events promised me a shelter from the coming storm, which I felt so confident was near at hand. I had not got for, mother, into this place, when I saw placed upon tressels a coffin, partially covered with a black velvet pall."

"Oh, my dear, what could you have been thinking of?"—"I must have been thinking of the dead, mother, surely."

"You must, indeed, my child. And that is all your dream?"—"Not all—not all," said Marian, with a shudder. "But yet, why do I tremble when it was but a dream, and Charles will soon be back again?"

"What has Charles to do with it, my dear?"—"I will tell you. It seemed to me as if some invisible hand was drawing me on in the direction of the coffin. I approached it, and looked at the inscription that it bore; it was this—'Charles Ormond.' Yes, mother, Charles's name was on the coffin lid."

Marian was silent now for some moments, and Mrs. Whitehead was afraid to speak, for fear of giving her some hint that her dream had more of the significance of reality about it than, in the half deranged state of her mind, she imagined.

"Mother," she added, at length, "you say nothing."—"My dear, what can I say? You told me your dream, and, as you know it was but a dream, it requires no comment from me."

"True—true—true. But why does he not come home? Send for him, mother; tell him that I am not well, and then I know that he will soon return. Oh, Charles, Charles, where are you now? it seems an age since I beheld you."

Mrs. Whitehead tried to soothe her as well as she could, and hinted something about going into the country, but it fell unheeded upon Marian's ears evidently; and after a time she dropped into a deep slumber, which had something so profound about it, and death-like, that Mrs. Whitehead, after it had continued for some hours without the smallest interruption, began to get a little alarmed at it, and determined upon awakening her. When she approached her for that purpose, she was still more alarmed to perceive that, to all appearance, she had her eyes open.

"Marian! Marian!" she cried, "are you awake?"

There was no answer; and, with all the terror upon her mind that her child was dead, she rang the bed-room bell furiously, and sent for the nearest medical man, who arrived in all haste.

"No," he said, the moment he beheld Marian, "she is not dead."—"Thank Heaven!" ejaculated Mrs. Whitehead, as she burst into tears.

"This is a kind of trance," said the medical man, after he had listened awhile to the action of the heart, and quite satisfied himself that vitality was going on. "This is a kind of trance, madam, which we call catalepsy. It may last some days, and perhaps for a longer period; but there is no positive, or immediate danger, to life in it, however distressing it may be."

"And will she remain thus?"—"Probably. You must attend to her. Have you any reason to think, that mental affliction, of any kind, has brought on this seizure?"

"Alas! too much—too much."—"Then I have good hopes of a perfect recovery, since it does not arise from any actual disease of the brain. You may entertain the most reasonable expectation of a cure. Medical science can do very little in the case; she will of herself awaken from this trance, which bears so strong a resemblance to death, but is, in reality, so very different a thing."

The medical man gave Mrs. Whitehead minute directions what to do, and when he was gone, she at once sent off for the attorney who had behaved so kindly to them.

That gentleman obeyed the summons as soon as he possibly could; and he was much grieved, when he came, to find what an apparent change for the worse had taken place in Marian's condition. When he was informed of the name of the physician who had been to see her, he at once said that he knew him, and started off to his house, promising to return as soon as he had had an interview with that gentleman.

He was, in a manner of speaking, better than his word; for he brought the physician back with him to see Marian. That practitioner at once confirmed the opinion which had been given by the medical gentleman, who had been by Mrs. Whitehead, in the hurry called in, and then he added,—

"Now, madam, will be the most favourable opportunity you could possibly have of removing Miss Whitehead from London."

"What, sir, remove her in her present state?"—"Yes, certainly. You may take my word for it, that if she is taken to the country now, as she is, in an easy carriage, it will do her more good than town."

"Then, Mrs. Whitehead," said the attorney, "pray leave all the arrangements necessary for such a purpose to me; I have a cottage some short distance off, which is now untenanted; you shall go there, and to-morrow I will remove you and

Marian, and you will at once be rid of the anxiety of this house, and all its heavy expenses and encumbrances."

Poor Mrs. Whitehead knew not how to thank the attorney sufficiently, but he stopped her in her profuse expressions of gratitude, saying,—

"Now, my dear madam, do not say another word upon the subject, I pray you; but when you hear somebody say, as people who are censorious will sometimes, that the lawyers are all rogues, pray do you contradict it, and only stand out for the majority of them coming under that reproach."

"You may depend upon me doing so, sir," said Mrs. Whitehead, with all the seriousness in the world, as if she considered what the attorney said to be a *bona fide* request, which he expected her, out of gratitude to him, to comply with.

He and the physician then left the place, and Mrs. Whitehead, with a full conviction that she was about to leave London on the morrow, proceeded to pack up some few personal articles which belonged to them, and which she intended to take with her.

Now she hoped, that until they got away, and had arrived at the cottage which the attorney had so kindly promised to them, Marian would not recover from her trance, since she had been assured that there was nothing positively dangerous in its continuance for some time.

She would not, however, entrust the task of watching by the bed-side of Marian to any one, but made up her mind herself to sit up by her, at all events, until the morning's light, when, with more confidence, she could trust some one else who had had a good night's repose, and then herself seek such needful bodily refreshment.

CHAPTER XXXIV.

MRS. WHITEHEAD'S NIGHT WATCH.—THE MORNING.—THE CARRIAGE.

IT is a weary and a miserable thing, sitting up to watch all night in a sick chamber, even when affection dictates the duty; but, in this case of Marian, it became more than usually lonely and mind-depressing, because of the condition of absolute stillness in which Marian was, which gave to the affair all the aspect of watching in the chamber of the dead.

Mrs. Whitehead felt this acutely; and now, with a rapid alternation of feeling, which, under the circumstances, we cannot feel surprised at, she felt that she would give worlds if Marian could but speak to her again, even despite all the prudential considerations connected with getting her, while in her present state, without any opposition, into the country.

It must not be imagined, however, that even Mrs. Whitehead lost all recollection of, and all sympathy with, Charles Ormond.

No! Notwithstanding all her own more immediate miseries and troubles, as well as those that were for her in expectancy, she still, during the long and weary hours of that night, thought, with genuine and deep feeling, upon the dreadful fate of the unhappy young man, who had, for her and her dear child, endeavoured to do so much, and had fallen, no doubt, a victim to those very endeavours.

She believed—indeed, we may say that she knew—he was innocent; and what a dreadful thing it was to reflect upon, that there he was, in a condemned cell, awaiting the dread sentence of the law, for a crime which he had not only never committed, but which he had never, even for one moment, contemplated the commission of.

And yet, Mrs. Whitehead could only pity and pray for him. The sacrifice which Marian had thought would have saved him, had not succeeded, although she, Mrs. Whitehead, had made it to the nearly absolute ruin of herself pecuniarily.

These thoughts were too painfully harrassing; and, after trimming the light, she took up a book, and strove to while away some of the long and weary time, by plunging into the realms of fiction.

She read as follows, and became much interested in the wild and strange legend which the tale recorded :—

The moon shed a gentle radiance upon the earth, and no sound disturbed the stillness of the night, save the light wind, that shifted the leaflets and caused a momentary bustle in the forest, and there were no other sounds met the ear.

In the distance were the blue mountain tops, but which now were hidden from human sight, for none could see through the moonlight to so great a distance—for the moon was on the wane, and, though she were unclouded, yet she shed not so full a light as at some other times.

Beneath the boughs of a forest tree, lay three men. They were clad as peasants —though somewhat better clad than most of them ; and they had with them long sticks, and were wrapped up in a large mantle of course materials, but by no means at all uncommon or unusual.

They remained there for some time in utter stillness, and no one man spoke to the other ; but long silence was tiresome, and men cannot long confine themselves to it, when they are not compelled to observe it.

" Will he be here to-night ?" asked one the men of his companions ; " this is the third night."

" The third is a magic number, and one that is always lucky. What will happen to-night, no one knows ; we must wait here, and see," replied one.

" It is near midnight—is it not ?"

" Yes ; but we have to earn our reward, for we have but a part of it yet ; we shall have the other when we take the girl to the fool, O'Connor."

" Ay, ay—so we shall ; but if the girl comes not, what then ? Shall we have to return the money we have not earned ? I say, comrade, we earn something by waiting here in the open air, exposed to the influence of the night."

" And who cares for the influence of the night ? Are we not Irishmen, and hate all foreigners ?"

" 'Tis so—'tis true."

" Then let 's banish all fears. The chief is generous ; but he likes to be faithfully served by those who take his bounty."

" And so he shall, for I will not hang back, though the Great Spirit were to rise up and bid me hold my hand in striking when it was at my enemy's throat."

" Be not rash," replied the first ; " see what vapour is that, that seems approaching us. I should not be surprised if the Great Spirit himself were shrouded in it."

There was a shroud-like vapour that seemed to be advancing towards the spot where the three men lay. On, on it came, without apparent cause. No wind was stirring, save what went in an opposite direction. The three men were amazed, and already had the fear of the supernatural crept over them.

They huddled up together as they saw this singular white vapour approaching towards them. A kind of instinctive knowledge seemed to seize upon them, that there were powers at hand with which they could not contend. They felt there could be no chance of meeting with any help from aught better than themselves, and their purpose was of that nature, that, in the presence of a superior power, they shrank from avowing it.

The white cloud came to the spot where they were, and rested for a moment or two; then it seemed to dissolve, and there stood the form of an old man of immense stature and proportions ; his hair was white, and his robes loose and flowing ; he had, too, an eagle eye.

He gazed upon the cowering party of assassins for a moment or two in anger and sorrow. A threatening frown seemed to hang on his brow, and he remained in that attitude they could not tell how long, for it seemed to them an age.

Finally, after some time, the cloud again arose and enveloped the figure, which glided away unseen by the three terrified men, who hid their faces from the dreadful sight that was before them.

It was some time ere they gained courage to lift their faces towards the spot where lately the spirit had stood, but when they did do so, they found it had vanished.

" Well," said one, " what think you of this, brother ? Have we not had a warning ?"

" We have had a warning, indeed. I will leave the province, and seek service elsewhere."

" Never will I," said he who had spoken boldly from the first; " what I said before will I say now, and stick to it. It shall not be said that I flinched from my work, spectre or no spectre."

" Well said, brother; and yonder come our friends, whom we are to carry to the great Connor."

The men rose up, and stood within the shadow of the tree, beneath which they had been lying, and looked in the direction pointed out by the staff of the foremost, who said,—

" Yonder—just on the brow of the hillock, do you not see the old ruin?"— " Yes, yes."

" Well, below that, to the left."—" I see," replied the same man; " I see them now. How many are there?"

" I know not."—" There are more of them than we bargained for, I'll warrant, and then there will be more blows than will suit some of us, and who'll stand the damage?"

" Who stands for a few blows, when such a prize is to be won by a few strokes from his hatchet?"—" Ay, put on your staff heads, boys, and be in readiness. I'll warrant they will make but little good, whichever way they attempt a resistance."

As he spoke, he produced a small axe, or hatchet; it was fitted to the top of his staff, and when wielded by a strong arm, was a most desperate weapon. The others did the like.

The travellers were now seen advancing towards them from the valley beneath, from whence they had a good view of them.

" There are but four."—" Five, I say," returned another of the bandits.

" Five—ay, but two of them are women, and of no moment to us; you know we have but man to man, and we never ought to shrink from that, especially as we take them at an advantage, for they expect not the attack we meditate."—" Then now for the onset."

" No, wait until they are within reach of our staves. I will give you the signal."

This being agreed to, the whole party stood as mute and still as the trunks of the trees that stood around. In the course of the next ten minutes, when the party of travellers neared the spot gradually, and when within some yards of the spot, they were heard to converse together, and then in a little time the sounds of their voices became distinct on the night air, and one of them said,—

" About three hours more, and we reach the town I spoke of; there you can rest in safety until you are met by your intended bridegroom."—" Alas! it's a long way to travel, and in this country very unsafe, and would I were there."

" There's none would hurt you, save O'Connor, and he knows not you intend journeying this way."—" No one else? We may meet banditti."

" We are well armed in your defence, lady, and can fight for you while we can wield a sword."—" I know you would; but I should lament such a necessity. I tell you I would sooner fall myself than any one should be injured for my sake."

These words were scarcely uttered before three men rushed out upon the unsuspecting travellers, and two out of the three were immediately thrown down, and killed upon the spot, the other drew his sword, and attempted to defend himself, but he was unable to do so, for one of the robbers attacked him behind, and his powerful weapon brought him to the earth a corpse.

The lady attempted to escape the savages who had killed her escort, but she was prevented, and the bridle of her mule was seized, upon one of the men saying,—

" Be satisfied, lady, you must go with us, but you are safe, quite safe. We would not hurt you. Beyond confinement you have nothing to fear."

* * * * * * *

It was near the dawn before the party arrived at a strong castle, which was a most extensive place, with strong fortifications, and a most massive place it was. Here the lady who had been thus unceremoniously captured was placed in a high and square room, in which, according to the custom of the times then, was but little furniture ; and, on the whole, it looked desolate and dreary.

"What place have we here, my lady?" exclaimed the attendant, for such was the other female who was captured with the first. "What kind of vault is this?"—"This, no doubt, is some great chieftain's castle. It's the fashion of the country."

"The fashion, eh? Well, such fashions must surely spring from necessity, and not from taste."—"There seems to be but little in this country that is not designed for some express purpose, either of concealment or of defence."

"And the people, one and all, seem but little better than brigands. Really I don't know that we are any better off than we should be had we been taken by infidels. Indeed I don't know what purpose we may be reserved for."—"We must wait, and see," said the lady. "Time will presently divulge all we would know on that score."

"True, very true ; but what a comfortable idea that is, to wait for miseries of all kinds ; nobody knows what's coming, nobody knows when."—"A truce to your gaiety—I am sad."

"I would we were well out of the country," said the handmaiden. "It's a sorry place to come to. They are half naked, my lady."—"Hark! here comes some one."

At that moment a heavy footstep was heard, and in another instant a door was thrown open, and a stout, red-haired man entered into the apartment. He stopped short when he perceived them, and then with some attempt at courtesy, he said,—

"Welcome, fair lady, welcome to the halls of the O'Connor."—"Indeed!" replied the lady. "I have been brought here by force. I know not you or your castle."

"You must have heard of the O'Connor, lady."—"If I have, I knew him not. But, tell me why I was seized by banditti ? and why my attendants were basely and cruelly murdered, and I myself thus imprisoned?"

"Call it not imprisonment."—"I do."

"Imprisonment then where you rule supreme? Lady, you were about to journey to wed my enemy. I watched, and had you seized, and brought here."—"Could you not face your enemy, and fairly fight him, that you must revenge yourself by attacking unprotected females, and murdering servants ?"

"You are angry."—"And well I may be at such treatment."

"What shall I do to wash away the remembrance of the past, and to appease a lady's anger?"—"To restore those to life you have slain, and to restore me to my friends," replied the lady.

"There were but little policy in that, lady, as little as there is possibility."—"Then at least restore me to my friends, and give me an escort to my journey's end."

"There you are already."—"Nay, I am not. I am far away from all. Cease to be an enemy to one who never thought even evil towards you. If you have the hearts of men, restore me."

"Lady, I would do so, but for one reason."—"And wherefore not ?"

"Because I should have to give up the object of my having got possession of you."—"And in Heaven's name, then, why did you that ?"

"Because I would make you my bride—the mistress of my people, and my broad lands. These are no trifle, lady, which the O'Connor lays at your feet."

"From such a trifle Heaven defend us," exclaimed the lady's-maid. "What, my lady marry a bear—an ill-licked cub—a wild man—a very Orson, without any saviour Valentine?"—"Maiden, I forgot thee. Thy mistress's presence must stand my excuse. The eye sees not the stars when the sun shines ; but let that speak for me ; I am not ungenerous—that fault is not O'Connor's."

"I didn't accuse you. But a substitution of bridegrooms is not one of our customs. The bride admits but of one bridegroom. La! la! the purse is heavy !"

She weighed the purse which the O'Connor flung her, and secured it about her person.

"I pray you," said the lady, "to permit me to return to my friends. We are not used to the ways of this country, and although the deed that has been committed——"—"Nay, think not of it. You are beautiful and young, and the O'Connor knows how to love."

"Ay, but we know not how to do so, when wooed in such a place or under such circumstances. We can never yield to force, save to death; but to nothing on this side of immortality do we yield."—"We shall see. Lady, I would have treated you as my guest: allow me to do so now."

"Treat as you will. We are your prisoners, in fact, and may Heaven watch over us! for we have no other protector—our escort has been murdered."—"I will give you three days to think over this matter; and if, at the end of that time, you adopt the only one that will procure you happiness, you will consent to become the O'Connor's bride.

"And if not?"—"Then force must be used, when persuasion will be of no avail. Take your choice."

The O'Connor left the room, and the lady sunk down on a rude seat, terrified at the threat that had been used towards her by the savage Irish chieftain. Her handmaiden was by her; she sank upon the earth at her mistress's feet.

"Shall we be all murdered?—shall we, indeed, be used in the manner that bad man threatens us, my lady? What a horrible fate is in store for us!"—"Horrible! most horrible!"

"Mercy on us! have we left England to be murdered, and used worse than brutes—to be treated thus, and no redress? Oh, I wish we had never come to this country."—"I would, indeed, we never had."

"But what can we do, my lady; can't we get away—can't we escape from this den?"—"No, no! There is no escape. Who could reach those high and narrow windows?"

"No human being," sighed the attendant. "Mercy on us! who could have supposed such places ever existed?"

"The doors too are strong and firm. There are no means of ingress or egress, beyond what are necessary, you see; there are none that will avail us."

"There's only room to scream in, my lady; we shall certainly be killed and eaten by these Irish."—"God grant that may be the worst," returned the lady.

* * * * * *

The Lady Alice Mowbray had been betrothed to the Irish chieftain; of a province of Ireland, he was king; but his authority was precarious. He desired to marry into a powerful English family, to support him in his wars and on his throne; and, to do this, he offered an immense tract of country to the parents of the Lady Alice.

The chieftain could not leave his dominions, lest, during his absence, his authority should be usurped by some other nobleman of his family or some other family. Thus there arose a necessity of sending the bride over the sea to his dominions.

She was sent; and that, too, with an escort fully suitable to her rank and family. There was a goodly train of men-at-arms and archers, to escort her fairly to her intended bridegroom, who was represented to be young, handsome, and generous, and, above all, kind and brave.

They had but a few short leagues to go, when it was deemed desirable that she should travel with celerity through a certain district, with but few attendants, as with many she would attract attention, and probably bloodshed would have been the result, for the natives would have deemed this a hostile inroad, and have resisted accordingly.

A few leagues more riding would have brought her to the town where she would have been received in the arms of her intended husband. This, however, was all learned by the spies and agents of the O'Connor: a wild and ferocious chief, who held absolute sway over a powerful clan or tribe, and who determined to possess the lady, thinking, if he once secured her, he should ally himself to her family, and secure their aid to aggrandise himself.

When he obtained possession of the lady, however, passion become the stronger, and he determined she should be either his wife or his mistress; and, in his own words, he determined to use force when persuasion failed.

It was elapsed—the three days had gone by, and the O'Connor stood before Alice Mowbray. He had been scornfully rejected, and stood with an eye red and bloodshot with anger and disappointment; and then, suddenly, he seized her by the waist, saying,—

"I see it—I see!—you are my prize!"—"Have mercy, Heaven!" exclaimed the unfortunate lady.

"Heaven may, but I will not," replied the ferocious chief; "you are my prize and my spoil, and as such I will use you. You are mine, irrevocably mine."

A shriek was the only answer that came from the Lady Alice, and a loud laugh responded to it from the O'Connor, but it was suddenly stopped. He released his hold, and staggered; his eye was fixed on some object, and he gasped,—

"The banshee!"

The same mist, or vapour-like cloud, presented itself to his eyes that had been seen by his followers the night they seized upon the lady. The same gigantic figure looked angrily on him; a deep, stern, and frowning aspect, it wore towards him—he shook like an aspen leaf, and could scarce support himself.

The spirit shook its white locks, and then, with a clenched hand raised as if about to strike, it stood stationary a moment, and then it gradually became enveloped in a mist, and disappeared from his eyes. The Lady Alice and her maiden were amazed at this sudden change, for they saw not, nor knew of the cause, but they did see the change.

"Lady," said the O'Connor, in a subdued voice, "you are free, since the great banshee wills it. I cannot fight against destiny; men cannot prevail against the spirit of his sins."—"Free!—free!"

"Ay, lady, to go where you wish."—"Send me back to my escort, so that I may leave the country, and return to England."

"You can be safely sent to your bridegroom," said O'Connor; "my people shall see you safely there."—"No, no; homeward, homeward," exclaimed the Lady Alice; "I will return to my own country, I have suffered enough the short time I have been here."

*   *   *   *   *   *   *

The lady was restored to her friends, and could never be induced to visit Ireland again, and she declared that the only friend she ever met there was a dubious spirit of the other world.

Mrs. Whitehead laid down the book with a sigh, and, on proceeding to the window, she fancied that the day was just beginning to dawn.

At the same moment, too, she heard the sound of carriage wheels, which paused opposite to the house, and she said to herself in surprise,—

"Surely, surely, they cannot have come for us, so soon as this."

CHAPTER XXXV.

THE JOURNEY TO THE COUNTRY COTTAGE.—THE CONTINUED TRANCE OF MARIAN.— NEWS FROM LONDON.

UPON drawing aside the window-blind, Mrs. Whitehead found that her surmise was correct. A carriage had stopped at the door, and, to all appearance, there was no mistake, for the driver descended from his box, and knocked and rung for admission. That it was a carriage which the friendly attorney had brought, for the purpose of conveying her and her daughter to their country abode, was then abundantly proved, by that gentleman himself alighting from it.

Mrs. Whitehead certainly had no idea at all that so sudden and so early a transit, from one house to the other, had been decided upon, and she descended to the dining-room in great surprise, to know if any extraordinary reason was about to be assigned for it. When she reached that apartment, she found the attorney, who, after the compliments of the morning, said to her, earnestly,—

"Madam, I see that you are very much surprised at my presence here so early, but I can give you some satisfactory reason, I think."—"Sir, we ought not to require reasons from you," said Mrs. Whitehead; "we have been so much indebted to your kindness, that your word ought to be a law to us."

"Not so, Mrs. Whitehead, not so. In the first place, let me tell you, that I am anxious myself to go with you to your new house, so that by my presence I may fairly install you in it, and show the woman, who will remain there to attend upon you, that you are really friends of mine, towards whom I wish every attention paid." —"Oh, you are too good to us, sir. And as for any one to attend us, it is what we cannot, and ought not, to expect."

"Nay, Mrs. Whitehead, understand me; it makes no difference to me whatever. The cottage to which you are going is one which I let furnished, and it is only in the height of the summer season that usually I have any tenant in it. So you will understand that I am forced to keep some one there always, who, in a manner of speaking, I let with the cottage."—"I understand, sir."

"Very good; it is empty now, and therefore you can occupy it until you find some place more suited to your liking elsewhere. And now, as my business engagements would not permit me to accompany you at a later period of the day, I have come now, you see, and will breakfast with you if you will endure my company; after which, as soon as may be, we will start."—"Certainly, sir, certainly."

"Then again, you see, Mrs. Whitehead, as poor Marian will have to be lifted into the carriage, it is better that all that should be done and over before any of the neighbours are about to stare at the proceeding, and find food for gossip in it enough to last them, Heaven knows how long."—"I see your reasons, sir, and approve of them all. Breakfast shall be got ready with all possible expedition, and then we will start."

This was done; and by the time the morning meal was despatched, and Mrs. Whitehead had got Marian ready to go, it was about seven o'clock, so that the attorney urged their departure, saying,—

"It is a good hour's drive to the cottage, and so, of course, an hour back. It will likewise take me, I dare say, an hour to see you put all to rights then, and I must be at business by ten, if possible: therefore, now, Mrs. Whitehead, if you are ready, I am."

Upon this hint the good lady bustled about, and soon declared all to be in readiness.

"But," she said, "how is Marian to be placed in the coach?"—"You wrap her up well, like an Egyptian mummy," said the solicitor, "in a blanket, and then I will carry her myself, and place her in the vehicle."

This Mrs. Whitehead did; and although the inert form of Marian was, as may be well supposed, a tolerable weight, the solicitor, who was a stout tall man, carried her down stairs with ease, to all appearance; and Mrs. Whitehead having, by his directions, got into the coach first, he handed Marian in to her, and then himself entered the vehicle. He had given the driver the directions previously, and so off they went.

Marian did not stir in the least; and had she been really dead she could not have been more thoroughly inert than she was.

They had got away exceedingly well. The only persons who had seen the corpse-like shrouded figure brought out of the house, were a milkman and a boy. They, of course, both stopped, but the whole affair occupied so short a space of time that the coach was off before either of them could make a remark upon the subject, although the milkman had immediately placed down his pails, and taken off his yoke, and the boy had sat down on the very step of the door.

"I say," remarked the milkman, when the coach was gone, "young fellow, did you see that, eh?"—"Do you think I've only got one eye," said the boy, "and that at the back of my head, spooney?—Of course I seed it."

"Well, I never! What do you think of it?"—"I hasn't began to think yet."

"Well, then, do begin. I'm flummuxed."—"Here goes, then. Do you serve this here house with milk, old sky-blue?"

"Yes, I does, but none of your names, if you please."—"Very good," said the boy; "then you may depend as somebody has died of the chalk and water you put in it, and that the body as they was taking away in the coach, to be what do they call it, *bisected.*"

See page 224.

"I tell you what, young fellow, if it wasn't for leaving of my milk-pails, mind you, I'd come after you, and give you a good hiding."

After this threat the milkman went on, but the boy was not going to be defeated in that way. What boy, with anything of a boy-like spirit, would, so he went after him, making sundry inquiries concerning his mother's pecuniary resources, and the extraordinary way in which she was suffered to sell one article of furniture, for the sake of purchasing another.

" I'll have you yet," said the milkman.—" Who stole the copper?" said the boy.

And so on they went, until they quite forgot the original object of dispute, and poor heart-broken Marian was far on her journey to the cottage home. Blessed and happy would she have been, and many years of suffering would she have been spared, had she been going to that " bourne from whence no traveller returns."

It was in the neighbourhood of the picturesque and pretty village of Ealing, that the cottage belonging to the benevolent attorney was situated, and Oxford-street was soon traversed, and left far behind.

Then came Notting-hill, Bayswater, Acton, and last of all, Ealing itself, through which the carriage went, and diverging to the left, instead of continuing the road to Hanwell, stopped before the gate of as pretty a little rural cottage as any one could wish to see.

" Here we are," said the attorney, " and it's only five minutes past eight, so that I consider we have done the distance in good time."

A decent looking woman in a widow's cap appeared at the door of the cottage, and in answer to the attorney's inquiry, she said she had received his note, and had prepared everything for the " sick lady "

When, however, she saw Marian lifted from the coach, so enveloped as she was, and so utterly to all appearance lifeless, she looked terrified; but the attorney soon reassured her by explaining the nature of the case, and then she shewed a most feeling and sympathetic nature, eagerly assisting Mrs. Whitehead, who, what with her general state of anxiety, and the flurry incidental to the rapid journey, was really scarcely able to attend to Marian.

The attorney carried her up stairs, and placed her in bed, and then he told Mrs. Whitehead that he must go to town again. He named a medical man resident in the neighbourhood, who she might call in to attend upon Marian, should any fresh symptoms appear, and then leaving her some money for current expenses, he promised that he would see her again in a few days. Before, however, he left, Mrs. Whitehead said to him,—

" Have you any hopes sir, as regards poor Mr. Ormond?"—" But very few and faint hopes," he replied. " Few and faint, indeed."

" Have you heard nothing further of him?"—" Nothing; but you may depend, should anything transpire, that I will let you know, and more especially, too, if it should be anything of a pleasing nature."

" Alas! if Marian should awaken from this trance into which she has fallen, and have sufficient sense left to make an inquiry concerning him, I shall be most sadly put to it to know what to say in answer to her."—" Say as little as possible, Mrs. Whitehead; but beware of giving her any false hopes upon the subject, because they, I fear, would but be eventually disappointed."

" I will be careful, sir."—" Do so; and I have the most sanguine hope that all will yet be well, as regards her health, both of body and mind. Time, you may depend, will do much for her."

He then left for London again, and knowing what we know, of how he had made an effort to save Charles Ormond, by providing him, at all events, with the means of attempting an escape, we can well imagine, as likewise can our readers, what a state of anxiety he was in.

We cannot accuse him of a want of candour in not telling Mrs. Whitehead what was his real and his most substantial reason for wishing to get back to town early, because his motives were correct and good.

The fact was that he felt most peculiarly anxious concerning Charles Ormond, and knowing that he would make the attempt to escape from Newgate, he wished to be in London to hear either of its success or of its failure, the latter being of course by far the most probable.

When he had given the particulars which he had done to Charles, respecting the route he was to take from the prison, he had done so with a conviction, that if he, Charles, or any one else were to escape from Newgate, it must be in that way.

He had not thought of the possibility of such an escape as was actually lately achieved by climbing the angle of a perpendicular wall. He likewise knew, that in the event of the escape proving abortive, Charles Ormond would be in no worse position than he was now in, because that was the very worst, and he felt certain that the authorities, upon the case as it stood, intended to hang him.

The attempt to escape could have no effect, therefore, one way or the other, because, if innocent, it was extremely natural that he should do all that lay in his power to escape an unjust punishment, and if guilty, why they could but hang him after all.

As for Godfrey relenting in any way, that was completely out of the question, because he was so far personally committed, in the evidence which he had given, that his own transportation must follow as a consequence his indictment for perjury.

The only chance for Charles, therefore, was in his escape from Newgate, and the only chance that that escape should be successful, consisted in its absolute terrifying boldness and singularity.

In order to render this part of our narrative, which is one of great interest, as clear as possible, we may as well follow Mr. Blake, the attorney, upon his arrival in town, to his chambers, where, as he seemed fully to expect, a young man of the name of Jeffries was waiting to see him.

This young man he had shown into his own private room, and after the double doors, by which it was defended from listeners, were closed, there ensued between them a short consultation, which will place our readers in a good position, as regards a knowledge of what the attorney was endeavouring to do for Charles Ormond, always provided he did succeed in gaining the street.

"Has anything occurred, Mr. Jeffries?"—"Nothing, sir; Mr. Clark, by your orders, relieved me at eight o'clock this morning, and is now keeping strict watch in the Old Bailey."

"Well, that's quite right; and when do you go back?"—"At twelve o'clock, sir."

"Of course you have made every other arrangement?"—"Yes; I took a number of old keys with me late last night, and as it was a very dark night, indeed, I climbed over the iron rails of St. Paul's, nearly opposite to Doctor's Commons, with a perfect confidence that I was observed by no one."

"That was right. It was a dark night. Did you find a key to fit the door?"—"I did, sir; and made my way through the very small low door you and I had looked at, if you recollect, sir, into the vaults of St. Paul's; and I will say, sir, that as a place of concealment, the least likely of all to be dreamt of by any of the authorities, there cannot be its equal. You perceive, sir, it is in the centre of danger, and yet presenting such features of perfect security."

"It is, indeed."—"I will venture to assert, that if Mr. Ormond once gets clear of Newgate, he will be as safe there until all pursuit is over, as if he were a hundred miles away, and perhaps a great deal safer."

"I am quite of that latter opinion of yours. Any hiding-place for an escaped prisoner should be as near as possible to the gaol from whence he has flown."—"It should, sir."

"Have you taken any further steps?"—"Yes; I have placed there provision enough, at all events, to last two weeks, or perhaps three, and Mr. Clark has now the key, which he will hand to me, when I relieve his guard."

"But this escape, you know, may be in daylight, and in that case, what is to be done?"—"Nothing particular; but just go to the parlour of some public-house not so close at hand, that it is likely to be frequented by any of the officers about the courts, or any of the officials of the gaol, but yet not so far off as to be much out of the way."

"That looks tremendously daring."—"It does, sir. It does look tremendously daring, and that is the very circumstance which will make it successful. Let him once get clear of Newgate, which, between you and I, sir, I don't think he will, and I will answer for all the rest."

"I hope to Heaven he may. You would then at night remove him to St. Paul's?"—"Yes, assuredly; and once there, I shall consider his life saved, unless he catches a cold in those horrible vaults, the dampness of which, even now, since my visit, clings to my clothes."

" Better die of a cold, than by the hands of the hangman."—" I think so, too."

" Well, Jeffries, you will be sure to let me know the moment anything occurs, or as soon afterwards, at all events, as you can do so with safety. I suppose Clark knows fully what to do ?"—" Oh ! yes, sir, quite so. He is an adept at these kind of affairs, and has been my coadjutor in a number of them, so you need have no fears on that head at all."

" I have none. You know that I repose in you. Your reward in this case shall be prompt and ample."—" We have never had any reason, sir, to doubt your libe-rality," said Jeffries ; " and now, if you please, I will go and lie down for an hour or so, before I go to take Mr. Clark's place ; and I do hope, sir, that all will turn out to your satisfaction in this affair."

CHAPTER XXXVI.

THE QUARREL BETWEEN GODFREY AND NEVILLE, AND THE NEW PARTNER.

SINCE the atrocious attempt which Godfrey had made upon the life of Neville, it was no wonder that a considerable amount of coolness had sprung up between those two worthies. It will be recollected that Neville had uttered a great many threats against Godfrey, and he was extremely anxious to get from him large sums of money before the execution of Charles Ormond, whose execution he, Neville, might certainly have stopped by a declaration of all the real facts.

He thus kept Godfrey in such a state of dread and agitation, that it was almost enough to lay him upon a bed of sickness through sheer fear. But when the news of the reprieve for a week transpired, which it did early on the Monday morning which had witnessed the departure of the Whiteheads from London, it gave Neville more time to angle with his victim, as the villain Godfrey might truly now be called, while it brought to the latter such an accession of nervous apprehension as nearly to kill him.

Under these circumstances, and as soon as he heard of the week's reprieve, he sent for Neviile, for he had a, to him, dreadful suspicion, that something must have arisen to throw serious doubts upon Charles Ormond's guilt, and in that case, his, Godfrey's, safety must be implicated.

Part, indeed, of that retribution which Godfrey, for his misdeeds, might be con-sidered to have most richly merited, might now be well said to have commenced in the many terrors which beset him, on account of this reprieve which had been granted to Charles Ormond. Could he but have guessed the motives which induced the reprieve, he would have been able to relieve himself from a world of anxiety ; but that he could not, for it never, for one moment, entered into his imagination to conceive that Charles Ormond owed the protraction of his existence for another week partly to the strong personal interest which the attorney had, and partly to the anxious wish of the authorities that he should be hung, according to precedent, on a Monday. It seemed to Godfrey an age before Neville made his appearance, and he had the additional horror, before that most virtuous character did come, of being a prey to the most alarming apprehensions.

Neville showed that he, too, had his fears as he walked into the counting-house of Godfrey, but when he had done so, he closed the door behind him carefully, and looked at Godfrey with an air of suspicion, as he said,—

" Are we alone ?"—" Yes," said Godfrey, giving a furtive glance around his own office, " we are alone, Neville, so far as earshot goes, unless you have any intention of raising your voice particularly loud."

" You are more like to raise your own," growled Neville ; " you have a greater propensity to do so than I."

" How know you that ?"—" It is useless to ask one like me what I know of a man like you ; we know each other, and therefore something like honour ought to be between us "

" Eh ?" said Godfrey.—" Honour among thieves, you know, since you want one to speak plain."

"To what do you allude?"—"You may as well tell me," said Neville, "what you want me here for? I came because you sent for me; here I am—but how long I shall have freedom enough to do it, you and some other friend only knows."

"I sent for you to arrive at some understanding about this affair of Charles Ormond."

"Well."—"How is it he has obtained a reprieve? he will not be hanged at least for a week, and then who's to tell what may happen to convert the reprieve into a pardon?"

"As to that, Godfrey, you know more of it than I; and it strikes me you'll burn your fingers in meddling with such a fire; you'd better let him hang, and rid yourself, and me too, of an inconvenient life."—"That is all very well," said Godfrey, with a diabolical sneer, "to talk in that manner; but you must know, as well as I, there must be something going on behind the curtain to cause them to grant a reprieve."

"Well, and suppose I do."—"Why, what can that something be, but what tends to injure us both?"

"Injure us both! what, do you imagine," said Neville, sharply, "that by sending for me, and telling me this, that I am to be blinded and hood-winked?"—"What do you mean?" inquired Godfrey.

"That you must be the cause of all you complain; you must have been the cause of all this bother; it'll all come upon your own shoulders—you're only heaping hot coals upon your own head, come what may."

"It is all very well to carry it off thus, Neville; but I tell you honestly, I believe you have been trying your hand at mischief."

"And wherefore?"—"Out of mere revenge against me; but you are mistaken, it will be your own injury as much as mine; for remember, whatever you may have done to throw any doubt upon the evidence, it must injure you as much as it can me; when I swing, you'll not be safe—your life won't be worth three minutes' purchase."

"Now you are trying to make me believe you have done nothing yourself. Now look here, Godfrey; you want the property, there's no doubt about that; you have got it, but you may endeavour to weaken the evidence by some underhanded move of your own; you have a revenge against me as well as Charles Ormond—you know you have."—"Well, and so you have against me; and when you have made me angry, you complain at my being so."

"Well, that shows plain enough how the case stands."—"Pho! pho!"

"Don't 'pho' me Godfrey; it's an understood thing; you are tampering with the execution; I am sure of it, and you want to put the onus of Ormond's affair upon me."—"You, Neville, are doing the same thing. You imagine that I don't know you well enough to take all this in good part, but we had better understand each other."

"Ah, I understand you, fast enough; you must not fob me off in this way, Godfrey; I know you."—"No, you mean, Neville, I know you."

"Then we may as well be confidential," replied Neville; "you had better be made fully aware that you are playing the fool in this matter; I will not be a sacrifice to your treachery."—"Treachery!"

"Yes, your treachery, Godfrey; I know you are well capable of anything like villany and treachery."—"Come," said Godfrey, "this is carrying matters too far; you are not the man to call names, at all events. I sent for you here in consequence of what has taken place elsewhere."

"Well, now I am here, what is it you have to say to me? I can listen."—"Very well. What is known in this affair?"

"To whom?"—"To you and to me, or any one else, if you have tampered with any one in this matter."

"Now, by God!——"—"Pho! pho!" said Godfrey; "that's all very well, Neville; but you know, as well as I do, that what implicates one, will and must implicate the other."

"I do know that, Godfrey."—"Well then, remember it; for you may depend upon it, that when one falls, the other sinks with him. I have made up my mind to that much."

"And so have I. Hark ye, Godfrey; you may imagine you can play your cards with me as easily as you could with Charles Ormond."—"Well."

"But you are miserably mistaken in your man, if you imagine, for one moment, you can succeed with me as you have with him: no, no, it will not do, Godfrey." "This is playing to cross purposes, Neville."

"So it seems."—"And one of us must be candid," continued Godfrey, quietly, and looking hard at Neville.

"Which of us is to believe the other ?"

Here was a pause, and Godfrey seemed puzzled what to say, or how to proceed; but after a few moments' pause, he said, in a low tone,—

"You must know, Neville, that we both row in the same boat." Neville nodded. "And that what will drown one will cause the other to sink also—there can be no doubt about that."—"None, whatever."

"Then, having agreed to that, we may as well come to this affair of Ormond's reprieve."—"I think we may," said Neville."

"Well, then, how comes it that his execution is put off for a week ?"—"I really don't know; but I suspect you know a great deal more than you choose to say. You don't usually confer in this way."

"I have not usually sufficient cause but to proceed; it must arise from some doubt as to the questionableness of the evidence, and so on."—"I thought so when I heard it."

"Exactly my own case; it is a thing they could not do, unless they had some doubt about the evidence, as I said before, and that doubt must be injurious to us."—"It will be, if it is to one."

"Eaxctly; and any injury arising from that quarter, will put our necks in jeopardy."—"So it will; if mine's endangered," said Neville; "you may depend upon it yours will be, for I will not fall unrevenged. I will bring you down with me; I remember more things of you, than you of me."

"I know enough to hang you; and if I had five hundred facts against you, they could do no more."—"Why, one hanging is quite enough for any man, Godfrey," said Neville, "as you will find when it comes to your turn, as it most certainly will, if you breathe a word about one of that. I am resolved—I am not fearful, for I always make my mind up, so, if you have anything to say about that, you had better do so at once."

"Well, well," said Godfrey, "as I said before, we row in the same boat; and when one sinks, the one will follow the other—that's my mind."—"And mine, too," replied Neville.

"You see," said Godfrey, "that though you may imagine that the first come is first served in these cases, it's not so much that, as those who have the most to tell."—"What do you mean ?"

"Why, if you should imagine, that, because you went and divulged the whole affair to the Home-office, you would get a free pardon, you would be mistaken; for, if I were to tell all, you would, of a certainty, be hanged."—"I don't doubt it."

"Therefore, do not imagine, that, because you may be first, you can gain anything."—"I haven't been."

"How is it he is reprieved ?" again asked Godfrey, with an uneasy glance; "that fact says something."—"It does."

"Well, then, I am unable to understand it otherwise than that somebody has been moving in it in a manner they ought not Now, recollect, that you have done more in this matter than I. You concocted and carved out the plan, and swore the forgery was not my handwriting, and that you know is the fact."

"Now, you think you are playing a very cunning game. You forget you have attempted murder."

"What do you mean ?"—"Did you not attempt to poison me ? And why did you make that attempt? Because you thought that I knew too much, a great deal too much; and while I lived, you believed you were not safe."

"Well."—"Well, indeed; and since we are not upon other than angry terms, I may as well tell you that you are not safe so long as you play these games. We know each other, Godfrey, and you would not trust me, nor I you, further than I could swing on by the tail, and that is not far."

"No, indeed."—"Well, then, as we both row in the same boat, let us do it to mutual advantage."

"I wish it to be so."—"Exactly; that's just and liberal; but you're very fond of making good propositions, Godfrey, but no beneficial practical result ever flows from them."

"That's the misfortune of being thwarted, and having no confidence in those whom I trust."—"You may have as much trust in me as you please, Godfrey. I have ever kept your secrets; they have been part my own, and yet I have never divulged them."

"I tell you what, Neville; after the last affair we had together, you don't think I could trust you?"—"And why not? I did all I undertook to do, amply and fairly, and most successfully. What more would you have from any man's exertions?"

"I don't complain of that—that was all right enough—it is of subsequent events I complain of."—"You don't mean to say you hadn't enough for your money? Look at what you had from the Whiteheads. Come, Godfrey, it's useless carrying on this kind of deception any longer. I am not the man you take me for, an easy fool, who don't mind putting his own neck into a halter to oblige another, and then feeling a power of gratitude if he gets a trifle in return. You've made a devilish good harvest out of my exertions, and ought to have more gratitude than to wish me out of the way."

"Who does when you do right?"—"You do. You have made one attempt to put me out of the way; and here's another; now, if that ain't proof, what is, I should like to know? It won't do, Godfrey—it won't, indeed."

"Well, it seems we can't come to any understanding. I suppose you won't confess, and repair the evil as far as you can; but, rely upon it, you will be as great a loser as I, by meddling with Charles Ormond."—"I know that, and I am not the fool to do it; but I suppose you are probably under the idea that I shall be sacked in guilty, and swallowed up. But no—no, Godfrey; don't imagine, for one moment, that I am such a man; you might hang me, but curse my heart if you don't hang too."

There was a moment or two's pause, and Godfrey evidently didn't know what to do. It was evident Neville was either innocent or obdurate. He couldn't believe in anything else; the latter was the most probable; but why he should do it, he could not tell. There was one thing, however, that Neville saw and admitted—his own danger. He appeared also—it might be appearance only—he appeared to be very uncomfortable, under the idea that all this affair had a doubt thrown over it, and a fear also, that he, Godfrey, had been playing the traitor.

But then there was no guarantee but that this might all be affectation; he might be the traitor he affected to believe that he, Godfrey was; there was no trusting to appearances.

Thus it ever is between two men, placed as these are, ever requiring each other's aid, and yet fearful of the consequences. A man who cannot trust his fellow man is unhappy, indeed; but how much worse is he who, having placed good name, fortune, and even life, in the power of a mercenary villain, yet fears each day he may be brought to ignominy and death.

Such, however, was the situation of Godfrey. He knew his position well; he knew what he depended upon, and heartily did he wish his companion in iniquity were out of the way, and he would, without doubt, have secured his attendance upon Pluto in the shades below, but for the dread of failure and detection, two very powerful motives.

"I see," said Godfrey, "we must come to an understanding for the future.'

—"Exactly. You won't believe me, nor I you. What now can we do?" said Neville.

"Well, be that as it will, what will injure the safety of one, will injure the safety of the other."—"Of the truth of that I am fully impressed," said Neville, "and I hope that you are so too, and that you will well weigh and remember it before you act, because it is very true, indeed ; and I shall make it so if my safety is endangered."

"Very well ; we both row in the same boat ; let us pull both the same way."—"Agreed."

"When this affair is all over, then we can breathe freely and safely," said Godfrey.—"Exactly. But as you observed but just now, we do row in the same boat, and we ought to row together."

"So we ought."—"Well, since I was here last, I have been unfortunate, and lost my money."

"Unfortunate," said Godfrey, in dismay.—"Yes, I am doing nothing—nothing at all. I have ample leisure, and will come and row in the same boat with you, to show my sincerity."

"What do you mean?"—"That I will come here and assist you in your business ; you must require aid."

"I—I—don't."—"Ah, but you do," said Neville.

"I tell you I do not, and will not have anybody. I know best what I want."—"Indeed you don't. I tell you, Godfrey, that you want somebody like myself to help you. I am about nothing. What can be more gratifying than one friend helping another? I will be that friend to you, Godfrey."

"You, Neville—you ———"—"Yes. Why, how you stare ! You wanted to be convinced of my sincerity—you told me we rowed in the same boat, and that our interest is one. I am fully impressed with this belief, and I am moreover fully prepared to act up to this belief, and show you how sincere I am in my belief."

"Well?"—"I say I will show you. I fully believe and appreciate the proposition that we row in the same boat. I see that you would like your safety insured. I will do it ; for I will come and row along with you, and be your partner in the business."

"My partner?"—"Yes ; and a very fair offer it is, to relieve you of half the cares and anxieties of your business."

"D——n !"—"Come, come, Godfrey, no exclamations. You know you ought to be grateful for the offer."

"I'll not submit to this. You had better leave the house. I'll not have it."—"But you must, and shall. Godfrey, understand me ; row in the same boat,—we share and share alike ; profit or loss, ease or danger, it's all one. Our interests must not be separated."

Godfrey, with a sudden impulse, rushed at Neville, who was by no means backward in a personal encounter with anybody, much less where he was sure of victory. They had hardly closed in a scuffle, when a footstep was heard, and the door handle turned. They had scarcely time to separate before the door was opened, and a clerk entered.

"What do you want?" inquired Godfrey, suddenly, and savagely.—"A letter, sir, for you," said the clerk, who gave a jump at the manner in which Godfrey spoke.

"A letter?"—"Yes, sir, for you ;" and the clerk handed it to him.

Godfrey took the letter, and said,—

"That will do."

The clerk retired, leaving Godfrey and Neville alone, much disturbed, lest they should have been overheard.

"Your stupid attempt at violence, Godfrey, has possibly resulted in the detection, or overhearing us."—"I think he could not."

"Indeed he could. I'll be bound he had his ears as well as his eyes open."—"Do you think so?"

See page 231.

"Indeed I would, were I in similar circumstances. I can tell you he's drunk all in."

"I'll see to that," said Godfrey; "but, in the meantime, you had better leave quietly. If anything goes wrong, you'll be the first that's taken."—"But not the first to be hung," said Neville, daringly.

"Be that as it may, you needn't make the time you have to live shorter than necessary."—"No, no," said Neville; "I'm not afraid of that; and I tell you what, Godfrey, when we both come out to the drop together, as I'm persuaded we shall, you shall see that I'll die like a man; see you do the same."

As he spoke he gave a leer of delight at the uncomfortable feelings he seemed to have caused in the mind of Godfrey.

"But I'll see you another time, Godfrey," said Neville, as he prepared to leave. "I suppose you have said all you intended to say?"—"Yes, yes," said Godfrey.

"Then I shall see you, I dare say, soon enough; but, depend upon this, that whatever you do to place me in danger will recoilon your own head ; for, as sure as you are a living man, I'll hang you."

Neville spoke with so much savage earnestness, that Godfrey, had he been inclined to do so, could not have doubted his sincerity of purpose. He left the counting-house of Godfrey, who felt much disturbed at what had taken place. He could now well see the spirit with which he was leagued, and which he had called up to his aid.

" I will call him in," he muttered, alluding to the clerk, who had so inopportunely entered the counting-house just at that juncture. " I will call him in, and ascertain whether he does or not know ; that will be some satisfaction, at all events, and a guide as to how to act."

He rung his office bell, and in a moment afterwards the same clerk who had before entered now came in.

" Well," said Godfrey, " what made you come in just now, when I was engaged with some one ?"—" If you please, sir, I didn't know you were engaged with any one, or I should not have come."

" You did not ?"—" No, sir."

" Now, tell me truly what you saw when you came in this room ? Tell me the truth ?"—" Yes, sir. I saw you and Mr. Neville."

" Well ?"—" That was all," said the clerk. " I saw nothing more ;" and he stood waiting to be dismissed.

" And what did you hear ?" inquired Godfrey ; " tell me that truly, as you hope for my favour ?"—" I heard nothing at all, sir."

" Nothing at all ? Why, I am sure we spoke loud enough to have been heard in the office."—" Indeed, sir, I heard nothing. There were, it is true, the sound of voices, and that was all."

" What did the voices say ?"—" Say, sir ? I don't know ; they were so confused, that I couldn't learn or understand anything."

" Are you sure of that ?" inquired Godfrey.—" Quite, sir."

" Then you must have listened," said Godfrey, suddenly turning to the terrified clerk.—" Indeed I didn't, sir. I assure you I wouldn't be guilty of the slightest attempt of the kind."

" Well, we will let it be so ; but, mind you, if you have heard a word that has been spoken in confidence between me and another, and if you dare breathe it again, remember, if not a dead, you are at least a ruined man. The fate of Charles Ormond, who was also here, shall be yours, depend upon it. I will follow you to the end of the world. You may now go ; but remember what I have told you."

CHAPTER XXXVII.

THE ATTEMPTED ESCAPE OF CHARLES ORMOND FROM NEWGATE, AND ITS RESULT.

HAVING thus far proceeded in our narrative, giving, as we felt bound to do, a preference in our descriptive scenes to the beautiful, but sadly persecuted Marian Whitehead, let us now turn our promised attention to the condemned cell in Newgate, where Charles Ormond remained, with the hope clinging to him that the attorney had imparted, by the welcome gifts which he had made to him.

It was something to believe in the possibility of an escape from the dreadful doom which was so unjustly assigned to him ; and, although he was able to dis-tinguish with an accurate judgment between what we might call the execution of the badly administered law in his case, and the law itself, yet, at the same time, he felt that the great principle of human nature, self-preservation was an amply sufficient justification for him in opposing by force all who might endeavour to retain him in his unjust imprisonment.

Charles Ormond was just the person to regret the necessity of having to use violence, for the purpose of endeavouring to effect his release. But he told himself that he could not sit down supinely, and put up with a flagrant injustice, because other men thought they were doing their duty.

"I, too, have a duty to perform," he told himself; "a duty to my Creator, who gave me life, and a duty to myself, which consists in its preservation."

He resolved, therefore, without the slightest hesitation—for he felt that he was right, and that to hesitate would have been unpardonable weakness—to seize the first good opportunity that occurred to possess himself of the keys of the gaoler who had the special charge of the court-yard adjoining the condemned cell.

This man evidently considered that his position was a peculiarly safe one, and he took his duty remarkably easy in consequence, lounging about in a free-and-easy, indifferent sort of manner, seeming not at all to dread an attack upon him, or to think that such a thing came at all within the bounds of possibility.

He usually swung the keys by a chain, to which they were appended, carelessly on his fingers; but whether or not he might prove a dangerous customer, if freely meddled with, was quite another question.

Charles Ormond watched him with the most intense eagerness; and little did he dream of what was passing in the mind of the prisoner. It was impossible that Charles could form any idea of what was the best time at which to attack this man; although he had a notion of course that, for him to get into the streets at broad daylight would be worse than as if he could get there about or after dusk, so he determined upon making his attack just about twilight, or a short time preceding it.

His first care then was to remain quietly in his cell, and set about, as calmly and deliberately as possible, freeing himself from the fetters, which it was then the fashion to add to the miseries of a condemned man, as if Newgate were not strong enough to keep its prisoners in safety, without adding such a needless aggravation to the ordinary disagreeables of imprisonment.

He found that the tools, such as they were (necessarily small, in consequence of their portability), which had been brought to him by the attorney, were of the very best material and workmanship, so that the file made its way almost as easily through the soft iron, of which his manacles were made, as it would through a piece of wood of similar thickness.

In less than a quarter of an hour he was comparatively free, and he could walk, at least for the short distance that such an exercise could be taken in his cell, with the pleasure of feeling that his limbs were at liberty.

But he was forced to use a precaution, in case his cell should be visited by any of the officials of the prison, before he was quite ready to undertake his enterprise. He cut some slips from his clothing, with which he tied the manacles round his wrists, so as to give the appearance of being in every respect in their original state, and yet leave him to get rid of them at almost a moment's notice.

This was a precaution which was not an useless one, as proved shortly after he made it, for the cell was visited by one of the principal turnkeys, who came ostensibly to ask him if he wanted anything, but most probably to see that all was safe and the prisoner secure.

This man had been friendly disposed evidently towards Charles, and Heaven only knows whether he had been tampered with in any way by the attorney; but certain it is, that, although he brought a small hammer with him, as was the custom, for the purpose of ringing the irons, for the purpose of discovering whether they had been tampered with, he performed that ceremony in so inefficient and bungling a manner that it could be scarcely said to be performed at all; and then he departed, really or apparently satisfied that all was right.

"Now is my time," said Charles, as, immediately he was left alone, he rose and got rid of the disgraceful shackles that had been hanging around him,—"now is my time to make one bold effort for my liberty."

He carried the irons in his hands, and walked slowly from the cell round to the entrance of the yard, where he saw the turnkey pacing to and fro. The man just glanced towards him for a moment, and remarked,—

" I think we shall have a stormy night, sir."—" No doubt," said Charles, and he strode into the court-yard.

thIt was a bold thing to do ; but he walked up to the latter so deliberately that e latter was thrown completely off his guard, and then, raising his hands suddenly, with the tolerably heavy shackles, he, with one blow, struck him to the earth, where he lay insensible.

" It has commenced," cried Charles,—" it has commenced !"   And he spoke in a strange voice, which almost might be called one of agony, for it went most sadly against his disposition to strike the man, as he had done, at a disadvantage. But the first step in any enterprise is the most important ; and, now that Charles had once commenced, it was not likely that, for lack of energy, he should not carry out completely what he intended to do.

To secure the keys now was the work of a moment ; and, casting down the chains, which had done him better service than ever he supposed, when first he felt his limbs encompassed by them, they would do him, he opened the gate, which led into a narrow passage, and, repeating to himself the attorney's words, " Keep to the right, keep to the right," he might be fairly said to be launched in his fearful enterprise. And an awfully hazardous one in was, too—that is to say, hazardous to succeed, although not in its results, for a chance to him was everything, and his failure could not make his condition worse than it was.

He went on in a sort of bewilderment, like a man walking in a dream, until he came to a door, and he knew not what induced him just to tap with his knuckles, when he reached it.

A key was turned in the lock on the other side, and, as if he were being welcomed and cheered on his enterprise, a rough voice said,—

" Come along, Charley."

Charles Ormond stepped through the door-way, and was face to face with a burly man, whose pimpled and inflamed countenance shewed how much he was in the habit of sacrificing to the rosy god.   So intense seemed to be the surprise of this personage, that, with his mouth wide open, and his great goggle eyes fixed strangely in their orbits, he glanced at Charles as if he had seen an apparition.

It was very strange, but not a word was spoken on either side, although in another instant they closed in a deadly embrace, and each strove for the mastery. Mere brute force, however, cannot do much against absolute desperation, and that word alone best describes Charles Ormond's state of feeling. A kind of wild insanity had possession of him. The burly man was hurled to the ground ; and Charles scrambled over him, and rushed onwards, without waiting or caring to do him any further injury.

Whether it was surprise, or that his great chuckle head had come in contact with the wall, or the stone floor, we cannot say ; but there lay the man with the pimply face, and he never attempted to get up for a good half hour.

Charles went on now for a considerable time without interruption, and, in fact, he reached the small room which had been mentioned to him by the attorney before he encountered any other of the officials of the gaol, and then he came face to face with a man who was proceeding in the other direction.

The man started back, but Charles did not ; he walked on, and passed him with as much calmness as he could command, saying, as he did so,—

" A fine evening."—" Why, why," said the man, " who are you ?"

But before the question could be answered, even if Charles had been inclined to answer it, he had passed through the room, and stood in the passage by the governor's house.

It was an anxious moment that ; and it was not likely that, for more than about a minute, this man would be so deprived of his energies by surprise, as not to be able to come after the escaping prisoner. Accordingly, Charles turned, and (mechanically, rather than from reflection) closed the door ; and, as he did so, he felt it pulled from the other side, and knew that the man was making an effort to open it. It was a strange struggle that took place between them, for an instant, and only for an instant—for, by the end of that time, Charles discovered what he had not before observed, namely, that there was a key in the lock, and that it was on the side next to him.

This was a most welcome chance. To turn it was but the work of a moment ; and then the man, who heard the click of it among the wards, began savagely shouting for assistance, and crying out as loud as he could,—

"An escape—an escape !"

It was too late, however. Charles was in the passage of the governor's house —the street, or outer, door was before him ; the prospect of liberty warmed his blood ; there was not a moment's irresolution.

"Success—success," he said, "for life, for liberty, and for you, Marian White-head."

Almost before the words had ceased to vibrate upon his lips, he was in the open air. He had a little difficulty, for a moment, about those awkward steps which descend from the governor's house ; for, at the bottom of them, was an impracticable kind of gate. It was only for a moment, though, that he was thus hindered, and then he overcame the obstacle, and was in the Old Bailey.

A man suddenly sprung forward, and laid hold of him by the arm ; and, in the dusk of the evening, Charles could scarcely tell whether he were an acquaintance or not.

"Mr. Ormond," he said, hurriedly, " I come from Mr. Blake, the attorney ; trust me, sir, and follow me instantly."

Without a doubt of the sincerity of the man, Charles said " Yes, yes ;" and then his friend walked with a lounging pace up the Old Bailey towards Newgate-street.

Our readers may imagine the strange, bewildered feelings with which Charles Ormond followed his conductor ; there he was free from one of the most formidable prisons in England, perhaps in Europe, in the short space of a quarter of an hour, after having been condemned to death, and considered as one completely lost to the world and its ordinary occupations.

It seemed to him as if he had been ages away from the public streets ; and, had he passed indeed through the portals of death before attaining his present position, his own feelings of strangeness and surprise could not possibly have been greater than they were.

"Am I, indeed, free ?" he asked himself ; " God of Heaven ! am I, indeed, free ?"

How strangely did it seem to him to see the busy crowd bustling past him, and never once dreaming that they were elbowing the very man who was doomed to death, and waiting his dreadful fate within the walls of that building, which they passed by with such heedless haste.

His guide never turned once, nor uttered the least remark, but walked on, and turned into Newgate-street, and from thence he shot down one of those narrow alleys, through which the uninitiated would scarcely ever find his way, but which conduct those who knew how to thread them to St. Paul's churchyard.

He chose this route, probably, from some good reason, best known to himself, instead of going the more direct one of Ludgate-hill, to the particular part of St. Paul's churchyard which he wanted to reach.

When he arrived at the end of the narrow alley, down which he had passed, he crossed hastily the top of Ludgate-hill, and then darting across the way, by the railings of St. Paul's cathedral, he paused at a point nearly opposite to a narrow turning called Paul's-chain. Charles Ormond was by his side in a moment.

" Whither are we going ?" said Charles ; "whither are we going ?"—" Hush ! not a word," said his guide ; " get over these railings."

As he spoke, he commenced clambering over the railings himself with great agility ; and then, again, in a subdued voice, urging Charles to do the like, the latter did so, and they both stood, in another moment, within the large area of the cathedral.

"Tell me—tell me," said Charles, "why are we here?—where are you going to take me ?"—" No where else but here," said his guide.

"Here!—you speak in riddles."—"Nay, I do not; you must have a hiding-place for some weeks, perhaps months."

"And that hiding place?"—"Will be the vaults of St. Paul's cathedral."

"You surprise me."—"Never mind that; I hope you will surprise your enemies much more. Come on; I look upon it that now you are in comparative safety. We have not been followed, I'm certain; and, in the friendly darkness of this place, we shall not be seen. Keep close to me."

With a delightful feeling of security, Charles followed his guide, and they both halted on the little doorway, which, it will be recollected, this man, Jeffries—for it was he—informed Mr. Blake he had found the means of opening.

"This door," he said, in a whisper, as he produced a key, and fitted it to the rusty lock, "this door is never opened, for I have ascertained, by personal inspection, that the vaults to which it leads have been out of disuse for many a year, so that you can remain in them in perfect safety. You will at once perceive the importance of a hiding-place like this, so close at hand, and yet one so improbable to be thought of by even the keenest imagination."

CHAPTER XXXVIII.

THE VAULTS OF ST. PAUL'S.—THE STRANGE SLEEPING CHAMBER.—CHARLES ORMOND'S HAPPY FEELINGS.

It was indeed a bold step to carry into effect the bold conception, whosever that was, of finding a refuge from Newgate in one of the largest and best known public buildings of its vicinity. It was not within the bounds of probability that any one would dream of looking for the prisoner in the dreary vaults of St. Paul's; and poor Charles Ormond, who had passed through so much misery, seemed indeed fully to feel the truth of this proposition, as he stepped out of the open air into this noisome atmosphere, loaded with damp exhalations, which hung about the narrow passages into which his guide led him.

Immediately within the door there was a step of about twelve inches in height, and of it Charles Ormond's companion warned him, for the darkness was profound and impenetrable, so that probably he would have fallen, if he had not been aware of its existence.

"Now remain where you are," said Jeffries, "and I will soon procure a light, by the friendly aid of which we may thread those passages with perfect safety."

"And where do they terminate?" said Charles, in a whisper.—"In a vast range of vaults, which again, by winding staircases, conduct to the body of the cathedral."

He carefully closed the little door as he spoke, and locked it on the inner side, leaving the key in the lock, both for safety and for convenience. He then took Charles by the hand, and led him some little distance from the doorway, observing,—

"There's a narrow grating, as you may have perceived in the door, so that if I were to procure a light close to it, it is possible that some of its rays might attract the attention of a passenger, in which case we should run a chance of being discovered."

This was too self-evident and wise a precaution to be neglected, and, in consequence, Charles cheerfully followed him for about twelve or fifteen paces, until he paused, and then with a phosphorous match procured a light, with which he ignited a piece of wax candle, which he took from his pocket. The candle burnt with a sickly and dim lustre, for the air was loaded with damp vapours, and of course as little favourable to combustion as to animal life. But still the flame was sufficient to enable Charles to see, with tolerable precision, the character of the place in which he was. It was a narrow vaulted passage, on the sides and walls of which hung cobwebs of an enormous size, the accumulation of the long-legged spinner for many a year. A quantity of sawdust was on the floor, which completely deadened the sound of their feet, as they walked, and into which they sunk deeply. Indeed, to an unromantic imagination, this place would more have resembled a wine-cellar than anything else, where the more accumulation of dust, cobwebs, and general dirt, there could be found, the greater was their recommendation.

" This entrance to the vault," said Jeffries, " has not been used for many a year. Indeed, when I say entrance, I'm wrong altogether, for it was never used as such, except on very extraordinary occasions, because it was down the staircase leading from the cathedral that the mourners at a funeral usually went."

" And what is all this sawdust for?" said Charles.—" I scarcely know, except to make something like a pathway, on account of the dampness of the ground ; but many of the vaults have a quantity of it. It is not so here, but in some cathedrals on the continent, which I have visited, the floors of the vaults of the dead are strewed to the depth of two or three inches with fine dust from scented woods, such as the cedar."

" I have heard as much," said Charles ; " what a hermitage this is—the condemned cells of Newgate are bustling, in comparison to the dreamy sort of repose which is about this place."—" I should imagine as much ; but then you must consider that you have the knowledge of the solemn and majestic pile which is above you, to add to the illusion."

" It is so. Go on, I'll follow you, with a hope that we shall get into some wider place than this narrow passage, and so be not compelled to breathe so confined an atmosphere."

They walked on, and, as they did so, the light burned dimmer than before, and Charles felt, from the state of his own breathing, that the air in that place was thin, and destitute of the vital principle to a serious extent.

" By some means," said Jeffries, " the ventilation in these places is always wretchedly imperfect, and yet one would hardly think it possible that such would be the case with the commonest knowledge gained by the most ordinary experience upon such a subject."—" It is indeed most oppressive," said Charles Ormond, " and I think a few weeks' residence here of any condemned man, would spare the public executioner the task of taking his life. I feel assured that I myself could not exist for long, pent up in this dreadful place."

" Nay, you shall have a resource. I will show you a narrow staircase which leads up to a gilt door in one of the aisles ; and, when all is still in the cathedral, and the doors closed upon the busy world without, you can steal up to that entrance, and although you cannot pass it, inasmuch as, had you the means to do so, it would be highly dangerous, you can, through the ornamental iron-work of which it is composed, bring in the cooler and purer air which floats about the vast area of the cathedral."—" I will do so," said Charles ; but he shuddered as he spoke, which Jeffries observing, provoked a remark that he hoped he was well.

" Yes, quite well," said Charles ; " but I was thinking that I must endeavour to fix my mind, as calmly and dispassionately as I can, upon some pleasant objects of contemplation, in order that I may get rid of the despairing feelings which otherwise will be sure to take possession of me, and haunt me in this dreadful place."—" Whenever you feel in such a state of mind as that,". said Jeffries, " I should advise you to let your mind go back to Newgate, and fancy some Monday morning there, and the brutal throng without, waiting for the victim to be dragged forth, to die before the eyes of thousands of his fellow men. Picture to yourself, when you feel dull and lonely here, such a scene as that, and it will go far, I think, towards reconciling you to a worse habitation than even the vaults of St. Paul's."

" Nay," said Charles, " my good friend, do not fancy that I was repining at my fate ; the remarks I made were but of an incidental character ; and I need not carry my imagination to such scenes as those you have described, in order to make me think this place perfectly endurable. I never can forget what I have escaped, nor can I forget those to whom I owe that escape."

" Nay, there is such a firm conviction of your innocence in the mind of Mr. Blake, that I am sure if he had not made the exertions that he has to save you, he would have found himself extremely unhappy. I must say, too, for myself, that I share the feeling with him, or probably I should not have been able with so much willingness to have engaged in this dangerous enterprise."

" I am innocent ; the great Heaven above, to whom the majestic pile now above our head is raised, knows my innocence, and the deep and terrific guilt of those parties who have forsworn themselves in an endeavour to effect my destruction."

The passage, narrow and uncomfortable as it was in which they had been walking, now suddenly widened out, and presented to their eyes a vault, in the walls of which were niches, calculated to receive a number of coffins.

His guide paused, and setting down the candle on the ground among the sawdust, so that it stood up, he said,—

"This is not the most comfortable bed-chamber in the world."—"Bed-chamber!" echoed Charles.

"Yes, you cannot call it anything else, as far as regards you, for it must serve that purpose for you. If you attempt to go further, you will, as is most commonly the case, fare worse."—"But here are coffins and dead bodies in this vault; cannot I find one free from those hideous remains of mortality?"

"No; there are a range of vaults, all of which I have explored; and I unhesitatingly say, that, for depth of sawdust, general salubrity, and pleasantness of aspect, this one is decidedly the best.'"—"Is it, indeed?" said Charles, as he surveyed the gloomy remnants of mortality that were around him. "What bundle is that lying in the corner? Is it a heap of grave clothes?"

"No, it's a lot of things we brought from Mr. Blake's house from time to time, to make up a bed for you. I think you may make yourself tolerably comfortable here; you will not be annoyed in any way by impertinent visitors, and a more quiet chamber, I believe, you could never find in London. You see one of these niches, from which I have displaced a coffin, serves for a cupboard, in which you can keep articles of provender, and so on; and here, in another, I have placed an oil lamp, which will give you, no doubt, a tolerable light. You will find a jar of oil in yon corner, which we have brought in, and you will be left plenty of matches, so that really, considering all things, and that you have nothing to pay, you will be amazingly comfortable."

"Oh, amazing, no doubt," said Charles. "However, I cannot be too thankful for even the chance of exchanging where I was for where I am. I think now, if I could see Marian Whitehead for a moment, and be assured that she was happy in the consciousness of my comparative safety, I should find this place far from being of the gloomy aspect it now is. Have you any news of her?"

"Not of my own knowledge, Mr. Ormond; but I was directed by Mr. Blake, if you asked any questions, to tell you that all was well, and not to vex yourself, but to reconcile yourself as speedily as you could to your position, as well as to hope for the best."

"That is but an ambiguous message," said Charles; "and yet its first words shall reconcile me to its latter ones; for if Marian Whitehead be not well, all cannot be well; and feeling, as I know that Mr. Blake does feel, for her misfortunes, he could not, would not, send me word that all was well if she were suffering. How often will you visit me?"

"Every day, I, or some one else, will come to you here; but it must always be at night, by-the-bye, and an opportunity must be taken to make the visit without a chance of discovery. You will find plenty of provision to last you for some time, and now I must bid you farewell."

Charles did not like actually to say to Jeffries that he would like him to remain yet awhile with him, although he would have been glad of his company, for he expected, as he well might, naturally to feel extremely lonely in those vaults when his companion was gone; and now, as Jeffries moved towards the door, he felt inclined to say something to him which should detain him yet a moment. A sense of shame, however, of the seeming cowardice of such a course, deterred him, so that when Jeffries said farewell, he echoed the sentiment, and, in another moment, he was alone.

No, not quite alone, not quite alone yet, while he could hear the sound, subdued as it was, among the sawdust, of the retreating footsteps of his companion. Not quite alone did he feel until he was certain he was quite gone, and that he was able

See page 246.

to detect himself, because he heard the little door which opened into St. Paul's churchyard close after him; then, and not till then, he said, in melancholy sadness,—

"I am alone, indeed; alone in these vaults, with the majestic pile of building above me I have so often looked upon with awe and admiration; oh, can there be a loneliness in this great city that is equal to this?"

He shuddered as he spoke, and although, as we well know, that Ormond's was not a mind embued with many superstitious fancies, but still the strongest-minded man on earth could not but have felt some tremour at knowing that he and the dead were the sole occupants of so vast a space.

The oil lamp burned with a steady but still with a dim lustre, and probably the want of oxygen in the atmosphere tended greatly to depress the animal spirits of Charles; a natural effect, for the flame of intellect burns but dimly and with an enfeebled lustre when the heart beats slowly and laboriously, and that gaseous matter which is the very principle of vitality is but limitedly supplied.

He stood where he had been left, nearly in the centre of the gloomy vault, and sad and philosophic reflections came across him, but he knew that he kept company there, an unbidden guest, too, as he was, with those who had walked the streets of London many a year before.

"Where, now," he said, " are all the hopes and fears of these men who lie around me in all the calm repose of death? Where, now, are their ambitions, their lives, their jealousies, their hatreds, and their brilliant speculations? Where, now, are all these things that made life to them a charm, while death seemed to them too far distant in the dim obscurity to form an integral portion of their high-reaching calculations?"

Impelled by a strange and irrepressible curiosity, he approached one of the niches where a coffin, apparently of gorgeous make and finish, as if in very mockery of the ghastly inhabitant it enshrined, was placed.

There was a handle exteriorly, but when he touched it, it fell off, and he found that the sides of the coffin, although they looked entire to the eye, were rotted and gone, and could not bear the slightest touch from the living, but, as if by magic, crumbled to dust.

He shuddered and turned aside, feeling disposed to chide himself for the momentary impulse that had induced him thus, in a manner of speaking, to profane the sanctity of death.

"Truly," he said, as he leaned against one of the moist walls; " truly such a place as this, after a time, would make a philosopher a madman."

CHAPTER XXXIX.

THE CONSTERNATION AT NEWGATE.—THE NEWS OF THE ESCAPE, AND MR. BLAKE'S SATISFACTION.

As may be well supposed, when we consider the rarity of an escape from Newgate, there was no small amount of confusion and consternation contingent upon this one of Charles Ormond's. The officials ran about in all directions, making confusion worse confounded ; and not knowing what might be the consequences to themselves of the apparent dereliction of duty which had resulted in the escape of one condemned to death with such apparent ease, as if Newgate were only a place to walk out of whenever it became uncomfortable to remain longer within it.

It was the man who was locked up in the small room adjoining the governor's passage, who made the first alarm ; and, as he could not get after the prisoner, he thought that his best plan was to go the other way and make as much disturbance as possible. And certainly that was a fact which he executed with remarkable skill, for, in the course of a few minutes, he succeeded in apprising every official connected with the place of the fact that something remarkably wrong had ensued.

His consternation, however, of a personal character was so great, that for a while nobody could get from him what was the exact nature of the catastrophe, as all he could say was, "He's off, and no mistake !" which was not a very explanatory speech. However, in a short time, the other officials who had met with such rough treatment from Charles as he escaped from the prison, recovered sufficient consciousness to give some account of the transaction, and then the higher authorities became fully aware of the escape of the man of all others upon whom they would have been glad to have kept a cautious eye.

An unconvicted man has no great inducements offered to him to make any violent or dangerous exertion to leave his prison-house ; nor has one convicted of a minor offence, the punishment for which is not of a very heavy character ; but a man condemned to death, a man against whom the laws are about to wreak their worst vengeance, may be well presumed to have every possible motive for endeavouring to better that condition which it is quite impossible he could make worse.

Hence the authorities of Newgate felt themselves peculiarly aggrieved by the escape of Charles more than they would have been by the escape of any other prisoner in Newgate, for there happened to be none just then lying under the sentence of death.

It was very mortifying to have to send for the sheriffs and say, " Well, we have let Charles Ormond go, and couldn't help it ;" and it was equally mortifying for the sheriffs to have to send to the secretary of state a similar communication, which certainly they were bound to do. But all this had to be accomplished, whether it were pleasant or not ; and, in the course of three hours, at the outside, every one in authority, who was interested in the matter, was perfectly well aware that Charles Ormond had escaped from Newgate, and that not the slightest clue to his discovery was in the hands of the police.

As yet, however, the news had not reached the public ear, and the authorities flattered themselves that it would not, for some time, and perhaps that, when it did, it would be co-existent with the news of his recapture.

But the minor officials of Newgate have a better appreciation of things ; they know very well that a morning newspaper has no violent objection to a capital piece of domestic intelligence even at the price of a few guineas, and the consequence was, that the escape of Charles Ormond from Newgate formed a nice snug little article, with a prominent heading, in all the journals published early on the morning succeeding his bold and successful escape.

In another hour it became the town talk, and of all the wild and varied conjectures that were hazarded, with respect to his place of concealment, not one pointed to the vaults of Saint Paul's, as a probable place in which to look for the man, who had baffled the sagacity of the Newgate officials, and who was in a condition to laugh at its massive stone walls, which had in vain attempted to clasp him in captivity.

Jeffries, when he left Charles Ormond, immediately made his way to Mr. Blake, and informed him, with a very pardonable amount of exultation, of the entire and unequivocal success of the plan which had been adopted, for the escape of the prisoner.

Mr. Blake was quite delighted, indeed more so than any attorney ever was before, in the law being thus outwitted ; he rubbed his hands, positively, with glee ; loaded Jeffries with expressions of satisfaction, and paid him a handsome sum of money, at once, as a reward for the fidelity with which he had acted.

" I should like, uncommonly," he said, " to go and see him ; but you know, Jeffries, I am not in the habit of clambering over those iron railings, and how dreadfully I tore my breeches, when I did it one night."—" You did, indeed, sir," said Jeffries, " and I thought I'd given you a helping hand too."

" Yes, you did give me a helping hand, with a vengeance—you laid hold of my foot, and soon turned me over, so that I fell upon a tombstone, with a force sufficient to break every bone in my body."—" Well, sir, you asked me for a leg up, you know—but, however, I think, that if you now feel really inclined, in the course of a night or two, to pay a visit to Mr. Ormond, that we can manage to get you over the railings without much trouble."

" I should like to go, indeed. Does he not think that he's remarkably safe ?"—" He does, but feels the dulness of his situation ; and, in truth, sir, although I would not say so to him, I must confess, sir, that I should feel it most acutely myself, if I were compelled to pass the night in that most uncomfortable place."

" Ay, you may well call it uncomfortable."—" I tried, sir, to do all I could to cheer him, by making light of it, and by talking of it as if it were a matter of no consequence ; but still, as I came away, I could see that he shuddered, and I anticipate that he will pass anything but a comfortable time in those gloomy vaults, which are, certainly, gloomy enough to drive anybody melancholy mad."

" Oh, it shall not last long ; as soon as the ardour of pursuit is abated, I will manage to get him on the continent ; and, after that, I will spare no pains to render his innocence very apparent ; so, that I may yet see the day when I may bring him back in triumph, and own the part that I took in his rescue, without incurring blame from any one good man. By-the-bye, what have you done with your coadjutor ?"—Why, sir, it's no fault of his, of course, that he has not succeeded as I have done myself, in performing good service to Mr. Ormond—he would have done so, doubtless, if he had had the opportunity."

"So you argue that he's as much entitled to the reward I promised, as if he had ?" —" I certainly must say I think so, sir."

" Well, he shall have it—I think you are right, and, at all events, I would rather make an error on the liberal side, than on the illiberal one, so you can tell him when you see him, that he need not feel vexed at his non-success, for that I shall not forget that he did his best."—" That will satisfy him, sir ; he is not at all a greedy man. Mr Ormond asked me concerning Miss Whitehead, and I told him what you desired me, namely, that she was very well."

" Ay, that's the best, though I'm sorry to say it's not the truth, but even the truth must not be told at all times, if we would save those we love from pain and misery ; so let him remain in the pleasant delusion, that all is well with her, rather than feel, with the despair which such a knowledge would bring, that such was not the case."

" Is the young lady very bad, sir ?"—" Not so bad, Jeffries, but that she might be worse, and yet, bad enough to give all who are interested in her fate apprehensions concerning her of a serious character."

" I regret to hear it. And now, sir, that this escape has ended so admirably well, let me beg you not in any way to mar it by precipitancy, in allowing Mr. Ormond to leave his place of concealment ; a few days, more or less, can make but small difference to him, and would make an immense one to his enemies, if that those few days were to produce his capture."—" Agreed, agreed ; you may depend that I shall be most careful."

Mr. Blake, when Jeffries was gone, could hardly keep himself from rushing off to his cottage, at Ealing, for the purpose of communicating the news of Charles Ormond's escape to Marian Whitehead and her mother—that is to say, if the former had sufficiently recovered from her dreadful state of apathy into which it will be recollected she had fallen, to listen to such intelligence ; which, upon consideration, Mr. Blake had every reason to doubt ; for he had heard of cases, similar to hers, which had been of long, painful, and protracted character, and he dreaded that hers was of that nature likewise."

Upon the whole, therefore, he made up his mind that he would not take any notice of the proceedings to Mrs. Whitehead, whose good feeling he did not doubt for a moment, but whose discretion, he did most enormously ; and it was something, likewise, to picture to himself the delight of being the first to communicate to Marian Whitehead the delightful news of the escape of Charles.

" I shall be able to tell her that, after all, the dreadful judicial murder has not been committed, and when she is sufficiently convalescent, and wants but such a piece of news to complete her recovery, with what an exquisite feeling of delight will she hear it, and what a happy meeting will hers be in some foreign land, with the object of her best and dearest affections."

These were the considerations which induced Mr. Blake to make up his mind not to tell Mrs. Whitehead of what had occurred, notwithstanding his great aversion to keep back what might be considered as good news, for he really entertained not the remotest doubt on earth of the ultimate escape of Charles Ormond completely from the toils which beset him.

He felt inclined quite to felicitate himself upon the choice of a hiding-place, which had been made for Charles ; and certainly if ever anything looked well in this world in such a respect, that did ; for no one could conceive it possible that for an instant any of the authorities should suspect where Charles was, so that the only possibility of a discovery would be in the fact of the secret being betrayed by some one, and that, he was quite certain, would not occur.

It gave him a little twinge, though, on the following morning, to find that a reward of no less than £100 was offered by the county for Charles's apprehension ; while £200 more was tacked to that by the secretary of state.

This was presenting a temptation to any parties whom he had trusted of rather a fearful character; but still he would not despair, but told himself, that after all, £300 was not to be placed in competition with a man's honour and honesty, besides the advantages which Jeffries and his associates might fairly expect to accrue to them from a combined connexion with him—Mr. Blake.

"No, no," he said to himself, "I will not believe for a moment that there is any danger, and least of all will I believe that there is any danger from treachery. Jeffries has been too well tried by me in matters of confidential import for me now to suspect him, therefore I will not do so, but rely wholly and solely upon his faithfulness."

But there are other parties to whom the escape of Charles Ormond became a matter of serious import; and we need scarcely say, that such an occurrence to Godfrey and to Neville would be likely to bear a most ruinous aspect, if it did not terrify them past all ordinary bounds, which it was more than likely to do.

In fact, under any other circumstances, we could almost have pitied Godfrey, considering the state of horror and anxiety in which he was kept ever since the condemnation of Charles, from one cause and another.

It is one of the penalties of guilt, that to a large extent it can seldom be committed without confederacy; and the inevitable consequence of such a state of things is that greatest agony of the mind—mistrustfulness.

Such a man as Godfrey could not lie down at night in peace, or rise up with any degree of satisfaction, because it was impossible for him to tell that he was not deceived and betrayed by one of his subordinates.

And, moreover, such persons feel that they are at the mercy of any accidental circumstance which may have the effect of proving their own guilt, and exposing the chicanery with which they have shifted it on to the innocent; and, inasmuch as everything which brings the truth to light is highly favourable to the innocent, so is it in due proportion unfavourable to the guilty.

It was a great shock to Godfrey to hear that the execution of Charles Ormond was put off even for a week, and a much greater shock was it to him to find that during that interval the prisoner had escaped.

He could scarcely be said to have recovered from the uncomfortable feelings which had been induced by his last interview with Neville ere this terrifying stroke of intelligence was doomed to fall upon him. The first intimation he had of it was from one of the morning journals; and as he read the commencement, the paper dropped from his hands, and he turned as pale as death itself.

It took him many minutes before he could recover sufficiently from the confusion into which his intellect was thrown by this circumstance to be able to reason upon it at all calmly or collectedly; and even when he strove to arrange the affair in his mind, and to ask himself how it was possible that Charles Ormond, of so many around him, should be the only one who had been able to escape from his prison-house, he began to suspect that he was made the victim of some juggle, and that more was known by the authorities respecting his own share in Charles's condemnation than at all met the public eye.

For such an idea as this once to take possession of Godfrey's mind, was sufficient almost to drive him to distraction; and again, notwithstanding his horror and dislike of the man, he felt compelled to throw himself upon the society of Neville as the only person to whom he could venture to talk upon the subject.

This time, however, Godfrey did not send for that villanous character to his house, but he sought him at the address which he had given.

What befel him there will form the subject of another chapter, and which we shall now proceed to record.

CHAPTER XL.

GODFREY'S ADVENTURES IN THE CELLARS OF ST. GILES'S.—THE PROPOSAL AND
THE REFUSAL.

GODFREY, as soon as he had despatched his morning meal, and he did that
with a lack of appetite which to him was an unusual circumstance, copied upon
a piece of paper the address which Neville had given to him, and started off in
quest of that notorious character.

The address simply ran as follows:—" No. 50.—27, Monmouth-street, St.
Giles's. Go to the cellar and ask for 50."

Singular as this address was, Neville had assured him, that whether he chose
to come himself or send a messenger, it would assuredly find him ; and accord.
ingly, with a full faith that it would do so, Godfrey started alone to go to a place
of which he knew little, or he never would have ventured to have set his foot
in it.

There was no difficulty, of course, in finding No. 27, Monmouth-street; and
perhaps little difficulty in getting into a thieves' den. If any trouble was likely
to arise, it was assuredly to be found in getting out again. But that Godfrey,
in his present excited state of feeling, did not consider; all he thought of, was the
frightful consequences to him, probably, or at all events possibly, of Charles
Ormond being at large.

" Who knows," he said to himself, as he hurried through the crowded streets
with a vehemence of manner and an excitement of gesture which brought upon
him the observation of many a chance passenger—" who knows but that almost
the first use he may make of his liberty will be to concert some plan of personal
revenge, which may bring with it most fearful and uncomfortable circumstances,
and which may take me by surprise in such a manner that I may not be
able to resist it. He must, he shall be found, and restored again to his dungeon,
or I shall not be able to sleep in peace."

Hard as it was to such a man as Godfrey to part with his money—that money
which he had waded through so many difficulties to obtain—still he now felt the
necessity of drawing his purse-strings, and dispensing some portion of his ill-gotten
wealth, if he would wish to preserve the remainder as well as himself from destruction.

He made up his mind, before he reached the locality in which he expected to find
Neville, to offer that worthy a considerable sum, provided he succeeded in discovering the retreat of Charles, and delivered him up to justice.

He made up his mind to offer fifty pounds, but not to stop at a hundred; for he
told himself that he should know no peace until that object was accomplished ; nor,
indeed, now, until death itself had interposed to protect him from any chance of
aggression, on the part of Charles, against him.

There was nothing particular in the appearance of No. 27, Monmouth-street,
which tended in any way to proclaim that it was devoted to any other than the
purpose of legitimate business.

The shop belonging to the house was occupied by one of those dealers in miscellaneous and faded wearing apparel, for which this street has, for so many years,
enjoyed a reputation, while an extraordinary collection of shoes, in all stages of
decay, adorn the head of the cellar, where, according to the directions he had
received, he was to inquire for No. 50.

The strange and anomalous nature of the inquiry came across him for the first
time as he paused at the house, and he hesitated several minutes before he could
make up his mind to attempt it.

He was, however, then brought to a decision by the man of the shop, who, of
course, was a son of Israel, darting out in a very frantic manner, and attempting to
drag him in, assuring him that there was an unlimited quantity of clothes to be sold,
a great deal better than new, at any prices whatever.

Godfrey's natural obstinacy and violence of disposition were roused into activity by this attack, and it tended greatly to relieve his mind from the throng of apprehensions which beset it, by withdrawing it to other objects.

He shook off the Jew, with a volley of curses, and then, without a moment's hesitation, descended into the cellar, where he was accosted by a woman, who began to be profuse in her recommendation of a heap of old boots and shoes, which she had for sale. This, however, he put a stop to by hastily saying,—

"I do not want anything, I only came to ask for No. 50."

"No. 50!" said the woman, and she shrunk back for a moment, and surveyed him with suspicion in her look. "No. 50—what can you want with him? Here, Joe, here's a man come and says he wants No. 50."

"Oh, he be blowed," said a male voice; "I'll soon settle his hash."

A ruffianly looking man approached, of herculean frame and build; he looked bloated and heavy from intemperance; and, as he confronted Godfrey, he seemed much inclined to make an immediate attack upon him, without caring for any explanation he might be able to give of the cause of his visit.

"And what," he said, with a brutal oath, "do you want with No. 50, or number anything else? I don't know you, nor anybody else here, I'm sure."—"I have the address from himself," said Godfrey, "and I can tell you his name, if you like."

"Perhaps it's right, after all, Joe," said the woman; "who knows?"—"You don't, of course. I don't want to know the name of No. 50 from anybody; it's your name I want."

"My name is Godfrey; and if he be here, when you mention it to him, it will be amply sufficient to induce him to see me, because he will know the business upon which I come."

"Godfrey," said the man; "oh, I knows you—you're the cove as swore away the green one's life the other day. Why, he's got out of the stone jug; how came they to manage that, I should like to know—not an easy job, I should say, considering all things? Well, well, I can take you to No. 50; he's here, sure enough; but there's the rules and regulations to think of first."

"Rules and regulations, where may they be?"—"Why, they begins with half a spangle, as you're a swell, and have got dollops of tin; so hand it out, and earn a character for honesty once in your life."

"But I don't happen to know what half a spangle means."—"It means half a guinea, since you are so jolly green; but you can make it a whole one, if you like; we don't stand upon trifles here."

"Well, if it be customary to pay something upon coming to a place like this, I've no wish to avoid it. I come upon business, and I suppose, as on many occasions, a man must pay what may be called his footing."

"Call it what you like, so as you do pay it."

To his mortification Godfrey found that he had not half a guinea about him, and he was compelled to give a whole one; but then his natural parsimony would not allow him to make the most, as he ought to have done, of a compulsory circumstance, for he actually had the absurdity to ask for the change, which, as Joe told him, spoiled the liberality of the whole affair; and, as he did not get the change, the asking for it was certainly a work of supererogation.

"Come on," said the man, "you've behaved like a trump, though you haven't done it in the handsomest way in the world; come on, and I'll soon show you where No. 50 is—give us a light, Bet."

The woman handed him a light, and then Godfrey followed him. As he did so, he became amazed at the extent of the subterraneous place into which he had got; for what, from the street, one would have imagined to have been only the common underground-cellar of a house, seemed, as he proceeded, to be but the commencement of a number of vaults, extending a long way back, under a number of houses."

They traversed a number of passages, the floors of which were composed of earth trodden hard, with here and there in soft places a tile or a brick laid down and imbedded in it.

The passages were intricate, and here and there Godfrey ascertained that smaller ones branched off from the main artery in which he was travelling. He was curious to know where these smaller ones led to, and he asked the man, who replied with a laugh,—

"D—n me if I do know where some of 'em lead to; but I believe the greatest number have pitfalls in them that would let you down into the common sewers before you knew where you were, if you were to attempt to come into these places without an official guide."

Godfrey shuddered, as he remarked,—

"I had no idea that there were places of concealment equal to this in London. Don't you think it probable enough that in some such place the escaped prisoner from Newgate has found a refuge?"

"No, I don't think any such thing; he is not one of our sort, which makes all the difference; he wouldn't know how to set about it; but mind ye, if he had he'd be safe, and not you or any dozen like ye would get any proper family cove to give him up."

Godfrey was silent, for he felt assured from what the man had said, that he had a sufficient knowledge of the history of the affair to contradict him, if he were to assert anything contrary to truth, so he followed in silence, preferring to endure the reproaches which had been cast upon him, to making an enemy where it would have been great folly so to do, in consequence of the ignorance of the force which could or might be arrayed against him.

The passages were profoundly dark, and but for the light which the man carried, probably, he, accustomed as he was to them, in all likelihood would not have been able to find his way in their intricacies.

After, too, Godfrey had heard of what danger there was from pitfalls, and had been enlightened as to where they led to, he kept much closer to his guide, lest by accident, when he least expected it, he should drop into one of those uncomfortable places, and so be a great loss to himself, if not to society at large.

Suddenly the man paused at what appeared to be the termination of the passage in which they were walking; at least, at the first glance it seemed like the termination of it; but upon closer inspection Godfrey saw that it was nothing but a heavy black curtain made out of some rough looking material which was hung from the roof to the ground, and so closely resembled the wall that it was difficult to detect the one from the other.

"Here we are at last," said his guide; "beyond here is what we call the common room, and as our chaps kept it up rather late last night, I have no doubt we shall find him sleeping, for it is a precious early time of the day to disturb a gentleman at. I can't think what people are thinking of to get up so precious soon."

"It may seem soon to you," said Godfrey, "because, probably, you've been up all night."

"Not I, by Jove. I knew it was my turn to be door-keeper, so I was forced to do the best I could; but for them as needn't come out unless they like, it don't seem at all comfortable."

"Nevertheless," said Godfrey, "my business is urgent, and such as must be attended to. I shall not be afraid of disturbing Neville, or of getting any violent reproaches for so doing."

It was an original scene, indeed, which presented itself on the other side of that curtain, and one that might well make Godfrey, as he did, pause, and almost forget, in his glance at it, the express object of his visit.

It was a large oblong shaped room with a vaulted roof. We give it the name of a room, because it was roughly boarded, and so was, perhaps, entitled to the designation. At one end was a fire-place, or rather the opening where one might have been put, for there was no grate, in which smouldered a quantity of wood. There were a number of tables and forms, similar to those in use in tap-rooms of common public-houses; and candles, some stuck in the necks of quart bottles, and some in more legitimate receptacles, but all of which were neglected and untrimmed, cast a meagre and uncertain light about the place.

At the first glance it was difficult to see that anybody was there; but, upon a minuter examination, Godfrey felt certain that there were not only occupants of that room, but a considerable number of them, say to the extent of between twenty and thirty; but they escaped observation at first in consequence of lolling about in all directions, as if sleeping off, as doubtless was the real fact, some debauch of the preceding evening.

"Hilloa," said Godfrey's companion, as he walked into the apartment, "curse ye all, don't ye see here's a stranger?—is this your manners, and be d—d to you?—lor, when will you all take after me? You see, sir, that I was brought up at a boarding-

ee page 255.

school myself, and larned to be sanguinary civil on all decent occasions; but these here know-nothing-vagabonds don't know the big end of you from the small corner."

"What do you want?" growled a voice;—"you're always kicking up no end of disturbance about nothing."

"Do you know where No 5 is?"—"Under the table, to be sure; where else

N   21

do you expect he is ?—didn't he make a fool of himself last night ?   Here, 50, you're wanted.   Here's the beaks have sent their traps after you."

" Eh ?" cried a voice ; " what do you mean by that ?" and Godfrey knew the voice was Neville's, so when he cast his eyes in the direction from whence the sound proceeded, he saw that gentlemanly character slowly emerging from beneath a table, where it appeared he had been taking his repose and enjoying a morning slumber after the proceedings of the over night, which, no doubt, had been of a sufficiently boisterous character.

" Neville, I wish to see you," said Godfrey.

" What's amiss ?" said Neville, springing to his feet, and striving to shake off the fumes of drowsiness and drunkenness which still clung to him ; " what's amiss now, I say ; who'd athought of seeing you here ?"

" Ormond has escaped."

Neville staggered back till he came to the wall, and then, with a drunken look of gravity, he stared in Godfrey's face, while the latter regarded him with stern ferocity.

It was evident that this was a piece of intelligence as unexpected to Neville as it was uncomfortable ; and, what with the state of confusion he was in with his overnight's excesses and the stunning nature of the intelligence, it was no wonder that he continued to glare at Godfrey in a manner which excited all the ire of that individual.

He glanced round him for a moment as if he wished to see who was within hearing before he gave utterance to the angry passions which were swelling at his heart, and then, when he saw that most of the men present were either in a state of hopeless drunkenness, or sleeping off its effects, he spoke fiercely.

" Neville," he said, " is this well of you, while yet there remained a chance of anything going amiss in a transaction fully as important in its results to you as it is to me, for you to be sitting here, instead of being upon the alert in case of any untoward accident ?   Is this well, sir, I repeat, that I am to be left to bear the brunt of every cross-grained circumstance ?"

" You—you don't mean to say he's escaped from Newgate ?" gasped Neville.— " I have said it ; and hardly should I have said it had it not occurred."

Neville, by this time, had a little recovered, and he by no means relished the admonitory tone in which Godfrey took upon himself to address him.

" Thank you, Master Godfrey," he said ; " this sort of thing may suit you, but it won't suit me.   I tell you I will not be spoken to, as you seem inclined to speak ; and if the devil himself had escaped from Newgate, what is it to me ?"

Neville likewise looked around him, and it was evident it was for the purpose of witnessing what effect this bold speech, or seemingly bold speech, had upon any of the persons present.

Godfrey saw this, and, after a moment's pause, he stepped up to him and said, in an under tone,—

" This is folly.   Is there no place in which we can speak in private ?   You know, Neville, that your safety, as well as mine, is intimately concerned in this affair ; we must not trifle with it.   The apprehension of Charles Ormond has become to us of vital consequence."

" Curses on him," said Neville, between his clenched teeth; " I had made a resolution."

" What resolution ?"—"A resolution to be drunk till the hanging was over. Hark ye, Godfrey, you know well enough that I'm not one to go snivelling about because something uncomfortable has happened, and making a fool of myself ; but I did think it would be more agreeable to forget the exact time, whether the young fellow's neck was to be stretched or not."

" It was a desperate and foolish resolution.   How could you possibly tell what might occur?   There's many a slip, Neville, between the cup and the lip."

" Hush !" said Neville ; " don't speak so loud ; I half trust the people here, and I half don't."

Godfrey started—for, coward as he was at heart, he was not at all a likely person to be heedless of any caution.

"But what am I to do?" added Neville; "what can I do?"—"Join in the pursuit—find him—hunt him up—drag him back to his prison-house, let him be ever so well concealed. You must come out of this place, and join in the hue and cry which shall be, and which, in fact, is now raised in pursuit of the prisoner, for there must be a gallows erected, and you may be assured, Neville, that it will be for Charles Ormond or for you."

"I beg your pardon there," said Neville; "for yourself, more probably; and if I really suffer by such a means, I will, at least, take most especial care that you are my companion. This news has sobered me, and, for my own sake more than for yours, I will see into it. In another half hour I shall be abroad and about, and if Charles Ormond is to be found above ground, I will find him."

"Do so. I have more faith in your exertions, backed, as they are, by personal interests, than in that of the hirelings, who have nothing but money to urge them on. You will not forget that your neck is in jeopardy—a tolerably important consideration."

"And I will be well paid, too," muttered Neville to himself.

"Farewell for the present," added Godfrey; "and remember I shall expect to see you in the evening with an account of what you have done; for, by Heaven, I shall not sleep, or eat, or drink until Charles Ormond be again within the walls of Newgate."

He turned round to look for his guide, in order to leave the place again, but he did not see that individual, and Neville said to him,—

"Walk on; keep the widest path; you can't go wrong; besides, you'll soon meet with some one to direct you."—"Nay," said Godfrey; "I'm rather afraid of the pitfalls, and other dangerous places, which, I am informed, abound here."

"Psha! There's no such thing; that's merely said to frighten fools."

Neville turned aside, and Godfrey, after another moment's hesitation, essayed himself to find the path out of the subterranean region into which he had been conducted.

Probably it was the excitement of his mind which made him overlook the strong probability there was of going astray, for his interview with Neville had by no means comforted him, and the look of consternation which the ruffian's face had worn when he was told of Charles's escape, added much to his, Godfrey's, disquietude.

CHAPTER XLI.

GODFREY'S ADVENTURE IN THE CELLAR.—THE FEARFUL SPECTACLE.

TAKING up the candle, which had been placed upon the table nearest to the black curtain which hung over the entrance of that large cavernous-looking room, Godfrey passed out by himself, with his thoughts all intent upon what was to be done in case of a failure in finding Charles Ormond. Risk and danger, of all sorts and descriptions, seemed to him most likely to arise from the fact of the escape of the innocent man from his bondage.

He felt confident that time to Charles Ormond was everything, and that his own principal safety lay in Charles being executed with as much celerity as possible, and the affair forgotten by the public, after the nine days' wonder which it was calculated to produce.

"My malediction on him," he muttered; "his escape will only tend to make the thing more notorious; there will be more inquiry than ever into the circumstances which have attended upon his conviction, and as there are a number of individuals who fancy they can see much further their neighbours, I shall be now exposed to a thousand dangers."

As he reasoned thus, Godfrey almost felt a pang of regret that he had carried the matter so far as he had done, but it was not that species of regret which resulted from any conviction of the great injustice he had committed, but, on the contrary, it was a purely selfish feeling, and looked no further than his own comforts, or his own danger.

Soon, however, he found that his reflections upon what was past, and upon what was probable to come, must be submerged into a consideration of the present, for he found himself involved in a complete labyrinth of gloomy damp passages, not one of which presented a more inviting aspect than another.

There was nothing of any character whatever to guide him in his choice as to pursuing any one of these passages in preference to another; and, indeed, as several windings had taken place in them, it was more than probable that he might have doubled upon his course, so that he could not tell whether he was proceeding towards the street or not.

This was a most uncomfortable dilemma to be placed in, and when again he considered what had been said to him of fulfilling the possibility of what he had been told of them might be correct, and that Neville, in his bitterness of spirit, and general love of inflicting injury for injury's sake, came so strongly upon him, that after a few moments of such hurried thoughts, he felt afraid to move, and stood trembling with the candle in his hand, more like a spectre walking through those dreary regions, than a man who had come out of the open light of day to visit them.

But still something must be done; he could not remain passive, for if he did, Heaven only knew how long his imprisonment might last. He must either walk on, and endeavour of himself to find an exit from that maze of intricacy, or he must call for the assistance of those who would release him from it. He chose the latter course, and not without some nervous misgivings, he called out aloud for assistance. The echo of his own voice in that dreary abode was the only answering sound that came upon his ears.

He then shuddered at the fearful feeling of solitude that came over him, for to such men as Godfrey, whose very souls are steeped in guilt, solitude always has the effect of awaking memory, which to them is the greatest of all curses.

Ten minutes reflection with a consciousness, or, at all events, a belief that no living soul was near him, were sure to be ten minutes of mental agony to Godfrey; anything was better than that.

"I will proceed onwards," he said, "and surely by taking excessive care I can avoid danger, even if it should be directly in my path; these pitfalls that have been mentioned to me cannot be so cleverly constructed, but that they surely may be seen, and to see them, of course is to avoid them. Yes, I will proceed, I will proceed—I shall either meet some one, or find my way out of this detestable place into which I never again will set foot, for any earthly consideration."

His plan of proceeding was now to hold the candle so close to the ground, and to walk on so slowly, that it was the next thing to impossible he should fall into any snare such as had been mentioned to him.

Thus he proceeded for some distance, paying no attention to the passages which occasionally appeared to the right and to the left of him, but keeping as much as possible to the main trunk or artery of the subterranean labyrinth in which he was.

He had not proceeded very far in this manner, when in consequence of looking more upon the ground than on what was before him, he very nearly extinguished his light by suddenly running against a doorway, as well as striking himself a severe blow upon the head, which, in consequence of the stooping position in which he was, projected considerably before him.

Anything in his then state of mind, was sufficient to give him great alarm, and this circumstance, trivial as it was, induced an exclamation of terror from his lips, totally inadequate to the occasion. He found now, upon a closer examination, that the door against which he had struck, was about as rough a specimen of that useful article as could well be imagined.

It seemed to have been some old door, which in consequence of numerous dilapidations, had required repairing, for there were a number of rough bits of planking and odd shaped boarding nailed over it in different places, so that it had great weight about it, and probably unmovable strength from those causes, which so materially impaired its personal appearance.

Godfrey moved the candle up and down, minutely inspecting this specimen of house architecture, and wondering much how it came there. He felt quite convinced that in his progress to the apartment, if it might be dignified by such a name, in which he had seen Neville, he had encountered no such door, nor ha l he passed through any space which had resembled a door-way, and therefore he c ame to the conclusion, an uncomfortable one under the circumstances, that most certainly, and without the shadow of a doubt, he had missed his way.

Athough this was more than probable before, yet Godfrey trembled when he felt positive of such a fact; and yet a great amount of curiosity came over him, to think where that door could lead to.

"After all," he said, "may it not be a short cut to the open cellar, that may eventually conduct me to the street? I will try to open it, at all events. He could see no perceptible fastening, and yet it seemed perfectly tight; as tight, indeed, as if it formed a portion of the very wall itself. He made several efforts with the hand that was at liberty to open it, but finding this ineffectual, he put down the light, and exerted more power by getting what hold he could with both hands, and pulling violently.

It was all in vain, he could not stir that door, although he felt confident, from the position of the hinges, that it opened outwards towards him.

Curiosity then, as well as a spirit of opposition being fully aroused, he took up the light again, and made a more careful examination of the place? and then he saw what he considered was the great cause of the difficulty that presented itself to his opening the door.

It consisted in a piece of cloth of some sort being wedged in so firmly between the door and the jamb, that it was almost impossible to think of moving the former. And, to his surprise, this seemed to be the only real fastening.

"Surely," he said, "it is one that may be removed. I will try to do so, at all events; who knows but some discovery, beyond this door, may reward me for all m y trouble?"

After a few moments' reflection, he thought the only way which presented the slightest chance of success in removing the obstruction, was to endeavour to cut it out. He took a penknife from his pocket, and found that the blade, had it been six times as thick, would have easily passed into the crevice, so that he instantly began, with great industry, to cut onwards upon the piece of cloth, with the hope of so getting it out piecemeal.

It was astonishing with what perseverance he set about this object, which really seemed rather foreign to his present purpose, inasmuch as he could not possibly tell, even were that door opened, that it would at all facilitate his escape from where he was.

But still he worked on, and he certainly had the consolation—if it might be called such—of finding that he made considerable progress in getting through the piece of cloth, which seemed to be two or three folds in thickness, and which he considered had evidently been purposely wedged into the door in lieu of a better fastening.

Now he had passed the penknife blade completely through it, and, after again and again repeating the operation, there seemed to him every prospect of completing his object successfully, for he got out a small shred of the cloth.

Then he considered that it was high time to see what strength would do, since art had done so much, and he placed the candle upon the floor again, where he found that it burned better, in consequence of some under current of air, than it did when he held it higher up.

One of the loose pieces of board, that was nailed over a large hole in the door, just left space enough uncovered to enable him to lay hold of it firmly with his hands, and now, throwing all his strength into one vigorous pull, he found that the door moved a little at its lowest part, although it was still held by that piece of cloth which must have been wedged into its place by some most vigorous slam to of the door. Partial success was encouraging, and he tried again—a third time, and the door moved more than before.

"At last," he muttered to himself, "I shall get it open."

Even as he spoke, he, with a mighty effort, succeeded in wrenching it from its hold.   It swung wide open, and then there fell completely into his arms, upon his face, and about his neck, a dead body, the throat of which was cut from ear to ear; a quantity of coagulated blood from which almost found its way into his very mouth.

So shocked, so positively horrified, was even the cold-blooded villain, Godfrey, at this unexpected denouement, that he fell completely backward, with the body above him, and there he lay for a few moments, as if held in its ghastly embrace—a few moments of such agony, that they seemed hours in passing away.

With a yell of terror, that awaked every echo in those desolate and murderous-looking passages, he shook himself free from the horrible incubus which pressed upon him.

And this was a work of no ease, for the weight of the dead body was enormous; and, somehow or another, the long arms got entangled about him, and it required the most frantic efforts to free himself from them.

"Murder—help—murder!" he shouted, and then suddenly feeling how indiscreet it was to make any riot or disturbance in such a den of murder, or even to insinuate the least suspicion to any one of his knowledge of the dreadful spectacle that was there to be exhibited, he shook with apprehension less his cries should have been now heard, and bring some one to the spot who might wish to add him, for common safety's sake, as a companion to the terrific object he had liberated from its confinement.

Now a dead silence reigned in the place, and there lay the corpse, mangled and terrific.   He could not help looking upon it, although he several times made an effort to turn away his eyes from so imagination-haunting a sight.   He felt that each moment he gazed upon the terrifying spectacle, the more firmly he was implanting its terrors in his fancy; and yet he looked on, as if he wished to register each minute particular, rather than to avoid storing up such horrors in his brain.

The corpse seemed that of a man of middle age.   It was respectably attired, but without a coat, and the head, as we before remarked, was nearly severed from the body, for there was a deep gash extending quite to the vertebræ, which alone had resisted the knife with which the dreadful deed had been committed.

The face was most ghastly and terrible in appearance, for the blood had naturally drained from all the vessels, and left it almost the colour of course, yellowish paper, while the eyes peeped out from beneath the half-closed lids, with a glassy, horrible, and lustrous opacity, that probably terrified Godfrey more than aught else.

"This is horrible—this is horrible!" he said.   "I shall not leave this place alive.   I'm certain of it now—quite certain of it.   Neville means to have me murdered!"

The moment this idea took possession of his mind, he seemed as firmly convinced of it, as if some one, on whose word he could place the most implicit confidence, had told him of it.

"Yes, yes," he groaned; "he means to murder me!   It is my life that he aims at—my life—my life—and that is the reason I was left without a guide.   What shall I do—what shall I do—what shall I do?"

Death in any aspect to such a man as Godfrey, was sure to present numberless terrors; but when he came to consider that it might come to him in the ghastly and terrific shape he saw before him, well, indeed, might he tremble, even to dream of such a doom.

And how utterly helpless he was; how far away, for aught he knew, from all assistance; how totally unarmed, even had he felt inclined to make a manly struggle for his life, and to sell it as dearly as possible!

"No hope—no hope!" he said; "I am doomed now—I am doomed now!"

CHAPTER XLII.

GODFREY'S INCREASED DANGER.—MORE PERILS, AND THE CONSEQUENCES OF CRIME.

Now he remained torpid for a time, as if deprived of all power of action. His mind was in a completely confused whirl, through which a thousand strange images kept rapidly passing, without anything tangible appearing, which should enable him to better his condition.

But that could not last for ever; and as the first shock gradually subsided, and he began to feel that at all events the alarm which he had himself given, was productive of no bad results, he gathered a little hope from the fact, that it was just possible he might succeed in escaping the suspicion of having seen the murdered body.

No doubt the best way to give himself the best chance of avoiding such a sacrifice would have been to have replaced it in the receptacle from whence he had enabled it to emerge: but that even for him was by far too horrible a task.

"No," he muttered, "no," in a low, groaning tone of voice. "No, not for my own safety's sake, dare I do that. I cannot—I cannot—I cannot!"

Slowly and reluctantly he rose to his feet, for, although he had rescued himself from the superincumbent weight of the dead body, yet he had not risen from the damp earth on to which he had fallen, on its so suddenly coming upon him.

But even, although he rose, he found that he could not take his eyes from the frightful spectacle. He lifted the candle from the floor, and held it shivering in his nervous grasp.

"If—if," he said, "I move away, it must still be with my face to this frightful corpse, for I feel that I dare not turn my back upon it. My reason tells me it is harmless—more harmless than as if it lived; but still is there something so horrible about it, that I must look upon it until some turning of these passages hides it from my view."

And so, backwards he retreated, keeping his eyes, as he had promised himself, fixed upon those gloomy orbs, which once, perchance, had beamed with all the lustre of intelligence, for the face, even denuded of all its natural colour as it was, had about it that indescribable appearance which bespeaks the man of good society, and of education.

It was some consolation, that, as he went backward with the light, the body seemed to disappear in the darkness which prevailed around it.

"I shall lose sight of it now," he said; "and then, when no longer the slightest vestige of it meets my eyes, I shall be able to turn, and pursue my way with some hope of safety, for safety now, and hope, and everything almost that I can wish for at the present moment, is but in getting out of sight of that spectacle, which, with a horrible fascination, chains me to look upon it. It is more dreadful than ever I could have pictured such an object. I have thought of a death, but never a death like this, so horrible—so horrible! Ay! I would not see it again for worlds—no, not for worlds—that is to say—not for a large sum, would I be tempted to look upon anything so terrific!"

He began to consider what it behoved him to say, if he should meet any one here who would ask him a troublesome question, a question that he might find it as inconvenient as disagreeable to answer.

"I would not confess having seen such a thing; indeed, dare not, for my life—no, not for my life. What would become of me if I were?—why, instant death, of course; and then ——"

A loud shriek burst from the lips of Godfrey at this moment, for he felt certain that he had arrived at one of the pitfalls which had been mentioned. The foot that he put behind him, found no resting-place.

He hovered for an instant, over what he considered, no doubt, some terrific abyss. He made a frantic struggle, but it was in vain. He could not save himself.

"Mercy! mercy!" he shrieked.

And then, down he went, a distance of about twelve inches, for he had only arrived at a sort of step, which, of course, he knew not the existence of.

The candle was extinguished, and the shock he received was severe; but when he recovered himself sufficiently from that, to feel what a mistake he had made, and that, instead of falling over some terrific abyss, he had, after all, only been precipitated down a step, the delightful consciousness of personal safety for a time almost overcame every other feeling.

"I am saved!" he said; "I am saved! Oh! what a moment of horror was that. Dreadful—dreadful!—too dreadful to contemplate."

He lifted his head, and wiped the heavy perspiration from his brow. It was the perspiration of mental agony which had collected there in large drops; and what an exquisite feeling it was for a few moments, to feel assured that he had escaped almost as terrific a death as that which the murdered man had suffered, whom he had seen liberated from the cupboard in which he had been confined.

Joy, however, is but a comparative passion, and human nature, relieved from any one great cause of personal terror, soon falls back upon the next subject of uneasiness in importance.

So it was with Godfrey; he found that his life was spared, that he had escaped the gigantic evil which, for a moment, had presented itself to his mind, and for a time he was abundantly pleased that he had done so; but then self felicitations soon withered away, and again he became aroused to a consciousness of how full of terrors was yet his situation.

"It is true," he said "that I have escaped death in one way; but may I not encounter it in another? It is more than probable all is darkness as to what will become of me; dare I move now an inch from where I am, when something, probably worse than even death may stare me in the face."

Terror, in every variety of aspect, now sat at his heart. He felt such pangs as he had never felt before; and if the wrongfully persecuted Charles Ormond had but then known what his arch enemy was suffering, probably in that generosity of spirit which so much distinguished him, he would have said,—

"Forgive him, Heaven! for even he has suffered enough."

But we are by no means so tender-hearted towards such a man as Godfrey; we are quite willing that he should suffer amply; for, of all the fiends that can appear in human shape, we look upon the man who could bear false witness against his neighbour, as one of the worst, if not the very worst.

There is not one redeeming trait that we can perceive in the character of Godfrey; gladly would we seize upon one, if we could find it, but it is not to be found; on the contrary, all is rascality, savage ferocity, combined with the worst feelings of grasping rapacity.

He was a man willing at once to sacrifice the best and most beautiful specimens of humanity, and who, regardless of all consequences, had always pursued his own evil course; and it was only that he happened not to be destitute of an imagination, nor of an immense amount of personal fear, that he felt so keenly upon the subject of that murdered corpse.

He rose now once again; for, upon a second thought, he considered that possibly he might remain there until the crack of doom, before any one would come to his rescue.

It was a horrible idea; but really it struck him that he might be left there to starve to death, which would be about as bad, if not worse than meeting with the fate of that poor man, some of whose blood, though he, Godfrey, knew it not, was still clinging to him.

"I must," he said, "now cry aloud for help. I must, let the danger of the proceeding be what it may, procure assistance from somewhere or from some one. I dare not move hand or foot, for my next step might plunge me into destruction fully equal to that which I thought I had come to, and an escape from which I have just been felicitating myself upon."

"Help! help! help!" he now shouted; and, even as he did so, he thought he heard a distant cry, or hilloa, in answer to his voice.

It might be fancy, and yet it was a very strong impression he had—an impression which was soon strengthened by a fact, for now, in the dim distance, he saw the faint glimmer of a light, and he said to himself,—

see p. 261.

"I am saved, or I am destroyed!"

The light came nearer, and the felicitous feelings, for they partook more of that character than of any other, which had first come across him when he observed it, began now, as it evidently approached him, to give way to the most acute uneasiness.

Over and over again he asked himself what he should say as an excuse for being there at all; and he made the most gigantic efforts to school his countenance to an expression of absolute calmness, so that there might be no suspicion in the mind of any one who should encounter him, that he had had an opportunity of making the dreadful discovery which he had done in those gloomy passages.

"I must seem to know nothing," he said to himself; "the slightest symptom indicative of a knowledge of the horrible secret which has been revealed to me, would, no doubt, prove my destruction; and I feel convinced that it will only be by assuming an ignorance, which I am far from having, that will give me the slightest chance, now, for my own existence."

It was with a sad and a sickly feeling that he now heard the sound of a footstep approaching; he drew his breath in long inspirations, and tried to assume a careless attitude, and then, as he felt assured that it was a man who was coming near him, and began to have an acute perception of the quarter whence he was proceeding, he thought it would be better to advance and meet him; so that, being as far away as possible from that horrible cupboard which had disgorged its loathsome contents, he might the better avoid the suspicion of having, what in this case might be called the little knowledge, which was a dangerous thing.

Acting upon this idea, he advanced, not quickly, but with a steady step; and, when he thought that the man was sufficiently near to hear his voice without it being loudly aggravated, he called, saying,—

"Hilloa! hilloa, there! I've lost my way in these passages; is there no one to show me the way out of them?"

"Who speaks?" cried a rough voice, and in another moment he saw a man advancing towards him, with whom, by his herculean proportions, he felt convinced that he should stand no chance in a personal encounter—"who speaks? what the devil have we here, a stranger? Are you sick of your life—eh?"

The man carried the light which he held high in his hand, in order to obtain an accurate view of Godfrey.

"Well, I am a stranger," said the latter, with assumed carelessness, which sat but ill upon him. "I am a stranger, certainly, so they ought not to have left me to find my way out alone."

"And pray, how came you here?" said the man, fixing upon Godfrey's face a searching glance, which he trembled beneath. "I say how came you here?"

"I came upon express invitation to see No. 50, and I trust there is no harm in that. I had a guide as far as the room, which was covered up at its entrance by a curtain of black cloth, and then, after I had said all I had to say, I was left to find my way out alone—rather a scurvy proceeding, I think, when I came to do a favour, and not to ask one."

"And pray, how long ago was that?" said the man, suspiciously.—"Oh, not long; about a quarter of an hour, perhaps."

The man was silent for a few moments, and then he said, in a tone of resolution, not unmarked by a considerable amount of ferocity,—

"Your story may be true, or it may not; for your sake it had better be true; for, should it turn out to be the contrary, you will find that you are not in so pleasant a position as you might be. We have secrets here, and those who chance to know them, we consider must be one of us, or else so useless to the world, as to be better out of it—you understand me?"

"Secrets!" said Godfrey, assuming an innocent look. "Well, I suppose everybody has his secrets; but, however, it's nothing to me. I don't want to know anybody's secrets, nor do I know them. All I require is a guide out of these passages. I have paid what money was required of me upon first entering them, and I do think, therefore, that, in common courtesy, I ought to be shown the way out."

"Come this way," said the man. "I don't pretend to say but it's all right, but, if it isn't—if you're in the habit of any such nonsense, you'd better say your prayers, for we don't stand upon trifles in a place like this."

"My prayers!" replied Godfrey. "I really do not understand you; and I can only say that you are much mistaken if you fancy me an enemy."—"Come on, come on."

The man strode on before, and Godfrey followed closely, feeling now very much assured of his own safety; because, of course, any inquiry must prove the truth of the tale he told, and so long as he kept his own counsel, who could tell of the frightful discovery that he had made?

So he told himself; but immediately he had done so his imagination became dizzy with a thousand terrifying fancies, and, as he followed the man whom he had thus encountered, he began indeed to feel that he stood in a ticklish position, notwithstanding of course that Neville would own him as an acquaintance, and confirm the tale he told.

He found that his guide led him by a short cut to the very identical room, before which hung the apparently ominous black curtain; but when they had passed that temporary obstruction, Godfrey saw that the room was untenanted, save by one man, who, by his alert look, and general air and manner, seemed like a sentinel more than the last of a quantity of stragglers taking their ease.

"Watkins," said the man who had encountered Godfrey, "where is No. 50?"—"In the next room; going out, I heard," was the reply.

"Will you keep this gentleman company till I return."—"Certainly."

Godfrey was left alone with this sentry, who walked up to him, and drawing a horse pistol from his breast pocket, tapped it with his forefinger, as he said,—

"Hark'ye, sir. I am so fond of good company, which I take yours to be, that I'll send a leaden messenger from this barrel after any one who, in an unmannerly manner tries to leave me. Do you understand?"—"I do," said Godfrey. "You need not be more explicit. I have nothing to fear, and, therefore, can await any inquiry, be it from what source it may."

"Very good," said the other. "That's no business of mine. I only tell you so that you may not be taken by surprise."

It may be fairly presumed that Godfrey was in a terrible fidget, and that feeling acutely the danger which he was in, he would have given almost any thing to have escaped from it. The next few minutes passed most laggingly to him, and it was with a feeling of exquisite relief that at length he heard the sound of footsteps, and, in the next moment, Neville, accompanied by the powerful man whom he, Godfrey, met in the passage, made their appearance.

"Know him," exclaimed Neville, as he came into the apartment; "ay, to be sure I do. There isn't a greater rogue unhung. Why, where have you been, Godfrey? I thought you were gone long since."—"I could not find my way," said Godfrey. "Meeting with this gentleman, he was pleased to suspect me of being here without leave, of which, I presume, you can acquit me."

"Oh, certainly," said Neville, with something of a sneer upon his countenance. "It's all right; you shall be shown out. Heaven forbid we should keep a gentleman like you away from his proper business."—"Well, if it's all right," said the other man, "I'll show him out myself. Indeed I'd rather than not; so come along, will you, sir. I'll soon put you into daylight."

"And you," said Godfrey, turning to Neville, "you will not forget the business you have in hand."—"It is one which too nearly concerns me," said Neville. "Be assured then I cannot, and shall not forget it."

With this assurance Godfrey was satisfied, and he followed his new guide, who led him by an amazingly short cut to the outer cellar fronting the street.

Ah! with what a feeling of intense satisfaction he breathed again in the open air. It was truly delicious after passing the time he had in those miserable subterraneous passages, to look once again upon the beautiful daylight; and, although he was far from being in the most salubrious district in the world, never before had he so much enjoyed the mere act of existence as he did upon that occasion.

What an escape too! It was from death! for death surely would have been his portion, had it been known that he walked into the upper air with the possession of so dreadful a secret as that which he took away with him.

"I know enough," he said, "to crush them all in that place, and they do not suspect me. If I were to give information, now, of that with which I am acquainted, I might root out this den of iniquity completely, and so purchase for myself quite an honourable name as a benefactor of society. But what care I for society? What has it ever done for me? and what will it ever do? People may murder each other as they please; it matters not to me, so that I have my turn answered, and make as much money as is necessary for my purposes, and deceive society"

"I beg your pardon, sir," said a respectable-looking man, stepping up to him, "but you seem in a state of excitement."

"What is that to you?" said Godfrey, suspiciously.—"Sir, I again beg your pardon," said the man, who spoke with great sincerity of manner; "but I saw you emerge from one of those cellars in Monmouth-street—a cellar, too, which I have some reason to believe communicates with vaults, wherein reside the worst of characters. I will be plain with you, sir; I am an assistant to the Bow-street magistrates, and have been engaged for some time in watching that very place. The fact is, a gentleman has disappeared, who, it is supposed, was inveigled into it; and perceiving at once that you were evidently not one of the characters who make such a place their home, I have made bold to speak to you."

While he was talking Godfrey looked at him, and first of all a suspicion, and then a certainty came over his mind that he was one of the men whom he had seen in the room, the entrance to which was covered by the black curtain; and, if such was the case, he felt assured that this was a mere manœuvre for the purpose of discovering if he had anything to tell of a dangerous character against the fraternity.

"You hesitate," said the man, "and very naturally too; but, however, if you'll come with me, we'll have a bottle of wine, and talk the thing over. I will tell you, sir, all that I suspect, and all that the authorities suspect, and I make no doubt whatever that you will be candid enough to tell me all that you know."

The more Godfrey looked the more he felt certain that he had seen the face of this man in the cavernous looking apartment, so that, with an appearance of great unconcern, he answered him, saying—

"Why, really, sir, I have nothing that will compensate you for the time consumed in the discussion of a bottle of wine. I do not for one moment doubt that you are just what you represent yourself to be, and if I had anything to communicate, which I really have not, I should do so with the greatest pleasure."

"Oh, well, indeed," said the stranger, "I'm rather glad, upon the whole, that there is nothing than that there should be something; but I tell you candidly it is suspected a murder has been committed there."—"Really!" said Godfrey; "you don't say so. How very dreadful!"

The man bit his nether lip for a moment, and then, with a sudden start, he exclaimed—

"Good morning, sir; good morning; I'm extremely sorry to have troubled you."—"Oh, don't mention it."

"I have the honour of wishing you a remarkably good morning, sir."—"The same to you," said Godfrey. "I merely went to visit a friend, and I must say I think you are wrong in your suspicions; but, however, the wickedness of the world is so very great, that, after all, you may be right, for all I know to the contrary."

They parted with a bow upon each side; and Godfrey, when he had got a short distance off, smiled to himself, as he said—

"So! they think that I am foolish enough to be taken by such a shallow pretence as this; but they will find themselves mistaken. What is it to me whom they murder? I have my own concerns to look after; and now that I have put Neville upon his guard, I will set about stirring heaven, earth, and—and—no matter where else, to discover the retreat of Charles Ormond."

CHAPTER XLIII.

CHARLES ORMOND IN THE VAULTS.—THE WEARY TIME.—ST. PAUL'S BELOW THE SURFACE.

CHARLES ORMOND never knew perfectly what solitude meant until he stood alone in those dreary vaults, whither he had been taken for the preservation of his very existence, and which, under any other circumstances, would certainly have been most insufferable.

Not the condemned cell in Newgate, that cell in which he had passed so many weary hours, presented to his mind such a solemn aspect of extreme desolation as did these abodes of the dead in which he now found himself.

We have said that he listened to the retreating footsteps of the man Jeffries; and no wave-beaten mariner, left upon a desolate shore, could watch more wistfully some vessel in the distance, than did he, Charles, listen to the last dying cadences of those footsteps, which, when they were completely gone, convinced him he was all alone.

He was not superstitious, he had no absurd fancies or vulgar fears, but he could not help feeling, what all well educated persons will feel under such circumstances, his imagination strongly, most powerfully, acted upon by the position in which he was placed.

And, yet, it was not altogether devoid of interest, for there is ever something, to cultivated minds, in a close communication with the dead which is of an exalted character, although pregnant with many fears.

The oil lamp which had been left him cast a steady glare around the vault, and as he looked into the various niches which contained the remains of the families who had owned that place of sepulchre, and counted no less than nine coffins in the various niches, he became somewhat curious to know the name or names of those individuals with whom he shared that rude, uncomfortable, damp, and noisome lodging.

Jeffries had left him plenty of candle ends, so that, without removing his lamp from the advantageous place in which it was situated, a place from which it cast a tolerable light over the whole of the vault, he was able to pursue any special inquiries that he pleased comfortably and easily.

Fixing, then, one of these pieces of candle ends at the extremity of a cleft stick, which had been left him by Jeffries for that purpose, he lighted it, and proceeded to institute his careful inquiry. It was no easy matter, in consequence of the great progress which decay had made upon the exteriors of the coffins, to ascertain the family name of their inmates.

Most certainly there were plates which had at one time borne both date and name; these were rotted away; and notwithstanding he went from coffin to coffin, with a hope of finding one which had been sufficiently recently placed within the vault to satisfy his researches, he found that the pursuit was a vain one, for the freshest of those receptacles of the dead had evidently been there for a sufficient number of years to render the progress of decay sufficiently complete to defeat his object.

" It is evident," he said, " that this vault has been for some time deserted, either by the complete extinction of the family who owned it, or by their removal to some distant place, which renders their use of this, as the last resting place of their dead, most inconvenient." He had a great aversion to touching any of the coffins, or, possibly, he might have facilitated his object.

"No!" he said, " I do not feel that I ought to desecrate this home of the dead more than I am doing by my simple presence."

Already, it will be recollected, he had laid hold of the handle of one coffin, and that the end of it had come out in his grasp; it was to this one that he came round last in his inquiries, and he found that, upon a closer inspection, he really had done no mischief to the narrow home of the dead, because within the wooden coffin he found there was a leaden one, which, except being discoloured, seemed as intact and entire as when it first came from the hands of its maker.

He held the candle close to this coffin, and then he found that if he had done so at first, he would have been saved all his trouble, and that his inquiries would have been at once answered. Engraven on the end of this coffin were the following words :—Eliza Brenton.—Ætat 22.—Died 1750.

"So," he said, "Brenton is the name of that family whom I feel I have intruded upon by becoming an unbidden guest in the vault which contains their mortal remains.

There seemed nothing further in this vault which was calculated to attract his curiosity ; but, situated as he was, night and day presented to him the same aspect, and as he did not feel inclined to repose, he thought he would pursue his researches, at all events, up to the grated door which had been spoken of by Jeffries, as looking into one af the aisles of the cathedral.

"It must be night," he said, "in that stupendous building, and, if the moon be shining, I shall catch a glimpse of some of its glorious architecture, so ridding myself of the teeming fancies which burst my brain amid these subterranean abodes of the dead."

He pushed open a door which had no fastening, and which creaked heavily upon its hinges, and entered a narrow passage, similar, in general appearance, to those by which he had approached the vaults along with his guide Jeffries.

Now, again, in consequence of the confined dimensions of the place in which he was, and the quantities of damp that exuded from the walls, the candle burned with a dim and sickly lustre. But he heeded not that, for, so long as he was not actually left in the dark, it was of little consequence ; and, even if he were, he had but to turn round and walk back again to the vault, with almost a positive certainty of not missing his way.

After he had gone a considerable distance, he came upon a narrow staircase, which seemed to ascend to a great height, and which he had no doubt terminated in the gilt door which had been described to him as looking into the aisle of the cathedral.

Before, however, he reached the foot of this staircase, he came upon several doors, opening to the right and to the left, which he had no doubt led into vaults similar to the one he had just left, and which, as he might explore at a more fitting opportunity, he now passed by, being far more intent upon reaching the grated doorway before mentioned.

The stairs were narrow and steep, and he did not wonder that it became necessary occasionally to reach the vaults by the more even entrance opposite to Paul's Chain, than encounter what must be the immense task of carrying a coffin down those stairs.

As he neared the top, he fancied that he saw some faint light, and he hastily paused, shrouding his own candle in such a manner that it could cast no rays upwards, and then, when the light was permitted to shine with its own lustre, he became convinced that it was the beautiful moon that was shedding its radiance in the body of the cathedral, while some of its reflected beams probably found their way through the grated door which now he hoped to reach.

Although no one at that solemn hour—for that, now he began to calculate, he found must now be near to midnight—was likely to be in the cathedral, yet the prudence of concealing the light he carried came strongly upon him, so he left it at an angle of the staircase, and walked up the remainder of the distance without it. A few moments sufficed for him to reach the grated door, through which he could see into the cathedral, by the most gorgeous moonlight that ever he had seen.

The beautiful silver beam that streamed in full upon the monuments and statutes of the dead, imparted to them a spirituality, and an exquisite touch and finish, far, indeed, beyond the sculptor's art.

Oh, what a longing desire came over him to walk free throughout the vast expanse of that beautiful building, reared to the worship of the great God of all !

"Surely, oh, surely," he said, "there could have been but little danger, if any, in trusting me to such an amount of liberty as that!"

And he looked wistfully through the ornamented grating, and fancied how pleasant it would be, during his sojourn in that place, to take his nightly walk along those stately aisles, while during the day he could have sufficient repose in the vault of the Brentons, to give him ample opportunity to enjoy such a nightly exercise.

"But I am interdicted," he said—"interdicted by those whose opinions I am forced now to make my law; so it may not be done, and I would not even ask for the means of doing it."

As he spoke, for the first time he laid his hand upon the grating of the door. Oh, what a sudden flush of pleasure and surprise came across him, as it yielded to his touch, opening noiselessly and gently towards the cathedral. He wasted no time in thought; he felt nothing, knew nothing at the moment, but that here was an opportunity of walking in the pure, cool air, beneath that magnificent dome which is unequalled in Europe, instead of stagnating, as it were, in the noisome vapour of vaults and passages devoted solely and entirely to the service of the dead.

"This is joy, indeed!" he said, and he stepped at once out into the aisle. "I feel as if I were really now free, while freedom before was but a mockery, a most unsubstantial something, which, while it seemed to belong to me, yet eluded my grasp."

A sensation of invigorated health came instantly across him; but, by the time he had passed half way over the aisle, he bethought himself, at all events, of some necessary caution, and paused to listen for the remote possibility of some one being in the cathedral.

All was profoundly still, but it was a stillness of a far different character from that which prevailed in the vaults; it orought along with it quite a different feeling; for, whereas, when he had been confined among the dead, in that damp unwholesome place, his mind felt depressed, now a feeling of exaltation, of fervour, and of the solemnity of devotion came over him.

It is true he started occasionally at the strange and grotesque shadows which were cast by some of the statuary; but those starts were rather of surprise than of fear, for of the latter feeling really he had nothing.

"Now," he said, "I shall enjoy the night indeed, for it will permit me—as I hope this door will remain unfastened—to feel that I live indeed, as I traverse the extent of this princely building."

To many men, most certainly, Charles Ormond's situation would have now been one of extreme terror, and shrinking nervousness; but it certainly was not so to him, for his intellect was just of that order which enabled him thoroughly to enjoy such a scene and such a place.

"Marian," he said, "my beautiful Marian! if I had but you here, how happy might I be for many an hour; then, indeed, should I almost bless the circumstance that had brought us together in so holy and devotional a spot; because, whatever words we should utter to each other, would seem to be sanctified by the place in which they were uttered." But this was a hope which he felt could not be realised.

"Oh, no," he said, "it cannot be. Here, alone, am I doomed to remain, and such consolation as I can find in this holy spot, I must find by myself, now."

He suddenly started, for he distinctly heard a sound that so closely resembled a human footstep, that he felt how impossible it was that it could be anything else; and yet the absurdity of such being the case came in another moment so strongly across his mind, that he could not possibly help thinking that his imagination must have most completely deceived him.

Still, however, he thought it worth while to listen acutely, and, with as much caution as possible, to get back towards the door through which he had emerged, so that in case of any one really breaking in upon the solitude of that place, he might have an opportunity of immediate escape. He crouched down by the side of a monument and listened attentively.

All was silent for some moments; and then, just as he had given up the idea of fancying that it could be any one, he distinctly heard a cough, which, if it came not from a human being, was quite as good enough imitation to excite all his fears.

"Gracious Heaven!" he whispered to himself, "I am not, then, alone."

Then the footstep sounded again upon his ears as if it were approaching him. Nearer and nearer it came, until he felt quite certain that it was coming towards him ; and so he was induced to crouch close down behind the monument to escape detection.

Then, just at the moment when he fancied that half a dozen more steps must bring the individual, be he whom he might, close upon him, the sounds began to die away, and all was as still and calm, in a few moments, as before.

This was most mysterious; and, for a time, Charles Ormond could scarcely believe in the evidence of his own senses. But still, how could he be deceived? He had not been thinking of any intrusion ; on the contrary, his mind was bent upon Marian Whitehead ; so that it could not be said that he was full of superstitious fancies, and had peopled even vacancy with terrors of the imagination.

He remained for a considerable time concealed; and it was not until assurance became doubly sure, that, whoever had been there, must, by that time, have completely left, that he ventured again to emerge from his hiding-place, and look around him freely beneath the dome of the cathedral.

Perhaps his solitude now felt worse to him, from this slight interruption to it, than it had done before. He certainly fancied that it did so ; and it was with more regret, by a great deal, that he prepared to descend into the vaults, for the purpose of endeavouring to seek some repose.

In vain he tortured his imagination to find some solution of the mystery connected with the singular footsteps in the cathedral. And, perhaps, had he been inclined to attribute them to his imagination, he could not so well get over the mysterious cough which had sounded in his ears, and of which there could be no doubt, for that was not at all romantic, or likely to be a subject of superstitious fancy.

And yet how, again and again, he told himself he could not be deceived! and with what a pang he began to think that those mysterious sounds which he had heard in the cathedral, might act upon his imagination to a sufficient extent to deprive him of the solitary, but delightful walks, he had promised himself!

"To-morrow night," he said, "I will watch for this again ; and, should it come, I will be more upon the alert to ascertain its meaning."

Slowly and cautiously he again descended to the vaults from whence he had emerged, and then arranging the clothing which had been brought to him by Jeffries, he trimmed the oil-lamp and sought for repose, even in that most unlikely place to find it.

And, had he been a guilty man—had an orphan's tears or a widow's moans, hung heavy at his heart, could he have laid down so calmly as he did to sleep amid the dead? Ah, no; it was his innocence of heart and purpose which gave him strength enough to lift his soul above even the crowding superstitions which form a portion of every man's character. He who would be without them, must be something more or less than man ; but still it does not follow that, although such fancies may exist, and come upon the mind with all the form and force of reality, that they are to be terrifying.

The man who admits the possibility of appearances, even in their worst garb, but who, at the same time, challenges their power of evil, or even of terror, is in a far better position than he who holds even a weak argument against such existences, while, at the same time, his fears too readily admit them.

Charles Ormond was most emphatically in the former position ; and truly might he have said, in the words of that immortal poet, who, while the English language exists, will descend with it to the remotest generation,—

> " Thrice is he armed, who has his quarrel just,
> And he but naked, though wrapped up in steel,
> Whose conscience with injustice is corrupted."

And so thrice armed was Charles Ormond against all that might befall him—thrice armed against all the most malignant shafts of evil fortune.

He slept soundly in that vault where never living, breathing man had slept before; and many a wretch, living in splendid iniquity, might well have envied the calm, child-like sleep which fell upon his soul. It was that sleep which "knits up the ravelled sleeve of care"—that sleep which a monarch in vain has sighed for beneath the canopies of state, until, turning philosophic in his restlessness, he has exclaimed,—

> "Then happy low lie down,
> Uneasy lies the head that wears a crown."

Charles Ormond had no means of measuring the time in that dreary abode, but when he awoke, he felt wonderfully invigorated; and, from the fresh and dawn-like feeling that came across him, he felt convinced that it must be morning.

This was a fact though which he thought, and thought correctly, he could ascertain easily enough by creeping up the staircase, and, without exposing himself to any observation, peeping through the gilt doorway, into the cathedral.

"Surely, I may do that much," he said, "without incurring censure from my friend Jeffries, on account of any presumed foolhardiness in the act. I will do it, too. It will be something even to look upon the daylight—if I may not, as seems to be the case, walk into it and enjoy it."

It was something, too, he told himself, to look upon living, breathing forms, instead of upon those sallow and time-worn memorials of the dead, with which he was surrounded; and, therefore, with an exquisite feeling of what a treat it would be to take this peep of humanity, even from behind the grating, with all the caution that it was possible to throw into his movements, he crept from the vault up the staircase, and looked out into the beautiful cathedral.

It was daylight; the sun instead of the moon was illuminating the place; and, oh, what a different aspect did it wear in that most different light in which he now viewed it!

What dearer charm could there now be in the whole world, but that daylight which we so little appreciate, because we so constantly enjoy it. Where could he found aught so really beautiful, or so calculated then to bring joy to the heart of the poor persecuted Charles Ormond, always excepting his own much loved and dearly cherished Marian.

With her, he could have been content to live in some wilderness of nature, with naught of the great world about them, but its immensity; and nothing whatever to call to mind all those jarring interests which make man what he is.

Secure, because he kept so far back that none could see him behind the gilded grating, of what might be not inaptly termed the cage in which he was confined, he saw the people who had paid their threepence walk about, and look upon the monuments, with that listless air that people regard those things with which they can see any day.

More than one chance visitor paused and looked at the grating, behind which the prisoner was; and one young man said,—

" I should like to go through that door-way—perhaps it leads to the vaults."

Involuntarily Charles drew back, and then, for the first time, the sense of a new danger struck him, and he said to himself,—

" What if some one should have the curiosity to push the door open, and finding every facility for so doing, then descend into the vaults, and so, if I even succeeded in concealing myself, find ample evidences of the presence of some one in the articles of comfort and convenience, which have been brought for my use?"

He felt it would be just such an adventure as would please him to do, and, therefore, why not others? He felt eagerly about for some fastening inside the door, and it was an exquisite relief to his mind to lay his hand, at length, upon a massive bolt, which he at once shot into its socket, and so shut out, as it were, the world from his solitude.

CHAPTER XLIV.

MARIAN WHITEHEAD'S INDISPOSITION.

Let us now turn our attention, for a brief space of time, to that place which should have been a pleasant country home, full of the dearest delights and domestic enjoyments. Let us see, while these eventful scenes are occurring in London, what variation, if any, has taken place in Marian's condition—that condition which was so lamentable, and so calculated to awake the tenderest sympathy in any mind capable of appreciating such a feeling.

Alas, she unfortunately remained as we last presented her to the reader, in that death-like trance, which poor Mrs. Whitehead said was a mercy, and so indeed it was. Heaven, perhaps, in its goodness, had enshrouded her intellect in the misty vapour which obscured all those painful perceptions, that else would most surely and vividly have acted with frightful earnestness upon her system.

Dead alike to joy and sorrow, she lay breathing, but still the very image of a corpse—there was no speculation in those eyes, which had once beamed with so much beauty and intelligence ; a something of the beauty was there, but the intelligence that lent them all their charms was gone.   Like some fair flower torn by the rude hand from its parent stem, she lay, presenting the principal features of her living loveliness, but carrying the sad impression to all who looked upon her, that the fragrance would be but fleeting—the blushing tints but evanescent, and that, in all her charms, she would, like the baseless fabric of a vision, fade, and leave not a rack behind.

Poor Mrs. Whitehead felt inconceivably lonely under the circumstances in which she was placed.   She could not find any consolation in the conversation of the woman who, to her credit be it spoken, attended really with great care and assiduity upon her and the helpless Marian ; but, certainly, she missed the sweet voice of that gentle girl, who, since the death of Mr. Whitehead, had been her only consolation, and the only being who could now lend a charm to her existence.

And what a dreadful thing it was to have her in that seeming trance of death—on the earth, and yet more fitted for an inhabitant of the grave to all appearances and for all purposes.

The principal occupation in which poor Mrs. Whitehead passed the day was in sitting by the bedside of Marian, and weeping bitterly, and calling her frantically by name, with the hope that she might get an answer from her at last, and so hear once again that voice, which had borrowed from memory a new charm, since she had become deprived of its beautiful cadences.

But, alas ! the gentle affectionate girl still remained in the fearful-looking trance, which, though it had nothing about it of a repulsive character, really, to the eyes, had too much of the calm repose of death in its aspect, to be otherwise than most heart-thrilling to those who loved her.

And yet, as hour by hour passed away, and Mrs. Whitehead felt that the period of Charles Ormond's execution, for she knew not of his escape, was drawing near, she almost blessed the trance in which her daughter lay.

On the following day, notwithstanding great pressure of business, Mr. Blake, the attorney, contrived to run down to the cottage, and he had a great mental struggle with himself to know whether or not he should inform Mrs. Whitehead of the chances, which at all events existed, of Charles's escape from the dreadful death that had awaited him, or still keep the affair a secret, until those chances had assumed a shape of greater certainty.

Think how he would upon the subject, he could not absolutely decide, but he made up his mind that when he arrived at the cottage he would be governed by circumstances, and he felt that if Marian had sufficiently recovered to heed the intelligence, that, indeed, it would be a sore trial to him not to give it to her.

When he reached the cottage, however, he found that she was in the same state as when he had left her, and that cataliptic condition had continued now so long that he began to get seriously alarmed for the consequences of it, and he at once proposed to Mrs. Whitehead that he should bring down a physician of eminence, who had not yet seen Marian, to give some sort of decision upon her case.

This suggestion wonderfully increased all poor Mrs. Whitehead's fears, for, to the majority of people, the very wanting of a physician is the symbol of approaching death.

" My dear madam, be calm," said Mr. Blake; "it would be the height of absurdity for me to give any opinion upon Miss Whitehead's case, for, of course, however I may feel for her condition, it is impossible for me to say whether she be worse or better."

" But you are alarmed at her condition, sir ?"

" Yes; but you may believe that alarm arises rather more from sympathy than from knowledge; so do not, I pray you, give yourself any additional uneasiness from the fact of my bringing a medical man of the highest character I can find to see her."

" You are too good to us, sir," said Mrs. Whitehead ; " you are too good to us."

"Oh, pho, pho, don't say anything of the kind ; you have been the victims of great oppression, and it is the duty of every man who knows of such circumstances to befriend you in every manner within his power.   I do not know, Mrs. Whitehead, that to-day I could bring you down any professional man upon whom I could rely, but to-morrow, be assured that you shall see me, and in the meantime, I pray of you, that you will want for nothing, and that if any particular symptoms should arise in the condition of Marian which should in your judgment require instant medical aid, you will afford it to her, and trust to me to be at the charge of it."

"Sir, how heavily we are already your debtor."—"Not at all, not at all ; I shall put it all down in a bill you know, and some day, when I think you are able to pay it, present it to you."

"Alas ! sir, that day will never come."—"I don't know that ; who knows that some day circumstances will arise which shall give you the power yet of enforcing restitution from Godfrey of those ample means which he has surreptitiously obtained from you.   If I could but get any other evidence but that of your own of the means which he used to extort from you the document that has placed your and Marian's fortune at his disposal, I would soon show you that it was yet to be wrested from him by the strong arm of the law."

"It was a shocking thing," said Mrs. Whitehead, "and more shocking now that my poor girl has fallen into such a state of health.   I think I could have endured anything and gone back to our poverty, if this heavy infliction had not fallen upon poor Marian."

"Do you forget the dreadful situation of Charles Ormond, madam ?"—"Oh! forgive me, sir, that for the moment the consideration of my own private grief made me forget it.   I should not have done so, for Heaven knows he was a good and kind friend to us, and alas ! it is to that friendship he has fallen a sacrifice."

"It is, indeed, madam, and that you see Heaven has brought with it this additional evil of your daughter's indisposition, which would never have occurred, doubtless, had not Charles Ormond been in his present dreadful and calamitous circumstances."

"But is there no hope for him ?"—"But little—but little."

"You say but little ; then there is some ?"—"Nay, it is more than I ought to count upon or speak of, and therefore it should not form a subject of contemplation, nor dare I mention it ; but yet if Marian should recover suddenly and speak of him, I think, Mrs. Whitehead, you might venture to say that his friends were doing all they could, and that there was just a hope of his escape from the dreadful doom to which he seems consigned."

"Oh ! sir, you would not say so much unless you knew more."—"Now don't think that—now don't think that," said the attorney, as he walked hurriedly from the cottage.   "If you think that, I shall regret I have said so much as I have ; so I pray you do not do so, but expect me here to-morrow."

Mr. Blake doubted his own prudence in saying so much after he left the cottage ; but still he reconciled himself to it when he considered he had acted from the best and kindest of motives, and he determined to be punctual in his promise to bring down with him some eminent physician on the following day to look at Marian.

A Sir Andrew Skelton was then about the first man of the day in the medical world, and he was deservedly so, for in addition to being profoundly skilled in all the known experiences of his profession, he was a man of a subtle intellect, and frequently hit upon original modes of acting with regard to patients, which produced the happiest results, although by no means according to the usages of medical science or what tmay be found in books.

Mr. Blake was informed by several friends, whom he consulted, that of all others Sir Andrew Skelton was the man to look at such a case as Marian Whitehead's, and accordingly on the following morning the attorney and physician might have been seen going at as rapid a rate as two vigorous horses could take them towards the cottage at Ealing.

In answer to the inquiries when they alighted, they were informed that no change had taken place, and the physician, whose time was valuable, at once desired to see his patient.

He was conducted by Mrs. Whitehead to the chamber of Marian—that chamber wherein she had lain so still and motionless from the first moment of her being carried into the cottage ; and Mr. Blake, too, after having obtained permission to do so, followed, to look again upon the form of one in whose fortune he felt almost as much interest as if she had been a dear child of his own.

And there she lay, so still, so calm, and so motionless—more beautiful than death, certainly, but presenting to those who gazed upon her almost as melancholy a spectacle.

The physician held her hand in his, and looked in her face attentively for a considerable time, during which his countenance was watched with all the scrutiny of anxious interest by both Mrs. Whitehead and the attorney, in the hope that they should be able to gather something from it which should, perhaps, give a better clue to his real opinion than any words he might think proper to utter.

Dr. Skelton, however, was too well versed in his profession to betray what he felt, so easily. His face was apparently calm and passionless, and not at all the tablet of thought which, perhaps, it might have been, under different circumstances.

The physician feels that it is a duty he owes to the sick, that his countenance should not be read too easily ; and the suppression of feeling that at first is an effort, at last becomes a habit, which it would require, perhaps, a greater effort of another nature to break off.

"Have you tried any remedies, madam ?" he said.—"Yes," said Mrs. Whitehead ; "warm baths were recommended, but they produced no perceptible effect."

Sir Andrew Skelton counted the faint pulsations of the wrist, and then he said,—

"We will not despair ; this is by no means the worst case that I have come across. You will understand, madam, that there is a vast difference when these sorts of effects move from an actual disease of some organ of the body, and when they are only sympathetic upon strong mental emotions."—"Yes, sir," said Mrs. Whitehead ; and she just understood about as much of it as the bedpost by which she held for support.

"From all that I can hear," added the physician, "this is a case which will yield to time ; at all events, this trance will go off, and I hope then that it will not leave behind it any permanent mental effects, but I warn you that such is possible."— "Oh, that is what I fear—that is what I fear," exclaimed Mrs. Whitehead.

"Then you have some cause to fear it. Did she, before lapsing into this swoon, betray any symptoms of mental aberration ?"—"She did, indeed," remarked Mr. Blake, who saw that Mrs. Whitehead was in a state of great confusion ; "she did, Sir Andrew. From the unhappy circumstances which I have detailed to you, her mind had evidently received a shock of the severest character."

"No doubt—no doubt ; it's a melancholy affair. And Charles Ormond is the name of the young man whose fate she takes so much to heart ?"—"Yes, yes."

"Well, I think we may try an experiment, if it be the fact that pure sympathy with him has caused this state of physical prostration."—"Oh, sir, don't—indeed, don't," said Mrs. Whitehead.

"I really cannot see, madam, what objection you can have."—"But it's so dreadful ; the idea of any body being dissected !"

"Dissected ! madam ; I said nothing of dissected."—"No, sir ; but an experiment's all the same thing, ain't it ? I always understood that when doctors tried experiments, they cut people up dreadfully ; and I'm sure I've heard they do it sometimes in the hospitals."

"I regret to say, madam, that such has been the case occasionally ; but give me leave to assure you that it is no experiment of that character I wish to try with your sick daughter ; on the contrary, my earnest wish is to do something which will tend towards her recovery, for I presume that your immediate object is, that she should be recovered from the state of collapse in which she has fallen."—"Oh, yes, yes ; if you can but let me see her open her eyes, and let me hear her sweet voice once more, I shall esteem it one of the greatest of favours."

"What can be done shall be done." The medical man stooped down close to the ear of Maria, and said to her, in loud and clear tones, "Charles Ormond!"

His voice was so uncommonly clear and distinct as he uttered these words, that even Mrs. Whitehead started and glanced round the room as if she almost expected to see Charles enter it.—"Charles Ormond!" again repeated the physician in the ear of Marian, and then, sliding his hand beneath her neck, he raised her up a little in the bed. A visible spasm shook her frame, and Mrs. Whitehead, clasping her hands, exclaimed,—

"She lives—she lives! oh, she lives again!"—"And she will recover," said the physician; "I think the spell that held her faculties enchained is broken."

A rapid change of colour took place upon Marian's countenance, and she evidently was making an articulate effort to speak.

"It is, indeed, astonishing," remarked the physician, "what a wondrous power there is in the name of one to whom we are much attached. You perceive that the mere utterance of the words 'Charles Ormond,' has produced an effect which we could not have hoped for with any known medicines whatever."—"It has, indeed," said the attorney; "I am astonished; I could not have dreamed of such a great result from so simple a cause."

"Give me some stimulant," said the physician; "have you wine or brandy immediately at hand?"—"Both, both," said Mrs. Whitehead; and she made such a rush to leave the room, that she nearly tumbled down the staircase.

"Do you really think that she will recover?" said Mr. Blake.—"I think we may go far enough to say that she has recovered," was the reply. "When once, in these cases, there is any symptom of returning vitality, we may look shortly for a complete restoration. Now, madam, what have you there?"

"Wine and brandy," said Mrs. Whitehead.—"Indeed! I see but one article."

"No, sir; but I put them both together in this cup to save time; I thought if one wouldn't do the other might."—"Good God!" said the physician, "what a singular idea! but it's of no consequence; I dare say there's brandy in the wine, and something worse than wine in the brandy."

"Yes, sir," said Mrs. Whitehead; "I dare say there is. Would you like a little laudanum? I've got some down stairs, and there's some medicine, too, I had for a cough, a little time ago. Physic's physic, sir, you know."—"Good God, madam! you don't suppose I'm going to give her a cough mixture?"

The physician held the cup containing the brandy and the wine to the lips of Marian; he allowed only a very small quantity of it to pass into her mouth, and turning to Mr. Blake, he said,—

"It's the aroma of the liquor, more than anything else, I expect the result from. I do not wish her to swallow any—probably, if she were, we should have some spasmodic attack that might be dangerous."

"Is she better?" exclaimed Mrs. Whitehead, rushing suddenly into the room—for she had left it—and carrying in her hand a small phial.—"I think she is, madam."

"Then give her this, sir, it's a very powerful thing."—"Indeed! what is it?"

"It's creosote, sir, for the toothache—a most powerful medicine; and a desperate case, sir, you know, wants desperate means."

The doctor looked at Mrs. Whitehead with a stare of amazement, and then he said,—

"Madam, have you any other abominable decoction or compound in the house? Mention it at once, if you please, and allow me the pleasure of throwing it into the fire; and I can only say, if this young lady's mind should turn out to be affected, I shall strongly suspect it's a family complaint on the mother's side."

"Yes, sir, certainly," said Mrs. Whitehead; "she had once a complaint in her side. It was a sort of kind of pain, sir, just round the small of her back, and going just down the large of the back, in a manner of speaking."—"Very likely—you see she is recovering."

Drawing in his breath for a moment, with a loud voice that shook the very apartment, he cried in her ear, "Charles Ormond."

" Yes," exclaimed Marian, speaking for the first time for many days   yes, yes, Charles; I am here—I am here."   And then she fainted.

" Oh! she's gone again, she's gone again," said Mrs. Whitehead.—" I beg your pardon," said the physician; " she's not gone again, and you will find that she has not; she will recover—this is a very different thing from what she has been afflicted with.   This is an ordinary fainting fit.   There, take your abominable mixture, and bring me some water."

Mr. Blake went to a washhand-stand, and procured the water required, and when some of it was spilled upon Marian's face, she recovered sufficiently again to open her eyes, and look around her.

" 'Tis nothing in the world but weakness," said the physician, " which produced this fainting.   She has been so long without the ordinary amount of nourishment to which her frame was accustomed, that she has not been capable of supporting what may be called a proper existence; but all that will pass away, and for the present we must be content to support her with stimulants.   Marian Whitehead, do you not feel better ?"

" Oh! where is Charles ?" she said.—" Oh! he's all right," said the physician.

" I hope indeed he is," ejaculated Mr. Blake.—" Hush, don't give her any alarm; she forgets his position, and we must not go out of our way to remind her of it. Let her be, Mr. Blake; memory will return soon enough."—" I fear it will, indeed."

" What has happened—what has happened ?" said Marian, hurriedly; " oh! Heaven, what has happened ?"—" Come, come, cheer up," said the physician; " you have been unwell, but you are now better.   There's no harm done—you have only fainted—you are not afraid of fainting ?"

" But where is Charles ?"—Even at the moment that she uttered the ejaculation, she uttered a shriek, for then, as the physician had said, memory came back to her, and she remembered at once all the perils of his dreadful condition.

" Oh! they have murdered him—they have murdered him," she cried; " he is lost to me for ever.   Have mercy, Heaven; this is worse than a dream, be it ever so terrible."

Mrs. Whitehead was inexpressibly alarmed at this sudden accession of grief in Marian, and she at the moment almost wished that Marian had remained in that trance which so much resembled death, but which, at all events, had about it no outward showing of mental misery.

" Now, Marian," said Mr. Blake, " you are jumping at hasty conclusions. Charles Ormond is yet among the living."

" Oh! sir, on your soul, is that true ?"—" It is."

She sank back upon the bed with a sigh, and an almost instantaneous sleep came over her—a sleep so deep and dreamless, that but for the different expression of the face, one might have supposed it to be but a relapse of the same trance from which she had been rescued so short a time before.

But that it was not, and the physician begged of them not to be at all alarmed at it, for it was nothing but what was natural, and might be expected.

" She will awaken much better and calmer, no doubt," he said, " and then you must be very careful for a time what food you give her; but I will leave you certain directions how to act, and let me beg of you, if you have anything, Mr. Blake, of a consolatory character to say to her about this young man, in whose fate she is evidently so deeply interested, that you will cause it to be communicated to her as shortly as possible after she awakens from her present slumber."

" It shall be so," said Mr. Blake; " Mrs. Whitehead, you can tell her, and please, my dear madam, to say that you have my authority for telling her so much, that I have a great hope of Charles Ormond completely escaping the dreadful fate to which he seemed by his enemies to be consigned."

" I will, sir, I will.   And do you really think he will be saved ?"—" I have truly the great hope which I have just mentioned to you, Mrs. Whitehead; but at the same time let me implore you to say nothing of this to any living soul but to Marian.   Of course I don't mind speaking freely before you, sir."

" Oh!" said the physician, " I never remember anything that happens before me in a sick chamber, except what is absolutely necessary that I should not forget, in consequence of its connection with the case of my patient."—"Of that I am well aware, sir. And now I will proceed to town again with you, for no doubt your time is as valuable as mine."

The physician, before he left the cottage, wrote down for Mrs. Whitehead, in pursuance of his promise, a kind of code of instructions as to what she was to do when Marian should awaken, and what she was to give her in the shape of food.

This was highly necessary, for, by the singular manner in which this good lady had behaved, it was quite clear that she was in such a state of mental confusion, that her remembering anything could not at all be relied upon.

Mr. Blake was very much delighted at the favourable change which had taken place in Marian ; and, during his drive to London with the physician, he gathered from him a tolerably decided opinion of her condition.

" She will do very well," he said, " if no relapse ensues in consequence again of any great mental shock. The intellect seems untouched, which I was doubtful of at first ; for these species of attacks are very often the precursors of something in the shape of insanity."

" Well, I do not really think that she will receive any other great mental shock. If she do so, it will be one of joy."—"Oh! that will do her no harm, you may depend."

" I should think not. We are much indebted to your skill and humanity, sir."—"Oh, don't say a word about that ; the medical men are fond, you know, of any such case as that which goes a little out of the ordinary nature of family disorders. Good morning to you, Mr. Blake."

" Ah !" said the attorney, when he reached his home that night, after the business of the day was concluded—"ah, I rather think that I have managed this affair remarkably well. Every hour that passes without a discovery being made, I consider adds to the security of my young friend, Charles Ormond ; and now I do really entertain a confident hope, which has almost amounted to an opinion, that he will escape altogether. What a defeat for the villain Godfrey, and what a triumph for truth and justice !"

The attorney, according to the aspect of affairs, had certainly great cause for self-gratulation. There did certainly appear to be every prospect now of Charles Ormond's complete escape, forl the hiding-place that had been chosen for him by Jeffries had evidently defied the scrutiny of all the official personages, who, no doubt, felt their own credit largely concerned in the re-capture of the escaped prisoner.

The very daring and extraordinary manner in which the escape had been achieved, put the officers connected with Newgate upon their mettle. But there, in the vaults of St. Paul's, did Charles remain in safety, although within hearing of the very footsteps of the men who were prowling about to apprehend him.

CHAPTER XLV.

THE SEARCH BY NEVILLE FOR CHARLES ORMOND, AND THE DANGER HE GETS INTO IN A PRIVATE MADHOUSE.

As soon as Neville could free himself from the effects of the debauch in which he had been engaged, he became more and more convinced of the necessity of finding out the hiding-place of Charles Ormond. The progress of recovering from the effects of intoxication was short with such a man as Neville, who was well used to all that kind of thing. After a plentiful application of cold water to his head, he threw himself on his bed to sleep. He had made several ineffectual efforts to think, which he found could not be done, unless he had less confusion in his brain than he had at that moment going on. A short sleep of a couple of hours seemed to restore him, and he once more applied to the cold water system, and was perfectly restored to all the uses of his faculties.

These might be said never to be put to a good purpose, for it could never be remembered when he did a good or even honest action, save upon compulsion."

"Now," thought Neville; "what is to be done, must be done at once. So, Master Ormond has escaped, eh? How could that have been managed? It must have been cleverly done; but it will be an ugly affair for me, and for Godfrey as well. While Ormond lives, of course there is a chance of something coming to light."

He paused in the midst of his own thoughts, and listened as though he had seen some one approach; but, apparently satisfied that no one was approaching, he continued.—"Now, if I had been caged up, I might, indeed, have remained there till the finish was put upon me, and nobody ever stirred to get me out of the way of the gibbet. No matter; I will cheat the world yet; but here we are, at the beginning of a chase.

"This young fellow must be found out; there can be no doubt about that, for if he remain unhanged, Godfrey may become frightened,—make off, or make terms of some kind or other, and I may very likely be let into the secret; but no

—no, that must not be; between two stools, it is dangerous sitting, and I will remove one of them, at all events; and if I can discover Charles Ormond, I shall, indeed, remove one of them.

"And now for Charles Ormond; where shall I find him, or where is it at all likely one such as he can be found; for, unlike others who are placed in such situations, he would not resort to the same mode of concealment. That is the thing; men know what kind of place to look for others in, but not for him. A good thought! Where are the Whiteheads? Wherever they are, there they can be found. No doubt he would visit Marian Whitehead; he could not help himself."

Neville paused, and a smile passed over his countenance, as he thought of the overwhelming misery he should cause, and the happiness he should destroy, by his success.

"Yes, they will little dream who is on the watch for them. It will be a rare sight to see Charles Ormond dragged from the arms of Marian, and be conducted to the gallows, despite all that could be said or done for him,—he must suffer. But where are the Whiteheads gone? that must be discovered, and then I will set a watch upon the place. I will haunt them day and night, but I will discover where he is. Yes—yes, that is the game. I will go and find out where the Whiteheads have gone, and then all that I have to do is, to exert some patience and vigilance; and I know well, when there is need, how to exert both."

Having come to the conclusion that, as a preliminary step, he must discover the abode of the Whiteheads, before he could attempt anything further, he determined to set about it at once, and for that purpose, dressed himself for the occasion.

"But where to go I hardly know. I'll go to their late lodgings; perhaps they may be able to tell me where I can find them. At all events, I will make the attempt."

Neville went to the lodgings of the Whiteheads, and having knocked at the door, said to the servant girl,—

"I wish to see Mrs. Whitehead."—"Mrs. Whitehead has left some time," said the girl.

"Indeed!" replied Neville, who expected no other answer from the girl, but affected surprise. "Indeed! I am very sorry for that. I wished to see them particularly."—"They are gone," said the servant.

"Do you know where they are gone to?" inquired Neville.—"No," said the girl.

"Nor where I can inquire?" said Neville.—"No," was the answer.

Seeing nothing was to be had here, Neville left the house, and turned over in his mind the next step he should take in the affair.

"Where shall I go now? Oh! I'll go to Blake's, and there I shall learn, I dare say, where they are gone to, from some of the clerks, though not from Blake himself. I must wait till he is out, at all events."

With this intention he walked towards Mr. Blake's offices, and, having ascertained that he was out, walked up to the door, and rang the office bell. A youth answered it.

"Is Mr. Blake at home?" he inquired, well knowing he was out at that time.—"No, sir," said the youth.

"I am sorry for that. Can you tell me where I can find Mrs. Whitehead?"—"They live somewhere down at Ealing," he replied.

"At Ealing?"—"Yes," said the youth; "in a cottage there of Mr. Blake's, somewhere in that neighbourhood."

"You don't know where it is, or the name of the cottage, do you?"—"No, I don't: all I know is, that she does live in a cottage belonging to Mr. Blake, at Ealing."

"Thank you, thank you," said Neville. "I'll come some other time and see Mr. Blake."

So saying, Neville turned away, and walked off, and disappeared from the eyes of the clerk, who began to have a notion he ought not to have given any information to a stranger, unless there were special reasons for so doing.

"So," he thought, when he had got some distance from the house,—"so they live at Ealing, do they, in a cottage belonging to Mr. Blake. Well, I will take up my residence there, too, for a time; for, if I find them, it strikes me strongly I shall find Charles Ormond."

He went to the coach-office, and having taken a seat on a coach that was going some part of the road, he consoled himself with the reflection that if he were suffering any inconvenience then, he would be secure when the object of his mission had ended in the recapture of the unfortunate Charles Ormond, and his return to Newgate.

The coach passed but within about two miles of Ealing, and he was forced to get down at that distance from the place; but this was rather advisable then otherwise, because he could walk into the town without any notice from any one.

"Can you tell me," he said, to the coachman, "whereabouts at Ealing Mr. Blake's cottage is?"—"No, I can't," said the coachman. "I never heard of the name before at all, sir."

"Do you know the name at all?"—"No, sir. Do you know the name of the cottage, at all?"

"No; I only know the owner's name; and it was empty but very lately."—"There have been a good many empty there, sir, of late; changing hands, and so forth. Sorry I can't help you, sir. Good day. The road is straight afore you."

The coach drove on, and the sound of wheels, and horses' hoofs sounded less and less distinct, and then Neville turned down the road, up which he walked, until he came near the village of Ealing, where he determined to stop. It was lighter than he desired to be seen about the place, as, if he should be seen, his presence would put the Whiteheads and Ormond upon their guard, and then, though he might be successful, yet he would have to lose much time. He, therefore, turned into a road-side public-house, and entered into a small parlour, where he called for some ale, determined to rest for a short time, until twilight made it safer to approach, and, at the same time, he could make certain inquiries, which he wished to make, and which he thought could not be better made than at such a place. When the landlord entered the room, he said to him,—

"Can you tell me where Mr. Blake's cottage is about here?"—"What, Ealing?"

"Yes, somewhere in or out of Ealing; but close at hand."—"Blake, Blake," said the landlord, endeavouring to recollect. "No, I can't remember the name at all."

"Very good," said Neville; "then it seems a bad job altogether. I can't find it out at all."—"Who lives in it?" said the landlord.

"A lady of the name of Whitehead."—"Mrs. Whitehead, eh? I don't know the name at all," said the landlord. "Never heard of such a name 'cept once."

"And when was that?"—"Oh! he was a sporting gentleman. His name was Whiteheaded Bob. That's the nearest like it as I knows on; but that's not them as you wants, I dare say."

"No, it is not so."—"Have you seen the news? Anything stirring in town, eh, this week?"

"No, nothing," said Neville. "What have you going on here, eh?"—"Oh, why," said the landlord; "nothing much 'cept this escape from Newgate."

"Indeed!"—"Ah! it is a strange affair that, sir! While such things go on, you may depend it's all not right. I mean it in the innerds of the country."

"Exactly."—"The constitution is in danger, depend upon it. What, break out of such a place as Newgate! I wonders they don't bring in a hact of parliament agin it."

"They ought," said Neville. "Have you had any new residents come here lately?"—"No, none, save the gentleman that keeps the land over the way, with the great house."

" Who lives in the house, then ?"—" His self, of course.   Who should ?"

" Who has come to him lately ?" inquired Neville, attentively.—" Why, he bought a couple of calves, but only one on 'em's come home.   That's the only new resident as I knows on yet awhiles ; leastways till somebody tells me of another, and then you shall know."

" You have seen nothing of two ladies, I suppose ?"—" Nothin' at all.   But, as I was saying about this escape from Newgate, don't you think it was a most owdacious proceeding, at all events ?"

" It was.   Have you heard of it ?"—" Oh ! yes ; the papers are full of it.   I am sorry he has broken out of gaol, though I am not sorry he got off ; because, you see I respects the country and its laws, and think that to break one on 'em is just the same as breaking the ten commandments, that I do."

" Do you ?" said Neville.—" Yes ; and what's more, I would never stand by and see it done any how.   Oh ! dear no."

" What, did you not say you were glad he had got off ?   How do you make that out ?"—" Why, I don't think he was guilty."

" But then both judge and jury pronounced him guilty, and the evidence was too clear."—" Yes, a great deal too clear.   I tells you what it is, sir, that what the young woman said, and what her mother said, completely settles it in my mind."

" Indeed !"—" Yes ; and, besides, that what's-his-name fellow, is a great scamp.   I should like to see him hanged.—I am sure he deserves it ; and so, as I said, I am sorry to see an escape from Newgate, although I am glad the young fellow is safe."

" Would you have harboured him yourself had he come to you ?" inquired Neville.—" No, not if I had known it, I wouldn't, certainly, because that would be abetting law-breaking.   But you may depend upon it he ain't guilty.   There's my verdict, and I don't care who says anything to the contrary."

" Very well," said Neville ; " we'll have it at that."—" If he can only keep out of the way for a time," said the landlord, " I should not be at all surprised to hear that somethin' had come out, and the jury's werdict has been rewersed, and he declared to be innocent."

" Very likely," said Neville, as he threw down some money ; " very likely. Take my score ; I must be off."—" Very well," said the landlord ; "thank'ee," and he handed him his change, and Neville then left the house to walk towards Acton.

It would not be long before it would be dark ; twilight was getting rather dim, and he had no fear now of being detected, except on a very close inspection.

" Well," he thought, " I am somewhat of the landlord's opinion ; that if Ormond can keep out of the way, something may come out, and make it dangerous to other people."

He walked onwards, seemingly lost in deep thought.   He meditated upon what Godfrey had said, and upon what he had just heard, and it seemed to confirm the opinion that had been gaining ground, that life to Ormond would be death to him.

" Yes, yes," he muttered ; " I must and I will find him.   He is sure to be met with somewhere near the spot where the Whiteheads live ; that will, at all events, be my settling point for a time ; then I must watch and lurk until I gain some information ; but, in the meanwhile, to find them seems to be the difficulty, for no one apparently knows them at all, or Mr. Blake's cottage either ; there are some difficulties to overcome."

The evening was growing dark, and the road lonely ; there were many pretty cottage residences on the road, and Neville looked at them one after another, but saw nothing in any of them by which he could recognise the one he was in search of, and he had made up his mind to go into the first, or rather every public-house he came to, to inquire.

" They must deal somewhere, and be known somewhere, by some one, one would think," said Neville.

Accordingly, he was about to make to one that was at a short distance from where he stood, when he saw a man coming towards him. It looked to him as if there was some hesitation in his manner, that struck him as being rather singular.

" Who is he—he seems as if he were ashamed of himself—he's not a runaway?" With more than a suspicion Neville approached him, saying, as he did so, " Good evening, friend. Where are we now?"

The man looked up, and both voice and feature at once assured Neville they were strangers to each other.

" Where are we?"—" Yes; whereabouts are we?"

" Oh! whereabouts are we? Oh! yes, whereabouts are we? Why, you see this is Acton."

Neville could not help staring at the man; his ways were so odd, and he seemed for moments lost in a fog or mist of a mental character, and it seemed odd, very odd, but it wore away after a few moments.

" Do you know anybody hereabouts?"—" Oh, yes; a good many people, and places, too."

" Do you know Blake's cottage?"—" Yes."

" Whereabouts is it?" inquired Neville, highly gratified at this lucky piece of information.—" Ah! yonder. If you'll come along with me, I'll show you, eh? it's not far, you know."

" Very well," said Neville; " I am very much obliged to you. Can you tell me who lives there?"—" Yes; I can."

" Who does live there?"—" I forget now; but I could easily tell it when I hear it—I can tell it again."

" Was it Whitehead?" said Neville.—" Ah! that was it; yes, Whitehead; that was the name, I remember it perfectly well. It is strange that I should forget such a name as that at all, it's so easy."

" Yes; mother and daughter."—" Yes; mother and daughter," said the stranger; " that's them."

" Have they had any visitor lately?" said Neville; " any male visitor, I mean; a young man?"—" Oh! yes."

" Indeed! perhaps you have heard his name?"—" I have, but have forgotten that, too; but it's not a common name, but I could tell it if I heard it."

" Ormond," said Neville.—" Yes, Ormond it was; he's at the house."

" What, now?" inquired Neville, scarcely believing in the blind confidence that must have seized both Ormond and the Whiteheads, if they could imagine that he was safe.—" Yes; now," said the stranger.

" Then lead on; I'll follow you, and am much obliged to you for the trouble you have taken."—" Don't mention it."

They walked up a narrow bye-path, and came to a house which he could not distinguish on account of the trees by which it was surrounded. The gate was opened by the man who conducted him, and he walked through several places till he came to a little door, and having opened this in a manner that Neville did not understand, they entered the house, and after some turnings and stairs, came into a large room, in which were a great number of men walking about, and talking to each other.

Neville stared, looked around, and in a moment comprehended his situation. He was in a private madhouse. He looked back, but there was no escape ; and, before he could move, he was seized by six or seven madmen, who carried him to the centre of the room, and pinned him to the floor by sitting on his extremities, and thus detaining him.

The man whom he had met was mad, but he had contrived to escape; he was not, however, able to get clear off, to make use of his liberty, but hovered about, and seemed to think if he could put anybody else into the madhouse, so as to make the number of inmates right, he should not be missed by them.

He had also a habit of answering yes, to almost every question that was asked him ; he would own to almost anything, and with a little cunning, he was not an object of suspicion, and in this instance he completely deceived Neville.

Now that they had him on the floor, they made various proposals as to what they should do with him. Some insisted they should roast him, and eat him, but the want of a fire was the reason alleged for not carrying the proposition out.

Another wanted to have some fun, and imitate an eastern execution, by dividing the persons present into four companies, each to pull at the four extremities, until one came away, and whoever pulled an arm or a leg out first, were to be considered as the conquerors of the game.

Neville groaned with terror ; struggle he could not, though he endeavoured, and four-and-twenty men made four parties, or gangs of six each, and would at once have commenced operations, but they couldn't agree as to who should pull legs, or who arms.

In the midst of all this a bell rang, and a cry went through the place that supper was to be brought in, and the keepers were coming. At this there was a momentary pause, and Neville then hoped he might be rescued.

" Throw him out of the window," said one, and the cry was taken up and repeated by all present, and every one seemed anxious to have some share in the business, and in less than a minute he was secured, and carried up to a window and pushed out head first, and with a loud hurrah he was thrown crashing and cracking through some fruit trees, till he came with a hollow thump upon the ground.

CHAPTER XLVI.

MILES ATHERTON AND HIS WIFE HOLD A CONSULTATION.——A SUSPICIOUS CIRCUM-
STANCE.——THE FIRE.——THE LOSS OF THE BLACK LADY'S DOCUMENTS.

AT this period, Miles Atherton paused in reading the documents of the Black Lady, and appeared for a moment or more lost in thought ; and then, looking up in his wife's face, he said to her,—

" Poor thing !—poor thing ! her sufferings must have been great, indeed—very great. What a scoundrel that what's his name is !"

" Who ?—Neville ?"—" No—yes. He is, too ; but the other man I meant—Whitehead's partner that was, you know."

" Oh, I know who you mean—Godfrey ?"—" Ah ! Godfrey's the man I mean. What a scoundrel he must have been to have persecuted any young creature."

" Scoundrel ! He would have deserved a slow death by fire, the awful brute," said Mrs. Atherton, wiping her face with her apron.——" Yes, my dear, you never said anything more true ; he does deserve it ; but for the poor creature herself, I am sure, it would be a real charity to aid her now. Do you not think so, my dear ? I mean to do any kindness for the Black Lady."

" Certainly, Mr. Atherton, we ought to do kindness to all people ; but yet it would require a whole lifetime and an immense fortune to do so," replied Mrs. Atherton.——" But who could contemplate such an act as this ? It would have been a piece of madness—I mean we ought to do such kindness as may come in our way to do ; and I was thinking, my dear, that that room up stairs is not occupied."

" Which room is that ?" inquired Mrs. Atherton.——" Oh, the back attic," said Atherton.

" Well ?"—" Well, my dear, that back attic is a very nice room, and one in which a person might reasonably be comfortable in, if they had the means and the will."

" So they might."—" Well, cannot we offer that room to the Black Lady ? She will, no doubt, be very glad of the offer."

" Yes, she would. I am sure I should, if I were placed as she is," said Mrs. Atherton. " Why, that room, and a few things that could be put into it, to make it comfortable, would be a very nice room for a lone woman, who didn't want any visitors."—" That is exactly what I was thinking of myself," said Miles—" the very thing. How strange, now."

" Isn't it ? But what do you think about offering it to the Black Lady now ?" said Mrs. Miles Atherton.——" Yes, my dear, I was thinking of it, and was about to ask your opinion upon the matter. She's a very worthy creature, and her condition is very much to be pitied."

"So it is, Miles; and I think it would be an act of great Christian charity to make her such an offer."—"It would be such, my dear," said Miles. "Shall we offer her the back attic when next she comes this way? She will be a very quiet, inoffensive woman, who would interfere with nothing or nobody, and that villain, Neville, dare not show his face here."

"No," said Mrs. Miles Atherton, with a peculiar energy; "he dare not, indeed; if he did, I should know what to say and what to do to him, I'll warrant you."— "No doubt of that, my dear; I might leave that to your discrimination; you are well able to give him a good reason why he should not remain in this house if he came."

"I should rather think, Mr. Atherton, that I just could, and, what is more, I would."—"Then we will consider that matter arranged," said Miles Atherton to his wife.

"Certainly, if you wish."—"Very well; now I suppose we had better give over reading the manuscript for the night, because you see the necessity for getting up in the morning for business."

To this arrangement there was no objection, and the manuscript being fairly folded up, and deposited in the usual place of safety, they prepared to retire for the night.

"I don't know the reason," said Mrs. Atherton; "but I cannot help having my suspicions that we shall all of us be the object of this man's schemes as well as others."

"What makes you think that, my dear?" inquired Miles, in a doubtful manner, as though he were himself half impressed with some notion of the kind.—"I can't tell, but I am inclined to think so; I almost fancy some kind of misfortune coming over us."

"Oh, no; I'll tell you what it is. It is because we have been reading this manuscript, and there are so many things of that character in it, that we naturally think and think until we don't know whether what we have read is to happen or has happened."—"Well," said Mrs. Atherton, hardly satisfied with this kind of reasoning, "I suppose it is so; but it is very uncomfortable for all that, and yet I am never out in my forebodings."

"That's true, my dear."

Now Miles Atherton had often listened to his wife's forebodings, but, at the same time, he could not say distinctly that he saw the truth of the observation, which was in itself very shadowy and capable of a variety of solutions, and each might be termed a wonderful fulfilment of her predictions.

However, this was a thing it was not worth to contest, since it might have disturbed the new found harmony that existed between the husband and wife. They, therefore, got up, and, taking the chamber candlestick, walked up stairs to bed.

"Now," said Mrs. Atherton, who was inclined to be more prophetic than usual; "now, Miles, place the candle and matches at hand, for it strikes me you'll have to get up."

"Eh?" said Miles, turning round.—"It strikes me, Mr. Atherton, you'll be disturbed to-night—you'll have to get up in the night."

"You're not going to be ill, I hope, my dear?" said Atherton; "because I'll sit up if you think so."—"No, no, no. I wish it may be no worse."

"No worse, my dear?"—"Yes, no worse, because my illness could be easily got over, but not so any heavy misfortune—if any happen, as I am sure will happen; but, let me see—ah! there are the matches and the candlestick; you'll recollect the place—won't you?"

"Yes, my dear, I shall remember them very well; but I think you are likely to be mistaken; look how late it is."—"There's time enough left for evil, Mr. Atherton, depend upon it; there is time enough left for evil."

"Yes, yes, there is."—"Well, well, Mr. Atherton, you had better come to bed and sleep while you may."

Miles Atherton did not exactly understand what was the matter; he considered Mrs. Atherton was peculiarly affected in some odd corner of the mind, that shadowed out dark objects alone, and the dismals were growing very powerful upon her.

"Now," thought Miles, "I shall be asleep in about a second, for I am woefully sleepy. Sleep, too, will allow the blues to escape from her brains."

With these thoughts floating lazily through his mind, he sank on his pillow and fell asleep.

* * * * * *

How long he had remained in this blissful state of forgetfulness of all things he could not well tell, but he suddenly felt a pain in his side, which was increasing, by sudden and violent efforts ; and then, when he shifted his hand to the spot, he found the pain was transferred to his knuckles. He partially awoke, and thought he heard his own name pronounced in a soft voice.

"Atherton, Atherton, awake !"—"Don't bother," murmured Atherton ; "don't bother."

"Atherton, Atherton," sang the chorus of mild voices.—"Disturb me not," he muttered ; " I'm asleep, and at home. Yes, don't bother, I tell you."

"Atherton, get up—awake, will you. God bless me, what a man you are to sleep, surely."

At the same moment the pain he felt increased in his knuckles so suddenly and sharply, that he was thoroughly aroused, and suddenly shifting his hand, he experienced a dreadful blow on the ribs.

"Yes, yes; hilloa! what's the matter?" inquired Mr. Atherton. "Who's this— what's this? Why, Mrs. Atherton, do you know what you are about—do you know what you are about?"—" Yes, Mr. Atherton, I ought to, when I come to consider the violent exertion I have had to awake you."

"Violent exertion, my dear?"—" Yes, I have been calling you till I'm tired. I was afraid to call out, and so I have been knocking you with my elbow till I have taken all the skin off."

"And made my ribs black and blue for a month or two to come, I'll be sworn." —"My elbow," began Mrs. Atherton.

"But what made you commit such an absurd act of violence?" inquired Miles. —"Because," she answered, " I couldn't awake you."

"But what did you want to awake me for?" inquired Miles, in a doleful tone.— "Because there is occasion."

"Occasion," said Miles Atherton. "What occasion was there to awake me, eh, Mrs. Atherton?"—" There's somebody in the house, Mr. Atherton. I'm sure of it—quite sure of it."

"Who?"—" How should I know, Mr. Atherton? but I am sure I heard somebody move about in the house."

"How very unfortunate," said Miles, as he turned to have another sleep, for he soon felt sleepy.—" Listen, Mr. Atherton. There they are—now don't you hear? I am sure of it."

Miles Atherton did listen, and he thought he heard something, and felt sure it might have been somebody or other ; but he didn't like to move, as that moment he was very warm, and the night was very cold, and very uncomfortable.

"There, Atherton, don't tell me ; I am sure you ought to get up and see what's the matter."—" There's no occasion, my dear. I don't hear anybody."

"There, now, what's that ?" inquired Mrs. Atherton, as the sound of some one moving about reached their ears.—" That is only the cat, or somebody going by in the street, my dear," said he, " you may depend upon it ; there's not anybody in the house, I am quite sure of it."

Just as Mr. Atherton spoke, there was the sound of a footstep distinctly heard below, much too plain to permit any doubt upon the subject, followed by the banging of a door.

"Now," said the lady, " can you say it is no one now? Get up, Miles, and see what's the matter. I am sure we shall have our throats cut, or something, if you do not. I cannot sleep—it's out of the question to sleep, and hear noises at the same time."—" Very likely, my dear," said Mr. Atherton.

"Then why don't you get up and see? I'll come down, too, but you must get a light first."

Whether it was the promise of company which the lady had promised him, and the consequent safety supposed to be desirable from numbers, I know not, but it is certain that Miles sat up in bed, and gave a rueful groan, and said,—

"Well, well, my dear, I will get up and see what is the matter, though, I hope, it will be less than you imagine."—"I hope it may, Miles; but you know we may better be too watchful than too heedless."

"Certainly, certainly; what you say is very correct, my dear," said Miles, and he got out of the warm bed, and staggered across to the drawers, where he had left the matches and candle. In a few moments a light was procured, and then Miles proceeded to dress himself, and then taking down a sword that hung over the mantel-piece, he said, "I will now go and look over the house, and see if it's a false alarm or not."

" I am sure, Miles, I don't want it to be anything else. I am sure it will be a gratification to me to know that it is so. Quite—quite."—" I had rather it was than it wasn't," said Atherton ; " but I must take it as it is."

" I'll come with you," said Mrs. Atherton, stimulated no doubt to this act of courage and devotion, by the fear of being left alone, and the consequences.

Slipping on some of her clothes, she quickly followed her husband down stairs, and into several of the rooms, one after the other. Closets and all sorts of hiding-places were carefully examined by the worthy couple, and yet no discovery was made. However, if no discovery had been made, they had assured their own safety, and Mrs. Atherton declared she could now sleep in peace and security.

" You know, Atherton," she said, " what a blessing peace of mind is."—" Yes, my dear, I do," he replied.—" Well, I couldn't have had it, if it had not been that I was satisfied there was nobody in the house."—" You see clearly, now, however, there is nobody in the house at all events."

" Yes, yes ; and very glad am I that it is so. It might have been worse, you know, much worse."—" That's very true, my dear ; and now we may get to bed again, I suppose, unless the cat should make more disturbance."

" Oh ! Atherton."—" Well, my dear, do you believe it was more than the cat that you heard ?"

" It was a footstep, Mr. Atherton."—" Whose ?"

" Ah ! that I can't say. I haven't seen anybody, or else I could have told you."—" If there had been anybody, my dear, you may depend upon it we should have seen them, else our search has been to little purpose, for it will have failed."

" Well, I don't know—I can't say," was all Mrs. Atherton said, and she followed her husband up stairs to bed again ; having secured the door, and placed the candle and matches in readiness as before, the worthy couple again sought their pillows.—" Well, my dear," said Atherton, " I hope we may sleep in peace till the morning, and have no more alarms."

" It's better to have many alarms, than one disagreeable event. I am quite clear upon that."—" Yes, yes, so it is ; but I should prefer to be without either," said Miles ; " but I suppose the event must take its course."

" Divine Providence," began Mrs. Atherton, " takes us in keeping, and watches over us, and—and ——"

Mrs. Atherton had began a very elaborate sentence, without any peculiar object in view, and then suddenly found out it was not to be carried out to the end, without such a previous understanding of what she intended, so she considered awhile as to how she could escape from the dilemma ; but her thoughts wandered, and she became drowsy, and fell asleep.

Mr. Atherton had done so some minutes before she was asleep, because as soon as he heard something about Divine Providence, he began to fear there would be a long list of moral apothems and maxims, which could go on just as well while he slept, as if he were really wide awake.

They didn't require anybody to attend to them, as many other things, for there was no necessity to affirm or deny anything, so he thought there would have been no need of him in the conversation his wife was about to carry on by herself. She was an excellent extempore speaker in this line, and as she herself got drowsy, she did not know the want of the responses in Mr. Atherton ; indeed, things would go on all the smoother, for that indicated great attention to what was said.

However, the case was hopeless, as far as regards fear that night, for Mrs. Atherton was very wakeful ; she felt as if a few moments were enough to refresh her for hours. It was very dreadful, but she was born to be wakeful on that night ; strange as it may appear, it was nevertheless true.

She gradually awoke again, about half an hour or three quarters after she had first fallen asleep. Some time before she was thoroughly awake, she had floating prognostications of evil, that kept up an incessant stream of events that were to happen some time or other. However that might be, she gradually awoke, and could distinctly hear Mr. Atherton snore.

Now, t ere was nothing particular in the snore of Mr. Atherton, more than in the snores of other people; but it was very disagreeable to Mrs. Atherton; she would not awake him, however, but she didn't like it at all.

There she lay, and thought of the vision, and the various evils that were to happen; but she really thought that there must be something in it, although it was not to happen then.

She lay awake for some time, and no noise was heard that she could not satisfactorily account for, until at length the same noise was heard again that had been heard before.

"There, now!" she exclaimed; "who would have thought of that? Well, I am astonished; who would have thought of that? How very aggravating it is to be sure. I'll wake Atherton."

However, she did not wake Atherton; but used a little patience for the occasion. She lay and listened to the sounds as they occurred, and wondered in her own mind what they could mean, or what could be the cause of them.

This, however, was no easy or pleasant task; she became more and more convinced that there must be some one in the house, and that all was not as right as it should be.

"I must wake Miles," she muttered; "this mustn't go on thus; if he don't like it, I can't help it."

And, as she spoke, she began to dig into the sides of the unfortunate cheesemonger, who turned round so as to shift his position, to escape the blows.

"Dear me, what a smell of smoke there is!" she exclaimed to herself; "I'm sure something is wrong."

Again Miles was incommoded as before, notwithstand'ng his altered position, and Mrs. Atherton shouted in his ears,—

"Miles!—Miles! fire!—fire!"—"Eh!" exclaimed Miles, starting up at this ominous sound.

"Fire! fire!"—"Where—where! for God's sake, where!—eh? where am I? —oh, I know—ah, very well. What's the matter, Mrs. Atherton?"

"There's a great smell of fire somewhere, and where the smoke comes from I can't say, but I think the house is a-fire; Lord have mercy on me, and fetch the engines!"

Miles Atherton jumped out of bed, not very conscious of what was going on; but being somewhat aware of the cause of the alarm, he soon threw on his clothes, and Mrs. Atherton did the same, at the same time the bed-room door was opened by one of them, and the smoke did then come in most unequivocally, and Atherton exclaimed,—

"By heavens, the house is on fire this time! hasten, or we are lost. Do you run down to the shop parlour, and endeavour to secure the papers of the Black Lady, and I will get my own papers and some money at the same time."— "Make haste," said Mrs. Atherton.

"I sha'n't be longer than I can help. Do you run down first, and see if you can escape."—"I won't go without you, Miles."

"I'm coming, then," exclaimed Atherton, as he lit the candle, and rushed to the chest of drawers, and pulled open one of them.—"Make haste, Atherton—make haste."

"I'm coming," he replied.

He pulled open one of the drawers, and possessed himself of some money that was there contained in them, and then he came to the door, and there he found Mrs. Atherton trembling and shaking from the effect of fear.

"Ah! Miles—Miles! we shall all be burned. Oh! goodness me, what shall we do?"—"Get out of it as quick as we can," said Miles. "Come on—come on, and mind the stairs."

"The girl—what will become of her?"—"Fire!—fire!—fire!" shouted Miles Atherton. "Fire!—fire!"

A scream announced to him that the servant was well aware of the evil she had to escape from, and when he heard her open the door, he shouted,—

"Come down, the house is a-fire—come down!"—"I ain't drest."

"You had better come at once, unless you want to be burned," said Miles Atherton; "the house is on fire."—"Come along at once, you good-for-nothing hussey, dressed or undressed; come at once, will you?"

"Im coming," said the girl, and she came floundering along, and at the same time, Miles and his wife hurried down stairs.

They had scarcely got to the bottom, when a dreadful knocking commenced at the street-door, and some persons then shouted out, "Fire!—fire!" in such tones, as very nearly made the whole party rush back again, under the idea that they were about to be burned from that quarter; but they reached the door, and opened it.

"Anybody asleep up stairs?" exclaimed one man, as he entered the passage. —"Nobody, all are down. Do you stop here, while I go and get the papers I spoke of."

"Shall I go?" said he.—"No," said Miles, "I know where they are, but I fear it is all too late to do any good."

As he spoke, he rushed back to the end of the passage, and then, as he opened the shop parlour, out rushed the flames in such force, that poor Miles reeled and tumbled over; but he soon scrambled along th passage, until he came to the street-door, more like a Newfoundland dog than anything else, for he came along on his hands and feet, for he forgot in his haste and flurry to stand up, but scrambled along like a donkey.

He soon altered his position and stood up, when somebody inquired if anybody was in the house.

"Nobody now," said Atherton.—"Then we'll shut the door. Now the engines will be here in a few minutes; they are sent for."

"The manuscripts?" said Mrs. Atherton, inquiringly.—"Are all burnt by this time," said Atherton, "and so should I, if I had got into the room."

CHAPTER XLVII.

THE RECOVERY OF THE BLACK LADY'S PAPERS, AND THE SECOND VISIT TO ST. PAUL'S.

"Wife," said Miles Atherton, when he and she had got a refuge in the house of a neighbour, who had kindly and at once opened his doors for them after the fire; "wife, we were thinking of giving notice to quit that house, and now it's given us notice, with a vengeance."

"The Lord have mercy upon us!" groaned Mrs. Atherton; "what's to become of us? and we not insured, either."

"Yes, we are; I beg your pardon, there."

"Insured,—insured, are we, Miles Atherton? Oh, good gracious! then we shall get all the money."

"Don't you flatter yourself, wife. It's true enough we are insured, and I paid the premium on the policy for the last eighteen years, always excepting this last payment, which has been over due now three weeks, that's all."

"You wretch!"

"Go on, go on; abuse me as much as you like, I can bear it all. There's all my stock of cheeses been made into Welsh rabbits at once."

"And can you joke at such a time as this, you unfeeling monster? Oh, what will become of us now? In such a respectable way of business, too, as we were. Oh, dear, oh, dear, I'm undone!"

"Then I advise you to do yourself up again," said Miles Atherton. "The fact is, wife, that I do not feel this misfortune so acutely as I should under other circumstances, because you led me such a dog's life, and always collared so much of the money, that I have often said to myself, I'd just as soon be somebody's shopman as have a place of my own; and now, Mrs. Atherton, that we are fairly burnt out, all I can say is, as we have no brats to plague our lives, we can separate, and each of us get the best living we can."

"What!" screamed Mrs. Atherton, "separate from your lawful wife, you Don Giwonny! You wretch, you want to seduce somebody, you do."

"Who—I?"

"Yes, you. Oh, Miles Atherton, you set the house on fire, I do believe, yourself; and, now I come to think of it, I know there's some woman at the bottom of it all."

"Then you may feel quite assured that she is smothered by this time," said Miles Atherton, with all the composure in the world. "The fact is, my dear, you have taught me to be quite a philosopher."

"A philosopher, sir, why, that's next thing to a fool."

"Perhaps it is, and perhaps it ain't, Mrs. Atherton; but, now that we are fairly out of business, mind I don't go into it again in a hurry, unless you and I have a much better understanding."

"Oh, dear, oh, dear; is this a time to allude to our understandings? Miles Atherton, you are a wretch. Who's that? Somebody is knocking at the door. Come in! What do you want? Somebody knocks again, and won't come in. Who can it be, Miles Atherton, who can it be? Come in!"

"It's only me," said Jem, as he popped his head into the room; "it's only me, missus. How do you feel by this time?"

"Oh, what a turn you gave me, to be sure, Jem!" said Mrs. Atherton. "What do you want? You know, as we have no shop, we cannot want you now."

"I knows that, missus; I only come to ask a question, that's all."

"What is it, Jem?" said Atherton; "you have been a faithful lad, although you have your faults, I suppose, like other people."

"Well, sir," said Jem, "I'm glad you admit I ain't quite an angel, but have some faults. Howsomdever, that's neither here nor there. What I wants all for to know is, what's become of the Black Lady's papers; because I ain't satisfied yet, nor going to be gammoned off by not knowing all the rest of it."

"Why, Jem, ain't Mr. Charles Ormond hanged? What more do you want?"

"I didn't want him hanged at all, if you come to that, master. But, as to what more I want, I'll just tell you I want to know what poor Miss Whitehead said when they told her of it, and what she didn't say. I want to know, too, what became of that vagabond, Godfrey."

"Then, Jem, I think your curiosity on those points must, perforce, go ungratified, for I really cannot tell you, and the Black Lady's papers are all destroyed."

"Oh, gracious! And the key of St. Paul's?"

"No, not that, I have the key."

"The blessed papers all burnt!" groaned Jem. "Well, I never! It's enough to make a donkey tie his tail up in a knot, and never undo it again, that it is. What shall I do? I tell you what it is, master, I won't give up hope. I'll have a jolly good hunt among the ruins, and see if any of the papers can be found."

"That you are welcome, Jem, to set about," said Atherton, "as soon as you like; and I can only wish you success without at all expecting it."

"We can but try, master; but when do you think of going into business, again?"

"Never, Jem, I am ruined; I was not insured, and have lost everything."

"The deuce," said Jem; "why, I ought to cut you, and never speak to you again as long as I live."

"Indeed! and why?"—"Oh! that's the way of the world, ain't it? When a chap is ruined, everybody always gives him the cold shoulder, don't they, rather?"

"It's true enough, Jem."

"Ah, well, now I'll be a fool, howsomdever. Now, master, I'll let you into a secret. I have been with you a matter of four years now, and what do you think I've saved up in that time? why, a little fortune, quite; I feels myself a independent man. I've got twenty pounds—don't go to swear, now—I'll lend it you on mortgage o' nothing, and no interest. That's settled, now. Now don't say another word about it; don't, I tell you it's settled."

Tears came into the eyes of Atherton as he rose and took Jem's hand.

"No, my good fellow," he said, "no. It gives me the first feeling of satisfaction that I have had since first the cry of fire sounded in my ears, to feel that you are not altogether destitute.   But I cannot risk the loss in business of your savings; keep your money, Jem, and don't lend your money to me, or anybody else."

"I suppose," said Jem, "I can do what I likes with my own."

"Well, then, take care of it."

"I sha'n't.   I tell you what it is, Mr. Atherton, if you don't take the money, I'll go into all sorts of extravagancies with it; I'll drink, I'll game, and I ain't sure but I'll keep one o' those gals as does the dances, and looks so insinivating at the Adelphi, with a lot o' white gauze cut short."

"Jem!" screamed Mrs. Atherton, "good gracious! do you know that I am here?"

"Yes, missus, I knows; but master shouldn't aggravate me to say wicious things, and then, in course, I shouldn't say 'em; that's all I've got to say, so you knows the consequences now.   Good-bye; turn it over in your mind, and don't be a fool.   Good-bye!"

Away went Jem, leaving Miles Atherton much affected at the generosity of his humble follower.

"Ah, wife," he said, "if there were a few more like Jem in the world, I could soon begin business again, without much caring for what had passed; but you may go a long way, indeed, before you meet another to make such an offer as he has."

"He's a strange lad," said Mrs. Atherton, "a very strange lad.   Who would have thought of him saving money?"

"Ah, who, indeed?   But, with all his eccentricities, you know, he was always careful; and four years is a tolerable time to save twenty pounds in.   However, I cannot take it from him; I will starve first.   It is not enough to make my going into business anything of a certainty as to success, and I should be continually harassed with the dreadful idea of losing his money, which would haunt me night and day."

"But how much, Miles Atherton, would enable you to start in business again?"

"Oh, a hundred pounds."

"Well, I—I—don't mind confessing, now—ahem!—hem! that I have got £42. 11s. 6d. in the savings bank—ahem! Miles Atherton; and so, with Jem's twenty pounds, you see, there will something near the amount."

"I'm a made man—I'm a made man, again!" said Atherton.   "There is a chance now, wife; and I thank God you had the prudence to lay by a little, which you will excuse me now for saying I always suspected."

"Did you suspect, Miles Atherton?   It would have been a good thing if you had been half as prudent and careful as I have, I can tell you, sir; but you never were, you were always too fond of guzzling with your low companions at the Blue Bull."

"Well, well, we won't quarrel now; that was not the sign of the house either, my dear; but that's no matter.   I'll go and look out for some new shop in a better situation, too, than the last."—"And so, you see, Miles Atherton, what a thing it is to have about you a wife who really, in spite of all your bad conduct, does her duty; a wife who looks to the main chance as I have done, and when a misfortune like this takes place, can be a fortune to her husband."

"Yes, my dear, I should be next thing to a cannibal, not to admit all that, in every full particular, I assure you. Won't she crow over me now," thought poor Atherton; "I shall not be able to call my nose my own."—"Very good," added Mrs. Atherton, in quite a dictatorial kind of manner. "Very good; I do hope then, and trust, that some people will look a little more to some people's feelings than some people have been in the habit of doing."

"Ah! I hope so too," said Atherton; for he was determined that he would not say, that cap fits me.—"And I hope," continued the lady, "that some people, when they shut up their own shops of an evening, will prefer the society of their virtuous wives to a set of low revelling sottish companions."

"So do I."—"Miles Atherton, you are a wretch."

" Now, my dear, my dear."—" Don't my dear me, I won't have it.—I say, too, I won't bear it ; so don't attempt to think of ever having my fortune, unless you intend to be a very different man to what you have been."

" Really ! did you mean me all the while ?"—" Oh, you hypocrite, you villain ; Miles Atherton, I'll have a separation if you go on in such a way. I believe a wife may get a separation if she proves—and, oh ! cannot I ?—that her husband is the most aggravating wretch in all the world."

" I wish husbands could get a separation on such grounds, my dear ; but I fear your idea of the law on those subjects is contrary to that of the judges, so that there is no hope ; but now, Mrs. Atherton, I have got something to propose to you, that I do think you would like."—" Indeed, I think I should like anything ; but what is it ?"

" Now, would you not be very much gratified indeed by making a visit actually to the very vault where Charles Ormond, poor fellow, stayed, while he thought himself so safe, when he wasn't, after he had escaped from Newgate ?"—" What ! I get over some high railings, Miles Atherton ; I wonder at you, I do, for proposing anything half so dreadful ; it's enough to make anybody's hair all stand on end ; oh, sure it is."

" No, no, no."—" But I say yes, it is ; you may think nothing of it, but I think a great deal, I assure you."

" My dear, I never meant you to attempt any such thing. You remember the little gilt door which is mentioned in the Black Lady's papers as opening into the cathedral ?"—" Ah, to be sure."

" Well, then, what's to hinder you from going in with the key that leads into the vaults by the entrance opposite Paul's Chain, and then getting up that very staircase which you have read of, and opening the gilt door, and letting you into the vaults?"—" Oh, what an adventure ! I shake all over ; and yet I should like to go."

" Of course you would. Any reasonable woman would ; I'll mention it to Jem when I see him again, and—bless my heart, what is all that disturbance about in the house ? What a racing about there is."

The door of the room in which Miles Atherton and his wife sat was now, with such a suddenness burst open, that the former caught up a chair wherewith to defend himself against any sudden attack, for it seemed like one, and the other, with a faint scream, thought of the propriety of fainting away. But when they saw that the intruder was no other than Jem, who, since his offer to lend the twenty pounds, had somehow appeared to them both in a very different light, Miles Atherton put down the chair, and Mrs. Atherton dismissed the incipient hysterics at a word.

Jem's countenance was quite radiant with delight. " Hurrah, one, two, three, hurrah !" he shouted.

" Good God !" said Mrs. Atherton, " what has happened ?"

" I've found 'em under a feather bed, all safe ; only one or two, and those the very ones that we have read, singed a little."—" He means the Black Lady's papers," said Atherton.

" To be sure I do. I told the firemen who had charge of the premises, that I came from you, so they let me hunt among the ruins as much as I liked ; and then, sure enough, under a feather bed that come whop upon 'em, and put 'em out of what they were in—a blaze, I found the Black Lady's papers, and here they are, all right."

" Well," said Mrs. Atherton, " I am as glad of that as if anybody had given me a ten pound note, I am. We shall hear now all about what became of everybody."— " Except Neville," put in Atherton ; " that villain has evidently yet escaped the penalty which he ought to pay for his crimes. And my own opinion is, that it is to him we owe the conflagration of my house."

" You don't say that," cried Jem ; " 'cos, if you does, we'll have him hung, as safe as bricks. I don't see what's to hinder us."—" Ah ! but I do, Jem ; we may have abundance of suspicion, but we have no proofs, you know. Something, however, may yet arise to bring him to an untimely end, and if he escapes the hangman, all that I have got to say is, that the gallows is sadly cheated of its real and proper due."

" Oh, never fear, master; he'll come to it soon, you may depend. He's not the sort of fellow altogether to escape it. No, no. The very way in which he has escaped some of the dangers that have beset him, is enough to convince everybody what will be his end at last."—"There's a good argument there, at all events," said Miles Atherton. " Jem, you were born for a lawyer."

" I beg your pardon," said Jem, " I hope I was born for an honest man, sir."

" Well, well; but Jem, you don't mean to say that there never was an honest lawyer?"

" No, sir, I don't mean to say that. I think there was one, and that, when he found it out, he died of grief."—" You are a droll dog, you are, Jem; but now we have two things to talk to you about; one is, that what with your twenty pounds, and what money Mrs. Atherton has, which I really knew nothing about, I shall be able, with every prospect of success, to start in business again."

" Shall you though, master. Hurrah! brayvo! that's the best news I shall hear to-day."—" Well, Jem, the next thing I wish to say to you is, that Mrs. Atherton would like very much to see that vault which poor Charles Ormond occupied in St. Paul's cathedral before his execution."

" I don't see any objection to that," said Jem; " you know the way, master, and so do I. Jem's your man for anything of that kind, you may make up your mind to. So, missus, if you like to come to-night, no doubt it will be all right."

" I'm in two minds about it," said Mrs. Atherton. " I really don't know whether to go or not. I should like, and yet I'm half afraid. What would become of us if we was to be seen, I wonder?"

" They couldn't hang us," said Jem. " It seems to me, they would have to do one of two things—that is, let us go or let us stay. It's not a likely thing anybody would go to the vaults of St. Paul's with a view of picking anybody's pocket, so it really strikes me as the blessed authorities would find themselves in a fix, and not know what to do at all."—" Yes," said Miles Atherton; " and they would be wise enough to see that the least said, in such a case, was soonest mended."

" Then I will go," exclaimed Mrs. Atherton, " if I die for it. I will go, that's settled, and to-night, too."—" Good," added Atherton; " and to-morrow I'll suit myself, I dare say, easy enough with another shop; and by to-morrow night we may be all settled well enough in it to go on reading the Black Lady's papers, for I must confess I do want to know what happened next."

" And so do I," said Jem; " for as I came along I turned over two or three leaves, and I can tell you that I saw enough to let me know that something did happen next, that perhaps neither of you at all expected."

This, then, was all duly arranged, and Jem and Miles Atherton made active preparations for introducing Mrs. Atherton, with such caution and secrecy as the case required, into the vaults.

Our readers, who have gone with us through the adventures of Charles Ormond, are sufficiently acquainted with all that was to be seen in that dreary abode of the dead to save us from the necessity of recapitulating any of it, so that we need only say, as regards the visit of Mrs. Atherton, that she, by the assistance of Jem and Miles Atherton, did actually contrive to get over the iron rails of the churchyard.

But then, what will not the ladies do when any adventurous and stirring object is in view? From the commencement of the world we have found that they have been capable of the greatest achievements, and so we will not call upon our readers for any great expression of astonishment, even at the fact of Mrs. Atherton clambering over the rails which separated the area around St. Paul's from the carriage-way.

With what she saw she was very much interested, and she fully examined all that was to be seen of the coffins with an intenseness of curiosity that quite convinced Miles Atherton—as he, indeed, whispered to Jem—that she was a woman of very superior mind.

When she was leaving the cathedral, however, Mrs. Atherton remarked to herself, in such an under tone that neither Jem nor her husband heard her,—

"Well, I think now I shall be even with Mrs. Green, at any rate. She fell down a common sewer once, and ever since then she tries to make herself a great person, by talking about it; but now that I have been in the vaults of St. Paul's, I rather think I can put her down."

Miles Atherton was successful the next day in getting a house and shop to suit him; and as the furniture he had had in his old place was all burnt, he had very little trouble in moving in.

On that very evening, he and his wife, and Jem, sat together in the back parlour of the new premises, where, at all events, they had a comfortable and cheering fire burning in the grate, and chairs to sit down upon, together with many other little matters in the furniture way, which some neighbours who knew them had kindly lent until they could provide themselves with all such requisites of their own.

No. 36.

No one, to look upon their faces, would now have supposed it possible that they had been so recently subjected to so heavy a calamity as fire; and now, as Miles Atherton produced the manuscript papers of the Black Lady, an air of intense interest sat upon the faces of his wife and Jem, which he himself quite sufficiently sympathised with.

CHAPTER XLVIII.

THE CONTINUATION OF THE NARRATIVE IN THE NEW HOUSE OF THE ATHERTONS.— RECAPTURE OF CHARLES ORMOND, AND CONSTERNATION OF MR. BLAKE.

IT was evening, and Mr. and Mrs. Atherton might be considered to be fairly settled in their new house, and it could not but be a matter of congratulation to them that they were so, since the fatigue and disagreeable feelings incident to the course of events that had happened to Miles and his wife, might now, at least for a time, be fairly considered at an end, and some rest was now to be afforded to them.

"Miles," said Mrs. Atherton, "I think we are very comfortable here, and we can make the hours pass quickly enough."—"So we can, my dear," said the cheese-monger; "the more easily is that to be done, since we have secured the papers of the Black Lady, which we thought were quite destroyed."

"We can. I am sure I thought they were lost for ever, and then we shouldn't have known how all that is to follow came about."—"We should not, indeed," remarked Miles Atherton. "Nothing more true. I am well pleased that they have been recovered, for I could have spared more valuable matters for the sake of knowing all that is to come yet."

"And so could I. Now, Miles, will you go on? But we may as well have lights, and that will prevent any getting up, and leaving off at an interesting point."

All the requirements having been complied with, Mr. and Mrs. Miles Atherton sat down with mutual good will to ascertain what would be the next event in this eventful history. Miles Atherton took up the manuscript, and began reading aloud as follows :—

And now the week has nearly elapsed, during which the respite for Charles Ormond was to have continued, and Mr. Blake began to congratulate himself, that after all, now there was the greatest possible chance of escape, since for such a period the hiding-place of Charles had not been discovered.

He well knew from experience in those matters, that if in the first flush of pursuit a prisoner were not discovered who had made his escape, he was seldom discovered at all.

The same general rule applies to persons who have committed heinous offences; we generally find, that if within a very few days after the commission of the act they are not in custody, their escape may almost be calculated upon as a thing successful.

Mr. Blake had made up his mind, that on the Sunday he would communicate to the Whiteheads the agreeable intelligence that Charles might be considered as rescued from the hands of death, and by that time, too, he hoped that as Marian had gone on progressing from day to day, that she would be in a state to receive such a piece of intelligence, without it producing any bad effect upon her nervous system, which had been so shattered. He saw Jeffries day by day, and heard of the condition of Charles, and that he had been reconciled to the loneliness of the place he was in.

"There is only one thing, sir," said Jeffries, "that he longs for continually, and that is for just a sight of Marian Whitehead, and I have almost thought that with safety some day she might be brought to the gilt grating of that door which opens to the staircase leading to the vaults, so that he might see her for a moment."

"No, no," said Mr. Blake, "we must try no foolish experiments of that sort. In a little time I hope that Charles Ormond will be enabled to leave his place of confinement, and then I shall take care that he gets to the continent as quickly as possible; after which Marian and her mother may go to him, and they may settle down comfortably in some place of safety."

"Yes, sir, I think," remarked Jeffries, "that in another week there can be no difficulty in saying that he may leave St. Paul's. There is only one thing that has surprised me in the whole transaction."

"And what may that be?"—"It is that the authorities have made so little efforts to discover his retreat. They seem to have been wonderfully supine upon the occasion."

"Well, do you know, Jeffries, the same thing has struck me. I have been surprised to think how the matter has been allowed to blow over as it were. To be sure, the offence of which he was pronounced to be guilty was not of a nature to excite any personal ill feelings against him."

"And then, too, sir," suggested Jeffries, "there may be, in quarters where they are very important, doubts as to Charles Ormond's guilt, and although, if they had kept him, they would have hung him, yet now that he has escaped, nobody, probably, is sorry for it."

"Well, I should not be at all surprised but that is a very just view of the case. I only feared, however, that upon principle, because you see he had escaped from Newgate which is supposed to be such a very stronghold for offenders, that the most strenuous exertions would have been made to recover him."

"And so did I, sir, but it's all for the best. I suppose you will not venture upon paying him a visit?"

"Oh, it's quite impossible. I never could get over those iron railings; you know I am not so active a man as you are, Jeffries, nor so young a one, so that what to you would be a feat of very little difficulty, would knock me to pieces to perform."

"True enough, sir; but you know I could give you a hand up, and after all, I do think you would manage it very well."

"Do you? I'm of a different opinion; you don't consider that I weigh somewhere about twelve stone, and that if I were to fall, I might damage the pavement of St. Paul's, which, under the circumstances, would be a very unfair thing to do, considering the good service we are getting from the old cathedral."

"Well, sir, as you please; but I never go near Mr. Ormond but what he charges me, in tones of the greatest emotion, to convey to you his gratitude for the great service you have rendered him. He calls you his preserver, and I think you, with Marian Whitehead, share the whole of his thoughts."

"Well, well," said Mr. Blake, "that's all right enough; I believe him to be as innocent of the crime for which he would have suffered death, as I am myself; so it became my duty, as well as my inclination, to do all in my power to rescue him. I say, Jeffries, there'll be rather a disappointment on Monday morning at the Old Bailey."

"Rather, indeed, sir, and I glory in it. The time will come when these frightful spectacles will become fewer and fewer in this country; and it is, indeed, something to have cheated the hangman of one of his victims, who, but for you, sir, would have helped to swell the dreadful list of judicial murders."

"Let us be just," said Mr. Blake. "I really do not think that that list is by any means a long one."

"Sir," said Jeffries, "if it contained but two names, it is a dreadful list."

"You are right, you are right—it is so; and at all events Charles Ormond shall not add a third. I suppose you've gone round among the police and made inquiries, to learn if there's any suspicions?"

"I have, sir, and they one and all appear to me to have given it up; they say they meet with no encouragement from the authorities, and that although the rewards have not actually been withdrawn, that the sheriffs and the magistrates are so lukewarm upon the subject, that they scarcely now mention it."

"That's capital; to-morrow's Sunday, and Marian Whitehead's getting better. I have promised to go down to the cottage at Ealing in the latter part of the day, and I shall certainly then do myself the pleasure of telling her there all that has occurred. I will give her the joy of fully believing, as I do myself, that the worst catastrophe is avoided, and that although fortune has been torn from her, still, he for whom she feels so acutely, and who, if he had been executed, would have been completely sacrificed, has escaped his impending fate, and may yet be happy with her. I am sure, quite sure, that the look of joy I shall see upon her countenance will amply repay me for everything, and for all the trouble I have taken."

"It will be a source, sir," said Jeffries, "of pleasant congratulation while you live."

"Yes, thank God!" said Mr. Blake; "I have made money enough by my profession to spend some of it how I please, at all events."

Perhaps, never had the honest-minded attorney spent any money which had ever returned him so much real gratification, as that which he was now expending upon the Whiteheads, and upon Charles Ormond. He was quite delighted at the success which had crowned his exertions to rescue an innocent man from death; and he often told himself, that let what would of a cross-grained character happen to him during the course of his life, that episode in it which comprehended the escape of Charles Ormond from Newgate and Marian Whitehead from poverty and misery, would be quite sufficient to reconcile him to himself and to the world.

He did, according to promise, go to Ealing on the Sunday, and he was much gratified to find that Marian Whitehead was much better.

She could sit up a little and converse quietly, but almost all the words she said to him, were :—

"Mr. Blake, it is to you I owe this partial recovery, for you have taught me to believe that there is a hope yet for Charles, and I don't think you would deceive me in such a thing; but, on the contrary, I am inclined to believe that that hope is a stronger one than you have thought proper to communicate to me."

"Well, to tell the truth," he said, "Marian, it is a stronger one than I have yet told you."

"Oh, he is saved," said Marian Whitehead, clasping her hands; "it is a certainty—a certainty."

"Now, my dear, don't run on too fast, but listen to me calmly and patiently, while I tell you exactly how the matter stands, and then you can draw your own conclusions."

With almost breathless anxiety, her lips slightly parted, and her whole soul concentrated in the act of listening, did Marian hear the detail which the attorney gave her.

She heard him to the end without the slightest interruption, for she would not, by a word of hers, mar any sentence which was coming from his lips; when he had concluded, she seized his hands in both of hers, while the tears streamed from her eyes.

"And you—have preserved him; oh, what do I not owe you—can a life-time of gratitude ever repay you?—second only to my thoughts of Heaven shall you be, sir. I cannot—cannot speak to you, for the grateful feelings which are swelling at my heart."

"Now, then—now, then, my dear," said the attorney; "that will do, that's more than enough—you see there's something flown in my eye just at present—don't you go fancying that I'm weeping or anything of that sort, it's no such thing—I never shed a tear in my life, and I don't mean to be such an old fool now."

Marian called loudly upon her mother to come and hear the blissful tidings, that Charles Ormond was saved from the dreadful death which they both considered inevitably awaited him.

"There, there," said the attorney; "you must tell your mother all about it yourself, for I cannot think of going over it again; and, when you awake at eight o'clock to-morrow morning—Monday, it will be, mind—just smile to yourself as you think of the safety of Charles, and compare your feelings with what they might have been, had that hour heralded him to another world by the hands of the common executioner."

"Oh, horrible idea!" exclaimed Marian; "I shall not smile, but I shall return thanks to Heaven on my bended knees, that he is saved from such a dreadful—horrible fate."

"And I, if I'm awake, you may depend upon it, I shall hear eight o'clock strike with remarkably different feelings to those which would have actuated me, if poor Charles had been led forth to execution."

"Speak not of it—speak not of it."

Mr. Blake left Marian to explain to her mother what he had communicated to her, and then he hastened to town, feeling as happy and as comfortable as any man could who had done a far better Sunday's work than as if he had given it up to sighing and groaning, and calling himself a miserable sinner.

Quite elated was Mr. Blake; he smiled upon every one he met, and looked so bland and confiding, that many people stopped to look after him, and to learn what made the stout elderly gentleman look so well pleased.

Truly, Mr. Blake could have tolerated almost anything on that Sunday night; and, when he got home, and found that Jeffries was waiting for him, he immediately insisted upon cracking a bottle of wine and drinking to Charles Ormond's future happiness.

They both said this with great gusto, and to one bottle succeeded another, for Jeffries was both a man of education and information, and one whom Mr. Blake could make a companion of when he chose.

"And so," said the attorney, "you say you left him quite in spirits."

"Yes, I'm happy to say I did, sir. We spoke of the great disappointment the mob would suffer to-morrow morning, in missing the execution, which, had all gone as the authorities wished it, they would have been gratified with."

"Ah, that's glorious; the bottle stands with you, Jeffries."

"Pardon me, Mr. Blake, it's getting late, you know."

"Late, man; why, what do you mean—what is the time?"

"Why, it's after eleven, sir."

"Well, what of that; time was made for slaves, and not for us; come, you shall finish this bottle. I'll have no excuses. It ain't every day in the week that I sit down in this sort of way; but when I do, I like to do it handsomely."

Jeffries smiled to himself, for he saw that Mr. Blake was getting on a little; but still he remained, and could not exactly screw up his courage to say that he would not stay and keep the attorney company any longer.

The bottle passed pretty briskly from one to the other, and, as might naturally be expected, the scruples of Jeffries got less and less each glass that he imbibed, until at length the third bottle was produced, and then the fourth, before either of them thought of moving.

By this time, it may supposed, that they were both getting exceedingly comfortable and happy. Twice they avowed eternal friendship to each other; and Mr. Blake told Jeffries, no less than five times over, how he had told Marian Whitehead that very day of Charles's escape, and present place of safety, and how she had so affected him by what she had said thereupon, that he had shed tears in spite of himself, and made her believe that it was something which had flown into his eye.

"My dear fellow," added Mr. Blake, "you're a man of discretion and judgment, and, consequently, I believe you will feel inclined to admit that that was about the cleverest thing you ever heard of."

"It was, indeed," said Jeffries; "and do you mean to say she didn't find you out?"

"Not she—not she; lor bless you, I acted it too well. She find me out! I think I see her—pass the bottle—lord, she's innocence itself; she wouldn't have found me out if I'd said there'd been something in both of my eyes—pass the bottle. Would you like anything else, by-the-bye? I tell you what's a nice thing, now."—"What?—let's have it."

"Why, a quart of new ale, with half a pint of brandy in it, just to settle your head."—"Oh, that's nothing," said Jeffries, "unless you boil it, and then add sixpennyworth of Devonshire cream to it."

"The devil! you don't mean that?"—"Don't I. I've said it; but I must be jogging."

"Why, where do you live, Jeffries?"—"Over the water."

"Oh! that's so indefinite."—"Well, then, sir, I go over Southwark-bridge, if you must have it; and from here I shall cut across Smithfield, get down the Old Bailey, and ——"

"The Old Bailey? ay, you dog; you pass Newgate; look at it as you go by. Ha! ha! I shall always laugh as I pass Newgate, d—d if I sha'n't, particularly when I see the governor's steps. Wouldn't it be a bit of fun, now, to go and knock at the governor's door, and ask him how he was—wouldn't it, you dog?" said Blake, laughing heartily.

"Yes, it would," said Jeffries. "I admit that of course it would, but rather hazardous. D—n it, it's half-past twelve o'clock. I must really go, Mr. Blake. I'm very much obliged to you, but I must really go."

"Oh! you are afraid of Mrs. Jeffries, are you?"—"No, indeed, I ain't; for there's no Mrs. Jeffries to be afraid of, if it comes to that. Ah! there was a Mrs. Jeffries once. It's a sad and a mournful tale."

"Well, then, the best thing you can do is to keep it to yourself; I don't want to hear it. Come, now, I tell you what we'll do, Jeffries; we'll finish this bottle, and then finish off with some soda-water, after which, I'll positively see you part of the way home."—"No, sir; I couldn't think of that, really."

"Think of what—finishing the bottle, or the soda-water?"—"No, sir; I couldn't think of your seeing me part of the way home; that would be too imposing."

"Impose—stuff! Don't talk such nonsense to me. I will if I like, and there's an end of it. I won't be contradicted, Mr. Jeffries."

Jeffries, on whom the wine had not taken quite so much effect as it had on Mr. Blake, consented to the arrangement. The bottle was finished, and some soda-water discussed; and then, at about half-past one o'clock, or rather nearer two, they both sallied out, about as jolly as any two gentlemenly men could be, who had drunk nothing but the best of wine, and whose habits were too good to permit them to show their exhilaration by any of the coarse methods in use among the lower orders of society.

They, certainly, talked rather loud, and were a little heedless of what they said, as they proceeded arm-in-arm across Smithfield and down Giltspur-street, towards the Old Bailey.

"There's Newgate," said Jeffries, "dark, frowning, and terrific-looking as usual; but it has no terrors for us now; the bird that wasted its sweetness in that cage has escaped."

"What a remarkably happy idea," said Mr. Blake, upon whom the open air had had a very bad effect, for, had it not been for his companion, he several times would have fallen. "What a happy idea that is of yours about Newgate being in a cage, and going bird-catching."—"I'm glad you like it, sir."

"Yes, Jeffries; and now that we are talking philosophically, allow me to remark that it's drunkenness that is a great evil among the lower classes. You recollect the old saying, eh?"—"What old saying, sir?"

"Why, this: 'Oh! that a man should put his brains in his head to steal away his memory!'"—"That's a most remarkable saying, Mr. Blake!"

"Yes, and there's a deal of truth in it."—"And a little obscurity too."

"Yes, to addle-headed people like you, who can't understand it. Mind the crossing. Ah! Newgate, there you are."

They crossed over from the end of Giltspur-street to the corner of the Old Bailey, and then Jeffries said,—

"What hammering's that, I wonder, at this time of night?"—"Stammering?" said Mr. Blake; "who's stammering?"

"I didn't say stammering—I said hammering. Good God! Mr. Blake, what's this? Do you see that long pole?"—"What long pole?"

"Why—why there by the—the debtors' door of—of Newgate. There's a fellow sticking up a long pole, and another helping him to do it."

Mr. Blake stopped, and a shudder passed across him. He walked up as steadily as any man could walk to the space immediately in front of the debtors' door, in the Old Bailey, and laying his hand upon a massive square piece of timber, which had just been placed in a hole in the ground, he said,—

"What in God's name is this for?"—"It's a bit of the gallows, sir. Ormond the forger's to be hung to-morrow. He's been caught about an hour ago, and brought into Newgate. I don't know if it's true, but they say as he was nabbed somewhere in the vaults of St. Paul's. Bill, just bring one of them ere wedges this way. Stand out of the way, sir, if you please."

CHAPTER XLIX.

MR. BLAKE'S CONSTERNATION.—THE DREADFUL MORNING, AND ITS RESULTS.

FOR a few moments Mr. Blake stood, after hearing this intelligence, like a man in a perfect state of bewilderment. Any one to look at him might have thought that in his sleep he had walked out into the Old Bailey, and then suddenly been awakened, and that all his surprise consisted in finding himself in the open air when he had thought that he was in his chamber.

But this state of things did not last long; he staggered back with a deep groan, and, no doubt, but for the assistance of Jeffries, he would have fallen. The shock restored him instantly, and probably had he even taken ten times the quantity of wine that he had, he would instantly have recovered from its influence in consequence of the painful and sudden revulsion of feeling that came over him.

"Gracious heavens, Jeffries," he said, "is this a dream, or can it be real, and after all the pains we have bestowed upon this matter are we doomed to this most bitter and cruel disappointment? Alas! alas! poor Marian, what will become of thee?"

"You're jesting," said Jeffries, stepping forward, and confronting the workman. "You know not what you say, man, nor to whom you speak."—"I mayn't know to whom I speak," said the man, "but I know what I say; and as for jest, if you wait till eight o'clock to-morrow morning, you'll find out at all events that it's no joke."

"Good God! do you mean to assert that Charles Ormond is taken?"—"To be sure he is."

"All is lost—all is lost."—"Can you tell me how it occurred?" faltered Mr. Blake. "I will reward you for any information you may choose to give me."

"Oh, I never tell tales out of school," said the man. "It would be as much as my place was worth to say anything."

"But you may speak confidently to us," said Jeffries, as he slipped half-a-sovereign into the man's hands.—"Ah," said the workman, "I know who you are now."

"Indeed, do you?"—"Yes; you're one of the newspaper chaps."

"Well, perhaps I am. Let me know all that you have learnt concerning the capture of Charles Ormond?"—"Well, then, you must know, sir, that I rather think the governor of Newgate and the sheriffs knew where he was all along. They say there was somebody as told them, and pocketed the reward a week ago."

"Do you know his name?" said Jeffries.—"Well, I did hear his name—let me see, what was it? I'll be hanged if I don't think it was Long."

"Your friend," said Blake, looking Jeffries in the face, and laying his hand upon his arm—"your friend, and the man you recommended so strongly to me for his fidelity."—"Kill me if you like, sir," said Jeffries; "I did all for the best, and I could do no more. This affair will make me wretched while I live."

"And myself—and myself; come away—come away, and let us think of some means of keeping this frightful truth, at all events, from the ears of Marian Whitehead. It will destroy her utterly."

At this moment a man stepped up and confronted Mr. Blake. He placed his arms a-kimbo, and looked him boldly and audaciously in the face.

" So, sir," he said, " what may be your opinion of affairs now ?"—" What do you mean ?" said Mr. Blake.   " I do not know you."

" It is the villain Neville," said Jeffries.—" Yes," said the fellow—who was no other than Neville—" yes, it is Neville, come to tell you what a nice kettle of fish you have made of this affair.   So you thought you'd get him off, did you, indeed—while I was above ground, too ?   But that game wouldn't answer, so you had better stay, now, and see him hung.   I have come here for that precise purpose, and mean to stay till morning, although I have got a good place at a window.   Don't the sound of these workmen's hammers come pleasantly to your ears ?   So, you thought you had managed it very nicely, did you, and that you could cheat the gallows just when you pleased ?   Upon my word, you must be a very nice sort of character. There will be an indictment against you next Old Bailey sessions, for aiding and abetting in the escape of a felon."

Mr. Blake knew this as well as Neville could tell him.   He hung heavily upon the arm of Jeffries, as he said,—

" Come away, Jeffries—come away; I am quite unable to talk to this ruffian. God, now, is our only hope.   Alas—alas! who would have thought of such a blow of fate as this.   Come away—come away."

" You black-hearted villain !" said Jeffries.   " So it is not enough that you have triumphed in your wickedness, but you must add insult to the injury you have inflicted.   But there will yet come a day of dreadful retribution for you, Neville."

" Do you threaten ?"—" As you please to take it.   I care not."

" Another word, and I will knock you down."—" Indeed ! I always answer such a threat in one way."

As he spoke, Jeffries forsook the arm of Mr. Blake, and with two tremendous blows, given in such rapid succession that he had not time to fall from the first one, he struck Neville to the ground, where he lay partially stunned.   Then taking the arm of Mr. Blake, Jeffries walked with him slowly from the Old Bailey, and no one—though several saw the knock-down blows given—thought of stopping him.

*   *   *   *   *   .   *   *

Alas! it is but too true, Charles Ormond's secret had been sold to the officers by the man who had been trusted by Jeffries.   That scoundrel had pocketed for his treachery no less a sum than three hundred pounds, besides a pardon for divers offences of which he had been guilty.   He instantly left England.

And now let the reader turn back some pages, and glance his eye over a fragmentary kind of document which was presented to his notice at the early part of these papers, at the top of which was the ominous word " Execution."

There he will find a dreadful detail of what occurred on the morning succeeding that Sunday night on which Mr. Blake and Jeffries were so merry.   The fate of poor Charles Ormond was sealed.   He was dragged from the cell of condemnation, and made to go through all the frightful formalities preceding his murder—for we can call it by no other name.

It was one of those frightful judicial mistakes, the only consolation concerning which we can give our minds is, that they are very few in number.

It was Godfrey—yes, it was the villain, Godfrey, who fell from the house-top among the crowd, as he looked upon the execution, enduring far more pangs than could possibly fall to the lot of the innocent and noble-hearted Charles Ormond.

Besides meeting with some severe contusions, he broke several limbs in his fall, and he was taken up shrieking with pain, at one moment calling for death, and at another upon Heaven for that mercy which how could he have the audacity to expect ?

Neville, too, was, as he said he would be, at the execution, the horrible details of which we shrink from.   But he was housed, and, through a window, he saw with far more indifference than Godfrey the whole of the terrific drama from its beginning to its end.

And there in the soft morning air, swaying gently to and fro, hung all that remained of the brave, the noble, the gallant, and the devoted Charles Ormond.   He who never, in thought even, had harmed a living thing—he who would have turned from his path, rather than tread upon the meanest insect—he who, in the emphatic words of an inspired writer, " Loved Heaven with a pure affection for the good it gave to all ; and respected the most insignificant of God's creation for the love of God."

That sad and terrible hour had not yet elapsed, though but a very short space of time remained to complete it, while still hung the body of the unfortunate Charles Ormond upon the gallows, in front of the debtors' door.

The rabble who had collected to witness the ceremony was, in a great measure, dispersed to their respective employments or amusements. Some few idlers remained about with the morbid taste for the horrible sight before them, and who would remain to witness the last moment the corpse remained out in the open air, in the humiliating condition it now occupied, not because there had been aught done that caused the fate to be deserved, but because others had taken so much care to entail consequences without Charles Ormond's being deserving of them.

The few who were about were only of the lowest class, save some few who may have been brought by other matters into that neighbourhood, and saw the condition of the place by accident, and not by inclination of their own for such sights as that before them.

Before the hour elapsed, a coach drove up to the foot of the gallows, on the side nearest Giltspur-street, while a few officers and constables were around to keep any one who might make any attempt to impede the delivery of the body at a proper distance from it.

They immediately concluded what was the object of the persons in the coach, though no one had made that object known to the officers. Having drawn up to the scaffolding, Mr. Blake stepped out of the carriage, for it was he, and seeing an officer close in attendance, he said,—

" I come to claim the body of Charles Ormond, as his nearest friend, now that the sentence of the law has been carried into effect."

The officer gave a glance at the clock of St. Sepulchre's before he made any reply, but then said,—

" I will inform the sheriff, sir, and your request will, no doubt, be immediately complied with."

He turned away, and was about to enter the prison, followed by Blake, but he turned round, and informed him he had better remain by the coach, saying—

" You will receive the body from off the drop, from the hands of the hangman."

Mr. Blake turned away, and gave a kind of shudder as the words were uttered, from the idea of coming in contact with such a person, but the duty that now devolved upon him he was resolved to execute.

He had scarcely remained there a minute or two when the sheriff appeared, accompanied by the governor and ordinary, upon the scaffold.

" There they are," said the officer; " you must now make your demand for the body, of them."—" I come to demand the body of Charles Ormond."

" The criminal who has been hanged, pursuant to the sentence of the law ?"— " Yes," said Mr. Blake.

There was a moment's pause, and then the sheriff again spoke to Mr. Blake.

" Are you a relation of the unfortunate man ?"—" No, but I am the nearest friend he has, and, as such, I claim the body."

" The body must be given up," said the sheriff to the executioner, who now appeared from below.

The sheriff and those with him retired, but still could see the ceremony of the delivery performed ; and the executioner came forward, and said—

" Are you willing to pay the fees, if I give it up to you as it now hangs, —clothes, rope, and all ?—I have had good offers for parts."—" Will five pounds satisfy you ?" said Mr. Blake, having no more notion of the sum requisite than the man in the moon, or a Chinese mandarin.

" Very well," growled the functionary.—" Be as quick as you can."

" The hour has not chimed yet."—" There it goes ; now you must be satisfied," said Blake, as the clock of St. Sepulchre's church chimed the quarters, preparatory to striking the hour of nine.

The man made no reply, but approached the body, and lifting it slightly up, he undid the end of the rope that secured it to the gallows ; and then, when he had so released it, he came to the side of the scaffold where Mr. Blake stood.

" The money," he said, as he supported the body partly on his own shoulder and partly on the scaffold.

Mr. Blake immediately handed him a five-pound bank note, and the coachman, apparently not liking the neighbourhood, or the proximity to the scaffolding, whipped his horses, and rattled off at a very rapid rate.

It was not very long before he arrived at Doctor Hesketh's door, where he stopped.

" All right, sir ?" inquired the coachman.—" Yes," said Blake ; " pull the surgery bell."

The coachman obeyed, and rang the bell violently; the door was opened, and a servant immediately came out, and was soon followed by a couple of porters.

"Carry this into the surgery," said Blake; "but Mr. Hesketh has given you orders no doubt?"—"Yes, sir, he has."

With some trouble they shifted the shell round, so as to get it out of the coach, for it had been so carried and placed to be as much concealed as possible; but once out, they carried it away, though it was heavy, into the house at once.

"Well," said Blake to the coachman, "what have I to give you, my man?"—"Why, yer honour, 'taint pleasant to go upon such a journey as this; hopes you'll make an allowance for the job; and I have come away very fast."

"You did so by your own good will, however, presuming you did it for me, what then?"—"Why, your honour will recollect it."

"Yes, I will; but how long do you wish me to do so? it is not a very important event."—"Well, sir, your honour will give me something for my trouble," said the coachman.

"If it is a trouble for you to undertake a job, why, you needn't have come out at all."

The coachman cursed himself internally, and dashed up the steps most recklessly; and, as Mr. Blake laid his fare in his hand, the driver turned it over, touched his hat, and said, "Thank you, sir," which was a sure sign that he was satisfied. Having settled that affair, Mr. Blake turned towards the house, and entered it.

"Well, Blake," said Mr. Hesketh, "how do you find yourself?"—"Why, scarcely so well as I could wish."

"I dare say not; it is a very disagreeable job altogether."—"It is, but I do not regret I have undertaken it."

"That is right; never do a thing deliberately, and then repent of it."—"No; I knew what it was, and have nothing to complain of; and yet it was a disagreeable event."

"You speak rightly," said Hesketh. "A most disagreeable task, especially to one of your habits."—"I never had to do with dead men before."

"I have often; they are natural enough to me. From the time I was a student, I have been accustomed to look upon the dead bodies of human beings as common matters. Had I not done so, I should have been very uncomfortable."—"No doubt."

"Use takes away the feeling of awe we naturally experience when we first view a dead body."—"I dare say," said Blake; "but the fact is, I have seen so much about this poor young fellow, that I cannot but feel much more uncomfortable than I should have done under any other circumstances."

"Ay, very likely."—"He was young and hearty, and, I firmly believe, innocent of the charge he was found guilty of by the jury; and to see him fall a prey to villany is more than one can well witness without feeling some sorrow."

"Very true; though now, as to these feelings, they are acquired, you see."—"Indeed! I think they are natural."

"Quite the reverse, I assure you. Why, I knew a young medical friend of mine—I say young—he and I were both young at that time; it is now years since we met."—"Yes, yes."

"I say I recollect a medical friend who dissected his own mother."—"Good God!" said Mr. Blake, with a shudder; "what an unnatural wretch he must have been!"

"Yes; but he did not know it was her."—"That, in some measure, alters the case; though, I must say, I should think he would feel very uncomfortable when he did discover the horrible truth."

"Well, he did. It was a long time before he would touch another body. But how it occurred was this; a few days after his mother's death a female body was brought him, and he at once paid for it, without examination. It was placed in his study, and, with some pupils, he commenced a dissection of it.

"A day or two afterwards, he was informed that his mother's grave had been broken open, and the body taken out. You may imagine his consternation at this piece of news. He ran to the body, and now, sure enough, he contrived to recognise the features of his deceased parent.

"After some trouble, he had the various parts of the body put together in a shell, and saw them decently interred in the grave which had been their original receptacle."

"Was that permitted to pass without some comment, or any angry discussion or rebuke taking place?"—"None," said Hesketh. "But the secret of that was, he had the prudence to commit the remains to their resting-place without the beat of the drum."

"He did it secretly?"—"Yes, he did. In the dead of the night, accompanied by a few friends, he replaced them, and then never afterwards bought a body, which was very absurd, you know."

"I dare say he was frightened."—"But, surely, he could not expect to meet more than one mother? People don't, usually, have more than one."

"I believe not," said Blake. "The law does not acknowledge more than one, and I expect nature is nearly the same in that respect. But about this young fellow?"—"He's all right."

"What do you mean by all right? You don't mean to say he is resuscitated?" —"Oh, no. I have had the battery prepared, and he's being laid out on the table, with blankets under him, and a few things, lest he should bruise himself."

"You don't think he will be violent, if he comes to life, do you?" inquired Mr. Blake.—"No, no; but galvanism is, you must be aware, a very powerful agency, and there is no knowing what may occur; and, to prevent accidents, I have so ordered it."

"Are we not losing time?" inquired Mr. Blake.—"No; you have not been here five minutes. But come this way; I dare say they have done all that is necessary now, and we may begin."

Mr. Blake followed his friend to the surgery, or rather a room fitted up in many respects as a medical theatre, in which operations could be performed, and many persons could be witnesses to them.

"Well, Mr. Gribble," said Mr. Hesketh, "is all ready?"—"Everything is prepared according to your orders, sir. The batteries are there, and the subject is laid out ready for the application," said Mr. Gribble.

"And have you stimulants, and all the appliances, in case we should cause a complete resuscitation?"—"I have, sir," said Gribble. "Hot water, spirits, fire, and beds, all ready at an instant warning."

"That is right, Mr. Gribble. I am much obliged to you. Here, Mr. Blake," said Hesketh.—"Do you really believe you can recall life in a case where life is extinct, as in this?" inquired Blake.

"Why, my dear sir, it is very difficult to say when life is extinct. Now, I will take upon myself to say that this is a case of simple suspension."—"Why his neck is broken," interposed Blake.

"Oh dear, no. Not in one case in twenty does a broken neck ensue; they die of suffocation merely; and, in some cases, it is difficult to say when it is complete; and while a single spark of life remains, however latent, it may, by some powerful agency, be recalled into activity."—"Indeed! and that agency, you mean to say, is galvanism?" said Mr. Blake, thoughtfully.

"I have no doubt but galvanism will do much—much more than is supposed; in fact, it is hardly known, and not understood by even one-tenth of those who study the subject, and they are very few."—"You have made experiments in this science?"

"I have, my dear sir, I have. Now, I will show you what it is capable of; I cannot command success, you know, though I will all that I can to ensure it."— "I am perfectly convinced of that, and shall therefore be satisfied, whether success crown your efforts or not," said Blake.

"You see the science is but in its infancy, and we do not know precisely all the conditions in which we ought to apply it; but experiment will rectify errors as we go on, until we have accumulated a volume of facts, and from them we can draw conclusions, and frame rules."—"I understand you."

"And now for the experiment, which I sincerely hope will succeed, for more reasons than one."—"So do I," said Blake; "but an hour is a long while—a very long time—to be bereft of sense and motion."

"In the case of persons suffocated by drowning, sometimes as much as two hours have elapsed, before animation has returned; and why should not the same occur in suffocation, by hanging?"—"Why," said Blake, "I cannot tell, save there is usually this difference: the body remains in the water but a very short time, while, on the other hand, the suspension, as you call it, continues for a whole hour," said Blake.

"I grant that," returned Hesketh; "but now the battery is charged, we will apply it. You will not be alarmed; your nerves are good—are they not?"—"Pretty well," said Blake; "I can bear some things better than others, and I dare say I can bear this; at all events, I'll try; I won't blame you, though, if I cannot."

"Very good. Now for it."

He placed the battery in a favourable position, where there was least danger of any accident occurring, and then brought a powerful charge in contact with the body. The effect was startling and awful. At first the body merely moved its arms, jaw, and eyes. Mr. Blake could not help shuddering as he witnessed this change.

"This is not powerful enough," said Hesketh; "we must unite two batteries, and thus increase its strength."

They immediately set about arranging the apparatus, and when that was complete, the application was again renewed, and the effect was proportionately terrific.

The dead man rose straight up at a single movement, in a manner so superhuman, that they all shrank back, aghast and terrified. Even Hesketh, acquainted with the effects of the battery as he was, retreated before the recovering body; the eyes rolled, and the jaws moved, while the lips were parted, showing the teeth as they were set.

The mouth moved several times, and the teeth came together with a loud clap that was truly horrifying to hear; and, to crown all, the body moved a pace forward, and swung the arms once or twice towards the individuals who were present, and who were terrified.

But one impulse seemed to animate them; and when the corpse was projected forward in a falling attitude, they all rushed out of the room, and Hesketh closed the door behind them, and secured it. They then paused a moment, and something fell with a crash upon the floor. They all shook; then a sound, the like of which never came from human lungs, was heard, and they all trembled excessively, looking in each other's faces.

"It has succeeded," said Hesketh, almost hysterically, which he endeavoured to hide.—"Succeeded in horrifying us, doctor, no more, I fear," said Blake, wiping the sweat off his brows with his handkerchief. "I never was so thoroughly terrified in all my life before. Never—never."

He repeated the last word several times, and the assistant said nothing. However, Hesketh, who wanted to see what had been done, turned to him, saying,—

"Go in, Mr. Gribble, and see what is the effect of our experiment, when you get in. You—you needn't be in a hurry; we are close here, and if anything happens, I can come to your assistance in a moment you know."

Whether this consolatory assurance prevailed upon the assistant or not, is uncertain; but he opened the door and peeped in, then walked into the middle of the room.

"Well," said Hesketh,—"well?"—"It is of no use," said Gribble; "he is dead."

"Dead!" repeated Hesketh, as he walked into the room, followed by Mr.

Blake, who saw the body extended upon the floor upon its face.—"So, the experiment has failed," said Blake.

"You see," said Hesketh, much perplexed, "the galvanic fluid is very subtle, and I dare say some conductor or other has touched the body, else if it had retained the fluid, I have no doubt it would have moved about till life returned; but there's the difficulty."—"I should imagine so," said Blake; "but I have seen enough of this room for once, to get very sick of it. Let us at once get out of it."

Mr. Blake then, accompanied by the doctor, quitted the surgery, and descended into another apartment.

The spectacle he had seen in the dissecting-room had much shaken Mr. Blake. He was not a man of weak nerves by any means; but his avocations were entirely different from anything that would lead him even to contemplate anything that would be an approach or introduction to such a horrible sight, as that which he had witnessed.

Still, though not a man easily frightened from his propriety, he certainly, on this occasion, felt an internal sickness, a feeling of great uncomfortableness, and even weakness of the limbs; it seemed as though he had suddenly lost the voluntary use of his limbs.

Doctor Hesketh himself did not feel so thoroughly composed as if nothing had happened. He had seen rather more of the effects of galvanism than he had witnessed before, and the result had been more startling and horrible than he had anticipated.

True it was, he was used to the appearance of dead and mangled human forms. He had himself done much of that work in the most scientific manner imaginable, and had given dissertations upon the beautiful complexity of the muscles, the confusion of movement, and the symmetry of bones, with the utmost *sang froid;* nay, he had even laid bare a human brain, and explored the presumed action of the nerves; but all this had not prepared him for what he had seen.

When the dead man opened his protruded eyes, the look was more than human nature could endure; the action of the arm, and the awful clap of the jaws as they came together with a loud snap were terrifying.

This was too horrible, and though they had been again in the room and saw the corpse, yet they could not recover their serenity, but stood gazing at each other as men who had seen something too horrible to speak of. It was the interchange of thought and feeling, without the intervention of words.

At length, Mr. Blake sank down in the arm-chair, close by him, with a groan. This was the first sound he had uttered audibly for some minutes; and it seemed a relief in him to do so, and he placed his hands before his eyes.

This sound recalled Doctor Hesketh to himself, and he said,—

"Blake, Blake, do you feel unwell?—faint, eh? Do you feel faint, eh? If you do, I'll bleed you."

Mr. Blake did not appear at all stricken with a due sense of the kindness of this offer, nor was his gratitude so lively as it ought to be, for he started, saying, in a hasty voice,—

"Oh, dear, no; I'm not faint; and if I had been, the thoughts of your kind offer would quickly restore me, for I have a great aversion to being bled."—"Oh, don't name it; I would do it in a minute," said the doctor; "in one minute. Only say the word."

"By no means," replied Blake, hastily; "you might as well galvanise me at once; you might, indeed."

The doctor shuddered.

"So, then," said Blake, after a pause, "you think, I suppose, there is no hope, none left—no possibility, however remote, of his being recalled to life?"—"None at all," said Hesketh; "every spark of life has quitted the body; and now that is gone, there can be no help for him; it is impossible, by any human agency, to implant anew the spark that was given it at birth. Had there been any latent, lingering life, I have no doubt that it would have been exhibited before this by the agency I employed."

"Alas! poor Ormond. But then the case was clear against him; there was no hope from the first."—"Ah! his account is made up. I think, however, that, to recall a body to life, is a most excruciating torture to the patient; as, for instance, when you recall life, after hanging till sensation is gone, the feelings of the patients are of the most horrible description."

"I dare say," said Mr. Blake; "but I never knew any one who had so suffered."—"Ah! I have heard them describe it; and so truly horrible were their sufferings, that I would not voluntarily undergo them to be recalled to life in such a manner; I would sooner be allowed to sleep on. It is a mistaken kindness to do this, and it is no cruelty to allow those who are insensible to pain and mischief to continue so; they can never know what it is to suffer more. But, then, the cant of the day is humanity, and humanity it must be, to please morbid sentimentality; so we recover all that we can, and shall continue to do so till the end of the chapter."

"I see; it must be a greater boon to the relatives, very often, when the apparently dead recover, than to themselves," said Mr. Blake. "I can understand that."—"And sometimes they are truly sorry for it," returned Doctor Hesketh. "I recollect the case of a man who had hung himself; he was cut down, and I was called in to restore him.

"After about a quarter of an hour's work, I succeeded. His family, at first, were terribly terrified, and showed great joy on his recovery, and declared they were eternally obliged to me for preserving the life of this man. He was after this a source of annoyance and misery to them all by his intemperate habits, having reduced them all to beggary and ruin. Often and often have they repented calling me in in such a hurry to aid his recovery."

"That may be in certain cases," said Mr. Blake; "but they cannot be known beforehand, and we must not play with human life. This, however, would never have been the case with so promising and honourable a young man as Mr. Ormond, poor fellow. What will be the consequence of allowing her, Marian Whitehead, to become acquainted with the fact of his decease, I know not."

"It will have a bad one, no doubt," remarked Doctor Hesketh. "Insensibility will supervene, I dare say. But I forgot; you have suffered a shock yourself, one that you are unused to, and one, to confess the truth, that surprised me not a little, and not at all agreeably. Will you have some brandy?"

As he spoke, he produced a bottle, from which he poured out a couple of glasses, without waiting for an answer.

"Here," he said, "you have some of the real pale. I acquired a taste for it while I walked the hospital; you know, young men, with strong stomachs, do such things."—"Yes, I have heard that you, while you are in your transition state, do many things you eschew when you are become the full-grown medical practitioners."

"There can be no doubt of that. Students of all degrees mix a little more with the world than, perhaps, they need; for that part they do mix with does not give them that knowledge and experience that they can boast of."—"I think not. Well, the brandy is good, and I find it is doing me good. To tell the truth, I was terribly sick and uncomfortable in my stomach when I came down stairs."

"Have another," said Hesketh, as he poured out another small glassful; "the occasion is an extraordinary one, and a sad one to boot, and sorrow, you know, is dry."—"Sorrow, indeed!" said Blake; "I cannot for the life of me drive from my mind the scene I shall have to go through with poor Marian. I protest to you, doctor, I have not been so taken with any person as I have with these unfortunates; for I may truly call them so."

"And you will have to break the news to her?"—"I shall, and that is an affair I shrink from, and yet it must devolve upon me. I would I could effect it by some means or other independent of myself; but I must and will not shrink from it. I have imposed it, as a duty, upon myself, and I will perform it despite of all that may happen."

"Where will you have the body interred?" inquired the doctor, after a pause.—

'I have not yet made up my mind; I may hear something more when I am down at Ealing to-morrow, and then I will see about it. In the meantime, if you will cause the body to be sent to my house in the shell, I shall be obliged to you; for the funeral, wherever it may go, will start from there. Any expense I will defray."

"It shall be done," said the doctor. 'I can do it in less than an hour; it is yet early in the day; scarce more than ten o'clock you know."—"Dear me, how this scene has confused me; there is ample time for me to get down to Ealing and inform Mrs. Whitehead of what has happened, and her daughter Marian also."

"It would be the better plan," said the doctor; "because you see the news would be there before you, and the shock may be indiscreetly given, and then the worst of consequences may be apprehended from it."—"Yes, yes, I will go at once. I will return to my house and give orders respecting the reception of the body, and at the same time I will write an order to a respectable undertaker to conduct the funeral, the expense of which I will defray myself."

"You are acting very generously, Blake."—"It is not in a case that does not call for it at all events," returned Blake; "and now, Hesketh, a good day; I am off for Ealing this moment."

"Good day, and good fortune in your undertaking; may it be more propitious or more harmless than it promises."—"Amen."

CHAPTER L.

THE FUNERAL OF CHARLES ORMOND IN THE VILLAGE CHURCHYARD, AND THE APPEARANCE OF THE BLACK LADY.

Mr. Blake left the house of the doctor and hurried off to his own, and there gave what orders he deemed necessary for the interment of Charles Ormond, and then he hurried to the coach-office, took his seat in the coach, and was, in less than an hour, on his road to Ealing.

Mr. Blake was a kind-hearted man and a generous one too; and it is not often that a professional man's sympathies are awakened to any extent. His intercourse with human nature is usually of that character, that it dries up the fount whence springs the genial flow of kindness.

However, his were thoroughly awakened, and he hesitated not to act upon them. His great endeavour was to conceive some plan or mode of making the dreadful communication of the execution of Charles Ormond, in the manner the least likely to produce the worst effects upon the weakened frame of Marian Whitehead. But this was a difficulty.

While he was forming one plan and then constructing another, he found he had arrived at the end of his journey, and the stoppage of the coach informed him he was at Ealing. Having paid his fare, he got out and walked to the cottage in which, by his kindness, Mrs. Whitehead and her daughter Marian were living. The garden gate was merely latched, and he walked up to the house, and entering the little parlour, he found Mrs. Whitehead alone and in tears.

"Ah! Mr. Blake," she said, "I almost dread to ask you the news; the worst is, I fear, all that you have to tell me."—"Alas! Mrs. Whitehead," said Mr. Blake, "the worst is, indeed, all I have to tell you; poor Ormond suffered this morning at eight—he is now no more."

Mrs. Whitehead shed tears; she was affected deeply, though she had fully anticipated the worst; yet it was too dreadful not to cause her tenderest feelings to overflow, and it was some minutes before she could speak. When she did, however, all she could say was,—

"Poor Marian, poor Marian; what will become of her, poor girl? It will surely kill her."

As the unfortunate mother spoke, she wrung her hands in all the bitterness of grief. She felt the full weight of the dreadful blow through her daughter. She felt all the desolation that a widow alone can feel, when she fears the dissolution of the last tie that binds her to the earth.

"Poor Marian! poor Marian!" were words that were often pronounced by her lips, as if she were regardless or unconscious of the presence of Mr. Blake, who, after allowing a reasonable time to elapse for this expression of feeling, said,—

"How is Marian to-day?"—"She is but weak and poorly," said Mrs. White-head; "and in a state of fear and anxiety I cannot describe to you. She is very weak, and I don't know what to make of her."

"Poor unfortunate creature," said Mr. Blake; "what misery has not this un-happy affair spread from one to the other. I do trust that the authors of all this will feel all they ought to feel, by way of punishment, for they richly deserve it."—"They do, indeed. How shall I tell Marian? I know not, I dare not do it—I dare not even be present. What shall I do, what shall I do?"

Mrs. Whitehead wrung her hands in the bitterness of her sorrow and grief. She was unable to proceed.

"Perhaps I had better endeavour to make her acquainted with the melancholy truth. She may not, perhaps, give way to so much before me as she would were you alone present. I might be a check upon her feelings."—"Do, do, Mr. Blake; do break the dreadful tidings to her. I am really afraid to do so. I don't know what it is that makes me fear to tell this dreadful news to her. I shall be more than thankful to you to do so."

"I will. Where is she, Mrs. Whitehead?"—"She is up stairs. I will send her down, Mr. Blake. Shall I send her down here?" she added, in a hesitating voice.

"If you please; or, if I can be admitted to where she is, it would be as well; for I dare say she is scarce well enough to rise, poor thing."—"Then come up stairs, Mr. Blake. I am afraid to go in by myself, and announce you, lest she should ask me the question I most dread to answer."

The truth was, Marian Whitehead was reclining in an easy chair near the window, gazing in sadness and sorrow upon the landscape around her, but at the same time she was hardly conscious of the objects her eyes rested upon; her mind was otherwise employed. She was absent in thought, but present in person.

She turned towards Mr. Blake as he entered, and for a moment she seemed not to understand clearly who was there. She looked, but saw him not. A dim consciousness of something, without any cognizance of what, was all that she felt.

Mr. Blake, too, was too sorrowful to speak; he saw the object of his compassion was not sensible of his approach, and then she turned again to the window.

"Poor thing," he muttered; "how dreadful it will be to awake her from this dream, to the reality of life—of death. I would it were over. So much beauty, so much loveliness, thus to be wasted and destroyed by the hand of fortune, is more than human nature can witness unmoved and unwept."

He approached her nearly, and taking her hand, seated himself upon the chair opposite to her. She turned her eyes upon him, and then, indeed, the light of intelligence beamed upon him from those sparkling orbs.

"Miss Whitehead," he said, "I come to see you. You have not forgotten your friends, I hope?"—"Oh! Mr. Blake, can I ever forget your kindness to me and my mother, and to poor Charles Ormond. I would it were a dream, and that I still slept on."

"Believe it a dream, Miss Whitehead; believe it a dream, and that you have but just awakened. It may confuse the senses, but yet all will be well, and life will at least flow on in an even channel. Yes, yes; believe it a dream."—"Alas! alas! I would I could; and yet, wherefore should I do so? Wherefore should I wish to believe that a mere shadow, the passing reality of which was so sweet? Besides, 'tis impossible to forget the original of the recollections that dwell upon my mind."

"And yet, Miss Whitehead, if you look upon the past thus, you will accomplish much; 'tis sweet to recall what has been in this manner—it tranquillises the mind, and is a consolation under the direst afflictions."

"But, without hope, it would be impossible to dwell upon the past without grief; it would be death. Were it not for hope, we could not live. I do hope, and yet God knows wherefore."

Mr. Blake's countenance fell, for he had hoped to find her somewhat inclined to receive the intelligence he had to impart, with a greater degree of calmness than he had at first anticipated; but now that hope was destroyed, for her last words convinced him she had yet hope that Charles Ormond would be spared, but why, he could not see.

"But, Mr. Blake, you have not yet told me how fares one, of whom I would sooner hear you speak than all else? Have you any news to tell me of Charles Ormond? Have they ——"

Here she paused, and a convulsive shudder passed through her frame, and Mr. Blake found himself completely aground, and very unprofessional feelings came over him. He was in a new light, and could not very well acquit himself with anything like readiness or cleverness. Here nature seemed inclined to take the lead, despite all his efforts to be master of himself.

"Miss Whitehead," he said, "forgive me, but the mere mention of that name brings to my mind many painful recollections. I would not for the world give you false hope, and then destroy it by the sad reality."—"What! what would you say? You will not tell me there is no hope? They will not destroy one so young, so noble, and so honourable as Charles? God of heaven, you do not mean to tell me that, Mr. Blake? Nay, nay, sorrow sits on your face. You would not appear so, if there were no cause. There is no hope then, that is, you won't give me any."

"I cannot. Though Heaven above is my witness how willingly I would do so, were there any to give you; but your wishes mingle with your hopes, and the result is, a sad and sorrowful disappointment. It will be a terrible blow to you, but we must all in our turn have some heavy misfortune to bear up against."

"What heavy blow, Mr. Blake?"—"Why—you see—that is—you—for instance—a-hem!"

Mr. Blake was nearly letting the truth slip out, but he got confused in doing so, and Marian, wakeful and suspicious, said,—

"What do you mean? Tell me, I pray you, tell me what it is you mean? God of heaven! have you any evil tidings to tell me of Charles? Oh! tell me while I can hear! tell me, Mr. Blake, tell me—in mercy, tell me at once."—"Miss Whitehead," said Blake; "Miss Whitehead, let me implore you to be calm, and to listen to reason."

"Reason, Mr. Blake; tell me the truth; I will listen, ay, as long as reason is left."—"Be calm."

"Hush! hark!—what noise is that?"

She pointed to the main road way that led through the village, and rose from her seat in a listening attitude, while every feature of her countenance betrayed intense emotion.

Blake listened, and instantly caught the cause of her alarm, and leaned back in his chair with clasped hands in calm despair; the worst he had anticipated was about to happen, but the intelligence he was labouring in vain to convey to her in the most delicate manner.

"It can't be helped, but I shall be saved a pang," said Blake, internally; "I hope it may not end badly."

There now came the sound of men's voices upon the air; not in conversation nor in quarrel, but a continued running commentary upon some event or thing they desired to obtain.

"Here you have it, my customers," said one; "here you have it, the last dying speech and confession. Here you have it, my customers, all for the charge of one halfpenny, the last dying speech and confession.

"Thank you, sir. Here you have it, my customers, with a copy of verses he wrote to his young 'oman, the night afore his execution this morning, at eight o'clock at the Old Bailey. Here you are, sir—sold again and got the money—the last dying speech and confession of Charles Ormond, who was convicted of forgery, and executed at the Old Bailey this morning."

The words had hardly reached the ears of Marian Whitehead, when she started as though an adder had wounded her; and, turning half round to Mr. Blake, she gazed earnestly at his features, and pointing towards the road-way, she uttered a scream of agony and fell senseless upon the floor. So suddenly had all that been done that Mr. Blake had not time to rise and save her. However, he immediately arose and assisted her to rise; but she was rigid, as if she were one mass of iron. He called for help, but Mrs. Whitehead was instantly by his side, and to her he left the insensible Marian, and went below.

"Well," he muttered to himself, "it has been done, but how, is the question? Certainly not as I intended it should be done; and yet I know not if I had conveyed the truth to her in my own way, I should have done any better. It is true the shock was great, hearing her lover's fate cried about in such a rude style, and with the additions they invariably give with these things. It ought to be put down by law, such abominable libels."

He paused and listened, but he could hear nothing of the unfortunate Marian; no sound came as though she had returned to life and sense; all was quiet and still, save the soft tread of female feet overhead. No word arose to convey any idea of her state; and when Mrs. Whitehead came down, she was too far gone in tears to be able to speak for some time.

"My dear Mrs. Whitehead," said Mr. Blake, kindly, "tell me how your daughter does; has she recovered from her swoon?"

Mrs. Whitehead shook her head mournfully, and she sighed deeply, though she could not speak—her heart was full. She had her portion of grief in her latter years.

"She is yet insensible," she said. "I fear I can do nothing with her, I must send for medical aid; she is gone beyond my means of recovery."—"I wish Dr. Hesketh was at hand."

"I rather expect him," said Mrs. Whitehead; "for when he was here last he promised to come down very soon; he has a patient somewhere on the road."—"I hope he may come, I am sure," said Blake; "his presence would now be of singular service. I wish now I had asked him to come down with me, but then he might have been required in some other quarter."

At that moment a carriage drove up to the door, and out stepped Dr. Hesketh, who immediately walked up to the house, and Mr. Blake himself arose and opened the door.

"Well, Blake, how do you get on here? How is Miss Whitehead—no occasion for my services I hope? I was close at hand, and thought you would be here, and we could return to town together, and perhaps I might be useful."—"You are indeed, especially useful," said Mr. Blake; "Miss Whitehead is quite insensible."

"Dear me," he said, "how fortunate I came. You have communicated to her the terrible event, I presume, and that was the cause of it, no doubt."—"Yes, that was it; at least it came in a ruder manner than that. I was upon the point of divulging the truth when some of the itinerant confession and dying speech venders came by, and vomited forth their stock of falsehood and absurdity."

"I see, I see."

By this time they had entered the parlour, where Mrs. Whitehead met them, and, seeing Dr. Hesketh, at once led the way to her daughter's room, informing Mr. Hesketh of what had occurred, and what had been done to her.

"And so, Mrs. Whitehead, she has remained utterly insensible all this time—quite motionless."—"Yes, she has been insensible all this time, doctor; but she has been in a kind of convulsion every now and then; her limbs have been set quite rigid, while her hands have been violently clenched, her teeth set, and foaming of the mouth."

"Upon my word," said the physician, "you have had some trouble since I saw ou last."

As he spoke, he walked up to the bedside of Marian, who yet remained insensible to all around her; but after a few judicious attempts to restore her, made under the direction of Dr. Hesketh, she gradually recovered her sensation.

"This is some consolation," said the doctor; "but she will require great care yet; she will not be well for some time, and the change being so sudden, from sensibility to insensibility, produces a shock upon the nerves that is not only injurious, but it leaves a great weakness upon the system."

There was now every prospect of her recovery, and Dr. Hesketh left the room, telling Mrs. Whitehead all she would have to do would be to soothe her when she came round, as well as she could; and, if possible, to bring her to a subdued state of mind, so that she could look upon what was past in the calmest manner possible, and as things that were done were now beyond recall.

Promising to obey these injunctions, Mrs. Whitehead let the doctor out, and walking down stairs, he entered the parlour in which sat Mr. Blake, awaiting the coming of Dr. Hesketh, whose step he no sooner heard on the stairs than he arose to make inquiries concerning the unfortunate Marian.

"Well, Hesketh," he said, "how do matters go on above? Does she show any symptoms of returning animation? Do you think she will recover?"—"Why, yes; she is recovering," said Hesketh, with a dubious shake of the head. "She has the symptoms of recovery, which will end, I have no doubt, in her complete recovery; but, at the same time, I know not what may be the ultimate effect upon her mind. It seems to me that she has received a most terrible shock, that has affected her whole nature."

"Poor thing! I trust that nothing may happen to injure her mind; she has suffered dreadfully and fearfully."—"Yes, yes. Let us take a walk. I must go to a chemist's shop somewhere here, and there obtain a few things I want; by the time I have obtained them, she will be recovered, I have no doubt, and then rest must do the remainder."

Blake immediately walked out with Hesketh, and they pursued their way to the apothecary's, where, after a short delay, Hesketh procured some matters he was desirous of leaving with Mrs. Whitehead for the use of Marian. These obtained, they both pursued their way back to the cottage, where they found, as Doctor Hesketh had predicted, that Marian had recovered.

"Has she been able to say much?" inquired Mr. Blake.—"Yes; she has spoken several times; she seemed to have recovered fully just as you shut the door, for she awoke, if I may use the expression, and inquired who it was that had left the house, and I then told her."

"Did she say anything about the unfortunate Charles Ormond, and his end?"—"She is perfectly aware of it, though she has not said so; yet she named the fact of his being dead in a subdued yet calm tone, and inquired if I knew where he was to be buried. I told her I had not heard whether any place had been fixed upon or not."

"No," said Mr. Blake; "I have not made any arrangement about that. What is the motive that induced her to make the inquiry? It is a singular one. Did she express any wish upon the subject?"—"She did say she hoped he would be buried in Ealing churchyard; for sometimes she would then be able to wander among the grave-stones, and there see Charles Ormond's last home."

"Poor thing! poor thing!" said Mr. Blake, much affected. "I am sure if I can gratify her I will; the burial shall take place at Ealing churchyard; it shall be there; it will be a quiet, secluded place, where there will be no bustle or annoyance of any kind; and, if she be able to go, she will, in case of accident, be not far from her home."

"That is decidedly desirable," said Hesketh. "What do you think of her yourself, Mrs. Whitehead? Do you think she talks quite as rationally as before?"—"I don't know what to say to her, doctor; she's too quiet over it to please me. I mean, her calmness appears to me to result from over distension of the mind. Her intellects are gone; not insane, or mad."

"Something approaching harmlessness and imbecility?"—"I'm afraid so," said Mrs. Whitehead, and a tear trickled down her cheek, as she thought of the wreck of beauty and loveliness that now was left her.

There was now a pause of some duration; each seemed so wrapped up in his or her thoughts, the current of which was not disturbed. They were of too melancholy a character to trifle with; and, as they afforded no consolation, they were not uttered. Doctor Hesketh was the first to break the silence.

"Well, Mrs. Whitehead," he said, "I can do your daughter, just now, no more good. I have a small parcel here; you will see how and when they are to be used by the directions. I hope they will do her some good; try nothing else, but let nature take its course, it is by far the best."

Mrs. Whitehead thanked him for his kindness, and assured him of her lasting gratitude while she lived.

"Be assured, Mrs. Whitehead, that Charles Ormond shall be buried at Ealing churchyard, as Marian wishes. I will have that all attended to; you may tell her that from me.   In the meantime, you must not be too cast down, for, recollect, that this and the next few days are the worst that she can have.   This is the consequence we shall feel now, and then, a week hence, all will be mere recollections of the past."—" Recollections that can never be banished, never be forgotten, and will, I fear, make but too lasting an impression upon my poor, dear girl's mind."

Mr. Blake and Doctor Hesketh now left Mrs. Whitehead's, and proceeded to return to town, having entered the carriage which the doctor had brought with him.

" Do you know, Blake," he said, after they had proceeded a short way in silence, " that, when you had gone, I thought over the matter, and began to think it possible that the communication you were about to make to Miss Whitehead would produce a scene of an afflicting character, and I immediately recollected that I had a patient who lived this road, and whom I must visit to-day or to-morrow; so I thought I would call to-day, as I might be wanted here."

" I am very glad of it," said Mr. Blake; " very glad indeed.   What is your opinion of this unfortunate girl?".—" I really can say little.   Grief, in general, is violent while it lasts, but, at the same time, the effects are various; in the worst cases, we find that a fit of illness produces great weakness, and then, after a time, grief becomes moderated with loss of strength; but as time increases, the lapse of it I mean, since the event grieved for, so the sorrow decreases in intensity."

" Indeed!   Well, there is much truth in all that, I must admit, and I hope it will be the case in this instance."—" I cannot see much in it that is different from other cases, save there is much to enlist the sympathies, I must say, and the case is, from beginning to end, one of unexampled affliction, and the parties concerned are gifted with high feelings."

" That is very true, doctor."—" I can well make allowance for the poignancy of feeling; but yet, be the class what it may, human nature is still human nature, and sorrow will decrease in its intensity; it is not natural it should always retain the same degree of severity."

" I hope it may be so, doctor; I hope it may be so, from my heart.   At all events, it is very afflicting while it lasts; but who can tell what may be the result upon a mind like Marian's?   She appears the very soul of grief."—" The mind, usually," said the doctor, " in my opinion, has very little to do with grief; it is the extreme of mental affliction, I will allow, but which, for the state of feeling and affection, would never, from the same cause, have assumed so intense a state of suffering as that she now labours under."

" You imagine, then, that this will cease to be what it is, as time goes on?"—" I do; it may cause a lasting melancholy, I'll allow, and she may even remain single all her life; but yet her feelings will be subdued, and allow her to enjoy herself to a certain extent; and recreation to any limited extent, in one so young, will have the effect of insensibly diminishing the intensity of suffering, and by degrees undermine the whole foundation of grief, and she may at once return to the joys of life."

" You think, then, grief cannot be lasting?"—" I do not say that; I am speaking generally.   There are cases which appear to be the reverse of all this—that I will allow; but these are exceptions to the general rule, and show more forcibly the effect of a general law."

" Well, I will endeavour to extract some consolation from what you say, doctor; though, I must confess, I am too low in spirit to be able to do much that way.   Since I have mixed myself up in these affairs, I have been as much interested in them as if they were really my own."—" There are people who are so interesting, and who are so particularly and singularly unhappy at the moment, that they enlist one's sympathies before one is aware of it."

" Yes; poor Marian Whitehead, so young and so fair!   It is a sad thing to see one so beautiful, so sadly wrecked and destroyed; it is a pitiable sight."—" She will recover, I hope," said Doctor Hesketh; " indeed, after this funeral is over, I shall expect to see signs of recovery, and those gradual and continual.   Change of scene and of life may do her much good; though, to tell the truth, I don't like the idea of her moping about Ealing churchyard."

"Do you think it would be safe to refuse compliance with such an expressed desire?"—"No, I do not, especially after the promise has been made. No, no; let it be fulfilled ; but, at the same time, in letting grief have its full swing for a time, we ought to guard against permitting anything that may assist in keeping up its intensity rather than in diminishing its violence."

"You would do the latter, if you could."—"Yes ; but what would do the latter in some stages, would, if improperly and unseasonably applied, only aggravate the former symptoms. No; permit the funeral to take place. I dare say it will soothe her mind for a time, till she becomes familiar and habituated to the contemplation of his death ; then this intensity of feeling will have subsided, I hope. Propose a change, and move her away ; this may cause a fresh flow of grief, but it will be of comparatively short duration, and is of no consequence."

"Well, Hesketh, I am personally obliged to you for all this," said Mr. Blake ; "it is, as you know, a matter of singular interest to me to see them safely over this unhappy period of their lives, for I deem it the worst."—"No doubt; but here we are in London. It grows late, I see, by the streets being lighted up ; how singular the effect after one has been on a country road."

"Yes, the change is great ; but now I will leave you, and thank you for the lift."

"You are very welcome. I shall see Marian in a day or two's time ; and then I shall ascertain if I am likely to be wanted. But I apprehend, beyond a little medicine, all must be left to the care of her mother's good nursing and tenderness."

"That she will do to the utmost extent in her power ; but the poor woman herself is sadness personified ; but her feelings being more merged into love for her daughter, she can school them better than any one else ; because, you see, her feelings towards the unfortunate young man were chiefly on her daughter's account ; not wholly, I dare say, yet in a great measure so."—"No doubt of that."

"Well, then, I have hopes of her, and those not of a very vague and uncertain description ; and yet I am free to admit that I may be mistaken."—"Farewell. We are all human, and liable to error ; but I hope all will yet be well."

Mr. Blake left the doctor, and proceeded alone towards his own house, filled with melancholy and sadness, for he could not drive from his mind the scene he had witnessed at the cottage. The extreme grief and misery there depicted was such that he had never seen its equal, and it had made a deep impression upon his mind, and he arrived at home in a state of mind he had never, before these unhappy occurrences, felt. He had been an entire stranger to all such impressions ; his life had been one of even prosperity, and he could have known nothing of what he now knew almost involuntarily.

* * * * * * * *

Several days passed, and Mr. Blake had given all the necessary directions to an undertaker to conduct the funeral in a respectable and even handsome style, at least so far as he deemed compatible with the circumstances under which the unfortunate Charles Ormond met with his death.

Everything was to be plain ; and, at the same time, it was not the plainness that arose from penury. As the time approached for the funeral, Mr. Blake determined upon going down to Ealing to see Mrs. Whitehead and her daughter.

In this determination he was strengthened, as he had not seen Doctor Hesketh for several days ; he was out so much on his professional duties, that he could not catch him at home, as the phrase goes, but he was constantly called out at the usual hours of his being at home.

He took the coach, and again found himself at Ealing, the day before the funeral, and there he found Mrs. Whitehead, in sorrow, trouble, and grief, with regard to her daughter.

"What do you think of her condition, Mrs. Whitehead ?" inquired Blake ; "do you think she will at all be able to attend the funeral ? Has she expressed any wish to do so ?"—"She has not said so," replied Mrs. Whitehead ; "and she is not well enough, that is also certain. She is confined to her bed, poor thing, and I almost fear she will never recover—never get up again."

"Have you seen Dr. Hesketh ?"—"Yes, I have ; he has seen her. He says she is very ill, but by no means desperately so. She seems listless and weak. I fear much she has lost her reason."

" Does she speak at all, or notice anything ?" inquired Mr. Blake, " or recognise anybody ?"—" Yes, she can do all that ; but she suffers anything to be done without notice, unless especially moved to do so. She seems to be buried in deep meditation, and deep sighs escape her ; and, altogether, she makes me sad and miserable. I know not what to do, Mr. Blake ; my heart is nearly broken ; I know not what we have done that we should suffer so dreadfully."

"Hush, Mrs. Whitehead ; say nothing upon that subject ; it is the misfortunes incidental to human nature that we suffer, irrespective of any reward or punishment for previous misdeeds or crimes."—"I think it must be so, sir," she replied, sadly.

Having done what he could to comfort the widow, he informed her of the day and hour at which the funeral would take place, in Ealing churchyard. He, then, at once proceeded to London, having satisfied himself of the condition of the unfortunate family in his cottage.

*   *   *   *   *   *   *   *

The morning came : the day was fine, but a deep gloom pervaded the air ; the sun's rays were impeded by masses of clouds, which, while they detracted not from the fineness and warmth of the day, yet cast a gloom over everything ; and it was not what an indifferent person would have termed an unpleasant day, nor yet a very fine one.

The funeral moved away from Mr. Blake's house, followed by but one mourning coach, in which was Mr. Blake himself, who, sad and lonely, followed, at a funeral pace, the body of the murdered Ormond, for such he really was.

When at a distance from the town, the hearse and coach slightly increased their pace ; and a few eyes were turned, with a curious gaze, at the unusual sight of a hearse and mourning coach going along the country road.

In due time, they arrived at Mrs. Whitehead's, where Mr. Blake ordered them to stop, a little way from the cottage, at a spot where they could not be seen from the cottage, and then he alighted and walked up to the cottage, where he found Mrs. Whitehead waiting for him.

" Marian," he said ; " how is she ?"

Mrs. Whitehead mournfully shook her head, and, with a deep sigh, as she adjusted her funeral hood and scarf, said,—

" Ah ! Mr. Blake, I know not what to say. She is still confined to her room, and apparently heedless or not understanding what is about to happen. She takes no notice hardly of any one. I fear she will never again be what she has been, poor creature ; and who can wonder ?"—" Not I, Mrs. Whitehead. But let us hope."

He said this, though he felt none ; and he led the old lady down the garden to the gate, for she would attend the funeral, as Mr. Blake was to do so, too—partly in compliment to him—partly in grateful recollection of the services of Charles Ormond, as well as respect, as, also, because she thought Marian, when she recovered, would feel pleased at her having done so.

And now they have arrived at the gate of the churchyard, and here the bearers lift the coffin out and adjust the pall, while the mourners brought up the rear.

The appearance of a hearse and mourning coach, and the tolling of the bell, had gathered many strangers and stragglers together, who all crowded around the grave, as the clergyman, with uncovered head, stood in the midst of those who had assembled, began, while the bell tolled heavily, to read the burial service.

There was a solemn silence pervading the very atmosphere ; the birds had ceased their song, and no sound disturbed the village churchyard, save the bell and the impressive voice of the clergyman.

The coffin was lowered to its final abode ; and then, for the first time, Mr. Blake looked round upon those who stood by, and was amazed to see a third person in black attending the funeral ; but he almost uttered a cry of surprise when his eyes rested upon the features of Marian.

Yes, no one had seen her enter the churchyard, and no one had noticed how she had glided among them to witness the last sad office performed for one whom she had loved so well.

She saw no one, and noticed no one. Her sad and grief-worn features were composed into an expression at once mournful and calm. She gazed upon the coffin, and seemed abstracted from all earthly considerations.

Dressed in sober black, but scarce a funeral costume—there were a few things that were not usual. She wanted the funeral hood and scarf; she had not been furnished with either; but she had dressed herself in black. But every one now knows the costume she wore to her dying hour. She cherished it; it was the same she wore at Charles Ormond's funeral.

Her presence was unexpected.   Her mother had believed her incapable of rising to come out.   How she came was unknown ; her presence alone was all that was understood.

She was looked upon by many, but her eyes met not those of any one who stood there.   She was mute and sad, but decent withal ; no sign or gesture betrayed the anguish that worked within ; even the melancholy and sadness of her countenance was no index to the strange feelings that clung to her heart.

The funeral ceased ; the clergyman himself gazed upon her.   There was something in her demeanour and appearance that seemed to fascinate, and the son of the church, for some moments, stood still, gazing with interest upon her.   Then the funeral was over.   She slowly turned from the grave as it was filled up ; the crowd made way for her.   She spoke to none—saw none, and walked out of the gate. Some one, as she did so, behind the crowd, asked audibly of the gravedigger, " Who is she?"   The man looked up for a moment, and then said,—

" The lady in black !"   This was said on the impulse of the moment, for the man was ignorant of who she was ; but it was heard by all, and all felt it was true and appropriate.

CHAPTER LI.

THE INTERVIEW BETWEEN GODFREY AND NEVILLE, AND THE ATTEMPTED MURDER.

THERE lay extended on one of the straw pallets the mangled and agonized form of Godfrey, who, as our readers are well aware, met with a serious accident on the morning of the execution of his victim, Charles Ormond, when he fell to the earth a mangled, but living, breathing man.

He was taken immediately to the nearest hospital, where he was placed in a side ward or room, it being understood that he was a wealthy man, and would pay for all that was done.   Therefore, Godfrey was well cared for, in comparison to other patients ; his bones and wounds were not rudely pulled about, but handled with all the care and tenderness imaginable, and the nurses were civil.

How different is the case of the unhappy being whose vices are not gilded with gold, and whose clothes betray no appearance of wealth, when he is carried in on a shutter ; few are the civil words he gets either from nurse or surgeons.

However, there lay Godfrey, in all the agony a man can endure.   Many bones had been broken, and terribly bruised was his flesh.   The pain he endured was great ; he groaned, and his breathing was hard.   No kind hand was near him to soothe the sick man's pillow, to moisten his lips, or cool his fevered brow ; no one was there to soothe the irritability of his temper, or the feverishness of his brow.

No one had a kind word ; no fondness—no tender solicitude was expressed by those who attended his couch ; no gentle murmuring of hopes and fears, and anticipations of his wants and desires.

No.   Godfrey lay there, unpitied, and uncared-for by all, save such care as those who expect reward have it in their power to bestow, or in their inclination to afford, to those who fall under their hands.

He had nothing within himself that could aid in chasing the long, weary hours away ; he had nothing he could look upon with anything like satisfaction ; all was a dark and gloomy picture, turn which way he would.

Godfrey had never done a good action—he could not at least recollect one, and that was tolerable proof he never had done one ; and while he lay there thoughts after thoughts chased the other away, but he could find nothing to dwell upon with satisfaction, and in that hour of mortal misery it was an aggravation even to Godfrey to find his character so very black.

It would have been something to have known, and to have been able to say, " I have done one good action."   Not that Godfrey cared for it abstractedly, but the moment of pain was to him the moment of fear, and that brought odd and strange thoughts into his mind, such as he would rather have banished, had it been possible ; but we cannot always direct our thoughts.

Thus lay Godfrey, racked with pain, feverish, and irritable, but no one was at hand to soothe or condole with him, and impart those nameless little attentions he could have received had he been at his own home, or any other than the one he was. But no, he was not doomed to feel and experience such delights.

The scene he had witnessed before his fall was present to his mind; the blackened walls of Newgate, their hard and harsh outlines, broken only but by many small irregularities. They had not anything in them but what was most gloomy, and most sad; but yet they were hardly so to him. They were terrible, and there was an undefined feeling at his heart, when he thought of them, that he could not well understand.

Much of what he had seen would return again and again to him, and the vision of that scene would flash in gloom and sadness through his mind. Great, therefore, was his disappointment when, in reviewing the past, there seemed to be an incompleteness about that he well understood.

"There is all there," he muttered, "save him. If I am to be pestered by this vision, why is he not there? Surely, surely he was hanged! I heard the bell tolling—I saw the drop erected, the crowd, and all, save the fatal act itself! Why, why was not my fall stayed until he came out? Curses upon the fortune that laid me so! Why was I doomed to such an accident? Mercy! my pangs are more than human nature ever felt! I cannot, without intolerable anguish, move hand or foot!"

Godfrey was in extreme pain; the injuries he had received were extensive, and very great; he could not turn from side to side; he lay a helpless mass of human misery.

His thoughts reverted to nothing so often as to the scene before the execution of Charles Ormond; there his mind seemed to make a stand, and moved not from it but to return to it again. He was always brought back to the same point, and the tolling of the bell rang in his ears as though it were palpable and present at the moment.

The gloom of night reigned around him; there was a dim light in the place; it just afforded an undefined medium to convey the impression of shadows rather than substances. He could not well tell the shape of objects many yards from him; he could not tell whether he was alone or not; there might be some one close at hand, or there might not; if he moved his head from side to side he could see nothing; the fire now and then, indeed, threw a bright flash upwards, and then but momentary; but it did so repeatedly.

Thus went on minute after minute; there was no change, save the change from light to dark, and darkness to light; such a light as pleases many, and in which one could sit by the hour, gazing upon the flickering flame that bursts out and dies away.

It was at this moment that he heard one of the nurses approach his bed. His hearing was painfully acute; he was sensible, too, to touch, most sensible, indeed, for he could tell the approach of any one by the least vibration in the floor; the least movement of the clothes that covered him produced a pang.

Oh! Godfrey was punished by living and recurring pangs, and his distorted mind was constantly dwelling upon his own sufferings. But he suffered physically and mentally.

"Mr. Godfrey," said the voice of the nurse, "here is one who wishes to see you below."

"To see me?" gasped Godfrey.—"Yes. He says he is a friend of yours, and desires to speak with you at once. Shall I admit him?"

"Do you know who he is?"—"No, sir. He would not give his name; he would not say who he was, save that he was a friend of yours, and had something particular to tell you."

Godfrey paused a moment before he made any answer. It was, he had no doubt, Neville, who had come to see him; but why he had done so he could not tell. Perhaps to tell him of the execution, or perhaps—but no, there could not be another reprieve, he thought. Surely, that could never be.

Perhaps something else had transpired, something at the last moment, and then all his well-laid schemes might yet be brought to nothing.

"Shall I let him come in, sir?" inquired the nurse, "or tell him to come some other time?"

But Godfrey knew Neville's character too well to think he would quietly go away as he was desired, or if he did, it would be to nurse some scheme of revenge against him that he would put in practice the first opportunity that was afforded him.

"Shall I send him away?" said the nurse.—"No, no," said Godfrey, in a low tone; "let him come here; I would speak with him. Let us be alone; I have a few words upon some private matters to speak to him."

"Very well, sir," said the nurse, and she quitted the bedside of the mangled man, and then, after a short interval, she returned with the man whom Godfrey, rightly enough, conjectured to be no other than Neville.

When the nurse had left the bedside of Godfrey, Neville approached, saying,—

"Well, Godfrey, how do you get on here? How do you like hospital fare? but then, you can afford it."—"Afford what?" exclaimed Godfrey.

"Afford to lie idle for a length of time. This is a bad job, but it might have been worse, you know."—"Worse!" said Godfrey; "nothing can be worse. I am in pain all over; I have not a limb or a bone that has not its own pain. God! what pain I suffer; it is agony, excruciating agony."

"Well, never mind, you will get over it one of these days, you know, and then you will enjoy the contrast in feeling. They say you do not know what good health is until you have suffered from illness, and now you know."

"What has brought you here?" said Godfrey, suddenly; for he liked not the sneering, heartless tone of Neville, who seemed to rejoice in all he suffered. —"Friendship," replied Neville.

"Have you nothing to tell me?" inquired Godfrey, not heeding the answer; ' for I cannot see you many minutes longer. The nurses won't permit it; I have not strength to endure it."—"Yes; I have something to tell you, and you must listen to me, too, even though the nurse should frown upon you."

"Go on," said Godfrey, impatiently.—"I am about to do so. You remember the moment when you caused such a smash on the stones, eh?"

"God! can I ever forget that horrible moment? I have thought myself falling, in my sleep, ever since; I fear to close my eyes, lest I should feel the same sensation again."—"It will go off when you are used to it; try it again, Godfrey; when you have felt the sensation very often, you will get indifferent to it, and then it will go off."

"Get used to it!" said Godfrey; "get used to such agony as that? Oh, no, no, no!"—"Well, you must endure it, then, without any hope."

"Go on," resumed Godfrey.—"Well, then, just at that moment, there was so much bustle and excitement among the crowd, and you were carried away, I was determined to see the hanging."

"Was he hung?" inquired Godfrey, eagerly.—"Yes, he was," said Neville. "He came out and was turned off: I saw him die."

"Thank God!" exclaimed Godfrey, for almost the first time in his life. "I have all along had some fear that he would not be hanged; but now, then, all is right; there is no longer any fear of him or his friends."—"I am not so sure of that; indeed, I am quite of another opinion to that, Godfrey."

"And wherefore?"—"I know not. I believe there will be now no effort lost to discover who are the authors of all this, and, if they do trace it home, there will be more hanging than either you or I may like to admire, Godfrey."

"Hanging can't be so bad as this," muttered Godfrey.—"I don't choose to try," said Neville. "I shall leave the country, and then you can have all the game to yourself, and no one to interfere with you. I shall be out of the way, and nothing can be traced to me, so that you will be extra sure, you know."

"I cannot see that we shall be any better off then than we are now," replied Godfrey. "Every one will now be quiet. The Whiteheads can do nothing; they have no means; they have no notion of what to do, if they had; but they have not."—" Then there is Blake."

" And what can he do? He is what is termed a respectable attorney; one who can do nothing but what is pointed out by sanction and by precedents. He can do nothing; he could not trace anything, even if he had a clue, and that he has not got."—" We know nothing about it," said Neville—" we know nothing about it. He may have more than we think for; and he will be perpetually watching for an opportunity, you may depend upon that, Godfrey."

" No, no," said Godfrey. " You have some scheme in your head, by which you want to effect some purpose of your own. You want to frighten me Neville; but, bad as I am, I shall not be so easily alarmed."—" I have no such object as frightening you, for you lay there helpless enough. But, I tell you, my opinion distinctly is, that if Blake were to obtain any inkling of what is the matter, he would have the secret out by some means."

" Impossible!" said Godfrey; " why, look you here, Neville; he has no interest in these people, and when the excitement of the death and burial of this man is once over, there will be no more heard or said about the matter. All will sink into oblivion, and be forgotten, save, perhaps, by the Whiteheads themselves; and even then, after a time, another lover may do much there."—" No," said Neville, shaking his head; " no, I say no to that; you don't understand these things, Godfrey. Blake seems to be much more deeply interested in the matter than you think for."

" How do you know?"—" I only judge of the fact, because I watched him arrive at the front of the gallows with a coach and shell, to convey the body away as soon as the hour had expired."

" Did Blake do that?"—" Yes, he did; I watched him. I was anxious to know what was done with the body, and I saw him come as I have told you; but why he should make such common cause with the Whiteheads, I don't know, unless he has some object which we cannot divine. At all events, I am now heartily sick of the whole affair."

Godfrey lay some moments in deep thought, though he could not suppress the expression of pain that every now and then would find vent in a groan or a shivering sigh.

It was some minutes before he spoke, and then he said,—

" Well, come what will, Charles Ormond is dead, and that is one very great point gained. Not only does it set the whole affair at rest, but it renders us more secure."—" It would appear," interrupted Neville, " from what I have seen, that it is a stronger inducement than ever for our enemies to bestir themselves in this matter. Blake having become interested, will, I think, have spies, whose object will be to discover something concerning this affair, and we know not how much he may know."

" We do; you may depend upon it, that all he knew, or knows, will not harm us; because, if it would have done so, why he would have made the attempt before Ormond was hanged, and so thrown a doubt upon the proceedings, which would, no doubt, have made an impression with the judge, and secretary of state."—" It might," said Neville; " it might, and yet he was moved to grant a reprieve, that could not have been obtained without a motive; and I believe, of course, it was insufficient to produce any permanent effect; yet it must have been something to the effect that there was a doubt, though we do not know on what point it was raised."

" We do not," said Godfrey, " nor are we likely to know; this, however, I know, you are troubled with a weak conscience. You are about to pray for forgiveness for the past, and hope to do better for the future; you are getting frightened, Neville. After this you'll turn methodist, and perhaps a preacher—who knows? Hadn't you better go to the head-quarters, and confess all, and be rewarded with a halter at once? Ha! ha! ha!"

" I tell you what Godfrey, if we were both to hang together, it strikes me I should be turned off in a more decent style than you. You would think you would want somebody to prop you up by the elbows; the thought that any one was placing anything uncomfortably tight round the neck ——"

Godfrey did seem to shrink from the bare contemplation of such a thing, for he said,—

" You don't know what you are jesting about; you may be nearer such an end than you can at all have any idea of; for if you have been overheard, now, in speaking to me, it strikes me forcibly you would stand a nearer chance of trying your courage than you may admire."

Neville gave a savage scowl around, as he said,—

" We are not overheard,—we cannot be; and if such were to take place, why, of course, you would be my companion in trouble; I would never think of going alone; I should be more comfortable in your company."

" Well, what more have you to say? I am tired, and wish to be alone," said Godfrey.—" I have something more to say, which concerns ourselves, and therefore I cannot leave you alone yet."

" I am tired."—" You may be, and so am I, but it is of living in this country, Godfrey. I can't feel here at all at ease; I feel myself in danger, and before the bubble bursts, I wish to leave the country, and be at a safe distance."

" Well, go. I think it would be as well; the more we are together, the more it may be noticed and commented upon," said Godfrey; " the plan is a very good one, and the sooner it is carried out the better. I am decidedly of that opinion."

—" Of course you would be rid of my presence, and that, you would allow, is a point gained. Well, so it would, but I don't go without the means. I can't go into a foreign country without means, and those I must have from you, Godfrey."

" Must you, indeed?" said Godfrey.—" Yes, I must," said Neville, savagely; " I must have the means to leave England."

" Now, look you here, Neville, I am not to be drained at every fool's pleasure. You have had your chances, and I have had mine. You have dissipated all your profits, and I have saved mine. Now, do not imagine that you are to drain me by threats, or anything, of money. I won't give it. You have been most liberally and handsomely paid."

" Have I ?" said Neville.—" Yes, you have; and what have you done with it? Why giving money to you is of as much use as drawing water up with a sieve."

" I have spent mine, and I want more."—" And you expect that I am continually to be ready to meet your demands for money, whenever your reckless folly may put you in a position to want it."

" Yes," said Neville, drily.—" Then I will not do it. You think because I am here shattered, broken, bruised, and helpless, that you can alarm me? but there you are much mistaken."

" Am I, Godfrey? Be sure."—" Yes, you are much mistaken, if you think that when I pay you most handsomely in the first instance, you are to be paid twice, or thrice, merely because you can betray."

" Well, do not pay me for what I have done, but for what I could do if I liked."—" No, no, I will not. You may betray me—that is you may make the attempt; but if you consider a moment or two, you will see how futile that is. You may confess all you have done in this matter, but you cannot injure me. You may say you forged the name, and you sent the letter, but you cannot bring me into the same net with yourself. You see that Neville, eh ?"

" Go on," said Neville, savagely. " You'll make a fine thing of it before you have done."—" You may confess all this, but I can say I know nothing about it. My character and respectability will shield me from suspicion, while you will either get hanged for your share of the trouble, or else prosecuted, and transported for attempting to extort money by false pretences."

" Now hark ye, Godfrey—you keep no terms with me—I need keep none with you."—" I care not," said Godfrey.

" This is a lonesome place," remarked Neville, as he gazed around, " and one well adapted to a murder. It is nearly dark, and I can see you very well. Can you see me, Godfrey ?"

Godfrey looked, and could just see the outline of Neville's person, and his two deep set eyes were glistening with unnatural fire at him through the deep gloom that surrounded him.

"Will you give me money?" he asked, in a deep but suppressed voice. "Will you give me money?"—"None—none."

"Then receive your fate at my hands, instead of the hangman's! It comes but little in anticipation of the time when you would have died by his hands!"—"Neville, what do you mean? I am here, helpless—I cannot move hand or foot. You would never attempt my life, at such a moment too? What could you get by such a deed?"

"Revenge!" said Neville. "If you were dead I could obtain security against your machinations, and I could rob your home; therefore die you shall!"

As he spoke he came towards Godfrey, who lay in a trance of terror, and yet he called not out for assistance, for he thought that Neville was merely endeavouring to alarm him thoroughly, so that he should be compelled to yield to his request, and be mulct in at least another thousand pounds.

However, he soon found that Neville's ferocity was equal to what he said, and he seized him, Godfrey, by the throat with one hand, while he placed the palm of the other on his mouth. Godfrey's limbs were broken—he could not use one to save himself. He writhed, and struggled; but what could he do thus at the mercy of a powerful enemy?

Suddenly he caught Neville's hand between his teeth, and with a convulsive grip, he almost made his teeth meet. For a moment Neville was startled, and released his hold, and then in that moment of mercy Godfrey uttered a hoarse shriek for aid.

Fortunately for him the nurse was not far off, and she came running up, when he again called out,—"Help! murder!"

"God help me!" said the nurse, "here's a pretty go! Who's hurt? What's the matter?"

There was much confusion and running about of people, in the midst of which Neville precipitately quitted the hospital, unnoticed by any one, most of the people being either asleep, or too much occupied to pay any attention to what was going on in any place but in their own.

CHAPTER LII.

THE MOURNER BY THE GRAVE OF ORMOND.—THE STRANGE DELUSION.—THE REMOVAL TO LONDON, AND THE SUCCESSION OF VISITS.

As had been foreseen by Mr. Blake, and expressed by him in his interview with Doctor Hesketh, the churchyard at Ealing became the only place frequented by Marian Whitehead. There alone, beside the grave of him she loved, was she found deeply buried in her own grief, and unnoticing all the world, she saw but the gravestone of her lover; there, with the bare initials and date, she would sit weeping and gazing upon them as if they brought to her mind the form and feeling of him who never could be eradicated from her heart.

The day of the funeral passed off in the manner we have described, and the unfortunate Marian left the churchyard, and proceeded homeward, and when she had reached the cottage, she shut the door of her room, and threw herself upon her knees before a chair, and buried her face in her hands, and wept.

How long she remained thus it is difficult to say, but Mrs. Whitehead became alarmed at the absence of Marian, and guessed truly enough that she was indulging to excess in grief, and also being justly alarmed at the appearance that Marian had made at the funeral in the morning.

On opening the door Mrs. Whitehead perceived her daughter in an attitude of prayer; she entered the room, and, unwilling to disturb her, she waited for some time, watching her as she knelt, but heard no words issue from her lips. Deep sighs came one after the other, as though her heart would burst with inexpressible grief and anguish.

Some minutes elapsed ere a sound proceeded from her, and Mrs. Whitehead, fearful of the consequences, thought she had better awake her from this trance-like grief, lest she should become worse, or lest some much worse consequence should arise than she had any idea of at that moment. She trembled lest some catastrophe was at hand, to meet which would require a new exertion on her part of that character which was incompatible with her powers.

Indeed Mrs. Whitehead was little fit to meet with energy the calls upon her care and watchfulness, that these sad appearances prognosticated. She grieved, and could sympathise with grief, especially with Marian, but she was unable to combat and overcome difficulties by mere force of character.

She herself had suffered much of late, and found herself much enfeebled by the weight of affliction that seemed daily to increase and become more heavy as she became less able to bear up against it.

However, she approached Marian, and laying her hand upon her shoulder, she said, kindly,—

"Marian, my dear Marian, look up, and speak to your mother. Marian, you will kill yourself and me with grief! I cannot survive you, dear Marian! You do not injure yourself alone, but you weigh down to the grave your mother too!"

After a moment Marian removed her hands from before her face, and looked up into her mother's with a sad but vacant gaze. She did not exhibit those tears of violent grief Mrs. Whitehead expected to see. For a moment or two she spoke not, but then she said, calmly and sadly,—

"Mother, saw you not the grave that contains all I love—all I can love? Ah! if it had but closed over me, what happiness would it have been my lot to feel! But no, I am a helpless mourner—a tarrier by the way—one who has a journey to perform, but cannot make the speed I would like! I would I were at my journey's end, then I might feel that the time was come when I was to become the bride of him who is now in heaven! Yes, mother, I shall see him again! Some day we shall meet, and then all past sadness and sorrow will be over! Then ——"

"Marian, my dear Marian, you are ill, very ill. Let me advise you to sleep. I knew not you were about to quit the house this morning, or else I had seen you."—"Could I be away from such a ceremony?" said Marian. "Could I who loved him so well be absent when he was placed in his last lone home? Oh! no! no! no!"

Then came on a succession of such long and deep-drawn sighs, but no tears, that Mrs. Whitehead was inexpressibly pained.

"Marian, dear Marian, do not speak thus! Let me implore you; 'tis your mother who has watched over you, who begs you to seek in sleep some rest from this dreadful grief! It will kill me to look upon you!"

She took her by the arm, and led her unresistingly to her couch, and obedient to the express wish of Mrs. Whitehead, she lay down, but not to sleep. She could not do that. Sleep could scarce visit her eyes, so full as they were of this mournful ceremony, of which she had been so conspicuous and interested a spectator.

Mrs. Whitehead left the room; she could do nothing but sit and gaze upon the pale, saddened countenance, which carried a pang to her heart too acute to bear. She returned to the parlour where she left Mr. Blake, who, after the funeral was over, had returned to the cottage, and stopped an hour or more to converse with Mrs. Whitehead, and to make some inquiries respecting Marian, whose appearance had no less excited his pity and curiosity than others.

"How do you find her now, Mrs. Whitehead?" inquired Mr. Blake. "Any better?"—"I fear none," said the weeping mother.

"Poor thing! Does she rave as we saw her? Is her grief more violent?"—"She has an unnatural calmness, and at times she appears as though she did not exactly understand all that has taken place. She is surely going wrong."

Mr. Blake was silent—he could not give the widow any hope, for he saw and felt none; and his tongue refused to give consolation, where there was none.

"She was, I thought, in violent grief; but there seems to be a settled calm-ness—a dreadful state of feeling that I cannot describe, more the result of a ruined mind than from excess of grief, though the latter were the cause of it. It

has been a most unhappy affair for all parties concerned; and none could have suffered more than the unfortunate young man. He acted from the purest motives, I believe; but how has it fared with him?"

"Poor fellow! God knows I regret all, deeply. I wish the deed had been signed, and I had never known the wrong that Godfrey intended to do me; then

No. 40.

Charles Ormond might have been a living man. It seems that was his fate, and he could not avoid it. May Heaven be merciful to him—he acted justly, and villany has prevailed; we know not why, but so it is. Yes, the young and the handsome are cut off, while the old and the withered remain a little longer to cumber the earth until they have run their race."

"Why, as for that," said Mr. Blake, "I can't say that I ever knew an old man who was desirous of dying; indeed, I believe he has a much greater disinclination to die than even a young man. But when old men have suffered what I have, and seen what I have seen, then indeed they may lose some of their love of life. Yes, yes, there can be no doubt but that great misfortunes have a surprising effect upon the mind as well as the body; and so you think poor Marian is no better?"

"I can hardly think so; there seems to me to be a great change in her demeanour. I never saw her in anything like the state she is now in; it's lamentable to see—I fear her head is turned. Poor girl! I think she has had enough of sorrow and affliction to turn a stronger mind than hers; but since I can do nothing more, Mrs. Whitehead, I must return to town."

"I have to thank you, Mr. Blake, and to express my gratitude to you for the kindness you have shown me in the midst of all my misfortunes—but for such a firm friend as yourself, sir, I and my poor daughter Marian would have been inmates of a workhouse—I can never feel grateful enough."

"Mrs. Whitehead, we will say nothing about that—I feel too deeply interested in this affair to deserve much praise for my disinterestedness; but, at all events, you may rely upon my doing my best to be a friend to you."

"I'm sure of it, sir," said the unfortunate widow, "I am sure of it; and such kindness is to me more acceptable than any other—I feel it, too, more deeply."

As she spoke, Mrs. Whitehead shed tears; for a sense of her terrible condition came over her so forcibly, that she could not refrain from weeping bitterly. Mr. Blake did his utmost to comfort and calm her; and then, after assuring her of his friendship, quitted the house, and proceeded on his way to London.

That day was one of anxiety to Mrs. Whitehead; but it passed off as many other long and anxious day had before passed off, in lengthened distress and sorrow. It was peculiarly uncomfortable—no day, perhaps, more so than that in which a funeral has taken place, especially under the unhappy circumstances that this had taken place; and, moreover, the further cause for sorrow and evil prognostications of the future. She sat in silence, and the thought often recurred to her mind as to what would be the end of this: would Marian ever recover, and be the comfort to her in her old age that she had at one time ventured to hope? She dared not answer this question in the affirmative, and she dreaded to answer it by the worst, her fears told her, was likely to happen. "If she would but recover," she muttered to herself, "I should be but too happy—all yet might be well—at least life might not be that burden, that scene of continual misery and cheerless existence it would otherwise be—I might yet hope to close my eyes in peace; but if she should not, my dying day will be one of terror and sorrow. Oh, Marian, Marian, what pangs you cause your afflicted parent! No hope, no joy—all sorrow and sadness in the past, present, and the future."

She wrung her hands in an agony of grief, tears fell fast, and thus closed a day so full of griefs, that she felt gratified when it drew to a conclusion.

The next day, Mrs. Whitehead sat down to a solitary breakfast with a heavy heart. She was well assured, by the little she had seen of her daughter, that she was likely to get worse rather than better; or, at the least, there was but little hope that she would ever be again what she was.

Mrs. Whitehead had been into her daughter's room, but at the sme time, she had not spoken to her: she lay asleep, so pale and wan—she appeared to have suffered much, as no doubt she must; but there she lay, tranquil, and Mrs.

Whitehead deemed sleep most beneficial, since there was an absence of all sorrow and grief, rather than awake her to a sense of her loss.

*   *   *   *   *

The sun shone upon the church-yard, and the tomb-stones cast their shadows westward, and the mild air was filled with the song of birds, when the figure of Marian, attired as she had been on the previous day at the funeral, entered the church-yard, and walked slowly towards the new-filled grave, that contained all she held most dear.

She knelt down, by the side of the turf that had been thrown over the spot, but said nothing for some time; tears flowed fast, and her lips moved as if in prayer. She clasped her hands in grief, and bent forward, in an agony of woe. "Oh, Charles!" she murmured, "thou injured and suffering spirit, hover round me, be near at hand, and see the sorrows of her whom you loved so fondly, and who cherishes your memory as the one feeling of her heart. Never, never, never, can it be erased, and never can it for one hour give way to any other feeling, however severe may be the affliction she may have to bear. Oh, God! have mercy upon my broken heart! I would my hour was come, that I might join thee in the realms of bliss. There never was such wickedness in man before, to doom my Charles to such a cruel end. What has he not suffered, and what have I, what shall I? Great is the wickedness of those who have done this!"

She wrung her hands, and arose, and slowly walked round the tomb-stone for some minutes, and then again she paused before the head-stone, to read the inscription, but she seemed not to understand the letters—or rather, her mind received no new impression. She leaned against a neighbouring monument, and gazed, sadly and steadily, upon the grave.

For the first time there were some persons coming through the churchyard; it was like many churchyards, frequented now and then; but it had a seldom-used path through it, and now two men approached the spot, and seeing a figure in black, motionless, they for a minute or two paused to examine it.

"Who is it?" said one.

"I don't know; but some one who has lost some relative, I suppose, and who seems to feel more than ordinary grief upon the occasion."

"Poor thing—she hears us not."

"No, she does not—do not let us disturb her; she is absorbed in her own sad feelings. Let us pass on."

They were about to do so when they heard a footstep approaching, and some one was whistling melodiously enough as he approached the spot where the two speakers stood, which was less than a stone's cast from that where the unfortunate and unconscious Marian stood.

He was a country lad, who, as he walked onward with a burden on his shoulder, whistled as he trudged along, thinking of nothing but his tune. When, however, he came to the spot where the two men were standing, he looked at them, and then around, but seeing nothing, he was about to walk on, when one of the men said to him as he was about to pass:

"Stop, my lad; do you know what that is yonder, by the newly-filled grave?"—"Where?" said the boy, staring around.

"You see—near the monument with the railings around it, do you not?"—"Oh! aye! I see."

"Well, then, can you tell me who she is?" inquired the man, pointing out with his finger.—"Oh aye! to be sure—she be the Black Lady."

"The what?" inquired the man with astonishment.—"The Black Lady; she came to the funeral yesterday in the same dress, and they called her the Black Lady."

"Who has she buried?"—"Dun' know."

"Her brother or sister? Man or a woman?"—"Dun' know;" said the boy again, and he moved on with his load until he was out of sight; and even then the merry tune with which he enlivened his walk rang sharp and shrill through the air; but it did not disturb her meditations; she was almost insensible of impression.

"Let us come nearer," said one to the other; "we shall see what she is. It is very strange. I have passed through this place often enough before, but I never saw such a thing."—"Nor I; but did you not hear the boy say she attended a funeral but yesterday. She has, therefore, never been here but once before, and at a time when the funeral was in course of performance."

"That is true enough—I will see—how strangely she stands—come this way, she will not see us."—"Do not disturb her, her grief is too great and too sincere for any interference."

"I mean none."

The two approached, and came within a few yards of where Marian stood gazing on the earth. Her lips moved, and words seemed to issue from her lips, but they reached not the ears of the strangers.

"How beautiful," said one.—"Yes, but how sad and sorrowful," replied the other.

"Her lips are pale, though she has a colour; but that is the custom of the time, and not the hand of nature that planted that there."—"That is true enough. Poor thing, poor thing! She makes one's heart feel sorrow and regret to see her stand weeping in that manner. As sure as heaven, she has lost some lover or other, and has been turned, and has lost her reason."

"It seems most probable that such is the case—but let us leave her, poor thing; if she were to see us, she might feel we had intruded upon her, and her grief would be none the less, because we had been unnecessarily curious."—"Very well, come away. I sincerely hope she may be better, and that time will restore her."

The other man shook his head, saying—

"No, no, she seems to me to have actually lost her senses; but we may as well leave her to herself."

They retraced their footsteps, and walked through the churchyard in silence, until they quitted it.

*　　*　　*　　*　　*　　*　　*

Mrs. Whitehead had missed her daughter that morning, and fearful lest some evil should betide her, she determined to follow her to the spot where she deemed it was most likely she should go, and that was the churchyard.

She had some fear of Marian's making away with herself; not but that her own principles of rectitude would cause her to abstain from any such act as that; but, at the same time, she could not be considered as answerable for her own acts—she was decidedly insane. If it were but temporarily so, she could not be held responsible for acts committed under such a concurrence of circumstances.

These, at least, were Mrs. Whitehead's ideas at the time; and she, in pursuance of them, arose, and dreading to find her worst fears confirmed, she went, in the first place, to search the churchyard; and then, making her way towards the spot where the grave of Charles Ormond had been made, she saw her afflicted daughter by the grave of him she loved so well.

Mrs. Whitehead approached her slowly and cautiously—she was curious to know what kind of demeanour she exhibited before the grave of her lover, as well as alarmed at the result of what she foresaw was likely to be a continued succession of visits to the burial place of Charles Ormond.

Marian was standing by the headstone, leaning her hands upon the stone, and her head upon them. She was motionless, save now and then a deep-drawn sigh escaped her, and she seemed as though her grief was by far too great for utterance.

It was with great sorrow that Mrs. Whitehead beheld the turn grief had taken with her daughter, Marian. She had almost fancied it would have destroyed her at the time; but now she saw worse than death hanging over the head of the only being on earth whom she seemed connected with; she appeared to have no other link that bound her to life. There was no other tie that seemed to connect her with society. Whom else could she confide in or speak to?—No one. Her daughter was to her all-in-all.

"Marian," she said, "what do you here? You will make me very unhappy."
Marian turned to her, and said—

"Mother, can we be otherwise than unhappy, when we have lost such as he,
and that, too, by such means? Ah! never more speak of happiness—for me, at
least, I am to know none while my heart beats."

"Don't talk thus, dear Marian; recollect your mother yet remains with you,
though it may be but for a very short time; for what I have gone through,
Marian, I feel has made me more feeble than I could have believed."

"Mother," said Marian, as she slowly raised her head, with a look of hopeless
grief; "mother, I have no hope or wish to live. I do not care to live—have I not
lost all? What is life to me now? the sun of my existence is quenched. Death
itself is not half so hideous and fearful as the terrible blank that now lies before
me—and what more joyful peace can I find than this? He is here—I know he
is here; and tell me, where shall I be, but where he is? No, no, I find a home
here."

"Marian, dear, come home; do not stay here."

"This is a home to me, mother."

"Nay, unless you wish to see me drop at your feet, do not stay here;
remember your health—your mother's hopes and wishes. Recollect, Marian, I
have none on earth to comfort me save you; I have no other soul that will close
my dying eyes, or watch round my death-bed."

"Oh! mother, mother!" said Marian, bursting into tears; "talk not of death,
unless it be to tell me when I shall be able to quit this world, of which I have
seen so much cause to hate. Dear mother, what is life now?"

"Time will show, my dear Marian," said Mrs. Whitehead; "time will show;
and should there not be happiness yet in store for us, we shall at least deserve it
by our conduct."

As Mrs. Whitehead spoke, she drew Marian's hand through her arm, and gently
led her from the spot.

*   *   *   *   *   *   *

It was useless to contend against a habit, that might almost be termed a
passion. She could not be dissuaded from her visits to the churchyard. There
was Marian to be found at all times; and, whenever she was missing, Mrs.
Whitehead was sure to find her at the grave of Charles Ormond.

True in death, as in life, was Marian's love; it knew no change; she was,
truly, the living bride of the dead. She seemed to haunt the place of repose for
the dead; and she was known to all who frequented the churchyard as The
Black Lady, who mourned at the grave of her lover; for such were people's
surmises.

Poor Marian, what hard fate was thine! Harder than even that of the dead.
Better far would it have been to have died while the sense of grief was most
poignant, than to have lived to become an object of sympathy and sorrow!

But we know not our fate, else some could anticipate it, and others would not
wait to have it accomplished. It is a wise dispensation which hides futurity
from us; and it is not till life is ended that we can tell for what we have lived;
and then, sometimes, the object seems little enough, compared with the troubles
nd the miseries that are to be, and have been, endured.

Thus it was with Marian, who had blossomed and bloomed; and in her prime
a blight had come, that destroyed the fruit that appeared so promising. Poor
Marian! a prospect so long and dreary, for even a short life, can hardly be
conceived, for one so frail in strength. So hard a fate seems to be ill-fitting the
back to the burthen it has to bear.

If ever pity was deserved, it was in the case of the solitary mourner in Ealing
churchyard; for there she went, day after day, to visit the grave of the dead.
Here she would be for hours—standing by the grave of Charles Ormond—sadly
sighing and murmuring at the decrees that brought him to such a fate as that
which he had so unjustly suffered.

There—alone, solitary and sad, was she to be seen mourning, in melancholy guise, over the hard lot of the dead. Sometimes she was silent; at other times, words would escape her lips; and then, she would kneel and pray beside the tomb —pray fervently for the welfare of him who lay beneath. Sometimes she would apostrophize the dead; and then she would wring her hands, as though she were in an extremity of woe.

Mrs. Whitehead saw there was no hope of weaning her daughter from the churchyard; that was her only walk, and when there she seemed to be more calm than when any attempt was made to interfere in her manner of disposing of her time; therefore, her mother now never interfered in that, but merely walked to the churchyard—when she thought she had been there long enough—to calm her feelings.

It was well known to many of the residents that Marian visited the churchyard, and there remained, mourning by the side of the early tomb of him she could never forget.

Yes, it was known; and ladies—ladies by courtesy—would come to the churchyard with motives of curiosity, to see the mourner, at what might truly be called her devotions. Yes; they could find something in that to gratify their curiosity, in watching the sadness and sorrow of Marian. It was something romantic to them, and furnished a topic for conversation; and they could indulge their morbid curiosity and sickly sentimentality, by taking the young of their own sex to see the broken-hearted one, and to surmise all that the peculiarity of dress and conduct might, in such people, give rise to.

Mrs. Whitehead was conscious of this, and it pained her; but Marian knew it not. She could not prevent it without putting a constraint upon her, which she was unwilling to do, especially as Marian was not susceptible to the feeling this conduct displayed; on the contrary, she heeded it not; and was, probably, even unconscious that she had become an object of comment and curiosity.

One day, however, the current of her thoughts took a different turn, and quite changed her habits and mode of thoughts. She had up to this time considered him as dead!—as lost to her for ever; with no hope in the future, and a satisfaction in the past—all dead, sad, and melancholy.

Mrs. Whitehead, feeling more than ordinarily sorrowful, walked out earlier than usual to fetch Marian from the churchyard; and when she got there, she found that she was standing in a musing attitude, and something had just happened to give a new turn to her thoughts.

"Marian," said Mrs. Whitehead, "I am very unhappy. Come back with me; I never shall know peace again."

"Unhappy, mother! Who is happy?"

Mrs. Whitehead sighed, and a new train of reflections seemed to take their course through her mind; for she thought, with truth, there were indeed but few who really were happy; but then she thought how few there were who had anything like the excuse for unhappiness she and her daughter had had.

"Mother," she said, suddenly, "he is not there—" pointing to the churchyard. "I have just discovered that."

"Discovered what, my child?"

"That he is not there. That was only a device to deceive them. No—no, he is not there."

"I do not understand you, my child. Who is not there?" inquired Mrs. Whitehead, in some alarm.

"Charles Ormond is not buried in the churchyard; no, he is yet living—yet living in London."

"Marian!"

"Nay, mother, you do not know what I do; they have not let you into the secret. Charles has escaped, and they seek his life—but he is not buried."

"Alas! Marian, did you not see the funeral?"

"I did."

"Can you doubt the sacred truth—that poor Charles is no more, and that you have been mourning him as dead? You have not yet thrown aside your funeral dress."

"Nor shall I, mother, until Charles is saved. They, too, will think him buried, which will give him more chance of escape."

"Escape, Marian! what can you mean?"

As Mrs. Whitehead spoke, she could not help feeling alarmed lest some new and more terrible exhibition of the misfortune that had befallen, and which Mrs. Whitehead deemed by far the severest, had presented itself.

"I mean, mother, that Charles has escaped the death that awaited him—he escaped and is now hiding from the officers, who think he is buried here."

"And is he not buried here?" inquired Mrs. Whitehead.

"No, certainly not, mother—I know he is not, though it is not every one who knows so much—if he can keep out of the way, there may yet be a chance of saving his life."

"Oh, Marian!"

"Mother—I know it; say nothing more about it—I must go to London," said Marian.

"Go to London!" exclaimed Mrs. Whitehead, lifting up her eyes and hands at the thought of returning to London after what had befallen them there, and their reasons for leaving it.

"Yes, mother, I may meet with Charles Ormond there, but you know I cannot here."

"No, no, you cannot."

"And there I may be of some service to him—there, you know, I should see him."

"Truly, if you were to see him, my dear," said the unfortunate widow, a fresh sense of her daughter's affection coming over her with more force than ever.

They returned to the cottage of Mr. Blake, and again and again Marian talked of going to town, upon that errand she had named. When Mrs. Whitehead perceived she was determined upon that object, she said to her—

"But you know, Marian, we have nothing to enable us to do so; we only live here upon the suffrance, and by the extreme goodness of Mr. Blake."

"I am sure Mr. Blake will see the propriety of what I say, and would not attempt to dissuade me, mother—he must know that Charles is not dead."

"Alas, poor Marian!" said Mrs. Whitehead, "I can no longer contend with you in words, for I do not know what to do; I cannot convince you, nor can you understand what I say—alas! I cannot even comply with your wishes, however they may tend to tranquillize your mind."

Mrs. Whitehead could not forbear to shed tears—she saw in everything her daughter wished her own poverty and Marian's incurable disorder.

"Why do you weep, mother?" said Marian, taking her hand, and looking up into her face.

"Ah, good Marian! do not ask me. My heart will break. We have nothing of our own, and yet you ask me to go to London. I know not how to do it."

"London is not so far, mother. Besides, mother, does not Charles wish it? I know that to meet him, and do what I can for him, is my duty. Has he not been our friend and benefactor? Has he not incurred the hatred of that dreadful man solely on our account? He would never have been persecuted as he has but on our account."

"Yes, my dear, but Charles is no more."

"Oh! I see you have been deceived as well as others; but, mother, I assure you Charles is alive. Look at me, and see if I grieve now."

Mrs. Whitehead did look at the placid face of her daughter, and her heart told her that the ravages she beheld there were never likely to be amended. She was, indeed, wan and sorrowful; but still she dressed and kept herself in precisely the same state she went to the funeral.

"Ah, Marian! let me beg of you, as you love me, to say no more upon this subject: I am too deeply grieved to speak of it. There is no doubt but poor Charles is dead."

Marian sighed, but said no more, and seemed wrapt up in her own thoughts. She seemed insensible to all that passed around her.

* * * * * *

Mrs. Whitehead, when she sat alone that evening—for Marian usually sat in her own room, wrapt in deep meditation ; or, if she sat with her mother, she was so absent in thought, she seldom spoke, while the poor old lady only worked on and sighed—she thought over the matter that her daughter had mentioned to her in the morning ; and she determined, as Marian had more than once named it, to write to Mr. Blake and inform him of what had taken place. She sat down, upon the impulse of the moment, and wrote to Mr. Blake ; and begged he would advise her how to act under such an emergency. This done, she felt somewhat relieved in her mind ; for to her it seemed that she had at least taken one step towards doing something respecting this sudden change in Marian's mind.

* * * * * *

The next day was not without its event ; and the post came down, and a letter from Mr. Blake was given into the hands of Mrs. Whitehead, who, with trembling hands, opened it and read as follows :—

"TO MRS. WHITEHEAD.

"DEAR MADAM,

"I am sorry I cannot come to acknowledge the receipt of your favour, but I am too busy. The only advice I can, I give you—it is the best I can think of—and that is, to humour the new conceit that Marian has taken to. Nothing can be done by thwarting her ; and she may eventually be much bettered by conceding to her all she wishes.

"In the meantime, I think the change of scene, and the removal to London, may conduce to the same ; and, as soon as I am able, I will procure you some lodging in town, which you can come to till you can find a place more suited to your own tastes and wants.

"I remain, yours very sincerely,

"S. BLAKE."

When Mrs. Whitehead had read this, she felt it was another instance of the thoughtfulness and goodness of Mr. Blake's heart. He could not but feel deeply and disinterestedly in their fate, or this would never have been done. It was, therefore, with great joy she consented to leave Ealing the next time that Marian broached the subject to her, which was in the course of the same day ; and, for the first time since the funeral of Charles Ormond, the churchyard wanted its solitary mourner. Yes—Marian now feeling convinced that Charles was not dead, but living—and that, too, in London—no longer visited what she considered a sham tomb.

"There, mother," she said, "I thought you would be convinced that Charles is living, and in London. If he were here, I would stay ; but, as he is in London, our duty tells us we ought to be there too."

"But how, if we cannot find him?"

"Then we must hope. I dare say we shall. Have patience. I am sure that there are means of finding him out, because he will be about at some time or other ; and if not, I will take the best means I can devise to find him out. London is a large place. And sometimes one part is more frequented than others. I can walk about till I do meet him. I am sure that, by so doing, within a certain time, I should meet with every inhabitant in that city, from one end to the other."

Mrs. Whitehead pondered over this strange assertion, and could not entirely comprehend it, and could find no answer to it, so it was passed by.

In about two days more Mrs. Whitehead received another letter from Mr. Blake, in which he informed her he had taken a lodging for her, and advised her to proceed to London, and occupy it until she could choose for herself.

This was a delicate intimation that he had done his best for her, but he by no means desired her to confine herself to his choice in a matter that was exclusively for her own use and benefit.

The invitation needed no repetition; but Mrs. Whitehead at once proceeded to make all the necessary arrangements for her immediate departure for London. Marian, too, was no less gratified, though she exhibited few signs of it, save her impatience to reach the scene of her future operations.

Calm and sad as was her demeanour, befitting the livery of death she wore, there could be traced an uneasiness of manner evidently betokening her being sensible she was waiting for some event that she most earnestly desired to see accomplished.

"Once, and only once," she said, "Mother, shall we get to London to-day?

Every hour may be of consequence. We know not at what hour I may be most useful to him."

"My dear Marian," replied her mother, "we shall go to-day, and be in London to-day, and that, too, with the utmost haste; we can walk, but we must await the coming of the coach that's to carry us away."

Marian said no more, but sat down before the window that faced the road; and there, occasionally rocking herself and now looking up the road, she sat thus for nearly two hours, without taking any further notice of anything. At length the moment came when the coach did arrive, and Marian and her mother entered it, while the small amount of luggage they had was fastened upon the top. When Mrs. Whitehead found herself really travelling towards the great city, her emotions were different from those with which she had come down. Then, indeed, her afflictions came new upon her, and she felt acutely enough; but then she, as a mother, had hope enough for her daughter, though she had none, or so little that it seemed but none, for the unfortunate and doomed Charles Ormond; but now, not only had his fate been sealed—and he was no longer a living creature—but her daughter was harmlessly deranged. She was no hope or comfort there.

A sad life for both of them, and neither of them had any prospect of any release, save such only as death afforded. It was a sad, a melancholy prospect.

Mrs. Whitehead came to town, and was met at the coach-office by Mr. Blake himself, who at once proceeded to take them to their new lodgings.

"This new change in Marian," he said, "may, perhaps, not be of long duration, but then, it may indicate her malady is not so incurable as we were led to imagine. We may have some hope, and yet I scarce know how to recommend you to indulge i it."

"I shall never hope again, sir," said Mrs. Whitehead. "I cannot look at Marian, without thinking she is an instance of living destruction, for she is certainly destroyed in all, save mere existence—that which made her the pride of my heart is gone—the intelligence which lit up her features is gone—a clear wreck of all mind is the evil."

"It is a very great evil," said Mr. Blake, "a greater misfortune I never knew, however, I would humour her as much as possible, for you may alleviate, if you cannot recover her; that much may be done."

"I will of course do my best, sir."

"Exactly—your living in town will enable you to consult Doctor Hesketh, should there be any need," said Blake. I do not know if there be any need, I hope there may be none. She seems so calm and serene but melancholy—to be thrown ill from her late afflictions—she seems insensible to the heaviest part of them. Poor thing! She seems to imagine Charles is living, her mind or recollection seems to have got as far as his escape from Newgate, and no further. She is ignorant of all the dreadful events that have since occurred, at least, since she has taken up the notion he is concealed in London. Ah, well! it is useless to fight against the notion, and you may benefit her by humouring her in the conceit—Poor thing! it is shocking to contemplate the state she is reduced to."

With many words of kindly sympathy, he beguiled the way to their new lodgings. They were comfortable and respectable, and Mrs. Whitehead could but express her gratitude to her benefactor for all the benefits he had conferred upon her.

Marian spoke not; she seemed occupied in observing all around her; she appeared to imagine it required much circumspection to deceive those who were endeavouring to re-capture Charles Ormond; and she had to take care she was not watched, and thus become the means of his destruction.

Harmless and quiet as were her manners, there was something peculiarly touching in them; her devotion to her lover, and the afflictions she had met with, were points that never could be forgotten by those who had once seen her.

Once established in their new lodgings, Marian Whitehead would leave her home in the morning, and frequent those places where she believed that her lover had formerly been in the habit of going upon business, and where she had more than once been with him.

Here she would wander about, sad and silent, amid the busy throng of men who worshipped Mammon.

Her appearance and dress excited much surprise at first, and some suspicion and comment; but that soon wore away, and she was considered harmless, and none looked upon her sad countenance without feeling emotions of sorrow and pity.

The places she used mostly to frequent were the Bank, and all the offices about there; the different banking and coffee houses of note about Cornhill, Lombard Street, and Lothbury.

At these places she might be seen daily wandering about as though her whole existence had been devoted to some penance or other, which she was compelled to perform in silence, in the midst of some densely populated district.

*   *   *   *   *   *

"Marian, my dear child," said Mrs. Whitehead, "you had better not go out to-day; remain at home with me—do not leave me daily to wander about thus."

"I must, mother—the very day I cease to do so may be that on which Charles Ormond would have passed me and then I shall have missed him."

"That cannot be."

"Ah, mother! you know not what I feel. I have the greatest anxiety to meet with Charles now, for I have made up my mind to take a new step in his behalf."

"A new step, Marian?" suggested Mrs. Whitehead, alarmed at the thoughts of anything fresh occurring to her daughter's mind, for she dreaded these changes.

"Yes, mother; I ought to make some attempts to save Charles's life."

"Indeed, Marian, but how is that to be done?" inquired Mrs. Whitehead; "how can you do it?"

"Thus: I must go round to those generally who have had anything to do with this affair, and interest them in Charles's fate, and then they may exert themselves to save him; but all this depends upon me."

"Upon you, Marian?" said her mother.

"Yes, upon me; for if I do not see them, they will never believe he lives."

Mrs. Whitehead thought so too, and in the sadness of her heart she had almost fancied a wish, that looking to the results of life she wished he never had; for his life, though filled with the most generous impulses, had proved most unfortunate to him, and to those whom he attempted to serve.

But the thought passed away, and she said to herself, that whatever had been the result he had been the principal sufferer.

"You see, if I can get them to interest themselves in this affair, and make representation to the secretary of state, as well as to obtain a petition, signed in his favour, I may succeed in saving him, while he remains out of sight."

"Oh, Marian, I would it were all as you hope, but it matters now but little—it is ridiculous to attempt to dissuade you from this useless attempt."

"Not useless, mother, when the object is to save the life of Charles Ormond!"

Mrs. Whitehead said nothing, she saw it was useless; and her heart bled afresh at every assertion made by her unfortunate daughter, and weeping, as she turned her head aside, she muttered—

"Oh, Heaven! this is a hard fate, indeed, to see my only child thus bereft of that which is the distinctive mark between ourselves and all nature."

*   *   *   *   *   *

It was but the next day, when Marian determined to set about the task she had assigned herself of saving Charles Ormond's life, by an intervention of all those connected with himself in the prosecution of the case, save and except Godfrey, of course."

It was for some time a matter of doubt as to where she should begin at, but having walked into the city, she determined to make the first attempt upon the bankers where Charles Ormond had presented the cheque for payment. She thought if she could get them to interest themselves about it, she would have less difficulty with the others; their example would have much weight with those upon whom she hoped to make a similar attempt. Her appearance now in London in the peculiar dress she wore made her conspicuous about the Bank and Cornhill, and many of the mercantile men of the day were familiar with her appearance; and when she entered the banking house she excited no surprise, but when she opened the little door which led to the private room in which sat several of the partners and managers of the firm, they were much amazed to see the entrance of the Black Lady into their private office. She dropped a curtsey, and approached the table at which they sat, and, as she did so, she said,—

"Gentlemen, I come to you upon an errand of mercy, which I am sure you will listen to, though it is in behalf of one who has been made to appear to offend against you."

"Madame," said the manager, "we have business to attend to."

The manager paused, however, in the midst of his speech, for he saw at a glance the state of the case, and any adjuration on his part would be thrown away.

"It is respecting the fate of the unfortunate Charles Ormond; he is more sinned against than sinning; his enemies and mine have made him appear what he is not —criminal."

"Charles Ormond! why, he is—"

"I know what you are about to say," she said, placidly and calmly; "but that is a mistake; he is not dead."

"Not dead?" said one of the gentlemen, looking up in surprise, for the first time, having been engaged in some calculation.

"No, sir—he has escaped; and I come to solicit your interest to save him from the fate that appears to await him. Let me assure you he is not guilty; I know his innocence is as great as my own, for I saw the letter come."

"Dear me," said one of the gentlemen, "this is truly distressing; she has not her senses, poor thing; promise her something, it will soothe her mind, and she will go away satisfied. It would be a pity to refuse one so harmless a mere promise."

"We will do our utmost to oblige you," said the manager; "what do you wish us to do?"

"I wish you to make some attempt to interest the authorities in his behalf, and make representation to the secretary of state, to the effect that Charles Ormond is a proper person to receive the clemency of the crown, that a pardon may be granted him."

"It is doing much."

"But not more than he deserves, if you knew his nobleness and disinterestedness, as I have known and experienced; then, indeed, gentlemen, you would not say it was much—but still my gratitude will be everlastingly your due if you will do this."

"Well, we shall be happy to oblige you, and will represent matters to the secretary, at his earliest leisure, in such a light that we shall have done all we can to procure a pardon for the young man," said the principal partner.

"Thank you, gentlemen—thank you; I have one more favour to ask you, with your permission."

"Certainly; proceed, madam."

"Will you sign a petition in his favour that I wish to get signed by the gentlemen of London in his behalf?"

"Yes, we will; have you got it with you?"

"I have," said Marian, and she produced a paper, setting forth the prayer of a pardon for Charles Ormond. The principal looked over the paper and immediately signed it, saying in a whisper,—

"The document is harmless."

"Thank you, thank you, gentlemen; I will let you know how I get on with the petition, and perhaps you will be able to inform me how you get on with the secretary of state?"

"Certainly," said the manager.

With much courtesy the manager arose and attended her to the door, and poor Marian Whitehead left the Bank.

"She is quite insane, harmlessly insane," said the principal; "th re can be no harm in humouring her, and, after all, hers is a very sad fate, indeed—I am sorry for her."

"Who is she?" interposed several of the gentlemen.

"She would have been the wife of that young fellow who presented a forged cheque here some weeks back."

"And she believes him still living?"

"It seems so, but it matters not; she does not feel the poignant grief she would have felt had she been more sensible of her loss. It, perhaps, is a mercy she is unable to feel as others do; for, since it has deprived her of her reason, it has deprived her also of the pain attending its exertion.

"That is very true; I have seen her about town these last few days, and always in that singular costume."

"Yes, I have heard that she attended the funeral just as you see her, and will make no change at all."

"Poor thing; poor thing!"

And so the matter was dismissed from the minds of the mercantile gentlemen.

*　　*　　*　　*　　*　　*　　*

As pleased as one in her sad state of mind could be imagined to feel, Marian sought out the next person to whom she should unfold the object of her wishes. Though no smile sat upon her lips, and she displayed the same grave melancholy she always wore, she felt something akin to satisfaction at having succeeded in this her first attempt.

But she was very far from feeling that this would at all insure her the object she most desired, the safety of Charles Ormond, but she knew it was one step towards procuring the attention of those whose consideration was of importance to his future welfare and safety.

The next party she turned her attention to was the Lord Mayor, who was at that moment presiding over his own court, and she at once entered the Mansion House, unimpeded by any of the officers, most of whom had already seen her about, and were aware of the nature of her malady.

The Lord Mayor was at that moment disengaged and the court empty, when Marian advanced to the bar, and made a similar appeal to that magistrate.

"Who is she?" inquired the Lord Mayor.

"She is, or rather was to have been, the wife of young Ormond, who was hanged for forgery the other day, my lord, and her brain is turned in consequence of grief."

"Poor thing!" said his lordship; "what does she want?"

"She wants, your worship, to sign a petition, she says, in favour of the young man."

"But he is dead."

"Yes, my lord," but she does not seem to understand that he is yet executed, but has some notion that he is not yet hanged."

"Poor thing; we will do our best," said his lordship, "for you; but I cannot see how I can serve you."

"You can do so essentially." my lord, said the unfortunate Marian, "by signing this petition. I assure your lordship every word of it is entirely true.

"I have no doubt about that," replied his lordship.

"Will your lordship, in addition, endeavour to interest the secretary of state in his behalf?"

"I will," said the lord mayor, who desired the officer to return the petition to her.

Marian next visited the sheriffs, and the governor and chaplain of Newgate, all of whom she endeavoured to interest in the favour of her lover. As may be imagined, they did not undeceive her, but received her statements with expressions of condolence and sympathy; for they in a few moments became conscious that she was bereft of that sense and consciousness that would have told her how useless were her present efforts.

Thus, too, day after day, she wandered about the city in her funeral attire, just as she had worn it at Ealing church-yard. She never ceased in her mission, and visited every one whom she imagined would be at all useful to her in her attempts to secure the life of Charles Ormond. Her constant appearance in the city was at length such, that she was considered as being one of the usual features of the place. Silent, sad, and earnest in her endeavours to attain the great object for which she so sedulously laboured, made her respected and pitied by those who were daily in the habit of seeing her, and who were well aware of the nature of her malady, and that love and sorrow had brought her to this state. Every one knew that she had been bereaved of a lover or a brother—they did not all know which—and that it had deprived her of reason, but they knew not the causes that led to that deprivation, for even the report of the trial was imperfect, and that was forgotten.

However, Marian endeavoured to see the secretary of state herself, but she never succeeded beyond his clerks and secretaries; she never did. Thus far shalt thou go and no further, say the officials of state, and their commands are better obeyed than those of King Canute on the sea shore. Often as she applied she never was able to see that almost invisible personage, and time after time she made the attempt but always unsuccessfully; the Black Lady was not admitted to an audience, though they all treated her with gravity and attention, always promising her whatever she required, with which she seemed well satisfied, and used to leave the office.

Thus passed the days of Marian Whitehead; between place and place in the city she was to be seen wandering about, sedate and sad, and moving at almost a funeral pace, in funeral attire, more unlike a thing of life than a semblance of death.

CHAPTER LIII.

THE KEY, AND THE VISIT TO THE VAULT BY THE BLACK LADY.—THE FAMILY VIGIL.

Next to Mrs. Whitehead herself, whose feelings, as regarded the melancholy mind of her daughter, must have been of the most painful character, we may mention Mr. Blake, as most truly sympathising with Marian's distresses.

The total failure of the means which he, in conjunction with Griffiths, had continued, for the purpose of rescuing poor Charles Ormond, had inflicted upon him more uneasiness than he was ever likely to communicate to any one.

Even his most intimate friends, however, observed for many months after those occurrences a melancholy about him, which they could attribute to no other cause; for he was a thriving man, and happy in all the various relations of life.

There was, too, a prosecution against him, for aiding in the escape of a prisoner, but the secretary of state quashed it, and the affair was allowed to rest; although, if it had been pursued, it might have resulted in the absolute ruin of the kind-hearted attorney.

When he fancied that poor Marian Whitehead had this strange mania upon her, of visiting any place which had in any way a relation to Charles Ormond's sad story, and everybody who was in any way connected with it, he made what efforts he could to wean her from such a course, until a judicious friend, of whose opinion he thought very highly, and to whom he was one day talking of the affair, said to him :—

" I cannot help thinking, Mr. Blake, that you take an incorrect view of this matter."

" Indeed ! how ?"

" Why, there can be no doubt that poor Miss Whitehead is quite insane, and that consequently her disordered intellect might adopt some cause of action ;

therefore the simplest and the least dangerous one she may adopt, is, I think, under these distressing circumstances, the best, and that, to my mind, is just what she has done."

"Certainly, there is truth in that," said Mr. Blake.

"Now," added his friend, "I would rather encourage her to keep her mind so occupied than set my face against it even to you. I would let her reap what satisfaction she might from that most harmless exercise of her tangled reason."

"I certainly have not before conceived the matter in that light; she often comes home, and I can assure you I grieve much to see her, and to hear her talk as if Charles Ormond was yet alive, and something might still, by persevering affection, be done for her."

"Encourage her; such a hope will keep her from dropping into a state of the most abject despair. You may depend that, but for that, she would become a gloomy and perhaps a dangerous lunatic. You and all who feel personally interested in her should be glad that the derangement of her intellect has taken such a turn."

"Well," said Mr. Blake, "I will endeavour to extract some comfort from that opinion, and when she visits me again I will adopt a contrary course to the one which I have hitherto done."

"You will find the benefit of acceding to anything she may say that favours the view which she sincerely takes regarding Charles Ormond being yet among the living."

"I will do so, you may depend."

There did not occur a long interval of time before Mr. Blake had an opportunity of adopting the new course which had been pointed out to him. On the following morning, when he reached his office, he found poor, heart-broken Marian waiting for him, attired in those same black weeds which she never laid aside again.

There was an earnest, eager appearance upon her countenance which made him much fear that some new, and perhaps dangerous, crotchet had taken possession of her. He welcomed her kindly, as he always did; and when he had conducted her into the inner office, she spoke quickly, saying—

"I have found out now where to wait for him."

"Have you?" said Mr. Blake, with a sigh.

"Yes, yes; a kind-hearted person who knew me, and who pitied my distresses, told me that if I waited in the vaults of St. Paul's he would come to me."

Mr. Blake groaned.

"They say he is there," she continued, "and they offered to show me a newspaper that contained a notice of the fact. Charles went there, you know, hoping to find me, and he was disappointed."

"But you know we cannot get admittance to the vaults of St. Paul's."

"Not get admittance! Then I will go to the Bishop of London, and force him to order me to be let in. I must and will. My brain will be on fire until I go there."

She clasped her hands as she spoke, and looked so much milder than usual that Mr. Blake began to think that even in that instance he could not do better than follow the advice which had been given him by his friend, based upon the theory of not contradicting her in anything she might do.

"Are you serious," he said, "now, in supposing that he will meet you there? And will not your disappointment be very great if he should not do so?"

"No, no; I will have patience. My misfortunes have taught me to have patience. I will then wait for him among the dead."

"If it be your fixed determination so to do, then it is likely enough that I may be able to assist you. Come to me again to-morrow."

Thus she, with meekness and patience, promised to do, and in the meantime Mr. Blake consulted his friend again, saying to him—

"I hesitate about this matter; but she seems so determined upon it, that I really know not whether to yield to her or not."

" Can she come to any harm ?"

" Why, no, the only harm any one could come to, would be to be very much frightened; and probably, the state of mind which she is in, would secure her completely from such a contingency."

" It would, you may be assured. She has no superstitious fears now, or she would not for one moment dream of going into such a place, even in search of Charles Ormond; and insanity not unfrequently destroys all those fine sensations and sensibilities of the mind, which would make such a place as the vaults of St. Paul's dreadful to an imaginative person."

" Then you mean seriously to tell me, that, having the means, as I confess I have, you would allow her to go."

" That is just what I would do."

" Then, reluctant as I am, I will follow your advice, because I know that I feel personally so strongly interested in this matter, that I am not so capable of judging calmly, and coolly conceiving it as you are."

" Why, the fact is, Blake," said his friend, " that poor young creature is now in such a state, that she can never know happiness again. If she were to recover her reason, you know it would only be to feel convinced, that he whom she has loved so well, is lost to her for ever."

" True, true, true."

" Therefore, I hardly myself, much as I pity and sympathise with her, would wish that she should do so. She suffers now, in the mental eclipse in which she lies, far less than she would suffer had her mind not yielded to the shock it had received, and she had remained possessed of all her reasoning faculties, along with the dreadful knowledge of what had really occurred to Charles Ormond."

" You are right, you are right; but you know one is apt to look upon insanity abstractedly, and to consider it the worst of evils, when, in reality, it is only so to those who look on, and not to those who are so afflicted."

Acting upon this determination, Mr. Blake sought out Jeffries, and told him what he wanted him to do. Jeffries was quite astonished; but when Mr. Blake had thoroughly explained all to him, he saw the matter much in the same light that the attorney's friend did, and he remarked—

" Poor thing ! it don't matter much where she goes or what she does, so long as she can fancy a chance of happiness, which really can never come to her. I will undertake to show her the vaults, and now I find that there is a small gate in the iron rails, which, from its appearance, I should say had escaped the observation of everybody for these last fifty years. It requires the closest searching to discover it; but, having once found it, and knowing where it is, she can get admittance into the churchyard whenever she likes. If I cannot find a key that will fit it, I will break the lock of it, so that she will only have to push it open at a time when no one is observing her, and then to be careful to close it always after her, and she may go and come with perfect safety."

" Be it so, be it so. I will tell her to meet you at my chambers at dusk, and the first night I should like you to hang about a little and give an eye to her proceedings."

" I will, sir."

Marian was true to her appointment, and when the attorney reached his chambers on the following morning, she was waiting for him, and the moment she saw him, she began speaking anxiously upon the subject which was so near to her heart.

" I must go to those vaults," she said; " you will not deny me ?"

" Not if you really wish it; if you come here an hour after dark, I will bring a person to you, who will show you how you are to make good an entrance to what you will find a gloomy place."

" Not gloomy, when radiant with the hope of Charles's coming."

" Well, well,—come, come again to-morrow, and tell me how you have passed your time there, and how long you remained."

" I will, I will; you have given me a new hope. I dreamt that I saw him last night, and that he said to me gently, but oh, in such a sad voice, Marian, look n for me in this world, for I am not of it." But I don't believe in dreams—no, no—I could not believe that such a vision is true."

Mr. Blake made no remark ; had he said anything contrary to her fixed belief in the fact, as she supposed it to be, of Charles Ormond's existence, he knew he would be giving her pain, and he could not, except passively, agree in the delusions she so fondly cherished. Jeffries met her at the appointed time, and he conducted her through the little gate he had mentioned ; he gave her the door-key, which had

admitted Charles within the precincts of the cathedral, and he taught her to unlock it and fasten it on the inner side. She thanked him so kindly, and in such a sweet voice, that the tears darted to his eyes, and he had hardly voice enough to tell her how she might go up the narrow flight of steps in the morning, if she chose, and make her way out by the ordinary cathedral doors. Thus he left her, and she sat down

No. 42.

with a quiet, resigned, holy kind of look ; he had left the same lamp for her which had illumined the darkness of that place for Charles Ormond.

"He will come," she said; " oh, he will be sure to come."

She sat down on an old coffin, which had been displaced from its niche by Charles to make a seat of, and then, taking a book from the reticule she always carried, she prepared to pass her time in reading, just as calmly and contentedly as if she had been awaiting Charles's arrival in an ordinary apartment of some house, with an attention that only flagged now and then ; then, as she looked around, and saw that he had not come, she read the following romantic incident :—

The gloom of gathering clouds deepened to an almost intense blackness, and the wind swept over the moor, and the elements seemed prepared for a coming strife. For some days the air had become gradually clouded with black, watery-looking clouds ; and now, as the sun sunk unseen in the west, there was a dashing shower of rain, carried along by the wind, which was cold and piercing to a degree.

Near the side of the road stood an old straggling building, and a few trees. There was a bright fire burning in the cottage, for such it was, though of larger dimensions than is usually seen in peasants' cottages ; yet it was not good enough for aught better. The large logs lay on the fire, blazing and crackling, throwing a huge light over the whole apartment, flickering and unsteady, throwing dancing shadows upon the walls, which changed in shape and attitude every moment, for the rude figures that sat before the fire were projected in much ruder forms on the walls. Four or five men, in a rustic garb, sat round the fire—they were absorbed in some object of their own meditations—they were still and motionless—their features were rude, but expressive ; and they might have formed a good picture for the pencil of a painter—their features were well worth preserving. For some time, however, they continued in silence to gaze upon the fire, which burned more fiercely than before, for the wood which had been recently put on it began to grow hot. The room was warm, and well lighted, though there was no other light than that observable from the fire, which, in the case of a large wood fire, was very great. The wind roared without, and the rain now and then beat against the windows and boarding. There was not much glass, only a few odd panes, and those of not the largest dimensions. Some open lattice-work did the duty of admitting light, when the weather was warm and fine, but now that was secured by a kind of shutter that was now placed up, and served the double purpose of security against intruders and the weather.

"The wind howls," said one of those present, who was a tall, athletic man; " it seems as though it would blow the ocean ashore—before morning, we shall have a pretty storm."

"You are right, a storm is brewing fast and furious, and one of no ordinary character ; it blows on the shore too, and if any unfortunate ship should be sailing on this coast, it will go to pieces."

"Yes, wrecks, more wrecks, more wrecks," said the eldest person who was present. "There never will be an end to these dreadful catastrophes—never, never, can I forget the one in which I took part."

"Aye, there are many things that we may encounter in life," said a young man, " which we forget, but some one or two events, that have afforded us great pleasure or more misery, will cling to the mind like a drowning man to anything he can close his grasp on."

"Right, boy, right !"

"I wonder if the lugger will be out to-night."

"The weather has been very bad these last three days. I should hardly think they would put to sea."

"It is very likely they would imagine the weather would clear up ; at all events we had better keep a good look-out, in case they succeed in landing the cargo."

"Yes, especially as the hawks are abroad. It strikes me very forcibly that the coast-guard have got an eye on this place."

"They have got their eyes upon every place, I think, that can afford concealment for an anker of brandy."

"So they have, but they do not time their visits; besides, they don't know the ins and outs of this place. It would take them some time to ascertain where they were, even if they got into the cellars."

"It is time," said a tall, handsome young man, to keep a look-out; "if they do come, they may put in early on such a night as this—expecting bad may be [worse, you know."

"Right, boy, so they may, do you keep a bright look-out, we'll come and relieve you before the night sets thoroughly in for the dark—it isn't late."

"No, it is not," replied the young man.

"But short watches, say I, this weather," said another weather-beaten looking man, "it's necessary to keep a good look-out such weather, and then the watches should be short."

"And they shall be," said the same old man.

The young man left the cottage, after wrapping himself up in a rough seaman's jacket, or coat made of tarpaulin, and painted over so as to resist the wet.

"I say, Nixen, that young 'un of yours will be a strapping fellow; he's as big and strong as a giant."

"He's not so big as you imagine."

"I mean for so young a man; why he is not yet twenty, I think, is he?"

"No, he's a big chap and strong too; but he's active and as fleet as the wind."

"I never knew you had a wife," said the lame man; "you don't mean to say the young one is yourn? I have often been puzzled to account for him being always with you; for I can remember him when he was scarce able to speak or to walk."

"Hush! say nothing about that before him."

"Not I; but is he your child, Nixen?"

"No, he is not."

There was a moment o two's pause, and the men seemed again lost in thought; they sat opposite the fire, their strong and embrowned features being lit up by the glare of the fire, and would have been, to an observer, a strange and marked picture.

"It is many years ago, Nixen, since you came to this spot. I can remember it as well as though it were but yesterday; you've had a rough time of it."

"Yes, I have, but I mustn't complain, indeed I can't; I haven't wanted any thing, and a man can but get enough; if he have more he cannot use it himself."

"Right, Nixen!"

"Then, as to roughness, why a man must meet that go where he will; but it was rougher where I came from, and a plaguy deal hotter."

"Where was that?"

"Wait till I tell you, lad; every man has his own secrets, and I don't mind saying I have had mine and have them still. Every man has a little to conceal."

"So he has—so he has."

"But I don't mind telling you mine, without, however, giving you name or place."

"We don't care about knowing, lad, and we wouldn't take any unfair advantage of it, even if we knew it; but that is not at all necessary, you know."

"Now, never mind them. Nixen, spin us your yarn, it will pass away the next hour's watch."

Thus admonished, Nixen proceeded :—

"About five-and-twenty years ago, I was a young man, about two-and-twenty. I was well-looking, and considered by many handsome, and had received a decent education for my station; and at that time I had a great notion of doing well in the world, and I endeavoured to improve myself as well as I could. I strove to rende myself more acceptable than I was, by every means in my power, but we don't always succeed."

"And you didn't?"

"At first, as you shall hear. Well, I entered the army—I had not means to obtain any promotion—I was obliged to act as a common man. However, that did not daunt me ; I was too well acquainted with my own merits to fear for a moment that this would eventually injure my rise—it might delay, but not destroy my rise. However, I entered my first step in life pretty early, for I was a somewhat marked object, for I soon displayed qualities that no other man in the ranks could, and I soon obtained promotion to a non-commissioned officer's rank."

"I never knew you had been in the army before, Nixen," said one of the smugglers, for such they were.

"Nor I," said another.

"You know it—know it all— ow, then," said Nixen ; "and will something more presently."

"Go on, we are all attention."

"Well, then, I became a non-commissioned officer; I wasn't satisfied, but determined to attain another step, not by any unfair means, but by exerting all the assiduity and talent I possessed in my duties, and being constantly ready for any extra duty or service that might be required, and by doing it always in the most creditable manner, and this was effectual. I was a serjeant in less than three years, which was a very rapid rise indeed. These things went on for several years, until the war broke out, and then I was ordered with other troops to take our parts in the troubles. This I was glad enough of, very glad indeed, because it gave me the opening I hoped to have—the chance of performing some meritorious action or another, which never could be done while at home. There was no scope to bring me out of the non-commissioned men ; I wanted to effect this. In our second engagement I had the desired opportunity ; my captain was sent with his troop to effect a certain point of duty which was important. He had not proceeded many yards when he was shot dead, and the officer next in command, was badly wounded and fell, in a few yards more; the other men were all disabled. I then was the only officer upon whom the command devolved. The men were hesitating : I cheered them on, and rushed forward myself, and in a few minutes more we altogether entered the spot where we were sent to destroy the enemy before us. This occurred within sight of the commander, and he inquired who I was. The answer was immediately, I was a non-commissioned officer.

"Then he shall have a commission," he said ; "if he lives till to-morrow, he shall be a captain.

"You a captain, Nixen?"

"Yes."

"Well, I could not have believed it—no wonder you could drill the men and place them on good look-out."

"I ought to have learnt something, and so I did.] I did live the day out, though wounded, but the next day I was a captain."

"Well, Captain Nixen was a very pretty sound, and this, together with some gratuities which I had to receive as prize-money, I was well placed in society. Then I began to form a few acquaintances among my present officers, but I saw there was a jealousy among them as to permitting me to associate with them upon any but distant and servile terms. This, of course, did not suit me. I spoke in the same terms to them, and one day they picked a quarrel with me. A challenge was a matter of course, and we met—swords were chosen, and after about ten minutes' play, I spread my adversary on the grass. After this, there was a little more cordiality, but not enough to make things agreeable, and I immediately set about picking a quarrel with the one who was to me the most disagreeable, and who endeavoured to slight me the most. I was not long without my opportunity— I soon saw that he was willing—we fought, and fortune was my way of thinking then, and he was wounded. On this occasion I acted with great forbearance, and he with extreme ferocity. I was triumphant and he discomfited, and as it often happens, the loser met with no sympathy even from his friends, and I was soon in favour."

You've been a fire-eater in your time, Nixen," said one: " I always thought you dangerous, but never so dangerous as you really are."

"Nor I."

"Ah! you don't know all, or you would say more about it. I am yet more dangerous than you think for."

"The devil!"

"I am: and, moreover, you'll say so when I tell you all, which I will do. Well, —we had a good deal of fighting and marching about from place to place, until we were ordered home. I was sorry for that; for it stopped my career of advancement, which I had hoped would have gone on. This, however, was not to be—and wasn't; accordingly we came home; and I got introduced to the family of my commanding-officer, who was very partial to me. There was in his family a young female whom I took to be a daughter, but who turned out to be a niece. Of course I knew she would have a large fortune. She was beautiful—very beautiful—and amiable too. I fell in love with her."

"You, Nixen!" said several of those present.

"What—you—old, iron-bound, ragged Nixen! You in love! I could never have dreamt of such a thing."

"Nor I."

Well, well—I wasn't then what I am now; and I was not subject to vice. But she, too, loved me."

"The deuce!"

"It is a fact. She gave me this brooch, in remembrance of her, some time before we last met. She loved me sincerely, and I her. But we were doomed to part. The moment my commander had an inkling of my desire, or my love for his niece, he forbade me the house, when he found I would not give up my object—that is, my pursuit of his niece—and leave her. The young lady was cautioned by her uncle that she would incur his severest displeasure if she attempted to see me. However, despite the most vigilant watch, we used to meet—aye, and meet often, too, I assure you. But we were found out, and there was a dreadful riot to get through; but it ended, as I thought, well enough, by her being sent away. I never attempted to see her again at his house; but I determined to follow her, should she be taken away—which was done in a few days. I did follow her, from place to place —but always too late. Nothing was to be seen of her, go where I would. I some-how or other always contrived to be too late. Well, this could not last long—nor did it. They soon forced the girl to marry"

"While she loved you?"

"Exactly. She besought them to take compassion on her—to have mercy—but all to no purpose. I heard the whole of the affair, and never shall cease to remember it as long as I breathe; and I swore I would have dreadful vengeance, even if I were to ruin every hope I had ever formed. And well have I kept the oath I then took. I swore, and I have done what I said I would."

"You are a man of your word, Nixen."

"And always have been. You may, therefore, well believe me when I say I did take a deep and bitter revenge upon those who were thus my direst and cruel enemies."

"Served them right."

"Moreover, as I have said, we loved each other. Her money I did not grieve over—it was herself I lost and I regretted. I hung about the house of my com-mander for some time, waiting the arrival of the moment when I could revenge myself. I waited many months. My commander caused my leave of absence to be recalled, and I at once threw up my commission. I was now dependent on my own exertions for support. I had enough to live on for a year or two, but no more. I was not now easily to be diverted; and my commander, seeing me hover about, prepared himself to quit the place, and get rid of me if he could. He tried it; but I came across the opportunity which I so much longed for. That was no other than to steal away his only boy, a child of about three years old. The boy was fond of me, and would come to me at any time; and I took advantage; while I promised him a ride in a gig, I placed him in, for the purpose of carrying him away."

"And did you?"

"I did," replied Nixen.

"What became of the child?" inquired one of the men.

"Oh, I kept him by me. I found he took to me kindly enough, and I determined to adopt him and bring him up as a child of my own."

"Indeed?"

"Yes; and well enough has he thriven, for he is now as stout and bold a smuggler—"

"A smuggler!"

"Yes."

"Where is he? not the young 'un who's just gone out to keep a look-out."

"The same."

There was a pause of some moments, during which the smugglers looked at each other in amazement and doubt, while Nixen gazed on the fire unconcerned, or at least in a reverie, and thinking about something else.

"Well," said one; "and does he know nothing of his birth, or the fortune that may be his?"

"No."

"Do you intend to tell him?"

"I hardly know what to say, or do about it; it will give him much trouble and me too, and after all his hopes and fears have been excited, he may be deemed an impostor: if, therefore, such were to happen, it might be very unfortunate for him, while he will be very well off here."

"How came you to be a smuggler, Nixen?"

"Why, I can hardly tell you, but I believe I knew the coast of France and the language well; I was master over a good yacht, and could make money."

"You have had many good runs across the Channel, and it ought to pay well."

"It does, but we have had some losses as well; we have had several taken of late."

"What sounds are those?" said one of the men.

"That," said Nixen, "is a ship in distress; this is a desperate night—a night, I fear, that will bring many to a watery grave; the wind blows in shore too."

"That may be the cutter."

"It may, and if so, it is just as bad as if the revenue officers had her, she can't live here at all, she'll be forced on the shoals."

"No, no, it is not, the cutter has no guns whatever; at present, therefore, you may depend upon it the cutter is not in any danger."

  *   *   *   *   *

There was a ship in distress, the smugglers were on the beach, and were ready and willing to do all they could to assist those who were in danger of drowning. By their help, the passengers were saved from a watery grave and were taken to the cottage, where they were all assembled around the huge wood fire that was burning. There were but few, some of them having gone further and sought refuge in the village, which lay at some little distance from the cottage. But here in the cottage was placed a family who had been saved from drowning, by Nixen and his adopted son, both of whom had exerted themselves to rescue the unfortunate from their perilous condition. When the rescued passengers had somewhat recovered themselves sufficiently to thank their preservers for their lives; when, however, the stranger who was present fixed his eyes upon Nixen, they remained stationary for a moment or two.

Nixen quailed not beneath the glance of the stranger, but returned it steadily, until the other said—

"Captain Maxwell—yes, it is Captain Maxwell."

"Sir John Norris."

"The same, Captain Maxwell. Tell me where my son is; you have saved my life; tell me where my son is. I have injured you deeply since. Do not carry your revenge too far; for you, and you alone can restore peace into the family."

"I, Sir John !"

"Yes, you, Maxwell. I am an old man now, and I have had years of sorrow since ; if you know aught of my boy, tell me for his sake as much as mine."

"The time is come," said Maxwell, for that was his name, "the time is come. Yonder, a lad stands ; that is your son, Sir John Norris," said Maxwell, pointing out the same person we have before named.

*   *   *   *   *   *   *

We will draw a veil over the scene, but relate what occurred afterwards. The son was found well worthy of his rank, for Maxwell had attended to his education, though he had not given him any idea of his rank. Maxwell, however, soon after died, but the father and son were united and pleased with the discovery.

Marian laid down the book, and with a deep sigh, she gazed around her.

"He does not come !" she said ; "oh ! Charles, why are you not here ?"

She crept up the narrow staircase, which led to the gilt-door, opening into the aisle of the cathedral, and sitting down upon the topmost step, with her head resting upon her hands, she there remained until the night slowly faded away. She slept a little ; and, now and then, she wept, saying to herself :—

"He does not come yet—he does not come yet !"

CHAPTER LIV.

GODFREY A CRIPPLE.—THE MEETING BETWEEN HIM AND MARIAN.

In the morning she quietly emerged through the gilt-door into the cathedral, and there she paused a few moments—shutting the door very quietly, heeding not even the presence of the man, who took the threepences at the door of those who came in—he stood with his back towards the unfortunate Marian, and was calculating in his own mind the probability of that day's harvest being a good one.

"Let me see," he muttered, "how many threepences make a pound ? Why, a pound is twenty shillings, and twenty shillings is—let me see, what pence. No, no, that won't do, for if I get into the pence-table I shan't be able to get into threepences again. How am I to tell ? All I know is—one pound is twenty shillings, of course it is—any fool knows that well—then twenty shillings is forty sixpences ; ah ! now we have it—now we have it—of course we have—forty shillings—no, forty sixpences make the sum of eighty threepences ! All that would be good—and too good for the time a-year. I wish I may get it, that's all."

As he spoke he plunged his hands into his pockets and felt to the bottom, but apparently there was nothing there, for he solemnly shook his head, and said gravely, as he buttoned up his pockets and put his hands under his coat-tails,—

"No, no, it's no use feeling there—no use at all. I haven't a mag, not even enough to buy a morning drain ; well, well, dear me—dear me—what a state of things ! what a condition the country has come to !"

This was an afflicting thought ; and the man of the threepences took a pinch of snuff ; after having done that, he snapped his fingers in the most approved style, and replaced his snuff-box, exclaiming as he did so,—

"I wonder what sort of morning it will be ; it's very dirty, and I expect we shall have a dull day of it—people aint in a walking humour when it's dirty. I wish there would be a mania for searching these old places and make it quite fashionable : if that were the case I should make a pound or two, but now I can scarcely keep myself in grog ! The honour of the Church is but poorly cared for if the servants are compelled to run up a score on account of their grog."

This was a terrible reflection, and one which carried with it some weight, especially if it had been fairly placed before the public. It was a national disgrace, and he felt it as such.

" Well, who's going to give me hansel ?" he said ; and then turned round and was about to walk away, when his eye rested upon the form of Marian Whitehead, who was slowly approaching him from the interior.

" Eh ? God bless me !" he exclaimed, stepping back several paces, and in fact performing a reel.

The appearance of Marian in her sad funeral attire, her down-cast melancholy look and slow movement—made him think some one must have risen out of the tombs below, and this was especially strengthened when he believed it utterly impossible anyone could get in.

The Black Lady slowly approached the door, and he, scarce knowing what to do, whether to believe she was living, or a thing of another life. After much trembling and attentive consideration, he came to the belief she must be a human being, and yet he was by no means sure ; what was she ? or, whence came she ? were questions that were rapidly proposed by his active mind, but his genius did not shine in the inventive, and he could propose no answer to them.

One thing, however, causing him to imagine that she must be human more than any other was, there appeared to be something like an encroachment upon his vested interest, and if this wasn't being a man, to regard matters in a commonplace light, it is difficult to say what is ; and the individual in question no sooner caught the idea, that there was something wrong in the shape of a defrauded threepence, than instead of falling back, he stepped a pace forward.

Still—as there was no observable change in the Black Lady's demeanour—he was sadly puzzled what to do.

" Hem ! hem !" he began, " mem, mem—did you come in, mem ?—hem !"

There was no answer. The Black Lady still moved onwards, and he still looked very hard in her face, and then muttered to himself, as he carefully scrutinized her :—

" Yes, yes, she is living !—she—she must be flesh and blood ! Confound— Heaven pardon me for swearing in the cathedral !—but consider the threepences —I'll speak again. 'Hem ! pray, may I ask, how you came in—did you come in by the doors, or—or—the—the—the —'"

He didn't like to say any more ; the fact was he could not very well, for he could not conjecture how she could have come in unless she had slipped through the keyhole, and that would have been an insult to have spoken it.

The Black Lady now gently opened the door and walked out calmly, quietly, and at a funeral-like step.

The money-taker at this clerical turnpike-gate looked after her till she turned an angle and got out of his sight, and then the amazed doorkeeper slammed the door too, and quietly sat down on the seat, wiped his forehead, groaned deeply, and began to consider the whole very like a vision that couldn't be explained.

     *   *   *   *   *   *

Marian Whitehead passed on several streets. She had not—as the reader well knows—met with the success she had hoped for in the cathedral ; and now she paced slowly and sadly away towards the lodgings of her parent. Poor Marian ! how sad at heart, yet how uncomplaining of all the trials and bitter disappointments that now, one after another, she experienced !

It seemed as though she were only capable of feeling hope to find every hope a fallacy ; but the bitter disappointments she must ever, in her state of mind, have felt, seemed but of short duration ; for a new hope sprung from the same sad foundation as the former, her own disordered imagination being at once the bane and antidote of her mournful life.

     *   *   *   *   *   *

Godfrey, too, had suffered terribly ; he had not gained wealth to enjoy it— he was a cripple—life would be but life for the future, and the ball and beauty— mere words—now became the nervous trembling cripple, always fearful, and always expecting harm from some cause or other, which, before this occurrence, he never so much as looked at or considered.

It is a dreadful thing when a strong man suddenly becomes deprived of his power—becomes wretchedly nervous and timid: a greater punishment could hardly be devised for any crime, and Godfrey was thus puished; aye, more than that, for he had not even a limb about him that had not been injured or broken in some place or other, and some he had nearly lost the use of.

This day he crawled out and contrived to shuffle along the streets, fearful of every one whom he met, lest they should run against him and fling him down.

It so chanced that Marian and he met—yes, Godfrey and Marian Whitehead met, face to face, in a quiet, bye street—Godfrey saw her coming and would have gone back, but he could not well do so; she would, probably, overtake him before he could get down to the end, and it might so chance that she might pass him without a thought, and, if not, what had he to fear from her?

And yet he shrunk from her, he knew not why, but he could not face one whom he had so deeply injured as he had this poor harmless creature.

Marian, however, saw Godfrey, and the thought entered her mind that she might be able to propitiate Godfrey in Charles Ormond's favour, and she walked up to him, though her very nature seemed to rebel at the vicinity of such a man.

Godfrey looked up at her in amazement, but when he saw her eyes fixed upon his own, he involuntarily turned them away, and sought to find some other way of escaping than by passing her; but this was no part of her purpose to allow.

" No, Godfrey," she said, calmly, " you have attained your object; will you now keep your promise and save Charles Ormond—you know you can, if you will?"

" Ahem !" said Godfrey, " I will do all I can, Miss Whitehead, but doesn't it strike you that I cannot save a man that is dead—I cannot do impossibilities."

" Never mind," said Marian, " the question as to whether he is alive, or not; I have information he lives. Will you do what I ask you? Charles Ormond, you know, is innocent, and I call upon you for a complete justification."

" I am afraid I cannot afford it to him," said Godfrey, who feared being overheard by any one; " you know, Miss Whitehead, I have done my duty."

" Your duty !" said Marian; " but I will not reproach you for your evil deeds—they bring their own punishment with them; but do, though late, an act of justice."

Godfrey shook his head and endeavoured to pass by, but Marian placed herself in front of him, and her eyes looked wild and she seemed to become suddenly influenced by strong motives.

" You must do what I ask you; you have robbed the widow and deprived the orphan of her inheritance; what more would you have? would you desire to imbrue your hands in innocent blood? I cannot look upon your guilty countenance without a fearful thought rushing through my blood."

" I pray you let me pass," said Godfrey; " I will hold no conversation with you."

" Do you wish the crime of murder to be added to the list of crimes? You have done all you desired and got all you wished or attempted, surely—surely—you can afford to be merciful to Charles Ormond. Go to the court and declare his innocence—do it all, and you will have relieved your soul of a heavy load of guilt."

Godfrey made no answer but attempted to cross the road, but Marian placed her hands upon him, and he shrunk back, exclaiming—

" Don't put your hands on me, don't do it! I can't bear it! I'm a cripple! I won't be taunted! keep off—I'll cry out for aid—be off—what do you do with me ?"

" I will tell you," said Marian slowly and solemnly, " I will tell you—I have asked your clemency for Charles Ormond."

" I have no power."

" I have asked you to save him," she continued, and he shrank back a pace at a time and she followed in the same manner—yes; I beg and implore you to save him."

" He is dead !" said Godfrey.

" He is not—you refuse your aid—recollect some of these days you will shriek for mercy, when it shall be denied you. Go and do this—justify him—declare he is innocent of a crime you know he would not commit, and you will have my earnest prayers for your health and safety."

" Oh," said Godfrey, " I can't wait here, I must be off ;" so saying he turned round, and in great fear began to move away as fast as he could, for he by no means liked the wild and excited appearance of Marian, which grew upon her as she continued to beseech him to interfere for Charles Ormond.

Excited she was, and, seeing him about to elude her, she sprang forward and seized him to compel his attention. Godfrey shrieked out and called " murder !" and then struggling fell off the pavement into the kennel, where he lay rolling about and calling for aid. In a few moments a mob of people had collected around and he was pulled out of the mire and set upon his legs, leaning against a wall, which served as a support to him, and then people began to make inquiries, " what was the matter, and who had done the mischief?" but the cause was nowhere apparent, for the Black Lady had passed through the crowd and was nowhere to be seen.

CHAPTER LV.

GODFREY'S OFFER TO NEVILLE FOR THE MURDER OF MARIAN.—THE ATTEMPT AND THE FAILURE.—THE STRANGE PROTECTOR.

THE recent events had made a great impression upon Godfrey's mind—not for the better, the reverse being the case; for he foresaw much annoyance from Marian, or, perhaps more truly, he feared what he so well deserved; he greatly dreaded the meeting with Marian; she was a living reproach, and he could not easily forget the expression of her eye when she found he would not do what she so earnestly prayed of him. There was all the fire and strange expression of the pupil of insanity about her that made him fear her; he thought he should one day suffer from her insanity, as he truly thought there was nothing that could or would not be done by an infuriated and maddened woman, and notwithstanding all the mildness of Marian's disposition naturally, yet there was so much provocation he well knew on his own part, that his fears painted the danger he ran in very vivid colours.

After much thought upon the subject, he could conceive no chance of rest for himself while Marian lived, and his object upon that would be of course to diminish her days by every means by which such an event could be accomplished. Godfrey was in no ways particular; the end was his sole consideration after the safety of the means had been duly disposed of. The way in which he was to get rid of the fears that haunted him night and day of Marian, was somewhat quieted when he had made up his mind as to what should be done. Marian might remain in this state for years, and he, Godfrey, would be the same defenceless cripple he then was all that time, and any one day he might be destroyed, were he only cast into the road, by some passing vehicle which might accidentally pass the spot.

"Yes," muttered Godfrey, as he thought of the bare possibility of such an occurrence, " I may be killed, and by her too. I shall never forget the expression of her features—she certainly meant to kill me : but I must anticipate a little—there's no help for it, I do it in self-defence—she must die !"

It was strange that he who thus doomed others to death so readily, and with so much coolness, should fear himself to face the death he had more than once doomed his fellow-mortal, and yet so it was ; like all cruel and bad men he feared to die ; there is something to them so horrible in the dark uncertainty beyond the grave—that is a consideration that completely destroys their equanimity. He could conceive nothing so horrible as being suddenly, and with violence, deprived of life, at a moment when he had just escaped a great danger. It was easy to say that Marian should die, but then how was it to be done became the next point of consideration, and an important one too ; and he set about the consideration with some degree of pleasure, because he had disposed of the consideration which involved death, and to him it was more pleasant to calculate the means of an exploit.

Since his quarrel with Neville, and the latter's attempt upon his life, Godfrey had not seen him ; he feared and hated him ; but at the same time he could take no vengeance upon Neville ; he knew not how, for Neville was still dangerous to him, and if he were to strive to inflict vengeance upon him, Neville might turn round and cause him not only much inconvenience but much danger; indeed, he believed he might cause his own complete ruin and disgraceful end; but then Neville would involve himself—though, in a struggle for vengeance rather than for life, it was questionable if he would care about that consideration at all. After much consideration he believed he must have recourse to Neville after all; for there was no one else he could so well trust in this affair. Besides, he would run the double danger of trusting another, who was not so much in his power as Neville, and, moreover, Neville would know no more afterwards than before; he did not involve the quiet of both, therefore it was less dangerous to trust Neville, he having already done such work before that occasion. Having considered the subject once very attentively, he determined he would not give any one else the same power as Neville possessed, by employing them upon this important affair, but seek out Neville and obtain his aid, which he was sure of for a sum of money; for he was well aware that Neville was in need, and could be bought over, after his late attempt upon Godfrey's life. The next thing was to see his coadjutor in iniquity, and detail to him his plan for the murder of poor Marian Whitehead; for it was no less than her that he intended.

*   *   *   *   *   *   *

After many inquiries, Godfrey learnt that Neville had left his old haunt about the Rookery in St. Giles's, considering the place was too hot for him, and that the officers would be sure to look for him here, when all other places were omitted; all the information that he could obtain was, that he was " down the water." To Godfrey, however, this was enough, and he determined at once to go to the place which " down the water " indicated, and which he knew well enough; but it must be evening before he could venture there, as he might be watched, and the great probability also that he would be unable to see him at all till Night came on and spread her sable mantle over all.

It was about an hour after dark that Godfrey approached the stairs, where some boats lay ready for him, when he was assailed by several boatmen with :—

" Boat, sir! boat, yer honour!—carry you safe anywhere and back again, all for the legal fare, and as much more as yer honour will give; a boat, yer honour? thank yer honour, I'll get it out in a moment, and carry you safe."

With much more of the same sort of talk the boat was got ready by the man who had Godfrey's preference, and as he was so engaged, Godfrey himself slowly travelled down the stairs to the water's edge, with some difficulty and pain, and then, by the aid of the boatman's arm, he got into the boat.

" Where to, yer honour?" exclaimed the man, when he had got clear of the boats that were moored around.

" Down the river, between the bridge," said Godfrey, " and the other side of the river."

" Very good, yer honour," replied the man, and he pulled down the river with good will, and away they went with some speed; the tide was with them, and thus, with but comparative little exertion, they sped down the river.

The night was not absolutely dark; there was much light though it was not what is usually called a moonlight night, and there was a glow of light that came from the various places and crafts on either side; the river was not crowded then with steam-boats as it is now, and there was no danger there or anywhere It was strange to see the motionless masses on the rippling water, and hear it as it passed by some huge bulk that lay quiet enough upon the bosom of the Thames; and as Godfrey saw and even felt the solitude and quietude of the moment, he felt miserable and wretched—every noise, however slight, and every danger his imagination conceived, was magnified by the stillness of the scene. This was painful, and he could ill bear it, and he began to repent having come by water: to dispel this train of thought and flow of feeling he commenced a conversation with the boatman.

" Do you often have accidents upon the river?" inquired Godfrey of the boatman.

" Yes, now and then, yer honour."

"Have you had one lately?" he inquired.

"No, not lately, yer honour; I expect to hear of one every hour though, now," he replied.

"Indeed! and why do you expect to hear of an accident before one has really occurred?"

"Because you see, yer honour, the time's up."

"What time?" inquired Godfrey, who began to think the boatman must be mad.

"Why, yer honour, we generally have an accident within a certain time, and when that time has elapsed without any, we say the time's up in which an accident of some sort may be expected; so, you see, if we were to sink, it would not be anything out of the usual way."

"Wouldn't it," thought Godfrey; and then he added aloud, "what sort of accident are we liable on such a night as this?"

"Oh, not much," replied the boatman; "we might run against any thing—a buoy, for instance."

"Well, what then?"

"Why, then we should be thrown out, and sucked under and drowned, without any hope of being saved."

Godfrey groaned; this was terrible, and for a moment he could barely sit upright; but the voice of the boatman recalled him to himself, and he heard him say—

"Never mind, sir; there's no danger with me. I wouldn't undertake to come if I thought I should meet with any accident at all."

"Boat, ahoy!" shouted a hoarse voice.

The boatman looked round, and Godfrey himself looked in the direction in which the boat was going, and then beheld a sight that made him stagger.

There was a vessel, a sailing-vessel, coming up the river with all her sails set, carrying all the canvass she could. Godfrey thought a collision inevitable.

The boatman, however, knew very well what he was about, and soon got clear of the vessel, and then proceeded upon the former course.

"There was much danger then," said Godfrey, "much danger, was there not?"

"Yes, if I had not heard the hail; however, I did, and all was safe. That's the worst of coming round a bend in the river, or a lot of vessels. You can't very well see what's going on; and if I hadn't seen that vessel, why, my boat would have been smashed, and we should certainly have been drowned."

"I saw," said Godfrey, "there was much danger in being on the river at all, and can see ——"

"Not more than in the streets, for I believe you may get knocked down at the corner of every street you come to, or any crossing—and even the falling of chimney-pots in windy weather."

"That we may escape; but one in the river," said Godfrey, "we can't escape."

"That's very true," said the boatman. "There was young Tom Sparks lost his life in the same way a few weeks ago."

"How?"

"I will tell yer honour. Young Tom Sparks, who was about to be spliced, and had the day named, and all got ready, and in two days more he would have had a wife, when he was taken down the river—somewhere below bridge—when, as they were going along, a vessel was coming up, and he run against her. They gave out no hail, and so he and his boat were sucked under in a minute, and before he was recovered he was a corpse. Everybody was sorry for poor Tom Sparks."

"Ah!" said Godfrey, "there are dangers that even you, who are supposed to be used to them, cannot escape."

"Oh, dear no, we cannot; we have our ups and downs as other men have, and as far as that goes, we are continually finding our way from one place to another."

"This will do," said Godfrey, as he gazed at a light on the other side of the river. "I want to be landed yonder, where you see that light."

"I see it," said the boatman. "Why did you not tell me before? I would have pushed across the stream earlier. We shall get carried past the place now by the force of the current."

Godfrey made no reply, and the boatman now pulled across the river as well as he could, but, despite all his efforts, he was carried past the spot, and placed in some danger, for in crossing they were nearly run down by a vessel coming down with the tide; they were, however, just able to reach their destination in safety, and that was all, when the boatman said—

"I thought the accident, which might be expected was about to take place, would have happened just now. See, it was a very narrow squeak, and that's all; hope you'll remember it in the fare, yer honour."

Godfrey felt it had been, in the man's own words, "a narrow squeak" for them; a few moments more and all would have been over with them; there would have been every chance of their being carried away past the shipping, and for weeks they might have remained undiscovered.

When Godfrey stepped out of the boat he gave the boatman some silver, saying, "If you choose to remain here for a couple of hours or so, I shall be back again, and have occasion to go back to London."

"Very well, yer honour; I will wait," said the boatman, who immediately began to moor his boat to the wharfing at which he had landed Godfrey, and then to seek some place where he could obtain something in the shape of supper.

Godfrey then stole along for some distance until he came to some low houses that were surrounded by different buildings, yards, and old stores of ship timber, and a variety of matters only known and heard of in such places at the water-side.

There was a public-house among the houses, on either side of which were several other houses, and behind it this kind of miscellaneous property, with a yard that led down to the water's edge, and gave, if need be, ingress or egress.

The house itself was a large rambling place, such a one as was probably built too small at first, and delayed at different times, and for different purposes. The front was long and low, with a row of red curtains all along, which prevented any one from looking into the rooms where the guests sat. There was much noise proceeding from the interior, and Godfrey paused, before he entered, to listen to what was going forwards; but he could gather but little from what he there heard, since there was so much confusion of words, that sometimes one man would have the ascendancy for a moment, and then another; so that a word or two from each was heard, which rendered the discourse none of the clearest. After a few moments more there was a little silence restored, and a sea song was sung by some one with stentorian lungs, that seemed to go through the ears like the report of a great gun. While this was in progress, Godfrey walked into the house, and found out the bar, but as some one was standing by, he refrained from making any inquiries; but, when they were alone, he inquired of the landlady, who was a fat, big woman, if Neville was there.

She examined him attentively for some moments, and then said, she didn't know such a name.

"You must be under some mistake, for I have come from the Rookery, and they told me he was here, and I have seen him here before now; if he is here, I want to see him particularly. Tell him, Godfrey wants to see him."

"I will see if such a person really is here, and if so, you shall see him," said the landlady, hesitatingly.

"You will find it all right."

The landlady now left the bar, and entered a room behind, and evidently consulted with some one else, and then she again appeared, as if she were waiting for a messenger to return; and Godfrey himself waited quietly until he had the satisfaction of seeing her called into the bar, whence she emerged in a few moments, saying,—

"He is here. Will you go round there to the right, and take the first door to the left, where you will see some one who will conduct you to the person you want to see?"

Godfrey was glad enough to hear this, for he began to be in doubt as to whether he should really get an interview with Neville at all. He had come so far, he did not like the idea of returning without having effected his object, for who could tell but the first person whom he might meet to-morrow morning might be Marian Whitehead? and then he should suffer from her violence and persecution as he had done before, probably, with much worse results than ensued upon that occasion; however, that was all avoided, and he was now about to have the desired interview with the fiend Neville.

CHAPTER LVI.

THE INTERVIEW BETWEEN GODFREY AND NEVILLE.—THE RECONCILIATION.— THE PROPOSED MURDER.

WHEN Godfrey had reached the door indicated by the landlady, he saw a man, apparently waiting for him, and who, when he had scrutinized him sufficiently, beckoned him to follow him, which Godfrey did, through two rooms and a narrow passage, at the end of which was another door; and, by the time he had reached that, he could hear signs of revelry, boisterous enough, but, at the same time, not the most refined that could be heard. When he had waited a few moments, to listen if there was any pause in the noise they heard through the door, but, finding none, they next opened the door suddenly, which displayed to view a scene seldom met with, and then only by those who have had, by strange incidents in life, the chance of seeing such characters at such a moment. There were several lights in the room, which was oblong, and a large fire in the middle, though for this there seemed to be no necessity, for the place felt warm as soon as the door opened; and, but for a dense cloud of tobacco smoke, all could have been as plain as midday; but a dimness hung over the room that was so dense, that it resembled some sublunary feast of the gods, and mortals by chance got a peep at them through the clouds below. The effect of this was the more striking, and the more-like, as the door which opened into the room was several feet above the level of the room, and Godfrey had to descend several steps before he found himself on the floor.

"Do you see your friend there?" inquired the man of Godfrey, as they stood looking into the room.

"Yes, I see him, not far from here—there, to the left, by the side of the man with the wooden leg, and sailor's jacket."

"Yes, that is him," said the man; "you may go to him—it is all right—go a-head."

Godfrey did go a-head, as the man expressed it, in a sort of shuffling gait, until he reached the place where Neville sat; before him was placed a glass with some liquors, and he had but that moment set it down, having finished the contents. The moment, however, that Neville's eye rested upon Godfrey, the former started as if he had seen something that he had not expected, but a moment more he was reassured, by his own consciousness, that Godfrey could come upon no hostile errand, else he had not trusted himself there. It was quite a matter of surmise between different motives that Neville could attribute the cause of his coming, though what he had no means of guessing, since all appeared alike improbable to his eyes.

One thing, however, was certain, and that was, Godfrey came not there to serve him, Neville, or to pleasure himself, since he never did anything of that nature, being essentially selfish and brutal to an extreme.

When Godfrey shuffled up to him, he made room on the bench upon which he was sitting to enable him to sit down, which seat he accepted, and squeezed himself in as well as he could, and he was yet fearful of being rudely touched, so sensitive were his recently healed bruises and fractures.

"Well," said Neville, "so you have found your way down here?"

"Yes, I'm here," said Godfrey.

"And how came you to find out I was here?" inquired Neville; "who told you?"

"I went to the old place, and there I learnt you had come down the water, and I concluded you were here, and so I came to see you as soon as I was able."

"Ah, how kind!" said Neville; "you came to inquire after my health, I suppose."

"Not exactly; you don't deserve that, since you would —"

"Say nothing about that," said Neville, suddenly; "you provoked me to it, at a time, too, when I was most driven, by many considerations, about to get away."

"Well, well," said Godfrey, "I did not come to speak about that now; but your glass is empty."

"Oh," said Neville, "we'll have it filled and another for yourself, and you shall pay for both by way of amends."

Godfrey made no reply, but pointed to the glass, and said to the waiter—

"Fill this and another."

The glass was taken away, and after a few moments was returned, and another placed before him, which, when paid for, were duly tasted; and then Godfrey looked round on the company assembled in the room, which was crowded by men of all kinds, that is, men who appeared to be engaged in all the lowest occupations which so large a city as London affords a necessity for.

Some appeared one thing, some another, while many of them appeared perfectly nondescript—some sailors, some costermongers, and some neither one nor the other; while many had that peculiarity of appearance which enables the stranger to declare they belonged to any class that most pleased them.

There was much noise and confusion; the place was very hot, and Godfrey found himself more than half choked by the density of the tobacco smoke that filled the room.

In a few moments, however, he became more accustomed to the atmosphere of the place, and began to see more distinctly, and saw that the company had placed themselves under the control of a chairman, who was seated in a chair somewhat elevated above the rest, and that long tables ran round the whole length and breadth of the room, while many were seated between the two rows of tables, seats or forms having been placed up the middle for their express use.

There were a vast number of persons here, and the noise of conversation was very great and general, so much so it was almost impossible to hear what any one in particular said, and certainly it was impossible to follow them for a sentence or two consecutively, however close they might be, unless they were speaking to you in a good voice.

"This is a strange place," thought Godfrey, "and filled fuller than when I saw it last; the sheep do not diminish in numbers; the shepherd of such a fold must make money at the least, for these men spend freely."

Such were his thoughts, when they were suddenly broken in upon by Neville, who said,—

"What brought you down here to-night?"

"I have something to say to you," said he; "I wish to consult with you upon a matter that I think ought to be looked to very shortly, else, we may feel the inconvenience."

"What is it?" argued Neville; "has anything transpired in London? Do they suspect anything?"

"Nothing as yet, I hope, and yet at times I cannot help having some fear of things going wrong; you see Marian Whitehead, since she has become insane, has excited much pity and commiseration, and I fear she may yet cause trouble and mischief."

"Indeed!" said Neville; "I have all along been of opinion something will turn up in this affair, that will make us uncommonly uncomfortable, if we don't hang."

Godfrey started as he heard the words pronounced by the lips of Neville with some emphasis, when the former said:

"I don't like it, I must say; and I think, if one was to get rid of Marian, there would be much danger got rid of too; but we must say more of that by-and-by."

"Why, I came to you for money, you know, to enable me to get away from the country altogether; there would be less danger to you and to me; they could prove nothing when I am not present, and you would be quite safe."

"So I am now," said Godfrey, "as safe with you here as if you were absent; they would not take your word at any price—they would not believe you."

"There you are mistaken, Godfrey," replied Neville, "most miserably mistaken indeed."

"Am I so?" replied Godfrey.

"You are; my evidence, when so strongly corroborated as it would be by others, and known facts, would be irresistible; I might get sent out of the country, it is true, but then you know I am an old stager, and you cannot get used to, or over anything that comes in the shape of hanging."

There was much truth in all this, and Godfrey saw it very well, but it was not his purpose to admit as much, and therefore he said, after a pause—

"Yes, yes: I know and understand all that; but you must be aware that you are the principal actor in that and a few other scenes that would inevitably tuck you up by the throat; but I do not wish, either for my own sake or yours, that anything of the kind should take place. Our strength ought to be exerted for one purpose, and with one object; we may be able to encourage each other to a great extent, but who is the gainer?"

"Neither," said Neville.

"That is true; now, if we pull together, we may have a chance of defeating all our enemies."

"And I am to do all the work, I suppose, run all danger, while you look on and endeavour to think you are safe and secure from any harm," said Neville.

"Certainly, I want you to do the work, else I had not come all this way, but you will have proportionate advantages," said Godfrey, " to say nothing of the fact that you will be more secure, for it will diminish the number of those who would injure you as well as myself; the advantages I allude too are a certain portion of the current coin of the realm, Neville."

"The best advantage a man can have under any other, since it includes all others.

"That is true enough," said Godfrey; "then you will undertake the job I have hinted at?"

"Yes, I will, but I must know more about it presently; but mind, I say, I will do so only conditionally; that is, if it be to my advantage, in the manner you speak of both as to safety and money."

"Exactly. When can you get out of this place? there's no saying anything here, at least, we are liable to be overheard, and then you have a pretty chance of hanging."

"They are all true enough," said Neville, "not that I would trust them for all that, far from it; they would be apt to let a thing out perhaps, in hopes of saving themselves, should they get taken."

"Aye," said Godfrey, "they are not to be trusted."

"Trusted, no," replied Neville; "I never trust any man further than I can swing an ox by the tail, and I reckon that aint very far; but come, we may as well get out of this into another room, where we can have some private conversation, and there settle our plans and return here afterwards."

"That is what I want," said Godfrey.

"Follow me," replied Neville, who arose, and they both quitted the room by a different door to that which he had come in at, and then Godfrey found himself close at hand with Neville, but in the dark, for there were no lights in the passage that he could see, and, having come out of a strong light, he was nearly blinded by the sudden darkness.

"Where are you?" he inquired of Neville; "I know not which way to turn, I am blindfolded."

"This way—give me your hand; can't you see the lamp at the end here? I can."

After a few moments more, he became accustomed to the place, and he did then perceive what he had not before seen, and that was a small oil lamp placed in a niche in one corner of the passage at a bend. The light was so feeble that after leaving the other room he could not see it; however, they walked towards it, but there was a step to go down, which, however, Neville took no notice of when Godfrey came to it; being ignorant of it; he stepped as if he thought it was all level, and he came down with a dreadful jerk, causing a thrill of agony to run through his body."

"I forgot the step," said Neville, "however, it's not steep. You are not hurt, I suppose."

"Oh no, no; but my bones as well as my flesh seem tender, and won't bear any sudden movement."

There was no doubt that Neville had hoped for this result; it gave him considerable pleasure to be able to see Godfrey in his agony.

"We had better remain here," he said, when they had got as far as the lamp; "the passage bends here, and we have a view down both ways while we stand here, and know that we cannot be overheard by any one."

"Very well," said Godfrey, "let it be here then; we are all to ourselves and need fear nothing. You know very well that Marian Whitehead has become insane."

"Yes, I have heard about it, in fact, I have seen her walking about; she is a queer body."

"Yes, but withal very violent; she vows vengeance against you and me."

"Ah, ah, ah!" laughed Neville, "she can do nothing, and now she's mad she is more harmless than ever."

"There can be no doubt, but in one sense she is more harmless than ever, that is, they would scarce take her evidence, but she becomes more dangerous upon personal grounds; she may be induced to commit deeds she would shrink from as being impossible when she was in her right mind, but now she is insane nothing is impossible."

"Very good, that seems all very well; but tell me what it is you are aiming at."

"Why you see," said Godfrey, "I want Marian put out of the way. I am sure you could manage it; it's easy done if you do but choose the proper moment for effecting your purpose."

"Yes, I know much is to be done when you can time your deeds, but the difficulty is to do that; however, what do you offer if I do it?"

"Why you want to leave the country, don't you?" inquired Godfrey.

"Yes, I should like to be beyond the reach of the Bow-street runners, in some place where I am not known, and can live free from all fear of this infernal business."

"Well," said Godfrey, "I will give you the sum you required when you came to me at the hospital, to carry you where you then intended going."

"A thousand pounds?" said Neville.

"Yes, I will; but mind that is to be the final settlement. If I pay you, you are not to demand payment again, for you only render me desperate, which involves your ruin quite as surely as my own, and probably a little sooner."

"We'll consider that matter at a future time," said Neville; "I am now only considering how to get money to leave England for ever with."

"Do this, then," said Godfrey, "and you have it at once; there's no fear of resistance, all you will have to mind is to do it carefully, and no one will suspect you; once clear off, and you never need fear, because there is no trace."

"I know all that very well," said Neville, "everything depends upon the way in which it is done; I must consider over the means before I make the attempt; but you know I have an empty purse, and cannot get to London."

"There," said Godfrey, as he counted out fifteen sovereigns into Neville's hands "there, that will last you till you bring me word the deed is done."

"Very good," said Neville, "very good; now we may as well return, else a longer absence may excite remark among these people, who are too much concerned for their own safety to allow anything to pass unnoticed, and they may come out to inquire into the cause of our non-appearance."

"Then it is agreed, then," said Godfrey, "that you shall make this attempt upon Marian?"

"I will—come on—it is quite a settled thing."

CHAPTER LVII.

THE ATTEMPTED MURDER OF MARIAN.—THE VISION, AND THE ESCAPE.

HAVING made up their minds that the murder should be committed, they returned to t e room which they left, and resumed their seats. Godfrey seemed to have relieved himself of some mental burden; he appeared to feel a relief after the business had been settled in the way in which it had, and he fancied he felt an additional security from the fact that Marian's days were numbered.

If there was one thing more than another that worried him—that gave him cause for fear—it was Marian Whitehead; he knew he had injured her irreparably, and therefore it was that he feared her; he knew his own deserts, and feared they would be visited upon him—he deserved the death he so much dreaded at the hands of the injured Marian.

It is true he knew her gentleness and amiability of disposition, yet he believed that she was now bereft of reason, and therefore, if the impulse seized her, she would not hesitate to destroy him, for he was well aware how very easy such a thing was to execute: he could be deprived of life in the easiest manner possible, and he was not fit to resist, were resistance possible.

" I might," he would say to himself, " be destroyed by the blow of a sharp knife; who knows, if given me in the back, it would reach my heart; under the ear a sudden gash would be quite as effectual, and deprive me of my existence as easily—as—as—I am afraid to think of it, and that's the truth."

" When do you come to London?" inquired Godfrey suddenly of Neville, who had been paying attention to some one who was speaking to him on the other side.

" Well I can hardly tell, but I suppose to-morrow, some time or other. Are you going to stay?"

" No—I'm going very shortly—hadn't you better come at the same time? you know well enough where to lodge for the night I dare say, and you would be the sooner ready."

" So I should; well, I have a great mind to come to London at once, though, for the matter of that, this is London; but never mind, how did you come down?"

" By water," replied Godfrey.

" And how do you intend to go back again?" inquired Neville.

" By the same means: I have a man and a boat waiting for me now. I told him to wait about two hours; my time's nearly up, I must return if you will not accompany me, but let me advise you to do so."

" Why?"

" Because you will only get more drink and that will unsettle your brains, and the sooner this thing is done the better, because there is less time for danger to come to anything. However, do as you like; night is better travelling for you than day, in my opinion."

" So it is," replied Neville, after some thought, " one more glass and I'm off with you; we shall consider all our accounts squared by this affair?"

" Very well, be it so;" said Godfrey, and he ordered the two glasses to be filled, and then, leaning back in his chair, he gazed around upon the mass of human beings by which he was surrounded, and found them all to be of the lowest class in the human scale—men dyed in crime of some sort or another.

They were fit companions, however, for Godfrey, for they were stained by the same hue of guilt by which he himself was contaminated—he differed from them only in station.

To an entire stranger these beings would have presented a very remarkable collection of heads. There have been, at times, all the genius and fancy of artists in delineating odd and grotesque features: such as long heads and queer noses; some askew; some flat from the bridge downward, but presenting a sharp front; some ike a lump of proud flesh jutting out about the mouth; some with them all askew; some one way and some this; indeed, all that could be called grotesque and forbidden, were to be found here, adding a hideousness to their aspect which they have not, and which, however, made them alone remarkable and suspected by all who saw them.

It was strange that Godfrey should sit and look upon these men as if he would shrink from contact with them—as though he were above them in morality—they only possessing the coarser features of the self-same class to which he belonged himself; and he was, moreover, one of the props and stays of such a class of men as this which he now saw, and from which he now appeared to shrink as though he had but been a visitor to, and not a partaker in their orgies.

By the time he had finished his scrutiny the glass of Neville was again empty, and taking the hint, Godfrey emptied his own, and turning to him, said—

"I think we had better now go, at least I must, else I shall lose the boat; are you in the same mind about returning to town, or are you going to remain here?"

"I am ready," replied Neville, who arose and led the way out of the place by the door he had entered, and then through some other passages, and they were, in a few moments more, in the street and in front of the house.

"This way, round here to the right," said Godfrey, "will bring us to a lane leading to the wharf, where the boat is moored and the man with it, for the time is quite up."

After a few minutes more walking they came to the wharfing and there found the man smoking a pipe and leaning his back against a post awaiting their coming.

"Rather after time, master," said the boatman, as he pulled his boat alongside the wharf to allow them to get in.

"Yes," returned Godfrey, "but then I have brought you double fare, and you can earn twice as much as you would have done had you gone a little earlier."

"Very well, your honour, I am satisfied, only the earlier the better; and, now then, we are off."

As he spoke, he pushed off into the stream, and then taking his oars in hand he began to pull for London. Fortunately for them all the tide had turned, and the stream was running up instead of down, so they went back at a rapid pace until they reached London, which they did in about the same time it took them to go down, which is usually considered a very rare thing, and only to be done when the tide flows and ebbs.

"And now here we are, your honour," said the boatman; "will you land here?"

"Yes," said Godfrey, "pull in, and we will get out here. It's very cold on the water; I'm tired of it."

"I am quite warm," replied the boatman, "rowing is hard work, and I am quite warm."

They both got out, and Godfrey gave the boatman his fare, and then turning away with Neville, proceeded up the stairs, and then along the street, when Godfrey said to him—

"Now, Neville, we understand each other clearly, I believe; you will get rid of this walking spectre for me?"

"Yes, upon payment of the one thousand pounds, certainly I will do it; you may rely upon me. I cannot fail, for to fail would be to be hanged."

"Yes," said Godfrey, "a half measure were ruin. Bring me the proof of her death and I am satisfied, and you shall have the one thousand pounds."

"Very good," replied Neville. "I shall stay here for the night. I am cold and tired, and shall find all I require, a quiet roost and a good drop of liquor."

They both parted; Godfrey walking as well as he was able to his own house, though he made but a hobble of it.

"Now, then," he thought, "I shall soon be at rest with respect to this affair; it is all in train, and the daughter once gone, I shall have no trouble with the mother; she will sink in the course of nature—that is a good thing. I wish the daughter would, by some chance or other, fall down dead, aye, to-morrow morning, that would save me a thousand pounds, and yet I could not very well put Neville off without something or other; however, I would give the money cheerfully, if it were to happen, for I should then be shot of her, and Neville would know no fresh matter to boast of concerning me; but I suppose the fates will be perverse and leave me to shift as best I may.''

With this consoling remark he reached his own house, which he entered with a steady step, and retired to rest without being seen or spoken to by a single soul.

*   *   *   *   *   *   *

Neville himself, however, sat up some time; yet, before he retired to rest, he, as intended, meant to enjoy himself by the fire of the tap-room of the house where he lodged, and to enjoy some of the best they had, for he now possessed money, and, as usual, felt disposed to spend it.

Here he remained till on the verge of intoxication, and then he fell asleep, from which he was awakened when the house closed, and then he contrived to crawl to his bed, where he lay until some hours of the day had dawned, and all the streets were filled with business and noise. Then Neville got up, and when out he began to frequent those parts of the city where he had heard the Black Lady was mostly to be seen.

It was some time before he could meet with her, but after some pains he was successful in the object of his search, and found her in the Bank. Neville did not stop a moment there, had he done so, it is more than probable he would have been desired to quit the place, and himself watched afterwards, and his whole plan frustrated; or he would have been very likely to have been taken, and then the consequences were what he would not like to endure if he had a choice.

After some thought he watched the Bank for the Black Lady when she should come out, and, as it was afternoon, she was not likely to be there long; and after about an hour he saw her leave the Bank, and then proceeding along some of the main thoroughfares she passed across some others towards her own lodgings where she resided with her mother. To this place Neville watched her at a distance, and saw her go in, and then he walked up, and then he noted well the house into which she had gone, and then again he returned to consider what was to be done.

"I must get in," he muttered to himself; "it will be the safest and the best. I have pistols, but I had better have recourse to cold steel; a long knife with a sharp point will at once do the business, and if the blow be well planted there will be no noise, and I shall make my exit without all that confounded row that rouses up the whole neighbourhood, and then a chase is the certain consequence."

"I am glad," he thought, "that I have found out where she does live; this will save many a long day and much danger too. Well, a thousand pounds hangs upon the point of my knife, and that will help me to strike home; at all events I'll try, and when did I fail?"

Having thus made up his mind to the murderous purpose he had in view, he next set about considering how he should be able to get in. This was not usually a difficult task; but upon this occasion he had no instrument with him, and hence the great difficulty he expected to experience.

After having maturely considered all his plans, he resolved to get in during the night, in opposition to the plan he had first formed of getting in during the day, and concealing himself somewhere about the house, and discovering which was her room. Without this knowledge he was completely at fault; and, if he passed into each room, and examined each bed, he might awake some of them, and thus destroy the chance he might have; and more, he might have the ill-luck to be seized, and get imprisoned for a lesser crime, which would be the more aggravating, especially as he could get no reward, and if he did split upon Godfrey, he would be no gainer by it, since, when he got free again, he was as good as a bank to him, for he must have money of him.

However, he determined to await until night before he made a determined effort to get in, yet, if an opportunity did occur, he would be sure to take advantage of it; and while he sat on a neighbouring door-step, under an archway opposite, he regarded the door with a whistful eye.

He stopped here for more than an hour, or perhaps nearer two, when the door opened, and out walked a servant-girl with a jug in her hand, and she left the door ajar, while she entered a public-house close at hand.

The moment Neville saw the coast clear he started across the street and entered the house at once. Here he paused a moment and then walked up stairs, and peeping into the first room he saw open, and finding it empty, he walked in there.

It was fortunate he did, for he had scarcely done so before some one came down stairs, and would have met him, and he had scarce time to ensconce himself behind some boxes beneath the bed, for it was a bed-room, when the same person entered the room with a slow, measured footstep.

Something assured Neville that he had actually concealed himself in the bed-room of Marian Whitehead, and that it was her who had entered the room. What an opportunity this afforded him of completing the tragedy he had in view at one blow, and in one moment !

But Neville could not move without making a noise and alarming her; and she would, as a matter of course, alarm the whole house, and that would cause him to abandon the plan altogether; and being quiet where he was, and allow Night to spread her sable mantle over all, and thus, when his victim was wrapped in the arms of slumber, suddenly to deprive it of its existence.

It was a terrible thought, and yet one which Neville never had any objection to coolly consider—not the necessity of doing it, for that had been settled in his own mind—he had a reward in view, and that was what he desired and what he worked for; and now his whole efforts were directed towards bringing about the death of Marian.

* * * * * * *

Night came on them, when the house generally were retiring to rest. Marian came into the chamber to sleep; but first, oh, how fervently she prayed for the safety and welfare of Charles Ormond, whom she believed to be living somewhere close at hand, but concealed from all, to save his life!

Her prayers were full of goodness and strong feeling, and he could hear by her sobs that she had shed tears that proved, were there any doubt, as to the sincerity of the feelings and hopes she gave utterance to.

There she lay on the bed under which he was concealed! For nearly two hours did Neville remain in what was to him a painful state of suspense; and then the deep though gentle breathing of Marian told him she had fallen into the arms of sleep, and now lay unconscious of the vicinity of the lurking foe who lay concealed to take her life.

Slowly and cautiously did Neville rise, and then approached the bed and gazed for an instant upon the unfortunate Marian; and then he grasped the haft of the knife that was to do its work so sure and deadly, that no sound, scarcely a sigh should escape her lips; and then he lifted his hand shoulder-high and held it point downwards to give a proper direction to the edge, and he was upon the point of striking the blow when his eyes rested upon the form of Charles Ormond, who slowly interposed himself between him, Neville, and the intended victim.

For a moment he was terrified and incapable of motion, but the pale shadow-form was so distinct to his eyes, that with a half-shriek he sprang back and rushed out of the room, and hastened the best way he could down stairs, and, with a trembling hand and quivering lip, he endeavoured to open the door, which, however, he could not effect for some time, owing to his hands shaking so violently that he might have been supposed to have had an ague.

However, he did get free of the house, not however too soon, for he heard the sound of footsteps, and it was with a wild terror he shut the door after him, and rushed down the street.

CHAPTER LVIII.

THE DEATH OF MRS. WHITEHEAD.—THE POOR AUTHOR'S SYMPATHY.—THE
PROPOSAL.

THE moment had now arrived when Mrs. Whitehead, borne down with heavy
and continued misfortunes. added to natural decay and feebleness, was brought to
a sick bed. She had long borne up against every misfortune—she had endeavoured
to combat the wild tide that was setting against her—but her strength decayed,
and she was no longer equal to the task. Had she been one of less submission
and more acute in her feelings, she would, no doubt, have worn herself out, and
sunk from the violence of her own feelings ere this.

Day after day she became weaker and weaker, until at length she could scarce
crawl about.

"Alas! poor Marian," she would sometimes say, " alas! poor Marian, I
scarce knew what will become of you if I am taken from you. I do not know
what to do. I am getting so weak and feeble, that I fear I cannot last much
longer. Heaven has granted me a much longer lease, and more strength to go
through what I have gone through, and to see what I have seen, without dying, than
ever I expected. Who would have expected that I should remain when the
young and strong have been snatched away?"

Thus the poor unfortunate Mrs. Whitehead would mourn day after day, and
yet unable to get better. However, she continued thus to get about for some
weeks; but she was unable, at length, to get out of doors, and then soon she
became too weak to get up and down in the house.

There were scarcely any signs of disease about her, properly so called; and when
Dr. Hesketh came, he shook his head gravely, and gave her no opinion.

"Do you think I shall ever get over this, doctor?" she inquired one day, as he
felt her pulse.

"Why," said he, " you must not expect much in the shape of strength again.
You must be content to rub on through the world in the way you do."

"But for my poor Marian, doctor," she said, " I should not care how soon this
weary time was over; but who will take care of her when I am gone?"

"Do not let that disturb you, Mrs. Whitehead," said Dr. Hesketh; " you
must be content to rub on in the best way you can. If you can get quiet and
refrain from indulging in grief and sadness, that would do you more good than
anything else. Ease of mind is the first thing to be thought of."

"Alas! doctor—that I cannot obtain. How can I, while I have such a sad
memorial of the past before me as my poor distracted daughter?"

Hesketh saw the case and said nothing, for he perceived there was little utility
i n doing so; but going down stairs he was waylaid by the landlady, who came
out to ask him a question or two concerning the unfortunate lodger of hers, Mrs.
Whitehead.

"Oh! if you please, sir," said the landlady, " I am very anxious about poor
Mrs. Whitehead."

"Ah!" said Hesketh, " she is a very worthy woman."

"Yes, sir, and so I ses to our Lizzy; and we both noticed how she seems to
break of late. I began to fear something would happen to her."

"She is very unwell, and therefore you cannot expect to see her very well;
besides, she has seen many years—she is what you may call an aged woman."

"Oh, above thirty. How old do you think she is?"

"I am sure I can't say," said Hesketh, dryly; " but old enough to be the
mother of her daughter."

"Oh, dear me, I dare say she must be. Do you think she can get over her
illness?"

"Yes, she can."

"Do you think she will?"

"It is difficult to say what can or cannot be done; but, as far as my opinion is worth anything, I think she is fast falling to decay."

"Poor thing! and then you think she'll die?"

"Under those circumstances," said the doctor, "I think it more than likely. She must be kept quiet and cheerful, if possible—nourishing and light food should be given her, and then all is done that can be done for her."

"She has friends, sir, who'll see her buried, I suppose? She seems a respectable woman."

"She is a respectable woman," said Dr. Hesketh, "and has friends; so you need be under no fear with regard to rent or trouble you may be put to."

"Oh, sir, I wasn't afraid of that, sir; I only asked out of respect for the poor lady herself."

Dr. Hesketh saw the motive, and at once appreciated it, of the inquiry that had been made, and then left the house.

The predictions founded by Dr. Hesketh were likely to be soon realised, for Mrs. Whitehead grew daily worse and worse, and was evidently sinking.

In less than a week she was unable to rise from her bed, but was confined to it; her strength gradually declined, until she became alarmingly weak.

One morning, as the sun peeped into the sick-chamber from between the curtains that were partially closed only, Marian arose, and was about to close it again, when her mother said to her,—

"Marian, my dear, do not shut the sun out; it will not be very long before I shall cease to see it—then, Marian, as you look upon the sunbeams, dear, will you think upon your mother."

"Oh, do not speak of it, mother; I hope the day will be far distant before I shall lose so good, and so very dear a friend and parent as you have been to me."

"The day must come when we must part—the aged must drop into the grave— their time is come at the end of many years—do not, therefore, grieve for what must be naturally; and when in the course of nature and of years we do die, why, we should not consider it a matter of sorrow and regret that we are to enter the life to come."

"Mother, we do not all drop off at such a time!"

"No, my child, no; I know that well. I remember the fate of poor Charles Ormond."

"Have I not told you that he lives, and I am daily expecting to find him—to meet him somewhere or other? And I have every hope I shall do so."

"Alas, poor Marian! what a hope!"

"It is, mother; but London, you know, is a large place, where there are many hundreds of thousands of inhabitants, and it may be a long while before I do find him; but then how joyful will be the meeting! but it may not be yet; I cannot tell when nor what day it will be, but sure I am it will be some day. He is obliged to keep so close, so very close, for if his enemies were to find him he could never again get free."

"Alas, Marian!"

"Yes, mother, it is very sad; but there is no help for it. I have seen many about the pardon for poor Ormond, and they have promised me to use their endeavours to do the utmost for him, and I am sure they will succeed."

"I hope they may, child. What would you do if I am taken from you, my child?"

"You, mother, you taken from me? What do you mean? You are not surely going away?"

"But I fear I am, Marian."

"Nay, mother, I will never leave you—I cannot leave you—it would be dreadful to part."

"And yet we must part!"

"Must part, mother?" said Marian, with something like energy in her sadness; "said you we must part? Oh! no—no; not even in death will we part. I will lie in the same grave with you—they shall not part us even then!"

"But we must part; as I said before, Death will have his own, and he has marked me for his prey. I am ill now, Marian, and I can see there is no hope for me; and, but for your sake, I could never form a wish to live. I have seen too little of happiness of late to have any longing for life."

"Do not speak so mournfully, mother. I am sad, but I have hopes; you are sad, do you have hopes; it will make you happy and wish to live."

"I have no hope!"

"None, mother?"

"None, Marian; but I could wish to live for your sake, and your sake alone. I would like to be by your side till you could exchange this life for a better; then, indeed, I might feel something akin to happiness—but that is denied me."

* * * * * * *

This conversation continued in the same strain for some time, and was resumed each day; but the strength of Mrs. Whitehead was visibly declining, and each day she was less able to continue the conversations she tried to hold with Marian—each day shortened their duration; and though Marian grieved and shed tears, she could hardly be said to be thoroughly acquainted with her mother's state, and her approaching decease.

The thought that Charles Ormond might and would yet be met with, and that she knew not which day or when the lucky moment might be, added to her mental alienation, seemed to prevent the full measure of grief from being fully felt; but her seared heart yet loved her parent tenderly, and she shed tears often when her mother talked of her approaching dissolution, but was easily directed from the contemplation when any mention was made respecting Charles Ormond.

There was, however, little doubt but the day was close at hand when she would cease to be. Mrs. Whitehead's strength was so far gone that she could not raise her head or turn in bed, and her eyes became dimmed—she could not see far.

Each time she left the room in search of Charles Ormond, her mother bade her farewell, lest she should not survive the day out, and see her on her return.

* * * * * * *

"Marian!" said Mrs. Whitehead; "Marian!" and she whispered the name several times; she could not speak above a whisper to her daughter, her voice was almost gone.

"Mother!" said Marian.

"Kiss me, Marian," she said with difficulty; "my dear Marian, I am dying—my last blessing—I cannot live long—take my last blessing, my dear Marian!"

"Mother, do not say that. Oh, Heaven! what new misfortune has now come upon me? Now must I lose the only being who is now with me? Oh! mother, mother!"

Marian flung herself upon the couch by the side of her dying parent, and she saw that she was indeed near her last gasp, and, poor thing, she knew not what to say or do. She was seized with a fit of trembling, as though an ague had seized her; and she was scarcely able to articulate a word.

"Mother—mother!" she said, her teeth chattering as with fear—but from convulsion; "speak, mother, I shall die if I do not hear you speak again."

"Marian, my dear Marian!" were the only words the dying woman could utter.

Marian threw herself upon, and kissed her lips, and bathed her face with her tears.

"Mother, mother! look up. Oh, do not fix that dreadful look upon me! I can't bear! Oh, 'tis horrible, most horrible! Oh, my mother, my mother! what can be done? What shall I do? Oh, my God, my God! do not forsake her!"

Marian held her hands up appealingly to heaven as she spoke, but she sank again on the bed she had risen from.

"You can do nothing, Marian, I am past the aid of man. Nothing can save me—I am dying, Marian—my blessing on you, child. May Heaven protect you, for human aid you will have none. Seek it there, my child."

"I will, mother."

"Do, my child. Keep far from those bad men, Neville and Godfrey—they are the authors of all. Oh, what an account they will have to render up when the last day shall come!"

"Think not of them, mother—think of yourself; moments are too precious to be wasted upon them."

"They are, Marian, especially when one's life may now be counted by moments. There can be no help—no hope from anywhere save from Him to whom I am going."

The sorrow and sadness of mother and daughter was great, but it became incoherent and broken; more was expressed by tears and sighs than words; but this could not last long, for Mrs. Whitehead's life was fast ebbing. Giving her daughter once more her blessing, she opened her eyes, to close them for ever.

She was dead.

" Mother, mother! speak to me, mother—speak to me! I cannot bear to see you so."

But Mrs. Whitehead answered not; and a loud scream alone gave notice that Marian was aware of the loss that had happened, and she fell, senseless, by the couch.

*   *   *   *   *

The door opened, and assistance was brought. Women entered the room and carried her away, and she was restored to consciousness of the deep bereavement she had suffered, but she refused the ordinary means of consolation, and was soon left to herself, while her mother's corpse was taken possession of by the people of the house, who had the ordinary customs adopted.

Marian, in the meanwhile, was placed in another room, and but little attended to by the females of the house, because of her condition, and because she was of a superior caste, and they were incapable of administering to her anything in the shape of consolation. Besides, she refused all offers, and would remain in the room where her mother was laid out.

But although there was little sympathy from the people in the house, after the first moments of grief and excitement, there was another being, who could and did afford her some consolation in the midst of her affliction.

This was no other than a man who had spent the best part of his life in administering to the amusements of others. He was, what is very common, a poor author.

John Alchet was an odd being—a good heart—but his head, maybe, a little ill-placed; he was kind—but odd; he would do any good turn for another; but he was an instrument often used, but none were thankful for his services, and few ever thought of returning them.

But yet John Alchet never hesitated to do good, if he could, though the good he did seldom benefited himself, and though he often experienced ingratitude; and the evil return which men make who fancy they have been served by one below them, never rankled in his heart—it was what it had been before, which at least gave him some comfort, for he felt not the pangs of ingratitude half so sharp, nor was his self-love so easily wounded. Kindness of heart is a much more effectual barrier against the world's rough usage than the most stony or stoical indifference.

John Alchet would often come down, and endeavour to console Marian under her affliction, and he saw she was mentally afflicted also, and this was a recommendation to poor Alchet's attention, and he made every attempt he could to divert her attention."

" You should not give way to grief—it will spoil your own happiness, and it will not help her who has left this scene of trouble," he said. " You should bear up against affliction, and not be cast down by any misfortune whatever—much less as you know your respected relative is gone to a better sphere."

" Yes, she was my mother."

" Truly she was; and, being your mother, it was in the course of nature she should go first—you must have expected it—but think of something else."

" I cannot."

Poor Marian, more than once, was diverted from the grief into which she was cast by this sad event, and only by the attempts of John Alchet; but it was only for a moment, yet it was not without its service."

By degrees she became communicative to him, and informed him of much of her history, and he more than once assured her, that, if it were written down for her, it would be the best thing that he had during his life attempted, and begged she would permit it to be done.

"But then all would be known about Charles Ormond," she said, sighing deeply.

"Not more than is known," he replied.

"Alas, poor Charles! when shall we meet? It may so chance that we may never do so, for I may not live."

"Nor he either; and if he do, he will know nothing of all you have done, or how you attempted to see him again," said Alchet.

That argument made an impression upon her, but he did not then follow it up.

"Come," said he, "the night sets in, suppose we pass an hour away in reading. I'll read you a production of my own, it will at least pass the time away, and that will be one point gained at least."

So saying, and having trimmed the candle, he began to read the following tale, one of his own productions, written with a view of passing some of the many hapless hours that hung on the poor fellow's hand:—

The forest leaves were rattling beneath the heavy drops of a thunder-storm, which was just at its commencement, when a knight, in plain black armour rode beneath the tall trees to seek the shelter they afforded. He was attended by two men in half armour; they were both tall and strong, and their visages betrayed more than one mark of the encounter in the field, for they were plentifully scarred by the healing of wounds received in battles. Their dress was, as we have said, half armour, but it was all plain and without ornament, or any badge of distinction being visible about them; moreover, all they wore showed that it had been hardly used and long. Their steeds were strong and good, but they, too, showed signs of years and travel. The three rode for some distance into the forest at an easy and ambling pace: there were no impediments near them, there was a bridle path through the forest, and huge rocks were seen in some parts, and the Rhine and its tributaries ran silently through some of its river-visited glades.

The thunder rattled over head, and leaped and crashed through the sky, as though the very earth were bursting; the air was filled with terrific sounds, while the sky, which was darkened from above, was every now and then illumined by the fearful flashes of the vivid lightning that followed the crashing peals, or appeared simultaneously with them, so close was the storm-clouds to the earth. The very air seemed disturbed, and the wind that swept through the forest was terrific, laying huge trees bare at the roots, and tearing up those monarchs of the forest that it had taken ages to produce. This was a storm, and one that would be remembered wherever it passed over as long as the inhabitants should live; but as it was, they were unable to stand against it, but fled, and many left their habitations, while many were buried beneath the ruins of their own homes. The rain all the while fell in such fearful torrents as promised to swell all the rivulets into foaming torrents, and swelling rivers to flooding, so that there was much fear that the fords in the Black Forest would be no longer practicable for man or beast, and many were in that storm lost.

The knight and his two attendants rode on, in the earlier part of the storm, in silence; and the sounds of their horses' feet were all that now reached their ears, save the howling of the storm, and the pattering of the rain.

The noise of the thunder increased to such a deafening extent, that while it lasted at its height, the air seemed incapable of conveying any other sound.

The knight drew his bridle for a minute or so, to allow of his attendants coming up to him, so that he might speak to them, for, at any distance, the attempt would have been perfectly futile; but even when close at hand, he was compelled to exert his voice to a high pitch.

"Hubert," he said, "canst thou hear at all in this storm?"

"Yes, Sir Giles, if you are pleased to speak loud enough," replied his follower, without any hesitation.

"Dost know of any place where we can have food and shelter for some time, at least so long as the storm lasts? It grows much too serious now. We cannot, with safety, keep our horses out in this dreadful storm.

"I was once a forester in the wilds, Sir Giles,'"

"I know thou wast, Hubert, and hence I ask thee if thou canst tell where we may lay by till the storm abates?"

"I can, but I know not if we can reach it in safety, Sir Giles; and, at best, it will only serve as a shelter."

"Never mind about that, so that we obtain a shelter for our steeds. What with the lightning and the falling of the trees, I think there is every likelihood of our journey being brought to a sudden and disagreeable termination."

"Will you take the path to the left, Sir Giles?"

"Ride forward, and we will follow you. The sooner we are out of this, the better."

Hubert rode forward, and not a sound could be heard save what came from the heavens above, where the thunder cracked and crashed in the air, and the sky seemed alive with fire, which streamed from all quarters of the heavens.

They rode on in silence, such as concerned themselves, for they heard not the sound of their own horses' hoofs upon the forest-road—they heard not the jingling of their own armour—and they heard not the sound of their own voices.

The heavens were filled with the most tremendous sounds; no moment was left unoccupied but had its appropriate sound—the roar of the wind, the creak and crashing of the trees, the rustling of leaves as the hurricane swept through the forest.

The air was illumined saddened with a tremendous and brilliant flash so strong and so sudden that they could not see, but suddenly shut their eyes, so dazzled with the brightness.

Then came such a cracking and crashing, and rolling through the heavens, that seemed as though the whole universe was splitting and becoming nought.

For some moments they heard nothing and saw nothing, the light was so vivid, and the horses stopped suddenly.

Sir Giles then looked up and saw that a huge oak-tree was falling to the earth in one blazing mass.

"By the mass!" said the knight, "this has been a narrow escape for me! A moment more, and man and horse would have been borne down by the weight of yon tree!"

"Aye, Sir Giles! it's ill-riding in the forest in storms—the lightning is attracted by the trees."

"Trees grow everywhere almost," said the knight, "and I expect we cannot travel far without them; it is one of the dangers we must incur, and therefore we need not make greater evils of it than is necessary. We must get round this impediment somehow!"

"This way, Sir Giles!" said Hubert, who had got to the other side before the tree fell, and had a yet more narrow escape; "this way—to the left!"

"The tree cannot burn long in such a deluge as this," said Sir Giles, as he turned round it in a clear space that was open but a short distance from it.

The party now rode onwards as quickly as they could, until they came to a small bridle-path, and here singly they trotted over the ground at a rapid pace until they came to an opening in the forest, and they could hear the rushing of water.

"What place is this?" inquired Sir Giles.

"It is one of the branches of the Rhine," said Hubert.

"And shall we not be overwhelmed with the torrent, if it rise, as it will most likely do?"

"If it rise high enough, Sir Giles; but this is the highest part in the forest, and never yet was flooded."

"Who is that man yonder who sits upon that crag that overhangs the river?"

The men turned towards the spot, and saw a hermit clad in sackcloth, seated on a crag that overhung the stream, which boiled and foamed below. The rain seemed to pour down in torrents on his white hair, and he stood unmindful of the pelting of the storm.

"That is the hermit of the Black Forest," said Hubert.

" Do you know him ?"

" I have seen him before; he can shelter us within his cave, and he will."

" Does he often so expose himself to the fury of the elements, or is this a solitary instance?"

" He is seldom seen on such an occasion as this. I thought he had been dead ere this; it is many years since I saw him, and he was then very aged."

" We had better ride on towards him," said Sir Giles. " Hark, how the thunder peals, and the rain descends in torrents!"

He immediately made towards the rising-ground, where the rock stood, and which, instead of being an isolated piece, as Sir Giles had at first supposed, was merely a portion of a bed of rocks that extended some distance by the bank of the river.

Hubert shouted to him from a distance, but he heard him not, and, despairing of doing so, he said—

" If you'll follow me, Sir Giles, I'll take you to a cavern where you can at least shelter yourself and horse from the weather, whence the hermit will come when he comes down."

" Lead on," said Sir Giles.

Hubert led to the base of the cliff, and then entered the cave he spoke of by means of a small path that wound round, and suddenly terminating in the cavern spoken of.

It seemed a large, spacious place, capable of sheltering a couple of hundred horsemen, supported at intervals, along the front, by solid pieces of rock, that acted as pillars.

" Here is space enough," said Sir Giles.

" Yes, Sir Giles, you may dismount here in safety, for here is, I dare say, some kind of food, and the hermit lives here, and we can obtain a fire and the means of changing and drying our armour and accoutrements."

As he spoke Hubert dismounted, and led his steed towards a place on the left, where there was a quantity of dried herbage, which served for bedding and food.

" Here Sir Giles," said Hubert, " they can rest here; and, if you please, we can find food here, somewhere. But here comes the hermit."

" You know so much of this place, Hubert," said Sir Giles, " that you must be my guide; but see we are not set upon at a disadvantage by any of the robbers of the Black Forest, for they are numerous and bold."

" They are, Sir Knight, but they are not likely to interfere here, at all events; the hermit, too, will be our protection; he is much respected by all."

The hermit came up to them, and said:—

" Sons, thou hast been overtaken by the storm, and seek shelter in these caverns."

" We do, holy father. We are travellers, and your hospitality will be to us a boon."

" 'Tis but little the hermit can give; but you are welcome, my sons, to such as I have."

" More could not be wished," said Sir Giles; " hard fare and a harder couch seldom come amiss to the soldier."

" Follow me," said the hermit, and he passed round a kind of pillow formed ou of the natural rock, and then entered a separate place of the cavern or apartment.

Here was a natural bench upon which they were seated, and they could see that this place faced the river, which they could hear rushing through its rocky bed.

" This is a strange place," said Sir Giles, as he looked around; " but it afford good shelter, Sir Hermit."

" It does, my son," said the hermit, placing before him some food and some wine. " It is a strange place, and was formerly tenanted by stranger people."

" Indeed!" said the knight.

" Aye, Sir Knight; there have been fearful deeds done in this now-deserted and peaceful spot."

"It seems as if made for shelter and concealment," said the knight; "it is perfect."

"Aye, Sir Knight, in my time I have seen a hundred-and-fifty men ready for any evil—daring and resolute men, who would never turn their back upon such odds as three to one against them; and when they were beset by yet greater numbers, never fell into their enemies' hands living men."

"They would have made good soldiers," said the knight.

"They would; but soldiers' pay and obedience to officers would not suit such men. They fought for gold; but it must be won in greater quantities than they can win it by ordinary warfare. Besides, their conduct in time of peace would not sit the townsmen and other peaceable people."

"What became of them?"

"I will tell you," said the hermit, after a pause.

"At that time (this is about sixty years ago), I was then over thirty."

"Are you ninety?" said the knight.

"Yes, stranger, I am over ninety—about ninety-five or six—for I know not exactly which; I cannot tell the year of my birth by one year or so; I am not less than ninety-five."

"It is a great age."

"Yes; I am now hearty, and capable of exertion to some extent. But my time will soon be come; I have not many more summers to gaze upon the sun.

"But—to return to what I was about to tell you—the events I relate occurred near sixty years ago, when this place was inhabited by a band of daring marauders —men who feared neither man nor devil."

"This band was termed The Forest Vultures, and they used to attack whole towns and villages without hesitation, and rob churches or churchmen.

"They were not restrained by the fear of God or man. None ever saw them turn their backs. They always succeeded in every attempt they made.

"The captain of this band of men was brave and skilful, and had the entire confidence of these men, who would follow him into any enterprise which he declared practicable, and offered to lead them onwards.

"He was called Black Hugh, or the Black Spirit, because he always wore a black plume and rode a black horse.

"But he was more cruel and heartless than all the rest—perhaps stronger and more daring than any one, and certainly more fortunate than any other commander.

"One night they determined to attack the cathedral; for it was believed that it would be full of plate, both gold and silver, to a very great amount.

"This was considered a very favourable moment to attack the church. True, it was filled with ecclesiastics; but then, they were only churchmen, and no more.

"The robbers were a hundred and fifty strong, trained to fight, and cared no more for robbing a church than many would thinking ill of a priest.

"It was a daring impiety, a piece of impious sacrilege, but which brought down its own punishment.

"Some of the men said they should be excommunicated, and the whole thunders of the Church would be launched against them.

"The captain of that band was one who cared not for the Church. He defied it and laughed at its power, and led his men on to the attack.

"The night was dark, and the rain fell lightly; it was suitable for such a purpose, and the robbers left their cavern in the Black Forest, and made for the cathedral.

"Some hours elapsed before they reached it. Mass was being celebrated at midnight upon some grand and solemn occasion, and the building was filled with churchmen, and there were many lights burning.

"This was unexpected, and there was a general pause among the robbers, and a consultation as to what should be done, and how the attack should be conducted; for some thought of going back empty-handed.

"The captain divided his men into three companies of fifty each,—one to enter each of the two doors, and the other to guard the doors, and the passages and the horses, while the others searched the building.

This having been done, the men were ordered to dismount, which they did quietly, and then the whole of the appointed number presented themselves in the body of the church, to the consternation of the priests and the terror of all who were present.

The captain of the band advanced to the altar, and began to strip it of its ornaments, its golden candlesticks, altar service, and the valuables belonging to the churchmen.

The consternation at this sacrilege and impiety was so alarming, that people sat immoveable, and looked on, until a venerable archbishop threw himself in the way, and interposed himself between the robbers and their booty.

He was cast down and trampled upon by the robbers, but he again arose, and said, in a voice that made the whole cathedral ring again—

"Sacrilegious wretches! you are despoiling the altar of your God, and you will reap the bitter reward of your crimes; the curses of the Church cling to you, go wherever you will; this gold and silver shall be your destruction, and you," he added, pointing to the captain of the band, "and you shall live many years to see and repent, in all the bitterness of your heart, the deed you now commit. Work your will, you are digging a pit for your own feet."

The robbers laughed at the churchman, and held up their booty in derision.

The wine that had been brought for altar-service was quaffed in huge goblets by the robbers, out of golden cups, to the health of the churchmen and the monks, until it was gone, and then the word was given to quit the church, and remount their horses.

The robbers strode throu h the venerable church, their armour clanking at their heels as they went along. The archbishop's niece, a beautiful girl, was in one of the pews, and the daring chief strode up to her, saying, he would salute her for her uncle's sake, as he had given them so many good words.

He kissed the trembling girl, and then walked out with his men, laughing at the occurrence.

They remounted, each man leaving a portion of the booty, which was heavy and cumbersome, for the quantity of plate was very great, for there had been much brought there from other places, as there had been a festival appointed in that quarter.

Hence it was so large a quantity was brought together, and the whole of the robbers were heavily laden, on horseback, and rode slowly back.

In the meantime there arose a tremendous storm of wind and rain; it had rained when they started out, and that rain had fearfully increased during their march, and while they were in the church they had not noticed it, but now on their return they could not avoid it.

The storm you have seen to-day, but which has now abated, was little in comparison—the rain fell for hours in great quantities.

The fords were swollen and impassable.

The robbers expected this; and, when they came to the banks of the river, they hesitated about crossing; they said neither man nor horse could stem the current. To stop on that side would be to risk all the terrors of detection, and being hunted out by the powers of the State; and the captain said it was fordable. There was some altercation about it, and the men refused to cross. They said there were plenty of places in the forest where they could pass a day or two, until the river had fallen again.

The captain laughed at their fears, and said that he would go alone; and he at once plunged into the stream, and arrived safely on the other side, where he stood and looked at the men, and derided their fears and cowardice.

Seeing he had successfully crossed, they immediately plunged into the stream in a body, and attempted to stem the waters, which at that moment came down with increased force and volume; and every man was swept away and carried down the stream, from which, being encumbered with the plate, they could not escape—and all perished.

"And the captain," said Sir Giles, "what became of him?"

"He was saved."

"To continue in his career of impiety?"

"No, Sir Knight; no, he lived to repent, in all the bitterness of his heart, the impiety which he had been guilty of. He lived for years, to remember the words of the churchman—to pray for the souls that were lost in the Rhine, and to hope for forgiveness in himself, and he yet lingers out a solitary and a wretched life."

"He yet lives ——?"

"Yes, Sir Knight, he now lives a repentant sinner."

"I should like to see him," exclaimed Sir Giles.

"You see him then before you," said the hermit.

"You the robber-chief," said the knight; "you!"

"Yes; I am he. Pray for me, Sir Knight: pray for the soul of one whose hour will soon arrive; but who, if he had a hundred lives, could not live long enough to repent sufficiently."

*   *   *   *   *   *   *

The storm had abated, the sun shone, and the birds sang, as the knight and his two attendants rode on, in their forest-path, deeply meditating upon the hermit's tale.

"There," said John Atchet, "I have done. Now, don't you think it was vastly amusing?"

There was no answer returned to the words of the poor author, who looked up and saw that Marian Whitehead had relapsed into a settled gloom, and she had most probably been so ever since the beginning of his tale. This was not gratifying, but John's self-love, as we have seen, was not easily wounded; at all events, the wound was not deep, and his natural goodness of heart was sure to find an excuse for it.

"Poor thing!" said he to himself, as he gazed upon her, while she was unconscious of what was passing in his own mind, "poor thing! grief has taken hold of her, and done almost its worst. I don't think death itself, after the loss of mind, can be making matters worse; though some people are so fearful of death, that they think anything better."

Let life be ever so wretched, ever so miserable, ever so painful, yet they tell you life is life, though your own senses will tell you it is not capable of producing one good or one solitary pleasure, nay, one hour's cessation from pain or sorrow.

But Marian became more communicative. She told the unfortunate author the misfortunes that had befallen her mother, whom she mourned. She related all the villany that had been practised against her; but yet she could not go any further than the escape of Ormond. She firmly believed that Ormond still lived

With the account of the death of Charles Ormond, and many of the incidents that were connected with the trial of the unfortunate young man, he could well perceive that Marian's mind was unsettled by the events.

However, he would not attempt to undeceive her in that respect, because, as he said to himself, it can do no good if it could be done; but he thought that if he could obtain some documents she said she had, he should be able to place the whole in a connected form.

"It is growing late," he said to Marian; "and I will bid you good night; but, depend upon it, you will be much the better for rest."

"Alas!" said Marian, "the only rest I could have, with any happiness, would be the rest that has so unhappily become the lot of my poor and afflicted mother."

"There, now, you cannot mean what you say. You would not desire that for yourself which you would mourn as an evil for your mother, would you?"

"I would only desire it when all was lost," said Marian, mournfully; "and have I not lost her?"

"But," said John Atchet, "you have forgotten Charles Ormond: you would leave him."

"Heaven above knows," she sighed, "as to whether I shall ever again see him —I may never do so, though I strive daily to meet him, but I have not been able to find him yet; nothing has hitherto staid me."

"No, no, I dare say not; but don't you think you ought to have recourse to some other means of letting him know—Charles Ormond, I mean—how you have endeavoured to find him out; how you have daily sought him in this great city?"

"How can it be done?" said Marian. "I feel my health is much worse; I am weak, and know not one day from another that I may not become a victim to the wickedness of Godfrey and his dreadful associate Neville."

"Then permit me," said the poor author, good-naturedly, "to write your memoirs—make a book of 'em, you know, so that in some future period, when you desire it, you can leave behind you the memorial of what you have done for the sake of Charles Ormond ; you would, perhaps, prepare the only means of letting him know how you had acted, and how you had striven to meet him. It might fall into his hands."

" So it might," murmured Marian, and she relapsed into silence, and seemed to ponder over the proposal.

" You have papers and matters relative to all these things you have told me ?"

" I have some, certainly, and some memorandums that I made at different times."

" If you will let me have them, I will write the memoir for you, and you can tell me what you wish altered, and that will form many an hour's amusement in reading and correcting the writing under your own eye."

" It shall be done," muttered Marian ; " while I live I will do what remains to be done. I will daily visit the most conspicuous places in London and search for him, and it may be, I shall yet find him ; and should I not do so, I will leave the means, should he ever meet it, of knowing that I have never forgotten him."

" Exactly," said Atchet ; " you act very wisely. You may depend upon it this is much better than giving way to grief, which, though you cannot shake yourself free of, you will find only makes you incapable of doing what you desire to be done under the circumstances."

Thus did John Atchet good-naturedly endeavour to employ the mind of the unfortunate Marian Whitehead, and prevent her from dwelling too deeply upon the loss of her parent, the last and sole relative she had.

This was a service that was but little appreciated, for Marian was scarce able to take notice of anything of the sort ; to him she became more communicative than to any one else, which was proof enough she at least felt, if she knew not enough to acknowledge it, that she was indebted to him for some friendly condolence. At such a moment, too, it was doubly welcome ; for, where the passions are divided, or where they are exerted upon different objects, it may be presumed that either may be more easily diverted than they would be if centred into one focus, as it were, and turned upon one object alone.

Marian was in this condition ; but her grief, though for more than one individual, was great, her sorrows were excited for more than one object ; but still it was but one class of feeling. However, her state of mind being of that character, she could be occasionally turned from deep and continued sorrow by reverting to the great object of her existence—the future meeting with her lover, whom she devoutly believed to be hidden in London.

CHAPTER LIX.

THE FUNERAL OF MRS. WHITEHEAD.

THUS passed several days—John Atchet doing all that lay in his power to alleviate the wretchedness and sorrow that enshrouded her heart ; his good nature, together with his oddity, serving more effectually to beguile the time than perhaps any other who might have been deemed better calculated to fill the post of comforter under affliction.

However, the best proof that he could receive, under the circumstances, was the fact that she listened to him, and this was all he sought to obtain. He would talk to her about Charles Ormond, when he saw her bending over the body of her mother with anguish and sorrow, and which thus unostentatiously drove her to speak and think of those objects in which she yet had hope ; and thus he was of service to the poor and forlorn Marian.

While the body was in the room, however, and the black coffin lay upon trussels, it was impossible to keep Marian from grieving over the body of her parent, especially when the friendly but poverty-stricken author was no longer by her side to draw her away by any sudden inquiry upon the one object of her life; then she would shed bitter tears of grief and regret for the loss of her who had so long been her only affectionate parent and friend.

The evening before the funeral took place, John Atchet came down from his apartment, as he was wont to term an apology for a garret, which he inhabited, and found Marian more than usual depressed, sitting by the fire, and shedding tears bitterly.

The poor author had some chops in his hand, and he came, in fact, to cook them by the fire that Marian had in her room, for he had none.

"Oh!" he said, "you are in tears, Miss Whitehead? Well, never mind, it may be all the better by-and-by; sunshine after a shower, you know."

Marian shook her head.

"You don't believe it, eh? Well, well, then there is no truth in the old saying! You are not to be eclipsed in that manner. I tell you what, Miss Whitehead, you mustn't grieve so much as this."

"I have lost my mother!" said Marian simply, but pathetically; "need I say more? I could not have a truer or more affectionate friend."

"I can easily see that," said Atchet; "but I have come to cook my chops, if you please—I see you have a nice fire—with your permission, Miss Whitehead?"

Without waiting for any reply—as if he were in the habit of doing so—he walked to the coal cupboard and took out a gridiron, which, having duly wiped, he placed upon the fire, and then placed his chops upon that.

John Atchet was very serious during the operation of cooking, which he tended with great assiduity and with a watering mouth as each morsel in its turn had a share of his attention, and then he consigned the whole to a plate.

Then taking a plate and knife out of the cupboard he at once proceeded to place upon it a very choice morsel, and placing it before Marian, he said—

"Come, Miss Whitehead, if you please, you must taste some of my chops; I know they are good, and I know you have not troubled yourself about food, and I will talk to you the while."

For some time Marian refused to eat, but the good-natured solicitations of Atchet prevailed, and she was induced to partake of the poor fellow's fare.

He made himself familiar and at home with the unfortunate Marian, and had he been a brother, or an elder female relative, he seemed to have little notion that there needed any peculiar kind of conduct on his part; his familiarity was that of a brother.

When he had finished his supper, he said to Marian, as she sat mournfully gazing on the fire:—

"When is the funeral to take place?"

"To-morrow," was her brief answer; and then she relapsed into the same sorrowful silence she was indulging in.

"Oh, well, there will be time enough between this and then, but the sooner it is over the better; you will find that when this sad ceremony is over, and a few weeks gone by, you will be much better."

"I never can forget the past—I have lost all."

"You have, certainly, and I would not say you have no occasion for grief, for I know you have; but still, self-preservation teaches us we ought not to indulge in it to our own injury, which I think you do."

"I cannot grieve less."

"Well," said Atchet, "I can't say anything about that, but who is going to follow with you?"

"No one that I know of," said Marian; "I shall be the only one that mourns her and the only one who will follow her to her last home."

"It will scarce be proper you should go alone," said Atchet, with some feeling, "there's no knowing the effect it may have upon you. You will, perhaps, require the assistance of some friendly hand—you had better not go."

"Not go?" said Marian, "I would not fail in following her : were I to omit doing so, I should believe I deserved all that I can experience, and that I may have to endure—yes, yes—I must and will go."

"As you please, of course ; but if you don't mind seeing me there, I'll go with you, and accompany you ; I will be a mourner with you ; nobody will know anything from the contrary, but will suppose I'm your brother."

Heaven save the mark ! There was not much affinity between the two ; there was a vast difference, not confined to the resemblance or non-resemblance of features, but even in air and manner ; not even in voice could there have been deemed anything that would have induced the slightest resemblance between them.

The poor author was lank and mean ; want, and a continual feeling of depression and dependence, had gone far to stamp the same upon his looks ; and, however free and good his heart might be, and certainly it was, it gave him but little promise in his personal appearance.

"Shall I go with you ?" he said. "I will take care of you, and you shall have the support of my arm. Besides, it will look better to have two mourners."

"Alas ! alas !" sighed Marian, "what have I done that my poor mother should be thus left to one so feeble and solitary as I am to perform the sad last offices required ?"

"Shall I come ?"

"If you please. I shall hardly require it, for I have seen so much misery and sadness that I shall not fail in what I have to do ; but I am grateful to you—you, as kind as though you were my brother."

"I mean to be so, if I can," replied Atchet. "I mean to be so, but I haven't got the means ; and, if you don't wish me to take care of you, I'll follow at a distance."

"Nay, I don't ask you to go," said Marian, turning and gazing in his face, with an expression which at once showed the sincerity of her feelings, "because you know it's a melancholy and sorrowful ceremony ; but if you wish you shall go with me, and I shall not be ungrateful for your friendly sympathy."

"Don't talk about that," said Atchet. "I am an observant man, and what I see on one occasion I may find cause to remember on another. I will go with you."

Here he began to consider some matters in his own mind, which he found expression for in the following manner, for he spoke out and began to talk to Marian, as though he were arguing the matter with her—

"Let me see, what shall I want? My clothes are black, you see, at least they were, and that's enough ; but I tell you what, I'll brush them up and make them look like new ; I know how to do it, for I have often done it. Then, as for a hat, when they lend me the band, it will look much better than it does now ; and my boots, with a little mending, will look quite new ; and I shall be quite respectable, and shall pass off very well."

Marian heard nothing of all this. She was deep buried in reflection ; and deep sighs, in spite of her efforts to prevent them, and an occasional tear fell from her pallid cheek, while her eyes would now and then steal towards the coffin in which her mother's body lay.

"Ah !" said Atchet, as he perceived her do this for about the thirtieth time "ah ! you mustn't give way to grief, you can't help it, I know ; but, at the same time, you mustn't do it, it won't do."

Thus he would talk sometimes, with no other result save that of filling up the time with something like conversation or chatter ; but, at the same time, he received no answer, and very often it was not even heard by the unfortunate being to whom it was addressed.

"When do you go to-morrow?" he said to Marian, inquiringly.

"At twelve o'clock."

"It's early," said the poor author ; "but so much the better—so much the better—won't the landlady go too?"

"I don't know, she has not said so," replied Marian, "and I don't expect she will."

"Oh! she's genteel, that is, after her own fashion; but I knew her when she kept a fourth-rate tripe-shop in the neighbourhood of Back-hill—that was in her husband's time. Ah! he was a careful man, I believe, and when he died she sold off and bought a larger concern, and now she owns a couple of lodging-houses."

"She has two, then?"

"Yes, this and next door; these people, who came from nothing, require an immense deal of swagger to keep it in sight, lest any one should not see it at first sight, and certainly I shouldn't I know, but they don't like it." Why, Lor' bless you! I recollect those girls—why, I have known those two go into a cellar to wash tripe, and make up bands of dogs' meat."

Again was Marian absent, and the information thus afforded her was lost entirely, so far as she was concerned; for she had not even heard the sound of his voice.

* * * * * * *

The day arrived at length when the body of her unfortunate mother was to be consigned to the earth, and when even the melancholy knowledge that, though dead, she was in the same room with her, was no longer afforded her.

It was a sad and gloomy day, and the more so to the senses of Marian, as she was well steeped to the lips in sorrow and grief, and too sad to receive comfort from any source. The attempts at comfort which were made by the undertaker came full upon her ears without producing any effect; she listened to him not, and remained standing by the corpse, and then threw herself upon it in the violence of her grief, and would not be persuaded to leave it.

"Well," said Atchet to himself and the undertaker—"well, this mustn't be, it will do no good, but much harm."

"It will, indeed," said the undertaker; "and worse than that, we shall be too late, and if not there in time the parson will not wait for us, and there will be a pretty to do."

"What would be the consequence of that?"

"Oh, we shouldn't get buried to-day," said the undertaker, gravely, "but have to wait for another day."

"Well, I would sooner wait for another day," said Atchet.

"But you want to be buried to-day, don't you?" he said, inquiringly.

"No, certainly, the corpse of poor Mrs. Whitehead we certainly wish to be buried, but I don't want to be buried at all; my time aint come I hope yet."

"Who said anything about burying you?" said the undertaker; "I didn't I'm sure."

"You said, 'we shouldn't get buried,' and I thought you included me; but screw away, and I will take care of Miss Whitehead."

As the poor author spoke, he lifted Marian from her mother's corpse, in an agony of tears and almost insensible. She endeavoured to resist the attempts to separate her from her deceased parent, but it could not be avoided, and Atchet took her away.

The undertaker's men soon put the screws into the coffin, and there was no more seen of the inanimate remains of the unfortunate mother.

"Now, Miss Marian," said Atchet, kindly, "do hold up, and pass through the ceremony without any excess. Remember you will do yourself much mischief; and it will be looked upon with cold indifference, or matter of mere curiosity, by strangers. And more—it may, in some measure, go to interfere with the very occasion you are called upon to follow; for you may cause, by delay, a refusal to bury your mother."

"I will—I will do my utmost," said Marian, "to be calm; but, alas! I feel the parting now more than ever. All the sorrow and loneliness that can be felt will now be mine."

"Nay, take it not to heart; you will be better by-and-by, and the event must have happened. It is hard to lose such a friend, but you cannot avoid it," said Atchet.

Thus did the poor fellow endeavour to soothe her, and in some measure succeeded in doing so; and when they were ready to leave the house the undertaker acquainted Atchet with the fact.

"Have you far to go?" inquired Atchet.

"Only to St. Mary's church, close by, it won't take a quarter of an hour to go."

"So much the better."

The undertaker nodded, and said in a low tone,

"I hope there won't be any bother when we get to the church—that it will be all right, and the young woman won't go into any fits, faintings, and vagaries."

"The young woman,'" said Atchet angrily, "has more sense than a dozen undertakers, and more feeling than all the trade put together; and you may, therefore, reckon you'll have no trouble or bother at all; you'll have your money, and that's all you care about. I wish I could earn mine as easily."

"I'll give you work," said the undertaker, "you'd make a very good mute at a door."

"And you'd make a good figure under a cross-beam and a halter; but move on with the funeral, we are ready."

This little interlude was carried on between the two in a tone that was not above a whisper, and in a few minutes more, the hats and cloaks being adjusted, the body was placed on the shoulders of the bearers, and proceeded down-stairs until they came into the street, followed by Marian and her good-natured escort.

There was no one else following save Marian Whitehead, and the unfortunate, but good-hearted John Atchet; the latter had taken the arm of Marian within his own, and well for her he did so, for she was so weak, and so dimmed was her sight, that she would have fallen to the ground.

The slow-measured pace which they trod through the streets gave ample time to think and brood over the sad end so common to humanity, as that which the unfortunate Mrs. Whitehead had just succumbed to.

The fate we must all meet seems to cause an extraordinary share of grief among the tenacious; they all know they must one day or other submit to the same thing, and bewail in anticipation the evil they dread.

Be it as it may, it ought now to be familiar to men's minds, as a thing that must happen, and not to be mourned as a misfortune and evil, unless premature or some cause helps to usher the person off before their natural day.

In the meanwhile, they approached the church-yard, and arrived in due season at its gates, and then proceeded until they met with the surpliced individual, who utters the well-known ritual, which he has by heart, and which he says for pay, and then he has done with it.

CHAPTER LX.

THE MEETING IN THE STREET.—THE LIKENESS.—THE PITYING STRANGER.

THE appearance of confirmed mania which poor Marian presented was such as to awaken in every sympathetic breast the most painful feelings of emotion. Those who watched her closely, and who from previous habits or study were enabled to come to correct opinions with regard to such subjects, shook their heads, with a mournful but thorough conviction of the hopelessness of ever again restoring that still young and still beautiful being to what she once was.

Yes, still beautiful we say, because, although there was but visible what might be called the wreck of her former beauty, there was sufficient of it remaining to show what she once had been.

No one could look upon her as she moved along with that sad and noiseless step, without speculating deeply as to the cause which had prostrated her in wretchedness.

The most indifferent observer could not but perceive that she owed her fixed and sad appearance much more to circumstances than to time. A passing glance was sufficient to enable any one to observe, that, had all gone pleasantly with her, she would have been a being of glorious aspect, and one in whom some of the choicest and most admirable beauties of the mind and person would have been combined.

But none knew the deep excess of mental affliction that at times came over her, although those with whom she preserved an intimacy guessed something of such a painful fact.

We shall gather best the opinion which was entertained of her at this period, by those who knew her well and wished her well, by listening to some remarks of the physician to Mr. Blake, in answer to an observation of the latter, which contained a feeling of regret that Marian Whitehead should have lapsed into the state of insanity which was evidently hers.

"Do not regret it," said the physician, "but rather join with me now in regretting that she has any lucid intervals."

"Indeed! do you regret, then?"

"I do most sincerely and deeply, for it is during then that she suffers. Can you not feel that it is a great mercy she should forget, even though lapsing into what we call insanity, those matters, the truths concerning which must be full of the most painful thought? Is it not a happy thing, if in imagination she can still persuade herself that Charles Ormond lives? Why should we wish that she should be awakened from a delusion that at all events brings with it hopefulness, and some considerable portion of joy? Again, I say, therefore, that it is in lucid intervals we ought to pity her, and not in those during which such strange fancies take possession of her."

"I cannot, of course," said Mr. Blake, "say that I consider you wrong, for there is too much abundant reason in what you urge, and henceforward I shall look with a less pang of regret upon that hallucination of intellect which makes poor Marian what she is."

"She is now, in the words of one who knew human nature well,

'The queen of a fantastic realm;'

but if that fantasy presents to her any image of consolation, let us rather consider it a merciful dispensation of a watchful Providence than a calamity; and much as insanity is to be deplored, viewing it as a disease, yet in some cases a partial mania appears to be but an adaptation of the mind to circumstances."

"You reconcile me much," said Mr. Blake, "to poor Marian's condition. It is true that she has nothing to hope for, for even if Charles Ormond's innocence were to be thoroughly proved, the grave cannot be made to give up again its dead, and injustice once perpetrated becomes an eternal fact. I expect her to visit me this morning, and near about this hour, too."

"I should like to see her, and will wait as long as convenience will serve me."

The attorney had given orders that whenever Miss Whitehead called she should be announced to him, and at this moment now he was informed she was waiting.

He ordered her instantly to be shown into the apartment where he was conversing with the physician, and that was the first time they had seen her with the artificial colour upon her cheeks, that afterwards became one of her chief characteristics.

There was an appearance of cheerful hopefulness upon her countenance, which any one could have perceived at a first glance, but a second would have been quite sufficient to proclaim to the observer, that it was that sort of hopefulness which arises, not from anything tangible, but from the chimera of a mind diseased.

What she said, therefore, could only have a melancholy interest—such an interest as attaches to even the wanderings of an intellect once of a high and beautiful order.

She approached Mr. Blake, and touching him gently upon the arm she addressed him in a voice which sounded most musically, saying—

"It is very fortunate that I find you within, for even moments may be precious when a human life is at stake."

Then turning to the physician she greeted him kindly, adding—

"Another friend too! I am indeed much favoured this morning. I shall get you both to sign at once."

"Sign what, Marian?" said Mr. Blake.

"Nay, you will not hesitate; the course of mercy is always a great and a good one. You know what is said of that quality by one who scarcely ever wrote a word in vain—'Mercy is like the gentle dew from heaven.'"

"It is indeed, Marian, and when I asked you what you wished us to sign, it was from curiosity, and not from an indisposition to accede to your request."

"I have it here," she said; "it is a petition for the life of Charles Ormond. It states that Godfrey is a villain, and that Neville, too, has done his best, by false testimony, to destroy the innocent. I must get many signatures to it; and when it is seen how many good and just men believe in his innocence he must be saved, and all will be well."

"What shall I do?" said Mr. Blake, in a whisper to the physician.

"Do sign it, by all means."

"It would be cruel to reason with her upon such a subject."

"That indeed it would;" let her hug to her mind the delusion that he still lives and may be saved, and let it be, as it will assuredly be, a continued source of consolation and of occupation to her, that she is doing something for Charles Ormond's liberation."

"Be it so, poor thing! who can wish her to live in such a state as this?"

"And this species of insanity wages no war against life, because, you perceive, it arises from purely mental causes, and not from a diseased brain."

"I understand the difference—it is marked and clear."

"Will you sign the petition?" said Marian, earnestly.

She unfolded it for their perusal, and they found that it contained a touching statement, to the effect that Charles Ormond was innocent of the crime imputed to him, and that, in the villany of Godfrey solely was to be found those causes which had led to his condemnation to death.

It was addressed to the king—that king who had so little of the god-like mercy in his composition, and it ended with an earnest appeal that Charles Ormond should be at once liberated from his prison, and enabled in peace and happiness to join his friends.

This mournful and touching petition was signed by herself, and it had evidently only been produced that morning. They could see her eyes glisten with pleasure as they affixed their signature to it, and then, on folding it up, she said with a quiet gentleness of manner—

"He will be saved now, he will surely be saved, and all may be well. We shall be very happy, so happy that we shall be able almost to forgive Godfrey the evil that he has done to us. In the cottage home when first we met, when Charles came to warn us of the evil that was intended, we shall pass long joyous hours, and then the past, which has had in it anything of misery or of wretchedness, shall be all forgotten, and shall present nothing but at times a felicitous remembrance, for the purpose of making the present happiness still greater by the power of contrast. I thank you, gentlemen, I thank you."

"And do you think," said the physician, "that you shall procure the pardon of Charles Ormond?"

"I must. Is it not here put down that Godfrey is a villain, and has wrongfully accused him; why then should Charles Ormond, who is innocent, suffer? How dare any king refuse to hear the truth? He must and will be saved; and, what is more strange than all—a fact which, to some extent, may excite your wonder—is, that I am to meet him in the vaults of St. Paul's. I do not know how we came to think of such a place; but that is to be the place of meeting by arrangement: and now farewell!"

She left them; and for some moments after she was gone Mr. Blake and the physician remained silent.

"Poor thing!" at length said the former; "I do hope now that no one will set about convincing her of what to her must be a terrific fact, namely, the execution of Charles Ormond. Did you remark how well pleased she seemed when we signed the paper?"

"She did, indeed, poor thing; but let us believe there is sufficient kindness in human nature to induce every one who sees her, and to whom she may prefer her request, to sign the petition. By such delusions she may rob the unhappy circumstances in which she is placed of their worst anguish; and, take my word for it, you will find that this is not the first nor the last of the petitions of Marian Whitehead in favour of one who, alas! is already far past all human aid."

"I fear not; but let her come here when she will I will humour the delusion, if it be but for a moment to see her wear that look of quiet hopefulness which beamed upon her face when she now left us."

*   *   *   *   *   *

We cannot but perfectly agree with the physician that the delusion under which Marian laboured was far more to be desired in its continuance than as if her intellect had withstood the shock of Charles Ormond's death, and she had lived on without a solitary hope to illumine the dreariest void of her existence.

If there be ever such a thing as a happy delusion, this of Marian Whitehead's was one ; and whether her years be few or many, it was a delusion calculated at all events to make them pass more pleasantly.

When she left Mr. Blake, she proceeded towards the City, for the purpose of calling upon the bankers upon whom the forgery had been committed, for the purpose of obtaining the signature of that firm to her petition ; and she was introduced to the old gentleman who was the senior partner, and who perceived at once the sad delusion under which she was labouring.

He had a scruple about signing the petition, even to humour her, which had not occurred to Mr. Blake or the physician, and that scruple was that it contained a direct and positive libel upon Godfrey ; so the old man said to her, with kindness in his looks and in his tones,—

" I cannot sign this ; but I will write a letter to the King, which will be all the same thing, you know."

This assurance satisfied her ; and she left well pleased with her interview, and glided along the streets towards her own home with that strange, odd manner and aspect that made her eventually so well known to the residents of London.

Many persons turned and looked after her in the streets, and some remarked to each other upon the strange facts of her history.

" She went mad," said a man, " because a young man to whom she was to be married was hanged for forgery. Don't you remember Ormond being hung at the Old Bailey ?"

" Oh, yes, I recollect," said another, " but I heard he was her brother, and had been a clerk in the Bank of England."

" No," said a third ; " you are both of you misinformed. They were married, that's the fact, and the forgery he was hung for was committed years ago. Her real name aint Whitehead at all, as some people say."

" Then what is it ?"

" Why, Godfrey, to be sure ; I have had it from an authentic source, and I can assure you altogether it is a most mysterious affair."

Such were a few of the contradictory rumours and reports which were circulated concerning this harmless, persecuted being—reports, each of them containing some portion of truth, but mixed up with so large a portion of falsehood and exaggeration as seemed quite wonderful, considering the very recent nature of the circumstances.

But she, little heeding what was thought or said of her, and little supposing that she was an object of attention, walked quickly on, But what new delusion now comes over her—she pauses and fixes her eyes upon one individual who has turned to look upon her with pitying curiosity. He is a man who has evidently seen much travel, but there is an expression on his face which has caught Marian Whitehead's attention—an expression which she cannot pass unnoticed, because it brings to her mind vividly the countenance of Charles Ormond.

She sprang forward and seized the man by the arm, exclaiming—

" You are not Charles, but your name is Ormond !"

" It is," he said, " and you are the unfortunate Marian Whitehead, of whom I have heard and read so much."

" Speak again," she exclaimed, " oh, speak again. Your voice is like his, and there are some of its tones that strike upon my ear like the memory of music heard long—long ago. Speak to me again, I pray you !"

" Alas !" said the stranger, " what a sad wreck is here !"

" Yes," she said, " yes, once more I seem to hear his tones. Go on, go on, I would listen to you the whole day and not seem tired of those accents."

"Take my arm," said the stranger, "I have much to say to you, and much information to gather from you, I hope. My name is Ormond, and there must be, although I was not aware of the fact, a striking likeness, I presume, between me and the Charles Ormond in whose fate you are so deeply interested."

She took his arm at his request, and heedless of the remarks of the bystanders, some of which were of a heartless and jeering character, he walked with that poor sad being along the public streets. As he went he spoke to her kindly, saying—

"I have heard something of your history, and in order that you may place confidence in me I will tell you who I am. My name is Ormond, and from family circumstances I am aware that the Charles Ormond in whom you are so deeply interested is my nephew. He is the son of a sister of mine, but as early in life, when quite a wild roving lad, I went to sea, and finally settled in Canada, I heard nothing of my family, and probably cared little; for by my own conduct in early life I had estranged them from me, and that begot estrangement on my part in return, so that I never made an inquiry."

"Oh, you should have known him," said Marian, "you should have known Charles—a being so full of high and noble sentiments, that he seemed more of heaven than of earth."

"The first thing that awakened me to a feeling that I should like—and I ought to hold some sort of communication with those who were akin to me—arose from the fact of reading in the English papers an account of the accusation against one Charles Ormond of forgery. A very strong impression came across my mind from the first moment that it was some relative of my own, and hour by hour I grew more anxious concerning his fate. At last, unable to endure suspense, I made up my mind to come to England, and although I could not have hindered his fate had I been here sooner, I found that I was too late even to make an effort to ward off the final catastrophe."

Marian looked at him with a confused air for a few moments, and then she cried, "Why should we not save him yet?"

"Save him yet!"

"Yes; I know there are some who will pretend to you that he is dead; but how can that be, when in dreams I look upon him? He is not dead; or he could not thus revisit me in the still hours of night."

"Alas!" said the stranger, in a low tone to himself, "I now perceive that her insanity, of which I was informed, is a melancholy truth; but if I am too late to save my kinsman from the fate which so unjustly has been his, I may not be too late to avenge him, and to accomplish that task I will now bend all my energies, and from this poor creature, even in her blighted state, I shall doubtless gather sufficient information to enable me to proceed."

"Yes," said Marian, as if she was pursuing some train of thought which she had not previously given utterance to—"yes, I have the key. They have kindly given me the key that opens the small door in the cathedral, and there I am to wait for him; and he will surely come."

"What door, what key?"

"Of the vaults of St. Paul's. Charles is to meet me there, and the light of love is to be so refulgent and so beautiful, that those dim homes of the dead shall look most glorious, and full of majesty and beauty. It is not the glitter of gilding, nor the richness of superb hangings, that shall truly make a palace; for if the heart be overclouded with gloom its shadow will be cast over all objects, while the poorest home that ever sheltered a human being from the elements may become most glorious and beautiful, if contentment has erected its altar beneath the humble thatch."

"Is this insanity?" said the stranger. "Can this be a disordered intellect? and yet I have heard that persons so afflicted will often, with a marvellous aptitude, hit upon truths that will escape those whose intellects are considered to be perfectly correct. Addressing her then in the same kindly tone he had before used, he said—

"What I want from your lips is, a distinct and clear relation of all that has occurred in respect to Charles Ormond. I want you to tell me every minute circumstance, even, because I am anxious to be able to come to a correct conclusion; my means are not great, but still they are sufficient to enable me to take up this cause warmly. The argument which may be used to me, that exertion now is useless, shall not sway me; there shall be time for retribution and for justice against the guilty, although the innocent may not share in the triumph."

"You shall know all; you have something of the face and much of the voice of Charles; kindred blood, you tell me, flows in your veins, and I will trust you. Come with me, and if there be any point in the sad history that I shall relate to you upon which you may desire more information than I shall impart, you must speak of it, so that I may know at what points to enlarge my narrative and where to condense it. We shall save Charles Ormond yet!"

CHAPTER LXI.

THE PROCEEDINGS OF MR. THOMAS ORMOND AGAINST NEVILLE, AND THEIR RESULT.

It was not altogether a strange and unaccountable accident, as at first sight it would appear, that meeting between Marian and the relative of Charles Ormond.

He had been but a day in London, and during that time he had been able to make inquiries of a nature that fully enabled him to understand what had occurred as regarded Marian. He was told of the accession of insanity that had come over her since the execution of Charles Ormond, and her singular dress and appearance now in the public streets were described to him, so that he could have no difficulty in recognising her; but no one could tell him where she actually resided, and therefore was it that he was walking in the City, with the express hope of recognising her—a hope that, as we have seen, was not disappointed. Although he felt, of course, that there was no expectation whatever of benefiting poor Marian, except by aiding others to keep from her the pressure of want, yet, with the natural feelings of a man of strong impulses, he was determined upon punishing, as much as it was possible for him to do, those who had so disgracefully leagued themselves together for the destruction of an innocent man.

"If," he said to himself, "if I really become convinced that the prosecutor, Godfrey, is the villain I suspect him, and if I find that he and his associate have managed matters so well that public justice cannot reach them, they shall certainly not escape private vengeance."

He listened with the most marked and deep attention to all that Marian related to him, and the facts were so clear and distinct, that he did not doubt for a moment that Charles Ormond had been made a sacrifice of completely, and that he was one of the, let us hope, very few persons indeed who in this country have lost their lives judicially, although entirely ignorant of any crime which should entail upon them such consequences.

He took the address of Mr. Blake and went at once to him, where he got a confirmation of what Marian had related.

"It does happen," said Mr. Blake, "that there are things which we fully believe, and, indeed, actually known, but which we are not in a position to prove. The innocence of Charles Ormond and the culpability of his accuser rank under that head."

"Alas! so it seems."

"You can scarcely suppose that without a full and entire conviction on my own mind of the innocence of Charles Ormond, I would have made the great effort I did to save him—an effort which compromised me much professionally, and has really done me a deal of harm, besides exposing me to the chance of a serious State prosecution."

"Then, sir, you fully believe with me, that my relative is a murdered man?"

"I have not the shadow of a doubt upon the subject."

"Gracious Heavens! can such things be in a highly civilized country such as this?"

"They can; and it strikes me, if you consider the subject well, you will come to the conclusion that although rare it is in a highly civilized country they are likely to occur, because you perceive that, in the administration of the laws, everything must go upon evidence."

"I see all that; but still I swear that neither the villain Neville, nor Godfrey, shall escape entirely free in this affair."

"Be careful what you do. You have bold, bad men to deal with, and if all that I hear be correct, Godfrey has already entailed upon himself sufficiently enough to satisfy any one."

"Then it shall be my endeavour to discover Neville. I look upon it that I have a sacred obligation to perform, as regards my relative Charles Ormond, and I must and will do it. Can you give me any information as to where Neville can be found?"

"Indeed I cannot; Godfrey's house is well known, and it is possible that there you might acquire some information."

"It shall be tried; and, at all events, nothing shall be wanting, on my part, to let that villain see that there is yet a retribution which may yet overtake him."

With renewed exhortations from Mr. Blake to do nothing rash, Mr. Thomas Ormond, for that was the name of Charles's relation, left the attorney with the address of Godfrey, and with the resolution to make an inquiry of that person's servants concerning Neville—an inquiry which he thought might be successful, if he backed it by a cogent reason in the shape of a bribe.

He walked direct to Godfrey's house, and as he reached it he saw some altercation going on at his door between some man and the servants. Before he reached the threshold the street-door was slammed to, leaving the man on the outside with whom the quarrel had been taking place.

He was a ferocious-looking individual of sinister aspect, and as he shook his clenched fist at the house he muttered such curses as were amply sufficient to convince any one of what a ruffian he was.

"So," he said, "Godfrey has put you upon your guard, has he, and given you all your orders not to admit me across the threshold? Be it so—I shall be revenged for all that—the time will come when with safety to myself I will do something, as sure as my name is Neville."

"Indeed!" said Mr. Thomas Ormond, as he shrunk back; "this, then, is the man I seek. He knows me not; and I will follow him, let him go where he may."

Neville still lingered some few moments, pouring forth bitter invectives. Perchance he thought that by getting into Godfrey's house he should have been enabled to appropriate something to his own use, and no doubt he would have done so, but that the servants were too much upon their guard to allow him. Then he turned away, and walked rapidly from the place, till he came to the corner of the street, when he paused irresolutely for a few seconds, as if he had not quite made up his mind which way he meant to proceed.

Then, however, he came to a fixed resolve, and muttering between his teeth words which Mr. Thomas Ormond could not catch, he walked rapidly on towards the Edgeware-road, up which he proceeded for about two miles, and then turning down a lane he paused at a low-looking public-house and entered it.

Mr. Ormond waited about a quarter of an hour, so that it should not appear as if he had closely followed him, and then he strolled up to the door of the little public-house and sat down upon a seat which was outside it.

He had not been there many minutes when a boy came to know what he required, and ordering some simple refreshment, he resolved, at whatever cost of time it might be, that he would wait until Neville made his appearance again.

In about an hour the ruffian came forth, and scarcely casting the slightest glance upon Mr. Thomas Ormond, who by drawing his hat over his forehead and pulling up his cravat had as much as possible destroyed the remarkable likeness he bore to Charles, his nephew, he walked still down the lane towards the open country.

Much wondering, then, what sort of expedition he was upon, Mr. Thomas Ormond followed him at such a distance that, while he could just keep him in sight, he avoided the suspicion that would have arisen had he too closely dodged his footsteps. After proceeding for about an hour in this way, during which, however, not more than three miles of country were traversed, Neville stopped at what appeared to be the wall of some extensive plantations or grounds belonging to a mansion, the windows of which could be just seen glittering among the trees as they caught the slant rays of the setting sun, for the evening was now rapidly advancing, and in a very short time gloomy shadows would overspread every object. Feeling convinced that Neville was somewhere near his place of destination, Mr. Thomas Ormond crossed the opposite hedge, and got into the meadow which skirted the lane. Then he ran along the soft grass until he came exactly opposite to where Neville was standing, and from whom the thick, tall foliage completely hid him.

He then saw that Neville was casting stones over the wall gently, as if with a view of giving a signal to some one who was within, and thus continued for some time without any reply, until at length one was cast from the inside, and then Neville leant his back against the wall, and crossing his arms upon his breast, seemed to make up his mind to wait patiently what might ensue.

Now the sun had completely sunk, and the sky, particularly towards the north and east, assumed a cold, leaden-like aspect, while a moaning wind swept among the trees, giving a melancholy aspect to the scene, which was only broken by occasionally the low, twittering noise of some bird as it retired to roost in the leafy covert of one of the gigantic trees that grew about the spot.

The spot was a romantic and a beautiful one, and one well calculated to awaken sad and serious reflections, as well as perceptions of the beautiful and the serene, in the minds of those capable of appreciating such feelings.

And still no one came to Neville, and he began to show evident signs of impatience. At length, however, just as he stooped to pick up some more stones for the purpose of repeating his signal, a small door in the wall was opened at some little distance off, and a short, stout man made his appearance. His face bore ample testimony to the fact of good living, and there was an angry look too about him, as if it were a great infliction to be compelled thus to make his appearance.

He walked directly up to where Neville stood, and when he reached him he exclaimed—

"God bless my heart and life, I thought I was never to see you any more!"

"Did you?" said Neville, "you are mistaken, you see; I don't like to give up old friends in that sort of way, it looks so shabby, I cannot think of doing it."

"Good God! what do you want now?"

"Well, that's not a very civil remark to make, after a fellow has walked all the way from London to see you; but I'll soon tell you what I want—I want money."

"I tell you I have none; look here—here's eighteenpence, and I tell you I have no more."

"But you have got money's worth, master butler; hand me out some more of the old heavy forks and spoons, or I shan't object to a silver candlestick or two—a dish-cover, or a soup tureen. Let's have no nonsense, but to business at once. We have done business in that way before, and I don't see why we should not do it again."

"I told you, the last time you were here, that I had gone to the utmost length I dared go in such transactions. There is only enough plate left now in the house for ordinary use, and I dare not take any more."

"I don't care for that, you must go a little further; I must have it, and will have it."

"Do you want me to take off the very tops of the pepper-castors?"

"You may take off or put on, just whatever you please. You have once begun to do business with me in that sort of way, and you shall go on."

" What ! to my destruction ? why, I tell you now, that if Sir George were to have a dinner-party, I really could not put plate enough upon the table for twelve people, and should have to take myself off at once."

" That's no excuse to me."

" I cannot and won't go any further : you may do what you like."

" Very well, I will do it, then. To-morrow morning I shall write a letter to your master, telling him to look over his plate and see what he has got of it and what is missing, and if he don't make some awkward discoveries for you, I must confess I shall be a little surprised."

" Hark ye," said the butler, " for God's sake listen to reason, and tell me what good it can possibly do you to ruin me in such a way ; I am quite surprised how a man of your judgment can think of such a thing."

" You may be surprised as much as you like ; I not only think of it, but mean to do it ; so you may please yourself as to the consequences."

" Good gracious ! if I give you something now, will you go away and never come back gain ?"

" Why, let me see, I think I will. Yes, agreed then, I will go away and not come back again ; I am hard pressed, and therefore content to make such a bargain ; but mind, I won't be put off with a trifle—it must be something worth my while."

" Well, well, I will do the best I can ; wait a little."

Working his hands up and down in a state of great perplexity, the butler, who at some former time had, no doubt, availed himself largely of the service of the ruffian Neville, in the disposal of plate and other matters, which he had stolen from his master, passed again through the small door in the wall, and disappeared from the observation of Mr. Ormond.

This gentleman at once decided in his own mind what he should do, and that decision was that he would follow Neville until they got near to town, and then at once attack him and take him into custody, for he was a bold and courageous man, and one of considerable physical power. as may guessed from the fact that he could at all contemplate such a mode of procedure.   He was armed though, and Neville probably was not ; that circumstance gave him increased confidence in his resources ; so, without wavering in the slightest from the resolution he had come to, he waited patiently until the butler reappeared.

In the space of about ten minutes this event took place, and that individual emerged once more from the small door in the wall, with something wrapped up in a towel or a dinner napkin.

" Here, then," he said to Neville, " here, you have positively all I can bring you, and, for all I know, they may be missed within twenty-four hours, and Heaven knows what may become of me."

" What the deuce do I care what becomes of you !" said Neville ; and, unwrapping the bundle, he saw that it contained some massive silver spoons and forks. " Well, this will do for the present."

" For the present !" cried the butler ; " you promised me that you would never come again."

" Oh, ah ! so I did. Well, you may depend upon me, I'll keep my word—so now good evening to you, and mind you make yourself comfortable."

The butler looked after him, and then muttered to himself—

" Make myself comfortable, indeed,—make myself comfortable ; yes, a likely job that I can do that, when such a vagabond feels himself at liberty to call upon me and walk off with some of the spoons and forks whenever he likes ; I shall never be comfortable again as long as I live, that's a fact."

As Neville walked rapidly down the lane, Mr. Ormond as rapidly followed him, only keeping on the other side of the hedge, so that he was not perceived, and could make very rapid way upon the villain ; indeed, he got some distance ahead of him, for it was somewhere near the top of the lane that he fully determined upon accosting him.   Accordingly, he got into the road from the hedge, about three or four hundred yards in advance of Neville, and then walked slowly forward to meet him.   As he drew near he took a pistol from his pocket, and when Neville, seeing the person before him, slightly slackened his pace and deviated considerably from the direct path in order to pass him, Mr. Ormond walked at once up to him, and, holding the pistol to his breast, said in a firm voice—

" You are my prisoner. I am not a man to be trifled with, and if I have any difficulty whatever in getting you along alive, I will shoot you, as sure as you now draw the breath of life."

" Who are you?" said Neville, stepping back and gazing fixedly upon Mr. Ormond's countenance, " I have seen that face before."

" You have seen one which, to all accounts, I understand is like it. Now, hark ye, I am a man of few words, but of steady determination, and I now tell you frankly that I am resolved you shall not escape with impunity, after the rascally manner in which you have betrayed and hunted to death Charles Ormond. If you choose to come forward, and confess your own share in the transaction as well as implicating your associate, Godfrey, and take the consequences of so doing, my private vengeance shall be satisfied; but otherwise I tell you most distinctly, that I will have life for life."

"You would murder me?"

"It is not murder, but an act of justice. I would rid the world of a villain, who has already done more mischief than the whole remainder of his existence could set to rights. Scoundrel that you are, retribution has at last overtaken you—you may escape the law, but you shall not escape me!"

Neville seemed to be measuring his antagonist with his eye, to see what chance a personal encounter would give him, but he did not gather much of a cheering character from that examination, for Mr. Ormond, although a man as old as Neville himself, was by far the more powerful of the two, and one with whom to risk a personal contest would have been, on the part of Neville, an act of positive insanity.

"You are mistaken," he said; "what have I to do with Charles Ormond except as a witness? I was forced to give my testimony."

"You know that testimony was false. Will you walk with me to town quietly, and then write a full confession of your iniquity, or do you prefer being left here with a pistol bullet through your brain?"

"Death," said Neville, "would be no man's choice; if it must be so, I will follow you."

"No, you will go on before; and mark me, if you attempt to escape in an unfrequented place, I will shoot you; if you do so where there is plenty of assistance, I will give you into custody for stealing the plate you have now about you."

"Curses on me for a fool," said Neville, "that I should not have thought of being followed under such circumstances! And what's to be the consequences if I tell all?"

"Possibly your escape; for, villain as you are, I don't wish, if I can help it, to dip my hands in your blood."

"Will you promise me, then, that if I implicate Godfrey you will let me go?"

"I will promise nothing; but if you come to town with me to the hotel where I am staying, and make a full confession in writing of the guilt of Godfrey, I shall at all events consider it as one act of reparation."

"I will do that at the first public-house we come to, if you will let me go afterwards. You may have what witnesses you please to my signature; I will keep back nothing in my written statement."

"I have already made my conditions. Proceed onward, or you will exhaust the small amount of patience which a recollection of my kinsman's wrongs has left me."

Dreading, then, that on the impulse of the moment his captor should carry his threat into execution, and take summary revenge at once, by shooting him, Neville walked onward, cursing in his heart the unlucky chance that had brought him in the way of such a man, and revolving in his mind some means of escaping from so uncomfortable a train of circumstances. From our knowledge of Neville, we may be well assured that no scruples could intervene as to any means he might adopt to rid himself of the troublesome customer that had come across his path.

Gladly, and without a moment's hesitation, he would have taken the life of Mr. Thomas Ormond; but the difficulty—nay, the almost impossibility—of effecting anything against a man walking behind him with a loaded pistol, struck him too forcibly to be resisted; and he therefore was compelled, although in dogged silence, and with a heart full of the most desperate feelings, to proceed onward towards London.

It was not a very pleasant thing to have such a man as Neville in such custody; and as they went, Mr. Ormond thought it would be better to avail himself of the first opportunity of getting the written confession from him, so, when they came in sight of a public-house, he ordered him to halt, and spoke to him, saying—

"You shall write your confession here, and it shall be witnessed by some person belonging to this establishment. After that, I shall let you go for to-night; but I will make no promise that vigorous efforts shall not be made to apprehend you immediately."

"These are hard conditions," said Neville, "and not such as you ought to think of; besides, I think that I do quite enough by giving up Godfrey, and incurring possibly his vengeance, without being called upon to do more."

"I have made my conditions, and will abide them. You know, as well as I, that this plate robbery, of which you have been guilty, would be amply sufficient to transport you, and to secure me getting you into custody whenever I pleased. I saw the whole transaction, and there can be no difficulty about it."

Thus urged, Neville found that he had no excuse left, but at once entered the public-house, and Mr. Ormond, ordering a private room and writing materials, sat down along with the scoundrel he now considered he had so completely in his toils.

CHAPTER LXII.

THE WRITTEN CONFESSION AND THE MURDER.

THE people at the public-house looked rather amazed to see two men, evidently not upon friendly footing, enter and require a private room and writing materials. Moreover, they saw that there was a remarkable difference in their costume, for whereas Mr. Ormond had all the appearance and outward seeming of a gentleman, his companion, Neville, presented an aspect most decidedly the reverse in every respect, being such a compound of the blackguard of a large city and of a sea-port, that it was evident that some strange and unaccountable circumstances could alone bring those men together.

The room into which they were shown was at the back of the house, and overlooked a large, old, rambling-looking yard, in which was a haystack, as well as a great quantity of rubbish of one sort and another. Into this yard a large window opened on to a rudely-constructed balcony, which was not above twelve feet from the ground.

"I will take some refreshments," said Mr. Ormond to the waiter, who brought in an inkstand, some pens, and paper—"I will take some refreshments afterwards which shall compensate you for this trouble, but do not let me be interrupted until I ring."

When they were alone Mr. Ormond turned to Neville, and said—

"Now there are all the materials for writing, make use of them at once."

"I can only write my own name," said Neville, "but I will sign what you write after I have read it, and I suppose that will be the same thing."

"Will it? I almost doubt that; but, however, I will take care that there are plenty of witnesses to your knowledge of the contents of the paper, as well as your signature."

Mr. Ormond then sat down, and commenced writing rapidly and briefly a short statement, to the effect that he, Neville, and Godfrey, had conspired together to make it appear that Charles Ormond was guilty of that forgery, concerning which he was so entirely innocent; that they had sent him the cheque with the doubtful signature, which had caused him to be apprehended at the banking-house, and that the whole affair had been a conspiracy artfully planned, and most diabolically and artfully carried out for the purpose of hunting Charles Ormond to destruction, which they had thoroughly succeeded in doing.

As he wrote, Mr. Ormond warmed with the theme that employed his pen, and alas! he forgot that want of caution which he ought never to have forgotten in his intercourse with such a man as Neville, for the villain watching when his victim's attention was occupied so intently with the paper, as to be scarcely aware of any one else's presence, drew from his pocket a clasped knife, the long double-edged blade of which opened with a spring, so as to convert it into a formidable dagger.

Raising it then in his right hand behind Mr. Ormond, as he stood by his side, he pointed with his left to the writing, saying,—

"You use strong expressions, sir."

"But not stronger," said Mr. Ormond, "than the case will warrant. Were they the last I had to use in this world, I should not modify them in the least."

"They are the last," said Neville, in a hissing whisper, and, before Mr. Ormond could move or look, or utter the slightest sound, or even think what those words signified, the blade of the knife sunk into the back of his neck, and he fell forward on the paper with a half-stifled groan.

"It's done—curses on him, it's done!" said Neville. "He would have it, and, by all the furies, he has got it!"

It was but the work of a moment then to snatch up the half-finished confession, to thrust it into his bosom, and then proceed towards the window, with the knife in his hand, that was still reeking with his victim's blood. He opened the casement, and stepped out of the balcony. The night was pitchy dark, not a star twinkled in the sky, for masses of dark clouds obscured the whole of heaven's arch, and not an object was discernible in the yard of the inn. He knew, however, that they were but upon one flight of stairs, and, consequently, that the depth from the balcony to the garden, if the piece of lumbered and waste ground behind the house deserved such an appellation, could not be great.

He clambered over the balcony, and then dropped the distance, alighting in perfect safety; after which, he ran on until he was stopped by the haystack, and then a sudden thought seemed to strike him, that he had better get rid at once of the knife with which he had done the deed, and that he might look in vain for a more eligible place in which to conceal it than that haystack.

He made a plunge with the knife at the side of the stack, and sent it so completely in that it was altogether hidden, and then, patting the hay down over the slight orifice, he felt assured that, until the stack was cut, which might not be for a year or more, the knife would remain undiscovered.

By this time, his eyes had got more familiar with the darkness around him, and he could just distinguish, with some difficulty, one object from another; but this enabled him to go on without accident, and finally, after surmounting a low paling, he found himself in the open fields, lying to the westward of the Edgware-road, and pushed on at great speed, he cared not whither, so long as he succeeded in removing himself to a distance from the spot where he had committed his last great offence, which, although it had temporarily relieved him from the consequences of other matters, still left him with an increased catalogue of enormities to answer for when the day of retribution should really come.

And come it certainly would, notwithstanding such a villain as Neville might congratulate himself upon putting it off for a time. Sooner or later it must arrive, bringing in its train all the most fearful consequences that might be expected to accrue from an amount of guilt almost unparalleled in the history of iniquity.

* * * * * * *

"William," said the landlord of the public-house to the waiter, after nearly an hour had elapsed, "William, did those people in the private-room order no refreshments?"

"No, sir, they said they would have some, when they had transacted their business."

"Oh, very well, I suppose we must wait."

"Yes, sir, I suppose we must. One of them, sir, is a very gentlemanly man, but I certainly can't say as much for the other, who is a very so-so sort of personage."

Another half hour elapsed, and then the landlord again spoke as he drew a small glass of brandy for himself at the bar, and this time it was to his wife; he said—

"My dear, I don't feel at all comfortable; I am all of a shiver, and I don't know why."

"All of a shiver! why, what does the man mean? I declare you have given me quite a turn—a small drop—that will do."

"Something has been coming over me," said the landlord, as he drew a long breath, " for more than kalf an hour; I really feel about as uncomfortable as any-body I suppose could possibly expect to feel, without exactly knowing why."

" You don't say so! but what's it all about?"

" Why, somehow or another, I can't help thinking that something is queer up-stairs. William, just go and listen at the door!"

" I have, sir, but I can't hear nothing; I peeped through the key-hole too, sir, and all I can see is the candle, with a deuce of a long snuff, and one of them asleep with his head on the table."

" Ah! I can't stand that," said the landlord, " I must go up stairs and see what it's about. Come along, William, we will go and see, and as you know I put great faith and trust in you, I'll let you go first; what do you think of that?"

" I don't think much of it," said William ; " of course I feel the compliment, but I couldn't think of going afore you, sir ; no, sir, you shall go first and I will follow arter, always perwided as there aint any danger, cos if there is I would rather decline following at all."

" I am afraid, William, you are a coward?"

" You needn't be afraid, sir, for I have known it for a matter of thirty-two years. I only profess to be a waiter, and, taking that view of the subject, I don't see why I shouldn't be as great a coward as anybody that ever breathed."

" Well, I suppose I must go myself; a nice set I have got about me that's afraid of nothing at all. I am quite ashamed of you, William, quite—I really am—I wonder at you!"

" Very good, sir, you can go on wondering as long as you like. You know, sir, as well as I do, that there's two things I can't abide."

'Two things, William! what are they?"

" Why, one of them certainly is danger, sir, and the other of them is cold wittals; howsomdever, I don't mind carrying a light for you and following you."

"Come on, then—come at once, I am not going to have people staying two hours in a private room of the 'Red Lion and Mousetrap' for nothing."

Before he went, the landlord felt a strong inclination to draw himself another little drop from the brandy-tap, but as he considered, if he did so, William would think himself entitled to a similar indulgence, he overcame the temptation, and so saved both the drops. He then proceeded up the staircase, followed by William, holding a light as high as he could, till he came to the door of the private room, and which he tapped several times, but received no answer. The most profound stillness reigned within, and, by peeping through the key-hole, he, the landlord, could just see the candle guttering down at a most fearful rate, while, as the waiter had reported, one of his guests certainly was leaning with his head upon the table, apparently asleep. Then, beckoning to William, he turned the handle of the door and slowly entered the apartment. William followed with more serenity than might have been expected, but perhaps curiosity now was getting a little the better of his fears. As the landlord walked into the room, he felt that his feet went with a slopping sound into something, and taking the light from William, he looked down, and with horror saw that he was standing in a pool of blood. For a moment or two terror had absolutely deprived him of the power of speech or motion; the waiter broke the spell, by saying—

"What the deuce are you looking at?"

And then the landlord, with a voice that made itself heard throughout the entire building, shouted "Murder, murder—murder, murder!"

Turning round as he did so, he made such a rush to get down the staircase that he upset the waiter, and with a tremendous clatter they rolled down together, candlestick included, into the bar below, which so alarmed the landlady that, in her agitation of mind, not knowing what she was about, she began screaming and working away at the beer-engine, as if a large order had just come in for porter, that must positively all be drawn within a given time.

" Help—thieves—murder!" cried the landlord.

" Fire!" shouted William, and scrambling upon his feet, he rushed out into the village, screaming 'fire' with all his might. That was a cry that was soon echoed by many voices, so that the first arrival that took place at the 'Red Lion and Mousetrap,' in consequence of the dreadful deed that had been committed within its walls, was the parish engine. As this piece of machinery had not been called out for a long time, those who had the guardianship of it were anxious to show what they could do on a push, so they pumped a stream of water right into the bar, which put out the only light there was there, and soon set everything afloat.

"Good God!" cried the landlord, "what are you about? Who is a-shying in pails of water here? We don't want to be put out."

"And there won't be a blessed chalk-mark left behind the door," said the land-lady, "and there was a matter of twenty-two pots put down to different people as I shan't know again from Adam."

Whiz went the engine, and at last, when the idlers who pumped it were exhausted, a man walked in, and looking over the bar, said, "It is gone out!"

"Curse you!" said the landlord, "it's only just come in; here's a pretty mess I am in! There's not only to be a murder done up-stairs, but as if that wasn't enough, I am to be pumped upon directly I come down. I suppose somebody will kick me next because there is not a fire."

"A murder? Did you say a murder?"

"Yes, I did."

"You are quite sure the kitchen-chimney aint on fire?"

"Get out, stupid! If you want to make yourself useful at all, fetch Mr. Snoggles, the constable. There is somebody up-stairs that twelve of the most respectable inhabitants will have to sit down upon, and that will be the first inquest we have had here. Oh! he is here. Mr. Snoggles, I am glad to see you; you will be petrified, sir."

"I petrified? Oh, dear no! it takes a devil of a lot to petrify me."

"There has been a murder done, and the gentleman is up-stairs lying rolling about in his blood."

"In his blood!" said Snoggles, and he took two steps towards the door; "you don't mean that?"

"I do, though; and what I want you to do is to go up-stairs and secure the murderer. I think he is hiding in some corner, ready to pop out upon anybody with a double-barrelled blunderbuss, or something of that sort."

"What," said Snoggles, "you don't mean that? Good gracious! I'll trouble you for a glass of the best gin. Do you mean that staircase? up that staircase?"

"Yes, of course I do; up that staircase, in the room above here."

"Well, I don't think I will go, Mr. Bromley. You know I have a wife and family all to myself; not that I shrink from my duty, oh, dear no! and I don't mind at any time taking up a little boy for grabbing somebody else's apples, or something of that ere sort; but as for tackling a murderer, Mr. Bromley, is quite another thing; not that I am afraid, you know, Mr. Bromley, but somehow or other I rather think it's a nice point of law; but I wasn't swore in to take murderers. If, however, all of you will go up and lay hold of him, and bring him down stairs, and hold him tight, mind you, I don't mind walking on before to the cage."

"What's the matter," said a stranger, who strolled in at the moment, "is there a fire here? I met a half-mad looking waiter down the road calling out fire!"

"That's William for a guinea," said the landlord. "You may well ask if there's a fire, sir, when you looks at the situation as we is in, and when a outrageous fire-engine has been pumping a lot of dirty water slap into my eye; but it aint a fire, sir."

"No," said the man who had charge of the fire-engine, "it aint a fire, it is only a murder."

"Only!" said the stranger, "you seem to think a murder a very insignificant affair."

"He does, sir," said the landlord; "but the worst of it is there's the murderer up stairs alongside of his wictim, and nobody won't go and take him."

"Indeed, give me a candle—I'll go and bring him down."

"Lor'!" said Mr. Snoggles, "mind, sir, he is a hiding in some corner, with a two-edged blunderbuss and a double-barrelled bayonet."

"Oh, never mind," said the stranger, "I am used to those sort of things; thank you, this light will do, I will be down in a minute."

"Well, I am d——d," said Mr. Snoggles, when the stranger ascended the staircase with all the coolness in the world. "He is used to them are matters—that light will do, and he will be down in a minute. Well, I never!"

All eyes were bent upon the staircase, and every ear was strained to catch the slightest sound, for the general belief was that some desperate struggle would take place above that would alarm the whole house, and show, not only what a terrible fellow the murderer was, but likewise how accustomed the stranger was to tackle such fellows; but minute after minute passed away and nothing was heard.

"I say," remarked the landlord in a whisper, "perhaps he has settled him too."

"I think I'll go home," said Mr. Snoggles; "somehow or another, I think my wife is getting anxious."

"It's rather odd," said the fireman.

"Hush!" said the landlord, "I think I hear something."

"The deuce you do! what is it like?"

"Well, I hardly know, but it sounds to me—mind you, I may be mistaken—but it sounds to me just for all the world as if the fellow as did the murder had settled him that went up last to him, and was creeping along just down the winding part of the staircase to settle us."

"D—n it," cried Mr. Snoggles, "why didn't you say so before?" and he rushed out of the door, pushing the fireman before him all the way with the greatest precipitation. He was quickly followed by the landlord and his wife, so that these valorous persons completely deserted the inn, and stood upon its exterior gazing up at the window and wondering what would happen next.

The alarm now had spread through the village like wildfire, and a tolerable throng of persons, for so small a place, reached the spot, and it really, to those who were of a speculative turn, seemed positively wonderful where so many persons could have come from all on a sudden.

But this is a peculiarity of all towns and cities, and all villages we may say likewise. Let but anything happen which has a tendency to excite the curiosity of people, and lo! from some unimaginable source will issue a crowd, that before one could hardly be aware, existed.

It has all the effect as if a number of persons were continually hiding until some occasion of excitement, and that then they all sallied forth to the surprise of everybody, and made up a large crowd, when one could hardly have supposed it possible to get twenty people together.

When, however, the people found that it was a murder instead of a fire that they were called upon to assist at, they felt the keenest interest, but still none ventured into the premises, which had been, as we have related, abandoned so completely to those who should have remained and faced any danger, if danger there really was.

While now all eyes were bent upon the inn, the door was opened from within, and the moment the landlord and Mr. Snoggles saw that, they, with one voice, cried "That's him! That's the murderer!" and started off at full speed, followed by the crowd, who only wanted some impulse to do anything or everything in the world.

The only person who remained to witness the advent of the supposed murderer from the inn, was a boy, and he sat his back against a pump hat was close at hand, and with great perseverance and courage awaited the result, which simply consisted in the man, who had proffered his readiness to capture the murderer, emerging from the inn, and saying—

"He's off completely, and I have gone over the meadows some distance after him, but I cannot find him. Why, where the deuce is everybody?"

"Oh, they have all run away," said the boy.

"Run away !"

"Yes, they thought, I suppose, as you was the murderer !"

"How very absurd ! Just run after them and say that some steps must be taken about the body, and that the man, who no doubt did the deed, has escaped by the back of the premises."

It took some time, however, notwithstanding this pacific message, to get any-

thing like confidence restored to the people. As for Mr. Snoggles, he fairly went to bed, and there was no such thing as getting him up again for anything or anybody.

The landlord was got back, and the stranger, who now for the first time announced himself as the well-known Anthony Sharpe, a Bow-street officer of great repute, made all the necessary arrangements, and then proceeded to town to make a report to the magistracy of what had occurred, promising that he would be back at the inquest, which must take place that day. Alas! Charles Ormond, it seems fatal even to try to avenge your death!

CHAPTER LXIII.

THE BLACK LADY'S ADVENTURE IN ST. PAUL'S.—THE BODY-SNATCHERS AND THE DECEASED ALDERMAN.—THE FRIGHT.

It was a strange idea of poor Marian's, that of her one day meeting with Charles Ormond in the vaults of St. Paul's. It was of all places, she thought, more likely to be that in which she should meet him, because it was the least likely that any one would seek him there. His enemies would have no idea of looking for him in the vaults.

Fully impressed with this notion she would steal along at her funeral pace until she came to the little door from St. Paul's Chain, and then rapidly and noiselessly open the door and walk in, closing it after her so as not to attract the observation of any one who happened to be at hand.

Thus she went night after night her rounds through the vaults—places, that even those connected with them would not willingly venture to perambulate; there they would not venture, unless, indeed, some strong incentive urged them on, and then the probability is they would have stuck fast on the road by fainting in the vaults or by coming to a stand and then a precipitate retreat.

But here poor Marian used to wander in the dull midnight hours, awaiting the arrival of him who was never to come again, save when all meet at the last day, then, indeed, she might meet with him whom she so constantly sought through life.

The quiet, unobtrusive character she bore, and her silent and retiring manners, made her less often seen than she might have been, and also rendered her somewhat suspected of having connexion with the world of spirits, to which she in many respects appeared to belong.

Night after night might she be seen going through St. Paul's Chain to the small door, at which she found entrance, and to which the key she possessed admitted her.

On this day there had been a celebrated alderman buried with all the pomp and splendour of a civic funeral.

Alderman Gobble was as great a man as ever presided at a city entertainment or at a Mansion-House dinner, many of which he had in his time partaken of, as well as Hall dinners.

He had been a successful man, and hence his dignity. He was a wealthy man, and had passed through all the various offices that were usually coveted by the ambitious citizens, and had been sheriff.

No human being could be more dignified or have a more profound sense of the importance of himself or his office, and these ideas, conjoined to his wealth, made Alderman Gobble no mean or common man. And Alderman Gobble must, like other men, die: it was a sad truth, and one that he thought as little upon as any man could desire; and moreover, his friends kept that out of his sight as much as possible—they said as little as could well be expected—even the chaplain spoke of death as a matter removed from the consideration of Alderman, and also in those soft, velvet tones that made the matter one of a far less terrific nature than usual.

It was spoken of as a thing somewhat removed from the present, and then touched upon the undying name that was left behind; so the matter was usually smoothed over and made palatable, like some made dish, that in its native state would hardly suit the appetite of lordly stomachs, unless made more piquant by the addition of some foreign matter. Thus lived Alderman Gobble, and his death was equally characteristic.

Seated at a private feast—we say private, because it was not strictly public—there were upwards of sixty guests. A turtle feast! The worthy Gobble was present, and voted to the chair. The delicious viands were much more delicious than they were actually, when they were eaten with the gusto of a Gobble. It was delightful to see him eat turtle; large pieces of green fat found no turnpike-like obstruction in his throat; no, they glided down swiftly, like the City barge on the bosom of the Thames.

Great was the envy of many of the aldermen when they saw Gobble's plate refilled, for they could not keep pace with him; and then he commenced the attack he made upon every dish with some sly joke, and if anybody cast their eyes towards the spot where he sat while the waiter was changing his plate, he turned him off adroitly, as he made some remark, or uttered some repartee that had the effect of causing others to fix their eyes upon the individual, who returned to his own plate abashed.

Yes, Gobble was envied, and upon this occasion he tried all his former efforts and even outdid himself. Alas! the power of nature, in all its capacities and capabilities, is limited, and great as they were in the alderman, yet he could not contain more turtle than would go in, though Gog and Magog both had taken him in their hands and rattled and bumped him to and fro, as a fishmonger rattles and bumps a small barrel of natives, to make the required quantity go in before it is nailed up.

Poor Gobble's eyes began to grow dim as he finished the eighth plateful. At the ninth he gasped and was observed to turn pale—he ate—he got through half of it, and then he took some brandy.

" More turtle and more brandy!"

" Ditto, ditto; as the doctors say, the draft repeated," and so it was.

Gobble's silver fork fell, and his head would have fallen upon his shoulder, but it was too short and too fat to admit of that, so he leaned back upon his chair.

" Gobble's ill! Gobble's dying!"

These words came from a dozen throats, and for the moment even turtle was forgotten, and a rush made to the worthy alderman, who was getting a blueish red about the lips and nose, which changed to a blackish tint.

They undid his neckerchief—he breathed again for a moment—and then he lifted his head up and said, in an inaudible tone—

" My friends, I die in the execution of my duty!"

" You do! you do!"

" And—and—I feel I haven't long to live." There was much sensation at this, and he resumed,—" I die amongst you. I have been your sheriff!"

" You have, Gobble, you have!"

" Then grant my last request and see it performed!"

" We will, Gobble, we will!"

" Then bury me with honour and let me have my chain of office buried with me; 'tis all I ask, promise me quick, promise me!"

" We will, we will, Gobble!"

" I shall be buried with the chain? say, say I shall, and I shall die happy."

" You shall, Gobble, depend upon it you shall; we can vote it, it shall be carried by a majority of the whole court. You shall have the chain—there—there he's going—he's dying."

" I am satisfied," he gasped, " and—"

" Offer him a plate of turtle," suggested one, " it will revive him, and if anything can bring him back to life, it will be the thought of turtle."

But Gobble was insensible to the charms of turtle; his eyes looked dim, and his mouth seemed propped open by some mysterious and not apparent means, very much like a large cod that had received some injury in packing. They laid him on some chairs, and medical assistance was of no avail—he was too far gone even to wag his tongue or wink his eye again.

The medical men said he died a martyr to his duties and to apoplexy.

So died Alderman Gobble!

The wishes of the deceased alderman were strictly adhered to, but there was an insurmountable difficulty in complying with that portion which related to the chain, seeing that it was one of the things that appertain to the office and not to the individual.

However, the genius of an alderman and an alderman's friends are equal to such emergencies, and the defunct alderman was buried as he desired, with his sheriff's chain around him.

Thus, on that very day, he was deposited in the vaults of the Cathedral of St. Paul's, with all the ceremonial and honour that befitted the dignity which belonged to the rank of an alderman of the City of London.

There can be no question but there are many circumstances which are coincidences—and they appear strange—but then again it oftener happens that some events are the parents of others, and an incident occurred on this occasion that fully justified this assertion.

The rumour spread abroad that Alderman Gobble was to be buried in St. Paul's Cathedral, and at the same time he was to have a solid massive gold chain hung round his neck, and to be buried in his coffin and there left.

This caused a sensation, and many persons asserted that in any other place the chain would not be safe; but the vaults of St. Paul's were as sacred, aye, as sacred as those of the Bank, though not quite so valuable by a great deal—old bones weighing as nothing compared with ingots of silver and gold.

That was the notion of many persons, among a certain class; indeed we will, to show the feeling and the sensation created, give a specimen of the feeling engendered by this affair.

*   *   *   *   *   *

Not far from St. Giles's is a public-house, the resort, of many characters not of the most exalted or the purest in thought and motive—but some of them were eccentric in their notions of right and wrong, and of the rights of property.

"Jem," said one, "I have a case on to-night."

"Are you alone?"

"No, I have one more with me, but we think two aint enough; we want a third; how do you stand to-night, are you out?"

"No, nothing to do; have no objection to turn the honest penny, if you know how."

"I'll talk to you more about it presently," said the first, as he glanced his eye around the room in which he was sitting.

"Have you heard of the alderman who died a-stuffing himself with turtle?"

"Yes; him as is going to be buried with a gold chain round his neck."

"The same, he was buried to-day."

"In St. Paul's?"

"Yes, in the vaults; well, it's about that same gold chain as I was about to speak to you."

"Indeed! but the vaults of the cathedral are not so good a place for plunder. Why now, if you've a mind for old bones, I can tell you where there's plenty."

"I want something better than old bones, I can tell you; but the vaults are not so hard to get in as most people think."

"Are they not?"

"No, indeed, they are not! Why, there are but locks and keys to contend with, and I should like to know what lock there is that I cannot open."

"You are a dabster at it, certainly. I don't think anybody is your equal at the use of the pick-lock."

"Few, indeed. Then why should the vaults of St. Paul's be any great difficulty? I can see none whatever, nor do I expect any."

"But who's to go groping about in the dark, and there are so many of them, and they wind about? and altogether it is—is—a—a—"

"You don't like it, eh?"

"In truth I don't like grubbing among dead men for only a chance, and no more."

"You needn't go if you don't like, there's no compulsion—only keep it dark. I know, however, to an inch where to pitch for my plunder."

"That alters the case. I don't mind going if you know where to pitch for the gilt."

"I know all about it very well. I went with the funeral into the vaults, and said I was a relative, popped on a cloak, and made one of the funeral party; I saw where the body was placed, I know the particular nook where it was poked."

"That is all right, if you can find it out in the dark; you know things look different then, and I dare say you won't get in the same way you went in," said the other.

"In truth, you are right there."

"Well then, if you can make sure, after all that, to find this particular box, that contains the alderman, why, I'm your man through thick and thin."

"That's all right—then we may as well go."

"Is it time?"

"Why, as for that matter, you see we had better leave here all in good time, but as it is, it is half-past ten, and it will be much past eleven before we get there —perhaps, twelve."

"It will be the safest hour to be there."

"Yes, but then I have to call for Hardware Joe—he's in with us, and that will take us some time, so we shall not be there so very soon."

"That is quite the dodge. Well, come along."

The two worthies went then to call upon Hardware Joe, who was found at another public-house; and, after something short, they turned out and made for Saint Paul's, and the hour of twelve boomed forth from the tower with solemn sounds, as they crossed Bridge-street, to get up to the cathedral, by an indirect route.

* * * * * * *

That evening, we should say night, Marian, as was her custom, had been in the vaults some time anterior to the striking of St. Paul's clock, and, wandering up and down the various passages and chambers that were there, and each passage and vault was well known to her, so often had she trodden them over and over in the search after that one loved object, which she was doomed ever to seek, but never to see, for he was no more.

Sadly and slowly she paced the cold, damp passages—dark and drear as some of them were, and many totally so, and yet she trod them in safety and in security, for she knew no fear, and the place had no terrors for her.

Yes, the Black Lady was an object much more likely to alarm any one else, than to be any way alarmed at her proximity to the dead. With them she was at home —they were to her the world, for all the world was nought to her, and she lived but to hope, that she might one day be blessed with the sight of him she thus sought.

At times she would emerge into the moonlight, and stand like a spirit come from the tombs of the dead, and stood alone like a shadow in the moonlight, breathing for a space the vitiated air of the vaults.

Then she would glide into some dark corner, and watch the moonlight passage, and thus detect, if possible, if Charles Ormond should pass.

It was a sad and melancholy sight—one that would have drawn tears from the eyes of one whose heart was as hard as stone, to see her, thus sadly and patiently sit or stand, and watch in this unhealthy spot for the appearance of one lo g since dead, but who she believed to be still alive."

" Yes, sadness could never meet an object so strictly, yet so unobtrusive in her melancholy, deserving of pity and of commiseration, than was poor Marian Whitehead.

Thus she was when a party of men, three in number, came up to the door, and there silently but quickly opened the door by means of a picklock.

They closed it again after them, and then, walking a few yards, the first stopped, and then the others did the same. The fact was, they were in the dark; and, when one stopped, the others were compelled to do so.

However, the pioneer had an object in view, which was the production of a dark lantern, which threw a gleam of light in the direction which it was turned.

Aided by this they pursued their way from passage to passage, now stopping at this place and now at that, but not quite sure of where they were.

"I am afraid you don't know where it is," said one of the men; "you aint so sure as you thought for—we may have our trouble for nothing."

"You'll wake the dead if you go on in that way, you fool you; can't you shut up your noise-box now you are in good company?"

"Well, but where are you now?"

"In the vaults."

"I could have told you as much—but as to your knowledge of where you are precisely, how far are you off the Alderman?"

"Just one turning more."

"To the right?"

"Yes; here it is now. The coffin is up here—there, that is it—you see by the size that he must have been a man of extraordinary dimensions."

"That will do; an alderman all over. I am sure if it were full of gold ten men added to our number would be unable to move it."

"So it would, but we may as well have him down, and wrench the coffin lid off."

"No, no—that will be harder work than you at all expect; that won't do."

"What will, then?"

"I will tell you; there is room for all of us on the top, in that hole."

"Well, we don't want to be buried there."

"I dare say not. At first I thought of breaking the coffin open, but I think we can unscrew it in less time than we can break open such a coffin as that—why, it is enormously strong."

"That will do; set to work, for I'm as chilly as you can wish. How cold the vaults are! God bless me, I think we must be in a dry well."

"It amounts to pretty well the same thing—but I can smell a most disagreeable odour."

"So can I; and it is so thick too, that I can almost bite it, and certainly I can taste it—make haste—it is horrible. What a lot of heavy it will take to wash this down: I am done almost now!"

"Here is some brandy; I came provided, for I thought no violets smelt like this place."

"Indeed they don't," said the other, "but the brandy is a refresher."

They now tasted the spirit all round, and in another minute they were employed on the coffin of Alderman Gobble, which in a few minutes they had unscrewed, and one of them put his hand into the coffin and withdrew it rather hastily.

"What is the matter, Jem?" inquired one.

"Oh, nothing; I only put my hand on the Alderman's face, and it was so blessed cold it startled me; I have got hold of it now, and won't leave go till out it comes."

He had scarcely spoken, before, from hard pulling, he broke it in two, and then with great precipitation, they screwed down the coffin slightly, and adjusted the fittings, and then, jumping down into the vault, he said—

"Well, let's examine the chain and see what we have got for our trouble; it is weighty, and ought to fetch us ten pounds each, suppose we were to sell it to a fence, and much more if we can sell it first hand."

They looked at the chain by the light of the lantern, and after a minute inspection the projector of the robbery let the chain fall with a hearty execration.

"Well, I'm d——d!" he exclaimed.

"Eh? what's the matter—what's the matter—what's amiss now?" said the other two, as they looked around to see if anybody was coming.

"It's a d——d counterfeit."

"Eh? What?"

"A counterfeit?"

"Who's a counterfeit, eh?"

"Why, the chain, fool; it's only copper and gilt."

Imagine the consternation of the three robbers as they looked in each other's faces; their surprise, consternation, and intense disappointment was very great, and as the light of the dark lantern fell upon their visages, they would have formed a picture that would have been worthy the study of a painter.

"Well, I'm done up all of a heap! Here's a pretty go! I'll come again with you!"

"Yes, into this place for a dead man's bones! How long are we to remain in this hole?"

"We may as well go at once."

"We may, as you say, but I should like to do some mischief before I go."

"So should I, for the trouble they have given us in coming to look after a copper and gilt chain."

The fact was, the alderman's friends were of opinion it would be quite a useless expenditure to bury so much gold as was contained in the sheriff's chain, and therefore prudently had had one made of baser metal, which they concluded could not be discovered by the deceased alderman or his spirit, though when alive he was a good judge.

However, the robbers found it out soon enough; they had just taken it up to examine it again, when they thought they heard some sound like a foot-fall or a rustling of dress, as if some one was stealthily walking near them. They looked up, and their eyes rested at one moment upon the form of the Black Lady, who stood within a few feet of them, gazing in their faces, as if she were desirous of ascertaining their identity. The robbers were terrified, too much so to speak or even to move; they sat staring, as though their eyes would burst in their sockets, while they broke out into a cold sweat.

The Black Lady, after pausing for a few moments, pursued her way and left them, and her footsteps were so light that, terrified as they were, they heard them not.

When she was out of sight they, with one accord, started to their feet, exclaiming, "The devil! the devil!"

They rushed along helter-skelter; but found themselves suddenly involved in a labyrinth of passages, from which they could not extricate themselves. Cursing and swearing, and trembling to an excess, the robbers rushed from place to place like caged lions; but on one occasion they met the Black Lady, but they dared not speak or endeavour to pass her; they turned back and proceeded in the opposite direction. This brought them to the door at which they had entered; and, with very little difficulty, they got out, congratulating themselves upon their escape, and hastening from the very vicinity of the Cathedral, and such was the effect of the fright, that they spoke not of their adventure that night, even to themselves.

CHAPTER LXIV.

THE ADVENTURES OF NEVILLE AFTER THE MURDER AT THE INN.

WITH what a mad haste Neville sped along the fields, with feelings of so mixed a character, but in which fear and terror were decidedly the most prominent! The night was dark, and Neville, had he been master of himself, so far as he had been on other occasions, would have conceived that no particular danger could result to him, seeing the darkness of the night was so great, that he could hear anybody long before they could reach him, which would give him ample time to secrete himself.

He soon after found himself near the Edgeware-road, up which he walked rapidly for some distance; he dared not go faster—he dared not run, lest he should be stopped. Most of his energies were spent, and his self-possession almost entirely destroyed. His only object appeared to be, that of putting as much distance between himself and the place where he had committed the murder.

After he had gone some distance down the Edgeware-road, the thought suddenly struck him that that road would, at all events, be the worst he could take, for he would have the whole of any pursuit upon him, for more reasons than one.

In the first place, the main road, in which he was then moving, was that most likely to be traversed by any one coming from that spot than any other, because they would think, that any person who was flying from justice would at once make for London, and they would also do it by the shortest and quickest road.

In the second place, there was not much chance of his being able to secure himself there from any one who might come riding along. At least, in places, it was not calculated for such a purpose.

At length, he determined to push off to the left, and make the best of his way towards London. The road was just calculated for such a purpose as that which he had in view, namely, concealment. He would probably be able to get as far as Hendon without meeting a single soul the whole distance.

That was an object to be desired, and he immediately crossed the road and made for the opposite side, and by the time he reached the windmill he knew there was a road, on the opposite side, that would take him where he wanted to go.

It was lonely—a cross-road, but that suited him all the better; he wanted it lonely for his purpose, it could not be too much so. Up he ran the slight declivity and pushed on up the road with a desperate speed. It appeared as though he had been fearful of being seen to run before this, but this was not the case now.

He darted forward for several hundred yards at a great speed, but soon found his breath would not hold good for any length of time, but he soon relaxed his speed; he felt somewhat more at ease—and yet he knew not where to go, but the thought struck him, if he could get to Hendon before he was seen by any one, they would not be able to trace him from Edgeware.

For Hendon, then, he made the best of his way. He walked along at a rapid pace, keeping beneath the hedge-rows, or as close to them as he could, so that he should not be even accidentally observed by any one at all.

Suddenly, however, he was brought to a stand-still by his treading upon something soft, which moved and seized him.

"Dom thee," growled a voice, "I say dom thee, what's thee mean by treading upon my inside in that manner? Cus thee, thee hasn't no bowels theeself, else thee wouldn't have done it."

At the same moment he was forcibly seized by the throat and thrown down.

"Hold!" said Neville, terrified and trembling.

"Hold, did thee say?"

"Yes—for God's sake—you'll choke me."

"Well, I dare say I shall for thee own sake, and as for holding I reckon I can hold with anybody in the county. I'll hold—beant I holding now, eh? beant I— dom thee!"

"Leave go! I am sorry I kicked you. I did not think that any one was there."

"I dare say thee is sorry!"

"I am—I am!"

"Well, thee will take more care in future, eh?"

"Yes, I will—I will—do but let go your hold of my throat—you'll kill me!"

"Well, an if I did, thee had nearly killed me?"

"I saw you not," said Neville, "I saw you not. How could I think of finding any one lying in the road at this time of night?"

"Well, but what made thee skulk under the hedge-rows and so kick me in the bowels?"

"I didn't creep under the hedge."

"But thee didst; I was under the hedge, and thee couldn't have touched me had thee not gone under there on purpose to do so."

"I did not; by Heaven, I did not. I could not have seen, and, however, I meant no harm. I had no intention of doing so."

"Well, I'll let thee go this once," said the man, "but never creep under a hedge to kick a gipsy in the bowels again."

"Never, never. You may depend upon that," said Neville, as he rose to his feet and looked at the man who so unceremoniously treated him.

He was a tall man, singularly ill-looking, but did not appear to possess the strength that he had exhibited.

"There," he said, "don't make any more attempts of the like nature. No man likes being awoke out of a sound sleep in that manner."

As the gipsy spoke he crept under the hedge again, and laid himself down beneath the shelter it afforded, upon some dry rubbish he had collected.

"There you see, I was here before you came. If you want to sleep you ca find plenty of hedges and sleeping room too, if you go on without your disturbing me.''

Neville waited to say no more, but turned away and proceeded onwards with all possible despatch; and now again he sped onwards with all the haste he could make.

There was nothing now to interfere with his escape, and he made the best of his way onwards. There was something in the occurrence that had just happened that sobered him in his terror.

He knew that he was not pursued, at least he had seen no sign of it, and that there was no need of any over-haste which might betray him to strangers.

He could not tell how it was, but he never felt in so much trouble nor so much terror as he did on this occasion. He appeared to dread being seen and traced. On many occasion had he been in great danger, but his presence of mind never so entirely deserted him as it had upon this occasion, which he considered by no means so difficult as some others he could name.

"Curses on that fellow for lying there," he muttered. "Who would have expected finding such an obstruction in one's road? and the fellow was like iron, or else I am weaker than usual."

He pushed on. He was coming to a place where there were some cottages; his object was to get by these as rapidly as he could, therefore he determined to exert himself and run past them.

This he did. He rushed past them at the top of his speed; and then, when he had passed by nearly all, a dog that was loose began to bark, and, seeing him running, he rushed after him, and jumping up seized Neville by the throat.

"Well, curse the thing," muttered Neville, "this infernal dog shall pay for this."

He endeavoured to shake the dog off, but it clung too tight; and in a few minutes more he would have been in some danger of being throttled; but, while he struggled, the dog shifted his hold, and Neville contrived to obtain the use of his hands, and, drawing his arm, he struck him with the knife he held in his hand up to the haft, and then the dog, with a half shriek, fell to the earth, having let go his hold of Neville.

"There, die, you brute. So you have been of some use to me in the way of annoyance and trouble. May your owner be as much plagued as I have been."

Then turning away he pursued his way towards Hendon, where he expected shortly to arrive, for it was scarce half a mile.

What his object was there was no telling, neither could he have told any one had he been asked and tried; but he had some distant notion that, if he could sleep anywhere in the neighbourhood and get to London before people were much about in London, he would be safe.

He came to Hendon—all was quiet and still—no signs of life were there: all was quiet—not a light of any description was to be seen, not even in the chamber of the sick.

He looked down the several roads, but saw nothing more one way than another to induce him to turn down either.

All was dark and still—there were scarce any shadows, the darkness was too complete—and he came to the side of an old barn, which was stocked with hay and straw to protect it from the weather, and the thought struck him he could enter that, and pursue his way at what hour in the morning he choose, and be observed by none.

This then he determined he would adopt. He crept into the barn, and at the same time he listened carefully to see that he did not fall into the lion's mouth in doing so.

However all was still, and he, with some difficulty, climbed up to the top of a lot of wheat, on which he deposited himself with the intention of sleeping out the night.

This place afforded a good shelter and a safe retreat to Neville, and he congratulated himself upon the excellent covert he had found.

"I can lay here for a week or two," he muttered, "had I but meat and provisions; I could stop here for many days and so baffle them all, if they should not pull down my hiding-place."

He then thought over many things; the past all came arrayed before him; and then the murder at the inn and his subsequent flight.

"They are now in full pursuit of me," he muttered, "and there they will continue at it till they grow tired and hunt all London through, and yet they will not find me; I am safe from them here."

He stretched himself out at full length in the straw with an apparent enjoyment of his liberty, as if in his own mind he contrasted his present to his probable position a short time back.

"Well," he thought, again and again, "I am glad I am free; I thought I was nabbed once again; and I expect I should not get off so easy; it would be for life this time if it were not shortened at the Old Bailey; but, as I said, I am free."

There was a loud whoop and scream uttered just above his head, and different voices began to whoop and scream in higher tones.

For a moment he was petrified, unable to understand the nature of the interruption, and broke out in a moment into a profuse sweat with fear and apprehension.

"What can it be?" he muttered to himself; "surely they cannot have traced me here and set upon me here in the barn; but that is impossible; it was overhead. But what can it be?"

That was a question iterated and reiterated by himself without any plausible answer being discovered for it, and thus he lay until the sound was repeated and a rustling in the straw above him.

Then it became apparent what it was that disturbed him. It was a nest of owlets; the old one was out in search of food when he first came in, but now the parent was returned there was a discovery in the barn, and the presence of a stranger was speedily discovered by the old one.

Determined he would not be disturbed by these animals, he got up, and after some trouble poked the whole nest outside, to fall or fly as best they might.

Having performed this act to his satisfaction, he got down to the same place where he had before laid, but this was not quite so easy as he at first imagined, for after a short attempt he fell down between the straw, where it had been packed end to end, for some distance, more than two thirds of the depth down, and then he stopped at some impediment.

This was very awkward, and then, after one or two desperate attempts, he gave it up as a bad job, for he could not pull himself up again.

"Now I am fixed," he muttered; "I can't move. Curse the place; I wish I had pushed on for London, I shouldn't have been locked up in a barn as I am here. Curse the place, say I."

He again made an attempt to get up, but it was only after pushing his way through the corn, which enabled him to reach the sides, that he was able to get up, for by the aid of the cross pieces he pulled himself up.

Once more upon the top of the straw he secured himself in his position, and then, after a long time spent in thought, he fell asleep.

*　　*　　*　　*　　*　　*　　*

How long he slept he could not tell, but when he awoke he thought he heard some one moving about below on the floor.

Neville listened with painful anxiety to the sounds. His interest was fully excited by the occurrence which appeared to be fraught with so much danger to himself at the vicinity of men.

This attention was soon rewarded, for he heard more than one person move about, and now they spoke, and from what he should gather, they were but little better than himself.

"Well," said one, "how are you to-night."

"Ah, pretty well—much as usual. Have you the cart with you?—had'nt you better back in"

"Well, I did'nt know what to do about it ; and yet, I think it safe, because you see we shall not be noticed by any one passing."

"There'll be nobody here I'll warrant ; but have you the meat at hand."

"Yes, all killed and ready for the market, but we'll fill the cart with straw— a load of straw will do very well as a blind."

"It will."

"Who would think that rich farmer Wilkinson was having his barn turned to such an account as it is? Why, it's quite handy."

"No, nobody has seen or not'ced anybody. Has any of the sheep in the neighbourhood been missed?"

"Nobody has missed any as yet, but it can't be expected to last out much longer. He is not to be done very long ; after a time, somehow or other, he is sure to find you out."

"Yes, we had better move the spot, and begin somewhere else, then we shall not be traced."

"How many have you this time?"

"A dozen."

"A dozen! did you say?" said the other.

"Yes."

"Why, you are getting into the wholesale line after all ; but load away. I want to get on the road before the patrol gets on this district. He waits, and watches about for you, and you cannot tell where he is, or when you are to expect him."

"He's not safe, that's my opinion," said the other. I would'nt trust him with the value of a straw. I am sure he would collar you as soon as look at you."

"You are right. I know he would, so I never give a chance away."

They now proceeded to load a cart with wheat straw, and then began to draw a number of sheep carcases that lay in the straw close to where Neville lay concealed. He made up his mind what to do. He determined that he would get into the cart and proceed onwards with it, unperceived by the men in charge of it.

After some time he slipped down and got up into the load just as it was finished.

A few more minutes and he was clear of the barn, and proceeding on his route towards London.

While proceeding on his journey, a thought suddenly recurred to him as to what he should do if the cart and its contents were at all examined by any of the authorities who might have some suspicion of the load. This gave him an agony lest he might be detained upon suspicion, and then committed while enquiries were made, and, at the same time, give time to have the charges inquired into, and then, long before that time, he would be committed upon the one of all others he would have to suffer most from.

This thought tormented him so much that he was resolved to quit the cart as soon as he could. It was very early, and the cart came along at a good pace for a walk, when Neville got up, and, on looking about, saw the sun was just peeping up in the east.

"It is time," he muttered, "I was in town too. I shall have no time to wait; for, if I get into London, I shall be seen descending."

Having made up his mind, he chose his spot, and descended very carefully, and got down, having first torn out some five or six kidneys for his breakfast.

He overtook the carter, and walked with him for a little while, and at parting he said,—

"Your sheep, friend, wants kidneys."

"Eh! what," said the carter, staring about him thunderstruck, and not knowing what to do." Neville repeated the words, and then suddenly disappeared in some of the streets on either hand."

CHAPTER LXV.

THE ROBBER AT THE CHEESEMONGERS, AND THE MURDER.—THE DESPERATE
ATTEMPT TO GET POSSESSION OF THE BLACK LADY'S PAPERS.

Up to this point, we have thought it more convenient to the reader to continue the narrative of the Black Lady, without any continued or particular reference to the papers from which they acquired their information.

But when any circumstance occurred which deserved particular attention, we feel it our duty in the course of editing and preparing those papers for the press, to make some mention of it at the proper time, and in the proper place, which it ought to occupy in our narrative.

And acting upon this principle, it now becomes necessary that we make something of a pause in the actual narrative of the Black Lady, which we lay before our readers, an account of what happened at the cheesemonger's house just at this juncture, and before doing so, it is necessary that we should say a few words about the situation of that worthy tradesman.

The fire which had occurred, and which the boy had remarked, had made Welsh rabbits of the cheese, had so much shaken the fortunes of Miles Atherton, that, although he could hold up his head as an honest man, and no one could feel disposed to say one word to his prejudice, he for a time, certainly, had some difficulty in making both ends meet.

This was rather a grievous state of things for a man who had been very differently situated indeed, and cost him and his wife a great amount of anxiety; and here we cannot help noticing one fact, which we think is to the advantage of Mrs. Atherton, who, for some time has presented herself to the reader in not the most amiable of lights.

That circumstance is, that she had with a cheerfulness submitted herself to her husband's altered circumstances, that could hardly have been expected, and that now when she knew he was in little difficulties and straits about money matters, she did not add to any such perplexities, by a single word of ill-humour or reproach.

On the contrary, she did all she could upon other scanty measures to restore the appearance of comfort to the place, which their old house used to bear. They both, likewise, did everything that could be done, for the purpose of economising; and, among other things, they let a portion of the upper part of the house, in the shop belonging to which, Miles Atherton was slowly, but surely, picking up a comfortable and prosperous business, which would ultimately (but of course such things are not done in a hurry), place him above the necessity of taking strangers beneath his roof. And the reader may well imagine that lodgings over a cheesemonger's shop, were not calculated to let to the most exalted portion of the British public; but, were necessitated to be cheap, and consequently, Miles Atherton was forced not to be over particular as to who he took in.

It happened then, that about a week before Atherton and his wife got to this portion of the Black Lady's narrative, that a man of the name of Zachary had taken one of the vacant rooms at the cheesemonger's, and from the first moment that he came into the place, he had made vigorous efforts to get acquainted with the cheesemonger and his wife, but they both resisted his advances, for there was a something about his appearance and manner which they could not well define, but which certainly gave them a disagreeable impression concerning him.

"I don't like that fellow," said Mrs. Atherton, "and it's like his impudence to pop his great ugly head into our parlour and say 'how do you do' of a morning, as it was anything to him how we did. I declare I won't answer him another time, for he's just the sort of wretch that I know would not mind smothering and eating a baby."

"Gracious providence," said Miles Atherton, "you don't believe so bad of him as that, do you?"

"Yes, I do, and a great deal worse."

"But what can be worse than smothering and eating a baby?"

"Never you mind what can be worse; I know, of course, that we are glad to get the second floor let, because in addition to the smell of the cheese and bacon, the soap boiler's copper at the next house sometimes do smell a little, but for all that I would certainly get rid of Zachary."

"Well then, my dear, since such is your impression concerning him, and as his week is up to-day, I will just give him notice to quit, and there will be an end of any further trouble about him."

When the disagreeable lodger came down to pay his week's rent, which he did with an annoying punctuality, Miles Atherton gave him notice to quit, which he received with some appearance of surprise, but made no remark about it, with the exception of simply observing, "that he was sorry he did not suit them, as from the fine air of the place he had taken a particular liking to it."

This sounded so dreadfully ironical, that if anything could have tended still more to induce Mrs. Atherton to wish to get rid of him, such would have done so, for the idea of talking about fine air in such a place as that, was certainly a little too preposterous.

Such then was the state of things on a Monday, when Zachary had only been in the house a week, and was expected to remain another, and then go quietly. But as will be seen, the fates ordained it otherwise, and on that evening some singular circumstances occurred.

Ever since the fire when the papers of the Black Lady were so near being all lost, it had been the constant and invariable practice of Miles Atherton to take them up to bed with him, and place them on the drawers, so that on any sudden emergency, he could lay hold of them at once, and be certain at all events, whatever else either fire or thieves might succeed in depriving him of, he had those interesting documents safe in his possession.

And we must say that both he and his wife were prompted to be careful of those papers from a feeling of quite another nature to mere curiosity connected with them, for they both, after what had already happened concerning poor Marian Whitehead and the villain Neville, conceived it to be not impossible, but that on some occasion the production of those papers, notwithstanding the prohibition of the poor suffering creature herself, might be absolutely necessary for her sake.

They could not help feeling that the circumstances there disclosed were of a nature that made the papers bear something more than a mere ordinary interest about them, and while they were amazed at the amount of the information which she had acquired respecting the movements of Neville, they felt that while he lived she ran a great risk of her life.

It happened then, that on the night of the day on which Mr. Zachary had been given notice to quit his rooms at the cheesemonger's, the heavens wore a very particular aspect indeed, and there was every appearance of a coming storm, such as the great city of London had not been visited with for some time.

The whole colour of the sky was altered, and as Miles Atherton stood at the door looking at the peculiar aspect of the houses, Jem spoke to him, saying—

"Master, I think there will be a jolly row soon."

"A row, Jem?"

"Yes, a storm that will knock some of the old houses about down here, and smash a few windows. You may depend it's a coming. Don't you see, master, that little odd red-looking cloud there?"

"Yes, I do. It ain't much bigger than a Gloucester cheese."

"No it ain't, but it looks like mischief for all that, and I should not at all wonder if —— oh, there's a splash!"

James's exclamation gave but a faint idea of the terrific flash of blue lightning that lit up the whole place for an instant, and which left its image for many minutes painfully imprinted upon the eyes of those who happened to be at that precise moment looking up at the sky.

"That was, indeed, a tremendous flash," said Atherton, as he covered his eyes with his hand for a moment, and then, before another remark could be made, there came such a sudden peal of thunder that it sounded as if a thousand heavy waggons were all rushing wildly over some sort of archway paved with loose iron plates, each one of which were broken into fragments in their passage.

Involuntarily the bewildered Atherton retreated into his shop, for he had no wish again to look upon such a flash of vivid forked lightning, as that of which even than he had not got the glare out of his eyes.

"Come in, Jem," he said, "you had much better come in. There's no knowing but cheese may attract the lightning."

"You may depend, master," said Jem, "if it does, that bacon will put it out; but I don't want to see any more such as we saw just now. Anything in the moderate way, I don't mind, but such a zigzag gentleman as that I don't want to make any acquaintance with on any account."

Both the cheesemonger and Jem now made their way into the shop, and closed the door, as they did so, they heard another thundering reverberation which awakened every echo far and near, and which seemed as if the very vault of heaven itself was split asunder.

Mrs. Atherton was so terrified that she ran out of the back parlour into the shop, and laid hold of Jem, who therefore called out murder as loud as he could till she let him go again.

Then there came down such a sudden and alarming deluge of rain, that it was absolutely terrific to hear it dashing upon the pavement, and come, as it did, roaring down the chimney, sweeping them all for *nothing*, as Jem said, only not having the civility to give you notice, so that you might stick up some old cloth with two forks to prevent the soot from coming intothe middle of the room. Then the lightning flashed still vehemently all through this heavy rain with unabated brilliancy, and the thunder continued in one interrupted peal, as if the claps succeeded each other so quickly that the echo of one ran into the actual sound of the other.

The cheesemonger, his wife, and Jem, all stood together in dismay, watching the progress of the storm through the half-glass of the shop-door, when it was suddenly darkened by a human form, and with one voice, they exclaimed—

"It's the Black Lady! It's the Black Lady!"

Miles Atherton flew to the door, from which he was some paces, and opened it in a moment, when poor Marian, draggled with rain, and looking terrified and exhausted, staggered into the shop.

"The wind and the rain," she exclaimed "are working even against me now. Oh, Heaven! let your red lightnings fall upon the guilty, and not upon the heads of those who have already suffered much, and yet would fain linger for awhile to quit those whom they love. Have you seen him? Oh, tell me, have you seen him? Have you—you, or you? Oh, speak to me, and tell me have you seen him!"

"Be calm, Miss Whitehead, I beg you will walk in, and be calm and composed," said the cheesemonger. "It's only a storm, you understand, and will soon be over."

"But have you seen him?"

"Seen who?"

"Charles Ormond. They say he is condemned to death; but is that possible, when we all know he is innocent of that which they attribute to him? He was to meet me about this time, and as he was so pale from much persecution he was to have a chaplet of flowers in his hand that I might know him."

"Worse and worse, poor thing," said Miles to his wife.

"Well, we must try to soothe her a little and get her to sit down till the storm is over; I have often heard that storms affect poor creatures whose wits are not quite right."

"You do not answer me," said Marian, in a low, wailing voice. "You do not answer me, and really that is not kind when I tell you he is innocent. Hark,

hark! do you not hear Heaven's thunder? Oh! let the guilty tremble, and the firm of heart and purpose admire, instead of fear that voice from Heaven."

"Come into the parlour, Miss Whitehead," said Mrs. Atherton, "and sit down till the storm is over. You know you are quite welcome here at any time, storm or no storm, but we are glad in such an emergency to offer you a shelter."

"I thank you," she said, in something of her ordinary manner, "I thank you. You have not seen him then? You could know him by the chaplet of young spring flowers that he wears; they are a passport to heaven. You have not seen him?"

"Alas! no; but compose yourself, I pray you, and take some refreshment."

Mrs. Atherton took her by the hand and led her into the parlour at the back of the shop, where she gave her a seat; but there, in consequence of the constant turmoil of the thunder and the splashing of the heavy rain, they found it no easy matter to carry on any conversation.

"You must have walked far in the shower," said Miles Atherton, "and if you will change any of your wet things I'm sure Mrs. Atherton will manage to accommodate you with others."

"To be sure," said Mrs. Atherton, "and if you will not wear anything but black I have a gown that I can lend you."

"No," said Marian, "no; these are fitting garments for me—the garments of woe. You see they think they have taken his life and laid him in the cold grave, but I know that he lives and that we shall meet again; but they must not think so, and therefore, you see, I wear a garb of mourning. Alas! alas! I have not seen him yet, but he comes to me in dreams, and I see him with the old familiar smile upon his face, and he spoke to me as once he spoke—so gently and so sweetly, while his eyes beam upon me like twin stars and I am happy. When, oh! when shall I look upon him again? How cruel are those who hinder him from coming to me, and they must be Godfrey and Neville. Yes, oh! yes, the villain Neville, who knows no touch of human sympathy."

"Ah," said Atherton, "I believe he is about as great a scoundrel as can be found unhung. But don't you be afraid of him; you let him try his worst; he shan't do you any harm, you may safely depend, while I am here, and so long as you are under my roof. I only wish you would come here oftener than you do."

"Alas, alas! why should I?"

"Because it would withdraw your mind a little from your own sorrows, you know; and you would feel all the better, I'm sure, for coming here and having a little quiet chat now and then, about old times."

"You have by this time read my melancholy history."

"Not entirely; and there are some things which, if you would not mind my asking you, we, that is my wife and I, would like to have cleared up as we go on, you know. Jem," added the cheesemonger aside, "you go away, I'll tell you what she says afterwards, but if you stay she won't tell us anything."

"All right," said Jem, "I'll stay in the shop."

"Ah, do so."

Jem accordingly started; and when he had done so, the Black Lady replied to the questions of Miles Atherton in a melancholy tone of voice saying,—

"I ought not, I am sure, to refuse you what you ask, for as I have taken you into my confidence I see no reason why that confidence should not be complete. Ask, therefore, what you will, and so far as I can I will answer you."

"Well then," said Atherton, "we want to know how you came to know all about the private proceedings of Godfrey and Neville?"

"That is easily explained to you. There was a poor girl, who was in her ignorance of the world and its ways deceived by Neville, and she having repeatedly heard from him that his intention was to murder me, took it much to heart, and sought me out to warn me from him, and then from time to time she visited me and told me how, when he became talkative in his cups, he detailed to her the minutest particulars of his life, and how he had persecuted me and poor Charles, and then I told them to a friend I found, who wrote them down for me in the state you now have them."

"Well, but knowing so much as you do of Neville, could he not be apprehended?"

"No, oh, no! I dare not for poor Charles's sake do that, for I should be put upon my oath, and then they would ask me if Charles Ormond was alive or dead, and I should be compelled to say that he still lived, and then would commence all his persecutions anew."

"How strange it is," said the cheesemonger in an under tone to his wife, "that after all these years she will still cling to the idea that Charles Ormond is alive."

"It is strange, poor thing, but it would be a thousand pities to attempt to convince her otherwise, so let her be in the delusion, which, no doubt, she will carry to the grave with her, poor thing."

"No doubt, indeed."

" You see what abundant reason I have," added the Black Lady, " to be silent."

" Ah! well, there is something in that," said Atherton. " We have just got as far in the papers as where Neville murdered a relative of Charles Ormond's at an inn near to Edgeware."

" Ah! that was a cruel deed—a very cruel deed. It was after that, Neville, fearing the consequences of the deed, went to sea, and was not heard of for a long time. Indeed, I did not myself see him until that night, when, in the dense fog, he tried to take my life, for he fancies that the poor girl who told me so much concerning him, did so, and that I had power to bring down upon him the vengeance of the law. So he would fain kill me, and by such means get rid of what he considers a great danger."

" That, no doubt, is his motive; but I cannot help thinking you ought to make an application to a magistrate."

" Oh! no, no, no. Do not urge me to that. Do not ask me to do so, and for your own parts let me remind you of your oath, sworn so solemnly and taken, when first I placed in your hands those documents which you so much wished to see. But the storm is now subsiding, and I think I may venture forth in safety. Accept my thanks."

" The rain," said Atherton, " falls heavily yet, and you had better remain yet awhile and dry yourself by the fire. Wife, why don't you give Mrs. Whitehead a little of that cherry brandy you have ?"

" Mercy me," cried Mrs. Atherton, jumping up. " Here have I been listening to what you have been saying, and never even thought of offering you anything at all. How very remiss of me to be sure. Why did you not, Mr. Atherton, remind me of it, but I never in all my life, did know such a man as you. You never recollect what you ought—no, never."

" And I always do recollect, I suppose, what I ought not."

" Now, don't begin any of your aggravating ways, Mr. Atherton. You know what a handful I have of you, and that if I were not a woman among ten thousand, I could not hope to live with you a quarter of an hour. It's a fact, Mrs. Whitehead, I assure you, although you really, to look at him, would not think it. But come, now just take one glass of cherry brandy."

" No, no; pray excuse me—I cannot, I dare not. There is already at times a mild fever in my brain, which makes me think that the day may come when my misfortunes may affect my mind. God help me if such be the case. They call me mad, and I can hear people, as they pass me, say ' She is mad.' But it cannot be so. Oh, no, no. I am not mad, not mad yet, and I still hope to look upon the face of Charles Ormond in this world."

" Well," said Mrs. Atherton, " if you would rather not take anything, I won't press you, although I think it could not possibly do you any harm; but I hope you will call upon us oftener than you do, for you know quite well that we are always glad to see you, and sympathize with you very much. Why, you have not been near us for I don't know how long until to-day, and then I don't know if you would have crossed the threshold but for the storm."

" Do not think me ungrateful for your kindness."

" Oh! you have nothing," cried Atherton, " to be grateful to us for. What little help we have been able to give you against that villain Neville I am sure you have been very welcome to indeed, and we should have done just the same for everybody or anybody, for I will say that much for myself, as well as for Mrs. Atherton, that we are not the sort of people to see any one put upon if we can possibly help it."

" Of that I am quite certain. Hush! hush!"

" What do you hear that alarms you, Miss Whitehead ?"

" There is a footstep outside the door of this room, in the passage. Oh! protect me! Save me from Neville—if it should be he."

" Of course we will; but you need not be at all alarmed, for we have several lodgers in the house, and I dare say it is one of them coming in with his key."

Miles Atherton had scarcely given the explanation, when some one gently tapped at the door of the parlour that led into the passage, and then without waiting for an invitation to enter, but seeming to think that a superfluous ceremony, Mr. Zachary, the disagreeable lodger of whom we have before spoken, made his appearance.

CHAPTER LXVI.

THE MISTAKE—AND A NIGHT OF GREAT TERROR TO THE ATHERTONS.

THERE certainly was something very disagreeable about this man's appearance, and we do not wonder that Miles Atherton wanted to get rid of him. We only wonder that he ever took him in. There was an odd sort of anxious silence for some minutes after Mr. Zachary thus unwelcomely made his appearance, and he could not but perceive that he was far from welcome.

"Oh," he said, "I see you are busy, so I won't disturb you, Bless me, is not that the Black Lady that goes about the streets, and attracts everybody's attention so much?"

"Well, Mr. Zachary," said Miles Atherton, "and what, suppose it is?"

"Oh! no offence, no offence. I only made the remark as I happened to see her all of a moment, you know, and was a little surprised, as you may naturally suppose. That's all, I assure you."

"Very well, sir."

"But, as I was saying." continued Zachary, "I see you are busy, so I'll just say what I came to say, and that is, that the rain has come in at the roof of my bed-room by some means or another, and the bed is almost swimming about. It's quite out of the question me sleeping there to-night."

"Well, then," said Mrs. Atherton, catching at the idea of getting rid of Zachary at once, "I have no objection to your going of course now, Mr. Zachary. I don't expect you to sleep in a wet bed, of course, so you can be off as soon as you like, and we won't charge you anything."

"Well," said Zachary, "that's very liberal and kind of you, marm, I'm sure, but it don't suit me at all."

"And why not?"

"Because I am not suited with another lodging; so all I have to say is, that while I stay here, which will be five nights and six days longer, I shall expect a bed somewhere, that's why."

"Will you, Mr. Zachary. Then I can tell you, sir, that you may expect what you like."

"Nay, nay, wife," said Atherton, "do not let us have any quarrel with the person; we can, I dare say, find some means of accomodating him while he stays, if he will stay; so Mr. Zachary, as you say you see we are busy, we will now bid you good day, sir."

"Very well," said Zachary, "be it so. Mind, I shall expect a dry bed somewhere in the house; I don't care much where it is, but it must be as good as the one I have had, or I won't pay so much money at the end of the week, so now you know what you have to expect."

It was with no small amount of difficulty, that Mrs. Atherton succeeded in controlling her temper, so as to make no reply to Mr. Zachary, and the probability is, that if the Black Lady had not been there, she would have told him, what she usually called a piece of her mind, and that would have been not the most agreeable piece of it."

As it was, however, Mr. Zachary got out of the room without such a collision with the oratorical powers of Mrs. Atherton, and that good lady turning to Miss Whitehead, said, "you see what disagreeables we have to put up with sometimes, but don't be alarmed. You look quite terrified."

"I am. Some unknown fear creeps over me when I gaze upon that man, I know that I never saw him before, and yet from the first moment that I heard his footsteps, I had a strange presentiment of evil."

"Oh! that's all imagination."

"It may be, and I hope to Heaven it is. I am subject, I know, to strange fancies, which make the people look back after me and call me mad, at times. Alas! alas! I may be so before my mortal race is run. But let me go now at once. The storm which compelled me to seek shelter with you, has passed away."

"Does it rain now Jem," said Atherton.

"Only a mizzle," said Jem, "like a cat sneezing. That's all."

"Farewell then," said the Black Lady, rising, "I am much indebted to you— very much, and let my last hour come when it may, I shall along with those few images that will occupy my thoughts at such a time, think kindly of the friendship I have had from you, and the words of sympathy you have spoken to me. May Heaven bless and prosper you, and may you go through life and never feel such unhappiness as belongs to me."

"It's quite affecting," said Mrs. Atherton.

"Yes," said Miles Atherton; "yes, yes. If you have any fear Miss Whitehead, I will walk home with you—now do let me for this once, for you seem quite nervous and unable to take care of yourself."

"No, no, I shall do very well; I will not take you out from your home at such a time, and you shall not, because you are kind enough to offer to do so—expose yourself to ridicule by walking with me!"

The Black Lady spoke these words with a firmness that at once convinced the cheesemonger that she really meant what she said, so he did not further press his offer to accompany her, but as upon a former occasion, he contented himself with having made it, and then he let her depart in peace from his dwelling.

"Well," said Miles Atherton, when she had gone, "poor thing, I pity her more and more every time I see her, and as for her having some sort of dread of Zachary, I don't wonder at it, for did you ever see what a look he cast upon her, as if he would have taken her life as soon as say good day."

"Yes," said Mrs. Atherton, "I saw that, and I declare, Miles, that if you had been half a man, which you are not, you would have turned him at once out of the place, that you would."

"But, my dear—"

"Oh, don't dear me. I know what I know, and I know—that is to say, I don't know what I don't—but of course, as you have said, he must sleep here to-night, I suppose he must, the odious wretch; for my part, I hate the sight of him, and he goes skulking up and down the stairs like a tom cat, that he does for all the world, and you never know whether he is listening or not to what you are saying."

"There can be no doubt but that he is a disagreeable lodger, and one we shall be glad to get rid of, but all I can say in such affairs is, let us get rid of him as mildly as we can, so as to give him no ground of complaint against us. After all, it is only for a few nights, and we must find some place for him to sleep in during that time."

"Well, I dare say I can find a bed for him, somehow, and he shall sleep in the spare-room while he stays, which is over the yard; of course, all his own things will do, with the exception of the damp bed, as Jem and me can soon put the place to rights for him."

"Very good; let it be so, then, and I'm quite sure that nobody will be better pleased than I shall, when the day comes for him to go, and we have done with him altogether. I think we have let him know pretty well that we don't mean to make any acquaintance with him."

"If we have not," said Mrs. Atherton, "and he attempts to come in here, I'll pretty soon tell him a little of my mind, or else my name ain't——"

"Oh, don't trouble yourself, Madam," said Zachary, suddenly opening the parlour-door, and walking in, "oh, don't trouble yourself, I know the whole of your mind already, and there is not much research required to become acquainted with such a small affair."

"You odious wretch, but I won't put up with such insults any longer, I—oh! it's a good thing for you that you have taken yourself off."

"Never mind him," said Atherton, "he is quite unworthy of your notice, I assure you, my dear; and the first thing that can ever be done with such a man is to let him have his rights and no more, and then get rid of him as quietly as possible."

"Just wait till his week's up, then, that's all; and I'll let him know pretty well, what I think of him, or I'll know the reason why. The vagabond, to come prying and peeping about our parlour—the man ought to be hung."

"Well, perhaps his time may come, some day, and when it does, I must say I shall not particularly regret that such is the fact, for he don't deserve any one's consideration, nor does he at all go the way to get it, I make bold to say. But I have been thinking, wife, now that we really have several rooms in the house, that we don't want, if we were to press Miss Whitehead very much, perhaps she might be induced, poor thing, to come to one of them."

"I'm willing, I'm sure," said Mrs. Atherton; "for after reading what dreadful misfortunes she has gone through, I'm sure a Turk would pity her, and she cannot, you know, be thought so much of anywhere where they don't know her as we do, for no doubt she is just looked upon, poor thing, as mad, and nobody thinks what dreadful misfortunes drove her mad."

"That's true enough, and since you concur in it my dear, I will, the next time she comes here, speak to her about it; or, suppose you were to do so, it would come best from you, and although I say it, perhaps who ought not, I will say that there is no woman who can say a kind thing with a better grace than you can yourself, my dear."

"Well," said Mrs. Atherton, with a simper, "I never denied Mr. A. that, when you liked you had as much sense as any man, that's my opinion, and I don't care who hears me say it, that I don't, and if you had been lucky in business, there would have been nothing to prevent you being a common-councilman, that there wouldn't. There's many a greater fool than you been made a common-councilman of."

"Well, I believe that."

"Ah, to be sure, a man has only to keep up a constant gabbling noise to be considered wonderfully clever directly."

"Ah, that's true; and I will say that I have heard you, Mr. A, speak of things much better than many an alderman."

"Oh no! oh really, oh now!"

"I mean it, my dear."

"Gammon!" cried Jem, popping her head in at the door which separated the shop from the parlour—"Gammon, on precious broad wheels, all that is, and no mistake at all I can tell you. Why, there's been a boy here for an egg, and he's been a listening to it all, and gone away nearly a splitting of his sides all along of grinning at you!"

"Oh!" exclaimed Mrs. Atherton, "I shall be hanged myself, I do think, some day for that Jem. He is the most out and out aggravating puppy as ever breathed. I wont endure it no longer, Mr. A., if you was half a quarter of a man, instead of being the poor miserable creature you are, you would knock your our own head clean off, and play at humble puppy with it, rather than you would see me insulted in this way."

"There she goes again," said Miles Atherton, as, after this speech, his decidedly better half bounded from the room, and went up stairs to superintend the arrangements necessary upon the damage the storm had done. "Ah! there she goes again; there aint a better tempered woman under the sun, when she ain't in a passion; but, some how or another that happens pretty often."

Miles Atherton knew it was of no use to say anything to Jem, for the spirit of fun was too inherent in that individual's character to enable him to fight up against it, so the cheesemonger had long since made up his mind to put up with Jem's vagaries, &c., out of the real feeling qualities he possessed, and which were certainly of a character in themselves to apologise for a multitude of minor airs.

And now we must proceed to a detail of some circumstances that took place that night at the house of our worthy friend Miles Atherton, which were of an extremely serious nature, and which altered many of the circumstances of affairs, and placed the cheesemonger in rather an awkward position as to what he ought to tell for the purposes of public justice, and what he ought to retain to himself in pursuance of the solemn promises, and indeed solemn oath he had taken, not to reveal the contents of the Black Lady's papers, until the time she had mentioned.

CHAPTER LXVII.

THE NIGHT ATTACK, AND THE MURDER OF THE SLEEPER IN THE SPARE ROOM.

It is night, and under an archway opposite to the cheesemonger's house a man is waiting—that man is Neville. How jealously he watches, and how careful he is not to be seen by any one, either a stray passer by or any one from the neighbouring houses. He cautiously draws into the recess when he hears an advancing footstep; at the same time, the deep gloom of the place favours such concealment, that, unless looked for, he would not be found by any one passing by.

How he watches the lights as they move about, and how he wishes for the shutting up of shops, and the last sounds that precede the close of the day's labour of all that are honest or nearly so, for now the hours that begin the reign of such as he are at hand, and the saturnalia of crime begins.

The hours of darkness have a peculiar degree of terror attached to them; and it must have arisen because by far greater part of the crimes committed against society are committed at such times, when men are least able to meet them and repel them; but, at the same time, it is at a moment when the thief and murderer have less risk to run from detection.

Darkness adds its terrors to the sum of others, and the consequence is, acts committed in the day lose much of their atrocity, and that which is merely considered a bold or clever act of dishonesty in the day, would, when darkness has sealed the day, be termed a daring atrocity or outrage, but it is because men are unable to withstand the torrent of lawless force.

The darkness of this night was great—the shadow which fell beneath the archway was complete—and Neville felt himself secure from observation while he stood there.

Often were his eyes directed up and down the street, and then at the windows opposite, but he saw nothing.

"It is not time," he muttered, "it is not time. Curses on the hours, how they drag their length along—minutes become hours, and hours ages; but they must be endured. I have watched ere now, and have never been in this state of fear and impatience; but the hour will come, though it were ages between it and this.

Then, with an impatient gesture, he endeavoured to assume a look of calm and steady watchfulness.

"Let me see," he muttered, "how often I have walked and crept about like a cat, watching an opportunity to commit some deed or other, and I have in general been successful; but this cursed Black Lady baffles me, at least she has done so, but that is no reason why she should now, far from it. Every fool knows that luck must change sides some time; fortune is always variable, and she will find that she cannot always baffle me. Circumstances may interfere with me now and then, but I shall steal a march upon her one of these times.

"The streets are bare, and few indeed are going about now. No man stays out such a night as this from mere pleasure; but here are two men. Who are they?"

As he spoke, two men came along talking very earnestly together, and when they came to the archway they both stopped, and Neville retired a few paces further back.

"Stop here, Jack," said one of the men; "I can't go any further now: come—I must go back."

"Very well, there's nobody here."

"Nobody at all," said the other; "we are safe here," and he gave a glance round, but saw not Neville.

"Well, now, you understand all about to-morrow night."

"I do."

"That is all right then, now you will remember. I shall have a good chaise cart, and we shall slap along the road like one o'clock: we shall be safe, and the moment the crib is broken into we shall be off."

"Where can you put the chaise while we are busy?"

"In a field hard by. We have only to lift the hinges off, and turn horse and and cart into the field until we want it, so it will be in nobody's way, but be safe from sight."

"I see—very good plan. Do you think there is much of a swag to be had?"

"Yes—plenty."

"There was that affair the other day that did'nt pay the expenses of the journey; that was thought to be a good crack, and yet it was a beggarly account of empty boxes."

"So it was, but I can't help laughing when I hear of it; it was such a miss: I really think they must have gone to the wrong house and mistaken the work-house for the parsonage; and that is stupid enough."

"So it is, but I want some money. I am quite out at this moment, and I can't shew myself."

"Well, you shall have what I can spare you; but, it ain't much as I have got: there are five half-crowns."

"That will do," said the man, who received the money, and pocketed the half-crowns, saying as he did so,—

"We shall have gold instead of silver to-morrow night. Good by till we meet again."

"To-morrow."

"Yes. Good night."

*　　*　　*　　*　　*　　*

"So, thought Neville, they are out upon the grand hop. They are likely to drop upon some cash. I wish they would let me into it; but, no matter, I'll have something soon. What can be done without money? Nothing, and everything with it. That is all the difference."

He paused and listened to the retreating footsteps of the two men as they both pursued different tracts, and disappeared at either end of the street, and no other sound came upon his ears. He gazed again upon the house opposite, and there appeared to him to be less and less moving about, until, at length, all seemed to be quiet, and no soul stirring. All was quiet and death-like.

"If I can but get those papers," he muttered, "then, all will be well, and I shall be free from these harassing fears and curses; and that Jem, too, he shall pay something dearly for his cursed mischievous dispositions. I'll have a deep revenge upon him.

"Should I not, he'll put the start upon me, as sure as I am a living man. I think that boy was born for a devil, he'd make a good Bow-street runner, but he aint got brains enough to try; but I dare say there will be plenty of work for him by and by. His skull is too thick to try experiments upon. It shall be a knife that make its way into a softer part than a mere blow."

He muttered to himself, and his keen eyes might be seen to watch the windows with great care. Every now and then casting his eyes up and down the street, and then, again, he looked upon the windows of Miles Atherton's house.

There was no human being about. No soul was to be seen. Not even the footfall of a distant passenger—all was hushed. No sound met his ear, and he rejoiced to find the streets thus lonely and thus deserted.

Who could be there that he watched so earnestly, and what did he watch so for? The signal for the deed he was to commit—to attempt to get certain papers which he believed to be inimical to himself, and to perpetrate a deed of the blackest vengeance upon the unfortunate Jem.

Presently he appeared to be somewhat more interested, and his attention became fixed, for he saw a light moving about in Miles Atherton's window, where it became fixed.

"Ah!" said Neville. "Ah! that is Zachary's signal. The time is come, then, and now for one good half hour's luck, and I will do all I desire to do. Secure myself and put the knife between Jem's ribs. I have it here," he added, feeling for the knife. "Yes, it is all right, safe, and in the proper place."

He waited a few moments and then crossed the road, and, by the application of a picklock, he was soon inside the passage, and had closed the door behind him.

There was now a pause, and he listened as he stood to catch the slightest indication of any one stirring, but no sound met his ears. He crept forward and leaned upon the stairs, as he again listened long and patiently, but no sound met his ears.

They sleep—all—they are all asleep, add soundly asleep; but they will awake by and by, quickly enough, too, I'll warrant, and now for Zachary's candle.

He crept softly up stairs and waited upon each of the landings for some time, to ascertain if all were quiet, and, in doing so, if any one's overhearing him.

"The papers," he muttered, "the papers! but now for Jem! The papers were locked up here," he muttered, as he undid the lock of a door, while he groped his way in in the dark, and felt about for a few moments.

"Curses!" he muttered, "curses!" and he started back to the door as he pushed against something that tumbled down with a crash upon the ground.

He paused for a moment, and then rushed to some drawers, which he opened, and pulled out a bundle of papers which he thrust into his bosom, muttering,—

"These are safe now at all events, and now for him—and now for Jem! Now for Jem! I'll risk all to have a fair blow at that young imp of the devil."

And with this furious desire he rushed out of the room up-stairs, in search of one who had given him deadly offence, and whose crime was to be expiated so fearfully.

In the mean time Mrs. Atherton had been disturbed in her sleep. She thought she heard something, but couldn't say what; but she was hardly awake and she might be excused for being somewhat confused in her intellects.

"Well," she muttered, "I thought there was something moving, but I suppose its only the cat."

Mrs. Atherton tried to console herself with this reflection, but at the same time she felt that it was inconclusive, and as she thought and turned over and over again her opinion of the matter, she became more and more disturbed, until at length she lay wide awake.

"I have a presentiment," she thought, "that somebody's in the house, and there's that Miles Atherton snoring like a pig; but there, that's just like the men, they aint half so watchful as women are."

Mrs. Atherton was now thoroughly awake, and turned round in virtuous indignation, when she suddenly exclaimed, as the noise that Neville made, smote her ear,—

"There! there! Miles Atherton; do you hear that?—do you hear that?"

At the same moment, as if to prevent his hearing at all, she shook him soundly by the shoulder, saying as she did so, very close to his ear—

"Miles—Miles! do you hear that—do you hear that?"

"Eh! no, my dear; yes, I do! Eh! what is the matter? anything? A bad shilling, eh?"

"A bad shilling, Mr. Atherton—a bad shilling—why you are a bad shilling—you are. Don't you know the house is being robbed, and thieves are running

about like rats in the cellar. Goodness me, Miles, how you take it! Didn't you
hear it, I say ?"

"I do hear you, my dear," said Miles; "but, upon my word, I do not hear
anything else."

"Didn't you, dear? I can tell you somebody has broken into the house, and I
heard something fall down below. I am certain of it, Miles, quite certain of it."

"Well, my dear, if you are, there can be no question about the matter—none at
all; but as they have fallen down, why, they cannot give us any trouble."

"Are you awake, Atherton ?"

"Not quite, my dear; but I shall be in the morning, depend on it."

Neville, in the meantime, had crept up hastily to the floor on which the room was, where the candle was placed in the window, but owing to his haste, believing himself discovered, and not wishing to go until he had wreaked his vengeance upon Jem, stumbled on the last step. However, he was soon up; but then it made a noise, and completely aroused Miles Atherton.

"There, Mr. Atherton, there, can't you hear that? Lord-a-mercy, we shall be murdered and *famished* in our beds, and you'll lay there and look on, I suppose."

"It's Zachary," muttered Mr. Atherton, who hastily got out of bed, but in doing so he mysteriously got entangled in the bed-clothes, and rolled clean out on the floor, at the same time he dragged down the washhand stand, and crash went the ewer and bason—splash went the water, and in an instant poor Miles rose up like a merman, shaking the watery element from his locks much like "Neptune," the favourite life-preserving animal of the Humane Society.

Mrs. Miles Atherton shrieked; and, gentle reader, we are sorry to say it, but we cannot hide the truth, Miles Atherton swore, aye, very energetically too—

"Oh, goodness! mercy, mercy! we shall all be killed. Save me—save me!"

Atherton tried to get a light, but could not at first succeed; and when he did, it was only after several attempts, and then he seized a large knife, and made his way to the stairs, Mrs. Atherton following close, it requiring more courage to stay behind, as the thieves, be they who they might, would be sure to find their way to a lone and unprotected female, as they always do, regardless of their own safety, only from an innate desire they have to trample upon the rights of woman.

Neville heard the noise and clatter, and heard Mrs. Atherton's voice, and he, too, heard the bed-room door open; but before he would attempt to escape, he determined to have his vengeance upon Jem.

With a bitter curse he put out the light, and then hastened to the small room, in which he believed Jem slept. The door was locked, and he made a furious plunge at the door, with the view to open it; but it resisted his efforts—it was too strong.

Zachary, in the meantime, hearing all the hubbub, and also the attempt upon his own door, rose up and opened it, saying as he did so,—

"What the devil's the matter now? Am I to have no sleep nowhere? Hush!"

"Curse you," muttered Neville, not recognising the voice of the speaker— "curse you, take that!"

As he spoke, he pulled open the clasp-knife, and struck at the man as he looked out of the door. The knife entered his ribs up to the haft, and the man staggered backwards until he fell to the floor with a loud groan, and then he, Neville, turned and fled.

By this time the house was alarmed; Mrs. Miles Atherton and Atherton himself were coming up stairs, hearing the noise, and having some notion that the man Zachary had something to do with it. They were on the stairs when Zachary fell by the hands of his accomplice; but Neville meant the blow for another, he knew not it was Zachary.

"Stand, whoever you are," cried Miles, brandishing his knife, "stand, upon your peril!"

"D——n!" muttered Neville, as he rushed down the stairs with all the desperation of a madman, heedless of Miles and his wife, and regardless too of his knife, which he brandished with terrific effect.

"Oh, the villain!" exclaimed Mrs. Atherton; "oh, the villain!"

Miles said nothing, but he stood firm when he saw the dark form of Neville on the top of the stairs making a rush at him; but before Neville reached him he was quite confused, for he had thrown a garment he found on the rails at the head of the stairs at his head, which confused Miles's vision, at the same time it put out the light.

"Murder! help! thieves!" screamed Mrs. Atherton.

"Curses!" muttered Neville, and at the same moment the whole three were precipitated down the stairs; for Neville, in trying to pass them, had, in the dark, rushed against them, and they all three rolled down together—Mrs. Atherton calling out ten thousand murders.

When they came to the landing, Neville got upon his feet, and bestowed a hearty kick upon the cheesemonger and another upon his wife, who set up a doleful scream, and then rushed down stairs and gained the street-door.

"Murder, murder! fire, fire!" screamed out Mrs. Atherton, as she perceived some things had taken fire and began to blaze away with a great flame.

"Fire! fire!"

This was echoed by Miles, and Neville, thinking it was time to be off, left the house, carefully closing the door behind him, and then he rushed as quickly as his legs would carry him to the end of the street, leaving Miles and his wife to get out of the mess as well as they could—to be burned or escape, as best they might; he made the best of his way to a place of safety, where he could hide himself from the eyes of honest people, and keep in safety his ill-gotten documents.

Poor Miles and his wife were in a dreadful state; they for some minutes thought the whole house would have been in flames, but the articles that caught fire were of that character that they soon burned themselves out, and left the place in darkness and smoke.

At that moment a knocking came at the door, and for the moment paralysed both Miles and his wife.

"Go, Miles, and see what it is."

Miles looked irresolute; but a second injunction from his wife was necessary, as well as his own sense, that it was useless to make any objection.

Miles did go to the door, and upon opening it he saw the form of one of his neighbours.

"Mr. Atherton," he said, "what has happened?"

"I really don't know," was Miles Atherton's answer, "but, for Heaven's sake, come and help me; there has been an attempt to rob the house, and we have been both knocked down stairs, and the house has been set on fire."

"Fire!" said another voice.

"Oh! Mr. Brown, come in and help me; there has been an attempt to rob and murder us. Did you see anybody run by?"

"I did. I saw a man run very hard up the street, and I heard your door almost immediately before open and shut; but, dear me, what a smell of smoke!"

"Then come on."

They all three now came to the end of the passage, and lights were procured, and there was Mrs. Atherton sitting huddled up in one corner, perfectly shocked and bewildered.

"Well, I'm ashamed of you, Atherton; but there, you don't mind, no other man would have done so."

"My dear, I couldn't tell where you were in the dark; at the same time, I thought you might have got back to your own bed-room, if you had desired to do so."

"How could I tell where the room was? I don't know where I am now, hardly. I have come, I am sure, I can't tell where from, and the house is so full of smoke that I don't know if it aint on fire now."

"We'll soon ascertain that," said one of the new-comers, and they and Miles Atherton went up stairs, and Mrs. Atherton made no more observations, but ran into her bed-room and rapidly attired herself, and then hastened after the men. She came up stairs and to the room just in time to witness with them the horrors of the room.

Here, extended on the floor, was the dead body of Zachary, laying out at full length. The whole of them stood aghast at this scene, for there was a pool of blood formed round the corpse.

Horror was depicted on the countenance of all present, and they started back in affright, and looked each other in the face, without uttering one word.

* * * * * * *

Neville, when he had got a certain distance from Miles Atherton's house, slackened his pace, but walked rapidly towards a house, he where he knew could obtain shelter and security after this newly-committed crime.

He soon arrived there, and then dived through some courts until he came to the public-house, into which he turned with all due precaution having first taken care to avoid being noticed, and then he rushed quickly into a passage, where he met a man with a pot in his hand.

"Any one in the little room, Jack ?"

"Nobody."

"Then let me in, and bring some drink."

"Yes, you are in a hurry ; but, no matter, I've got the key, and will take care on you—you is a precious chick—but you are of the right sort, anyhow ; and there's no skulking, half-and-half breed about you, is there ?"

"Curse you for a fool! open the door."

"Well, aint it open ?" said the man, as he pushed the door open, and Neville entered a small room, which was completely dark, and he threw himself into a chair, which he appeared to know very well, for he said,—

"Bring me a light."

"Yes, in a minute, and the lush, too."

The man left the room, and relocked the door, and went away to satisfy the wants of Neville, who took his hat off and wiped his forehead, for the perspiration bedewed it pretty freely. He had come very quickly, and besides, his case was one of some excitement, for he had committed a murder ; and even a man of Neville's callousness could not do that without a feeling that he had done something fearful.

"And now," he muttered, "I will examine these papers that have cost me so much trouble to get from that cursed cheesemonger. I have them safe now, at all events."

At that moment the man returned, and placed light and liquor before him, saying, as he did so,—

"Here we are, you see. Here's your health—you drink mine when I am gone."

The man left, but Neville made no answer ; but when he was gone, he drunk nearly the whole of the liquor off at one draught, and then he pulled out the papers, muttering, as he placed them on the table,—

"Here, then, at last, I have them. I cannot tell what these cursed things have cost me ; but I will now rest satisfied for a time, at all events. These papers and that rascally boy done for, I am well satisfied. There is but one other I care for— she disposed of, and all would be well."

Putting the candle beside him, he snuffed it, and then carefully unrolled the papers, and began to examine them with care. At first he looked very hard at one or two of them, and then he opened the whole ; but they fell from his hand as he looked at them with a bluish expression and dazzled eye.

Neville groaned, struck the table with his clenched hand, and growled between his teeth,—

"And for these have I done all this ? Curses !"

The papers were not those that he wanted—they were merely some old bills and invoices of Miles Atherton's, which he had rolled up and put away, in case he should ever be called on to avouch for past transactions.

CHAPTER LXVIII.

THE CAPTURE OF NEVILLE.—THE INQUEST AND THE VERDICT.—THE LAST PAPER
OF THE BLACK LADY.

THE welcome dawn of the morning at length came, after all this night of terror and excitement had passed away, and never to the weariest watcher, who ever counted the minutes and wished for day, did the first faint flush of the coming morn feel more welcome than on this occasion it did to Miles Atherton.

Such a night of fright he nor his wife had certainly never in all their lives passed, not even making the least exception of that occasion when the fire had taken place, which had so nearly reduced them, without a hope of any extrication, to irredeemable poverty.

"Thank God," said Miles Atherton, "it's getting daylight, and now, I suppose, at all events, we shan't be dull."

"And why not dull?" said his wife, "I am sure what has happened is enough to make one dull as long as one lives."

"But I means you won't be dull as regards company, for you will have the coroner, and the beadle, and all sorts of people, to hold an inquest upon Zachary, as sure as fate."

"Well, I never!" exclaimed Mrs. Atherton; "I did not think of that. Of course twelve of the neighbours will have to come in and sit upon him naturally. The idea of me not thinking of that at all! I wonder if the jury will want any refreshment, because if they do, I'm sure they could not do better than have a little bread and cheese, or a slice or two of grilled ham, which I could dish up in a minute."

"Mrs. Atherton, you are always thinking of the shop."

"Well, Mr. Atherton, if I was not to think of the shop, perhaps the shop would not think of me. But you may depend upon it, Miles Atherton, that talking of this murder, there are wheels within wheels; ah, and lots of 'em too, however you may think there aint; and if it wasn't that vagabond, Neville, that I saw in the house last night, it was the devil himself in his likeness, Miles Atherton."

"I am," my dear, "inclined to be of your opinion; but you cannot help seeing that we are placed in very troublesome circumstances by this affair, because if I say too much, we shall be ordered to give up the Black Lady's papers, as sure as fate, and what would poor Miss Whitehead say to that?"

"Fate be hanged," exclaimed Mrs. Atherton; "I won't give them up, so there's an end of that at once. I rather think I should like to see the coroner or anybody else who could get them from me, if I said they should not. I don't mind saying that, in my opinion, there is wheels within wheels, but they won't get any more out of me."

"I'm afraid they won't think that very satisfactory then, my dear, but we shall see what we shall see, and, as I have sent Jem off to the nearest watchhouse to say that a man has been murdered here, we may, for all I know to the contrary, be all taken into custody in another half hour or so, I shouldn't at all wonder."

"Into custody? Why, we didn't kill him."

"But that's no rule. Have we not been reading about how poor Mr. Charles Ormond was hung, and he all the while as innocent as the youngest baby as ever was. What, then, would there be wonderful in our being taken into custody and all of us hanged, which I fully expect now is what will happen, and I think the best thing we can do is ——"

"To get ready," put in Jem, "our last dying speeches and confessions—'Good people all, take warning by me, and more particular you young men of London. I have come to this here disgraceful end through sabbath-breaking and bad company—so mind all young women's eyes, will you?"

"Ah! well, 'tis not a bad idea, that," said Mrs. Atherton, "so you have been and given notice, Jem, about the murder to the police and the coroner, and all that sort of thing."

"I believe you. Here's the beadle a-coming. He would have been here before, only he ran home to put on his coat and hat; because he said, somehow people didn't think so much of beadles when they only looked like common ordinary people."

Even as Jem spoke, that dignified functionary made his appearance, arrayed in his full official costume. And when he got into Miles Atherton's shop, he did look grand and imposing indeed, and made a tremendous noise, coughing and stamping for fear any of his dignity should be lost. Some of the Guildhall police, too, now made their appearance, so that there began to be an aspect of much bustle in the cheesemonger's house; and Mrs. Atherton became anxious to know if anybody wanted any cheese; and the beadle seemed rather inclined: he could just take a little bit—he heard Mrs. Atherton say that it was as cheap as could be got any-where—and then he declined, for he had fully expected it was an offering at the shrine of hospitality.

We need not relate what was done, or what was said, by these not very conse-quential parties—suffice it, that, within four hours, an inquest was duly summoned, as the bruit had got all over the neighbourhood that there had been a murder com-mitted, the whole locality, as the newspapers say, was thrown into a state of the greatest excitement and consternation.

The cheesemonger's house became literally invaded by all sorts of people, and the police had to take possession of the door, in order to exercise that discretion in ad-mitting people which is always exercised in this country, and where peculiar defer-ence is invariably paid to the sort of coat a man may happen to have on his back.

There were, however, quite sufficient people unexceptionably appareled to fill the room in which the inquest was to be held, and that was the apartment imme-diately behind the shop.

To be sure the coroner did suggest that the front room on the first floor would be better, he thought, on account of being longer and lighter, and an attempt was made to get possession of it, but in vain, for it belonged to an old lady who had it with her own furniture in ; and when the application was made to her, she gave it a prompt refusal.

This was an uncomfortable idea, but there was no helping ; for, as the beadle remarked, " a person's first floor is a person's castle, and you cannot turn a person out of it, try what you may, in any shape whatever: so we must let the old woman remain, and just hold the 'quest here, subjected to all the annoyance in the shape of butter and cheese, that can be possibly given to us."

" Really," said the coroner, " I am extremely sorry, but, gentlemen of the jury, something must be wrong in the law of the land, for whoever heard anything so preposterous as an old woman keeping twelve of the most respectable citizens of London that ever I saw assembled together, out of a first floor."

" There wants an act of parliament, sir," said one of the jury, " there wants an act of parliament, sir, for the abolition of old women entirely, and then they could'nt be in anybody's way."

" That's a very excellent suggestion," said the coroner ; " and now, gentlemen, if you please, we will proceed to business."

The first act of the jury was to view the body of Zachary, which presented what might be called a terrifying appearance ; for, at the moment of death, some strange convulsion must have swept across his features to distort them, so hideously were they contorted, as to place the body altogether in so terrific a position as it assumed.

The fixed and tender eyes, too partially closed only as they were, appeared to be regarding the different members of the jury with a stern and terrible expression; and many of them who, from intense curiosity, had pressed most eagerly forward to look upon the corpse, now shrunk back quite terrified at the fearful aspect it presented. Even the coroner and the beadle, who were old hands at such matters, evidently did not like the job of going too near the corpse of that mur-dered man, and they were glad to leave the room entirely in its possession, and the possession, likewise, of a medical man, who did not seem to care particularly whether the dead subject looked at him or not.

He was requested to make his report as soon as he had sufficiently examined the body to enable him to do so ; and as there was no obscurity about the mode of death whatever, he said that that was a scrutiny which he should be able very quickly to bring to an end, and that they should have the result of it, at all events, by the time the other evidence that had to be produced, was fairly gone over.

It is doubtful now, whether the indignation of the old lady, in not allowing the use of the first floor, did not altogether subside in the feeling, that it was better to be at as great a distance as possible from the dreadful object that was above stairs.

Before the inquest commenced in all its formality, a note was placed in the hands of Miles Atherton, which contained the following words :—

"It cannot be necessary, in detailing the circumstances concerning the death of Zachary, to say anything of other matters which have nothing specially to do with the inquiry ; and although the name of Neville may be mentioned as the probable murderer, it cannot be at all necessary to allude to one whose misfortunes have been so great that she considers her grief may and ought to be sacred from common observation."

Miles Atherton could have no doubt in the world but that this note, although it bore no signature, came from the Black Lady, and that it was an admonition to him to mix her up as little as possible in the affair that was in progress.

He showed it to his wife, and they mutually resolved to be extremely careful in what they said, for they could extremely well conceive how such a creature as she was likely to shrink from public attention being drawn towards her at such a juncture.

In his deposition, therefore, the first thing he said was, that he knew of no motive for the murder being committed. He stated how Zachary had become his lodger, and how he and Mrs. Atherton, not at all liking him, and highly disapproving of the continual attempts he was making to become intimate with them, had determined upon getting rid of him as quickly as they could.

Then he proceeded to detail as much as he knew of the events of the night, and that was not a great deal ; because, as we are well aware, there had been so much hurry and alarm about the whole affair, that the narrative he could give was anything but a very clear and tangible one.

His identification, however, of the body was, of course, quite complete ; and then came the evidence of Mrs. Atherton, which was rather more important, because it tended to fix the guilt upon a particular individual.

When she had gone through that part of the evidence which we need not detail, but which described how she had been disturbed in the night, and so on, she proceeded to state how it was that she came to suspect any particular person.

"I laid hold of a man," she said, "on the staircase, who would, no doubt, have murdered me if he could."

"Now, madam," said the coroner, "this is very important; and what we wish to know is, if you can swear to this man you laid hold of?"

"I have no hesitation," she said, "in declaring that, to the best of my belief, it was a man of the name of Neville ; and there isn't such a rascal in the whole world."

"Pray, madam, confine yourself to facts," said the coroner.

"Well," said Mrs. Atherton, "that is a fact."

"Yes, but I mean facts that you know, and can produce as evidence."

"I do know it, and produce it as evidence ; and it would be great gammon if I were to say anything else."

"Really, madam," said the coroner, who liked sometimes to be very fine, and not understand illiterate witnesses, "really, madam, I wish you would explain to the jury what you mean by gammon."

"Oh, everybody knows what gammon is."

"I really do not," said the learned coroner.

"Well, then," said Mrs. Atherton, "if I were to tell you you were a handsome man, I should be gammoning you dreadfully."

The coroner looked very black, and the jury laughed ; and the former thought it better to resume the examination in chief, and not again be so handy in withdrawing Mrs. Atherton's attention from it.

"Are you quite certain," he said, "that this man whom you had hold of is named Neville? because, you will perceive, a mistake, under these circumstances, would be an extremely serious matter indeed."

"Of course it would," said Mrs. Atherton. "Do you think I'm such a goose as you are?"

"Really, really," said the beadle, "that's too bad—too bad by a great deal. Madam, you must not call the coroner a goose, or we shall have to take you into custody."

"A-fig for your custody. What is it to me? I am asked a question, and I reply to it. I say it was Neville who murdered Zachary; but I don't think he came to murder him, but on the contrary, that he came to murder all of us."

"Then how do you account for his making such a mistake?"

"Because the rain had come in at the roof of Zachary's room, and he made a noise about it, and insisted upon sleeping somewhere else, and that's the reason why I think he came by his death."

"Who is this Neville whom you suspect of the murder?"

"We don't know who he is, or what he is exactly, except that he has been here once or twice, and that we know he would like to murder the Black Lady."

"The Black Lady! Do you allude to that strange creature who goes about London attired in mourning weeds, attracting the sympathies of some and the derision of others?"

"Yes," said Mrs. Atherton, "that's the individual, and now you know all I have got to tell; and all I have got to say is, that if you or any of the jury would like a slice of cheese, there is plenty in the shop, and as reasonably as it can be got anywhere."

"Really, really," said the coroner, "this is trifling with the court; and the idea of endeavouring to sell cheese, at a moment when we are painfully considering the circumstances connected with the death of a fellow-creature, is to my mind perfectly dreadful—I say perfectly dreadful, gentlemen of the jury; and I have not been a coroner fourteen years now without, I should think, having a pretty good idea of what is perfectly dreadful and what is not."

"A-fig for you," said Mrs. Atherton. "I don't care what you think or what you say; and it's quite as correct for me to try to sell my cheese, as it is for you to be continually sitting down upon dead bodies. So, Mr. Coroner, you may make the best of that you can, and, what's more, if you say another word I'll pretty soon let you know who you are and where you are."

"Will anybody be so good," said the coroner, "as to stop that woman's tongue? It's a very odd thing, gentlemen of the jury, but I have always remarked that, as regards female witnesses, you invariably get too little or too much evidence out of them."

At this moment, Miles Atherton, who was standing near the door, was pushed aside by some one entering the room, and, upon turning round to see who it was, he observed a portly-looking woman, tolerably well dressed, and who, with very little ceremony, pushed aside whoever was in her way, in order that she might get sufficiently forward to hear the proceedings.

Atherton, of course, would have resented the formidable elbowing that he received had it come from a man, but, as it was, he could only grumble at it and put up with it; and it so happened that, while Mrs. Atherton was returning from giving her evidence, she came quite face to face with this bulky female intruder, and, in a moment after, she uttered a loud scream that alarmed everybody in court; and, to the surprise of all who witnessed such violence, the large female turned round and kicked down two people in a vigorous attempt which she made to leave the room.

Then Mrs. Atherton found voice to speak, and in accents that rung loudly through the apartment, she cried—

"It's Neville the murderer! seize him, seize him—it's Neville the murderer!"

The sensation which these words created, as may be supposed, was immense; and the efforts which the disguised Neville made to escape were of the most frantic and terrific character. Almost every one near to the door received some injury or another; and finally, it required the united endeavours of as many persons as could possibly lay hold of him, to capture him. The bonnet was torn from his head, and with it a woman's cap and a wig, and then the ruffian stood confessed to the eyes of all present.

Anxiety to hear exactly what was said at the inquest, and perhaps a confidence in a disguise which may before have served his turn, had brought him with such audacity to that place, where, most contrary to all his expectations, he had been so immediately captured.

The whole aspect of affairs now was changed; and, from an inquiry involved in great doubt and difficulty, the thing assumed quite a different aspect, because the very conduct of the suspected man gave the strongest possible presumption of his guilt.

Had he been innocent, why should he come there disguised? and then, when the disguise was discovered, why should he, unless with a consciousness that his capture must result in his condemnation, make such violence and frantic efforts to avoid it?

It was not safe to leave him a moment without handcuffs, for the expression of his countenance, now that he found himself taken, was perfectly demoniac and of the most horrible character. He glared upon the crowd of eager countenances around him as if he would gladly have been the destruction of every one there present; and, such was the compressed fury within his breast, that he bit his lips through and through, and the blood that flowed from them added much to his terrific and ghastly aspect.

There seemed to be so much danger lurking in his ferocious looking eye, that the jury were hardly satisfied when they saw him even handcuffed and held firmly by two police officers, who were not likely very easily to let go such a prize as that. But it was when his eyes fell upon Mrs. Atherton that the greatest amount of fury flashed from them, and then, indeed, he looked scarcely human.

No doubt that, at that moment, he well remembered how on a former occasion, with the assistance of the red hot poker, that lady had completely foiled him in his attempt upon the life of poor Marian Whitehead; and now that he had, in addition to that reminiscence, to attribute to her the fact of his capture, it as not to be supposed but what he should regard her with the most violent and malevolent feelings.

Indeed, it was tolerably clear to all those who noticed the looks which he cast upon her, that her only safety must consist in his condemnation; but as that seemed to be an event of a highly probable nature, she did not feel great apprehension from a thought of anything that Neville might wish to accomplish.

"Gentlemen of the jury," said the coroner, "we have, now, an accused person before us, and after hearing the remainder of the evidence, it is for you, by your verdict, to place me in a position, or otherwise, to order that he be continued in custody. If you think the evidence against him sufficiently strong to warrant his committal to prison, I shall, of course, issue my warrant; but, if you do not, the police-officers can use their own discretion as to what further steps they take regarding him. I perceive that the medical gentleman, to whom has been entrusted the examination of the body, is now ready with his report, and, after hearing his evidence, I believe that, as there are no more witnesses, the case will be left in your hands for consideration."

The evidence of the medical man we need not trouble the reader with in detail. Suffice it to say, that it was amply sufficient to satisfy the mind of any one that a murder had been committed; that is to say, that the deceased had neither died from natural causes, nor by his own hands, and, consequently, must have come by his decease during the eventful night which had preceded that deeply interesting inquiry.

Mrs. Atherton was again called forward, and she positively swore that Neville was the man whom she had encountered after the murder.

It took but a small portion of penetration for any one to perceive at once what the verdict was likely to be. The coroner, to do him justice, summed up with considerable perspicuity, pointing out to the jury that the evidence against Neville was of two kinds: first of all, very positive and direct, as regarded Mrs. Atherton's recognition of him; and secondly, strong and circumstantial as regarded his own conduct on the occasion, which was certainly strongly indicative of guilt, for no innocent man would ever, for a moment, have thought of conducting himself in the manner that Neville had.

He was asked his Christian name, which he indignantly, and with scorn and derision, refused to tell, and, although from the manuscripts of the Black Lady, Atherton and his wife could have supplied the deficiency, they thought it was best not to do so, and prudently said nothing upon the subject.

A verdict was accordingly returned of wilful murder against ——— Neville, and the coroner at once signed a warrant so as to place him with all due formality in custody.

For a moment, then, it seemed as if Neville were about to say something, and then he altered his mind, and with a kind of scornful laugh, he allowed himself to be led away without making any remark upon the proceedings.

He was conveyed at once before a magistrate, and, to save trouble, the depositions of the witnesses at the coroner's inquest were read over and sworn to, when the magistrate at once committed the prisoner to Newgate, to take his trial at the next Old Bailey sessions, remarking, as he did so, that he had no hesitation in taking that step, for he had never seen a clearer case against any one; but that the prisoner, if he chose, might make his own statement, although he warned him it would be taken down in writing and used for or against him, according as its purport might be.

Neville was silent for a few moments, and then he spoke.

"A man," he said, "may put on a woman's dress without being the murderer. I know nothing of the occurrence, and shall be prepared to prove that I was somewhere else the whole of last night. In fact, I was at a masquerade."

"Indeed," said the magistrate, "and where was that?"

"At an assembly rooms near Brentford, and I can produce witnesses, although not just at this moment, to prove that fact."

"Of course," said the magistrate, "if you can prove an *alibi* you may do so, and, if you had mentioned it before, I should have remanded you for a week, in order to give you the opportunity."

"No," said Neville, "as it's gone so far let it go to a jury, and we will see what can be made of it. I am an innocent man, but the principal witness, Mrs. Atherton, has a grudge against me because I played a trick upon her once by giving her a bit of glass, and telling her it was an emerald. I have got no more to say, except that I shall be able to prove both Atherton and his wife to be bad characters, and that they are not content with robbing the living, but I am in a condition to prove that they steal the very bones of the dead. This man, Atherton, cannot deny that he has more than once burglariously broken into the vaults of St. Paul. He knows it's true; look at him."

Miles Atherton certainly looked staggered at this remark, which was strictly true, and consequently he did not attempt to deny it—a fact which the magistrate was not slow to perceive, and which rather puzzled him as regarded the case generally.

"I will withdraw the committal," he said, "and remand you for a week, if you like, so that you may have a full opportunity of proving all these things that you state, if you think it desirable so to do, but if you choose rather to be committed and reserve your defence for a trial, you can do so, and I shall not interfere with your selection."

"Yes," said Neville, "let it be so;" and he was at once removed, but it will be seen how, by the brief statement he had made, he had most materially injured Atherton and his wife, who now began to see what a troublesome thing it was to have other people's secrets in their keeping, and perhaps it would have been better for them in the long run, if they had repressed their curiosity to become acquainted with the melancholy story of Marian Whitehead. It was too late, however, now to retract, and if any uncomfortable consequences were to arise, from a relation of that sad history, they felt that they must just bear the brunt of them in the best manner they were able, for they quite despaired in getting her permission to relate the causes which had made the visits to St. Paul's so deeply interesting and so guiltless.

"My dear," said Miles Atherton to his wife, "it's no use vexing yourself about this affair, and it's quite ridiculous for any one to suppose that we went to St. Paul's with a bad motive, because, what is there to be had there that is worth anything to take away?"

"I grant there is nothing, but still it is not very pleasant to be told such a thing and not be able to say it is not true."

" I grant you all that, and before Neville's trial comes on, which will be some time yet, we can try and get the Black Lady's leave to clear ourselves."

" Ah! that will be hopeless," said Mrs. Atherton, " and besides, poor thing, it will put her in such a fever to ask her, that really, for my part, I should not like to do so, and would rather, by a great deal, put up with any inconvenience, for Heaven knows she has had enough to bear in her time, and don't need anything else now to torment her."

CHAPTER LXIX.

THE CHEESEMONGER AND JEM TRY TO FIND THE BLACK LADY, AND MEET WITH AN ADVENTURE.

No wonder Miles Atherton was troubled in his mind respecting this affair of the murder of Zachary, for the testimony he would have to give would, most probably, if not for certainty, touch upon the safe keeping of the secret of the Black Lady. He was much troubled upon this score, and his conscience was, in what an American would call, a fix. If he divulged the secret he thought he committed something so very like perjury that he could not tell the difference, and, moreover, if he observed strict silence upon that matter, which it would be difficult to do, he would be making a material reservation, which, in itself, was a crime.

What to do he knew not; turn which way he would he was met by some objection or other, and there was no alternative left to act upon. She had a choice of evils, neither of which he conceived could be borne, and after mature deliberation, all he could do was to attempt to seek the Black Lady for the purpose of ascertaining if there were any possibility of obtaining her consent to his revealing, when on oath, some of her secrets.

The next difficulty that occurred was the obtaining of an interview with her, indeed there was some trouble in that matter; if they were quietly to wait until she made her appearance *then* they could make the necessary request of her, but there was the uncertainty that she might not come at all before that period, and it was very likely, because Miles wished to see her, she would not come; at least events often happen after that fashion, and they appear as if they were ordained upon contradictory principles, and thus it was he feared to leave the thing to its own course.

" No, no," said Miles Atherton, " no, no, that will never do, I must seek her, and I may, as I hope, find her, besides, I shall have the chance of her coming again; as well as the probability of my finding her in addition. So I have two chances instead of one. I must say, though that her coming here is at best a poor and uncertain chance, for I do not know why or wherefore she should do so, and it would not be difficult to find her in some of her usual haunts in the city."

He determined in his own mind that to do the thing effectually he must devote a whole day to it, so that he should have perfect freedom of action and no care upon his mind.

" I shall lose the day," he said, " but having made up my mind to that there is no further need of thinking about it. It is done and settled, and then I will take Jem with me. Jem knows something that other people don't, and may, after all, be very useful to me. I can often make inquiries by him without being seen by any one."

This being settled, Miles Atherton's next step was to obtain the full consent of his wife, which, under the circumstances, was conceded, and then Miles informed Jem of it. Great was this worthy's delight when he saw there was a chance of what he called a day's pleasure,—a spree out with his master.

" It will be a good chance," he said; " I shall go and take care of the governor, and he'll stand treat of course, and there will be a glorious job, and all out of missus's sight; though she aint much like what she used to be anyhow, now."

This was true enough, and since certain passages in this narrative, Mrs. Atherton had been a much more pleasant helpmate than heretofore. It was early in the morning when Miles Atherton and Jem sallied out on their voyage of discovery.

"Which way are you going?" inquired Jem, after he had gone the length of the street, and given a customary or habitual look back.

"That, Jem, I hardly know—but I think we must make somewhere towards St. Paul's—the Bank—and other places, where they say she is usually to be found, or occasionally to be seen."

"Well, governor," said Jem, "I'll follow you where you please, but you aint going to remain all about there, are you, for the whole day? It will be a precious long job, and we'll be taken for suspicious characters if we aint very careful—very careful indeed!"

"Why so, Jem? I can't see any reason why we should be taken for such."

"We shall be considered so, having no good object in view, when we are noticed hanging about the Bank all day and other places in the city, they'll think we want to rob somebody."

"I have lived too long in London and paid rent and taxes too long, also, in the city, to be much afraid of that; they'll not do that, Jem, I pay towards the support of the police."

"Do you?"

"Yes, I do, Jem, and you ought to know that pretty well by this time. I wish I had all the money I have paid away in the shape of taxes and rates, it would be a small fortune, Jem."

"Aye, I dare say it would, but if the government were careful of the shop-keepers they might put all these sums in the saving's bank and when you get old you would have a good annuity to live on, but they don't do that, they only drop it into a sinking fund."

"That is true enough, Jem."

"Yes, governor," continued Jem, "and I am afraid you will never be recognised as a rate-payer even in the city by a constable, even if you were to put your receipts in your pocket, you'd only get taken up as having stolen them from some person or other, and so get detained for the robbery."

"Come, come, Jem, no more of that; you know you are going it too fast just now, we mustn't spend our time in this way else we shall not get any way advanced on our adventure to-day."

"Very well, governor," said Jem, "but we haven't lost time as yet as I see, because we have been walking along at a pretty good pace, and here we are at the Mansion-House."

"She used to walk around here, Jem," said the cheesemonger, "do you look out upon the passengers and if you see her tell me directly. You know her, don't you?"

"I do, I believe you. If anybody ever set their blessed eyes on her they'd never forgot her. I aint been so frightened yet but I can recollect her very well."

"She's not about here. We'll go and see the Bank, some of the porters will tell us something about her, I dare say; if they cannot tell us where she is now, they will, at all events, be able to inform us of some likely place where she is in the habit of going to and where we may possibly find her, though we can't tell where she lives."

"Very well, governor," said Jem.

They now crossed over from the Mansion-House until they reached the Bank, into which they turned, until they reached the body of the building, when they paused and looked around for some moments until some one came, and perceiving they were only looking about them, accosted them in a somewhat peremptory tone.

"What do you want here?" inquired a big fat man, looking with some contempt upon Atherton and Jem.

"I want to find the Black Lady," said the unconscious Miles Atherton, looking around him.

"Do you? then you must look for her somewhere else, she don't live here. It strikes me you had better Black Lady it somewhere else—you don't want any good here—be off!"

" I want no harm of you or any one else. I am a citizen of London and don't expect this kind of treatment here, or elsewhere."

" We haven't anything to do with that. We is bankers, Bank of England, and nobody comes here for nothink, and since you don't want anythink, of course you can't be arter no good."

" But I do want something," said Miles Atherton, " I didn't come here without an object in coming."

" What is it ?"

" Why, I told you, I wanted the person who is usually called the Black Lady."

" Very likely, but that is nothink to us ; and what is nothink to us is nothink here ; so you see you are arter nothink—nothink good—so you had better go about your business."

" A nice old codger you'd make at a tea party," said Jem. " I wouldn't mind wagering a bad farthing against your cocked hat that you are nobody at home, great as you are here."

The beadle was furious—his rubicund visage appeared of a dusky purple, and he was preparing to make a seizure of Jem, but the latter was as wary as he was daring, and he made for the door and was out of reach in no time.

Miles Atherton followed Jem at leisure, and then left the indignant beadle to his fate—apoplexy or an inflammation of the face, which could probably never be subdued.

When Miles Atherton got out, he espied Jem on the other side of the way, but before he crossed over he saw a man walking about before the Bank, with a familiar and confident air. Now the cheesemonger thought he had seen this man before, and concluded he was some one who was employed about the Bank, either to answer inquiries, or some officer in disguise.

" He will be just the man I want—I will put the question to him at once, and he will give a satisfactory answer, I have no doubt ;" and he accordingly made up to him, saying :

" Pray, sir, do you know anything of a strange figure in black—known about here as the Black Lady ?"

" I have seen her very often," replied the stranger.

" I cannot find her to-day, anywhere ; and yet I want to do so for an essential purpose. Perhaps you may happen to know where I may meet with her."

" She doesn't like her place of abode known to any one ; but I happen to know, accidentally seeing her go in. You don't want to know from a bad motive, I suppose ?"

" Oh, no, no."

" Well then, I'll tell you. You are charitably inclined, eh ?—you want her for a good purpose ?"

" I do so."

" Ah, well then, you must go down one of the long steep turnings out of Watling Street, that runs down towards the river."

" Which ?"

" I cannot properly tell which ; but you'll know the place I mean—it is one that is as steep as any in that neighbourhood ; you will see a green door, over which is chalked a gridiron, so you can't miss it."

" What part of the house ?" inquired Atherton.

" Ah! I don't know, for I never was in there, and know nothing of the place ; but I think I saw her push the door open herself, so I dare say you will not be required to knock ; and if I might give an opinion, I should say go in until you meet with somebody or other, capable of telling you what you wanted to know."

" I thank you," said Miles Atherton, when the stranger had finished his communication.

" Ah! you are very welcome," said the stranger, and he walked away. And Miles Atherton crossed over the road to where Jem was standing waiting for him, and watching him all the while with an air of curiosity and suspicion combined, and when he came over, Jem said—

"Well, governor, what news?"

"I think I have learned where she may be found, after all, Jem; and if it should turn out so it will be very lucky."

"So it will, governor; but who did you learn it from—from that cove you were speaking to outside?"

"Yes.'"

"Well I don't know why, but I don't like his looks at all. I fancy I have seen him hanging about before to-day."

"And I thought so, too," said Atherton; "he is probably somebody employed by the Bank to keep the peace, should any disturbance take place, or any attempt to rob the bank or those going in and out; there are many people going in and out with large sums of money—and there are many who know it."

"No doubt they do," said Jem.

"Well then, they get set upon and robbed, and they don't know how it is done—for you don't know who these men are."

"I dare say not," said Jem; "but it strikes me that the man you spoke to was as much like a thief as a horse; perhaps, as he's a thief-taker, that may account for his looks; but have you learned any thing, governor, of the Black Lady?'"

"I think I have, Jem; we must make the best of our way to those steep streets or lanes running down from Watling Street or somewhere thereabout, and there we shall find her. She has been seen to go into a house there which I shall know when I see."

"That is consolation, at all events," said Jem. "Let us push on to the house; you know, governor, it will be about your lunch-time, won't it?"

CHAPTER LXX.

IN WHICH MILES ATHERTON AND JEM ARE IN FEAR FOR THEIR LIVES.

MILES ATHERTON replied not; he was deep in thought, and pursued his way towards the spot indicated by the obliging stranger, and it was with some industry and trouble that he sought out the house with a gridiron chalked over the door. House after house he went to, and looked hard at the doors, but he saw not the desired mark, and at length Jem, who had been attentively looking for the same, said—

"Well, governor, I think we may as well look for a frying-pan as a gridiron, now; it will only be a change, you know."

"Well, I am tired; I shall go and sit down, and have my lunch before I go any further. I'll try again by-and-by. We aint had much fortune this morning, at all events."

"We aint had none yet at all," said Jem, "but perhaps a liberal outlay at the Nine Tuns here will purchase some. Depend upon it, governor, there never was yet any thing good come of an empty stomach. I never did myself, and never heard of anybody who ever did."

Miles Atherton pushed open the door of a low public-house. It was a decent-looking place on the outside, with good parlour and skittle-ground at the back. This was the amusement that was presumed to be so tempting to the passenger.

They entered, and walked into the parlour, Jem keeping close to the governor; for he considered the adventure was to be a joint one, and therefore he was fully entitled to be considered as in partnership on this occasion, and he expected liberal treatment.

"Now, Jem," said Atherton, "go to the bar, and order a pot of ale and some cold meat; they must have some, I should think I am very hungry."

"And so am I, governor."

" Well, then, make haste, and after that we'll try what we can do again; we may by chance find her now."

Jem waited not to be told, but ordered the ale and cold meat, and then returned to the parlour, where the eatables soon made their appearance, and then commenced the work of destruction, which both shone in, for they had been walking about for some hours, and disappointment had sharpened the cheesemonger's appetite, but Jem's wanted no artificial aid. It was always good, and on this occasion he did justice to himself.

They remained here an hour, by the end of which time the ale was gone, and their hunger appeased, when after some further consideration they arose, and Atherton having paid the charges was about to quit the house, when a rough-looking man said—

" You are wanted a moment, governor."

" Who ?" says the cheesemonger.

" You, to be sure ; you were in the parlour just now."

" I was ; but I cannot understand what you want with me on that account. It is not unusual for anybody to do so, I suppose ?"

" No ; but if you have no regard for your own property, other people have, and so you can go and take it, or leave it alone."

" My property," muttered Atherton ; " what can it be ?" and he immediately turned round to retrace his steps, followed by Jem, who kept a good look-out, as if he expected something was wrong, but couldn't tell what. They, however, took the wrong door, and found themselves in a passage, into which they were followed by some persons, and before they could make an attempt to return.

" Come, push on," said the man.

" Rather not," said Jem. " Will you go first ? I dare say you are going further this road, and know it better."

" I'd sooner you go on first," said the other. " You are first already, and know more of the place than I do."

" I shall go no further," said Miles Atherton, turning back.

" Won't you now ?" said the man, when he and another man rushed upon them, and began to fight and strike out right and left, and knocked them along in this manner for some yards, and then succeeded in forcing them through a door ; after which they fell down some steps until they came to the bottom, and then found themselves alone, standing in some place they knew not where, and all in the dark.

" Well," said Jem, " this is a pretty go, and I'm thinking we are very much like the babes in the wood ; we don't know where we are."

" No," said Miles Atherton ; " but what does all this mean ? They want to rob us, I suppose."

" Something worse than that, master," said Jem.

" Worse ! what can be worse, Jem ?"

" Murder," said Jem ; " they aint put us here for nothing, depend upon it ; for if we were only robbed, and they are welcome to rob me if they can ; but then, if we get away, we should ruin the house. No, no ; it isn't for robbery alone, governor, they have pushed us into this black hole."

" And what else, Jem ? You don't think they would murder us, do you ?"

" I do."

" What ! in the city ? You must make some mistake."

" Not a bit of it, master. We should do very well to dissect as well as anybody else besides. There are our two bodies," said Jem, as if he were about to enlarge upon the misery of their position ; " they'll fetch them something, them thieves ; our clothes—they are worth something, especially mine, for they are my Sunday ones ; and then there is the money you have got about you, so, taking all things together, they will get plenty by the job—they'll be well paid."

" We must try and get out of this, Jem," said the cheesemonger, " if we can ; for it will not do to remain here longer than we are really obliged, you know."

"Not longer than we are obliged or can help—but we are all in the dark, and have no light."

"None!" said the cheesemonger, mournfully.

"Well!" said Jem, "we are in a pretty fix! Have you got such a thing as a cigar and a piece of German tinder?"

"Well! I dare say I have—indeed, I know I have; but what made you ask such a question, Jem? who could smoke a cigar under such circumstances as these, I should like to know?"

"I will, if you won't, governor; it will give us something of a light, and that will perhaps show us about a little, and enable us to see where we are, and when we can get out of this place."

"Two heads are better than one," said Miles, and he began to light his cigar, and, by dint of much blowing, he got a view of the place. It was a long passage, the end of which he could not see; seemingly of brick, and very damp. However, they walked along until they came to the end of the passage, and then they came to a door, which they found wide open, and went through into another passage and through another door.

There was a sudden blaze of light which met them strongly, and having taken a false step they were suddenly thrown down some place, and did not recover themselves until they came with some force against something soft.

There was a loud bang of a door over their heads, and then all was still. Miles Atherton and Jem lay on their backs, between some bales of goods, that appeared to be lying about in great profusion.

They did not move for a moment or so, and then they heard a voice say, in low but deep accents,—

" What was that ?"

" I don't know," said another, " those doors have been left open, and a gust of wind has blown through."

" Then damn them ! I wish they would take more care, or one of these days we shall all be sold ; that's my opinion. Somebody will come poking along those passages and they will find out our warehouse, and we shall find our way to prison."

" If any one finds his way here, he had better settle his account with this world, for I'll do for him ! There will be no use in showing him any mercy."

" None ! we should only bespeak our own imprisonment for life."

There was a sound as of some one going away, and the sounds of voices ceased ; Jem and Miles Atherton lay perfectly still for some time, believing their lives were in great danger, but when they felt they were alone Jem whispered,

" Well ! we have got somewhere now, governor ; I'm thinking that we shan't get out of this very safely—we are in here for no good purpose, look what a place it is !"

" There does seem to be something very much like murder," said Miles Atherton, as he looked around ; but his vision was limited, and he could not see far, because there were piles of goods and packages, to an extent scarcely conceivable

" Well !" said Jem, " I'll get up and see if I can get out of this place—there may be some means of getting out as we got in, and there appears plenty of places to hide in."

Jem got up and scrambled, and saw that they had got into some large, long room, up and down which, on either side, was filled with bales and casks from one end to the other. It was evidently a depôt for smuggled goods.

At that time, heavy duties were paid upon all things, and it made it worth while to engage deeply in these smuggling transactions, for they soon enabled those doing so to retire with large fortunes.

They crept along for some time, until they came to a turn in the room, which was caused by another room running across the end of it. They followed the course of this with some trouble ; and at length they heard the voices of men talking together, close at hand.

Carefully and stealthily they crept along, when they came to some goods that were piled higher than others, and on coming to the end of the bales, they looked over upon the heads of four or five men, who were playing cards, and drinking brandy and water of the best quality, as could be told by the scent that arose from it.

" Well, Bill !" said one, " how many more voyages do you intend to make ?"

" Not many."

" Remember the fable of the broken pitcher !"

" Yes, but I have been too careful, and we have our secret in the hands of a few only."

" That is good certainly—very good. What will your last voyage bring you, eh ?"

" A good sum, I hope."

" What do you think, upon a rough guess ?"

"About five or six hundred pounds, at least; possibly as much more. I have done this some fifteen or sixteen times, and have, as yet, always succeeded in running my cargo."

"You have been lucky."

"Yes, pretty well!"

"When you get out to sea, I dare say you don't care how soon you are in some of the foreign ports?"

"Not a bit, if I only get a cap-full."

The remainder of this sentence was stopped by the fall of Jem's cap, from off his head, right in the midst of the smugglers, who gaped at it in utter astonishment, and then they looked up and beheld the features of Jem and Miles Atherton.

"Damnation!" shouted one of the men, who jumped up from the seat in which he had been enjoying himself.

"Betrayed, by God!"

"Cut them down!" said the seaman, "or run them up to the yard-arm, don't be fools—have them!"

Jem and Miles Atherton, for a minute or so, appeared to be fascinated to the spot, so much so, that they could not get back for some moments, till the words 'cut them down,' acted like the sound of an enchanter, and they both endeavoured to scramble back, but, in doing so, they pushed the bales from under them, and down they rolled, Atherton and Jem on the top of them, with awful destruction to the table, glasses, and bottles, and the lights, which were extinguished.

The smugglers swore—the bales of goods rolled and bumped about from place to place, and Miles Atherton and Jem were both so confused and terrified, that they knew not what they were about, though Jem did try to get back again, but the smugglers threw themselves in a body upon them, and soon succeeded in securing them.

"Spare our lives!" said Atherton, "spare our lives!"

"Yes, we will! as long as it is convenient to do so; but just be quiet, or you will be settled and done for at once."

"Gag and bind them!" said one, who gave the order very peremptorily; and he was at once obeyed by the others.

In a minute more Jem and Miles Atherton were both safely secured; their hands and feet fastened, while a gag was thrust in their mouths, which prevented their making any noise, save a low groan, or something of that sort.

There was a short consultation held among the smugglers, among whom a diversity of opinion appeared to exist.

"Knock them both on the head at once," said one, "there will be no further trouble about them."

"No, no! there will be trouble about the bodies. Let's take them below and see what they say to it. Something must be done, or they must be sent somewhere, where they'll never speak of what they have seen here." So saying, he led the way, while the others, seizing their prisoners, dragged them along after them.

CHAPTER LXXI.

THE TRIAL OF NEVILLE, AND HIS CONVICTION.—THE OFFER TO IMPEACH GODFREY.

IT was with feelings of reluctance and great fear that Miles Atherton and Jem felt themselves thrust forward, and wholly in the power of these people, who had every inducement to take their lives. It was their interest to do so, and Miles could not but think it was more than probable they would be destroyed—nay, that it would be improbable that it should be otherwise. Even Jem appeared to think that he stood a very poor chance of escape.

" Master has no chance," thought Jem, " for he couldn't speak, and I don't know how much of a chance I have got—none I'm afraid, and yet, who can tell? I may be able to persuade 'em I am likely to be useful to 'em, and will do anything they want me."

However, there was not much time given for reflection, before they were thrust into a room where there were several other men, who were similarly employed to the first, but soon ceased as the intruders appeared, who now with little or no ceremony pushed them into a small closet, and a council was immediately held upon them, and conducted for some time in whispers, and then they spoke out,—

" I tell you what," said one, " there can be no silly feeling of humanity in this matter, as we shall be transported, perhaps hanged—life and fortune are at stake."

" No, no; they must pay the penalty of their curiosity; they are spies, no doubt, and have been caught in the fact."

" But they had better not be settled here," said one man.

" What can be your objection, Smith?"

" I will tell you," replied the man. " You will, by killing them here, bring upon us certain destruction. Indeed, I am sure it would be a hanging matter, and, so far, it would be a settler for us all."

" Who do you think would split?"

" It isn't necessary that any one should do so ; but there would be the difficulty of getting rid of the bodies, and something or other would turn up to betray us while we had them ; depend upon it, it will be by far the best plan to take them both out to sea and throw them overboard, and then they are only killed, because they won't swim ; that is the whole of the case."

" Well, well, there is something like reason, for, I am sure, I thought you were going to propose that they should be let off altogether—a thing that could not be done with any safety to ourselves."

" No ; it would be total ruin and destruction not only of ourselves, but of all connected with us, to whom we have sworn to observe, and have so long observed, faith."

" Well, then, the next thing to be considered is how to take them on board the vessel which is lying off Gravesend."

" But how to get them there is the difficulty."

" No ; that need be no difficulty : pack them both up in a crate, and put them on board the lighter, and she will be along-side the brig in a very short time ; we shall make the run to-night, and we can hoist them over about the Nore, or off the Foreland, and, if necessary, they can be tied together, neck and heels, so that no accident can save them."

" Yes, that will do, and tie shot to them, so that they may be kept down until they are past recognition, and then they can take their chance."

" Agreed.   We'll consider that settled."

" Exactly, and now to business."

*   *   *   *   *   *   *

In about an hour they came to the closet, where Jem and Miles Atherton were confined, and took them out, and, after uttering the most horrible denunciations against them, and threatening them with an instant and cruel death if they stirred, they forced them into a large crate, which was packed up with straw.

They were incapable of motion, or of uttering a single sound, no matter how loud it might have been, and, moreover, they were almost insensible ; Miles Atherton especially so, for, from his superior bulk, he was unable to move, and was moreover so bent that he ran great danger of being killed.

They were carried they knew not where; but they were tossed about a good deal until they were finally placed upon what they supposed to be a cart, and so it eventually turned out, for shortly after it began to jolt along the stones, until they got on to what they supposed to be a country road, for they got rid of the jolting, or much of it.

They were a long while thus, and how they lived was a complete mystery to themselves; indeed, it was a miracle how it was they preserved so much sense as to be enabled to tell or feel any change whatever.

Jem, all the while, was completely upside-down, the whole weight of his body being thrown upon his head and shoulders, while Miles Atherton lay upon his knees and his head, his body being bent up like a hoop.

They felt they were being carried along on a waggon, or some slowly-moving vehicle, which they had no doubt was filled with goods, or rather which was going to be filled with some contraband articles, which were to be brought to the store-house for smuggled goods, from which it was to be distributed all over the metropolis in the ordinary course of business.

But why had they who knew nothing, and who even suspected nothing, why should they be thrust into it? There was no object to be gained—nay, they were going to be murdered merely because they were intruders and spies.

Perhaps they thought our looking about the neighbourhood was the motive for pushing us forward in the way they did. We were considered spies, and it was thought only safe to act as they had done. They had excited the suspicions of the people in the house, who took the best manner they could to dispose of people whom they deemed busying themselves to their injury.

Suddenly, however, they felt a change in their motion and position; they were quietly turned over, and, after one or two movements, they felt the jolt of the cart cease, and yet they thought they were being carried along at a slower pace with a gentle motion, the meaning of which they couldn't understand, but were in dreadful fear lest they were about to be precipitated into the Thames, crate and all, and so sink in a mass, without the possibility of an attempt at even a struggle for life and liberty.

How long they were thus carried about they knew not, but there were several rests or stoppages, and they thought they heard some whispering, though they were not sure; but that afforded them no hope.

Suddenly they felt a violent motion, as if the crate had been flung down with some force on the ground, and the crate jumped up and burst open to a small extent, giving the prisoners a little ease, but not restoring them or releasing them.

"There," said a voice, "I never had such a load as that before."

"Nor I; my back is almost broken. If Bill and I hadn't been two bricks, we never should have had the pluck to have brought it all the way here; we should have ripped it open and brought the contents, or part of them, and so gone back for the remainder."

"You would be liable to be caught."

"Yes, we thought of that; but it has been an awfully hard pull, and ought to be something good to repay us."

"Well, I tell you, I was told at the office there was a large package going containing some valuable goods, chiefly silk."

"Then, if we have three or four hundredweight of silk, we shall make a good thing of it. I dare say we shall have one or two such jobs as these on this road. It will never be suspected."

"And if we are, we had better shift our ground after every fresh fakement we make, or we may have one or two loads before we shift our place of abode."

"Well, well, open it before you do any more, and let's see what you have got there. We can't carry it away in that shape, and the crate will do to light the fire; and then we'll have a rousing glass of grog as we overhaul the booty."

"Here goes, then," said the other.

At that moment Jem and Miles Atherton felt the strokes of the axe as the man struck it, blow after blow; and at every stroke some part of the crate gave way, until at length both Jem and Miles Atherton rolled out into the space before the robbers.

It is difficult to describe the utter consternation and amazement of the thieves when they saw the unfortunate individuals roll out before them on the floor of an old barn. Some whistled, some swore, and a third laughed outright.

"Well," said one, "you have made a good job, you have. Why, you've been a body-snatching."

"D——n, where did you come from?"

It was now observed that they were bound and gagged, and one of the men drew his knife and cut the cords in two, leaving the unhappy cheesemonger and his aide-de-camp, Jem, at liberty.

However, it was some time before they could speak or even stand, so cruelly had they been used; but they lay on their backs, gasping and glaring about them, until one of them threw some water over their faces, and poured a large dose of brandy down their throats.

By these means they somewhat revived, and Jem, having suffered least, being the least, and not quite so long and so bulky as "the governor," was the first to find the use of his speech.

"Oh! we aint off the Nore now, are we?"

"He's mad. How the devil did you get there? Who put you there? What have you done that you want to be smuggled out of the country like that?"

"Don't know," said Jem. "It's all done against our will. We wouldn't have been put up in a basket."

"Who did it?"

"The smugglers," said Jem.

"The smugglers!" reiterated the man. "Well, I never heard they smuggled men before. Surely they must have desired your services on the next Guy Fawkes-day?"

"No," said Atherton; "though that wouldn't be the worst. We were seized by some smugglers, who thought us in the way, or were looking out for them."

"Aye, excisemen."

"No, no; we had some other object in view: we have no connexion whatever with the excise or police, and were not even aware that we were near them when they thrust us into their place of concealment; and yet I take Heaven to witness we had no design against them whatever."

"What did they put you in there for?"

"To put us on board a smuggling vessel, and then to throw us overboard below the Nore."

"By Jove! you would have had a damp bed of it, to say the least, and a little more water than you could drink."

"Ah!" said Jem, "and not half so good as this brandy; but you've saved our lives, and no mistake."

"Well," said Miles Atherton, "I can never repay you for what you have done for us. What money I have about me you shall have, and be most welcome to. But where are we?"

"This is called Plaistow Level."

"Goodness me, I have no idea where that is."

"Below the Isle of Dogs—near the Thames. You are some miles out of London now, and it is there you want to get back to."

"It is," said Miles Atherton.

There was some conversation among them all. Miles Atherton at once gave up all the money he had about him to these people, who, having inadvertently saved his life, felt some compunction in injuring him; and the upshot of it was, they gave them some refreshments, such as they had, and conducted them across the fields to the main road, having made up their minds that they would make another expedition that night, as it was early, and the first had turned out so badly.

This they did, and Jem and Miles Atherton returned to town on foot, almost wearied out and crippled, and being compelled to rest repeatedly; only, they were scarce able to do that without ordering something for the good of the house and themselves, which ended in their being very unsteady and tottering when they reached town, but in a most deplorable condition, both as regarded atigue and sobriety, in which state they succeeded in finding at a late hour.

CHAPTER LXXII.

THE TRIAL AND CONVICTION OF NEVILLE FOR THE MURDER OF ZACHARY, AND HIS OFFER TO SACRIFICE GODFREY.

THE day upon which the villain Neville was to be tried soon came round, and with it much anxiety to the worthy cheesemonger and his wife, who were unable to make up their minds what to do in this matter as regarded the Black Lady s secret, which they had already sworn to observe, and they were of opinion that no subsequent oath ought to interfere with the due performance of so sacred a promise; but then they must take and break the second oath, which they were both unwilling to do.

Betwixt these two alternatives they stood equally unable to tell what they should do to release themselves from such a dilemma as that in which they were so unexpectedly placed by the possession of a secret.

However, there was no help; no aid that day came, and they and others were kept in suspense in the neighbourhood of the Old Bailey the whole of the day; but it so happened that the day appointed for the trial did not come on, but it was to come on the first thing the next morning, and to the end that he might be there in good time, Miles Atherton and Mrs. Atherton, attended by Jem in as respectable a dress as was deemed necessary or possible on the occasion, went to an inn in the immediate vicinity of the Old Bailey court, indeed, almost directly opposite— a place much frequented by the legal profession, and at the same time by clients.

Here they had breakfast, to which they all did ample justice, Jem conspicuously so; and here they remained for an hour and a half.

"There are a great many people here," said Atherton, "and most of them connected with the Old Bailey trials."

"Then there are a great many people who are related to those who are taken up for crime of one sort and another?"

"Yes," said Atherton, "there are some unfortunates in every family, and their relatives, if they be not very hard-hearted, will generally do them some good at such a moment as that, when they are in peril for life and liberty; and also to avoid the disgrace of having one connected with them subjected to a disgraceful punishment."

"However, I should hardly have expected to see so many people here; the place is all alive with people. Ah, but they are all passengers."

"Most of them have been passengers by coach, for many of them are country people, farmers and others; but many of them are employed about the inns, the court and prison of the Old Bailey and Newgate; besides the usual traffic belonging to the place as a thoroughfare."

"Ah!" said Jem, "but there are many more who come on a Monday morning when there's a grand show over the way."

"A grand show, Jem! what do you mean by that?" inquired Mrs. Atherton, for a moment believing he meant the Lord Mayor's show.

"A hanging treat," said Jem.

"A hanging treat! Goodness me, what can that be?"

"Why they hang 'em over the way," said Jem, "when they find them guilty of murder and the like, you know; it's the place of execution, as you may have heard in the papers."

At this moment an attorney entered the room, saying as he did so to Miles Atherton,—

"Your presence, Mr. Atherton, will soon be required in the court. This is the first case to be called on, and you will be required early. I hope you will not be detained long."

"You are very good," said Miles. "Have you breakfasted?"

"Oh yes, I have taken care to guard against the damps of London. It would never do for a professional man to expose himself in that way. There's a carriage going into the yard. I dare say that is the recorder, or one of the judges—most likely it is the latter."

Upon this they all arose, and Miles Atherton, having paid the charges, followed the attorney, and entered the court of the Old Bailey.

There were many people present; indeed, it is usual to find them there when there is a capital trial going on, that is, when there is any one about to be tried for an offence that endangers his life; but there were many more than usual, as it was generally anticipated that it would be a long and interesting trial.

The judge soon after entered the court, which was crowded with counsel and many attorneys. The usual proclamation for silence having been read and the prisoner arraigned at the bar, the jury were called over, and the counsel on both sides, objecting to some and admitting others, until the jury were complete.

Then the prisoner was asked to plead guilty or not guilty: the latter was, of course, the answer in a deep, gruff voice, and then the usual formalities having been gone through, the counsel for the crown arose to commence his statement.

After some few preliminary remarks he said,—

"The crime with which the prisoner at the bar stands charged is one of the deepest and the most heinous in the whole catalogue of human iniquity. The guilt of blood-taking is the first great crime punished by man, and the one for which no reparation can be made to the deceased or to his relatives, or, in fact, to society—none save that of rendering up his life for his offence.

"But, gentlemen, I need say this is no reparation—it is merely a consequence—an awful one, but it is the only one that will meet the exigencies of the case—the crime is an extreme one, and it requires an extreme punishment.

"Society requires it—we should not be safe without it, neither would it be safe or just that the murderer should be maintained for his life at the public expense, while so many honest men starve for the food which he would be plentifully supplied with.

"But, gentlemen, God forbid that I should make his case worse than it is—it is bad enough.

"The prisoner stands charged, gentlemen, with entering the house of Mr. Miles Atherton, a respectable tradesman—a cheesemonger—for a felonious purpose, and while in the house, in the pursuit of that object, he slew one Zachary, a lodger, who had for a short time previously lived there.

"He broke into the house at midnight—he stabbed the unfortunate man to the heart, and when he was discovered he was quite dead, and his room set on fire by the prisoner.

"Then the alarm being spread, and knowing the people in the house were about, he made what haste he could to escape from the house, and in doing which he assaulted and struck down both the witness and his wife, the latter of whom at once recognised him again.

"The prisoner at that time escaped in the confusion of the moment, and got clear off; but somehow or other, for a good purpose no doubt, he was afflicted with a curiosity to witness the proceedings of the inquest on the body of his victim, when he was recognised and secured.

"I shall now call witnesses to prove to your satisfaction, gentlemen, all that I have stated to you."

Miles Atherton was then called, and the counsel proceeded to ask him some questions, and then he desired him to tell the court all that had happened on the night in question.

"I will," said Miles; "I was in bed with my wife—"

"You must not trouble the court with anything concerning your wife," said the judge; "just tell us what took place."

"Yes, my lord," said Miles, rather confused, "I will. As I was saying, I was in bed fast asleep; I was alarmed at some noises that seemed to come from some parts of the house, I couldn't tell where. My wife insisted there were robbers in the house, and that I must get up and see what was the cause of all the disturbance."

"And you did," said the counsel.

"Yes, I did."

"And what did you see on that occasion?"

"My wife and I got up. I came out first, and she followed me; we had a light, and I was ascending the stairs, when we heard a noise overhead, and saw a man moving about. I called out to him, but I can hardly relate how it occurred, but something was thrown that knocked the candle down, and the prisoner rushed down upon us, and we were both thrown down with great violence."

"Then the prisoner escaped," said the counsel.

"Yes."

"And what took place afterwards?"

"We got up and went up stairs, and went to this man's bed-room."

"Which man?"

"Our lodger Zachary."

"What induced you to go to his apartment?"

" Because there was a light and smoke issuing from the room, and then we thought we heard a noise, so we went in."

" And what did you see there ?"

" I saw Zachary lying on his back quite dead, in a pool of blood, and, at the same time, the candle was placed under the bed so as to catch light of the clothes and set fire to the room."

" You got that under ?"

" Yes, and then assistance was obtained, and the murdered man was examined by a surgeon, but he was quite dead."

" Do you recognise the prisoner as being the man who entered your house and committed the murder you have related ?"

" I cannot do so positively, though I have no doubt about it—yet I cannot swear to him."

" Can you give any account how the man Zachary came by his death ?"

" I cannot—but I suppose he must have been murdered in coming out of his room. We did not like our lodger, and he was about to move in a day or two; and I really think he must have let him in, because, when we went to rest, the doors were all fastened, and he must have been murdered by mistake, or to conceal his own crime."

" You cannot swear that the prisoner at the bar is the man who broke into your house ?" inquired the prisoner's counsel.

" I cannot."

" You had not light enough to enable you to do so—it was knocked out of your hand ?"

" It was ; but as I held it in my hand, it was before my face, and I could not see distinctly."

" And you were flurried ?"

" I was not very cool and comfortable upon the occasion."

" Was your wife more so than you ?"

" She stood behind me."

" And less able to see."

" I cannot say that."

No more questions were asked. Miles Atherton and the counsel sat down, and Mrs. Atherton was called, and that lady came up and was examined at some length with regard to the occurrences of the night of the murder, all which she very circumstantially related, and declared she could see the prisoner very well, as she was in the shade behind her husband, and the light fell upon the prisoner, and she had seen him before."

" Before, madam ?"

" Yes, he had been there before, and attempted a robbery when my husband was out : he has come in and made inquiries, I have no doubt with a view to the robbery of the place."

Many questions were put to the good woman, with the view of extracting some contradiction, or some important admission, but she stuck to the main facts of the case.

Her examination closed the case, and then the counsel for the defence rose, but as it happened that there was no one point that could be urged in the prisoner's favour, his speech was a mere matter of course, and he endeavoured to throw some dust into the jury's eyes ; but the judge in his charge soon set this matter to rights, and though he said the prisoner was entitled to any doubt that they might reasonably entertain, yet the jury appeared to have none at all, for they at once brought him in guilty.

The prisoner was asked, in the usual formalities, what he had to allege why judgment should not be pronounced.

This done, the judge proceeded to pass sentence upon him in the usual manner, telling him he had been convicted upon clear and satisfactory evidence of the crime he had committed.

" There was no sort of doubt remaining upon his mind but that the prisoner had been the murderer, and he feared he had been the perpetrator of many other crimes. There could be held out no sort of hope of the commutation of the sentence, for he (the prisoner) was not one of those who could hope for mercy—it would be an injustice to society, from which no benefit would be derived."

He was then sentenced to be hanged on a gibbet until he was dead, with the ordinary recommendation of his soul to Heaven.

There was a pause in the proceedings, and every eye was turned towards the prisoner, who stood with a deep and marked scowl upon his brow, which bid defiance to all investigation, and it was impossible to say what were his feelings— he appeared to be meditating—and at length said, in a constrained voice, to the judge :—

" If your lordship has so much love for justice, I could bring to justice one of the greatest villains in London—a man named Godfrey—but I must be a gainer by doing so. If you will save my life, I can tell you that which shall be enough to hang twenty men, and it shall not rest upon my testimony alone—it shall be proved by others. What say you to my offer ?"

" Remove the prisoner," said the judge.

" Will not you give me an answer ? or am I to expect one by-and-by ?"

" Prisoner," said the judge, " lest you and others think that we can bargain here for the punishment of criminals like yourself, know that though you were to point out such another as yourself, yet would your own crime be just the same, and you would deserve the same punishment. You have no right to purchase immunity from punishment at whatever price you may offer. Were it once done there would be an end of justice altogether. Such an abomination would be the scorn of all good men. Jailor, remove your prisoner."

There was an instant commotion in the dock—Neville uttered a curse, and his pale, haggard features appeared worse than before, and his hardihood was scarce sufficient to enable him to keep his feet; he had evidently treasured this hope to the last, that he could purchase life by sacrificing Godfrey—but now, indeed, he had lost that.

With the removal of the prisoner the court broke up.

CHAPTER LXXIII.

THE CHEESEMONGER AND HIS WIFE AGAIN REVERT TO THE MANUSCRIPTS, AND FIND THE TALE OF THE POET'S DEATH.

THE last event of the trial of the notorious and villanous Neville afforded to Atherton and his wife far more food for conjecture than it probably did to any one else, for no one not acquainted with the story of the Black Lady could know what it really was that he (Neville) had to tell of the villanous proceedings that had resulted in the execution of the innocent and deeply-to-be-regretted Charles Ormond.

The anxiety of Atherton to know whether or not Godfrey was in existence, was extreme ; and he thought it a most provoking circumstance, that, at this juncture of all others, Marian Whitehead should have disappeared from her usual haunts, which in fact she had done ; for no one of whom he inquired had seen anything of her for many days.

" My dear," said Atherton to his wife, " if that rascal Godfrey be alive, it is a thousand pities he is not hung along with Neville, and then the gallows would have as pretty a pair of customers as any one would wish."

" I should think nothing," said Mrs. Atherton, waving her arm and nearly upsetting the candle, " I should think nothing, Atherton, of hanging such a fellow as that Godfrey, myself ! and if there was nobody else to do it I would do it too."

" Well ! if anybody ever deserved hanging, he is the person, without doubt."

" I do wish, Miles, you could find the Black Lady ; for you may depend something will come out, before the execution of Neville, that perhaps nobody in all the world would be able to confirm but herself."

" Alas! I wish I could find her, my dear; but you know the great exertions that Jem and I have made, and how unsuccessful we have unfortunately been."

" Do you think anything has happened to her?"

" Heaven forbid, poor thing! At all events, we know that she has been safe from Neville."

" Yes   But if Godfrey is alive, there's no knowing what his fears might not make him do."

" I own that such a thought has most disagreeably crossed my own mind, more than once; and notwithstanding all the risks I have already run in hunting for her, I would do so again, if I had the least idea (which I now have not) where to go and look for her."

" Well! well! it's a sad thing; but we can do no more than we are doing, unless we were to tell all that we have read in the Black Lady's papers."

" I have been thinking of that," said Atherton, " and you see, if we were to tell, it would do little good."

" I don't know that!"

" Why, you see we cannot swear to any of it; because, for all we know, it may not be correct, although we have all the reasons in the world to think that it is correct every word of it, so we could not produce it as evidence, you see, of the matter."

" I understand, now; of course there's a great difference between what you know yourself, of your own knowledge, and what you are told by any one else, however you may believe it.

" Yes! that's just it, of course; you're quite right my dear; and so you see, if we were to give our solemn oath to the Black Lady not to reveal what is in her papers, on one side, we should not be really doing anything by telling it all."

" I see.   Well! well! Who knows? Poor Marian Whitehead may herself come forward; and my idea is that she would, poor thing! if it was not for that strange notion she has that Charles Ormond is alive yet."

" Yes! that notion clings to her still, and it would be a thousand pities to disturb it, for if she thought him really dead, and that there was no longer any chance of their union, Heaven only knows what despair would come over her."

" It would be the death of her!"

" I fear it would, and therefore it is that, when we have seen her, I have not, as you know, tried at all to disturb her in that strange and wild belief."

" No! no! and we won't disturb her in it, if we see her again, poor thing, which I hope we shall.   But what do you say, Miles, to looking at her papers, and seeing what they say next?"

" Oh! with all my heart, my dear! The fact is, that what has now happened has only made, to my mind, every word of her papers much more interesting, because the conduct of Neville affords a kind of practical proof that all she has there put down, poor thing, is neither more nor less than the exact and strict truth."

" Yes, that's just how I look at it, Miles; so get the papers at once, and let us see what they say next."

Miles Atherton at once proceeded up stairs to his bed-room, where, as we have remarked, he, for security's sake, kept the Black Lady's papers, and brought down the packet to the parlour.   But before he could open it, Jem, who must have overheard what had passed (he was so uncommonly shy, that Jem) popped his head in at the parlour door, and said —

" Come now, missus, you don't mean all for to go for to say that I aint to hear what comes next."

" Oh, bless me," said Mrs. Atherton, with a jump, " I declare you gave me quite a turn. How dare you put your head in here so suddenly, Jem, I should like to know?"

" Well, missus, don't be in a passion," said Jem; " but the fact is, when I hear your voice, it sounds like ever so much music to my two precious ears—it does indeed, missus."

"Oh, you flattering villain," said Mrs. Atherton, with a scarcely suppresse smile at the idea of the musical nature of her voice, which she certainly had not heard of before, "you flattering villain, I believe, Jem, if you had been Lord Somebody or another, you would have been a sad deceiver. But come in if you must, only sit near the door, so that, if anybody wants anything out of the shop, you can pop out in a minute. It was but the other day I saw with my own eyes ——"

"I should think so," said Jem.

"What should you, think?"

"Why, that you saw with your own eyes, missus—I don't suppose you see with anybody else's."

"How dare you interrupt me? I was going to say that I saw a lady."

"*Saw* a lady, ma'am—saw her into two bits. Oh, lor', where did you begin, missus?"

"Now aint this unbearable, Miles Atherton? Are you a man or a nothing that you sit there and see me insulted in this horrid way? Oh, good gracious, when I was only going to say I saw a lady try the shop door, and go away again in a minute when she found it wasn't easy to open."

"Why, my dear," said Miles Atherton, "I think what Jem said was very funny —he was only joking, and I wonder you don't laugh at it. The idea, now, of sawing a lady—that is good!"

"Oh, you are each of you just as bad as the other," said Mrs. Atherton. "There's six of one and half a dozen of the other of you—that's a fact."

"I really," said Jem, "beg your pardon, missus, but I saw the lady, too, and I know her. I tell you what she does for lunch."

"Does for lunch? I suppose she orders it at home."

"Oh dear no, missus, she don't do no such thing—she comes out with a penny biscuit, and then she goes into some cheesemonger's shop, and goes on tasting till she has had as much as she wants, and then she says she will consider of it. Do you think if I hadn't knowed her, missus, I'd have kept her waiting?"

"Is it possible, Jem?"

"Oh I believe you. Lor' bless you, missus, you don't know one-half the tricks that genteel people have to make out a living—I knows 'em, I can tell you—I sometimes, when they come into the shop and asks for a taste, I gives 'em a dollop of something that makes 'em screw up ever such a face."

"It serves 'em right, Jem."

"Yes, missus—then I says to 'em—that ere," says I, "is the best genteel cheese, ma'am—it's nothing a pound—how do you like it, ma'am? and then away they goes spitting and spluttering—it's enough to do any one's heart good to see 'em, that it is."

"Well, Jem, I did always say as you was a *genus*," said Mrs. Atherton, "only it aint always easy to make you out, but, however, as you have heard so much already about the Black Lady and her papers, there can't be much harm in your knowing a little more, so I think, Miles, we may let Jem stay."

"I am decidedly of that opinion myself," said Atherton, who had a good esteem for Jem, and knew that, beneath a strange manner and an oddity of speech, he had very many sterling good qualities.

So Jem was fairly installed in the parlour, but in a chair very near to the door, so that Mrs. Atherton might feel quite satisfied that he kept an eye upon the shop.

"Well, my dear," said Miles Atherton, "it appears to me that we have got as near as possible to the end of the Black Lady's papers."

"What makes you think that?"

"Because the one which immediately follows that which we last read, has upon the top of it these words, "The Last Paper of Marian Whitehead.""

"You don't say so?"

"It's a fact; but we shall soon see what it says. Shall I begin reading it at once?"

"Yes, to be sure, of course ; begin reading it at once. Why, what did you open the packet for else? Are you a goose, Mr. Atherton?"

"I hope not ; but however, here goes."

Miles Atherton then, with a preliminary ahem! to clear his throat from nothing at all, commenced as follows, reading that document which purported to be "The Last Paper of the Black Lady."

*   *   *   *   *   *   *

This is the last chapter of my eventful life, with the exception of one, which will have to be added to it by some kind Christian soul, and which will describe, to those who may feel any interest in such an event, my last moments.

The kind friend, who spared time from his own sorrows and his own wants to pity me, and who wrote down for me much that has preceded this paper, making the events, as his fancy suited him, into a kind of narrative, without destroying any of the incidents which were real, is now no more.

"What!" exclaimed Mrs. Atherton, "is that author man dead?"

"I suppose so," said Miles Atherton.

"Poor wretch!—well, I never—oh, dear me ! Perhaps it's just as well. He was not of much use, and those sort of people, of course, can be much better spared than folks who really are of some use to society. I dare say he was a little cracked too, for I have heard that most of those people are, besides being a dreadful handful to their wives, and everybody who have to put up with their horrid whims and fancies."

"Well, but poor man, perhaps he had no whims and fancies."

"Perhaps he had, and perhaps he hadn't," said Jem. "But, however, as the poor devil is dead, there's an end of him, so go on with the reading, master, and do let us know what it's all about. How can we tell you know, missus, but what some out-and-out blood curdler is a coming?"

"Oh, good, gracious! you make me feel all over of a coagulation. Really, Jem, you have such horrid ideas about you, you are enough to turn anybody's system."

"Well, I'll go on," said Miles Atherton. Attention—si—lence!"

In an audible voice, then, the cheesemonger commenced again where he had left off :—

Yes, he is no more, and that generous heart, with all its excellences, and with all its errors, has gone to the grave. Before he died, he spoke to me, saying,—

"Miss Whitehead, I am not long for this world now, and I shall be satisfied if I leave behind me one heart that will pity me. My life has been a series of bitternesses and disappointments. Where I have expected to find sympathy, I have met with heartlessness and cruelty—where I expected to be appreciated, I have been ridiculed ; but I forgive freely all who have added one pang of bitterness to the lot of the poor poet ; and rather, much rather blame my own susceptibility than their scorn for the sufferings I have from time to time endured."

I tended upon him, for, alas! he had no one else to do so ; and towards midnight, on the evening when he breathed his last, he called to me in a low, gentle tone of voice, and I went close to his bed-side—

"Marian," he said, "God bless you! good night."

It was with these words he yielded up to God one of the purest, happiest natures that was ever created. I could not but weep—I who had not wept for years —I who thought that the fount of tears had dried up within me for ever—I wept like a child over the corpse of that kind but eccentric being, who, with his best endeavours, had chosen some time from his own sorrows to make mine lighter. He is with God, among that blessed throng that know no pain, but with whom bliss is eternal.

Mrs. Atherton was really much affected at this paragraph, and unable to control her tears, although she certainly made an effort so to do, she got up such a hideous face, and finally burst into such an odd sort of woful sound, that the cheese-monger was really alarmed, and Jem pretended to be so.

"Lor' missus, what's the matter?" cried Jem. "Don't do that again."

"What again? you unfeeling brute."

"Why, make that dreadful noise, and the *ekally* dreadful face? I'll tell you what you put me in mind of, missus, neither more nor less than somebody a going through that ere interesting experiment of being sawed in two, as you spoke of a little time ago. I should say that face was just the sort of one they would make up, and that sound was just the sort of one they would say."

"If you, Jem," said Mrs. Atherton, "have got no bowels, other people have."

"Bowels!"

"Yes; bowels of compassion I mean. You see that mentioned in the Scriptures I rather think, so don't say I'm wrong there. It was very affecting about the poor wretch saying good night, and then going out like a lamp and the snuff of a candle. I only hope we shall all of us go out as comfortable."

"A-men!" said Jem. "I don't much mind how I go out, so as I go out quick. But is that all of it, master?"

"Oh, no; listen and I'll go on. But really, what with you and what with your mistress, and one's feelings and another's feelings, I must say that it's a very difficult matter to get on at all."

"Oh, don't say it's me—I could have stood the face as missus made very well, but I couldn't stand the odd noise, that was what upset me altogether; but how-somdever, you go on, master, and don't mind nobody; I want to hear what comes next, I does."

Mrs. Atherton made no reply to this speech of Jem's, which we cannot but construe into an act of great magnanimity as far as she was concerned, for there certainly was matter in it which ought to have provoked some rejoinder.

In another moment Miles Atherton continued the narrative :—

He was not buried as he would have been, with the scanty rites of a pauper's funeral. No, no; Heaven stirred up some friends for me, and enabled me to place him in peace beneath the verdant sod in a rural spot, where his pure spirit could wander among pleasant trees and hear the song of the happy birds. He was satisfied. I have seen him since at the soft twilight hour, and there was a look of joy upon his face which told me that his spirit was pleased.

"His ghost has been a walking!" exclaimed Mrs. Atherton.

"It looks like it," said Jem. "I wish he'd walk in here, if it was only for the curiosity of the thing."

"Don't say that, oh! don't say that," cried Mrs. Atherton.

"What, missus! do you think as the ghost will take me at my word? And besides, you know you did not ask to see him, so he had no business to come to you. If he comed at all, he'd come up stairs, you know, to my attic; and I'm sure, so far as I am concerned, he's welcome enough to do so. But ghosts now-a-days are so precious shy that there's no getting hold of one for love or money. I only wish as we could. How it would take as an exhibition! A real ghost, only a shilling, at the Egyptian Hall! Only think, master; that would be better than cutting butter and cheese, wouldn't it?"

"I should most decidedly say it would, Jem."

At this moment there was a strange sound in the passage just outside the parlour, door followed by a single shriek of so terrific a nature that it was horrible to hear it.

CHAPTER LXXIV.

THE UNEXPECTED VISITOR.—THE ALARM AT THE CHEESEMONGER'S.—THE CRIPPLE CULPRIT.

THIS sound from the passage filled Mrs. Atherton with dismay, and it had some effect upon the nerves of both Atherton and Jem, who looked at each other with astonishment, while the latter was not without a suspicion that the ghost of the poor author had been listening, and had taken him at his word, and really was about to walk in.

" Oh ! gracious powers !" said Mrs. Atherton, " what can that be ?"

" I—I—can't think," said Atherton. " The—the—I don't know who must be in the house ?"

" Why," remarked Jem, " there's no lodger, now, so who the deuce can it be ?"

" Don't mention the deuce," said Mrs. Atherton, " you don't know but what he may be at your elbow. Don't mention any such person, I beg of you, Jem. If either of you had the courage of fleas you would go out into the passage and see what it was, and not leave me here all of a stew."

" I don't hear anything now," said Atherton. " Suppose you and I go, Jem?"

" Come on," said Jem, as he armed himself with the poker. It's something or somebody, that's for certain, because nothing can't make such a horrid noise as that we heard just now. Come on, master, I think you had better take the tongs, and if missus keeps an eye on the shovel we ought, I think, to get the better of anybody with all the fire-irons on our side."

" Come, come, Jem," said Atherton, " I insist upon going first. Don't you push your way before me, you know, and go first, 'cos, if you do, you know I can't help it."

" Oh ! I won't. You may depend upon me," said Jem, " I won't do anything of the sort. You shall go first, master, I won't, you may depend. You shall go first, then I'll follow you, while missus comes after with the light."

" Well, well," said Atherton, " I know it hurts your feelings, Jem, not to let you go first, so you shall."

" Not at all," said Jem ; " the fact is, I'm a little afraid, and, as you aint, you see, it makes all the difference, so you shall go first, master, and I'll come close after."

" Oh ! then," said Atherton, in whose hand the tongs shook to and fro in a very peculiar manner—" oh ! then, we will both go together, Jem, so come on; and you, my dear, be so good, will you, as to hold the light up as high as you possibly can ? Now, come on, and don't you be afraid, Jem. I—I—aint a bit afeard myself ; a—a—hem !"

" No ; nor I. Ahem !"

" I think you are both afraid, to tell the truth," said Mrs. Atherton, " or else you wouldn't stand, the one talking against the other, there, but you would go into the passage at once, you two abominable cowards, and see what was really the matter."

Thus urged, and their courage so strongly doubted, they both walked towards the door leading into the passage, although they took good care that neither of them would be an inch before the other in so doing. Mrs. Atherton herself followed with the light, which she just held on a level with Miles Atherton's head, so that, when he turned suddenly to say something to Jem, he would either receive a severe blow with the candlestick, which made him think that he was attacked in some mysterious manner by the ghost behind, and he accordingly cried murder!

" What's that ?" said Jem.

" I don't know, but something is nobbing my head behind."

" How can the man be such a goose ?" said Mrs. Atherton.

" A goose ?"

" Yes. You nobbed your own head against the candlestick ; you might have known that well enough."

" How should I know the candlestick was there ?" said Atherton. It must have been very near my head, I'm sure, or else I could not have touched it. However, I don't see anything—do you, Jem ?"

" Yes," said Jem.

" Yes ? What—who—where—why—eh ?"

" There," said Jem. " There—right a-head, on the staircase. Are you blind ? There's somebody a sitting down there, like a heap of old clothes—don't you see ?"

" Gracious ! yes," cried Mrs. Atherton. " Mind it don't make a spring upon you. Mind, it's a moving—it's a moving.'"

"Have mercy upon me," said a deep, sepulchral voice, "oh! have mercy upon me; I have suffered enough already, Heaven knows! Have mercy upon me now, and let me go!"

"Who are you?" said Jem, advancing with the poker.

"Do not ask—do not ask; but, if you are so inclined, and think you can do the deed with safety to yourself, the most merciful thing you can do will be to dash

out my brains here, as I sit at your mercy. Do it; and beforehand, I tell you, I am quite willing to forgive the deed. You will not find my spirit stand forward to accuse you at the judgment-seat of God."

These words were spoken in a tone of such strange, wild agony, that no wonder Atherton and Jem, as they did, should both shrink back aghast from the strange object that spoke.

Why he sat upon the stairs and made no effort to go away, they could not tell; and why he came there at all seemed to be a profound mystery, since he had taken the trouble to proclaim his presence by uttering that shriek which there really seemed to be no possible occasion for.

He looked aged. The small quantity of hair he had upon his head was of a dirty-looking white colour; his cheeks were sunken and full of wrinkles; and his deep-set eyes looked preternaturally bright and blood-shot.

"What do you want here? and who are you?" said Atherton.

There was an odd sound, as of some sticks being knocked together, and then the stranger rose from the stair on which he had been sitting, and they saw that he was supported by crutches, and appeared as if he was a complete cripple. He groaned as if with pain, as he advanced a step or two towards the door leading into the street, and then, in a strange tone, he said:

"Do not ask who I am, but let me go—oh, let me go."

"But how came you here—what do you want here?"

"Enough! enough!—Ask me no questions, but let it suffice that I have been disappointed—bitterly disappointed in a foolish errand: I ought not to have expected anything else."

"I can't let you go, you old sinner," said Mrs. Atherton, "till I know who you are, and what you want here. Jem, go and fetch a policeman directly: how do we know but he's some desperate character?"

"Be it so," said the cripple, "be it so, then; if you will enforce me to tell you who I am, I must. Let me sit down in your parlour, and I will tell you truly who I am, as well as why I came here. Will you afford me a glass of water?"

Mrs. Atherton impulsively made way for the stranger, and he hobbled into the parlour, and sunk upon a chair, letting his crutches fall to the floor with a clattering noise, and uttering a deep groan; suddenly, however, his eyes fell upon the figure of the Black Lady, and they became lit up with a dazzling brilliancy, as, stretching forth his hands, he said—

"Give them to me; oh, give them to me; let me have them!"

"Have what?"

"Those papers—those damning papers. You were reading them, and that was how I failed to find them, after such a toilsome journey as I had up stairs for them. Give them to me, I say, give them to me!"

"I beg your pardon," said Mrs. Atherton, "we don't mean to give them to anybody, so you need not expect it. Who are you, I wonder, that want other people's property in such an off-handed manner? Marry come up! What next?"

"I will pay you well for them. Name your own price, and you shall have it."

"Good gracious! how much?" said Mrs. Atherton.

"Wife, wife," cried the cheesemonger; "we must not traffic with what is not our own. Those papers are given to us to read, not to sell. The matters they contain are secrets which we must not reveal."

"£100! £500!" cried the stranger. "Only give them to me, and do not let them come up in judgment against me. Of what service can they be to you? while to me they are all—all the world. They must be mine."

"I begin to suspect," said the cheesemonger, "that I have got a man beneath my roof that I never thought would have polluted a dwelling of mine by his presence."

"You—you suspect," said the cripple. "What—what is it that you suspect? Do not utter the—the name of—of—"

"Of Godfrey! you mean," said Atherton. "And I feel convinced that you are that villain."

"The villain Godfrey!" cried Mrs. Atherton.

"The villain Godfrey!" exclaimed Jem.

"Yes, yes," gasped the cripple; "you are all right, and you give me my proper name. I am the villain Godfrey; and I say again if any of you will kill me it will be a thankful deed: I am Godfrey, of whom doubtless you have read and heard much, and you see now my horrible state. You say how very successful I have been in—in my wickedness. Look at me well, and then ask yourselves if you ever saw a more pitiable object than I am now—I, the villain Godfrey, who is forced to shriek out with pain sometimes, and who can know no peace here or hereafter!"

There was a deathless stillness for a few minutes in the cheesemonger's parlour, during which all eyes were bent upon the cowering form of the wretched man, upon whom had fallen such an awful amount of retribution.

"Do you not curse me?" he said. "Why do you not curse me?"

"We leave you to Heaven," said Atherton; "wretched, guilty man, we leave you to Heaven!"

"And Heaven," he cried aloud, "leaves me to hell. Ha! ha! Yes; that is my fate, and it has begun already here—yes, it has begun already here!"

He struck his breast violently as he spoke, and then he let his head drop, and almost seemed as if he had suddenly become insensible, so still was he, and such a striking contrast did he present to the violence of manner which only a moment before had characterised him.

"I tell you what it is," said Mrs. Atherton, "we don't want you here, so go away at once."

"Yes, go away," cried the cheesemonger; "there's the door."

"There," said Jem, picking up his crutches and handing them to him, "be off. We don't want to know you, and on the whole we would rather you never came down this street any more, for we don't wish to breathe the same air with you, Godfrey. Take your sticks, and then cut your stick as soon as you can."

"I—I am going; I am going. I came for the papers, but I am disappointed. You need not visit any further vengeance on me than Heaven has already wreaked upon this wretched worn-out frame. Look at me: one glance is surely enough; and yet I am rich—rich—yes, oh yes! I am a rich man. Envy me, you houseless wretches, who crawl at night for shelter to door-steps and beneath the eaves of houses! God, how I envy you!"

"And is this, indeed," said Atherton, "all that your evil deeds, Godfrey, have done for you?"

"No, no; not quite all—not quite all. I—I sleep sometimes. Yes; exhausted nature will sometimes claim her due, and then I sleep; and—and then I dream. Yes, yes; then I dream!"

"And serve you right, too," said Mrs. Atherton; "I hope you do dream, and bad dreams, too. You know very well you deserve them, you old white-headed sinner."

"Hush, wife, hush!" said Miles Atherton, "hush! I implore you. We must never add anything to self-accusation."

"That's right," said Jem, "that's right; nobody can make Godfrey feel more than he can make himself feel, when he thinks of what has been done."

"And has it come to this?" groaned Godfrey, wringing his hands, "has it come to this—am I an object of such abject pity that even those who would otherwise use harsh words towards me refrain from doing so? Alas! alas! has it come to this? Oh, God! have you no lightning to launch at the head of such a wretch as I am?"

"Don't call for lightning here," cried Mrs. Atherton, "as if that element was as easily called for as you would a cup of coffee. Don't call for lightning here, if you please; we don't want it, though you may."

"I suppose," said Jem, "you got knocked about so as to be forced to use crutches in consequence of falling from the top of the house when you went to see poor Charles Ormond hung."

Godfrey made several efforts to speak before he could gasp out the word "Yes," and then he added,—

"The villain Neville came to me in prison—the worst of prisons, a hospital—and nearly killed me. Since then I have been in constant pain. They tell me that he forced the fractured end of one of my ribs into my lungs, and that there it remains, so that whenever I draw a deeper breath than common it is terrific. You see I can only breathe as if I were fainting. Oh! what have I not suffered!"

"You don't seem comfortable," said Mrs. Atherton.

"I should wonder if he did, missus," said Jem ; "how would you feel if you had tumbled off the roof of a house headforemost, you know?"

"Don't mention the idea, I beg, Jem. And now Mr. G. (Mrs. Atherton was fond of calling people by the first letter of their names, whether they were friend or foe) and now, Mr. G., the sooner you go the better. You cannot pretend that you are unable, because, if you could come here, you can go."

"I—I will go ; but tell me first if you think that she could be brought to forgive me for the evil that I have done her?"

"You mean Marian Whitehead?" said Atherton.

"Yes, yes. Do you think she could be brought to forgive me? You know her well, I am given to understand ; and perhaps, because you have behaved kindly to her, you may have some influence over her. Will you exert it in such a cause?"

"I would much rather not interfere," said the cheesemonger. "Poor thing! her wits are not just as they should be, and I don't want to make her worse—leave her alone, and get Heaven to forgive you if you can, Mr. Godfrey; we do not wish have anything at all to do with the matter, so far as you are concerned, although we know all!"

"You—you—know all?"

"Yes, we do," interposed Mrs. Atherton, although her husband made several telegraphic signals to her to say nothing. "Yes, we do know all ; and after that I'm sure you can't wonder at us not wishing to make much of your company, and being much better pleased if you would take yourself away. I can tell you that if you were walking about on your own proper two legs like a Christian, and not in the state you are, with a couple of crutches, you should be given in charge."

"Well, well!" said Godfrey, mournfully, "well, well, I will go. I am going now. I had a hope that when you saw what an abject wretch I had become, you would have had some pity even for me."

"We have," said Atherton, "we have some pity for you ; but still we cannot interfere, because we have more pity still for poor Marian Whitehead ; and we fear that the hint of such a thing as you seeing her on any pretence whatever, would be so highly exciting and injurious to her that, poor thing! it would make her ten times worse. So we decline, not because we don't pity you, wicked as you have been, but because we feel more for her, poor thing!"

"That's right, master, that's right," said Jem ; "you never explained anything better in all your life, and that's a fact. Bravo! Do you understand that, Mr. Godfrey? Oh! I say, what a precious—but never mind, I don't want to say anything to you—not I—go along. The worst we wish you is that we may not never see you no more."

"Jem, Jem," cried Mrs. Atherton, "there's somebody opening the shop-door."

"I'm going, missus—oh, oh, oh, oh!"

"Why, what's the matter with the boy? What are you standing for there like a stuck pig for, and turning up your eyes like a duck in a thunderstorm? Can't you speak?"

"I—I believe you, missus; but only look there!"

"Look where, you horrid booby ; really you are enough to drive any one out of their seven senses, you are, Jem."

"I thinks as how," said Jem, "to the best of my judgment, there will be a blessed skrimmage before long, for I'll be hanged and done up in heaps if there aint the Black Lady!"

CHAPTER LXXV.

THE UNEXPECTED MEETING.—GODFREY'S TERROR.—THE DENUNCIATION OF
MARIAN.—HER PARDON.

THE moment Jem uttered these words the effect upon all parties in the cheese-monger's parlour was marked and conclusive.

Mrs. Atherton, as usual, made a noisy demonstration of what she felt upon the occasion, and uttered a loud scream, which of itself was sufficient to have created a great amount of alarm among any number of people.

As for Miles Atherton himself, he screwed up his lips with a decided intention of whistling some popular melody, but, as he seemed completely to forget the first note of it, he made no sound.

But these effects of the appearance of the Black Lady were nothing to what came over Godfrey, for from the first moment that he heard Jem announce her presence, a kind of terrific panic seemed to have come over him, and he was wholly unable to speak or move, while he stretched out his trembling hands before him, and shook in every limb; his lips, too, moved convulsively, as if he would fain have said something, but wanted the power of utterance.

"Yes," added Jem, "yes, by Jove! it's the Black Lady, and now, I suppose, all the fat will be in the fire."

With her usual slow and noiseless step Marian Whitehead glided into the shop of the cheesemonger. She then paused as the cry of surprise, uttered by Mrs. Atherton, came upon her ears, and was evidently discomposed for the moment.

"What's that?" she muttered, "what's that? Surely I heard a cry of alarm!"

"Yes, you did," said Jem, running out, "that is to say, no you didn't—stop—I say Black—I mean Miss Whitehead, you had much better go home again."

"No, no," cried Atherton, "that must not be—I cannot have her repulsed from any roof of mine, let the consequences of her continuing under it be what they may."

"I do not understand all this," said Marian; "what does it mean? Am I unwelcome? God help me! I will go again at once."

"There now," said Atherton, "that's what I was afraid of. You are quite welcome, Miss Whitehead, and always will be, let me assure you—nobody can be more welcome. Jem?"

"Yes, master."

"Go and bundle Godfrey out somehow."

"I'll try; but he looks a tolerable weight, master. It's better to persuade an elephant than to push him any day."

Miles Atherton managed to keep the Black Lady in talk for some short time in the shop, while Jem went into the parlour to try his persuasive powers upon Godfrey, who still sat in the same strange attitude of horror he had at first assumed upon hearing the, to him, dreaded name of Marian Whitehead pronounced.

"I say, Godfrey," said Jem, "we all want that chair as you are sitting in. Do you understand, you old reprobate? We haven't got half a word more to say to you, and the door leads out this way into the passage, and so on by the private door, right away into the street, old boy."

Godfrey evidently had not the least idea of what was said to him; but continued glaring at the glass door which divided the parlour from the shop, with such an intensity of gaze that it was quite dreadful to look upon him.

"Come," added Jem, "are you out of your senses? I know you, Miles. Why don't you move, eh?"

"Hush, hush!" he now said, "who spoke of the Black Lady—who spoke of the Black Lady? for she is the much-injured Marian Whitehead. Who spoke of her to me?"

"I did. And, once for all, we don't want her to see you, so will you go? I say, master, he's gone clean stupid, and won't move half an inch. I can't stir him."

"Then it's of no use attempting further concealment," said Miles Atherton. "Miss Whitehead, I beg you will use your own discretion, and act as you think proper; but Godfrey, your old enemy, is in the parlour."

The Black Lady clasped her hands, and a half-suppressed cry of surprise came from her lips. Then, in another instant, she darted into the apartment, where sat her old enemy, deprived of all power to harm her, and, casting far back from her face that funereal-looking veil which now for so long she had worn, she looked stedfastly at him, pointing, with the fore-finger of each hand, in his face.

Mrs. Atherton got behind a chair, as if she feared that some personal collision would take place, and Godfrey slowly dropped his hands, and sat like one paralysed, gazing upon the face of his accuser.

There was a pause of some moments' duration, and then Marian Whitehead spoke.

"Godfrey," she said, "Godfrey! Betrayer of innocence! Suborner of justice—perjurer—murderer—Godfrey!"

He uttered a deep and awful groan.

"Villain—false witness—miserable trickster—wretched, wretched man! The day of judgment is near at hand—nearer, perchance, than you imagine. Give him back to me! Give him back, I say. Where have you hidden Charles Ormond?"

"In the grave," said Godfrey.

Marian started.

"No, no, no!" she shrieked, rather than cried. "No! oh no! You dare not—you have not murdered him, Godfrey. Tell me that in accordance with your general habit you then spoke what was not true. Tell me that he lives!"

"I—I cannot."

Marian passed her hand, with a dubious, distracted gesture, across her brow, as she muttered,—

"That is no evidence—that is no evidence. No, no! The word of Godfrey is nothing—nothing whatever; but—but shall I not be revenged upon the betrayer—upon the perjurer?"

"Save me from her," cried Godfrey, "save me from her! I can see the wild fire of insanity in her eye, and I cannot resist her. Oh, do not let her murder me, for life, with all its terrors, is better far than the horrors of what must be an eternity to me."

The Black Lady had, indeed, thrown herself into a threatening attitude, so that Godfrey might well enough have some fears of what might be the result of her enmity against him; and, from the state of extreme agitation he was in, it was evident that those fears were of the most excessive description.

"She will not harm you," said Atherton.

"No," she said, "no. Vengeance shall be God's work. Heaven does not make its best and choicest creatures to be the sport of such men as this. Bitter and terrible, Godfrey, will be the account exacted of you. Your death will be terrible, as your life has been wretched and detestable: no burial rites shall herald you to the tomb; no coffin shall be fashioned to hold your mouldering remains; no prayer shall gently usher you into the presence of an offended Divinity.

"Cease! oh, cease!"

"No, no! The gift of prophecy has come upon me at this moment, or rather Heaven has chosen, through my lips, to pronounce a portion of your doom. You will die a death of horror, and no friendly hand shall be stretched forth to save you. You will implore in shrieks for the aid which will not come, and your end shall be madness and desolation."

"Oh, horrible! horrible!"

"Yes, Godfrey, I have said it. That is my denunciation of you; and so, leaving you to Heaven's justice, I have done."

Marian sat down, overpowered by her own vehement feelings, and, covering her face with both her hands, she shook as with a violent mental emotion which could not find vent in tears, and so convulsed her whole frame.

And there they sat facing each other, that pair of persons—the destroyer and his victim; for if any living person could ever have been said to have been a blight and a desolation to another in this world, Godfrey had been such to poor Marian Whitehead.

Unless he had stepped in to mar her destiny, what a life of pure happiness might have been hers! If he had not been the evil spirit that had brought the clouds of disappointment and despair over the sunny sky of her felicity, surely there were no other circumstances that could have made that sky so dim and cheerless as it had become.

But, alas! he had, by an exercise of the most evil passions that appertain to humanity, made her wretched, murdered Charles Ormond, and reduced himself, notwithstanding all his wealth, to such an abject state of misery that, as he had himself said, he might well envy the poorest wretch that crawled about the public streets seeking a temporary shelter from the fury of the elements when in their wildest state of mad commotion.

Slowly he got hold of the crutches, without aid from which he could not move, and endeavoured to rise, as he muttered, in a low, indistinct voice,—

"Let me go! I must go! Let me go!"

"As soon as you like," said Jem; "and damned glad we are to get rid of you."

"Yes, yes," he continued, "she has launched a bitter curse on my head, and I will go now. Wretch that I am, I still cling to this—even to this painful existence! Farewell, Marian Whitehead. You need not heap curses on my head, for, Heaven knows, you are already avenged."

"Speak!" she suddenly cried, as she rose from her chair, and advanced two steps towards Godfrey. "Speak again, and tell me where you have hidden Charles Ormond!"

"This is her madness," said Godfrey, turning his eyes on Atherton.

"Poor thing," said Atherton, "she has cause enough to derange the best brain that ever was."

"Where is he?" added Marian. "I demand to know where he is! Where have you hidden Charles Ormond?"

"Let me go," said Godfrey. "I have nothing to say to you. I have no answer to make to such a question. I know nothing. You—you have cursed me, and should now let me go."

He evidently spoke under an impression of the most abject fear, for, in his condition, he felt that a child might overcome him, and each moment he dreaded some violent accession of insanity on the part of Marian which would prompt her to do him some serious bodily injury.

Therefore was it that, with a painful and a sidelong movement, he made towards the door opening into the passage, still keeping his eyes fixed upon Marian, who stood in something of a threatening attitude before him.

"Where is Charles Ormond?" she repeated. "I will know where Charles Ormond is hidden. Give him to me, and then even I can forgive you, Godfrey, for all the suffering you have inflicted."

"Oh! would to God I could," he said. "Would to God I could! You should not have to ask twice for such a recompense, nor I twice for such a forgiveness. But, alas! it may not be. The grave will not give up its dead! No, no! 'Tis all in vain! The next time I see Charles Ormond it will be as my accuser before the judgment-seat of Heaven, but never again in this world—never again! Oh, never—never again!"

"'Tis false!" cried Marian—"false as your own heart. Who shall convince me that he is dead, and I still living? No, no, that could not, cannot be. Is there no justice above? Does Providence allow the wicked to triumph, not only for an hour, but for ever, so far as regards the misery and anguish of the innocent?"

"Rather," said Jem. "You may depend, Miss Whitehead, that Providence don't interfere with family affairs."

"I suffer, I suffer," groaned Godfrey. "Do you fancy, Miss Whitehead, that I do not suffer?"

"And do you fancy," she replied, "that your suffering is any recompense for what I have suffered? Can your pain obliterate my anguish? Can your remorse affect my heart's agony? No, no; I will, I must have news of Charles Ormond. Speak, Godfrey, I charge you! Speak at once."

"Help! help!" said Godfrey. "I think she is armed."

He made a quick movement into the passage, which was too quick a one for his state of lameness to enable him to keep up, or even to undertake at all, and catching his foot or his crutch in some obstacle, he fell heavily, and with a horrid shriek of pain, just outside the door which led from the parlour.

"Good God!" said Miles Atherton, "he will kill himself. Here, come with me, Jem, and let us pick him up, and get him outside the door somehow or other: and I do sincerely hope we shall never look upon his face again."

Jem followed Miles Atherton into the passage, while the Black Lady sunk trembling into the chair again, from which she had so recently risen. They found Godfrey lying apparently lifeless in the passage; but Jem ran into the yard and got some water, which he dashed upon his face, and that restored him, so that he opened his eyes.

"A prison! a prison!" he cried. "Is this a prison?"

"No," said Jem; "but it ought to be. You may think yourself lucky that we are willing to let you off. Come, get up, and go your way; we don't want you here."

They lifted him to his feet again, and gave him his crutches; and as he looked with a terrified aspect towards the door from which he had just emerged, Jem thought it would accelerate his movements to tell him that the Black Lady was still there; and he was right in that supposition, for the moment Jem pronounced her name Godfrey, with looks of terror, made his way out, and glad were they both when they got the private street-door closed upon him.

When they returned to the parlour they found poor Marian nearly fainting, and Mrs. Atherton kindly attending upon her; for now that the sudden excitement of the presence of Godfrey had now passed away, a reaction had taken place in her mind, and she had become frightfully depressed.

As long as he had been there she had been supported by her indignation and a remembrance of the wrongs of poor Charles Ormond; but it was when she was only in the presence of those who had ever been kind and friendly to her that she sunk, and allowed her pent-up feelings to have full sway.

Alas! poor, poor Marian! happy will it be when the friendly hand of death leads you from a world which to you can present no joys, and which, so far as you are concerned, is indeed but

"An unweeded garden."

Happy will it be for you, and a source of not painful reflection to all who wish you well, and who feel for your deep distress, when the grave has closed over you, and you have gone to that better world where pain and sorrow are things unknown, and where, in those realms of everlasting bliss, you will again meet with him, the chosen of your heart—the noble, generous, just, and gentle-hearted, but, alas! frightfully, wofully, sacrificed Charles Ormond.

May that consummation be soon; for who would wish you to linger in life, the ghost, as it were, of your former self, the sad apparition of what you once have been!

It took all the unremitting care and attention which Mrs. Atherton could bestow upon her for some time, to restore Marian Whitehead to perfect consciousness, and to anything like her usual composure of spirits.

At length, however, she was able to speak, and to look about her with something like calmness, and she said in low, sweet accents, which afforded a sad reminiscence of what her voice had been in the sweet spring-time of her youth,—

"Was it a dream, or did I really see here that man, whose name I may well shudder to pronounce? Was Godfrey actually here, in this very room?"

"It's true enough, I am sorry to say," replied Mrs. Atherton; "for I did not, I am sure, want my door to be darkened by such a villain."

"Is it possible—can it indeed be possible?"

"Yes," said Jem, "he came here; and we should not have found it out, I dare say, if one of his pains had not seized him in the passage, and made him cry out in spite of himself."

"And his motive was to kill me?"

"Oh! no," said Atherton; "I think, do you know, you are mistaken there, for, from all I can see and hear, I am quite sure that Godfrey is much more afraid of you than you are or need be of him. Besides, God knows, he is not in a condition to venture upon doing harm to anybody, poor wretch!"

"But wherefore should he seek this house?"

"Because he has found out that we have all your papers, and, no doubt, he fully expects that there is plenty of matter in them that has a tendency to ciminate him ; so that I look upon his coming here as an audacious attempt to steal them."

"Yes," said Mrs. Atherton, "and he would have stole them, if we had not got to the end nearly, and brought them down stairs, just a short time before we found he was here, to finish."

" But how could he know you had such documents?"

" What ! don't you know all about Zachary, and Neville, and the murder?"

" Indeed I do not : you know I am so completely out of the world."

" Well, certainly, I began to think you were out of it altogether, and so did Jem, for we tried hard to find you, and got into some great danger in so doing, from which we were not a little glad to escape with whole skins."

"I believe you **master**," said Jem. "I don't know but what I am really murdered, and I'm only now mistaking my ghost for myself."

Miles Atherton now proceeded to relate to Marian all that had occurred as related to the murder of Zachary, and his firm impression that all these circumstances had resulted from the exertions which Neville thought it necessary for his own safety's sake to make, in order to recover possession of any documents or papers which might be criminatory to himself.

" You may depend," he said, "that Neville's idea has been, that you placed all those papers in our hands for us to consider which would be the best way of prosecuting him and Godfrey. By some means he has found out that we have such documents, and I have no doubt whatever in my own mind but that Zachary was actually sent by Neville to live here, on purpose to get what information he could for that scoundrel."

" But Neville murdered him, you say."

" Yes, in mistake for Jem, I have no doubt, against whom he had a great spite ; and what I wanted so particularly to find you for was, to get your consent to tell all I know."

"Oh ! no, no. It was better far that you should not. You see Charles Ormond is hiding somewhere, and the day will yet come when we shall meet again."

This idea was so firmly fixed in the mind of the Black Lady, that there was no eradicating it ; and after a time she left Atherton, congratulating himself that he had kept still secret the contents of her papers, notwithstanding the great temptation to do otherwise which the trial of Neville for Zachary's murder afforded.

CHAPTER LXXVI.

THE LETTER OF NEVILLE FROM NEWGATE TO MILES ATHERTON.—THE CONSULTATION.

WHAT abundant food for gossip and conjecture now had Mrs. Atherton ! Could anything have been devised, if the thing had been arranged on purpose, better than that accidental meeting of Godfrey with the Black Lady at the cheesemonger's, to afford the really worthy, but somewhat prolix Mrs. Atherton, with an endless theme?

And Mrs. Atherton was one of those people, as the reader is very well aware, who, when they do once begin to talk about anything, never know exactly when to leave off. In fact, although the good lady was really a very good lady, she was likewise what many very excellent people are at times, a most intolerable bore.

She would talk and talk until Miles Atherton would be fairly compelled, in absolute self-defence, to run to some public-house for the sake of peace and quietness ; and on this present occasion, when the Black Lady and Godfrey were both gone, she found out an immense number of things which he, Atherton, ought to have said to Godfrey that he omitted saying.

"Why didn't you ask him," she exclaimed, "if, in all his repentance, he intended to give poor Miss Whitehead any of her money again that he cheated poor old stupid Mrs. Whitehead out of?"

"Well, I really didn't think of it."

"You didn't think of it! I know that well enough, Mr. Atherton. That's what I say. You need not tell me you did not think of it: what I ask is, when do you ever think of anything? That's what I should like to know, Mr. Atherton."

"Oh! I can't tell you," said Atherton.

"No; I should wonder if you could. When did you ever tell me anything, I should like to know? It is a joke, indeed, the idea of your telling me anything. You, indeed!"

"Then why did you ask me, if you knew so well that I could not tell you? I wonder at such a sensible woman as you taking up your valuable time in such a way."

"You wonder, do you? Oh! you double-faced crocodile of the Nile. Oh! you Bengal and Bombay tiger on his hind legs—you wonder, do you? and call me a sensible woman—but I know what you mean. You think I have not got eyes in my head, and did not see you wink at Jem."

"Now, my dear, I assure you you are mistaken. I did not wink at Jem; and I appeal to him if I did."

"Oh dear, no," said Jem; "I believe you, master, you didn't. You wink at me! Lord bless you, missus, he couldn't do such a thing."

"Yes, yes," said Mrs. Atherton, "hang together. 'Like master, like man.' Of course, what one says the other will swear to—I expect that; but I do say, and I will say as long as I live, that you ought, Miles Atherton, to have said more than you did say to Godfrey when he was here, for you won't catch him here again."

Atherton saw that the storm had blown over: in fact, from the first moment that his wife began to speak in the tone admonitory, he perfectly well knew what she meant, and that she was only getting rid of the bottled-up wrath which she had been prevented from launching at the head of Godfrey.

"My dear," he said, "you are quite right as regards Godfrey fully deserving everything said to him that could be said; but you must remember how he disarmed us by presenting such a pitiable object as you recollect he really was. To say anything harsh to him seemed almost like shaking a man who had already been beaten down almost completely."

"Ah! well," replied Mrs. Atherton, who was quite convinced, but who certainly no more thought of saying so than of flying—"Ah! well, that's your idea, and I have got mine, which makes all the difference, you see. But we won't talk about him any more, and I hope you feel how very wrong you have been?"

"Oh! yes; and as I always am."

"None of your sneers, Mr. A.—none of your sneers. Jem, there's somebody in the shop."

"Hilloa!" cried a man in the shop; "does one Miles Atherton live here?"

"Yes, to be sure, stupid," cried Mrs. Atherton; "have we gone to the expense of having the name put up in gilt letters over the door for people after that to come in and ask?"

"Bless you," said the man, who was rather a rough specimen; "bless you, what a sweet voice you have got, to be sure! Why, I never did come near your ekal. It sounds like a pig having his tail sawed off with a oyster-shell."

"You wretch!"

"Go it again, old 'un; I'm a-going. Here's a letter as I shall leave; it comes from one of the coves at Newgate what is going to be hung on Monday morning next. It's cost him some trouble to get it here, and some money; but you see, a pal of mine is a-going all for to be lagged this ere session, so I went in to see him, and the cove as is going to be hung—no, my pal—no, the cove—let me see, where is I?"

"That will do," said Jem; "I wouldn't try back again if I was you, cos if you do, you may injure some of your teeth, you know, by trying to remember too much at once."

"Shall I? You are a nice article in a small way, you are. What's your mother? or did you come over in a cocoa-nut?"

"A little of neither," said Jem; "when did you get out of that ere travelling van as you was showed in last at a penny a head?"

How long this war of words would have lasted it is hard to tell—for the combatants were pretty well matched as to skill in the use of their weapons—had not Miles Atherton interfered, saying,—

"Come, come, I can't have all this. Are you sure the letter is for me?"

"Look at the address, and then give me half a bull; that's what I expects."

"Half a what?" cried Mrs. Atherton.

"A bull, ma'am. Lord love you! I suppose this here poor devil is your seventeenth husband; he'll soon be in his grave. Why, you'd talk the steeple of a church into a lobster's claw, you would, I can see."

Atherton pushed a half-crown into his hand, and drove him out of the shop before Mrs. Atherton had an opportunity of replying, and then he turned her thoughts into another channel, by saying,—

"My dear, I have no doubt but this letter is from Neville, and it will be very curious to see what he can possibly have to say to us; so never mind what that impertinent fellow says or don't say, but come into the parlour and let us read it at once."

"From Neville!" exclaimed Mrs. Atherton: "well, I never thought of that; at least, I did think of it, you know, a—but then I—I—you see—didn't—that is, I—"

"Yes, exactly, my dear; it is from Neville. Listen. Shut the shop-door, Jem."

"Yes," said Jem, "but bar beginning till I come back, now."

"Very well, very well, be quick."

Jem shut the shop-door and was back in an instant, by which time Miles Atherton had got the letter fairly spread open before him, and commenced reading as follows the communication from the rascally Neville, who, it will appear, was willing to sacrifice anybody for his own preservation from death:—

"'Mr. Atherton,—

"'If I was to put no name to this you would know who it came from; but I tell you at once it comes from me, Neville, now condemned to death in Newgate. Who likes to be hung? I don't, I can tell you; so in plain language I want to get off if I can, even if I get lagged for something else. Understand me; here's the point:

"'If it hadn't been for your wife swearing to me I should have got off, cos there was nothing else agin me. I shall get off still if she makes a "davy" that when she considers of it she aint quite sure about me, and can't sleep in her blessed bed all along of having some doubts about it.

"'Good. I don't expect you to do this for nothing, but I think I can do something that will please you by way of a kind of a sort of a recompence. I'll say enough about old Godfrey, and prove enough about him too, to get him transported, perhaps hung. Will that suit you? I know you haven't any great liking for him on account of the Black Lady; and she's been the destruction of me. But no matter: I'll damn Godfrey as well as confess all myself, so that we shall be transported together, only I don't want to be hung. Who the devil does?

"'A fellow as is lagged has some hopes—a fellow as is scragged can't have none.

"'You do what I ask and I'll do what I promise. If you won't, you may all be d——d.'"

*   *   *   *   *   *

"Well," said Jem, "I think that would do to put in a book as I have heard of, called the 'Elegant Epistles.'"

"What do you think of it, my dear?" said Atherton to his wife.

"What do I think? I only wish I had the villain who wrote it here, as I had him once before with a red-hot poker close to his face, he should have such a singe as he never had before in all his life. The vagabond, to think that I would make an affidavit to save him from being hung!"

"It's not likely."

"Likely, Miles Atherton! I should say it was not likely indeed, when I would think nothing of making affidavits all day long, and every day for a week, to get him hung. The vagabond—to suppose, after what we know of him, that we would stir half an inch to save his life!"

"Then shall we, or shall we not, take any notice of this letter?" said Atherton. "That becomes a question, you know, worth considering."

"It seems to me," said Jem, "that without doing anything for Neville, that letter will go some way, if you choose to use it, master, towards convicting old Godfrey; and, don't you think it would be a good thing, now, to prove to all the world that poor Charles Ormond was an innocent man, and to have a tomb-stone put over his grave, poor fellow, to say as much? I aint very rich, but I'd rather subscribe my shilling to that than to a subscription for any artist that might cut his throat on account of mortified vanity, or to a political leader, who, for his own ends and the ends of his own party, worried a weak minister into doing something that he didn't like, but that he thought would spite somebody else."

"Well," said Jem, "well said."

"Bravo!" cried Mrs. Atherton—"bravo! You are quite an orator, Jem, and I only wish somebody half as sensible as you was in the House of Commons."

"Thank you, missus. It aint often as you and me agrees exactly, but we does in that ere sentiment; and if I was in the House of Commons I'd soon do something for the cheesemongers."

"Good again," said Atherton. "Good again."

"As for that letter from Neville, master," continued Jem, who felt himself growing quite oratorical, "I wouldn't take any notice of it just now; but whatever I did afterwards I'd let Neville have the mortification not to get any answer to it at all, and I should not wonder a bit if, at the last moment, when he finds himself disappointed completely, and that no living being comes forward to say one word for him, he'll tell everything."

"That's what I think too," said Mrs. Atherton.

"Well," said Atherton, "I must confess that's a likely enough supposition. And we will consider then, my dear, I think, that the best thing we can possibly do with this letter from Neville is nothing."

"That's it," said Jem. "Let it lie on the table, master, or under, just as it happens. It will keep very well; and if Neville does go out of his way to accuse old Godfrey, we have nothing to do with what comes of the poor old cripple: I'm sure I shan't in a hurry forget him as we picked him up in the passage. He looked more like a corpse than anything else."

It was then finally settled that the letter of Neville should be treated with that species of contempt which is implied by absolute, so that the villain was left to all the horrors of hope deferred.

CHAPTER LXXVII.

THE CHAPTER FROM THE BRAIN OF MARIAN'S FRIEND, THE POET.

THIS being arranged, and the letter from Neville having been carefully put away by Atherton, in case at some future time it should chance to become of importance, Mrs. Atherton suggested the idea of looking at the conclusion of that paper, which had been declared to be the last of that deeply-interesting series which the Black Lady had placed in their hands.

"We may as well," she said, "make a finish of that, you know, A."

"Very good. Here are the papers; and let me see, here is just where I left off. she was saying something, I think, about her poor friend, the author."

"Not exactly, was she? But, however, go on."

"Well, it goes on somewhere hereabouts, I'm sure, for I don't recollect this."

"'You must not suppose—ye who peruse these papers—that the various facts here collected were all got at and ascertained with ease; but you must know, as indeed you may well suppose, that great pains and labour were bestowed by my poor friend, who is now no more, in the completion of the papers, so as to make them assume the form of a regular narrative, in case, when I am no more, they should be presented to the public in print.

"'For example, I will now state to you, that it was only after much inquiry that we ascertained beyond a doubt that it must have been Neville who committed the murder at the inn near to Edgeware, and then it was needless to denounce him for the deed, for it was thoroughly discovered that he had shipped himself as a common sailor, in an American ship, and had left England some time.'"

"Then," said Mrs. Atherton, "that accounts for his long absence, during which poor Miss Whitehead thought he was dead. Go on—go on."

"'The first time I knew of his return was, when he attempted my life in the fog, on the 9th of November, on which occasion I was indebted to you and to Mrs. Atherton, most certainly, for my preservation; and although, Heaven knows, my life is of little value, still your merit in saving it from being taken by a ruffian's hand is as great as if kingdoms had depended upon its preservation.'"

"What an uncommonly just remark!" said Mrs. Atherton.

"Very," said Jem; "we certainly did save her life. Do you recollect how old Neville bundled over my back as he was coming out, missus, while you were coming after him with the red-hot poker?"

"Ah! I do, Jem."

"And then, what a shout he gave, when you sawed his head nearly off with it!"

"To be sure. To be sure."

"And don't you remember," said Atherton, "how I served him out with the cheese-knife?"

"To be sure; we all served him out. But go on, master—what does she say next?"

Miles Atherton resumed the reading:—

"As some sort of tribute to the memory of my deceased friend, and to give you some idea of what his style and manner is, I have transcribed a short tale of his writing, which amused me at the time he read it to me, and which may do so to you, my kind friends, who, I believe, will take an interest in whoever has spoken a gentle word to the unhappy Marian Whitehead."

"Oh, read it, by all means," said Mrs. Atherton.

"Oh," said Jem, "let's have it, and we shall feel our spirits a little smoothened down. after the blessed row there has been here to-day, one way and another."

"Well," said the cheesemonger, "as you are both of one mind, and as I confess I am myself of the same opinion, I don't see why I should not read it at once; it's only a few pages, so here goes."

So saying, Miles Atherton carefully arranged the Black Lady's papers, and having directed Jem to keep the candles snuffed, he duly proceeded as follows:—

During the early part of the reign of King Henry the Eighth, when the rights of property were not so well defined or understood as they are now, and when guardians possessed an almost despotic power over their wards, there were many evil deeds perpetrated, and which could never be righted save the lady had some lover or other relation who was willing to do so with the edge of the sword.

The well known case of the Lady Emily Shaw was of this description, and arose in the following manner:—

Sir Thomas Shaw, her father, was an old and tried soldier; he had fought in many a bloody battle, and often received deep and honourable wounds: and whether it was in defeat or victory, Sir Thomas was always respected for his prowess and bravery ; and he never sullied the motto on his arms.

This hero had but one daughter—the subject of our tale—a lady of great beauty and amiability of temper. She was his only child, and dearly did her father dote upon her ; and never was a father's love more sincerely or better repaid by the devotion of a child.

Her mother died in early life when she was eight years old, and it was said that Sir Thomas Shaw abstained from more than one matrimonial alliance which offered him more than the usual inducements to form such connexions—youth, beauty, and wealth, being at his disposal ; and it was even said that feelings had even been sacrificed on his part to the superior one in him, of parental affection.

He determined to remain a widower for the remainder of his life, that his beloved daughter should not be subjected to any of the vicissitudes of life that are brought about by the presence of a mother-in-law.

He knew well that a soldier's life was precarious, and he might be cut off, and then his beautiful and only child would be subject or liable to all those evils he would wish to save her from.

This was the only motive that induced him to remain single : however, death put an end to the old man's life at an earlier time than he had anticipated. He had been often sorely wounded in battle, but always got off : whether defeated or victorious the old soldier was respected by the men whom he commanded, and this was the secret of his safety, for they often provided for his safety before they thought of their own, and they would usually bear him out of the field of battle if wounded.

Thus it was he was often rescued from what to others was inevitable death ; but he was often, as we have said, sorely wounded, and some years after his last encounter in hostile force, his old wound broke out again, and he was laid up ; and, despite all that the medical skill of the age cou'd effect—the prayers of his friends, and the sorrow of his daughter—the wound turned to a gangrene, and the old soldier closed his career.

Sir Thomas Shaw was not more than forty-eight when he died ; but yet he was often styled the ' old warrior' by his friends, because he had been actively employed in service from the age of sixteen, and his experience was very great in military and national matters.

He had one friend to whom he bequeathed his most darling treasure, and that was his daughter, the Lady Emily. This friend was Sir Rupert Walsingham, a gentleman of good estate, likewise a widower and an old companion-in-arms of his late friend, Sir Thomas Shaw.

This gentleman had several daughters—the juniors of the Lady Emily and her future companions.

This bore, to all appearance, as being the best arrangement he could by any possibility have entered into for the happiness and peace of his daughter, for the families were intimate, and the ladies were sincere friends.

We have said they were younger than the Lady Emily. This is true. Sir Rupert Walsingham was a younger man by many years than Sir Thomas, and he married much earlier in life, and after a few years he was left a widower with three daughters.

No doubt Sir Thomas thought that there was no inducement in such a family to force his daughter into any alliance they might think proper. They would be wanting the usual motive—the common incentive to such acts, which was gain : they could gain nothing ; there was no means of bringing the property in the family.

Not that Sir Thomas Shaw for one moment thought that such a thing would have been done had there been ample means. No ; he had too much candour and honesty in his own disposition to give others credit for intrigue when he never saw anything of the kind. He loved his friend, and he believed his friend had the same feelings towards him ; but upon so serious a matter he thought it only his duty to do all that a parent could do to secure the happiness of a beloved child.

Therefore it was that he confided to Sir Rupert Walsingham the care of his daughter, fully and freely, and taught her to look up to him as a parent, and follow his counsel in all things.

Such were his last words; and with a blessing on his lips he sank nto that state of forgetfulness from which the human spirit never awakens in this life more.

The grief of such a daughter may be readily imagined. She was inconsolable for the loss she had sustained. It was a shock to her delicate frame that took months to recover, and to bring her round to her former state of health, bodily and mentally.

However, the extreme kindness and even tenderness of Sir Rupert Walsingham, and the kind solicitude of his daughters, eventually brought her round to look upon life as yet having something in it to live for—to sorrow less and to hope more.

And yet there was a tinge of melancholy about her that promised long to be a distinguishing trait of her character, even if it were ever freed from it; but yet it was not so strong as to be by any means a cause of displeasure to her friends.

Sir Rupert Walsingham was most assiduous in taking all opportunities of supplying the place of her father to her, and succeeded in gaining her confidence and respect to a very great degree. She looked up to him as her protector and her guide.

There was, however, one matter to which all were strangers save to herself. She was possessed of the secret of her heart, which indeed she had not divulged even to her father.

But there was one reason for this, and it must be held as being good under the circumstances, and certainly it cleared her from any charge of want of duty and confidence towards her father, and that was, she herself was not aware of the extent to which her affections had been engaged.

Besides, there is a natural diffidence in young love to reveal itself to the eyes of others. It is such a fearful operation that the loved one shrinks from it as the passion-flower from the touch. At first it will not admit itself. The imagination alone shrinks from contemplating the fact of its existence at all until it becomes more and more self-evident—until the first flutterings of the flame in the breast become strengthened and formed by time are blown into a flame.

Then indeed strength of passion gives confidence, and enables the subject of such feelings to brave all danger and pass through flames of fire rather than it should be deemed unworthy of its object.

This was the case with the Lady Emily Shaw. It was but the first flutterings of a breast new to such emotions, and who was scarcely aware of their nature, before a load of sorrow was thrown upon her, beneath which, for a time, all other feelings were subdued and stifled.

However, the longest day has an end, and there is a time when the most poignant grief must wear itself out; and this was the case with the Lady Emily. Either she must sink or get over it. Youth and health decided for her, and the return of the object which had once caused these new and charming emotions in her breast ere other griefs began, completed the work so desirable in one so young and so beautiful.

The young knight, her lover, a warrior of scarce five-and-twenty, was one well qualified to bear the minstrel's harp in the hall, the lute in the lady's bower, or the sword and battle-axe in the field.

But even such qualifications have been bestowed in vain when viewed in some lights, and this we consider as the case with an unsuccessful but deserving lover.

The youth who had the happiness to excite the tender passion in the heart of the Lady Emily was one who possessed all the qualifications suitable for such a heart as that he aspired to, save one, and that was a fatal one among such men in hose days, when the affections of the heart were not so much thought of or so much attention paid to, as in more piping times of peace. Our lover wanted what was very common in such characters, and which is nothing more than what Burns calls

" Worldly gear and a' that ;"

but which is an essential in the bread and cheese part of the business.

However, to speak seriously and sadly, he was an adventurer, whose sole qualifications, beyond what we have enumerated, were an unblemished name and descent, and his known honour and bravery.

Great qualifications these, and well calculated to procure, with some favourable circumstances, a great fortune, perhaps the foundation of house ; many a family of great distinction was originally raised by less worthy ancestors than such an one as that which we have described.

Young Herbert Gordon, for that was his name, had served with credit, and not without profit ; he was favourably noticed by his superiors, and was considered in the light of one on whom fortune might smile, upon any lucky incident that was to arise.   Such an one never wanted a courteous reception wherever he might go, though the same fathers who so received him might keep their daughters out of the way.

But to do Herbert justice, he would have been slow to take any advantage of any such occasion, unless where the heart had entangled him; he would never have condescended to raise himself by such means, he had too much confidence in himself to do that.

However, he accidentally visited Sir Thomas Shaw, and there he met with the incomparable Lady Emily, to whom his heart swore fealty and love, whom he looked upon with a devotion that could never be equalled by the devotion of any lover to the object of his darling affection.

His visit continued for some time at Sir Thomas Shaw's, for he had served under that old warrior's command, and he respected him for his bravery and spirit as well as talent, all which he had seen him display in situations which had called them forth.

The walks and grounds round about the house of the knight gave ample opportunity to Herbert Gordon to show his attention to the beauteous Lady Emily.

The time passed by very quickly and pleasantly enough there, among the green glades and forest depths; there, indeed, they found each other's taste to coincide. She looked upon him as the model of a young warrior, a brave man, and a gentleman of his day, and one well calculated to raise the tender emotions she felt towards him; she now acknowledged, even to herself, that he was the only one who could ever make her happy.

He, on the other hand, saw in her all that was good and beautiful, and bowed the knee in adoration of such charms, and such a heart.

Thus things went on; but neither of them had time to speak upon the subject that was growing in their hearts. The lady could not—indeed, her thoughts and feelings were not advanced enough to take a definite form—they were merely taking their first shape: but had they been strong and clear, she could not have opened them to her lover.

That lover, however, knew her superior station in life; he knew she was the daughter of his host, and had large property; this to him was an inducement to pause before he did so. He could not bear the idea of his love being considered as mercenary; he would wait till some stroke of fortune placed him above such an accusation; but yet he could but permit his heart to linger near the spot, and there to adore the object of his affections.

Just at that time he was called away to perform some service for the nobleman under whose patronage he had placed himself, for that in those days was the only road to preferment.

When he reached his patron, it was to undertake, he found, a dangerous foreign service, to which there would be attached more credit than profit.

This to such a one as Herbert Gordon, indeed that was no objection to his undertaking the service. He was young and ardent, panting with the desire to distinguish himself, and therefore would not refuse any opportunity that offered a field for such an object.

"I will go," he said, "and do my best to achieve your grace's desires, and may they credit me as they may pleasure your grace!"

"If you succeed in this matter as I wish, I shall endeavour to stand your friend upon any honourable occasion in which you may need my countenance."

This promised, Herbert Gordon took himself to the shores of Normandy, where he remained for many months, during which time he had the good fortune to perform one action of gallantry, for which he was highly commended by those who witnessed it.

After about a nine months' absence he returned to his native land, where he soon made himself welcome by the account he was enabled to give of his success, which was more than was expected, and his patron was so well pleased with him, that he sought and obtained the honour of knighthood for him.

It was at this juncture that he returned to the scene where he first loved, and where he again hoped to have the happiness he had before found there.

Great was his sorrow at finding Sir Thomas Shaw no more; he was an old soldier, and young Herbert had fought with him in more than one bloody engagement—however, he saw the Lady Emily—he met her accidentally, and then they renewed their intimacy at the point where it had been broken off by his expedition.

Now, however, there was not the hesitation on the young knight's part there had been at one time. So far from that being the case, he urged the Lady Emily to give him a husband's right, by a secret marriage.

This, however, she refused, on the ground that they were both young—her father's recent death—and the want of confidence she would show towards her guardian, whom she respected, not only for his own good qualities, but because he was her father's friend, and her father had confidence in him; so much so that he had placed her under his care in preference to all others, and therefore she should injure the memory of her father if she did so.

Finding that these were her opinions, he abstained from making any further attempt to induce her to comply with his wishes, or to alter her determination.

This much he besought her—that she would enter into no alliance whatever; and that, as she would not alter her state for three or four years, she would at least preserve her faith towards him.

" It was to the interest of both," he said, " that his time should be employed usefully and honourably, and that he should not waste it, even in paying court to her—they both well knew their own hearts, and absence would not endanger their love."

The Lady Emily was so thoroughly aware of her lover's sincerity and honour, that she at once pledged her faith to him; if he at the end of that time returned to claim her hand, fortune or no fortune she would at once grant it to him.

Thus he was at liberty to pursue what course he thought most conducive to his own benefit. This he at once determined to consult, by accepting the command of a foreign expedition which had been offered him, and the command of a foreign province. This was a high honour and lucrative post; and he at once, after a tender leave-taking, hastened to accept it.

Nothing was, however, hinted at to Sir Rupert Walsingham, as, at the end of the period spoken of, the Lady Emily would be her own mistress, and would be at her own disposal; besides, she did not consider it at all necessary to bare all the feelings of her heart to one whom she could not do more than honour and respect; she had not the same endeared feelings she could have felt towards her father—indeed, her love appeared to be too sacred a thing to be spoken of to any other save her lover.

*   *   *   *   *   *   *

A year had gone by since her lover's departure, and she had more than once heard of him, always with honour, but often in danger; but she said nothing; she cherished the memory of such a lover with fervour.

However, there was a complete change in her happiness, for the conduct of Sir Rupert Walsingham was singular in the extreme; he had all along treated her with the greatest kindness; he had even evinced great tenderness and consideration towards her; but this was what now alarmed and annoyed her.

His attentions were more marked, and of a character that gave her much uneasiness: it was more of the attention of a lover than aught else; and this she speedily found out was the case, for Sir Rupert completely altered his character, and at once broadly asked her hand.

This at once she declined, stating that she looked upon him in the light of a friend and father, and not as a husband and lover; she could not alter her feelings.

But Sir Rupert was not so easily dissuaded from his suit; he persisted in courting her for a whole year, and at the end of that time he hoped to have made some change in her determination.

This, however, was impossible; and when he found that he could not succeed by fair means, he determined upon adopting other means more in accordance with the hopelessness of his own case, rather than suitable to a love-suit.

He was resolved to compel by force what he could not accomplish in the ordinary method, and at once informed her that she was his ward, and he would compel her obedience.

"And is this worthy of you, Sir Rupert—worthy of my father's friend, to coerce his daughter for his own profit?"

"My love is concerned."

"Your love of gain."

"Not at all so," cried Sir Rupert; "but it is worth the prize, and well worth the attempt. What we cannot win by court, we take by force."

"You dare not do so," said Emily."

"I dare do more than you think for. Remember, I am absolute master here, and whatever I command will be done. I shall be obeyed in all things, and you shall not be the only one who sets my will at defiance."

"God of Heaven! if my poor father were here, would he believe the evidence of his own senses? Would he believe his friend could act thus perfidiously?"

"He would have done the same himself if he felt as I did about this affair."

"Slanderer! he never could feel as you do; he could never feel he was the craven to break faith, to injure his friend's child's happiness. No, he could never feel that he was the oppressor of the orphan—he was a brave and honourable man."

"Nay, if you waste words in this way, you will have none left to ask my clemency."

"No, I never will do that, but I will do my best to call for justice to those who can give it me."

"Your voice must reach a long way if you think it will be heard beyond the walls of your apartment; and rely upon it, should you refuse to be my wife, my strength may compel you to be something less."

"Monster!"

But it was useless to remonstrate. He had her confined in a part of his mansion from which she could not escape, and here she was tormented by the visits and importunities of Sir Rupert, who did not fail to threaten her with every species of cruelty he could devise."

He, however, abstained from laying hands upon her, lest it should ever be in her power to seek justice; such an act would possibly only be expiated on the scaffold.

It was amazing how confidently he pursued his suit, and yet he was on the brink of ruin—for Sir Herbert Gordon had returned from his governorship and command —returned with honour, and not without some more substantial proofs of the approbation of those who employed him, and he was comparatively rich.

As soon as he had discharged himself from his command, he received the thanks of his sovereign, who conferred upon him an estate that had just been forfeited to the crown, not far from that of Sir Rupert Walsingham.

The latter welcomed his neighbour, unsuspicious of whom he was harbouring. At the same time Sir Herbert said nothing of the Lady Emily, but waited until he found that she was not to be seen, when he inquired for her.

"She is very indisposed, at a distance," replied Sir Rupert.

"Then I should like to see her—I was an old friend of her father's, and I am anxious to see her."

Sir Rupert found that he was obliged to comply; but determined to make the young knight acquainted with his plans, and to obtain his consent and countenance, which he thought would be of the utmost service to his cause, and he appointed a day for their meeting.

This came round, and no sooner did the Lady Emily see her lover, than she rushed into his arms, to the consternation of Sir Rupert, who, when he had recovered from the first shock of surprise, called all his vassals around him, to secure them both.

But this end was defeated, for Sir Herbert Gordon had posted a body of veterans to be with him, in case of an accident, at the blowing of his horn; and though few in number, they were men used to conflicts, and well trained, so that none durst meddle with them.

They left the house and proceeded to his own—the marriage feast was soon given, when they were made happy—not before Sir Herbert had challenged and chastised the wicked guardian; but spared his life at the intercession of the Lady Emily, who did so for his daughters' sakes, for they had always been kind to her.

"Well?" said Mrs. Atherton, finding that her husband paused at this point—"well, Atherton?"

"Pretty well," said the cheesemonger. "Might be worse, and might be better."

"Well, but why don't you go on?"

"Just because I have got to the end of the story, that's all. Why, you don't expect to go on for ever, do you, Mrs. Atherton? Come, come, be contented for once, and remember that we have come from the past into the present."

"What do you mean by that, Mr. A.? You really do sometimes speak as if you were going to set up for a conjuror in a small way. But please to explain yourself."

"I dare say now," said Atherton, "that Jem could explain all about it. What do you think now, Jem, that I meant, eh?"

"Why, master," said Jem, putting himself in quite an oratorical attitude, "I think you mean that as we have got through the Black Lady's papers, and as they all related to the past, and as we had got, in a manner of speaking, you see, quite mixed up with Godfrey and Neville as belonged to the present, we had gone from what was to what is."

"Exactly," said the cheesemonger; "you have hit it, Jem; you have hit the right nail on the head. Now, Mrs. Atherton, you know what I meant when I said we had gone from the past to the present; and if I don't mistake very much, the present will turn out to be something of a more exciting and a more interesting character than the past."

"As how, Mr. A.?"

"Why thus. First of all, there's poor Marian Whitehead herself: I am certain she is not long for this world, poor thing! and I only hope that her end will be peace. Then there's Neville, who, although I certainly hope he may be hanged, certainly is not hanged yet. Then there's Godfrey, who, if I mistake not, will yet, poor wretch—for a poor wretch he is, in spite of all his money—has not suffered all he will suffer; and then there's Jem may do something extraordinary, for aught I know. And then——"

"Stop, Mr. Atherton, stop! I am quite satisfied that something or another may happen at all events, and I'm half in the mind to go to No. 3, in the Alley, just to know."

The countenance of Miles Atherton assumed an aspect of great annoyance as his wife spoke of No. 3, in the Alley; for he knew that those words alluded to a fortune-teller who had recently set up in the neighbourhood, and who had succeeded in getting himself a large reputation among the (sometimes) gentler sex.

"My dear," he said, "if you go again to that impostor, you and I will quarrel."

"Impostor? How do you know that he is an impostor, Mr. A., I should like to know?"

"Of course he is, in consequence of professing the very art by which he gets a living. You cannot, Mrs. Atherton, really be so foolish as to think that anybody can possess the power attributed to that man. You know it was only the other day, as we were taking our coffee, and talking about conjurors——"

"There you are, wrong again, Mr. Atherton. We were taking our tea, and not our coffee."

After this, can any married man wonder that Miles Atherton snatched up his hat, and went off post haste to the nearest public-house, where he did find agreeable company, and where, if he was contradicted, it somehow or another had not that vexatious air with it that a domestic contradiction has.

If a man can bear to be contradicted, and set right at his own fireside by his wife, he has either an abundant amount of philosophy, or abundant amount of stupidity, which in this world answers precisely the same purpose. But we do believe there are few such, and that one-half the domestic disturbances that take place between man and wife, take their rise from that one fact, that the wife wants to put her liege lord right, when her liege lord has an undoubted and inalienable right to be wrong, if he likes.

Yes, wrong. We uphold the doctrine to all husbands that they, in their own houses, by their own domestic hearths, have a right to say that the moon is made of green cheese, and no one, particularly a wife, ought to think of saying otherwise, or of bringing forward a single astronomical fact in favour of a contrary theory.

And here some ladies may say, is it not a strange thing that you men will bear contradiction from others, but make such a tremendous fuss about it from your wives? and we answer,

Ladies, it is because you are wives that the contradiction from your lips does become of importance. It is because we can get away from other people when we please that their contradiction becomes of no importance. If Mr. A. B. or C. offend us in any way, and make his company otherwise than agreeable to us, we can cut him—yes, cut him dead—but we don't want the disagreeable, expensive, and troublesome process of getting out of the way of a wife.

Hence is it that people put up with more from their wives than from anybody else, and hence is it likewise that they feel it more, and make the greatest possible riot about it. A man may run against an iron chain and get bruised without saying aught about it, because he knows he can be more careful another time, and not renew the collision; but if he be compelled for life to wear one, let it gall him anywhere, and what a perpetual source of annoyance it shall become!

And although we have taken, in this instance, a strong case, yet we would say to the ladies that it is in their own power either to be the iron chain which galls or a wreath of roses, holding the wayward nature of man by the combined influence of love and beauty.

CHAPTER LXXVIII.

NEVILLE SENDS ANOTHER PRESSING MESSAGE TO MILES ATHERTON TO VISIT HIM IN NEWGATE.

MILES ATHERTON, when he reached the God-knows-whose Head or Arms round the corner, where, now and then, he went to solace himself with a glass of something after the fatigues of the day, found the whole conversation turning upon Neville and his expected execution.

Indeed the whole affair possessed an interest at that house of entertainment beyond that which would have ordinarily belonged to it, because its painful events had actually occurred in the house of a neighbour, and that neighbour no other than Miles Atherton the cheesemonger, who might be seen all alive for nothing at the public-house occasionally.

And such is popular curiosity, that people came from a number of streets off on purpose to look at Atherton, because he was the man who kept the house where the murder was committed. And they would order a glass of something and sit as nearly opposite to him as they could, really taking a great interest in what he said and did.

Of course the landlord of the house had no objection to this, and if, without offending Miles Atherton, he could have offered him an unlimited number of glasses of grog " free, gratis, and for nothing," to come every night to talk about the murder of Zachary, there can be no doubt but that it would have paid him, the landlord, very well in the long-run.

"Well, Mr. Atherton," said an old, portly-looking man who sat in a corner close to the fire-place, and who never would sit anywhere else,—"well, Mr. Atherton, I suppose there's no news, sir?"

"No," said Atherton, "none that I know of."

"I suppose, sir, that fellow will be hanged."

"I should think he would; and what is more, he amply deserves it for—but no matter—no matter."

Miles Atherton did not utter these disjointed sentences for the purpose of feeding or of awakening curiosity, but he, in the open frankness of his nature, was continually upon the point of saying something which would have been a breach of that solemn promise he had made to the Black Lady, and which he was as anxious to keep as any man could possibly be.

But for all that, and notwithstanding he had no real intention of doing so, these words that he had uttered awakened such an amount of attention as was almost annoying to him, and he certainly very much regretted that he had let them slip from his lips.

"Gentlemen," he said, in an apologetic tone of voice, "gentlemen, I am really very sorry, but the fact is, you see, that—that, in a manner of speaking, I have nothing to say at all upon the subject further than what you yourselves know from the public reports, and ——"

At this moment a man came into the parlour, and said rapidly,

"Is Mr. Atherton here?"

"Yes, yes," said everybody, pointing to Atherton. "Yes, that's the man."

"Oh!" said the stranger, "I have been to your house, sir, with this note, and a lad there told me I should most likely find you here. I believe it wants an immediate answer."

"Indeed! who is it from?"

"The governor of Newgate."

It is quite superfluous to say that this news created what might be called quite a sensation in the room, and there certainly was not an individual present who would not have given something handsome, in the shape of drink, to have discovered what it was that the governor of Newgate had to say to Miles Atherton in such a wonderful hurry that a messenger must be despatched, and it should require an immediate answer.

Miles Atherton had just lit himself a pipe, but he now laid that down, and with painful expectation upon his face, opened the letter which had been thus sent to him from a personage of whom he knew nothing.

The letter contained the following words :—

"The governor of Newgate presents his compliments to Mr. Miles Atherton, and begs to submit it to his judgment, whether it would not be better to visit the man, Neville, who is condemned to death, since he expresses so strong a desire to see Mr. Atherton.

"Of course, in saying this much, the governor can have no desire to dictate in any way to Mr. Atherton, but in his opinion, unless there are some private reasons for a contrary cause, which he, Mr. Atherton, may know, he thinks the visit would be as well made."

Miles Atherton pondered for a moment or two over this communication, and then turning to the messenger, with the air of a man who had made a sudden resolution, he said,

"Give my compliments and respects to the governor, and tell him that I will come at once. Get yourself something to drink at the bar and say it's for me."

"Thank you, sir," said the man,—"very good, sir."

How the parlour guests did stare to be sure! How they longed to say something and did not like to do so! How they hoped, against all kind of probability, that Miles Atherton would be communicative, and let them know what it was the governor of Newgate could possibly want with him. But when they saw him rise and button up his coat, and take his hat off the peg on which it hung, the grew desperate, and one at length exclaimed,

"God God ! Mr. Atherton, won't you tell us what it is all about ?"

"Oh! nothing particular ; only the governor of Newgate wants to see me, that's all, about something.   Good night, gentlemen, good night."

This was very unsatisfactory indeed ; they could easily, every one of them, have guessed as much as that, of course.   A letter comes from the governor of Newgate, and Miles Atherton tells the messenger to take back his compliments and to say that he will come directly ; so it was no news to say to him afterwards, that the governor wanted to see him.   It was provoking,—it was very provoking. But away went Miles Atherton to Newgate for all that, and left his companions wondering.

The distance from any part of the city to that sad and grim-looking building, which rears its rough stone front as a terror to all evil-doers, is but short, and Atherton soon stood beneath the shadow of its massive walls ; he proceeded at once to the small wicket gate at which visitors are admitted, and on presenting himself he was, as usual, asked,—

"What now ?" that being the common mode of salutation to a stranger, from the officials of the building.

"I have come," he said, "to see Neville."

"Well I'm sure," said the turnkey, as he looked Miles Atherton in the face ; "well I'm sure, that's cool, at all events.   And so you fancy you have nothing to do but to come up Newgate steps, and say you want to see Neville, and then be handed in at once."

"I did not want to be handed in,—I was sent for by the governor."

"Yes," said another of the turnkeys, stepping forward, "if this is the gentleman named Atherton, he is to be shown into the governor's room at once, and every attention is to be shown to him."

At these words, the wicket door was opened in a moment, and Atherton was invited to walk in at once, which he did, contrasting in his own mind this treatment with what he had at one time experienced, when he went to visit a poor fellow who was innocently confined, and when he was bullied about whether he had any tobacco about him or not, and his sides thumped while the interesting question was propounded.

He was conducted to the governor's private room, where he was in a few moments joined by that gentleman, who, with great courtesy, said to him—

"Mr. Atherton, pray be seated ; I have, under the circumstances, taken the liberty of sending for you, sir, because the wretched convict, who, whatever may be his serious offences before God and man, will suffer for them, has expressed an earnest desire to converse with you."

"Heaven forbid that I should, if you think it proper, sir, refuse to see a man who is in such an awful position.   If I had any idea of not wishing to see him, it was on account of not desiring to enter into such contention with him as I was afraid he would enter into."

"You have some reason to suppose, I presume, that such would have been the case ?"

"I have unhappily some reason to suppose so ; but my lips are sealed against the utterance of what that reason is, or I should willingly inform you, sir, of it. The fact is, that I have reason to suppose he wants to engage me in a scheme of revenge."

"Indeed, sir !"

"Yes ; and as the party against whom he wishes for that vengeance is already punished sufficiently, I do not, in common Christian charity, think that I ought to have anything to do with the matter."

"I cannot tell, Mr. Atherton, if he have anything of the sort to say to you or not.   Perhaps he may have taken it into his head to confess something, and we have frequent experience of criminals pitching upon particular persons to whom they are to make their revelations, and sending for them accordingly.   If I may presume to give you any advice upon the matter, it would only be to abstain most particularly from making any promises of secresy to him."

"Sir, I thank you, and I assure you that I shall be most particularly careful in that matter. He shall fully understand that; let him say what he may to me, it shall be repeated again."

"That is the best plan. You cannot go wrong then, Mr. Atherton, and if you will be so good as to follow me, I will take you to one who will show you the way to the cell in which we have him confined."

The governor now preceded Atherton to a small apartment, which was situated between that part of the building which he occupied, and that which was devoted to the reception of criminals, and addressing a turnkey who was there, he said—

"You will show this gentleman to the cell of Neville?"

"Yes, sir," said the man; and, rising, he took a small lamp from a bracket which was on the wall, and preceded Atherton through some of those strange and gloomy passages of Newgate, which led to the condemned cells, of which there are eight, and in one of which the villain Neville lay, awaiting that doom which, if any one richly deserved, he did **most** unquestionably.

"He's a strange fellow, sir," said the turnkey, as he went along: "and we have our suspicions of him that he would be mischievous if he could, so we will put him in irons, and you need not see him alone unless you wish."

"Oh, I don't suppose there is much danger," said Atherton; "perhaps if he has any revelation or confession to make to me, he will object to making it in the presence of another."

"Most likely, sir; but that can be tried at all events. This is his cell."

The turnkey stopped at one of the small doors of those most gloomy receptacles for humanity, and, having removed the ponderous bolts which held it fast, he turned a key that he carried with him, in the lock, and the door yielded slowly on its hinges, showing its great weight and thickness as it did so. The turnkey held up the little lamp he carried, and thus Atherton saw Neville sitting at the further end of the cell, with his arms crossed upon his breast, and his eyes fixed upon the door.

"Who's there?" he cried; "what do you mean by coming and disturbing a man continually? If it's a parson, tell him I don't want him."

"He's a visitor," said the turnkey; "Mr. Atherton."

"Ah!" cried Neville, rising, and rattling his fetters as he did so—"Miles Atherton, and has he really come at last? You are welcome, sir, and from what you think of me, you will hardly guess what I wanted you for!"

"I have no wish to do so," said Atherton, "and therefore do not intend to attempt it. Moreover, as this interview is of your seeking and not mine, I shall be glad when it's over, and beg you will say at once what you wish to say."

"It's just this then," said Neville. "I know my fate is sealed. I know that I am a doomed man, and I don't think anything can now save me from the gallows; so I have taken a fancy that you wouldn't have expected in me. I shall like to see everybody who has any reason to complain of me, and get them to say that they forgive me."

"Well, for my part," said Atherton, much relieved in his own mind to find that this was what Neville wanted, "I forgive you with all my heart."

"I thank you; for I know I have given you some trouble, and by your saying that it knocks off one from the list of people that I wanted to see on such an account. And now if, to-morrow, you will be good enough to let your wife come, it can be all settled comfortably, so far as you and she are concerned; for I feel that I require her forgiveness more than I do yours."

"You may make yourself quite satisfied upon that head; for I can now, as you ask it, assure you of her forgiveness, and I am only very glad to find that now, in the last moments as one may say of your life, you are so well inclined."

"Oh! don't mention that. Everybody is not so bad as they look, you know; but I shall not be satisfied, unless I hear it from your good lady's own lips, that she is willing to look over what has passed, and forgive a poor fellow who is now sorry enough for all that he's done that's amiss."

The turnkey gave his head a very dubious shake, as if he could not help thinking that there was something amazingly suspicious in this sudden sort of conversion to such a Christian line of conduct on the part of Neville.

"I think," said Atherton, "that this is no proper place for women to come to, and so I shall decline bringing Mrs. Atherton; but, if you cannot believe me when I assure you she will forgive you, I will get her to write as much upon a piece of paper, and sign it with her name, and have it sent to you, so that you shall have no doubt upon the matter."

"It's a hard case that such a small matter should be denied to a dying man, for such is what I may consider myself."

"It is not denied to you, I tell you, that you shall be assured of the full and entire forgiveness of Mrs. Atherton; and, as you say that is all you desire, I'm sure you ought to be satisfied."

"I think she would not refuse to come if she were really asked."

"She might not, but I shall decline mentioning it at all to her except in the way I propose."

" You will not ?"

" Certainly not."

" Then you shall have yourself what I intended for her, and it shall be all in the family, at any rate !"

As he spoke these words the ruffian made a rush upon Miles Atherton ; and most probably, if the officer had not been present, and, with great courage as well as presence of mind, thrown himself in between them, would have inflicted upon him some very serious injury indeed ; for by some means he was armed with a gimlet, which, how he became possessed of in such a place, appeared to be most mysterious.

The officer was a powerful man, and, moreover, used to such customers ; so he soon succeeded in disarming and placing upon Neville a pair of handcuffs which he took from his pocket. And all this was done with such immense rapidity from the first moment that Neville had rushed forward with his murderous intentions to that in which he had been handcuffed by the officer, that poor Miles Atherton stood in a perfect state of bewilderment, looking as if he did not know whether he stood upon his head or his heels.

" You scoundrel !" said the officer ; " I thought from the first that you had some scheme in view, but what it was I could not tell, for I little suspected you had any weapon."

" Curses on you all !" said Neville. " The bitterest curse that tongue can utter light upon you !"

" Ah ! you may amuse yourself by cursing as long as you like," added the turnkey ; " but you have no power now to do any mischief. He had very nearly done you an injury, I think, sir. You see, you really cannot be too careful with such fellows."

" Good God !" ejaculated Miles Atherton, " and at such a time as this too, he would actually have taken my life."

" He would, sir ; but you see his object, no doubt, was to get Mrs. Atherton here, and to have murdered her for the evidence she gave against him on his trial. But in that he has failed, thank the Fates, for, if she had come, and this villain had taken her life, it would have been such a thing as never yet took place in Newgate. We generally consider we have such gentry safe, at all events, from doing any more mischief, when we turn a key upon them."

" I'm all of a tremble," said Atherton. " It looks rather a long gimlet."

" Long enough for mischief. The cells have been recently repaired, and one of the workmen must have left this behind him. That must have been the way the vagabond got possession of it, and it's a thousand mercies that he has done no real mischief.

" Well," said Atherton, as he held up his hands, " I ought to have known that such a man was bad enough for anything. What an escape I have had !"

" Yes, sir ; and what an escape your good lady has had, for if she had come he would most assuredly, I should say, have murdered her. But come away, sir ; we will now leave him for a time to his own reflections."

We cannot transfer to our pages the frightful curses which the discomfited villain now launched at the head of Atherton, who was really glad when the door of the cell was closed, and he could no longer hear the wild, raving voice of Neville, who, no doubt, felt most bitterly the pangs of disappointment ; for not only had he failed in his attack upon the cheesemonger, but he had, as a consequence of that failure, become deprived of a weapon which no doubt he would have been glad to keep, for with it he could at all events have done some mischief to somebody, and so gratified, perhaps at the last moment almost of his existence, his evil passions.

When Miles Atherton was once more with the governor, that functionary looked amazingly chagrined at the result of the interview, which really might have been of such a different character, and which, if anything serious had occurred, he certainly must have blamed himself, as without his interference it would not have taken place at all.

"Mr. Atherton," he said, "I am extremely thankful that the affair has gone off as it has; for had you come to any damage, I should not only have blamed myself, but I should have been much censured by others. It was a most unpardonable thing for any one to leave such an implement of defence in the hands of the prisoner."

"Oh, never mind it," said Atherton, who saw that the governor was much vexed—"never mind it, sir; these things will happen, I should say, at times with all the precaution in the world, and you did what you did in the matter, I know, with the kindest and the best of motives, so you ought not to blame yourself."

"It's very kind of you to say so, sir; but if the event had turned out otherwise I should not have felt so easy as I do now about it. I feel that I am much indebted to your kindness."

The cheesemonger and the governor parted with mutual expressions of good-will towards each other.

But although Miles Atherton had made light of the affair before the governor in order to remove from his mind any uncomfortable impression concerning it, he by no means in reality thought light of it; and he congratulated himself, when he was once more beyond the walls of Newgate, upon his escape from perhaps one of the most imminent dangers that had ever beset him, for that Neville would have murdered him if he could, he did not entertain the slightest doubt.

He debated within his own mind whether or not he should say anything to Mrs. Atherton upon the subject, and although he did not like exactly to be made a subject of gossip among her lady acquaintance, he thought it would be better to tell her at once rather than it should ooze out on some other occasion, and then he should fairly enough be asked why he had kept it so long to himself.

This was a highly prudent view of the subject to take, in a matrimonial point of view, and we cannot but applaud Atherton for feeling as he did upon such a point, for out it would have come some day, perhaps to his great discomfiture; so directly he got home he informed Mrs. Atherton of what had occurred, to which she listened with dismay, mingled with indignation, and when he had concluded his narration, she exclaimed,—

"Oh, the villain!—oh, the wretch!—the monster! to think of settling me with a gimlet. I have a great mind to go to Newgate, and gimlet him—the murdering vagabond—and you, Miles Atherton, to be such a goose."

"Such a what, my dear?"

"A goose, Mr. A.—a—goose. If you had but come and told me that Neville wanted you at Newgate, I could have spared you running the risk of making me a widow."

"Why, how could you have done that?"

"How could I have done it! Do you think I should not have guessed in a moment that he had a gimlet with him? Do you think it possible I could have been mistaken in his intentions? No, I should have said—no, Mr. Atherton, that fellow has got a gimlet."

"A gimlet, ay, my dear, he certainly has got; but how you could have thought of his having a carpenter's gimlet with him, is certainly beyond my power to say."

"Oh, pooh! you don't know what people may think of; and it only shows you what a wrong and foolish thing it is to go and do anything without consulting me in the first instance about it."

Miles Atherton did not exactly see how this applied to him, or to the affair, the particulars of which he had just related; but here again he showed his prudence, for he said nothing, but allowed Mrs. Atherton to suppose that she had uttered something of a very straightforward and logical character indeed, instead of a mere unmeaning string of words which could have no such pretensions whatever.

CHAPTER LXXIX.

THE BLACK LADY FOR ONCE AT HOME.—THE ATTEMPTED THREAT.

WE have never yet properly introduced to our readers the Black Lady in her own abode. We shall proceed now to do so.

A little way on the outskirts of the town, over the water, was, and in fact is still a narrow street, peculiarly constructed. There are gardens in the front of the houses, and there is no carriage or road-way, for these gardens meet in the middle of the street, with the exception of a little paved slip of a walk down the centre from which, at right and left, the garden gates open.

It was in one of these little quiet houses that the Black Lady had found a home. The house was in the occupation of sober, industrious people, who just had one room to spare, and, as it peculiarly suited the Black Lady to reside where there were no other lodgers, she at once took the place, although it must be confessed that at first the people had some sort of reluctance to take her.

They thought that she must be mad, and the good woman who kept the house had an impression that, as regarded mad people, you never knew when they were going to kill you; but that, assuredly, they were continually on the look-out so to do.

But about the manner of poor Marian Whitehead there was so much real gentleness, that, contrary to all their impressions, they did let the room to her, and as our readers may well suppose, they never found any reason to regret doing so, for a more inoffensive, quiet, harmless creature they could not possibly have got into their house than she, so that after a very few weeks, they began actually to congratulate each other upon being so lucky as to get her.

They gave her a key to the street-door, for they found that they could entirely trust her, and that she always was extremely careful to fasten the place up if she was a little after dark before she came in. She seldom spoke to them, but if they addressed her, she always answered them in the most courteous accents, and take her all in all, they began to feel quite proud of their new lodger.

Then her little room, which it was her fancy to see to herself, was quite a pattern of neatness and order. Everything was placed just where it ought to be. There was no litter, no confusion, and, perhaps, it was one of the few amusements of that solitary being to be careful in tending that apartment. Alas! poor thing! when she had placed it all to rights sometimes, in quiet order, she would say,—

"If Charles Ormond should escape from where he is, and chance to come in here, he will be pleased to see everything so neat and orderly, in this my humble home, and I shall have the pleasure of hearing him make a commendatory remark upon that subject, for come he will some day ; but I must have patience. Yes, I must have great patience yet.

This, as the reader is aware, was her continual delusion, and how she managed to keep herself from utter despair. It would indeed have been cruel of any one to have robbed her of it. What, though it was a delusion, yet it was one which kept alive in her heart that blissful hope, without which life would indeed be nothing better than a barren waste.

She was very seldom out after sunset, for she had always had such a dread of meeting Neville—a dread, however, which now there certainly was no necessity for, knowing, since he was so well taken care of in Newgate, that she might freely have wandered now about the streets.

Of Godfrey, of course, she could have no fear, for she was much more an object of dread to him than he to her; but still in the same way that she gave, in her madness, a vitality to poor Charles Ormond, which in this world he could never know again, she gave a power of action in her imagination to Neville which the stone walls of Newgate most effectually prevented him from exercising.

It so happened, however, that on that very night of the evening on which she had met Godfrey at the cheesemonger's shop, she felt her spirits so much fevered and oppressed, that she lingered long upon the bridge which she had to cross before she reached the street in which she resided, in order to cool her fevered brain with the fresh breeze that blew off the water.

She had noticed that a man passed her more than once, but she did not think much of that circumstance, inasmuch as she was used to being an object of idle curiosity ; and sometimes even people, who had no regard for any one's feelings—and there are too many of such—would actually impede her progress, coming full in front of her to stare in her face ; so she thought nothing of this man passing her more than once, and stealing a furtive glance at her.

But when at length wearied of her own promenade upon the bridge, she turned to leave it, and found that the same man followed her, she did feel some little sensation of alarm in consequence ; and she quickened her pace in order to avoid him, and reach home as speedily as possible, for although, when she did reach her own door, there was no smiling face of kindred to greet her, she called it home.

It was a very great relief to find that he did not follow her quite close to her door, or attempt anything in the shape of interruption, so she began to think that her fears were groundless, and that nothing but idle curiosity had prompted him to be any annoyance to her at all on that occasion.

"Yes," she said to herself, mournfully, as she made an effort to find her key ; "yes, I am, I know, a subject for idle remark as well as for idle curiosity. But no, I would not that any of those who, from time to time, have followed me through the London streets should suffer what I have suffered. Can I really have lost my key ?"

She searched in vain for her key, until she was satisfied that she had it not with her ; but as it was possible enough she might have left it at home, she did not much concern herself about it, but knocked for admission to the house, and the door was opened by her landlady, to whom she said, in her gentle, quiet way,—

"I suppose I have forgotten to take my key with me, or else I should not have given you this trouble."

"Oh! it's no trouble at all, Mrs. Whitehead—I hope you are well to-day?"

"Yes, thank you, I am am as usual—as usual."

Marian Whitehead uttered these words with a deep sigh, and then passed on to her own chamber.

It must be premised that she had not been for a long time in this lodging, and that consequently the people knew no more of her than common rumour made them acquainted with. They knew nothing of the loss of her friend, the poor poet, to whom she had behaved so kindly in return for the generous sympathy with which he had treated her ; for, when she had taken the lodging, she gave no reference, but merely said,—

"I dare say that by sight I am known to you. The story of my misfortunes may likewise, in some respects, have come to your ears. If you feel inclined to let me live in your house in quiet, take me, but I have had too many rebuffs from the world to be much touched even if you should say nay to me."

It was, therefore, merely from their own good feeling that they had taken her in, and never had they any reason to repent of having so done.

Well, as we have said, she proceeded to her own chamber, dreaming of no evil, and dreading none in particular, just at that time; she was weary, and she hoped to be permitted to lie down in peace, and rest herself after the fatigue, both of body and mind, which she had endured in her encounter with Godfrey.

She had hoped never again to meet that man, but the Fates had ordained it otherwise, for her fears had brought him precisely into a position that made him come into contact with her, and had enabled her to say some things to him, which, if he had not a heart of stone, must have cut him to the quick.

And here it may be as well to state how it was that Godfrey in his wretched, debilitated state had thought it so absolutely necessary that he should take some measures for his personal safety.

It has been often remarked by all persons who have reflected upon the subject, that there is no condition of life, however abject, and however troublesome or painful, that people will not cling to in preference to death—that is to say, the majority of people, to whom death does not indeed appear as the very king of terrors. There is a minority who look with much greater philosophy upon that subject, and prefer the repose of the grave to many evils that might afflict them in the course of their earthly pilgrimage.

But Godfrey was not one of these latter: the wicked never are. They cling to life under any circumstances, with a pertinacity unkown except to them, and to absolute cowardice. The dread of that retribution in another world, which they have been taught is to come, makes death always terrible to them; for any one who goes to the grave with a soul loaded with the consciousness of guilt, is not able to believe that a few sighs, and groans and prayers, towards the termination of his existence, will suffice for his regeneration.

Even the most stultified wretch ever brought out for execution at the Old Bailey finds it difficult to believe—as the Rev. Mr. Carver, the ordinary of Newgate, once told a criminal—that he would be welcomed by ten thousand angels in another world, because he had faith in revelation.

The rev. gentleman might as well have told him how he managed to count the heavenly host, and have promised him that he would be first of all shown the way to glory by a donkey, which would have been typical of the Rev. Mr. Carver himself, who is or was as little afflicted with intellect as any person that ever breathed.

But do not let any of our readers suppose we have no respect for "the cloth," as it is called; we do respect it as an useful article, but we very rarely found the man wrapped up in it other than a fool or a knave.

Godfrey, then, had all his fears awakened since the arrest and condemnation of Neville; for the fact is he had had a visit from that individual, who had urged him to attempt the rescue of the Black Lady's papers from the custody of the Athertons.

"These papers," said Neville, "are highly criminatory no doubt of you and I: they are dangerous documents, and should be got possession of at any cost."

To all this Godfrey had only intimated his disbelief altogether in the existence of such documents, and had concluded by bitterly and firmly upbraiding Neville for the attack he had made upon him in the hospital.

"You know well, Neville," he said, "that but for certain considerations I would this instant give an alarm, and have you taken into custody, charging you with an attempt to murder me."

"I am quite easy on that score," returned Neville, "for I know what those considerations are."

"Indeed!"

"Yes, considerations for your own personal safety of course alone prevent you from acting in the way you mention, and so I am perfectly safe. Your life or your death now are nothing to me, and I am not so hasty in my temper as I once was, so you cannot so easily aggravate me, although it may be, after all, a little dangerous to go too far with me."

"I defy you—you taunt me with being moved, in what I do and say, by considerations for myself—of course I am, as all men are; but I have taken such precautions now, that if anything happens to me suddenly——"

Godfrey paused, and Neville, fixing his keen eyes upon him, said,—

"Well, well."

"I care not if I tell you; but papers will be found behind me, which will sufficiently point you out as the author of my death; if I should die by violence, and if even otherwise, I leave behind me a full confession of all."

"You do, do you?"

"I do; and I think, with this debilitated frame of mine, it is likely enough that you will outlive me. I tell you that you may have the pleasures of expectation of what will some day happen. I have adopted that plan of avenging myself upon you, and at the same time making you afraid to touch me. The confession is sealed at present; but it is in the hands of a sharp solicitor, who has orders to open it, and act upon it the moment I am no more."

" I suppose you think, now, that's very cunning ?"

" I know it will suffice. There is in the sealed packet a cheque for £1000, which I declare payable to him, the solicitor, on your conviction for the capital offences with which I charge you ; and if he don't stir heaven and earth to accomplish that object with such a stimulant, he is something more or less than human."

The expression of Neville's countenance, while Godfrey spoke, was positively that of a fiend ; but still, although his passion was roused to its utmost, he gave a striking proof of the correctness of Godfrey's calculations, and of the efficiency of the scheme he had concocted for his protection.

On any other occasion, when he had not been aware of the danger of touching Godfrey, one-third part of such an amount of provocation would have been more than sufficient to induce Neville to take vengeance upon him. The matter for which he had attacked him at the hospital was slight and insignificant, compared to this ; but now, although he uttered some of the most violent language, and swore some of the most terrific oaths, he was evidently afraid.

He glared upon Godfrey with eyes of intense hatred ; but the latter made him no reply, being content to enjoy his triumph, for a great triumph to him it was—one which he doubtless enjoyed more than he had enjoyed anything since the time before his accident, when he so much exulted in the execution of poor Charles Ormond.

At length Neville left him ; and although Godfrey had told him that he disbelieved the asserted fact that the Black Lady had possessed any papers, or that the family of the cheesemonger in the city had any documents criminatory of him, he was painfully and at once convinced that such was the case when he heard of the particulars of the murder of Zachary.

Godfrey had no doubt at all but that Zachary had been sent into the house of the Athertons by Neville, as a spy, to attempt to get possession of the papers he spoke of, and that he had either failed in so doing, or his instructions had gone no further than to desire him to find out where they were kept, and to let in him, Neville, in the night to get them.

That Zachary thus had fallen a victim to Neville, by mistake or by design, he was assured ; and although he had no sort of commiseration in the fate of that individual, he began to have a thousand fears lest he should turn the tables upon him, and confess all—pointing to those papers as a confirmation.

Godfrey then thought, that if he could get possession of those papers, it would be one piece of evidence against him dispensed with, and hence he had resolved to make an attempt himself to do so.

He had lingered about until he saw the private door of Atherton's house left a moment open, by chance, and then he had made the attempt, which, from its very boldness, really might have succeeded, had not the manuscript been in the parlour at that very time in the hands of Miles Atherton, who was concluding the perusal of what to them had contained details of so great interest and such immense importance to Godfrey himself.

He had actually been into every room in the house, and then, failing in his search, his next great object was to make his escape, which he endeavoured in vain to do ; for a sudden and violent pain, in consequence of his making a slight slip on the stairs, caused him to utter the cry that had alarmed the Athertons.

The after-meeting with Marian Whitehead was one that he would have done anything to avoid that he possibly could, but in his helpless state he was quite at the mercy of almost any circumstances that could occur.

CHAPTER LXXX.

THE ALARM.—THE VILLAINS FOILED.—GODFREY'S NEW CONFEDERATES AS TROUBLESOME AS THE OLD.

WHEN Marian reached her chamber, she felt a great relief in the fact that the day was at length over on which she had been doomed to have an interview with Godfrey.

She had, as far as in a christian spirit it was necessary to do so, entirely and completely forgiven him, villain as he was, for the great evil he had wrought her; and she did, from the abundance of her gentle nature, absolutely pity the suffering wretch, who, whatever might be the amount of physical woe he endured, certainly, as far as desert went, ought not at her hands to have looked for anything in the shape of pity or commiseration.

But if ever there was a self-denying, forgiving, kind spirit in this world, it was Marian Whitehead; for who but she would have prayed as she now did, that Heaven would have mercy upon Godfrey?

Yes, she actually knelt in prayer for him—for the man who had destroyed all her hopes of earthly happiness—for the man who had been the cloud in the sky of her otherwise free and happy destiny—for him who had played the part of the canker-worm in the bud of her young heart's best affections.

If ever a prayer ascended to the throne of God hurried and wafted on its way by a million of blessings from angels' lips, surely such a prayer as that was of that description.

And, would it have moved Godfrey to know that she, Marian Whitehead, actually prayed for him! would it have awakened any slumbering sensations of bitter remorse in his heart! Alas, no! He was not formed of such penetrable stuff. He might, if he had heard her utter the prayer, have listened with intense surprise, and then he would have attributed the pious abjuration to insanity, for it would not have lain within the province of his mind to imagine it possible there could be so much goodness in human nature as that she should pray for him.

No. It is not in the nature of some human beings to understand the pure impulses of others; and they borrow from their own bad hearts and from their own corrupt imaginations, motives, which those whose conduct they attempt so to scan have no sort of conception of, and never dreamt of in all their lives.

And Marian Whitehead did not utter a prayer for Godfrey in that vain-glorious spirit that your evangelical people pray for their enemies in, and in which they almost seem to say,—

" Pray take notice, Heaven, how pious we are!"

No: her prayer was a spontaneous effusion of her own fine and beautiful benevolence of heart, and such it must be regarded, although she might well have been excused, and it would have been no detraction from her merits had she so far shuddered at the thought of Godfrey, as not on any account or on any occasion to mix him up with her pure devotions.

Before she retired to rest Marian usually wrote or read, but upon this occasion she was too much wearied both in body and mind to do either, so, in the course of less than half an hour, she had lain down to rest.

  *   *   *   *   *

It was about a quarter to twelve o'clock on that night when two men made their appearance stealthily, and with caution, in the little street where was situated the house in which Marian Whitehead resided. They had about them all the appearance of being, no doubt what they were, viz., London thieves, of that class who rely upon what they consider a respectable appearance for getting the better of the unwary.

They were attired in black, probably because it was the least noticeable colour they could assume, on account of its being the most usually worn.

They paused at the entrance of the narrow path leading up between the small gardens in front of the houses, and began to converse together in whispers with respect to the undertaking in which they were involved, and which certainly was one which did not seem exactly in the usual routine of their business.

" I don't half like the job," whispered one, " this is a devil of a disagreeable place to get into any trouble in. Only look—a brick wall at the further end—no thoroughfare, and nothing to escape by but this slip of a walk that one man might stop us in. How do you like it?"

" Not over well, I can tell you: but we have said we would do it and fingered some of the reward; so our honour, Jack, you see, our honour, and our gentlemanly feeling is concerned. Don't let us be snobs."

" That's all very well, I grant you; but let us be as careful as we can. You have got the paper, I suppose?"

" Yes. It says in it that she, Marian Whitehead, fully and duly acknowledges that all she has written or caused to be written and placed in the hands of Mr. Miles Atherton is a mere connivance, and has no truth in it, for that Charles Ormond confessed to her the justice of his sentence, and that moreover she had been on more than one occasion told by Neville, that he would lay a deep plot for the ruin of Godfrey by pretending, provided he ever came to the scaffold for his own offences, that he was making a confession with his dying lips, and that then he would invent something that would bring him, Mr. Godfrey, into trouble, although there should not be half a word of truth in it."

" Well! what do you think of all that ?"

" I'll be hanged if I have thought about it !"

" But you know it's a dodge."

" I suppose it is. All I think of is our honour and our gentlemanly character. We have promised to get into No. 4 here and to frighten or coax the Black Lady out of her signature."

" Good !"

" But upon my honour, as I was about to say, I think it's a ticklish job."

" So do I."

" And if she makes a squalling, upon my reputation and gentlemanly feelings, I don't know what to do."

" You wouldn't like to cut her throat ?"

" Upon my honour, no. Cutting purses is in my line, but cutting throats is most decidedly out of it, so I should unhesitatingly decline doing so, I can assure you. You can do so if you like, and if you think your honour at all concerned in doing it !"

" Oh, no, no."

" Well, then, I tell you what I was thinking. If there is any alarm, we must not attempt to leave by this way, for it would be much too hazardous to do so. But by the back I think we could get away tolerably easy. There are some gardens of an adjoining street there, in which there are several houses to let. Now, what I propose is, that we get away in that manner, if there be any disturbance."

" Agreed. You have the key."

" Oh yes, I picked her pocket of the key on the bridge. That was easy enough. You might rob her before her face ; and she is the blessedest simpleton ever I came near."

" Why, they do say she is out of her wits ; and, if she is so, poor devil, I don't see what good her signing any paper can be to old Godfrey, or any one else "

" Well, my friend, you know that's no business of ours ; our honour is concerned in doing the job ; and, what's a damned deal more to the purpose, we are to get £50 a-piece for it if we succeed."

" Ah, and only the £20 between us if we fail."

" True ; so come on, and let's try the caper. It's a good night's work if we can get through with it, and I don't myself see why we shouldn't. Besides, when you come to consider there is only one man in the house, and if he will hear anything going wrong, and will come in and make a disturbance, he must be muzzled."

" Good again ! our honour will be concerned in muzzling him, I should say ; so come along, and let's see what can be done. We may earn £50 a-piece in the next half-hour, and then again we may—not."

" Ah, you are a rum 'un—you are. Upon my life, you are enough sometimes to make a cat laugh."

" A curious zoological phenomenon, that. If you can find me the animal, I'll exhibit it at the Egyptian Hall, for that seems, now-a-days, the grand place for all sorts of humbug."

" Good again ! You are a genius, you are. What a rum street this is, to be sure!"

" You may say that. I don't know whose genius it was that built it ; but it's an odd, and after all, no bad place, I should say, for peace and quietness, when we do come to consider the infamous nuisance of cabs."

" They can't get down here, that's one comfort to the people, at any rate.

Only consider living in a street, rough paved, near a station of a railway, and being woke up in the night, every time a train comes in by the railway cabs, built strong for luggage, and every one of them making as much noise as a cart-full of old iron coming down the street."

" Don't mention it. My nerves shake at the very idea; but this is No. 4, and in this blessed, innocent region the people seem as if they had all gone to bed long ago."

" No doubt of it. There aint a light anywhere to be seen."

They opened the little garden-gate of the house in which Marian resided with extreme caution, and when they had walked up the path that led to the house, and stood upon the door step, they paused, and narrowly scrutinised the whole street, in order to be certain that they had not been observed.

" All's right," said one; " have you brought your cat's slippers with you?"

" Do you think now, I could forget?" said the other.

" Oh, well, I don't say you would. Pop them on at once, then."

These cat's slippers, as they were called by the thieves, consisted of socks made of very thick worsted, which they drew over their boots, and which completely muffled all sound arising from their feet. A velvet shoe, treading upon down, could not have been more quiet than was their tread, when so provided.

Possibly then never, since the lock had been placed upon that street-door, had it been opened with such tact and skill as upon the present occasion. There was no rattling of the key, no blundering, but gently and with precision the lock was turned, and then the door yielded—a little.

" Oh," said he who had used the key, " there's a chain."

" The deuce there is! Have you got a wriggler with you?"

" I should think so. Do you think I'm such a goose as not to think of all these obstructions beforehand? I'll soon move the chain out of the way."

The fellow as he spoke produced from his pocket a beautifully made and very curious looking steel instrument, which he laid hold of the chain with. There was a slight grinding sort of sound for a few minutes, and then the chain dropped into two pieces, and fell away from the street door.

This falling of the separate pieces of the chain was inevitable, and the only noise of any importance which had to be dreaded in the matter. They stopped and listened attentively, to discover if it had made any alarm; but as the silence continued, there could be no doubt but that all in the house were sleeping, and that the noise made had not been sufficient to break their repose.

" All's right," whispered one to the other.

" Upon my honour! I think it is, and that you have managed the chain with your usual, or with more than your usual talent."

" Bah! none of your gammon, but come on."

" My dear friead, don't use that horrid word, bah! It's decidedly low—one of the ugliest and one of the most ill-tempered, ill-mannered brutes I ever knew used to say bah! and it has given me a distaste to it ever since."

" Well, well—damn it, you are as full of odd fancies as an egg's full of meat—come on, and let us shut the door gently behind, and then we can get a light."

" Uncommonly correct, upon my honour."

The door was then closed with such care, that a fly slumbering upon it would not have been disturbed; after which they at once made their way into a little parlour that was upon their left hand, and where they procured a light by means of a phosphorous box which they had brought with them.

By this light they saw that the remains of a frugal supper were upon the table, but there was nothing sufficiently inviting or delicate to suit the palates of these gentry.

" Oh!" said one, " I do wonder how people can live in the way they do! Bread and cheese! aint it monstrous? the idea of nething but bread and cheese for supper? and yet, upon my honour, I know some people that call themselves respectable who have it."

"Oh, bother you! I never came near such a fellow as you are; you are one of the most LUXURIANT dogs I ever came near."

"Now, my dear fellow, excuse me, but you said luxuriant, when all the while you meant luxurious. Really now it's awful to make such a mistake, quite awful."

"Is it? Make the most of it, then—I haven't had your edication, you know."

"I know that: but, upon my honour, you must be aware that these sort of blunders set my teeth on edge most fearfully, and give me a shiver."

"Plague take your shivers! Come up stairs: do you know the proper room?"

"I humbly insinuate that I do. A little judicious inquiry enabled me to know any room in the house. I called in one day and asked the good woman (who by the way is most frightfully green) who keeps the house, if she had a bed-room to let for a single gentleman, and when she said she had not, I got her into such a line of talking, and I gammoned her in praise of the house to that extent, that she showed me all over it."

"You don't mean that?"

"I do, though; and so I can take you direct to the room we want without any further trouble."

"Well, you are a rum cove, and you have got some odd ways about you, but I always did say you was a GENUS and no mistake. I always gave you credit for being a GENUS."

"A genius, my good friend—a genius, if you please."

"Well, a janus."

"Oh, good God! say no more about it; I will forego the praise if you cannot put it into good English, most willingly."

This extremely polite and honourable character now led the way, and his friend followed him up the narrow staircase, which was composed of too small pieces of wood to allow of any creaking, so that, as far as that went, it was an advantage to have a very little insignificant staircase to go up, and it answered their turn well.

The conversation we have recorded, had taken place in low tones in the little parlour below, and it was astonishing what a tact in whispering they both seemed to have—a tact which could only have been acquired by downright practice; for they contrived (which is very difficult) to throw into a whispered conference all the energy and variation of tone, as if every word of it had been uttered aloud.

Now, however, they did not say one word, for the staircase was much too hazardous a place to converse in, but they proceeded in perfect silence, with those absolutely noiseless footsteps, which they were enabled to step with, in consequence of what they called the cat's slippers, that they had put on with that object.

The distance up that little staircase was, as may be imagined, very inconsiderable, and they soon stood upon the landing close to the door of the chamber occupied by Marian Whitehead.

There they paused again, to listen; but the house was profoundly still. Not a mouse seemed to be stirring, and they quite inwardly congratulated themselves upon succeeding so far in their enterprise. The one who carried the light had, as they proceeded up the stairs, with great tact so shielded it with his hat that not the least ray from it could find its way at any keyhole of a bedroom-door, and so expose the fact that there was a light upon the staircase to any one who might be waking.

"Do you know who else," whispered he who carried the light to the one who boasted he had been shown over the house by the imprudence of its mistress—" do you know who else sleeps on this floor?"

"Yes; the master and mistress themselves do."

"The devil!"

"Well, I don't know; but I think not, for there is not a spare room for him."

"Oh! bah!"

"There you go again! Hush! hush!"

They thought that from one of the bed-rooms there issued a slight noise; but it was so slight that it might be nothing but a sleeper turning in bed, and as it immediately ceased and nothing ensued, they thought that it must be so.

"Now," whispered he who evidently took the lead in the affair, "now upon my honour, it strikes me that she will scream if some means are not taken to prevent her."

"But what means?"

"Stop her mouth for a moment, and then tell her she has nothing to fear."

"You may try that, but it sounds difficult. I only wish we were both well out of this job, for I tell you candidly that I don't like it at all, and I fancy ———"

"Hush! I fancy you are a fool. Come on and hold your tongue, and mind that you fasten the bedroom-door on the inside the moment we get in."

Marian Whitehead's door was not fastened, or even at this point the ruffians might have been disappointed.

———

CHAPTER LXXXI.

THE ESCAPE OF THE THIEVES, AND A GENTLEMAN IN A DIFFICULTY.

THE bedroom-door was opened cleverly. The fellow turned the handle, and then being well aware that all doors make the least noise if opened quickly and steadily, he had it quite wide in a moment, without the least noise in the world. They had shielded the light so that all was darkness within the chamber; but for a moment they paused to listen again upon the staircase-head, and to satisfy themselves that all was still, and then they entered the chamber.

The one who came last closed the door with the same caution with which it had been opened, and fastened it by shooting into its socket the little finger-bolt that was underneath the lock.

They then heard the low, regular breathing of one asleep, and approaching the bed they threw some of the rays of light upon it, and saw Marian Whitehead lying wrapped in repose.

Yes, she, that poor persecuted one, slept more soundly at that time than any of her enemies. Godfrey would have given £100 for one calm and serene, painless, dreamless, night's repose; but he could not get it, for when, by the aid of narcotics, he did succeed in lulling the acuteness of bodily pain, his mind would become preternaturally active, and he would dream such horrors as would make him start from his feverish and excited slumber with a scream of agony.

He frequently in that way would disturb the whole house in which he resided, and bring the servants into his bedchamber to know if anything had happened to him.

On these occasions, then, he would dread being left alone, and would get some one to sit down by his bed-side, until he should again lapse into repose; perhaps, again to repeat, before the night was gone, a similar scene.

But Marian Whitehead slept the calm, and holy sleep of innocence. She was of the few who, in this world, can lay their hands upon their hearts, and say with truth,—

"Heaven knows there is no guilt here!"

Such, and only such, can lie down like young children, to repose in perfect confidence, that, although they may dream of that which is most distressful, they will not awaken, as the guilty awaken, to a consciousness that the vision of the night is but a portion of that retribution which they have earned of an offended Heaven.

"She sleeps sound enough," whispered one.

"Ah, but we have no time to lose, and must awaken her."

He took from his pocket a silk handkerchief, and doubled it into a number of folds, and then, while his companion held the light, he suddenly placed the handkerchief over the mouth of Marian.

The touch awakened her, and she strove to utter a scream, but could not do so, for the pad of silk that was upon her mouth, and he who held it there said to her, in an impressive whisper,—

"No harm is intended you, Miss Whitehead, upon honour, if you will be quiet; but, if you make any noise, you will involve both yourself and us in trouble, and with this admonition I leave you at freedom."

He removed the handkerchief, and, as he had anticipated, Marian was still, and only looked up in his face with intense astonishment, to know what it could be that had occasioned such a visit. Her imagination immediately flew to Charles Ormond, and, in her wild and insane belief, that he still lived, she could not wholly divest herself of the idea, that the two men, who so mysteriously had found their way to her chamber, might be capable of aiding her in discovering where Godfrey had hidden him, for that that villain had Charles Ormond somewhere in durance, was one of her firmest fixed notions.

"Speak, oh, speak," she said, " tell me of him."

"Hush!" said the fellow, "we must not be overheard. You have nothing to do but to sign this paper, and we are off again."

"What paper?"

"Oh, it's all about nothing. But time is precious, so do it at once, I beg of you, miss, for upon my honour it must be done, and we cannot stay any longer."

"Is it from him—is it from Charles Ormond?"

"Oh, yes, of course it is. How could you doubt it? Here it is, and here is a pen full of ink. You see, Miss Whitehead I (believe that's your name) what pains I have taken in this matter. I have actually, all to serve you, brought a pen with me, and a portable inkstand. Upon my honour I ought to have a piece of plate presented to me by the clergy of this district, for doing the thing so well. Come, all we want is your signature."

There was a blackguardism about the fellow's manner which struck poor Marian, and she said to herself, " These are not messengers that Charles Ormond would choose, but rather such as might be charged with the perpetration of some foul deed by the villain Godfrey."

"Show me the paper," she said aloud, "show me the paper. Let me hear, or rather, let me myself read its contents, and I will sign or not sign it then, as I shall think proper."

"Oh, it's nothing particular. Come, be quick, time is precious."

"It may be to you," said Marian, " but it is not to me. Give me the paper, and let me read it, or the chances of my signature are small indeed, as you will find."

"We shall then," said the fellow, "be under the disagreeable necessity of cutting your throat; for, to throw off all disguise, I tell you, upon my honour, that we have promised either to get your signature to this paper, or to cut your throat; and we are such slaves to our word, and such d——d gentlemanly fellows, that we positively must do one or the other, so you had better comply at once, and make an end of it. Do you understand us, now?"

"I do."

"Well, then, don't let us have any nonsense, but sign the paper at once, if you please, and then you may go quietly to sleep again, for we have no inclination to stay a moment longer than necessary."

"Let me see the paper."

"No, no, what's the use? Come, now, don't be a fool; we know what we are about, and we mean what we say. Do we look like men who are to be trifled with?"

"I will not sign the paper; and, as for your threat against my life, alas! you must know little indeed of what I have suffered, or you would scarcely fancy it was such. If the will to murder be in your guilty souls, murder me; I will forgive the deed, for God knows, if it be a delusion that Charles Ormond lives, how desolate I am,"

"Very good," said the fellow, who, although he had no intention of doing such a deed, still clung to the idea that Marian would be easily terrified at the prospect of death. "Very good, then here goes."

He produced a knife as he spoke.

"Heaven pardon me," said Marian, "and forgive all who have injured me."

"Damn it! it's no go—Miss Whitehead, will you allow me to say that you will be doing me a very great favour indeed by being so obliging as to sign this paper,—upon my honour, it's a fact."

At this moment some one rapped on the outside of Marian's chamber-door, and a voice said,—

"Miss Whitehead, is that you talking to yourself? my wife is afraid you aint well, so she has made me—a-hem! that is to say, she has asked me to get up and speak to you—eh? what do you say? eh?"

"Nothing particular, my duck," said one of the housebreakers, in an assumed woman's voice; "how are you off for spectacles?"

"What?—eh?—what did you say, Miss W.?—eh?—what?"

"Give it him," muttered one of the men; "or shall I, while you hold him?"

"Just as you like—you can muzzle him."

They opened the door so suddenly, that the landlord nearly tumbled into the room, and he would have fallen, but that they seized hold of him in a moment, and one held him by the back of the head, and the other by the throat, while they forced into his mouth a peculiar sort of iron gag, which would open by a key, so that, in a few moments, his mouth was propped wide open, and he was unable to give the least alarm.

"I don't see any reason now why we should not be off by the way we came in," said one of the fellows, with perfect composure; "it's quite clear we shall not get the signature; she's too mad to be frightened."

"Damn it," said the other, "do you hear that we shall have to go and gag the man's wife, or else she will alarm the place?"

"Joseph!" cried a female voice, "Joseph, I say, Joseph, where are you, you stupid hound? Joseph, I say,—oh, if I come to you, I'll teach you not to answer me; Joseph!"

The gagged man made some frantic gestures, and the thieves took hold of him and led him into the bed-room he had so recently left, and when there, one of them said,—

"Here he is, ma'am!" and then they lifted him up on to the bed, and threw him on it with a vengeance, that was enough to break every bone in his wife's anatomy. The lady uttered a loud shriek, and began drumming upon Joseph's ribs with her fists at an alarming rate, very much surprised all the while that he said nothing.

"This way," said one of the thieves to the other, as he darted back again into Marian's chamber, "this way!"

They opened the window, the lower part of which was only about eleven or twelve feet from the little pocket-handkerchief of a garden behind, and out they jumped. They then made their way over the small low brick wall at the back, into the gardens of another row of houses, some of which they knew were to let, and, trusting to seeing, from its aspect, when they came to one that was vacant, they went on clambering walls, and treading down little flower-beds, until they did reach the object of their search, viz., an empty house, from which they easily made their escape into the street, and were off to a notorious thieves' public-house in the neighbourhood of Westminster.

When they reached here they were rather tired, for, in addition to walking fast, their caution, during the progress of their escape, had been of no trifling character, and they were glad enough to get somewhere into shelter at last, where, too, they could feel that they were quite safe.

"What's to be done, now?" said one.

"Upon my honour, I hardly know. You cannot but admit that I did all that it was possible for any human being to do, to ensure success. After you have threatened to cut a person's throat, I don't know, really, if that don't have any effect, what more you can say."

"It's a damned hard job, I'm sure, to have gone through all this for twenty pounds."

"Well, now, my good fellow, listen to me: I promised Mr. G. that we would make this little attempt to get the signature of Miss W. to the little document which Mr. G. thinks he would like to have."

"Well, of course you'd id, and so did I."

"Agreed: and have we not been slaves to our word?—have we not made the attempt most honourably and failed? so we are free, now, to adopt any course, having vindicated our honour, that can be pointed out by either of us, as likely to result in so very satisfactory a conclusion, as the fingering by us of fifty pounds each."

"Fine talking; but how is it to be done?"

"Why, I propose that, since Miss W. is so obstinately selfish, that she will not to oblige us, sign the paper, that we sign it for her;—eh? what do you think of that?"

"What do I think of it? why, it's prime; why the devil didn't you think of that before, and so save us all the risk and all the trouble we have had? You are a clever fellow, but I only wish you had been a little sooner."

"Softly, my friend, pray excuse me—you don't know what you are talking about; the fact is, I did think of that mode of doing the business from the first, but then there were two objections. In the first place, Mr. G. may know the hand-writing of Miss W., and so detect the fraud; and, in the second place, our honour was pledged—our honour!—think of that. We could not sacrifice, you are well aware, our honour in the transaction."

"Well, of all the rum devils ever I came near, you are the rumesest."

"Now, now—really, there is no such word in the English language as rumesest."

"Well, that's no matter, I'll introduce it; but come, sign the paper, and let us see what effect it will have upon old G. Ho, ho!—It will be a glorious thing if he is taken in by it."

"It will; but mind, I don't at all build upon it: it is only a last resource, you see, so here goes. Let me see: of course when she wrote it she was very nervous, and much agitated, so it's rather a scrawl. Oh, I think I can manage it, if he don't know her hand, but if he does, it's a thousand chances to one against us."

"So it is, to be sure—so it is; but we can't be hanged for trying it on, you know; old G. can only abuse us, you see, after all, if so be as he finds it out, and we don't much care about that."

The rascal who was so very particular about his honour spread out the paper before him, and, in a very good imitation of a female hand, tremulous from fear, wrote the name of Marian Whitehead; which, when he had concluded, he looked at with some amount of satisfaction saying,—

"Ah, well, that's not so bad. I have some hopes now; and as I have pledged my honour to myself, to get, if I can, fifty pounds from G., I shall do my best to keep my word, for the man who does not keep faith with himself cannot be fairly expected to keep faith with anybody else whatsoever, I should say."

"Oh, it's capital!" cried the other; "it's out-and-out—it's first-rate; come on, and I don't doubt at all but that we shall get the money—come on, and if we do get it, I'll stand out of mine as much champagne as you like to drink at a sitting. You are a clever fellow, and I always said you were an honour to the profession—come along, my boy, come along!"

These two precious rascals partook of some refreshment, and then they proceeded arm-in-arm towards the house of Godfrey, whom they hoped to be able, successfully, to impose upon, by the signature they had appended to the document, that he thought would be some sort of justification of himself, in case Neville should confess, under his present circumstances of peril, all the wickedness which they had concocted together and actually perpetrated.

"It would be something to feel to be able to throw a great doubt upon such a confession, and such doubt might enable him to spend the remainder of his days, at all events, free from a prison."

But while the thieves were making their escape from the house in which Marian lodged, a fierce, untoward *fracas* was taking place between Joseph and his wife, and the great aggravation of the lady was, that Joseph never said a word, but after a time began to defend himself as well as he could against the ferocious assault which was made upon him.

At last, an unlucky blow of Joseph's lighted upon the most prominent feature in the lady's face, from which it drew an ensanguined stream, and then she commenced shouting murder, with a power of lungs that soon alarmed the whole neighbourhood. The police were shouted for from at least twenty windows, and at length, when there had been time enough for half-a-dozen of the most deliberate and savage murders on record to have been committed, a policeman made his appearance, and coolly rubbing his nose with the end of his truncheon, asked "what was the matter?"

With one accord he was directed towards Number 4, the door of which, as he heard the cry of murder continued at intervals, he broke open, and going up to the chamber from whence the sounds proceeded, he cried,—

"Hillo! hillo! What's all this about? Come, young fellow," to Joseph "don't be insulting."

And then, as Joseph said nothing, he knocked him down at once, for aggravating conduct. Whereupon Mrs. Joseph sprung out of bed, and, seizing something or other, made of earthenware—of course a jug—she flung it at the policeman's head, against which it broke into a thousand pieces, exclaiming, as she did so,—

"I'll teach you, you infamous raw lobster, to come here intruding yourself in family affairs. Take that, will you?"

Then Mrs. Joseph picked up the tongs from the fire-place, and beat such a tune about the bewildered policeman's ears with them, that he thought himself bewitched, and for a time was incapable of moving. At length, when the great unboiled did recover himself, he got his rattle out of his pocket and began to spring it with all his might, and that put Mrs. Joseph in mind that she too had a rattle in the cupboard, so she procured it, and commenced springing it in opposition to the policeman, so that their combined efforts made a noise that, as the newspapers say, filled the neighbourhood with consternation, horror and alarm.

Various policemen from distant beats hurried to the scene of operations, and in a short time nearly one-half of the Z division was in Number 4; such a rattling of truncheons was never heard, and so many "bulls' eyes" were turned upon Mr. and Mrs. Joseph, that the glare was quite insupportable.

Finally, it was discovered what prevented Mr. Joseph from speaking, and a medical man was sent for, who examined the gag for some time without having the most distant idea of how to get it out of his mouth.

"Is your mouth open as wide as it will go?" he asked.

Mr. Joseph nodded violently.

"Well, if you could conveniently open it a little wider, I think we could get the gag out, do you know."

"A clever fellow that," said an inspector of police who was present, "don't you think, sir, you must be a relative, a good way removed, to some conjuror?"

"None of your insolence," said the doctor; "that's a very curious case, and I should advise saline draughts, to see what effect that will have upon the patient."

The inspector made no further remark, but getting a cab, he took Mr. Joseph off to the nearest hospital, and then a cunning workman in locks and metal springs was sent for, who fitted a key to the gag and wound it down again, so that, to the great relief of Mr. Joseph, he was able to shut his mouth once more.

That very identical gag now is in the possession of the Archæological Society, who have had it twice engraved on wood and inserted in the Literary Gazette, when it held a good place in an equally wooden article of the usual staple materials that adorn that wonderful production of Scotch ingenuity.

Whether or not the housebreakers succeeded in inducing Godfrey to believe that the signature they took to him was the genuine one of Marian Whitehead, we shall shortly perceive; but we grieve to say that the alarm of that night had a very prejudicial effect upon the imagination of poor Marian.

And it was not altogether the actual proceedings of the housebreakers themselves, that produced this effect upon her nervous system; for, to do them justice, they did not carry their threats very far, but desisted as soon as they became quite convinced that they could not induce her, from fear, to sign the dreadful paper; but it was the dreadful open riot made by Mr. Joseph that alarmed her, and made her think that something serious was really occurring. Those cries of murder, nearly drove her to the verge of madness.

CHAPTER LXXXII.

THE THIEVES' VISIT TO GODFREY, AND HIS GUILTY FELICITATIONS.—THE
REVULSION OF FEELING.

THE thieves were quite as anxious to finger Godfrey's money as he could be to
pay them for the document which he hoped would give him some amount of
satisfaction.

They had his directions where to meet him, and that was, not at his house, but
at a tavern, where he had hired a private room, and where he remained waiting
the whole of the night, in the most anxious state of suspense, for their arrival.
The people of the tavern wondered what a man in such a miserable state as Godfrey
could possibly be waiting for, with such anxious looks; and, every now and then,
he rang for the porter, who sat up, to ask him if any one had called for him.

When he was replied to in the negative, he would give a sort of groan expressive
of great disappointment, and sink on to a chair, again to wait with what patience
he could call to his aid.

At length, the welcome intelligence was brought to him, that two men—gentlemen, the porter, from courtesy called them—asked to see him; and he eagerly
exclaimed,—

"Show them in,—show them in here, at once; and be within call, in case I
want any wine."

"Yes, sir, certainly."

In a few moments the two housebreakers were introduced to him, and he would,
if he had been able, which he most certainly was not, have rushed towards them for
the purpose of questioning even by their looks, if they had been successful or not,
in their enterprise; but, as it was, he could only cry out,—

"Have you got it?—have you got it?"

"I have the pleasure of stating," said he, who prided himself upon his education,
"I have the pleasure, Mr. G. of stating, without anything in the shape of verbo-
sity or circumlocutory remarks, that we have succeeded."

"Right—right. Thank——Heaven," Godfrey was going to say, but he stopped
himself, for even he felt how out of all character it was for him to make such a
remark in reference to such a transaction; as if Heaven could have anything to do
with his rascally and nefarious proceedings, except to thwart them, which, somehow or other, it forgot to do.

"Yes, sir," added the spokesman of the two ruffians, "I have the extreme
pleasure of stating that such is the case; but I can assure you it required no
ordinary share of impudence, as well as, I may say, talent, to succeed in this
matter."

"No doubt—no doubt. I am willing to give you credit for anything, now
that you have succeeded."

"Ahem! That is kind."

"Give me the document."

"Thank you, Mr. G.; you have said that you were willing to give us credit for
anything; now, we regret extremely that we really cannot return the compliment,
by giving you credit for anything. So, if you will hand us the cash we are to
receive for this job, we will hand you the document; but not before. Oh! dear
no; not by any means, my dear sir."

"You are far more suspicious than you need be; my money is certain always,
and you may rely upon receiving it as a thing of course, without any trouble.
Here are two notes for fifty pounds each. You see I can keep my word, gentlemen. You can put them in your pockets, and then give me the signed paper
which you tell me you have ready for me."

"Really, Mr. G. this is handsome conduct; but it is no more than what we
fully expected from a gentleman of your acknowledged standing and high moral
character."

" Bah !" said the other, as he put his £50 note in his pocket. " Bah ! When you have done complimenting each other, I should like to have something to drink."

" Now really," said the first speaker, " I never did hear a more vulgar remark than that in all my life. It's positively atrocious. If Mr. G., as no doubt he does, intends to stand something handsome upon this occasion, he ought not, and shall not, be hurried by anybody."

" The paper—the paper. Business first," said Godfrey, " and then we will talk about drinking. Give me the paper, I say."

" It is here, sir, properly signed to your satisfaction—Marian Whitehead in full. I can assure you, Mr. G., we had some trouble throughout the transaction. First of all, there was an infernal chain fastening the door, and that had to be got rid of; and then, when we did get in, we found the Black Lady so precious mad, that a voluntary offer to cut her throat had no effect upon her whatever—not the least in the world."

" You—you have not murdered her ?"

" Murdered her ! Do you fancy we could do anything half so absurd ? Really if people are such positive, horrid bunglers, that they cannot do anything but murder, there's an end of the more polite branches of our profession. A man who cuts a throat I consider to be a hundred years behind the age, positively !"

" You are quite a philosopher."

" Well, Mr. G., I hope and trust that, in a small way, I may call myself a philosopher ; but, as regards the Black Lady, sir, we have not injured a hair of her head, sir. I could not have allowed it. As soon as she saw I had a knife, and that I began to sharpen it on the sole of my shoe, she signed the paper."

" You went as far as that ?"

" We did ; but no further. Oh dear no. If she had persevered in her obstinacy, she must have got clear of us, for we must have gone ; but she kept up such a constant bother about one Charles Ormond, that I really don't think, when she signed the paper, she knew what she was doing, Mr. G., and, at the same time, we must in candour own that she did not make use of some of the most complimentary phrases towards you."

" That matters not—that matters not. She is mad, and mistaken !"

" Exactly."

" How precious dry I am, to be sure !" said the other. " I wonder what they charge here for a jug of spring water? Oh, Lor, how dry I am, to be sure !"

" I had forgotten," said Godfrey—" I had forgotten again. Ring the bell close by you, and order up a couple of bottles of champagne. I have no wish but to do what is handsome and liberal towards you both. It is not likely that I shall need your services ever again, but if I should do so, I wish you to have an impression on both your minds, that you are certain to receive from me liberal treatment."

" You are a perfect gent, and no mistake," said the fellow, as he rang the bell, and at once ordered the champagne ; " you are a perfect gent, that's what you are, sir, and no mistake. I say, young fellow, just be quick with that wine, will you ? I'm as dry as dust, I tell you, do you hear ?"

" Coming, sir,—coming, coming."

The two bottles of champagne were speedily produced, and as speedily the corks were released and flew to the ceiling with a pleasant pop. The generous and invigorating liquor was drank freely, and if the two reprobates did not lay up a good champagne head-ache each for the morning, it was no fault of theirs.

As for Godfrey, he just sipped at a glass, shaking his head as he did so, and saying, in a sad voice,—

" Time was when I could have drank with you ; but now I am in such a state of decrepitude, and am such an invalid, that I dare not do so."

" Well, it's a pity, Mr. G. ; but all we can do is to drink for you. Here's your health, sir, and may your shadow never be less ! May you live a thousand years, and transmit all your virtues to your posterity, free of legacy duty !"

"Bah!" said the other, "he may easily do that, without the trouble of making a will."

"Thank you," said Godfrey, "thank you. I'm sure I don't know which of your compliments I prefer the most."

"You are a nice article, you are," remarked the more refined of the thieves to his companion. "Here you pocket a gentleman's money, and drink his wine, while you can't let me say a civil thing to him, by way of a recompense. I'm positively ashamed of you, that's a fact!"

"Oh, never mind, never mind," said Godfrey. "It don't matter: I am not a man who pretends to be any better than my neighbours, and I can bear a left-handed compliment as well as most people."

"Sir, you are trump; and now that we are so cordial together, and understand each other so well, will you, just for the fun and curiosity of the thing, permit me to ask you how you came to be so dreadfully knocked about, as to be forced to walk upon crutches all your life?"

A dark scowl came over Godfrey's face as he replied,—

"I had a fall."

"So he had, so he had," exclaimed the other thief, "I thought from the first that I recollected him. Why, you fell off a house-top when you were looking at an execution. I was below, and one of the mob that you nearly fell upon, and who helped to pick you up, when you seemed all broken to pieces, I declare."

Godfrey groaned at the very remembrance.

"I recollect all about it. It was at the execution of a young chap for forgery. Who the deuce is kicking me under the table for in such a way?"

"Why, it's I," said the other. "Have you no more feeling than a water-butt? Don't you see that Mr. G. aint partial to being put in mind of all that? Hold your row."

"Bah!"

"Yes, bah! is all such an ass can say, when he has put his foot in it. Never you mind him, Mr. G., you know one cannot make a silken purse of a sow's ear."

"It's no matter," said Godfrey, "it's no matter. I was that poor, shocking mangled wretch who fell on that occasion. I was the man—I was the man; and never, were I to live the thousand years you have wished me, shall I forget the agony of that frightful moment when I fell over the parapet, and felt myself going to, as I thought, inevitable destruction—I—I often wonder I did not go absolutely mad."

"Never mind, Mr. G.," said the reprobate, who had a kind of mild and strange philosophy of his own—"never mind, Mr. G.; keep on never-minding to the end of the chapter, and you will do famously. As for what my pal here says, why he is nobody, and if you know him and respected him as I do, you would pay as much attention to anything that came from his lips, as you would to the braying of a donkey."

"Thank you all the same," said the other.

"Yes, yes," added Godfrey, pursuing the terrible train of thought which had been awakened in his mind—"yes, I remember when, with a frightful smash, I came upon the paving stones. Oh, horror, horror, horror!"

"Come, I say, Mr. G. you are enough to turn anybody's milk."

"I heard my bones crack, and felt them at my joints, with a sudden plunge, fly from their natural sockets, and I lay a mass of bruises, of broken bones, of lacerated muscle. Oh, horror, horror!"

"Damn it, that's enough. I haven't got a bone in my own body now that ain't aching, and all my flesh has turned goosey."

"Horror, horror, horror!"

"I know it—I know it. Oh, I'm glad you are tired of it at last. Upon my soul, you are more fond than I should be of such matters."

"Ah!" said the other, "these may be called Godfrey's tender recollections."

"Tender be hanged; he has made me feel tender all over me."

Godfrey was completely overpowered by the dreadful picture memory had presented to him, and he let his head sink upon his hands, and shook like one in an ague.

"Come, come, Mr. G.," said he who was the most erudite of the two house-breakers, "we won't say anything more about such disagreeable matters now; let's drop them, and, as we have trespassed quite long enough upon you, we will now take our leave of you."

Godfrey made no answer.

"We have," added the fellow, as he motioned his companion to go with him, "we have the remarkable pleasure, Mr. G., of wishing you good night—eh?"

"Bah! He didn't say nothing."

"Oh, very well; these are not times when a man can be made to speak, if he don't feel inclined. As the lady said, however, when she went to worship her Maker, and found the church closed, we have done the civil thing, and that's all that can be required of us; so good night again, Mr. G."

They then left the wretched and guilty man to himself, and, when he was sure he was alone, he looked up.

"Gone, gone," he said. "I—I am glad they are gone—I am very glad they are gone—very glad. Oh that I were like them—oh that, like them, I was only a thief!"

Yes, Godfrey actually felt how superior even a thief was to him. What an ambition! What must be that man's state of mind who would be glad to be *only* a thief?

For a time he was silent; but when he spoke again, it was with something of hopefulness about his tone that he said,—

"At all events, the document which I have purchased at the price of one hundred and twenty pounds, will surely be of some service to me—it will do to produce as something in the shape of a justification; and I will say that it was in a lucid interval one day freely given to me by Marian Whitehead."

He took it from his pocket, and looked at it, but as he looked, suspicions gradually arose that after all he had been played with at his own game, and the signature was not genuine. Suddenly he uttered a cry of despair, for he made a discovery that convinced him it was not in the handwriting of the Black Lady.

There were actually two errors in the orthography—errors which she could not have made: her own name of Marian was spelt with an " o " in the last syllable, instead of an " a," as it ought to have been, and in the name of Whitehead, the first " e " was omitted.

These discoveries Godfrey considered as final testimony against the genuineness of the document. Errors of orthography in any other words would have been of no consequence; but people, if they are in ever such a hurry, or ever so much agitated, generally spell their own names right enough.

"Foiled again! foiled again!" he groaned; "deceived by all—deceived by the villains whom I paid so well. What recourse have I left me but death itself?—yes, death!—death! Oh, if I had but the courage to rid myself at once of this trouble-some existence; but I have not, I have not—I do not mind confessing to myself that I have not; oh, weak wretch that I am!"

We do not, we cannot pity Godfrey. We could not, as Marian Whitehead had done, pray for him; for, if ever a guilty man deserved to suffer, he was that man most unquestionably. And although we will not say that against even such as he the gates of Heaven's mercy are closed, we cannot beg that they may be opened for him.

It is scarcely in human nature not to feel an amount of resentment against such a character that makes anything in the shape of affected pity almost a piece of hypocrisy.

He slept at the tavern that night, for he had not strength to proceed homewards if he had wished, and the jolting of any kind of vehicle was always most painful to him; and had been so since the frightful accident he had met with, and the nume-rous injuries he had received.

CHAPTER LXXXIII.

GODFREY AT HOME.—THE NEWSPAPER, AND DETERMINATION TO POISON HIMSELF.

The home of Godfrey! What a sound, and how associated! Could, indeed, such a wretched and loathesome creature have a home? Could the sound, that brings to mind all that's dear and sacred to the heart, have any being for him? Could a home, indeed, belong to such a man? The inquiry might well be made when we recollect the hearths made desolate by him. He was worthless and undeserving. Should he then have a home? Should he have that which brought joy to the hearts of millions? Should he have that last spot or refuge, to which men usually hie when all the world looks black upon them, and shuns them? Should he have all this?

Ay, let him have it. It may appear unjust, but it is not so. It is said that a rose by any other name would smell as sweet. There is no denying the truth; but the rose may be withered—nay, its leaves calcined, and nothing but ashes remain. It would be scentless, useless, and all its beauty would then be destroyed.

A home is a home; but it may be rendered a curse rather than a blessing. It is the heart only that makes it the joyous place it is—the refuge from care and sorrow—and the heart, too, makes it a place to brood over fears and terrors, that the mind can never shake itself free from.

Therefore, we say, let Godfrey have a home—a place where he could sit, ogre-like, with eyes glistening and glaring around at the slightest sound—stricken with terror as with a palsy — a place of punishment — a very hell upon earth. It is the doom of such a man. It could truly be said that he had reaped as he had sown.

There sat Godfrey in his room—ay, his home. By his side, leaning against the mantel-piece, stood the crutches or sticks, by the aid of which he contrived to crawl, for he was yet maimed and unable to get about—save to look an object of decrepitude and wretchedness.

On his right was the breakfast-table, slovenly set with the half-finished cup, a toast just tasted—all showed a breakfast begun but not yet finished—it stood, and Godfrey, pale and ghastly at best, was now much more so than ordinary.

The fire burned low before him; the paper which he had been reading but a few moments before, had fallen from his hand, and was lying at his feet, and his whole appearance showed the greatest suffering, terror, and agitation; and he looked round the room with that slow motion and stealthy glance, that betrayed a world of terror, lest his eyes should meet some blasting sight which he feared, yet dared not shut his eyes to.

Thus sat Godfrey the day after the trial of Neville for the murder of Zachary, and after his condemnation and sentence.

He looked round from side to side at the least noise that was heard, no matter of what sort, that would cause him to start and tremble, as though it had touched him by some unseen electrical means.

"Yes, yes," he muttered, "the time has come—he will do it. Curse, curse, curse him!—he will do it—he will impeach me. May all the agony I endure be his! all that I may or can endure be his! may I be—but ah! what noise was that?"

He turned round, and the door came unhasped, and the cat walked in at the door, while Godfrey gazed on it with suspended breath, parted lips, and eyes that appeared to attempt piercing the very wainscoting, as though he had expected to detect what was beyond.

Yet will do it! hell and fury! The miscreant! I would his throat were in my clutch; I would never relax it, till I had deprived him of his life! Villain; wherefore impeach me—it will not save you? Ah! ah!"

These latter exclamations were uttered in consequence of great personal peril for a sudden movement of the body put him in most exquisite anguish. He had clenched his hand, and struck his knee, in the impotency of his rage and terror, and had exerted his body too much, for he was immediately attacked all at once as though by an universal spasm, and he leaned back in his chair.

"Oh! oh! what can be done—where can I go? How can I hide myself? Where can I remain secreted? There are none who will hide me. They all know I have money, and they will rob me, and then sell me."

This was a bitter reflection with such a man, who after years of successful vilany had now not one individual who would shelter him from his enemies; he had obtained nothing but wealth, and that was not enough to purchase immunity for the purpose; indeed, it seemed to increase his enemies.

"Curses, curses on him!" muttered Godfrey.

But muttering curses shows impotency, and this was the utter impotency of Godfrey, who, when he looked around him, saw nothing save the dingy and neglected furniture in his own apartment—everything he could rest his eyes on betrayed gloom and discomfort.

The very windows were dingy, and cobwebs hung over the room, the dust in many places was undisturbed, and a thorough air of discomfort appeared to range around and preside over everything.

"What can I do?" muttered Godfrey.

He relapsed into silence for some minutes, and then he slowly stooped down, and lifted up the newspaper which he looked over with such an eager, greedy aspect, yet haggard and horror-stricken gaze, as though what he looked for would blight him when he found it.

He turned the paper over and over again, as though he had lost and couldn't find what he was looking for.

"Strange," he muttered; "I couldn't have been mistaken—I saw it as plain as ever I saw anything in my life."

He turned over the leaves of the paper until he came to one part upon which he fixed his eyes.

"Ah! here it is!"

He ran his eye over the paper, speaking as he went,—

"Trial of Neville for murder—ah! fool—ah! there it is, plain enough. Yes, if they'll save his life, he'll give me up; ah! to be sure, he will; but they won't do that—they won't spare his life—he is too well known for that; on that score I might rest safe—yes, safe."

"But—but," and here Godfrey paused.

"Curses on the hound! curses on him!—he'll never die without giving me up. I know that too well; he will be sure to split upon me—I know he will, if it's only to hang me, and doesn't produce even a respite to himself. I know he will—I am sure he will!"

Godfrey uttered these words with a whine almost amounting to a cry—what a state for such a man to come to! He dropped the paper, and rested his head on his hand, and groaned heavily, while even tears ran down his face.

"Oh, oh! there is no hope—no hope—no hope! What will become of me? What shall I do?"

There was such exquisite anguish and grief in his voice and actions that any one, who knew not the extreme selfishness of the cause, would have pitied him; but this was only the beginning of a just retribution.

Suddenly, however, he paused, and, with both hands clenched, he raved and cursed in a horrible style, calling down all the imprecations of heaven and earth upon the head of Neville for his impeachment, which he considered as good as made.

"Curse him! curse him!" he said, vehemently, "and may all the evils and terrors that can cling to his heart hang thick about him to the last moment of his life, which is but a short one now."

Again he paused in his grief, and looked round, and at that moment the woman who attended upon him, or, more correctly speaking, his housekeeper, entered the room, and suddenly appeared before his eyes.

"What do you want?" he said, roughly.

"Have you done breakfast?" she inquired, without taking any notice of him.

"No—yes."

"Oh, I see you haven't eat or drunk anything this morning; are you worse than you have been, eh?"

"No—who told you I was worse?"

"No one."

"Then, what business is it of yours?"

"I thought you were worse, you look very bad, very bad indeed; you don't eat and your eyes are very red."

"Curse you, you old hag, take these things away, and give me none of your remarks; you are a corpse," said Godfrey, grinding his teeth.

"Corpse!" said the old woman, angrily.

"Yes, beldame, yes."

"I reckon you are nearer a corpse than I am."

As the old woman left the room, she muttered to herself, and this added to his terrors, and he listened to her mutterings as though they boded him evil.

"A corpse, said she? Ay, I have not long to live; turn which way I may, I am met on every side by evils from which I cannot escape. I shall certainly be hanged. Neville will tell all, and then I shall be hanged,—hanged."

He dwelt upon these last words with a whining tone, that added to his deep haggard, and ill-looking set of features, and which was like the cry of distress uttered by an ogre to lure passengers to come to his rescue, and then drown them when they come within his reach.

But Godfrey's cry of anguish was real; it was for himself, because he saw his own utter helplessness; he saw that he was enclosed on all sides, impeached by an old confederate, who could give too many evidences of all he chose to accuse him of, and there was enough to hang a dozen men.

He saw there was no escape; he saw that he was hemmed in by danger and mischief, all of which he must endure. He must suffer, and the end must inevitably be hanging on the gibbet.

Godfrey had this end staring him in the face; he could not shut his eyes to this great palpable fact.

"What is the use of living," muttered Godfrey. "What is the use of such a life to last some few days, and then to be ended in such a manner?"

Thus it was, that Godfrey came round to a point, that at other times his cowardice would have caused him to shrink from, with affright and horror. The thought that now crossed his mind was Suicide.

"Yes," he muttered, "I can't see any other way out, I can't escape, I am fixed. My shattered body would be but a mark to know me by; it is a mill-stone tied to me, to prevent my escape. If I did escape, I should be robbed, and subject to all kinds of imposition—all my money taken from me, and I should die of star vation, for I could never more earn a penny piece. f

"But I can't even get away. I shall after this be watched and followed, even i they are not after me to-day. Ay, they will be sure to be here. I know Neville too well; he will know what he has said will be found in the papers by me, and I should take every means in my power, to escape at the first alarm of his impeachment."

Godfrey groaned, and wrung his hands, when he saw the terrible state to which he was reduced.

"Yes—yes; poison—poison—it must come to that at last, and the sooner I set about it the better. Oh! oh! oh!"

He wrung his hands again, and even tears fell from his bloodshot eyes—tears, scalding—wrung from his soul, for though he had resolved upon a desperate course, yet it was to escape a worse evil; an evil, that to him presented so many horrors, and of such intensity, that he was almost paralised, and that made death more hideous and horrid.

"I will anticipate them," he said, with a desperate air, endeavouring to throw off the terrors and sorrows he had been indulging in; "yes, I will anticipate them, and when they do find me, I shall be a corpse. I will baffle them all, yes, and never yet failed in doing so, and my last act shall not be one in which I am baffled by them; no, I will be what I have been!"

Thus Godfrey made his resolve as to what course he would pursue, and he began to think of the means.

"Poison! ay—what poison? let me see. I can have a choice from prussic acid to ratsbane, but neither of them will do. I will not die like a rat; and, as or prussic acid, I can't get it—they won't sell it. I wish I could, that would do the business very quickly, but they are too cautious. Laudanum or arsenic? the first may be uncertain in its effects, whereas, the latter is sure. Ah! then I will have that. Arsenic is the poison for me!"

This was a desperate resolve for Godfrey, but, nevertheless, if his object was to escape the gallows, it was decidedly the only one that remained for him to attempt.

The next thing was to get it; he determined upon trying at every chemist's shop he came to until he succeeded in obtaining his wishes.

For this purpose he determined at once, while the coast was yet clear—if it were clear—to go and make an attempt to procure the necessary article.

He called to his housekeeper, and as soon as he could get ready—and preparation was to him one of pain and toil—but at length, with a haggard and downcast look, he rose from his chair, and taking his crutches from their corner, walked across the room to the door.

He had scarcely got so far, but there was an unwillingness to move, when a sudden indesition seized him, and he hesitated, but there was no hope, a moments consideration told him there was no other prospect for him, his only choice was the mode of his death.

CHAPTER LXXXIV.

GODFREY IN SEARCH OF POISON.—HIS ATTEMPT AT SELF-DESTRUCTION.—THE RESULT AND THE ARREST.

It was not without great fear and trembling that Godfrey desired the housekeeper to open the house door to let him out, and narrowly did he watch it as the aperture became larger and larger, and admitted more and more of the street to view.

Eagerly did he gaze from right to left, and left to right, to ascertain if his abode was not beleaguered by the officers of justice, who, he thought, would in all probability be ready to pounce upon him the moment he made his appearance in the street, and within sight of his own house.

" It is all clear," he muttered, with a sigh of relief.

He left the door, but each step was one of great exertion to him; it was against his will, and yet he was compelled to do so; it was an alternative, if it could be called so; but one of those dreadful choices from which the mind shrinks to contemplate until some fearful end has appeared which is far more dreadful, and renders the alternative of voluntary death preferable.

However, he saw no one about, and walked slowly down the street—but in what torture of mind and body did he not move! What dread of meeting some one who would seize him in the king's name as a prisoner, as a felon, to die the death on a scaffold!

" At all events," he said to himself, " I have my own fate in my hands now; I can surely obtain my poison now; I have but to go to some chemist and buy it; when I come to some small needy-looking place, I shall be able to get it without question or trouble."

However, he knew of none such just about there, and determined that he would go on until he came to one.

Godfrey thought that money was omnipotent with all the world, he knew it had been so with him. He would have sold his father's life for money at one time, ay, at any time. It was no wonder, then, that he thought he could have purchased anything, much less poison.

" At all events, I'll try," muttered Godfrey; " it will be the first time I ever found money to fail."

He still went onward, and at length found that there was a small chemist's near the corner of the street in which he was at that moment walking through, and he determined to walk up to it and examine its interior before he ventured into the shop to make the purchase

He hurried along until he came to the shop, and then was mounting the area rails to peep over the red curtain by which the shop was surrounded, and as he attempted to do so, his crutches went through the rails, and he fell with a loud groan.

In a moment somebody came by and tendered his assistance, and the man in the shop ran out ; in a moment more he was placed upon his legs, and had the crutches well placed in his hands.

"I hope you are not hurt, sir,"

"Not much," said Godfrey.

"Had you better not come in and rest yourself a while," inquired the chemist.

"Yes, I will, if you please," said Godfrey.

"Take my arm, sir," said the chemist, and he offered his arm ; but Godfrey found his crutches most useful and handy, and when he entered the shop the owner placed a chair for him, saying,—

"I dare say you are much shaken, sir."

"I am," said Godfrey,

"You are, I have no doubt, for a fall at any time upon such railings would shake you or anybody."

"I have no doubt of it, and my experience tells me that is the truth. I was coming up to the shop when I fell."

"Indeed, sir."

"Yes, I wanted to get something."

"What can I have the pleasure of doing for you, sir?" inquired the chemist's assistant, with some politeness.

"I am much infested with rats."

"Are you, sir?"

"Yes ; I want some white arsenic to poison them."

"Very sorry, sir, but we are forbidden to sell it to strangers."

"Very well," said Godfrey, "I am not a poor man, and therefore have no need to resort to an improper use of such matters, and I am terribly tormented with vermin in my place."

"Then buy a trap, sir,"

"I have, but it loses its efficacy after a time."

"I am very sorry, sir, I can't help you, but we are liable to severe censure for selling poison, and for the small sum of a few pence, you see, it would not be worth our while to get into trouble."

"I tell you," continued Godfrey, "I am not a needy man, and therefore I have no need to wish myself out of the world. You are a stranger, and of course you have only my word for what I tell you."

"Certainly, sir."

"Well, I will prove to you I am what I say ; that will alter the case, I apprehend."

"You would prove, sir, what you say, certainly."

"Exactly, I should. Well, I am willing to pay you gold instead of pence, that will at once prove to you I can pay, and do not want to make an improper use of it."

"I cannot say it would, sir."

"Will you sell it ?"

"No, sir, I cannot do so."

"Then good day," said Godfrey, who seized his crutches and began to leave the shop with haste, that made the man smile.

Godfrey left the shop and walked on further, passing by several chemists' shops, and refused to enter, because they did not appear to be what he thought at all likely places.

At length he came to another, and being recovered from the vexation caused by the refusal of the first, he entered the shop, and advancing to the counter he inquired for some white arsenic.

"White arsenic, sir?" said the man, looking very hard at him.

"Yes."

"What do you want it for ?"

"Why, you don't think I want it to eat ?"

"Don't know, sir, but we always ask the question."

"Well, then, I want it to poison rats with ; I have a very great many, and wish to poison them off."

"Oh, sir, there's so many accidents happening, that we can't sell it at all to anybody, no matter who. '

"Then, why didn't you say so at first ?"

"I thought you might want it for some purpose for which we could sell you something else that has the same effect."

Godfrey said nothing, but left the shop, cursing in his own heart the care and caution of the shopkeepers, and again left the place with a desperate and determined air. He could now see he would have much trouble in obtaining even the means of death, and he felt his situation each moment grow more and more desperate than before, and each minute of time thus lost, or unsuccessfully employed brought him nearer the gallows.

"I must have it ! I must have it !" he murmured, " else all I would avoid will happen, and that would be dreadful in the extreme. What shall I do, what shall I do? Where shall I get this infernal poison ? Why is it so hard to be had? What is it I should like to know to anybody else if I do choose to kill myself? Nothing, I should think.

It seems certainly an arbitrary kind of thing that people should be interfered with in this manner, and gentlemen are not even allowed to kill themselves when they have had enougth of the world.

But such is the perversity of the laws that a man may not do of himself that which the law would sanction, or admit as justice, only it chooses to have the luxury of punishing in its own hands.

However, there was no hope ; and yet he hated the task of going into the shops and asking for poison, for he got refused shop after shop, until he felt that his very looks caused the refusal ; and yet what could he do ? Poison he must have, or hang.

It appeared as if the penalty of his non-success would be death, by hanging, which catastrophe he could avoid by the purchase of a small quantity of white arsenic.

Godfrey went from street to street, from shop to shop, to inquire for white arsenic, and he found that a day had been consumed, and yet he had not obtained the desired compound.

At length in a fit of desperation he entered into a large chemist's s hp, where there were several assistants, and, recollecting for the first time, he had a prescription about him, he determined to have that made up first and purchase some other things besides.

Accordingly he entered the shop, and gave the prescription to the young man saying at the same time,—

"Will you make me up that ?"

"Yes sir ; do you wait for it ?"

"Yes."

The young man set about it immediately, and then in the course of a few minutes he succeeded in completing the order, and then inquired if there was anything more, and upon this Godfrey ordered a number of other articles, and among them some white arsenic ; all which were made up into a package, and then the young man said,—

"Where shall I send these, sir ?"

"I will take them," said Godfrey.

"You will find them inconvenient and heavy."

"I will take a coach, if you can stop one, or send for one. I am fatigued at this moment."

"Certainly, sir ; the boy will get you one."

The boy did get one, and Godfrey got into it with gladness, for he was very fatigued, and fearful of being stopped on the road, which he thought he would be better able to avoid by taking a coach.

He arrived safely at his own door, and hastened in with precipitation, and havg paid the man, he shut the door suddenly, and then, turning to his housekeeper, he said to her,—

"Let no one in, and don't open the door until I bid you."

He then walked into the parlour and seated himself down in his chair, and by some strange chance the same newspaper lay on the table, with Neville's trial uppermost; and the words of his own impeachment palpable before his eyes.

"I am determined," he muttered, "here, bring me hot water, sugar, and some gin, brandy, or rum."

The old woman looked at him very hard, but said nothing; she appeared to be very much surprised at these orders that had been given, but proceeded to obey them without any comment, but she more than once looked upon Godfrey with surprise.

What he had ordered was brought

"Will you want anything for supp ' she inquired.

"Nothing."

The woman said no more, but left the room, and then proceeded to enjoy herself, while Godfrey himself proceeded to do the needful in his own case; but here he paused.

"How shall I take it? How shall I mix it?"

These were questions he asked himself without being able to answer them; at length it occurred to him that if he were to mix a certain quantity up in a glass in a small drop of water, he should be able to swallow it off, and take some spirit and water after, which he thought would have the effect of causing it to take effect the sooner upon him, and put him out of his misery.

No sooner said than done; he put out as much of the white arsenic in a glass as he thought necesssay and then poured some hot water upon it; after which he mixed some gin-and-water to drink after it.

He trembled, and suddenly his eye glanced to the report of the trial, and the fear of the gallows was even superior to the fear of death in the wretched man who hastily drank off the poison, with a face so ghastly and horror-stricken at what he was doing, that he would have terrified even himself had he been able to see his own visage.

He gulped it down, and as he did so, he let the glass fall from his hands, and it was shivered into a thousand pieces.

Then taking some spirits, he gulped that down too, and then threw himself into his chair, and tried to sleep. The state he had been in all day, no food and much fatigue, mental and bodily, soon gave him the required forgetfulness for a time.

* * * * * * * * * *

That morning another scene had taken place. The offer of Neville to impeach Godfrey was justly reprehended by the judge, yet was not lost upon the authorities, who were willing enough to receive such communication.

There was an interview in Neville's cell on that evening, and what occurred, or what passed, did not transpire, but the consequences were more palpable, for a warrant was placed in the hands of two officers, with instructions to proceed to Godfrey's house, and arrest him at once.

* * * * * * * * * *

In the meanwhile Godfrey, whom we had left asleep, was in the course of an hour or more, awaked by horrible pains in his body, sickness, heat, and thirst, which added to his helplessness, and left him a prey to all the pains that can attack the human frame.

It seemed the poison he had taken he had in a great part vomited, and what he had taken was scarcely enough to take effect fatally—there was enough to put him in great danger and excruciating pain, and after about an hour-and-a-half's agony of body, almost indescribable, he with great difficulty got to his bed, and sunk upon it, exhausted and insensible.

At that moment a knock came at the door—his housekeeper seeing he was not to be consulted, opened the door, which the two men closed again as soon as they had entered.

" We want Mr. Godfrey," said one.

" You can't see him—he's ill, up stairs."

" We must see him—show us his room."

The old woman was about to object, but they silenced her by saying they were officers and would go ; therefore, she at once led the way, and there lay Godfrey insensible and exhausted on the bed, incapable of motion ; he uttered some words, but they were the effect of his wandering imagination.

" He can't be moved, that's certain," said one of the officers, as he looked at Godfrey, and then looked at the table and room.

" No ; he's been trying to poison himself," said the other.

" Very likely," replied his companion ; " but I tell you what to do."

" What now ?"

" You had better go back and tell them that I am staying here ; the man cannot be moved, and that they had better send assistance ; and as you go along you had better send the first surgeon you come across."

The other assented to the justness of this, and proceeded upon the instant to act upont hese directions.

———

CHAPTER LXXXV.

THE DESPERATE ATTEMPT OF NEVILLE TO ESCAPE FROM NEWGATE.

The cell of the condemned in Newgate is no place in which the unfortunate and highly criminal wretch can hope for peace and comfort, and to us it appears impossible that the evil deeds of a long life can in a few days be recalled and repented of, and sufficiently shuffled off from the mind, so as to enable it to meet eternity with a full assurance that forgiveness and future happiness awaits the unhappy wretch.

It must be strange way-wardness of intellect that can induce men seriously to urge what they hope rather than what any one can seriously believe. We may believe in mercy, and we may be forgiven for believing in justice ; at least, such notions of justice as it has pleased Heaven we should have the power of understanding, and no other can we believe in if we are not permitted to understand.

It seems very singular, but it is a common doctrine, that he who has led a wild life—a life of crime, of wickedness, and injustice—such an one may, at the eleventh hour, as it is called, repent of all he has done ; and we are assured that there will be more rejoicing on his account than those who have been from principle just, and who have, as far as human capabilities, that is, the power that has been granted to them, spent a long life in doing good. Truly, the balance in favour of sinning seems great in the extreme, and it requires all the good there is in human nature—and there is some—to resist it. But doctors may be wrong, and the parable of the prodigal son may be but an exception.

That such a nature as Neville's should recoil with horror from his doom is not to be wondered at. Sunk for years in the lowest debaucheries, in the worst of crimes, and used to the commission of the most determined villanies, it is not to be wondered at that he could not turn from looking forward to life.

Yes, he loved and longed for life ; he had hope too, but why, we cannot say, simply, because he loved it—because his nature clung to it, and not for the chance that aught could happen to prevent the just consummation of the law's doom, no reasonable being could, for one moment, imagine.

Neville's nature was cowardly and brutal, and his brutality was accompanied by great strength, and desperation might give him courage and energy, which he would, under other circumstances, have wanted ; and rather than stay and be hanged in an orderly manner, it is quite certain he would have made an attempt to rush through a file of soldiers, ready to bayonet and shoot him; he would have run such a desperate chance, when a worse fate would befal him; but no dangerous odds would he attempt, unless urged on by some such stimulus.

He lay on the seat that was fixed near the wall, and looked at the window of his cell all day, and would converse with no one; he was morose and savage, a real misanthrope, and incapable of thinking of aught, save his own wants and wishes.

"What can I do," he muttered, "what can I do? I see nothing—no chance, not the remotest. Who could it be that would keep me now? Not any human being. Curses upon them all, they have had my money, and yet they aid me not."

The cell door was opened by the gaoler, who looked at him.

"Well, no better, yet?"

"What do you mean?" said Neville.

"I mean, have you thought anything of your state? You aint long to live, you know; you had better make up your mind to die like a decent Christian than a dog. Come, come, let me persuade you to do better things than this. I am sure you know you have but little time left you."

"I do know it."

"Well then, make use of your knowledge; our parson, I know, has a peculiar way of telling you all this, but I am a man like yourself; be a man."

"There's time enough to talk of that," said Neville.

"There is no time to spare."

"Curse you," muttered Neville, "do you think I don't know it—leave me alone, I would sooner be left to myself than be medded with by you."

"Oh! I tell you what it is," said the turnkey, "you aint the pleasantest chap to deal with at any time, and it strikes me you'll require help to prop you up as you go in the last procession to the drop; you might have more regard to your own safety than you have."

"My safety! where is it?"

"I mean your soul——"

"Who'll save my life?" said Neville; "do that, and you will do something worth talking about, but as for your talk about dying resigned and all that, why, it is sickening. I want to live, not die—and you are trying to cry a man down, torment, and tease him; it is of no use only to make a man miserable; you give what you call consolation—that is, you try to frighten."

"You are hardened."

"You are a fool," said Neville, with a growl more like a beast than a man, and at the same time he glanced at the man in a manner that made him recoil.

"Well, you are a man after a fashion, certainly, but I tell you what, you won't die respectably; you'll die like a dog; you won't do Master Ketch credit; your halter won't be worth a shilling after you've done with it, I see; you'll have no pluck."

"You'll die a violent death yourself, and if you don't make the best of your way out, I'm thinking you will not find yourself so well as you might be if you went out of your own good will; so be off as quickly as you please."

"Very good. The law says an Englishman's house is his castle, and I suppose you think this was built for you; but no matter, I only came in to say a civil word to you, and to ask you if you want anything, before you are locked up for the night."

"I do."

"What is it you want."

"My liberty," said Neville.

"Then in that small matter I cannot assist you. It is your doom to remain here until you are hanged; and now, as you are not the most comfortable neighbour in the world, I will leave you to your own reflections during a long night, that is not the most agreeable position in the creation; but never mind, do you enjoy yourself after your own fashion."

As the turnkey spoke, he shut the door, and he whistled a lively tune to himself to show how little he cared for the want of civility on the part of his prisoner. He locked and double-locked the door, and jingled the keys against the iron doors, in a manner that almost wrung a groan from Neville.

The wretched man lay in the same position. The sound of the locks and bolts appeared to bring a stronger sense of the misery of his wretched condition before him. The sounds of the locks spoke in an iron voice to his soul, and told him more plainly where he was.

Yes, he was sentenced to death, no sound could speak plainer than that, and Neville shook as though an ague had seized him,—not a hope, not a chance appeared to be left him. Such bolts! such locks! what could be the use of even making a survey in his own mind? it was useless; there was no such place of safety for man-keeping as in the condemned cell in Newgate.

And yet if he remained there, he must die, that was a certainty. He had been told so, and he was well assured that such would be the case.

Horror upon horror to meet death there, to wait for it, to count the minutes as they pass, and as they diminish the space of life, while health and strength remains! This is indeed horrible, yet more so when there is no resource of mind left, no one consolation either derivable from a life already spent, or from strength of nerve—courage or fortitude.

But what was to be done? Could he escape from the prison?

That was a question which he put to himself over and over again, but could find no answer that could give him hope; the very iron bars seemed to say "No;" they appeared to tell him that there was no hope to be found there, and that had he been placed at the bottom of a well, he should not have been more secure, or could there have been a less prospect of an escape.

"And yet," thought Neville, "I have heard of some things that appeared to be impossible, yet they have been done after all; men have got out of worse places than even this, though I cannot tell how they did it; it is impossible here to do anything of the kind."

Neville lay gazing at the little cross-barred window which emitted a dubious light from a lamp that was suspended in the passage, an oil lamp in a wall, or hung up by a wire, or something of the sort, he could not tell which.

However, he heard few or no sounds; there was a gradual stillness and quiet stealing over the prison, for the night was setting in, and men were placed at certain posts, like sentinels, to keep watch and ward from one end of the prison to the other. No chance seemed to be afforded for a cat to escape past without being seen, and there was no passage that had not its appropriate warder.

It seems strange that a place of such strength and so zealously guarded, should be in such a place as London city, in the very heart of this busy metropolis. More singular yet is it still, that it should not be attempted from the outside; it has been barred, but the friends of the men confined are often numerous and desperate; and could, upon a sudden emergency, we should think, make a sudden and successful attack upon the place, and yet no one dreams of it.

At least it has never been done, never attempted; the building is strong and powerful, and no stone insecure about it; and then the possiblity of getting immediate assistance from the Horse Guards and the Tower would deter many from aiding their friends.

These thoughts passed through Neville's mind, and he groaned—

"No, no, there is no chance for me, I am doomed to the gibbet; but I'll never submit, they know not my strength, and I can yet do some mischief, and I will."

It was a scowl of fearful satisfaction that passed over his hideous countenance as he thought of the dreadful attempt he would make to inflict pain, and which must to a certain extent succeed.

He rose from his seat, and paced up and down his cell for some minutes, and then he looked at the grated window.

"If I could get the bars out, I could not pass through," he muttered, "and if I got through there would be the man at the corner of the passage. No hope, curse it, no hope!"

As he muttered these words to himself he threw himself with violence against the walls of his cell, and it returned him a sound that caused him to pause in his furious lamentations. He sounded the wall, it shook only when he flung himself violently against it.

"What can be the meaning of all this!" he muttered.

He turned to the wall, exerted his whole strength, and found it shook. It was certainly brick, but it appeared as if it had been put up against some wainscoting or door, a place bricked up and considered as safe; most probably no one living knew anything about it at all.

"This may lead to something," he thought.

The best thing would have been to have got down the bricks, but this appeared to be quite impracticable: they moved and yielded, but it was not possible to shake any of them out. What was to be done? Here was a chance at least.

Neville was now alive and desperate; it seemed as though his nature had suddenly changed ; he was all energy and spirit. There was hope of life before him. He thought he could escape, and, once free of the walls of Newgate, he was safe, an d would never be retaken.

" What shall I do," he muttered, " to pick out the mortar ? Displace one brick, and I am safe ; I could get the others down with my own hands."

He paused and looked round.

" My very life," he muttered, " depends upon an old nail."

But no old nail was to be had ; and Neville was just about to relapse into a fit of maledictions, when his eyes rested upon his own fetters, and the thought struck him, that he might be able to make them subservient to his wants upon this occasion. He therefore made a desperate effort to break them, and after incredible efforts, he succeeded in causing them to snap, so that his legs were unencumbered, save the rings round the leg ; he had now very efficient tools.

The rough ends of the fetters enabled him very speedily to scrape away the mor- tar round the bricks, and to get at the wood-work beyond. This was all well enough, but the wood-work was very powerful, and secured by an old lock, that there was no possibility of turning, and besides that, there were, no doubt, bolts, rusted by years, if not generations.

" This must be got over, too," muttered Neville.

In a minute more he turned the brick-work from the hinges, and examined them.

There was hope! the hinges were much decayed, though of great strength originally.

" They must now be worn down to the thickness of a shilling," he muttered, " and I can overcome that ; at all events, I will soon try."

No sooner said than done, for Neville inserted the end of the small steel bar, for such it now was, into the crevice between the door and post to which it was attached.

This, however, was difficult and tedious, and he in a moment afterwards aban- doned the idea of doing this, but after a few unsuccessful attempts, he thrust it in between the post and brick-work, which in a short time gave way entirely.

This was a great achievement and the whole door came out, which with a little care hung gently, leaving a passage exposed to view. A very small passage, with some stairs at the end, or rathe r steps, for they were of stone, led to the underground cells which are never used now,

" This," he muttered, " is good, I shall get off."

Neville's spirits which had been so bad all along, so hopeless, were suddenly brought up to a pitch they seldom or ever reached before. He was like a madman in a frenzy of hope.

But every now and then as he looked back a shadow crossed his brow, and he saw clearly, the possibility of his being again secured was not a mere naked possibility.

It was, to all intents and purposes, a very great probability, for if they were by any accident then to visit his cell and detect him in the act, this would be worse than all. What could he do to avoid such a fate? Why, he could fight and die.

" And I will die," he muttered, " before I will be taken. I shall but die if they do take me, and I only die in a better manner as I like, and not as they please. I die not according to their sentence ; I die, escaping, fighting, and I am not led to a public execution."

Again he paused, and hopes revived.

" If they come while I am searching my way down below, they will come after me, and I shall be again secured ; but I must provide against that."

He looked around him, and then seizing some pieces of brick and mortar, he thrust them into the lock to prevent the key going in.

" But this will be better," he muttered, as he seized upon the door he had just wrenched out of its place, and then with great exertion he placed it before the cell door in such a manner that it would take the united force of several men to displace it.

" That will do," he thought, and then he plunged into the passage.

He walked down some distance ; there was no sound that met his ears, but he walked on very cautiously, feeling the sides of the passage as he went along, which was easy enough, seeing that it was but very narrow, until he came to the stairs.

However he could see nothing, all was dark, and could he have obtained a light, he would have done much better ; but as it was he would be able to grope his way along only by means of his hands, and he could not tell when he met with an impediment, until he came full against it.

This was inconvenient, and yet it was all the chance he had, and perhaps it was better after all that it should be so, seeing a light might have betrayed him.

How far he wandered about he knew not ; he had passed through more than one door, he felt the walls were all damp and slimy, and a disagreeable smell seemed to arise from the soil, and the rotting walls and things lying about in places.

Altogether it was a most uncomfortable search, and one which he feared would each moment lead him into some great danger or other from which it was his object to escape.

"Where am I ?" he muttered more than once.

This was a question, difficult to answer, unless in a very general manner, indeed ; there he was in every sense of the word, metaphysically and literally, totally dark.

The places were dark and damp, noisome smells, and impure vapours, that collected there, and had collected there for years perhaps, and which only slowly enhaled. These more than once caused him to hesitate and pause, lest he should sink unable to bear them.

"Where does this lead to ?" he muttered to himself.

But he merely put the question to himself, and began to set his wits to work for a probable answer ; but he could not do this. At one time he thought he might be getting into some of the cellars of the surounding houses, and in that case he could soon make his way into the open air.

But all hope of that, he felt, was fallacious ; and that the best thing he could do was to make his way towards the roof of the house or prison.

"It's no use staying here," he muttered, "I am in no better state than in my cell, and the longer I am in this cursed hole, the longer I shall be in escaping, if I escape at all ; at all events they will be closer on my trail if I should get out.

He groped along until he came to a door that seemed to be shut, but after some trouble he got it opened, and to his joy found that they led their way upwards.

"This will do," he muttered, and he sprang forward, but his haste was repressed, for he struck his head a violent blow against something that projected over head, which brought him to his knees, and stunned him for near a minute, and appeared as an admonition to be cautious.

"Curses," he muttered, as he ran his hand over the part affected.

But he determined to proceed and with caution ; induced by so severe an admonition, he went up stairs in a very gentle manner. He made several turnings— the stairs, or steps were narrow and winding. It was very strange, but they appeared as though they went upwards spirally, or something approaching it.

After having gone up some distance, he was thrown into a state of alarm by hearing some one close to him call out, saying,

"Hoy ! hoy !"

He was almost petrified, and stopped short in an instant, and heard some one walking about towards him at the same time.

"Well, what's the matter ?" said a strange voice.

"The matter, I can't sleep a wink, that's the matter, and matter enough aint it."

"You aint put there to sleep are you ?"

"There's no use in my keeping my eyes open here all night long."

"Then, why don't you shut 'em ?"

"Because I can't. I can't sleep, the infernal rats make such a noise ; they are worse than usual to-night, they run about like coach horses. There's one or two on em behind me as would take the shine out of a good many, Lord bless you, he came up just now the wall, and made such a noise that I was obliged to call out to put an end to the riot."

"What a fool you are!"

". Well, you have grown civil, you have."

"Well, you know that the rats don't understand what you say."

"He left off, what more can you say?"

"Very little, have you heard how that chap's getting on?"

"What chap?"

"Him as is to be hung"

"No, I aint."

"Well, then, I'll tell you, he is an out-an-out rascal, brutish, and cowardly, he aint half a man though, I dont think he'd tackle one fairly."

"Don't you—why?"

"Because he aint got any of that steady calmness and fearlessness that I have seem some men have; he's only savage, and will cry like a child. I am sure of it. Nobody likes hanging, I know, and yet there aint many who show much of the hite feather when they come here."

"Well, they don't."

"They have made up their minds to it."

"What does our parson say to him?"

"I don't think he says much about him."

"He aint done no good with him, I see, else he would have talked about him, for a month, and the papers would be chock full of the repentance and piety of the prisoner, all owing to the clergyman; nobody else would have thought of it, if it hadn't been the parson."

I should think not, and so he'll be afore he's done; but I must go back again now. I dare say it is time to pay him a visit, or at least very soon."

"He won't say thank'e for the honour."

"No, but its the rule, you know. Good night."

"Good night."

Neville listened till he heard the man out of sight; and now, being assured that he was on the right road to escape, he determined to make the best of his way out. Everything depended now upon speed. That was all he had to hope in. His cell would be invaded, and his absence discovered; then an immediate search would be made; all would be lost, and he would be dragged back again to his cell, but in the meantime moments were as precious as drops of blood.

He cautiously crept up stairs, but he could not avoid scraping his feet against some parts, which produced a noise.

"Get out you varmints," muttered the angry turnkey, "curse you. ain't you no respect for the rest of decent people? you ought to be all poisoned."

Heeding but little the mutterings of the sleepy turnkey, he got up some distance beyond his hearing, and then he came to a door which he found it necessary to force. This did not take long, but he could not tell where he had got to. It was a bed-room; there was nothing but hangings and curtains and furniture; he had come into the lion's den no doubt.

He paused a moment: he saw he was in an apartment that was in use; he examined the door he had come through, and it appeared like a piece of wainscoting first like the rest of the room, and any one might have been there for a hundred years, and yet never have known the existence of such a communication with the vaults below the prison.

"However," he muttered, "if I can put this back, it will cut off all traces of what has become of me; and that may be to my advantage."

In a minute more, he had pushed the wainscoting back and it was all right.

"Who's there?" said a voice.

"Goodness me, Robert, what can be the matter? Oh dear! oh dear! we shall all be murdered in our beds—I know we shall—I am sure of it."

" Be quiet."

" I can't. Get up and see."

" What's the use? the door is locked, and if I open it, I may be knocked down to please you See—I dare say I shall—open it yourself."

" Goodness gracious! I can't lay here! what shall I do? This will be dread to be woke out of one's sleep in this manner. I do believe something's going wrong. I hope it aint fire."

Neville found he had emerged into somebody's bed-room, and he had awoke them out of their sleep. What could he do? he couldn't stop there, and yet to move would be to reveal himself immediately. The only thing was, if either of the people in bed were to get out, he must at one blow silence them, before any alarm could be given to others in the prison.

It was accident that this was an unguarded point, for no doubt the avenues had been well guarded, and there was no approaching it without obstruction, and therefore here he was likely to be safe.

" I am in the governor's house," he thought, " and that has been some passage used formerly for the purpose of privately visiting the cells.

The conjecture was near the truth, but at that moment the alarm bell sounded, and he heard the man jump out of bed.

" Something's amiss—I must be off."

He came towards Neville, who levelled him senseless on the earth; he felt as if shot by a bullet.

" Murder—what's the matter? " screamed the woman, who, however, received in answer, a blow on the head which left her no inclination to indulge in screaming.

In another moment he had quitted the room with the light he had found burning, and began examining the place, and went to a room above. Here he found were the leads; if he could get out there, he could cross over to the opposite houses, and then get out of them into the streets.

All the while the alarm-bell kept ringing, and he could hear people running about from place to place, and after great efforts he opened a door, by pushing it open with his shoulder, and then he determined that he would make one desperate attempt, and force in the roof.

He saw no other means, for if he ventured about he would still be liable to be caught; whereas, in his place of concealment, he was not likely to be molested by accident, but only in case of a search; therefore, he was safe where he was, and he could employ himself in getting through the roof, after which he would be free, he hoped.

" Now then," he muttered, as he made an attack upon the ceiling near the window, which before seemed the best. " Now, then, I'll have a trial."

The plaster flew about, and the laths were soon knocked in, but then he found rafters and cross-pieces still were much stronger and closer than usual, and which was surmounted on the top by lead; this was difficult to penetrate, and yet, in about ten or fifteen minutes he had forced this up, and made an opening big enough to let himself out.

To do this, indeed, he had to exert a giant's strength; he had worked like a maniac—with the strength of one whose powers were increased with the knowledge of the necessity of such exertion as that, and nothing but that, would secure him.

He got through with enormous exertion, for the hole was too small, and he had forced himself through after wounding himself, and then he stood upon the top in the moonlight, and he cast for a moment his eyes below and could see men and lights were hurrying to and fro.

" I am free," he said, half aloud.

But he stood not there alone, and when he uttered the words, he turned round, and was immediately confronted by three stout turnkeys.

" You are our prisoner," said one stepping forward to seize him.

For a moment he was stunned, completely paralised that he could not move for a moment; but as soon as he felt a hand upon him—he made a desperate attempt to rush by them, and make his way over the houses at any hazard.

"D——n" he muttered, and he felled one of the turnkeys to the earth, but the other two rushed upon him, and each one seizing an arm flung him down and threw themselves upon him, while the other, recovering from the effects of the blow, aided his companions, and after some trouble they succeeded in putting the hand-cuffs on, and then secured his legs in like manner, for he was so desperate that these men were unable to hold him unless so secured. That done, they dragged him, as well as they could, back to the prison, where he was safely secured, and order and quiet restored, and Neville left to think upon the misadventure of his all but successful attempt at escape.

———

CHAPTER LXXXVI.

THE ARRIVAL—THE NEW CHARGE AGAINST GODFREY.

IT was hardly possible that such a man as Godfrey could go through life and commit no greater an amount of injustice than he had done to poor Marian White-head and her lover.

We may well imagine that his whole career must have been marked and sig-nalised by may such acts, although generally with that success which, we grieve to say, in this world too often attends upon rascality. No immediate retributive conse-quences arose to him from such bad action, except the stings of conscience—always provided Godfrey was in possession of such an article.

We shall, however, seize this opportunity of bringing to notice one of the events of his life which he little thought would ever make its way to the light of day to confound him.

In order that this matter may be quite intelligible to our readers we shall present it to them just as it took place, in the midst of the stirring incidents which it has recently, in pursuance of this narrative, been our duty to lay before the reader.

It happened, then, just at the juncture we are at, that one evening late there arrived at an old hotel, or coach office tavern, more properly speaking, a young lady, or what appeared to be such.

The house was one of those very old fashioned ones which are fast disappearing before the march of improvement, but some specimens of which still remain in out-of-the-way, odd places in the city, where one would hardly expect them. Pro-bably some archway, looking as if it led to a vault or cellar will appear in the street and if any adventurous traveller will plunge down such an entry, he will emerge into daylight again finding himself in an old inn-yard.

It is to such a place we wish to direct the attention of our readers.

In one of the strange, winding, back streets, lying behind the new post-office, was the inn to which we have to draw, at this time, particular attention.

It is approached by such a narrow, dark, arched entrance as we have described, but when once within, a considerable space presents itself for the stranger to admire if he happen to be an admirer of antique house architecture.

There is a paved courtyard, and the old-fashioned building occupies two sides, while the third is devoted to stabling, the fourth being occupied by the strange, inconvenient, and gloomy-looking entrance.

At the height of the first story of the house there is a gallery, curiously supported by timberenough to build half-a-dozen more wooden residences, and into which open innummerable doors and windows, and it likewise has several flights of stairs, by which the gallery may be approached from the courtyard, or by which many of the bed-rooms may be left without involving the necessity of going through any portion of the house.

The last coach which was to halt at that inn had made its appearance, and been duly booked, and the horses conveyed to rest. The coachman was enjoying himself with something warm in the bar, and the few passengers who were strangers in London were in what was called the coffee-room, although not a cup of that beverage had ever been within its precincts, enjoying themselves after their fatigue, and talking over the little incidents of their journey.

Suddenly, the swinging door which led to the bar was opened, and a light footstep was heard. The landlady looked up inquiringly to see what sort of customers had come, and observed a young lad, respectably dressed, but who looked so faint and so dreadfully weary and travel-worn, that it was evident he could but just keep on his feet.

"What do you want?" said the landlady. "Bless me, who are you?"

"May I" said the youth, in a weak, exhausted voice, "rest myself here a little while, madam, for I am so wearied I cannot move another step?"

" Oh, certainly, of course you can rest here ; you do look tired enough to be sure."

" I—I mean, may I not—without—without——"

" What—what? Of course you can rest. This is an inn, and on purpose for people to rest at. Don't you know that ?"

" Yes," faltered the lad, " but I thought I ought to let you know at first that I have no money."

" Oh, never mind that," said the coachman, who had been shaking his head as if he were wonderfully interested in the matter,—"never mind that, my boy. You seem run off your feet—a long stage you have had, I supposes. Are you off your feed, or will you take anything ?"

" Well, Mr. Jones," said the landlady, " if so be as you take compassion on him, why in course it will be all right. Just come into the bar, boy, and sit down, will you ?"

The invitation was obeyed with alacrity—at all events such alacrity as the wearied limbs of the boy could manage to exert, and he accepted a proffered seat by the coachman—who observed that his shoes were covered with dust, as well as many portions of his apparel, and that it was quite evident he must have travelled far.

" Why," continued the coachman, " you do seem as if you had come far. Where have you come from ?"

" From Watford."

" Watford ? Do you mean to say you have walked all the way from Watford?" Yes—two miles beyond Watford."

' You may well then look all over dust and feel tired, my lad ; why, what could have induced a little fellow like you to come such a long distance as that, and on foot, too. You must be fagged to death. Why, I change *osses* once in such a drive.".

" It was necessary that I should come," said the lad, " to do an act of justice. Can you tell me where Mr. Quentin lives ?"

" Quentin ! Quentin ! No, I never heard of such a name afore, not I. Do you know, ma'm ?" said he to the landlady."

" No. What street does he live in ?"

" I do not know. The only address I am aware of, is London."

The coachman shook his head, as he said,—

" That's rather a wide direction, my boy, but I don't mean to go for to say that you won't find him by it. It's rather an odd name too, and that makes it all the easier ; but come, take a drop of this ; it will do you good. Oh, don't be afraid of it."

The coachman would very good naturedly have given the lad some brandy-and-water, for he considered that compound as a kind of panacea for all evils; but the boy so decidedly refused that it was evident he did so from a much stronger feeling than bashfulness, and he said,—

" I am more in want of food than anything else."

Upon this, the coachman, although he did feel a little hurt at the positive refusal of the brandy-and-water, desired the landlady to cut the boy some sandwiches, and those with a glass of water, for this young stranger would drink nothing else, constituted his repast. Then he rose, and in a stronger voice, for he was both rested and refreshed, said,—

" I thank you, and will now pursue my journey."

" Pursue your journey? What do you mean. Aint this the end of your journey ?"

" No ! you know that I came to London to seek for a Mr. Quentin, and that I have not found him. I thank you very much, and must go."

" No, no—stop a bit, my lad. You will wander all over London to little purpose if you went off by yourself. There is ways of finding out people, I can tell you, as you don't know of perhaps, my little fellow. I say, ma'm—have you got such a thing as a Directory."

The landlady averred to having a Directory, which was at once sent for out of the before-mentioned coffee room, and then the kind-hearted coachman desiring the lad to sit down by him, began to look among the Q's for the name of Quentin, which he happened to want.

"Oh," he said—"here we are—Quentin, Quentin! Oh, there is only four of them. One of 'em is at Mile-end; another of 'em is in Tottenham-court-road; another of 'em is at Paddington; and another of 'em is in Old Kent-road; so you have got a tidy lot of ground to go over, my boy, afore you can see all the Quentins, I can tell you."

"But all those places are in London?"

"Oh, yes!"

"Then, I can walk from one to the other?"

"Yes, you can—but you, perhaps, haven't a very good idea of the size of London, my lad. It would take you a good long summer's day to do all that walking in, and then I don't know that you could do it. Why, if you think London is like Watford, that you could run over it in a quarter of an hour, you are much mistaken."

"What am I to do?" said the lad, in evident grief?

"Wait till the morning."

"Oh! no, no—there is one whose sufferings have been too long protracted already. She was all of consequence, and yet I know that if the distance be such as you say, and it should chance to happen that the Mr. Quentin I want should be the last I require, I am at present quite incapable of taking so much more fatigue.—What will become of her?"

"Her!—Who do you mean by her? Who is her, boy? Upon my word you are a very extraordinary lad!" exclaimed the landlady, who, although she was not one of the most liberal-minded persons in all the world, was decidedly one of the most curious.

"I do not know," said the boy, that I gain anything by keeping it a secret."

"Oh dear, no, you may depend upon it you don't. Pray tell us all about it. What have you come to London about? Who is Mr. Quentin, and what do you want to say to him, when you do find him? Come, you are evidently too tired to go anywhere to-night, as I dare say we shall find half a bed for you somewhere."

"Oh, to be sure," said the coachman, and as to-morrow ain't a driving day of mine, I don't mind if I help you a little in hunting out Mr. Quentin, if he be your father?"

"My father? oh, no! I have a father, I grieve to say, but not Mr. Quentin. I don't know him, but I wish he was."

"Well, you are the oddest little fellow ever I came near. You have a father, and yet you wish a man was your father that you don't know. I say, my boy, I hope as you aint a humbug!"

"A what?"

"A humbug! Come, now, if you don't tell us all about yourself, I shall think as how you comes to London arter no good."

"Alas!" said the boy, "am I, after all my exertions, to be regarded as an object of suspicion?"

As he uttered these words, there was a sound of horses' feet in the inn yard, and immediately that he heard them the boy sprang to his feet and looked very much alarmed, saying—

"Oh, if that be any one in pursuit of me, let me beg of you to conceal me and protect me; I have done nothing wrong, but there may be a pursuit for me, because i wish to expose the wrong that others have done."

"You make yourself easy," said the coachman.

"Yes, yes! but I hear a footstep coming. Oh, hide me, hide me, I implore you."

The terror of the boy was so real that the landlady, who by this time was in a perfect agony of curiosity, opened a little door which led into a small chamber behind the bar parlour, where she herself slept, and told him to go in there, where he could not only feel confident of effectual protection and concealment, but be able to overhear all that took place, so that if the horseman had nothing to do with him he could at once emerge.

This arrangement was readily acceded to by the boy, and just as a heavy footstep approached the swing door of the inn, he darted into the landlady's chamber.

CHAPTER LXXXVII.

THE MAD-HOUSE KEEPER.—THE DECEPTIVE STATEMENT.—THE COACHMAN'S PLOT.

IF, indeed, it was necessary that the little lad who had made so mysterious an appearance at the inn should get out of the way of the horseman, he only just accomplished that object in time; for scarcely was the door of the little inner chamber shut, than a tall, rough-looking man, attired in a large cloak, made his appearance at the bar. It was evident he had ridden some distance, and he at once said,—

"I suppose I can have accommodation for myself and my horse here to-night?"

"Yes," said the landlady, as she rung a bell, which let the ostler know that he was wanted,—"yes; will you walk in, and sit down, sir?"

The man accepted the invitation; and when he took a seat by the side of the coachman, the latter thought he had never seen such an ill-looking specimen of humanity as he really was.

There was a most malignant-looking expression upon his face, and a peculiarity about his eyes, which, although not exactly a squint, very nearly approached one, made him look anything but engaging.

"Rather dusty travelling," said the coachman.

"Yes," replied the stranger; "but I don't mind what the roads are when I have not a disagreeable errand to come upon."

"Oh, you have a disagreeable errand then?"

"Rather—a young boy has eloped from me. He is my son, the scamp, and has taken with him a large sum of money; I have ridden from home to look for him, as I had certain information he was seen upon the London road."

"Lor!" exclaimed the landlady, incautiously, "you don't come from Watford, do you?"

"Watford! yes, I do. How came you to know that? Damn it, perhaps you have seen the boy, and can tell me where he is?—I do come from Watford—he is a lad about fourteen, well dressed, with curling chesnut hair. Have you seen him?"

"I should think not," said the coachman, coming opportunely enough to the relief of the bewildered landlady. "How should we know anything of him? The fact is, a coach always stops here that comes through Watford, and as it had not come in yet, the landlady wanted to know if you came from there, and had passed it, as it was uppermost in her houghts."

"Oh, that's it."

"Ah, to be sure. And so the lad has robbed you?"

"Yes, he has, confound him! and the worst of it is, he is such a liar, for to secure himself from the robbery, he will, no doubt, invent some of the most atrocious stories about me. You must know, sir, and you, ma'am, that there is not a more humane man than I am in the kingdom."

"You don't say so," remarked the coachman, rather ironically.

"And may I ask what you are, sir?" said the landlady.

"Oh, yes, I have no need to be ashamed of what I am—I keep a mad-house."

"The devil! you do," said the coachman, "you don't mean to say that the boy you spoke of is out of his mind, do you?"

'Oh dear no not he, he's too vicious and clever by half. Only you see how a respectable man in my situation may be said all sorts of things of. Why he'll think nothing of telling people that I ill-use the patients, that's what I look at you see."

"And," said the coachman, "you need not mind that, if so be as you don't ill-use them, 'cos you see if so be as he says you do, and there's never such a row made about it, you will come out of the affair with clean hands."

"Oh, oh, yes, as far as that goes of course I have nothing to fear, but you see it aint at all pleasant, and so I don't mind a reward of five pounds for him.

"You don't?"

"No."

"Then of course you'll get him; who wouldn't give him up to you, if you were ever such a humbug, for five pounds I should like to know?"

The coachman winked to the landlady in order that she might take notice how he was making game of the madhouse-keeper, at the same time that he kept the boy's secret quite well and safe.

"Yes," added the man, "and would give five pounds to any one who would produce me the boy, because though he is such a bad 'un, of course I have a sort of natural affection for him, as you may well suppose."

"Yes, a sort."

"What do you mean by saying 'a sort' in that kind of way—do you want to insult me?"

"Oh dear no, not I. Perhaps if I was, you'd put me into one of your cells, and say as I was a mad coachman."

"What an idea! Hilloa, how came this Directory open here just at Q."

"Just at Q," said the landlady, "oh! you mean just at Q. That's it. You want to know why it's open just at Q, do you?"

"Yes, I do, but I need not ask. I had my suspicions from the first. I tell you the boy is here, or has been here, and you will find it's all the worse for you if you don't tell me where he is to be found."

"You are a rum 'un," remarked the coachman, "to say that a boy has been here, 'cos you sees a Directory open at Q. What the deuce do you mean by that, I should like to know?"

Before the madhouse-keeper could make any reply, one of the men who assisted in the inn-yard popped his head into the inn-yard, and said,—

"I begs your pardon, missus, but Sam says, as he see'd a boy come in here a little while ago, and as he aint in the coffee-room, and as he hasn't come out, Sam thought as you ought to know, 'cos of the swell mob, you know, missus, and all that 'ere sort of thing."

"Thank you," said the madhouse-keeper, rising, "thank you. You shall have a glass of brandy-and-water at my expense before I go. I'm much obliged to you for your information, I assure you. He is here, then, and no mistake, I will have him, so you had better at once tell me all you have got to say."

"Will any man do that," said the coachman, "for it amounts to nothing at all?"

"Nothing!"

"Not a word, old fellow; what do you think o' that, eh?"

"I shall stand then outside the house, so that evasions shall not save you, and I will set my lawyer to work to see what can be done to make you smart for concealing a boy that I have a right to take back with me when I choose."

The landlady was so alarmed at the loud voice and the threats of the madhouse-keeper, that she sat down upon the chair that was nearest to her, and looked as if she was ready to faint away, but the coachman was of a very different mettle, and he had no opinion of either the courage or the power of a bully."

"Turn him out, ma'm," he said to the landlady. "Turn him out."

"Turn him out, I conldn't do it."

"Try, ma'am, try, it's your house, and you've a right to turn him out, while he has no right to prevent you by resisting at all. Just you lay hold of him, ma'am, by the collar, and don't you leave go till you get him into the street. Now for it, old fellow."

"You had better mind what you are about," said the fellow. "I'll have the law of you, and what's more, when I do find the boy, he shall remember it."

"Oh you limb," said the landlady, "get out."

Encouraged by the coachman, she laid hold of the madhouse-keeper, who raised his hand to strike her, but before he could inflict a blow, the coachman interfered for her defence, as he had fully intended to do. In fact it was quite a little plot of his, to get the madhouse-keeper, as he called it, into such a line, that he (the coachman) could feel himself justified in interfering.

He at once now interposed by laying hold of the nose of the madhouse-keeper, who happened to possess that organ of an unusual length, so that it presented itself rather temptingly to assaults, and so tempting was the clutch which the coachman held upon it, that it seemed to its owner as if it were in a vice.

"So you would strike a woman, would you," exclaimed the knight of the whip. "Oh, you are a pretty rascal, are you, to be sure. Come, get out with you—get out!

The want of real courage is always at the first moment exhibited by those who have shown the greatest disposition to bully, and the man who, but a few moments before, had spoken so largely about what he would do, now suffered himself to be led by the nose to the door, and then and there kicked out.

"Take that," said the coachman, "and you may go and tell your lawyer all about it whenever you like, and see what good he can do you. I don't believe a word you have said while you have been here, you humbug. Be off with you now, and mind you don't show your face here again!"

The coachman did not wait to see what became of his opponent, but walked back quite triumphantly to the little bar-parlour again.

Had he waited he would have noticed that no one had happened at that moment to be in the inn-yard, and that, favoured by the darkness which had now crept over all things, the madhouse keeper did not leave the premises, but crept up one of the staircases leading to the gallery, of which we have before spoken.

What his motive was in so doing, and what he achieved by it, we shall presently soon see.

When the coachman got back to the parlour, he found the landlady quite in a state of agitation, which he did his best to allay, for he had certain notions, with regard to the said landlady, and the old landlord which made him certainly wish to keep on excellent terms with both.

"Don't you make yourself uncomfortable, then," he said; "you may depend upon it that vagabond won't come back here again—he's had a sickener."

"Oh!" said the landlady, "it is at such times as these here that I feel what it is to have lost the dear departed Mr. Barclay."

"Ah!" said the coachman, "when we feels the loss of anything, we ought to try to get a new one."

"What can you allude to?"

"Why, all I was a thinking of was, that if Mr. Barclay had been Mr. Jones, I shouldn't have loved, and you wouldn't have been a *widder*."

"Oh! Mr. J., how can you make such remarks."

"Nothing easier ma'am; now if I hadn't a been here who knows but that fellow might have murdered you, but I can't be here always, you know,—hum—'cos I'm a coachman; but if I was the landlord, I could. What do you say, Mrs. Barclay, to having of me? I've admired you now for a matter o' seven years."

"Hush! Mr. J., you forgot the boy."

"By Jove, so I do—then he won't say nothing about it. I know he's too good a-looking little lad to be hard-hearted. I say, my little chap, come out.'"

The boy, thus admonished, made his appearance; the traces of tears came upon his cheeks, for he had overheard all that had taken place, and he was evidently in a great state of agitation in consequence. He trembled, so that the coachman again suggested his universal remedy of brandy-and-water, but the boy would not be persuaded to drink.

"Well, if you won't you won't," said Mr. Jones; "and this is Liberty Hall, but howsomdever as you is here, you could be a witness you know."

"A witness to what?"

"Why a witness, that Mrs. Barclay here promises to be Mrs. J. in a fortnight."

"Now, really," said the landlady, "what a man you are."

"I should rather think I is, ma'am, and so now that all that's settled, my little chap, I think you cannot do better than tell us, as you know us will be friends to you—what you came to London about, and what you have got to say to Mr. Quentin, if so be as you should find him to-morrow morning, when you go out along o' me, as you shall, on a grand hunt for him."

CHAPTER LXXXVIII.

THE NEW INIQUITY OF GODFREY.—THE LONELY LITTLE CHAMBER.

The lad rather hesitated about making confidants with the coachman and the landlady; and often a little time he seemed to have made up his mind to do as they wished him.

Still however, he kept casting the most uneasy glance, towards the bar, as if he could not thoroughly make up his mind that the mad house-keeper was gone, but expected each moment to see his eyes glaring upon him, and to hear his harsh voice commanding him to return.

"Come," said the coachman, "don't you be afraid of anybody while you are here. He won't interfere with you any more, and if he was to attempt to do so, don't you think that among us all, we should be too many for him? What are you crying at now, eh? Why what a soft-hearted boy you must be."

"Yes," said the landlady, "he is more like a girl in his manners."

"Much more like," said the lad, "for I am a girl."

The coachman let his pipe fall out of his mouth, and upset his brandy-and-water, while the landlady stared with all her eyes, and could hardly persuade herself that she had heard correctly what had been just said.

"A girl, did you say?"

"Yes, madam; I feel that I ought not to keep up any disguise before such kind friends. I am a girl, although you see me in boy's clothes, which I have worn as long as I can remember, in consequence of some reason for my so doing, which my father always said he had, although he never told me what it was."

"My eye!" said the coachman, as he looked at the young stranger, "and so you aint a boy after all. No wonder you wouldn't take the brandy-and-water. Give us a kiss, my dear girl, as a lover."

The coachman kissed her, and made her sit down by him, seeming to be wonderfully amused at the whole affair, and he looked at her as if she had been some curious specimen of natural history, instead of merely a tolerably good-looking young girl, dressed in a suit of boy's clothes.

"You must tell us all about it now, my duck," said the coachman. "Lord love you! do you think I'd let anybody hurt a hair of your head? No! not I. You make yourself easy and comfortable, my darling; and so you are a girl, are you?—Well, I never."

Thus urged and encouraged, the girl commenced accounting for her appearance thus, by saying,—

"I have been for so long a witness to the cruelties in my father's lunatic asylum, that my heart was nearly broken, and I could endure them no more."

'No wonder; but what's your name?'

"Harry—that is to say, I have been always called Harry. I don't know of any other name. I have not been at any time within my recollection called by a female name."

The coachman took out a huge crimson silk handkerchief from his pocket and wiped his eyes, declaring, as he did so, " that he never—no he never did hear of nothing half so affecting in all his blessed life."

"Go on," he said, "go on; never mind me. You go on, Harry, and tell us all about it.'

"I never knew a mother," continued the young creature, " but my earliest recollection goes back to scenes among the mad people and to being beaten by my father."

"Oh, the wagabond! Confound his long nose, but never you mind, my dear, its a little longer now, I'll warrant."

"Go on ; you left off at where you was whopped."

"Yes, before—"

"Before ! Behind, you means."

"I was going to say, before that period, I remembered but little."

"Oh, I thought you *deluded* to the whipping ; I begs your pardon ; go on, and never mind me at all. Drive on, my dear."

"I was often years ago quite made ill by what I saw, and yet it was not till lately, when I found there was a poor woman, who had been a prisoner there for twelve years, and who declared to me that she was not mad, that I made up my my mind to endure it no longer, but to do something to put an end to so much wickedness."

"Right, go on."

"She, this poor prisoner, told me that her name had been Quentin, and that her friends lived in London; and she had been twelve years ago persuaded into a marriage with a Mr. Godfrey, who had no money ; but at his death there was to come to whoever was her heir, a sum of £10,000, and she thinks that that was Godfrey's inducement to marry her."

"Well, but she aint dead?"

"You shall hear all," she said ; "that after she had been married a short time, her husband tried to pursuade her to sell the right to the money, which she could do if he joined in it, as she might leave it to whom she liked ; but she refused, as she had made up her mind, that her child, or children, should have it."

"And quite right, too."

"She then went on to tell me, that one evening, just about two months before she expected to become a mother, she was persuaded to take an airing in a carriage her husband pretended to have purchased for her convenience, and that they drove out of town until the shades of night gathered around them, and she became anxious to return.

"This, however, was objected to by Godfrey, and when she got more clamorous on the subject, she says he silenced her by a blow, and she lay at the bottom of the carriage nearly insensible, until she heard it stop. Then she was lifted out, and when she recovered sufficiently to know where she was, she found she was an inmate of a madhouse."

"Well, I never !" cried the coachman, " your father is a nice article. Go on— drive away."

In vain she implored for her release : she was distinctly told that a good plan had been got up, by which she would be considered by everybody as dead, and that even if now she would sign away the expected money, it would not do, and so for twelve years she has pined in that dismal imprisonment."

"What a dreadful thing," said the landlady, " and what became of his child ?"

She said "she did not know, but that she had had a long and 'severe illness, and they told her it was dead. But I was so touched by the story of her wrongs, that, after in vain asking my father to do justice to her, I made up my mind to come to London, and seek out this family of Quentin and tell them all I know."

"And very right of you—too," said the coachman, " you have done what you ought, my dear, and as you drive through life, that will always be a pleasant reflection to you when you comes to a bad bit of road. You are an out and outer, and no mistake, and before any harm should come to you, I'll gobble up my coach and osses. You make yourself comfortable. I will see in the morning what can be done."

These words, from the coachman, seemed to inspire the young girl with fresh hopes, and she certainly looked more assured than she had done before, and indeed if she had known as much of London as those who afforded her such kindly shelter and assistance knew of it, she might to a still greater extent have thanked her stars for bringing her into such good hands.

Perhaps, at her age, the risks she ran were not so great as they might have been, and then, besides, she was everybody's care, who had the smallest particle of generosity in their dispositions.

We will not think so hardly of the world, as not to suppose that go where she would, a young creature bound upon such an errand as this young girl's would have found sustenance and shelter.

But still it is gratifying to feel a moral certainty that she had fallen across so admirable a friend as the coachman, for certainly he was not one at all likely to desert her.

"And do you mean to tell me," said the landlady, "that for twelve years any poor creature has lived in a cell?"

"It is a lamentable fact, and if you saw how wretched and worn she was, you would easily believe it. Many and many a time I have visited her when no one knew it, and taken her what comforts it was in my power to bestow upon her, and she was so grateful that I have at times awakened in the night and cried myself to sleep again at the recollection of the kind words she had bestowed upon me."

"And she knows," remarked the coachman, "that you have come to London to try to do her a service."

"Oh! yes, yes, she knows that well. I made her the promise, and I thought she would have gone mad indeed with very joy; and then at times as she thought of the danger to which I might be exposed in the enterprise, she would cling to me, and beg me not to undertake it; but I was determined, and so I slipped out by the garden gate, and walked for many miles enquiring my way as I went until tired and travel-worn, I came into the streets of London."

"And do you mean to tell me," said the coachman, "that you walked all the way from Watford without stopping?"

"I did, indeed."

"What, with those little bits of feet—well I never—wonders won't never cease—no how. I say, Mrs. Barclay, I say, mum, what a thing it would be, wouldn't it, in one's blessed old age to have a little'un like this here, wouldn't it?"

"How can you speak in that sort of way, Mr. Jones? I'm quite ashamed of you, and before a young girl too. Come, my dear Harry, since that must be your only name—you shall have something nice for your supper at all events; perhaps I ain't so quick as some folks in taking fancies, but when I am satisfied, I believe I can do the right thing."

"And you think," said the girl, "he will not come again."

"It's not very likely," replied the coachman, "I'm agoing to sleep in the house to-night, and if so be as there's the smallest amount of apprehension, just you call out to me, and I'll soon put it all to rights. I think I see the fellow, curse his impudence, coming here offering £5 for anybody, as if we were such a set of wretches as to give up people for £5—a likely job indeed—oh dear no!"

The landlady was as good as her word, for she had cooked for the young girl who, we must really call Harry, for want of any other designation, a very palate-tickling, and comfortable repast, and then she conducted her to a pretty little chamber where she was to pass the night, saying to her, as she left her,—

"Now, don't fancy that because you'll be lone, and hear no noises, that you're in a lonesome sort of place, for it isn't so, to be sure, nobody sleeps exactly in the next room, but still there's plenty within call in case anything should take place; so make yourself quite comfortable, and good night to you."

"Good night, madam, but I forgot to state, that I hope neither you or Mr. Jones think me guilty of taking money as my father imputed to me."

"How can we think that, for a moment, when you would hardly come into the house 'till you had explained to us you had no money to pay for what you might receive."

"It was so indeed—good night, good night."

CHAPTER LXXXIX.

A NIGHT ADVENTURE AT THE INN.

No wonder that this young girl who had undertaken so arduous a journey in the cause of humanity, felt care-worn and depressed, as she found herself alone in that little chamber at the inn.

Probably she would have lain down to rest with more confidence, if it had not been that she knew her place of refuge was known to him, who, instead of bei g, from the relationship that subsisted between them, her chief protector, was, in reality her greatest enemy.

But so it is, ever as a consequence of criminality, the man who could behave to anyone, as the father of this young girl had behaved to the hapless creature, in whose behalf she had come to London, could scarcely expect the respect or veneration of his children.

Notwithstanding the assurances of her landlady that she was in safety, vague and undefined feelings of apprehension flitted across her imagination, and her first act was to satisfy herself that she was really alone by making a most minute examination of the apartment.

This was quickly done, for it was a very small room ; and she satisfied herself to absolute demonstration that she was its only occupant.

This restored her to some degree of confidence, and yet from some lingering feelings of alarm that she could not entirely suppress, she could not bring herself completely to undress.

Divesting herself then, only of her shoes, and the lad's jacket and waistcoat that she wore, our young acquaintance, whom we must still call Harry, crept beneath the bed clothes, and laying her weary head upon the pillow, began to feel those confused and dream-like impressions which precede deep slumber.

Several times, before actual sleep stole upon her, she started into watchfulness as slight sounds came upon her ear, but finally fatigue conquered all other feelings, and she slept that calm, unbroken sleep which none but the innocent can know.

*   *   *   *   *   *   *

"Well, bless her," said the landlady, as she placed an extinguisher over the flame of the chamber candle she brought down from the room of the young girl— "well, bless her ; she'll at all events have a comfortable night, and much she needs it, after undertaking such a journey on foot."

"Ah, she's a rum'un," said the coachman, eulogistically, "that 'ere girl, Mrs. Barclay, if she grows up to be a woman, will be one of the out and outers of human nature."

"She, certainly, has a noble spirit."

"Yes, Mrs. Barclay, but as for her sleeping comfortably all night, I've got my horrid suspicions as she won't."

"You don't mean that, Mr. Jones,—why shouldn't she?"

"That's just what I should like to find out, but can't. I feels uneasy, Mrs. Barclay, as if something was a going to happen that I don't know nothing about."

"You alarm me."

"I'm alarmed myself, mum ; just let me have another glass of brandy-and-water. I always drinks a *hextra* glass to clear my faculties, when I suspects as anything is going wrong."

The extra was mixed, and between each sip the coachman thought over matters with a very serious aspect, and then at last without at all enlightening, Mrs. Barclay as regarded the result of his cogitations, he merely said,—

"That'll do, ma'm, and now I think I'll go to bed."

"Well, but Mr. Jones," said the landlady, as she handed him a chamber candlestick, " I can't see what harm is to come to the young girl ; she's safe enough here in the little room marked No. 11."

" I hope she is, ma'm, and as for saying what harm shall come to her, I say there shan't come any—a likely thing indeed—oh, dear no! Good night, Mr— good night.   I suppose I'm to go to my old room, No. 8?"

" Yes, Mr. Jones, that's your room ; and I believe it's a room you've had now in this inn almost entirely to yourself for a number of years."

The coachman turned, and winked slowly and solemnly, and then muttering something to himself, about having somebody soon to share it with him, he walked off, carrying with him his great box coat.

This he deposited in his apartment, and then he strutted down into the stable where there was a boy of the name of Ben, stopping the horses' feet, and performing other little offices connected with the menage.

" Well, Ben," said the coachman, " how's the brown mare ?"

" Pretty well, thank you," said Ben, who considered any inquiry about the horses as an implied compliment to himself ; " pretty well, thank you, but the bay 'un is off his feed."

" Indeed, we must see to him to-morrow ; I suppose you've been all alone, as usual, Ben ?"

" Very nigh, sir. I did'nt know there was anybody staying at the place besides you ; there's a lurking fellow though been looking over the banisters of the gallery, and he didn't look over pleased neither."

" Oh, indeed, well it's of no consequence, Ben ; I suppose you sleep in your old loft, and always remember, Ben, that I made a man of you ; didn't I pick you out of the streets, and show you what a horse was, and bring you into 'spectable society, Ben."

" I believe you, Mr. Jones, you did," said Ben, " and I always do say, that if you was to come to me in the middle of the night, and say, Ben, you're wanted, I should jump up and say, ' Here you is.' "

The coachman made no further remark, but walked off to his own apartment, where, strange to say, instead of going to bed, he, too, only took off a portion of his apparel, and propping up before him a large, old-fashioned watch that he always wore, he sat winking and blinking at it, and trying to ward off sleep in the best way he could, although, now and then, the soft influence would creep over him, despite his endeavours to the contrary.

It was half-past ten when he commenced this curious vigil, and he seemed to be determined to keep it up till twelve o'clock, for every now and then he looked at his watch, and said,—

" Well, I never ! how precious slow that hour and a half does go, to be sure !"

Then he would rub his eyes furiously, and wish very devoutly that he had a pinch of snuff.

In this kind of way he did manage to keep himself just on the wakeful side of sleepiness till within a few minutes of twelve, and then he heard sounds indicative of the shutting up of the inn, and he roused himself more than before.

The unequivocal closing of the great gates that led into the outer street convinced him that he was not wrong ; and then he gave himself a great shake, and got up feeling very cold and chilly, and most uncommonly sleepy.

When he began to move about, though, he got the better of this drowsiness, and having snuffed his candle, he began to look more like himself.   There was an expression of curious thought upon his face, which now and then gave way to a sparkling of the eyes, seemingly indicative of some tremendous piece of cunning which he intended to perpetrate within a short space of time.

" It's all right, twelve o'clock, and the place shut up.   Now for it—we'll see what we shall see.   I'm not going to be done by any fellow, be he ever so lanky— not I."

With these valedictory words in his mouth, the coachman left his chamber, which opened almost immediately upon the gallery, and walking slowly along it in the dark

—for he did not carry his candle with him—till he arrived at that point which was nearest to the stables. He tried the latch of a little door that was at his right hand; it yielded readily to his touch, and admitted him into a small, dark room, the floor of which was evidently covered with a quantity of straw, for he felt it rustle under his feet. He paused when he got a short distance, and inclined his head forward to listen.

The regular, and rather tremendous organ like snoring, of some one fast asleep, came upon his ears; and then, advancing a pace or two, he nearly tumbled over a mattress that was laid upon the floor.

"Hist, hist," he said, "Ben—Ben, get up, I want you at once and immediately."

"Here you is," said Ben, in a sleepy voice, "according to promise."

"Get up at once, and follow me, and make as little noise as you can. I'm going to have a game, Master Ben, it'll be as good as a play, and one may as well have a share in it; but make no noise, and be careful."

By this time Ben had thoroughly roused himself, and fully comprehended it was Mr. Jones, his patron, who wanted him to get up; he did so with the greatest possible celerity, and expressed his entire willingness to take part in any adventure that gentleman might dictate to him as desirable and pleasant.

Mr. Jones replied by another injunction to silence, and then led the way slowly along the gallery, till they came to a door which opened into a corridor, from whence several chambers opened right and left. Mr. Jones was quite familiar with all the locality, and probably with an idea of his future mastership of the inn, he had made himself perfect in the knowledge of its plan.

We may well suppose with what wonder Ben followed him, indeed several times he made an attempt to attain information, but was as often checked by the "Hush" of the coachman.

At length the latter paused, and a whispered conference began to the following effect :—

"Ben, there's a young girl sleeping in No. 11, and I want you to slip into her bed."

"Lor!" said Ben, "you don't mean that, Mr. Jones, do you? Don't you think that would be coming it rather strong, sir?"

"But you don't understand me—do you think I meant anything wrong, you rascal? I mean to take her out first, and carry her into mine."

"My eye," said Ben; "that's tidy for a person as doesn't mean to do anything wrong. How can you think of such a thing, Mr. Jones? At your time of life you ought to be ashamed of yourself, too."

"Pho, pho, what a goose you are. I mean you to be in her bed, so that she shouldn't be missed."

"Oh! I know well enough what you mean. Don't you think I'm as green as grass? Bother take you, Mr. Jones; you're to get out of your bed, and get me out of my bed, to put me into a gal's bed, to keep it warm while you put her into your bed. Damn'd if I do it, Mr. Jones."

"I've a good mind to be the death of you, Ben. Ben, she's a mere child."

"More shame for you then, you old sinner."

"Hark ye, Ben, once for all; it's to save this young girl from some one who may make an attack upon her in the night, that I wish to take her away from where she sleeps. The tall, ill-looking fellow you saw looking over the gallery railings wants to take her away, and I want to play a trick upon him."

"Oh! that indeed," said Ben; "come on—I'll do it."

This affair being then sufficiently understood between Ben and the coachman, they proceeded towards No. 11, from beneath the door of which apartment there beamed a faint light, which showed that the young girl had not put out the candle that had been left her. The coachman tried the door, and it yielded to his touch, and then he and Ben walked into that apartment, which certainly was the sanctuary of both innocence and beauty, unalloyed by any of that selfishness which belongs to frail humanity, even under the best circumstances in which it is to be found.

"There," said the coachman, "did you ever see such a little beauty; aint she quite a picture? Only look at her mane—I mean her hair—curling on her blessed bosom."

"Yes, that's all very well, said Ben, "but I've got no breeches on, and its precious cold."

"Lor! so you haven't," said the coachman; "now you'll see how I'll manage."

With this he stooped over the young girl, and before she could sufficiently awaken to know what he was at, he had rolled her up bodily in the bed clothes so that she was completely smothered like an Egyptian mummy, then carrying her in his arms, he strode from the room, saying to Ben as he went,—

"Get into bed at once, Ben, and let me know what happens in the morning."

"Yes," said Ben, "it's all very well to say get into bed, but where's all the blessed clothes gone? Here I'm in a fix. I think what'll happen by morning will be that I shall have caught an out and out cold—damn'd if I can make it out."

CHAPTER XC.

THE HIDING-PLACE.—THE MISTAKE, AND ITS CONSEQUENCES.

So utterly astonished was the young girl at being thus snatched from her bed, and carried along very quickly in the arms of somebody, that she was taken quite as far as the coachman's bedroom before she could find strength enough to speak, so overcome was she with terror and amazement.

"Mercy! mercy—oh, have mercy upon me, and do not kill me," she cried.

"Why, don't you know me? I'm Mr. Jones, the coachman—don't be frightened, my dear; you have only come out of one bed, you know, into another. You make yourself comfortable, and I'll tell you why you've done so in a minute."

Turning down his own bed clothes, he placed her within, rolled up as she was, and it was only at her own urgent remonstrance—for she was nearly smothered, and could neither move hand or foot—that he unrolled the bed-clothes from around her, and allowed her get in, partially attired as she was, to his bed.

He then drew a chair to the side, and proceeded to explain to her why it was he had thought it desirable to remove her from the chamber in which the landlady had placed her.

While this is going on, we will take a glance at another part of the premises.

We have before stated that when the madhouse-keeper was turned out, Mr. Jones, stopped short of seeing her fairly out of the great gates, which he ought to have done; and that, in consequence, the scoundrel had an opportunity, which he embraced, of ascending one of the staircases leading to the gallery.

This step of his may be called quite an impulsive one, for certainly when first he came to the inn, he had not anticipated being turned out by force of arms, and and consequently could not have pre-arranged hiding himself in any part of the premises.

As it was, however, hiding himself now became his first resource, and finding the door leading to the corridor in which the coachman and Ben had held their conference only upon the latch, he opened it, and at once proceeded into every chamber until he came to one which was evidently only used as a lumber room.

In this, then, he really made up his mind to stop, until night should either present to him some opportunity of finding where the young fugitive was hidden or enabling him unobserved to leave the inn, should that, upon consideration, present itself to him as the more prudent alternative.

It was very shortly after this, and when not the smallest vestige of twilight remained, that he ventured out upon the gallery, and was really about to leave, but, seeing Ben, was forced to pass off his appearance as best he could, and upon reconsideration he determined upon another course.

What that course was, we shall best perceive by watching his actions, which will soon develop themselves sufficiently to give us every information.

It happened strangely enough that he was making as violent efforts to keep himself awake, till twelve o'clock, as Mr. Jones, the coachman, but with a very different object in view. Most unlike Mr. Jones, the madhouse-keeper who has not yet favoured us with his name, wanted to commit an iniquity instead of preventing one.

He afforded abundant presumption of his guilt that he should be so very anxious to get possession of the young girl who had undergone what to her were great hardships, in an endeavour to do justice. The room in which he was waiting was almost as cheerless, and uncomfortable a place even in daylight, that could very well be imagined, but at night it was much worse, and, it had from long disuse collected within it a kind of damp, mouldy atmosphere that was really anything but an agreeable addendum to it.

But it is a melancholy fact as regards human nature, that people will undergo much greater inconveniencies in pursuit of their bad intentions than of their good ones, so that the madhouse-keeper waited with tolerable patience until it got nearly twelve o'clock.

He was then about to emerge from his hiding-place when to his great discomfiture, he heard the sound of voices in the corridor, and was afraid of making his appearance lest he should be discovered. Those voices as our readers may well suppose, belonged to Ben and the coachman, who were then holding their brief, but rather expressive little dialogue, which we have duly recorded as having taken place between them, before Harry was removed from the little bed-room to the coachman's rather larger dormitory.

The madhouse-keeper thought, that whoever it was talking, they would never leave off, but at length hearing that all was still, he did venture to peep from his shiding place.

On a previous portion of the evening, he had peeped out, and by such peeping thoroughly satisfied himself that he was not waiting upon a fool's errand, but that the young girl whom he sought, was really in the house, for he saw him taken out of the room by the landlady. Being then well assured that he was on the right scent, and that he had his prey secure, he watched patiently enough, until the time should come, when he might make an attempt to carry him off, with some prospect of complete success.

He was a man more likely to succeed in such a plan than the generality of people, because, he was, from his business, in the habit of encountering ntractable people, and forcing them to do divers things which otherwise they would not have done on any account.

He had provided himself with the means of gagging his victim, and likewise had brought with him one of those ingenious contrivances called straight waistcoats, which if put on with the skill and rapidity he could bring to bear, would at once put an end to all available opposition.

"Surely," he considered, "all this will be sufficient to overcome such a resistance as a young girl can offer."

After then waiting for some time until he felt assured that all was still in the house, and that now or never was the time to commence his enterprise, he slowly and cautiously stole forth from the lumber-room, and crept along towards the door of No. 11.

He had with him the means of procuring an instant light, but he thought that it would be imprudent to avail himself of them until he already got into the chamber, lest the reflection of a flame such as he could produce by the aid of phosphorus matches, should make its way into any other bed-room, than the one he wanted by visit, and so raise an alarm where he least wished it.

To his surprise however, when he did get to the door of No. 11, he found by a faint light that streamed through the key-hole that a candle was burning in the apartment, so that he would have no trouble on the score of seeing.

All was profoundly still, and, with a grin upon his ugly countenance, he cautiously tried the door, and found that it opened at once beneath his touch.

"All's right," he muttered, "all's right. Now my young lady, I'll teach you to steal such a watch upon me another time. The moment I get you back to the Benevolent Asylum, you shall be placed under lock and key, and it will be one while before you see daylight again.

With these kindly expressed intentions regarding the young girl who was safe and snug in the chamber of the coachman, the madhouse-keeper stepped inside the room, and closed the door behind him. There was certainly a very dim light burning, for the candle, although still alight, was untrimmed, and sent forth but a very sickly lustre. Moreover it was so placed that it threw the bed very much into shadow.

So softly did he tread that his footsteps would hardly have disturbed a mouse, and more than once he smiled to himself as if quite pleased with the vast amount of his own cleverness. For this reason he advanced towards the bed, and he was certainly, when he reached it, rather surprised, to find that its occupant had chosen to have the feather bed above and to sleep upon the mattress.

"A strange whim," he muttered, " this. She was cold I suppose after the fatigue of her journey. It wouldn't be a bad plan to tie her feet together, just by the ankles first. But perhaps the gag is the best thing after all, and we will try it at all events."

Taking from his pocket a rather curiously shaped little iron instrument, defended here and there by pieces of leather, he approached the sleeper, and leant over him. The moment however he touched the face, up sprung Ben, with a shout that so astounded the man, as to render him incapable, for a moment or two, of speech or motion. During that time Ben gave him two or three hard knocks on the face, calling for help all the while.

The madhouse-keeper on the whole, however, was a man about as accustomed to surprises as could have been found, and discovering that he had made a mistake, he felt that to make his escape was the only course open to him.

Dealing, then, several random blows at Ben, he darted from the room, and, running down the corridor, made his way into the gallery. When there, he found that the cries of the party whom he had mistaken so sadly, as he thought, for the young girl he wished to take away with him, had created an universal alarm. A rattle was sprung in the yard by somebody, and then the night-watchman ran up the stairs leading to the gallery.

It was high time for the madhouse-keeper to look after his own safety. The height of the gallery from the ground was not more than sixteen feet, and he was a tall man, so that if he hung by the length of his arms he knew he should not have a long distance to drop.

There was no time to lose, so raising himself over the gallery balustrade, he hung down as low as he could, and then, while the watchman was above, he dropped down into the inn yard, from which there was no difficulty in making an escape, inasmuch as there was a small door in the large gate, which was only secured by a latch and a bolt inside.

In another moment the madhouse-keeper was free, and putting on good speed, for fear of pursuit, he soon placed a good mile between him and the inn.

In the meantime Ben, who really had just before the attack was made upon him dropped into a light slumber, was quite sufficiently alarmed to make a tolerable disturbance, so that in the course of five minutes everybody in the inn was thoroughly awakened, and there was such a flashing of lights and banging of doors, as never had been heard in the place within the memory of the oldest inhabitant, all of which was very amusing to the coachman, who was keeping watch and ward over his *protege*, and not a little congratulating himself as he heard the tumult upon the success of his plan.

CHAPTER XCI.

THE JOURNEY IN SECRET OF MR. QUENTIN.—THE CHARGE AGAINST GODFREY.

THE coachman was not a little delighted to hear the sounds of riot and confusion in the inn, because these sounds were sufficient to convince him that he had made no error of judgment, in supposing that the madhouse-keeper would make an attack upon the young girl's chamber.

He chuckled amazingly as he pictured to himself an interview between Ben and the man, who expected to find so different a customer.

As for the young girl, whom we must still call Harry, for want of another name, she soon understood all the peril which she had been rescued from, and was quite as thankful for that rescue as the coachman could possibly desire her to be.

He sat down by the foot of the bed, and there they talked as if they had been quite old acquaintances, and had known each other, as the coachman himself observed, since they were " babies."

Of course, among the other persons who were disturbed by the outcries of Ben, Mrs. Barclay may be numbered, and that good lady's first impression was that the house was on fire, so she sprung a rattle, which she always kept in her bedroom, very violently from her window, and added not a little to the general noise by that ingenious contrivance.

The door in the large gate being left swinging open by the madhouse-keeper on his exit, was quite sufficient to convince every one that he had left the premises, and as pursuit would, of course, be useless, from the total absence of all knowledge as to which way he had gone, it was not attempted, and in the course of about half an hour the inn was restored to its ordinary tranquillity.

But still Miss Harry was too much alarmed to return again to her own bedroom, and Mrs. Barclay accordingly accommodated her with a share of her couch for the remainder of the night. Ben returned to his own bed in the loft, and the coachman, chuckling amazingly to himself at the highly successful manner in which he considered he had managed the whole affair, retired to rest on perfectly good terms with himself.

The love of gossip must surely be an inherent principle in human nature, for certain it is, notwithstanding their alarm and disturbance on the preceding evening, the whole household of the inn rose considerably earlier next morning than usual, solely because they wished to compare notes concerning the last night's adventure, and each to start his or her conjecture respecting it. And the coachman and Mrs. Barclay were no exceptions to this general rule, for they met in the bar parlour along with Miss Harry a good half hour before the usual time.

The young girl looked considerably refreshed by her night's rest, and really looked so good and loveable that the coachman insisted upon giving her sundry kisses, each of which made a report almost equal to the sound of a cart whip; then addressing himself to Mrs. Barclay, he said, " I've been thinking, mum, what I'll do this morning."

" Very well, Mr. Jones; but whatever you do, I won't have any more kissing of this young girl; don't you see that you've made the side of her face quite red already."

" I wasn't a thinking of any more kissing, mum; it's Mr. Squinting as was engaging of my thoughts."

" Quentin—Quentin," said Harry; " you mean Quentin."

" To be sure, I does; I wonder what made me call him Squinting ? and what I was going to say is just this here, that I'll go with you and try and find out where the proper Mr. Quentin lives, and when we do find him, I shall just speak up my mind, and say to him, Mr. Squinting——"

" Pray call him Quentin," said Harry.

" Lor, what am I thinking of? Quentin, to be sure, is his name, and no mistake; well, then, what I am going to say is this, that after breakfast,—I'll take another cup of tea if you please, Mrs. Barclay—after breakfast we'll have a fly, and go and see all those Quentins as is put down in the Directory till we find the right one."

" A fly," said Miss Harry, in surprise, for she never heard glass coaches called flies."

" Yes, my dear : don't you know what a fly is? It,s a glass coach, but your thinking it's a regular fly puts me in mind of a Frenchman as was writing something about England, and he said as they were so particular on the Parade, at Brighton, that there was a board up, to signify that the magistrates would not allow more than three *flies* to stand there at one time."

Miss Harry laughed as well as she could, for her heart was ill at ease ; and she was well pleased when the coachman rose to go.

" I do sincerely hope," she said, " that we shall find the right Mr. Quentin. Oh ! if you had seen the look of hopeful joy upon the countenance of the poor prisoner, when I told her that I would go upon her errand of mercy, you would never have forgotten it. Twelve years of grief and confinement have worn her almost to a skeleton; her voice is so thin and weak, that you can hardly hear it; and I do not think she will live long unless she be released."

"Don't say no more about it," cried the coachman; "if Mr. Quentin is above ground, we'll find him out; you may depend upon that."

They went away with the good wishes of the landlady, and they took the Directory with them; so that there should be no mistake about the places they had to call at. It was rather a sad disappointment to find that the first Mr. Quentin they had called upon had removed; that the second was not named Quentin at all, but *Quilting*, he having been put down Quentin by mistake in the Directory; the third direction they went to was upon the suburbs of London; it was a quiet, pretty cottage sort of place, and the young girl's heart beat high with hope, as it were, at an acknowledgment that a Mr. Quentin did live there.

"But he's very unwell," said the servant, who had replied to the ring at the garden-gate—"he's very unwell indeed, and I don't think he can see anybody."

"We must see him;" said the young girl, "it's upon a matter of the first importance; is he old?"

"Well, I'm sure, young gentleman, you're very curious to know all about him, but, if you must know, he is old, and you will be old yourself some day."

"Come, come," said the coachman, "just put a snaffle rein on your tongue; we don't want none of your imperance; we comes to see Mr. Squinting, and Mr. Squinting we will see."

"Hush, hush, there is no offence," said the young girl; "we should recollect, Mr. Jones, that we are perfect strangers here, but we really have business of importance with Mr. Quentin; we bring him information which, if he be ever so bad, will certainly make him better to hear."

"I don't think," said the servant, "that anything will make him better; he has never been himself, poor old gentleman, since the loss of his daughter."

"His daughter! his daughter!" exclaimed Miss Harry. "Oh! I'm so glad to hear that."

"Are ye, ye little viper?"

Yes, yes; but not from any bad motive. But can you tell me what was his daughter's name?"

"Why, of course: her name was Miss Quentin, until she married Mr. Godfrey."

"We are right, we are right. I must see Mr. Quentin; introduce me to him at once; I have that to tell him which would rouse him up, were he at the gate of death—let me see him, I implore you."

The servant was really here terrified at the vehemence with which the young girl spoke, and she retreated within the house, closely followed by Miss Harry, who kept reiterating her request to see Mr. Quentin, and in the midst of all this, a bell was rung violently, which the servant said was his bell; and, promising to mention to him that somebody wanted to see him, she hurried off to attend the summons.

"We are right," said Miss Harry, with the tears standing in her eyes,—"we are right at last, and perhaps shall really have the happiness of restoring to poor old Mr. Quentin his long lost daughter. Oh! how little do I regret the fatigue and the terror that I have gone through."

"Lor!" said the coachman, "I feel all of a heap—hark! here's somebody acoming."

The servant returned to say that Mr. Quentin was very unwell, but that if it was anything of very great importance he would see the party.

"It is, it is!" said the young girl, "of the very first importance. Lead me to him—lead me to him at once. I long to tell him that which will take a load of grief from off his heart. Come, Mr. Jones, come. I wish you to be present at the interview. Oh! this will be a day of heavy accusation against somebody."

"Drive on," said the coachman, "I'm acoming. Which way are we to go, young woman, up these here blessed stairs? Oh! thank you, I see there's a banister on the off side. Now for it; I suppose there'll be never sich a row."

Mr. Quentin's servant had not mentioned the fact that along with the young lad who waited to see him, there was a great fat man, so that that gentleman might well be supposed to be taken by surprise.

The room into which they were ushered was a dark one, although spacious; there was a bed in one corner of it, and a very dim sort of light was let in through the crevices of a Venetian blind. In a large easy chair, drawn up close to the fire, was an elderly man, with a silk nightcap upon his head, and attired in a very large brocade dressing gown.

He certainly looked at the visitors as they appeared, but it was not with any great degree of interest; in fact he had all the manners and appearance of one from whom this world and its affairs were gently but surely gliding away.

He looked up, and his eyes rested upon the form of the young girl. She sprang towards him, and, taking his hand, exclaimed,—

"Sir—sir! I bring you news—good news of your lost child."

The old man uttered a deep groan, lifted up his hands, and fainted away.

Miss Harry was inexpressibly alarmed, and the coachman looked on with his mouth and eyes wide open, evidently in a state of the most intense surprise and interest.

"Oh! his fainting is nothing," said the servant; "he does so sometimes ten times a day."

"Are you sure he is not dead?"

"Oh! you'll soon see that."

She took a small phial from the mantelshelf, and opened the old man's mouth very cleverly, by giving him rather a smart knock upon the chin: she poured a a little of the contents down his throat. The effect was almost instantaneous; he drew a long breath, and looked about him like a man awakened from a dream.

"Where am I," he said, "and what has happened,—did any one mention my daughter?"

"Yes, I did," said the young girl, who had gathered more caution, and was now not so disposed to speak to the old man in the hurried manner she had formerly done. "I did, Mr. Quentin, and if it is not too much trouble to you, or too much pain, I wish you to tell me how it is that you lost her."

"How very, very strange this is!" said old Mr. Quentin; "come hither and let me look at you—tell me, boy, for God's sake, tell me, where you got those features and that voice? But no—no, all that must be a dream—a mere vision. I know not what impels me to speak to you, but I will tell you how I lost her."

"Well, I'm blessed if it isn't better than a play!" said the coachman.

"Eh," said the servant, "what did you say, sir?"

"I said you lived in a nice airy situation, that's all, and an uncommon comfortabl bedroom this is."

"Why, we keep it as comfortable as we can, of course, for old Mr. Quentin; it' always clean and neat, as you see it now."

"So I should say. No fleas or bugs, I suppose?"

"Good gracious!"

"You shall hear," said Mr. Quentin, "you shall hear. My daughter wa entitled to leave £1,000 to whom she liked; that sum was to be paid at her deatl and, much against my will, she married a Mr. Godfrey, a bad man—a very ba man. I pressed her to make a will, disposing of the £1,000, but she always refuse to do so, for fear she should have a child to whom she could leave it.

"Yes, yes—go on, sir, go on."

"I knew that there had been misunderstandings between her and Godfr regarding this money, but one day he came to me with all the appearance of dee grief, and told a singular story. He said that they had taken a long walk dow to Hammersmith and some distance beyond; and that getting tired, and findi no other conveyance ready, he being tolerably well skilled in rowing, they h hired a boat in order to get pleasantly and quickly up to Westminster: he th said that they had fouled one of the bridges, that the boat upset, that his wife daughter was carried away by the current, and he himself got to shore with t greatest possible difficulty. I would say nothing to him, but set every inquiry foot for the purpose of testing the truth of the story, and I did ascertain that he had with a woman embarked on the Thames, and that he had been picked up himself from the water. It was in vain that the most active search was made, and the highest rewards offered for the recovery of my daughter's body; it was never found from that day to this, and I am a miserable man. I've held no communication with Godfrey, for I look upon him as little less than my daughter's, murderer and I desire to hear nothing of him, so that if your speech be of him, boy—go at once—go at once."

The old man now took such a violent fit of trembling, that it was quite impossible to say anything to him with effect; and his servant was forced to administer to him a cordial for the purpose of recovering him.

CHAPTER XCII.

THE ATTACK UPON THE MADHOUSE, AND ITS RESULT.

MISS HARRY waited until the old man had completely recovered before she commenced relating to him that which she had come so far to tell him, and then upon his assurance that he would listen to her with composure, she told him the sad tale of the alleged lunatic in her father's madhouse. It would be quite impossible for any pen to do justice to the world of emotion which displayed itself in old Mr. Quentin's manner when he heard this narration, it was with the greatest difficulty he could restrain his feelings at all within bounds, and when the singular story was concluded, he exclaimed in a loud voice,—

"Oh, Heaven! can this be possible?—do but convince me that this is not a dream! speak to me, boy again and tell me that you are really my good genius."

"Yes," cried the coachman, "and what's more this little boy turns up to be a girl."

"A girl,' cried old Mr. Quentin, "can it be possible that there is so much heroism to be found in one so young?"

"It's true sir—that's a wery good word for it, though I don't understand it: she's an out-and ou-theroine, as you say."

"Come to my arms, and let me tell you that in restoring me my own child, you have likewise made yourself so dear to me that I shall consider you a second daughter; Heaven's blessings on you. Here Martha, Martha, order Thomas to get out the chaise."

"Lor, master, what for?"

"Am I not going to bring home my daughter?"

"You, master? why you've not been out of the house these ten weeks."

"The more need then that I should go now—quick, quick."

"What is it, sir, that you intend to do," said the young girl; "be careful, let me implore you; the house is well guarded, and without a sufficient force, it will be impossible to force an entrance."

"Stop a bit," said the coachman, "afore you drives any further, just let's see what these papers is all about."

"Papers, papers," cried Mr. Quentin, "what papers do you mean?"

"Why, everything was in such a hurry skurry at the time, that I forgot 'em till just now; but the fact is just before I came away, Ben comes up to me, and he says, I say, Mr. Jones, while that ere fellow was atrying to pull me out of bed, I should say he must have dropped these' ere papers, for they aint none of mine, and as I wasn't never never brought up to be a scollard, I don't know nothing about 'em."

"Let me see—let me see, what have we here? A letter ready for sealing and addressed to Mr. Green, solicitor; what does it contain? I shall make bold to read this epistle."

"DEAR GREEN—Meet me at our old place as soon as possible this evening. I have come up to town upon a disagreeable errand, for the fact is the young girl who has been humbugged so long into believing herself my daughter, but who is as you know Mrs. Godfrey's child, has taken herself off; there's no knowing what mischief may come of it, so we must meet and talk it over.   Yours, &c.

JOHN DAVIS.

No sooner had these words fallen from the lips of old Mr. Quentin than with a positive shriek of joy, the young girl flung herself into his arms.

The silence that ensued was more eloquent than any words could possibly have been, the old man's tears fell like rain upon the head of his grandchild, and when he did speak, all he could say was,—

"Oh, how I am repaid, oh, how I am repaid!"

"I say," said the coachman to the servant, "doesn't you think as this is gallows affecting?"

"It only shows," said the servant, "the inscrutable ways of Providence, that it does."

"Screw what, screw a table with Providence, what do you mean by that, young woman? I say, Mr. Quentin, my advice is just this here: that we all go to that ere madhouse four-in-hand, and begin at the roof, and regularly take off all the bricks, and let out everybody. Come on at once, and I'm your man; just let me come across that fellow again with the long nose; the idea of such a wretch as that pretending to be anybody's father, but a pigs, it's enough to make anybody swear, that it is."

"There is a magistrate resides immediately in this neighbourhood," said Mr. Quentin. "I will seek his assistance at once. Martha run off to Mr. Lewis's, and give my compliments, and say that I'll be there myself in about a quarter of an hour—for I want to see him upon business of the first importance. We will go armed with a warrant, so that we dare not be resisted in that which we shall attempt to do. Put on your bonnet, girl, and go at once."

Thus arranged, Martha immediately left the room to carry out her master's instructions, and it was wonderful what a new life seemed to have been given to Mr. Quentin by the circumstance that had taken place. He was quite a different looking being to what he had been, and without any assistance he took off his great brocade dressing gown, and put on a coat.

He seemed to be never tired of embraces and showering kisses upon his newly found grandchild; and one can easily imagine, with her feelings and opinions, what must have been her joy at finding herself free from the reproach of being the daughter of a man whom she could not but despise, and with whom she had not one feeling or principle in common.

The dread thought of her poor mother's situation could scarcely banish the joy which showed itself in her beaming countenance.

By the time Martha returned to say that Mr. Lewis, the magistrate, was within, they were all ready for the journey, and Mr. Quentin's phaeton, which would hold four, was at the garden gate.

We need not procrastinate matters by relating what passed at the magistrate's; but suffice it to say, that upon the sworn information of her whom, we regret to be forced to call Miss Godfrey, he granted a warrant, and sent two strong constables with the little party to execute it.

With this addition, it was hoped that the attack upon the madhouse must be successful, for although it certainly was possible enough that the parties interested in keeping up that nefarious establishment might be in greater force, there was something about the majesty of the law which certainly had a right to be looked to as an assistance in the matter.

And it is most true, strange as it may appear, that such is the habitual regard for authority in this country—the mere production of a constable's staff, in weak hands, is sufficient to overcome by moral force an amount of physical resistance, which, under other circumstances, certainly would not succumb.

It might therefore be fairly concluded that the two constables, Mr. Quentin, and the coachman, backed by the magistrate's warrant, formed a strong party, which it would be difficult indeed to resist.

The worst of the matter was, that Mr. Quentin's little phaeton would not hold them all, and consequently they had to go by detachments.

This they managed though pretty well, for the officers contrived to get upon a stage coach, and although Mr. Quentin did not drive quite so fast as the public vehicle went, he was not very far behind it, and the officers agreed that they would wait in the road when they got to Watford until he came up.

After Mr. Quentin had got some distance, Mr. Jones touched him on the arm, and spoke to him, saying,—

"If you please, sir, as we're going to a madhouse, if you goes on a doing what you're doing, you may as well leave me there."

"What do you mean by that? Are you a candidate for a lunatic's cell?"

"No, sir—I isn't in an ordinary way; but if anything more than another is likely to drive me out of my senses, it certainly is somebody driving, and doing it all wrong. You'll excuse me, Mr. Squinting, but I never seed sich a muff in all my born days—do you call that driving?"

"Well, my friend," said Mr. Quentin, good humouredly, "if you would be so good as to drive, and leave me to talk to my newly-found grandchild, I shall be really much obliged, and not at all offended."

"Thank you, sir," said the coachman, as he seized with alacrity the reins and the whip; "thank you, sir—one of the horridest things in the world is being drove by anybody. You'll excuse me, sir, for calling you a muff—'cos it was true; but you aint more of a muff than lots of other people, who have no more notion of driving than a cat has of eating perriwinkles."

As Mr. Quentin had observed, he was not averse to the arrangement of letting Mr. Jones sit upon the driver's seat, and taking all the responsibility of getting the pony along, inasmuch as it left him ample leisure to talk to Miss Harry.

"My dear child," said the old man, "have you no feminine name by which I can address you?"

"No," she said. "I've been always called Harry, because, I suppose, I was always dressed in boy's clothes, and therefore it was thought necessary to give me a boy's name."

"I can well understand the disgraceful plot, from the working of which both you and I and your poor mother have so long suffered. Godfrey must have dreaded the risk of putting her to death, and so dooming her, through the agency of the man whom you have been led to believe was your father, to a confinement, which it was no doubt hoped and expected would soon terminate her existence."

"Alas! grandfather it must have been so; but answer me one question, and make me one promise."

"Speak—speak freely, my dear child, and anything in the world that I can promise you, or do for you, you can look upon as already accomplished."

"What I wish to ask is, does my—does Godfrey live?"

"I do not wonder at your hesitation to call him by the name of father, for he does not deserve that title at your hands, and if that is the question you so particularly wish to ask of me, I grieve to say that he does live."

"Then, grandfather, let me come to the promise I wish to exact from you, which is that you will keep my existence a secret from him, so that I may never look upon him nor he upon me."

"Be quite easy upon that head, my dear child; I will take especial care that you shall never encounter him, and from what I have heard last of him, he is not in a condition himself to take any steps by which he can be an annoyance to you. I have heard that he is not long for this world, for that some great amount of retribution has overtaken him in consequence of his bad conduct to a family of the name of Whitehead. I am not well acquainted with the particulars, but I can very easily imagine that Godfrey has executed some piece of villany which has met with its proper reward."

"Heaven have mercy upon him," said the young girl; "I grieve that he is my father, and only have to hope that let whatever may be his fate, he will by a repentance of the evil he has done escape the vengeance of Heaven."

"My dear," said Mr. Quentin, "there is no vengeance in Heaven : it is a bad word, for Heaven is only just, not vengeful ; but see, the coach stops to put down a passenger, and I think, after all, we shall not be far behind-hand with the officers."

In such like conversation as this, they passed the greater part of the road; but it was evident as they neared Watford, that old Mr. Quentin was getting very agitated, so much so, indeed, that his granddaughter feared he would never be able to go through the scene which would too surely await them.

Having seen him faint, likewise, once at his own house, she had a great dread that he would do so again, when the official assistance that was there rendered to him would not be at hand; but happily this did not occur, and when they came near the outskirts of Watford, they saw the two officers standing in the road-way waiting for them.

"My dear," said Mr. Quentin, before Mr. Jones drew up, "I must have some name to call you by, for I don't like Harry at all."

"Let my name, then, be the same as my poor mother's, whatever that was."

"Do not say was, for it sounds as if she were no more, her name is Agnes, and that I will call you ; it is a name endeared to my recollection, and one which has ever been enshrined in the inmost recesses of my heart."

Since Mr. Quentin has thought proper to give a name to her whom we have called Harry hitherto, we will adopt it, and say at once, that Agnes directed now that they should take their course down a lane on the right hand side of the road just before they entered the town of Watford.

"The asylum," she said, "is situated one mile down this lane, in a very lonely spot, and if we can get round to it, by the back entrance, to which I can show you the way, perhaps we shall succeed in getting in, without giving an alarm."

Mr. Jones reduced the pony's pace to a walk, so that the officers strode along by the side of the little vehicle, while old Mr. Quentin's agitation grew each moment more and more observable, and a greater amount of alarm for Agnes.

CHAPTER XCIII.

THE RESCUE, AND THE SECRETS OF THE MADHOUSE.

"I MUCH fear," said Mr. Quentin, "if I may take my present feelings as an index of what they are, that I shall be far too agitated to take any part effectively in this enterprise."

"That is what I have been thinking, grandfather," said Agnes, "and therefore would it not be much better for you to remain outside while we go to carry on the enterprise ? You know it will be necessary for some one to take care of the pony."

"Yes," remarked one of the officers, upon hearing these words, "and we are not in such force as to spare any of our efficient members for that duty. I should strongly recommend you, sir, to remain where you are ; and you may make up your mind that every thing that can be done will be done, but it will be a very awkward thing, indeed, when we get inside, to have you upon our hands as well."

Mr. Quentin did not seem to like the idea of abandoning the enterprise himself, but he was not so unreasonable as not, at all events, to see the full force of the arguments that were used to persuade him not to make one actually of the party.

"My judgment consents," he said, "if not my will ; and all I have to implore of you is to consider that I shall be enduring the greatest possible suspense, so I charge you to accomplish your object as quickly as you can."

"Oh, you may depend," said the other officer, " that we are never longer over our work than absolutely necessary : we shall get over it in a very short time — you keep yourself easy."

"But if you should fail ?"

"Fail ! oh, we never think of that ; we've got something to do, and do it we must ; it's no part of our business to fail."

"I am rejoiced to hear you talk so hopefully, and shall wait with better patience."

No doubt the old man would have liked Agnes to remain with him, but he did not hint at such a thing, because he knew how useful she would be to Mr. Jones and the officers as a guide through the house, of which they must necessarily be in ignorance. He therefore kept his seat in the little pony chaise, and although he looked after them with wistful eyes, his reason told him how much better it was that that arrangement should be maintained rather than broken.

But however great may be our sympathy with Mr. Quentin, we must leave that gentleman to his own thoughts, painful and anxious as they unquestionably were, while we follow his friends in their certainly somewhat hazardous enterprise.

The madhouse was pretty well protected from without; there was a brick wall of considerable height, and, at many places, where it would seem in consequence of the contiguity of trees, there might be a possibility of scaling it, some very ugly spiked railings were set up, which looked as if they would revolve upon the slightest touch, and so precipitate to the ground any one who might be confident enough to trust to their support.

Young Agnes led them on till they came to a door in the wall, which from the closeness with which it was shut, and the manner in which some ivy grew over the crevices, had evidently not been opened for a great number of years.

"This door," she said, "has never been opened in my recollection; it is firmly secured within, and seems always to have been considered as a portion of the very wall itself. I know, however, from personal observation, that although its bolts and bars are tolerably strong, and would resist any attempt to break them, the hinges are quite rotten; and, therefore, from that side I think the door may be forced.

"A very good idea, miss," said the officer; "it's a great pity you aint a boy in earnest, instead of a make-believe one. We shall soon find out what we can do with this door; I suppose it opens into some sort of a garden."

"Not exactly; but into a paved yard adjoining a kitchen, where there is a woman, who will give an instant alarm if she be not secured."

"Oh, we'll manage the kitchen then,—let us once get in, that's all."

The officers consulted together for two or three seconds, and then they produced from their pockets some housebreaking implements, which in the course of their vocations had come into their possession, and in the use of which they appeared quite at well skilled as probably the disturbers of the public peace from whom they had captured them.

One of these was a small steel instrument, which they inserted very skilfully between the door and the doorpost close to one of the hinges, and that by turning a screw a crackling noise succeeded, and the officer said,—

"The hinge is rotten, for it's going to pieces; there, it's off now; and we shall get such a leverage that we shall be able to pull the door outwards directly."

They were certainly slower in their operations than they would have been, but that in the first stage, they considered caution absolutely necessary; for although they knew they must come into collision eventually with the keepers of the establishment, they wished to effect an entrance fairly into the premises before they did so,—for if they were kept out while any parleying was going on, probably some means would have been devised effectually to conceal from their observation the unhappy prisoner they had come to rescue.

The officer who had used the housebreakers' implements was handing them to his companion, and then, taking a tolerably powerful but small crow bar in his hands, he succeeded in wrenching the door open sufficiently to get a good grasp of it; and then the powerful leverage of its whole length and weight, acting against the bolts, fairly wrenched them from their holds, while the bar that was across the door on the inner side was no impediment, because it simply went from one doorpost to another.

Thus, then, without much noise, and evidently without creating the least alarm, they were within the premises; at that moment, however, and just as one of the officers was about to make some remark, a loud bell began tolling, and it struck them immediately that it was to give an alarm, but Agnes told them otherwise.

"It is the keeper's dinner bell," she said, "and that is a favourable circumstance, because they will all be assembled together in one room."

"Capital," said the officer; "lead us to that room at once."

By Agnes' advice, however, they waited a little while, so as to give due time for the keepers to assemble,—of whom Agnes said there were eight.

The officers did not appear to be alarmed at encountering such superior numbers; but, on the contrary, after waiting a sufficient time, until it could be reasonably supposed the keepers were assembled, they walked on, accompanied by Mr. Jones, and preceded by the young girl, who looked very pale but very determined.

It was absolutely necessary they should go through the kitchen; and when they got to a glass door, through which there was a view of that culinary apartment, she placed her finger on her lips, and pointed to them to look in.

They did so, and saw a powerful looking woman, whose back was towards them, pouring some boiled liquid out of a saucepan.

The foremost officer made his way into the kitchen at once; and, laying his hand with a forcible grasp upon the shoulder of the woman, said,—

"Well, cook, how do you find yourself to-day? We mean to blow your brains out, if you make the slightest noise."

The cook was so astonished for the moment that she remained transfixed in the same attitude; but then, recovering herself, she swung round with the saucepan in her hand, and fully intended to discharge the whole of the boiling contents over the officer; but in this benevolent design she was frustrated, for he stooped, and the scalding cataract went over his head, falling full in the face of one of the establishment, who happened to be coming into the kitchen at that moment through an opposite door.

This was a man; and he gave such a yell of pain that any farther concealment that something was amiss was out of the question,—so leaving him and the cook to fight it out between them, which they began to do most heartily, the officers followed Agnes rapidly through some winding passages, until they arrived at a very large vacant apartment.

"In the next room," she said, "are assembled those whom we seek."

"Very good," said Mr. Jones; "let's drive on."

The officers needed no stimulating, for they went about the business as a matter of course. A door was flung open, and they marched into a room where at a very well spread table they sure enough found seven of the establishment, the eighth having gone into the kitchen on some message, and being he who had, unfortunately for himself, but not at all to our regret we must confess, received the scalding contents of the cook's saucepan.

Consternation and astonishment were depicted upon every countenance; and then, before any remark could be made, one of the officers spoke, saying,—

"Is the master of the house at home?"

"Why, how came you here? He's not at home; what do you want here? Are you thieves!"

"No, we're officers; here's my staff, and there's my warrant; we come to search this house for one Agnes Godfrey."

"Oh! this sort of thing won't do here," said one of the men; "we can't give up any of our patients, and we won't."

These words were scarcely passed the man's lips, when the officer sprang upon him with a suddenness and a force that set resistance at defiance, so that he was flung to the floor in a moment, and then, with a dexterity that could only have been acquired by very long practice, a pair of handcuffs were clapped upon him, and he was certainly for the time *hors de combat.*

"Has anybody else any objection?" said the officer, "because we are well provided with these little articles."

The keepers were evidently stout, powerful men, but it was astonishing what an effect this bold and initiative conduct had upon them; they were evidently thoroughly conquered, and although still numerically superior to the little party opposed to them, the success of the officers was no longer doubtful.

"Hark you, my men," said he, who assumed to be the spokesman, "as your master is in town, your wisest plan is to let this affair take its course quietly. You cannot and must not resist the law ; so one or two of you come at once and show us where the party is we seek."

"We don't want to resist the law," said one of them ; "our master isn't here."

"Let me out of these handcuffs;" said the one who had been knocked down ; "and I'll soon show you the man you want ; but there's Master Harry, he knows all about it and can take you over the place as well as we can."

"Very likely ; but we prefer you, and to show you that we are not at all afraid of you, I'll take the handcuffs off you on your promise to be quiet."

This was accordingly done, and two of the dinner party left the room with the officers to conduct them to the cell of the unhappy being who had been so long separated from all the comforts of existence, and who it was surprising had contrived to drag on so long and miserable an existence, under such dreary and calamitous circumstances.

Agnes did indeed know the way well, and preceded the man along some narrow and dingy-looking passages where here and there in a niche in the wall, there was a light burning ; there was heard the clank of chains and now and then a loud shriek burst upon their ears, coming from the lips of some poor wretch who had bid adieu to reason for ever.

As they proceeded, poor Agnes grew more and more agitated, and when finally they paused at a small door, she was so deeply affected at the thought, it was her mother she came to rescue, that she could scarcely support herself.

One of the keepers produced a bunch of heavy keys, and selecting one from among the number, he fitted it to the lock,—the rusty wards grated back with a harsh sound, the door yielded, and the cell was opened.

CHAPTER XCIV.

THE AFFECTING MEETING.—THE ATTEMPTED MURDER.

AGNES was the first to rush into that lonely place ; her heart was too full for words, and she could only fling herself upon the straw couch where she knew rested that being towards whom without knowing the closeness of relationship that existed between them, she had ever felt the tenderest sympathy.

The place was very dark, and one of the keepers entered for the purpose of removing a shutter which was placed across a grating, and when he did so remove it, a stream of light came into the cell, and Agnes found words to say,—.

"Success ! success !—you are rescued—you are rescued—you are rescued. Mother, mother you are saved."

There was no response, and when one of the officers stepped forward and looked upon the couch, he said,—

"The poor creature is dead !"

It was too true,—the victim was no more; but, by the expression of the face even in death, it would seem as if she had just lived to hear the gladsome tidings of liberty ere her spirit had winged its flight to those realms where there can be no tyranny, and no oppression.

The grief of poor Agnes was overwhelming, and it was with the greatest difficulty that the officers could get her from the cell, seeing that she clung with all the frantic efforts of despair to the senseless form of that being whom she had hoped to have welcomed to the world by the endearing name of mother.

This circumstance, untoward as it was and totally unexpected, placed the officers in an awkward predicament, for they certainly knew not exactly what to do ; one of them certainly hinted the propriety of taking everybody into custody in the place; but then it was a very awkward thing to do so, inasmuch as the really insane patients required attendance.

After some consultation then it was determined to wait until the madhouse-keeper himself came home, and at all events walk him off to durance vile.

The cell was closed again upon the lifeless remains of Mrs. Godfrey, and Agnes professed her intention of going to her grandfather for the purpose of informing him of the catastrophe that had occurred.

There did not seem to be any likelihood of danger to the young girl, as the officers allowed her to go alone, as she was of course familiar with the place, and with a saddened heart, she walked towards the door in the wall, a short distance beyond which she knew Mr. Quentin would be waiting.

In this route, of course she had to pass through the kitchen, but she received no interruption in doing so, and was just traversing the courtyard, when from behind a projecting piece of wall she observed a very small portion of the rim of a man's hat, as if some one were hiding for the purpose of taking her unawares.

Of course it would have been madness to have exposed herself to the chance of receiving a very serious injury, and accordingly she drew back, but without exhibiting any alarm, and acquainted the officers with what she had seen; at the same time she stated, that there was a window in the upper story, from which, whoever was standing in the situation she supposed they were, could easily be seen.

To this window then they at once repaired, and upon looking down, there, sure enough, they saw the madhouse-keeper himself, splashed with mud from top to toe, and hiding himself most securely, as he thought, while in his hands he had a brass-barrelled blunderbuss, ready no doubt to do whatever mischief he could with it, to any one who might appear.

"That's awkward," whispered one of the officers to the other. "How are we to get at him?"

"It isn't the pleasantest thing in the world to go up to him. He may not mind being hanged for shooting some of us, but he must be taken notwithstanding all that."

"Oh, yes, of course; but there's a good way and a bad of doing all things. I'll tell you what you do—stay at this window, and drop something upon his head, in about two minute's time. You see this is a bedroom, and here is a jugful of water, which will answer the purpose. Don't be in a hurry about it, but in about two minutes drop it comfortably upon his head, and leave me to profit by the little confusion it will produce in him."

The officer, who had suggested this course, now walked away to the ground floor of the house, and crept as close as possible to the angle of the wall, round which stood the scoundrel Davis with the blunderbuss.

It was a period of rather anxious suspense, and the officer who was above at the window, being anxious to give his companion ample opportunity to take his measures, waited rather over the prescribed time, so that about three minutes elapsed, which certainly seemed much longer in duration, considering that they were watched by all parties with such extreme anxiety.

The water jug was quite full, and a very large one to boot, so that it went through the air with a swinging sound, but somehow or another it swerved a little in its descent, and only touched Mr. Davis slightly on the shoulder, and then scraped all the way down his back, smashing, when it reached the ground, with a tremendous noise.

The effect was instantaneous, for, in his fright, the madhouse-keeper pulled the trigger of the blunderbuss, and bang it went.

In another moment, the officer, who was near at hand, closed with him, and he was a prisoner.

"You're a nice article," said the officer, as, after handcuffing Davis, he took him by his collar, and dragged him to his feet; "so you thought you'd take somebody's life—you're my prisoner."

Thieves, thieves!" cried Davis; "you're come to rob the house, and I had a right to use firearms."

"Stuff! you know better than that; it's quite another thing; but, however, if you think that defence will answer your turn before a jury, why you can make it."

"Jury! why do you say jury to me? I've done nothing. I didn't keep Mrs. Godfrey prisoner."

"Why, nobody mentioned Mrs. Godfrey but yourself. How came you to find out we come about her? but this is all nonsense. You're my prisoner, and you'll come to London as soon as we can find a conveyance in Watford to take you."

In a few minutes, the officer was joined by his comrade and Mr. Jones, and Agnes, so that the whole party proceeded into the lane, where Mr. Quentin had been left waiting their arrival.

They saw the little horse and chaise standing quietly on the spot where it had been left, and then, indeed, Agnes shrunk from the task of informing her grandfather of what had happened. She dreaded, as well, indeed, she might, the gush of feeling that would ensue.

And yet she hesitated to transfer that task to another, who might possibly execute it roughly, so, to her perception, it became a duty to be the bearer of the melancholy intelligence of the death of her mother to the only other relative, she believed she had in the world, excepting Godfrey, whom she was reluctantly forced to admit was her father.

When we have a disagreeable task to perform, we either hurry towards it, or recede from it; but Agnes preferred the former alternative, and although her eyes were blinded with tears, so that she could see nothing distinctly, she made her way towards the little chaise, followed by the officers and their prisoner at a few paces behind.

"Grandfather," she said, "I have something to tell you that will grieve you."

The old man did not answer, and, before she could ascertain the cause of his silence, she felt one of the officers take her by the arm, and endeavour to turn her away from the spot.

"What is this for?" she said. "Let me speak to my grandfather."

"You can speak to him, miss," said the man, "but you'll get no answer. I am sorry to say, this morning, you have lost another relation as well as your mother."

Agnes comprehended him in a moment, and, completely overpowered by this fresh grief, she would have sunk to the ground, had she not been upheld by Mr. Jones, who strove to console her in his way as well as he could.

"Well, you know, Miss Agnes," he said, "all this can't be helped. We must all on us go some day, horses as well as human beings, and no mistake. You'll get the better of this here crying in a little while, and when you comes to think, Miss Agnes, them as is dead is, arter all, the betterest off. Only think what a world we lives in, Miss Agnes, and how people gets drove about—think of that, and you won't be sorry as your old grandfather has walked his chalks."

There was certainly some practical wisdom in the coachman's consolations, although they were not couched in the most elegant language; and then again we must bear in mind that, as regards her grandfather, Agnes's acquaintance with him was very slight.

In such a case, there were no ties of association to rend asunder, and the grief she felt most rather arose from that natural sympathy which was an inherent portion of her disposition, than from any other cause.

But what she felt for her mother was of a far more endearing nature, and she told Mr. Jones, mournfully, that it would be long indeed, if ever, she recovered the shock which that sudden death gave to her.

It was a strange and melancholy-looking cavalcade that which now marched into Watford. Mr. Jones, with a very lugubrious face, drove the pony, while Agnes followed close behind, as if she were chief mourner in the funeral procession.

Then there was Davis, very pale, and very ghastly-looking, his hands manacled, and one of the officers walking on each side of him.

No wonder that such a procession excited in the little town a large amount of conjecture, and soon collected a considerable concourse of spectators.

A glass coach was procured from one of the inns, which, by the assistance of the chaise, managed to carry the whole party.

Agnes preferred taking a seat on the driving-box of the chaise along with Mr. Jones, to sitting in the chaise alone, for we should have remarked, that the dead body of Mr. Quentin was left at Watford, there to undergo the ordeal of a coroner's inquest.

"Now, my dear," said the good-tempered coachman, as they drove along, "what are you thinking of doing?"

"I can tell you far easier," she replied, "what I am not thinking of doing."

"Can you! and what may that be?"

"A fixed determination never to see my father. I know what may be said to me, that I am destitute. I know I am, but would rather toil in any shape or manner for my daily bread, than be beholden to him for the means of existence."

"I tell you what, my dear, if anybody was to say to you as you was destitute, I'd just take the liberty of telling them that was a sanguinary untruth."

"But I am, Mr. Jones, indeed, I am."

"You aint."

"I assure you, Mr. Jones, I have no source whatever, except a wish to be industrious."

"You has, you has. Did you fancy that I was such an out-and-out wretch as not to do something for you? Now I tells you what it is, Mrs. Barclay and me has made up matters, and I shall soon be landlord of that here inn, and coach-house; so I tells you what, as we aint got no children yet of our own, I don't see any objection to having you as a ready-made one to begin with."

"This is too kind and generous. Why should I be a burden to you?"

"A burden! what do you mean by burden? It's no such thing. I just fancy I sees myself sitting in the bar, and you a slicing me a bit of lemon to put into my grog, and asking me if so be as it's sweet enough. Lor' bless you, you talk of a burden, indeed! I think I sees it."

Need I say that, with the utmost gratitude, until something shall happen by which I can acquire a livelihood for myself, I accept this kind proposition, and——"

"Don't say another word about it. I won't hear no more. I know old mother Barclay will like it; for, though she has her tempers, it isn't always the worst horse that now and then gets over the traces, so just make yourself comfortable."

"I cannot do otherwise with such friends."

"There's a blessed lawyer, too, mixed up in this here affair, and that's what I calls quite a *wisitation* of Providence, that one of them, at all events, will be got rid of."

CHAPTER XCV.

THE ALTERED PROSPECTS OF AGNES, AND HER GRATEFUL FEELINGS.

It was getting rather late in the day by the time they reached again the inn, which the coachman was so soon to call his own, for it was the freehold property of Mrs. Barclay.

The landlady was all impatience to arrive at a knowledge of what had taken place, and neither Agnes nor the coachman could recount to her with sufficient quickness the various eventful circumstances.

Before the narration was concluded, a little odd-looking man came in, and nodding familiarly to the landlady, took his seat in the bar-parlour, as an old acquaintance, which in truth he was.

"Well, Mr. Silversides," said Mrs. Barclay, "how do you do, sir?"

"I'm very well, thank you, madam; and how are you, Mr. Jones?"

"Why," replied Mr. Jones, "I aint so much amiss, and now I'm a blessed deal better."

In an interval of this speech, Mr. Jones contrived to drink off a good portion of a glass of brandy-and-water, and then he added,—

"I will say this much for you, Mr. Silversides, that you is about the only lawyer that ever I could bear, though you does come out of *Thieves* Inn."

"Really, Mr. Jones, I've told you a great number of times, that that inn is called Thavies' Inn."

"Well, well, well, that may be your way; of course I don't expect a lawyer to call his own place *Thieves'* Inn."

"But this, Mr. Jones, is not one of your journey days, and yet you are as splashed as if you had been far; how is that, Mr. Jones?"

"Why, Mr. Silversides, I don't objectify to tell you, but the real fact is, I've had quite a *hadwenture.* First of all, there's Miss Agnes here—"

"Agnes! why that's a young gentleman, is it not?"

"So I thought, sir, once upon a time, but she turned up to be a little girl."

"You surprise me!"

"Wery likely, sir. And then there was a Mr. Davis, and then there was a Mr. Squinting."

"Squinting! what a strange name. I thought my name of Silversides about the oddest anybody could have, but Squinting beats that. I know a gentleman of the name of Quentin, a client of mine."

"Quentin, Quentin," said Agnes, "did you know Mr. Quentin—was he aged?"

"Well, rather so; but he was a broken-down man—that is to say in health and spirits I mean, in consequence of the loss of his daughter."

"It is—it is the same."

Mr. Jones dropped his pipe, and looked hard at the lawyer, as if with his natural suspicion of that craft, he still had his doubts that some swindling was going forward.

"You don't mean that, sir! you don't mean as you know Mr. Squinting?"

"Mr. Quentin, whose daughter married a Mr. Godfrey, and then was supposed to be drowned in the Thames, I do know."

"Then you don't know him no more, for he's gone uncommonly dead."

"Dead—Mr. Quentin, dead! Then who is to inherit his property, I wonder?"

"Property! Mr. Squinting's property?"

"Yes, to be sure; he must have died worth 12,000*l.* or 15,000*l.*, and I never could get him to make a will, for the life of me."

"Then you're a *hindependent* brick," said the coachman, turning to Agnes, who burst into tears.

After this, of course no secret was kept from Mr. Silversides, but he was duly informed of the whole of the circumstances.

He warmly congratulated Agnes, and then added,—

"There can be no question whatever but I shall be able to procure for you the 1,000*l.*, which was the subject of dispute between your father and mother, and which he, on the assumption of her death, has taken possession of."

"But what, suppose he has spent it?" said Mr. Jones.

"That won't much matter. I know all about it: the money was in the public funds, and as there was so much doubt cast on his story of his wife's death, he did not get the cash for some years, and when he did, it was only by giving security to return it in case it should be legally demanded of him again, so that you must have it somehow or another."

"Oh, never mind it—never mind it," sobbed Agnes, "there is more than enough for me already."

"Oh, nonsense," said the lawyer, "never despise wealth; it is a foolish affected philosophy to do so, for if there be any surplus above what you may require for yourself, you may be perfectly assured of always finding, with the trouble of looking for, some very worthy recipient of it. So I say, take all you are legally entitled to, and use it in your own way. "That's very sensible," said Mr. Jones. "I hope, Miss Godfrey," added Mr. Silversides, "that you will honour me with your confidence, and draw upon me for any sums of money you may require."

What a peculiar pleasure now it must have been to Mr. Jones, to feel that in the apparent hours of her adversity, he had been liberal and kind to Agnes. The look she now cast upon him was quite sufficient to make him see how fully she appre-

ciated that kindness; and, had it not been for the dismal recollections which her recent bereavement pressed upon her attention, there would scarcely have been a happier person at that time than Agnes, who found herself surrounded by such kind friends.

Even Ben came in for his share of gratification, for Agnes thanked him warmly for the part he had taken on the preceding evening, in saving her from the clutches of the madhouse-keeper. It was dreadful to think what might have been her fate, had she fallen into his hands ; impressed as he was with the belief, that, in all likelihood, his utter ruin would be the consequence of the revelations she might make.

And we can fancy what sort of feelings are likely to be awakened in the breast of the villain, Godfrey, when all these circumstances, which we have felt it to be our duty to detail, came to his ears, and he finds, that in another event of his life, as well as in that connected with poor Marian Whitehead, he stands confessed before all the world as a villain of the blackest die.

If such a man be wealthy, let no man envy him his wealth ; if such a man be capable of surrounding himself with luxuries, let no one envy him those luxuries ; for that undying worm, conscience, must yet at times attack him, making him feel and know himself to be a man, wretched in all the wretchedness of a seared conscience.

We again imagine what an interview (if it should ever take place) would be between the pure, the innocent, and the high-minded Agnes, and the grovelling man who, for this world's lucre merely, had made himself the wretch we know him to be.

Surely, even before such a man as Godfrey dies, there will come an hour when his past life shall pass in fearful array before him ; and at that dreadful time, surely, the intellect which enabled him to carry on so ruthlessly and so successfully his schemes against the good and the innocent, will likewise be sufficient to point out to him the terrible mistake of his whole existence.

There will come such moments of due and intense suffering, that he shall envy the veriest beggar that ever crawled from door to door for alms.

But is not this a deserved retribution upon such a man as Godfrey ? Can we forget, that, in addition to his treatment of his much-injured wife, he was virtually the murderer of poor unfortunate Charles Ormond, and that, but for him, the light of reason would still be illuminating the path of Marian Whitehead ?

Fully and easily can we sympathise in the feelings of Agnes, when she wished not to be introduced to such a father.

We rather give her credit for the forbearance of not, by her presence, adding, perhaps, the bitterest of all pangs to those which the wretched man had already endured, and was enduring.

But now that our tale is so fast drawing to a close, we need not anticipate any of its incidents, either of joy or of sorrow, but leave those incidents to speak out trumpet-tongued for themselves, and to show, that even in this world, within our own cognisances, and consequently without any cavil or disbelief, there is a retribution which, if even it be compressed into the short space of a few hours, for a life-time of iniquity, may well be the terror of evil-doers—ay, such evil-doers as Godfrey.

CHAPTER XCVI.

THE VISIT OF THE ATTORNEY AND MR. JONES TO GODFREY.

THIS circumstance of the fortunes of Agnes being brought about by them both, in a manner of speaking, got up quite a friendship and a correspondence between the coachman and the attorney of Thavies' Inn. Indeed, the former declared to Mrs. Barclay in a whisper, that he really thought there might by possibility be such a thing as an honest lawyer.

This proposition, as regarded Mr. Silversides, was one that the landlady was quite in a position to agree with, for she had on more than one occasion been beholden to the honesty of the lawyer, and the good faith, which formed an important part of his character, for her escape, not only from disagreeables connected with her business, but from being occasionally downright swindled by unprincipled persons who would have gladly taken advantage of her open, upright character.

"Yes, Mr. Jones," she said, "there is an honest lawyer, and if there is not another, that is Mr. Silversides.

"I agree with you, mum—my dear, I mean."

"Go along with you."

This little conversation took place in the bar-parlour on the morning succeeding the events we have already recorded, while the coachman was partaking of such a substantial breakfast, that one could not help thinking, if he had nothing else at all until the following morning, he certainly would not do amiss.

But then Mr. Jones was blessed with an appetite, and three or four good cuts off a round of beef at breakfast time enabled him to swallow his coffee with a greater relish. While he was engaged in that operation, a rather singular-looking personage made his appearance at the bar, and passed into the parlour beyond with an inquiring air.

He, for it was a he, was a young man who certainly must have been of opinion either that he was so obscure-looking naturally, that it was necessary to attract the attention of society in some way, or that he was such a wonderful personage that it behoved him to make what he considered the most of the personal gifts of Providence.

After this we need scarcely say, that he was a fop in a small way. His complexion was of that chalky-looking white which is seen in consumptive-looking girls, while on the cheek bones was the vivid patch of red, likewise a characteristic of such persons. His forehead projected, and about the point of his chin and the angles of his jaw-bones were some singular-looking tufts of hair, to represent whiskers, but they looked precisely as if they had been stuck there without regard to the intervening spaces which were left destitute of that manly ornament.

His hair was uncommonly long, being a sort of practical caricature of the sort of locks attributed to "*Jeune France.*" His apparel was of the most outrageous fashion of two years before that period at which he wore them; and altogether there was a silly, good-tempered, weak-headed, girlish look about him, as if he coveted being thought pretty, much rather than in any respect manly.

This individual asked for Mr. Jones.

"Well," said that gentleman, "what does *it* want with me?"

It was was only after a rather long look at the sprig of fashion, as he thought himself, that Mr. Jones came to the conclusion that "it" was the most proper term to apply, in speaking to such a creature.

"Oh, if you are Mr. Jones, I come from Mr. Silversides; I'm his clerk. He wants to see you, if you can step over to Thavies' Inn any time within an hour or so."

"Oh, you is his clerk, is you?" said Mr. Jones, eyeing the animal before him; "and you are a rum 'un, and no mistake; I say, my boy, wait a bit, will you? Mrs. Barclay, just obleege me with a loan of threepence, mum, if you please, for a short time."

"Threepence, Mr. Jones, what can you want with threepence?"

"Never mind, mum, never mind; let's have it, if you please, mum. Thank you, here, young feller,—no, damn it, I can't call you a feller, that would be too great a compliment."

"What do you mean, sir? Did you address those words to me, sir?"

"Yes, to be sure, I did; who else do you suppose I addressed them to, eh?"

"Oh, very good—I—I shall—I shall——"

"Do what?"

"Nothing, oh, nothing, sir; I didn't say I'd do anything, sir. Don't hit me, sir, come, now, don't hit me. Hilloa, hilloa, now, come, come!"

"Why, who's agoing to hit you, I should like to know, you poor creature, eh? I should be ashamed of hitting such a thing as you."

Somewhat reassured by this, the young gentleman put on a more valrous look, and bridled himself up a little, so that one would have thought, rthat if Mr.

Jones had really any belligerent intentions, there would have been a most horrible resistance.

"Come," said Mr. Jones, sliding out of the bar parlour with the threepence in his hand, "take this, will you?"

"What! I take threepence? No; oh, gracious! no."

"You won't? Then I shall be under the disagreeable necessity of making you swallow it. It's in them old George the Third penny pieces, so you can do it easy."

"Oh, no! oh, no! have mercy upon me, sir. I'll take it."

"Oh, you will; very good. Now, I'll tell you what you are to do with it. You will go down Fetter-lane, till you come to the first turning on the right-hand side of the way."

"Yes, sir."

"And then a few doors down that turning you will see a barber's shop. Do you understand me, you odd-looking animal?"

"Oh, yes, sir; certainly, sir; don't hit me, sir, if you please."

"Well, you will there lay down the threepence, and tell the man to cut your hair close, and then you may come back here, if you like, to show us that you don't look quite so like a ring-tailed monkey as you do now. Do you understand all that?"

"Ye—ye—yes, sir; I'll go at once, if you'll be so good as not to hit me, or shake me; oh! I couldn't stand a minute if anybody was to give me a shake. Thank you, sir, I'll go at once, sir; much obliged, sir."

"Very good; then you may tell your master that I shall come over to him as soon as I have had my breakfast; and now be off with you, you ape. It's such puppies as you that lead poor little servant wenches astray, who haven't courage to speak to a man, but pick up with a monkey instead. Isn't that the case?"

"Yes, sir, if you please, sir; that's just it."

Mr. Jones, who had the greatest contempt in the world for foppery in any and every shape, accelerated the movements of the dandy clerk by a tolerable kick, so that he went out at a good rate from the inn, and ran off as fast he could.

"I hate such fellows as that, Mrs. Barclay," said Mr. Jones, as he sat down again to finish his breakfast. Upon my life, mum, they is enough to make one fall out with what they call human natur, mum, aint they? Now, you see, Mrs. Barclay, that fellow who, unfortunately for him, has a great, stupid, girlish look, instead of trying, as he might do, to make himself something more of a man, just goes the other way; and the most ridiculous thing in the world is to see such puppies fancying as all the world must admire 'em; and that's why I always likes, whenever I comes across one of 'em, to take him down a peg."

Mrs. Barclay could not forbear smiling at the indignation of the coachman; for, after all, the contemptible and dandified clerk of Mr. Silversides had done nothing to him; but as the punishment he had inflicted upon that fascinating individual was not very severe, she made no comment about it.

When he had duly finished his morning meal, Mr. Jones put on his wide-brimmed hat, and walked to Thavies' Inn, to call upon the lawyer, and see what it was he wanted with him.

One can easily imagine the perturbation of the dandy clerk at this expected visit of the coachman, for he, the clerk, had no more idea of going to have his hair cut, than of flying, and much he dreaded some sanguinary vengeance on the part of Mr. Jones, when he found himself not obeyed.

Of course Mr. Jones never for a moment expected that the clerk would go with the threepence to have his hair cut; great would have been the surprise of the coachman if he had; and when upon reaching the chamber of Mr. Silversides, he saw that the dandy had carefully twisted his long hair behind his ears, Mr. Jones affected to be solid, and said,—

"Oh, it's all right, I see you have had it cut off."

"Yes, sir," replied the clerk, quite delighted with the success of the *ruse* he was playing off. "Oh, yes, sir."

"And don't you feel all the better?"

"Oh, of course, sir, of course I do! Mr. Silversides is in his room, sir; I will tell him you are here, if you please."

"Ah, do—do. I wonder what he has got to say to me now," added the coachman to himself, for he had a very natural fear and misgiving at going into an attorney's office.

In a few moments, the clerk returned to say that Mr. Silversides would be disengaged directly, and sure enough almost as he spoke, the coachman heard a gentlemanly voice bidding good morning to the attorney; and then there passed him a person whose anxious looks could not conceal the excellent aspect of his face.

When the coachman entered the private room of the attorney, he found that gentleman alone, and after the usual salutations of the morning, Mr. Jones, said,—

"I suppose, sir, now as that gentleman as just went out leaves us some unpleasant business; he didn't look very happy."

"I dare say not; I dare say not. He has been victimised by a money-lender, whose clutches he cannot get out of."

"Indeed! Oh, I know something of those wretches."

"Well, this gentleman knows assuredly of them likewise; the fact is, that he borrowed fifty pounds of one of them, and they won't let him pay it back again."

"Won't let him, sir?"

"No, they won't let anybody pay them back, if they can help it, Mr. Jones."

"You astonish me, sir! I thought that was what they wanted; but if they don't want the money back, sir, what do they want?"

"Interest and expenses."

"The deuce! I begin to understand now, Mr. Silversides."

"Yes, it's easily enough understood: a money-lender accommodates the man whom he thinks will make a good victim with, we will say, fifty pounds, upon his own acceptance, at the rate of sixty pound per centum interest: he, the money-lender, knows that his debtor cannot pay the fifty pounds back all at once, but he agrees to take it by instalments, and he finds by putting on the screw as nearly as possible what the victim can drag from his current resources, weekly."

"Go on, sir, I begin to see."

"Well, he takes good care that the whole of that shall be absorbed in interest, and if by chance the debtor brings a few pounds off the real debt, he has a writ immediately, so that those few pounds should be absolved in expenses, and the debt still remain exactly where it was."

"I understand, sir—I understand."

You perceive then by that, how the creditor will not let the debtor pay him, and the greatest disappointment he could experience would be the bringing to him all his claim.

"The wretches! Well, if there's a hotter place than another down below, it will surely be set apart for them, I should say, Mr. Silversides; don't you think so?"

"I don't know what to think about that, Mr. Jones, but all I can say is, that if there be such a place, I certainly don't grudge it to the money-lenders, and any amount of luck they meet with there, they are quite welcome to, as fas as I am concerned."

"Yes," said Mr. Jones, "and worth £60 per cent. interest too."

"Do not mistake me," said Mr. Silversides. "The interest a man agrees to pay, were it twice £60 per cent., he ought to pay; but the grand iniquity consists in the money-lenders always dissolving by legal expenses any sum that is offered off the principal."

"I understand you, sir. Of course, that's the *pint*, that's the *pint*."

"Well, Mr. Jones, as we so well understand each other about that, I will explain to you why I sent for you just now. I have been making the most careful inquiries about the villian, Godfrey, and I have ascertained that he is in the most pitiable state, if we can feel any degree of pity for such a man."

"Lor! is he?"

"Yes. He lies upon a sick-bed in pain and misery, so that I have been thinking that his physical suffering is quite sufficient ; and that if, by paying him a visit, you and I could awaken him to a sufficient sense of his criminality in this affair of his wife, so that he would do justice to her, we should be conferring upon him a favour, and perhaps accomplishing all we wish without further publicity."

"I'm willing, sir, to anything you like. If the vagabond has been already sarved out, why, in course, that's all I care about ; so I'm your man, Mr. Silversides. Drive me anywheres you likes, sir, in a manner o' speaking."

"Very good, very good. I could not but feel, my friend, that you had the best right in the world to be consulted about this matter ; and that, considering the noble part you had played in it, you ought to have your feelings with regard to it partly carried out. It, therefore, as you may very well suppose, gives me much pleasure to find that we think alike about it."

"Oh! don't mention me ; I haven't done nothing."

"Well, well, we won't dispute about that ; but, if your leisure serves you, we will start in one hour from this time for Godfrey's house, where, as I am informed, you will find him in a most wretched condition, and fully as miserable as anybody could by any possibility wish him as a retribution for his many crimes.

CHAPTER XCVII.

THE VISIT TO GODFREY.—AN AWAKENED CONSCIENCE.

LEAVING Mr. Silversides and the coachman to make their arrangements about the visit they proposed making to Godfrey, we will, with the kind leave of the reader, take up a station by the bed-side of that most despicable man.

There is a room very much darkened by the blinds being drawn nearly to the bottom of the window, for the sole inhabitant of the apartment is in that miserable state that he cannot have much light—that inhabitant is Godfrey.

The villain is lying on his back in bed, groaning and looking up at the ceiling, for he is compelled to adopt that one posture, which enforces such an observation, continually. Every one but himself is aware that now he cannot recover from the wretched state he is in, but he, to whom death is invested with no hopefulness as regards a future, but a thousand unknown terrors of what may be, clings to life with shrinking ferocity.

He is muttering even now to himself.

"No, no, I cannot, dare not die! No, no, I shall, I must recover ; I will do so. Death, death! what has death to do with me, oh, horror, horror! Hush! what sound is that? My throat is parched—drink—drink—drink."

These last words he called out so loudly that they at length attracted the attention of an old woman who was in an adjoining room and who was his nurse.

"What now?" she cried, "as she made her appearance ; "am I to have no rest?"

"Drink, drink."

"Here, take it," she added, as she held a jug of some liquid to his lips. "Don't I wish it would choke you."

"Why do you leave me?" said the wretched man, when he had quenched for a time the thirst that consumed him : "why do you leave me alone? You ought not. You do not know what dreadful sights I see."

"Oh, bother! A person aint to be made quite a prisoner of because you have had dreams ; I should think not. A nice idea that would be, to be sure."

"But stay! oh, stay! Look in that corner. Is there not some one there crouching down ?"

"Bother, no! who should there be? There is a coat thrown over the back of a chair, that's all I can see in the corner."

"Thank you, thank you; is that all? is that really all?"

"To be sure."

"Well, it's a great relief. But you will stay by me now, will you not? Oh, what agony I suffer at times! You do not know what agony."

"Yes, I do, I've known such cases before; you have got some ribs broken inwards, and the jagged ends of the bones have dug into some part of your inside. How do you like it?"

"Oh, Heaven help me!"

"Oh! you are going to begin to pray, are you? Well, that will last some time, so you won't want me."

"No, no, stay! How can you treat me with such brutality! oh, how can you, when I suffer so horribly?"

"I tell you what it is, there's not one nurse in a hundred would stay with you at all; I don't wonder at no less than five giving up the situation; what you say of a night is enough to drive anybody out of their senses, unless they have strong nerves, and something to drink perpetually, as I am forced to have."

"Oh, horrible condition!" moaned Godfrey. "Before any one will even wait upon me, they must be bribed by drunkenness."

"Yes, that's about it; you should not make yourself so disagreeable."

Godfrey was silent for a few moments; and then, when he did speak again, it was in whining accents that he said,—

"What did the surgeon say last night?"

"He said that a miracle might cure you, but that he didn't think this was the age of miracles."

Godfrey groaned aloud.

"As for my part," continued the nurse, "I am only surprised how a man, knocked about as you are, wants to get well at all; you would never be able to work, I am sure; you would only be a burden to yourself as well as everybody else; you must be quite aware of that yourself."

"Oh, no, no, no!"

"Oh, but I say yes, yes, yes! Why, you know it, or ought to know it; you have been told it often enough, I am sure."

"By you, by you only."

"Ah, but—well, what do you want?"

These last words were addressed to a servant, who made her appearance at the door of the sick chamber, and who said, in reply to the interrogation thus put to her,—

"There's two gentlemen want to see Mr. Godfrey; they want to be admitted, though I told them how bad he was."

"Well, I don't know that it's any harm whom he sees! it aint in his head, altogether, that his complaint is."

"Then I suppose I may show them up?"

"Oh, yes! oh, yes! I generally look for something when visitors come to see a sick man, whether I get it or not," muttered the nurse to herself, as she smoothened the bed-clothes, to make the place look as tidy as possible."

In a few moments the servant, who had already received something liberal from the attorney and Mr. Jones, made her appearance again, ushering in those two personages to the sick chamber of Godfrey.

He cast his eyes inquiringly to the door, but, although he was well accustomed to the dim light of that apartment, and could see pretty well in it, he did not know either of the forms that presented themselves to his notice. To the guilty, however, the appearance of any one is a matter of alarm; and Godfrey, despite the pain that it really gave him to do so, trembled from head to foot, as these two strangers approached his bed.

How did he know but that they might be officers, determined upon taking him in charge for some of his delinquencies, and dragging him to prison, notwithstanding the wretched state of suffering he was in. Nearer and nearer they came, and the attorney, taking half-a-crown from his pocket, gave it to the nurse, saying,—

" You can leave us with him a short time—we have something to say to him."

" Very good, gentlemen, and if so be as he should be at all obstropulous, you can just call to me, and I'll soon come and put him all to rights, I'll be bound."

So saying, the nurse, after casting an admonitory glance at Godfrey, left the place, and the wounded, wretched criminal was at the mercy of what his visitors chose to say to him.

" Mr. Godfrey," said the attorney, " do you know me ?"

Godfrey turned his glaring eyes upon him, and gazed for a few moments, as if he were trying to remember the face.

" No, no," he said, at length. " No, you are no friend of mine. What do you want here ? Tell me at once what you want here."

" I certainly am no friend of yours, Godfrey. Do you really flatter yourself that you have a friend ?"

" What is that to you ? Speak your errand, if you have one."

" I will speak my errand, and I hope it is one that you will listen to, as I wish you. You are as bad a man, Godfrey, as ever I heard of, and my errand here is to hope that you will repent of your deep and numerous iniquities, and endeavour, while you still linger in this world, to make what atonement you can for them. It is an errand which you would indeed do well to listen to.'

" And you ?" said Godfrey, with a strange calmness, turning to Mr. Jones.

" Oh ! I came to see what a horrid old rogue you is, and to help Mr. Silversides."

" Then may my bitterest curses light upon you both !" cried Godfrey. " You take advantage of my not being in a position to kill you, or I would do so with all the pleasure in the world."

" Thank you all the same," said the coachman.

" Hush, hush !" said the attorney. " Godfrey, do you ever think of your wife, the daughter of old Mr. Quentin ?"

Godfrey winced a little at this question, but he made no reply to it, and Mr. Silversides, after a pause of a few moments, added, in voice of solemnity,—

" I ask you again, do you ever think of your wife, Godfrey ? because, if you do, I can add something to your reflections ; and if you do not, I have come here to recal her to your mind. Your villany, as regards her, has become well known, all is discovered ; and you will, provided you recover sufficiently from your present desperate condition, have to answer at the bar of justice for that matter as well as for the numerous others that stain your soul."

These words evidently produced a great effect upon the villain, Godfrey ; and his fit of trembling came upon him again as he said, " Wife ! my wife, I have no wife. What do you mean? I have no wife."

" You might have had even now about you a wife and child, and you might have been happy ; yes, Godfrey, you might have escaped all that you now suffer, for it is not disease that racks your frame, but the consequences of accident, brought on by your own wickedness ; and, as sure as there is a Heaven above us, you will yet suffer much in the shape of retribution."

At this moment one of Godfrey's raving fits came on him, and he shouted aloud,—

" There, there—oh, save me from them ! Do not let them glare at me in that hideous fashion. There have been bad men before my time, and they have not suffered all these pangs. Save me from them—oh, save me—save me ! Look there—can I live and endure the sight of those dreadful faces ? See, see ! they come nearer to me ; and there is a skeleton form, too, rattling its bones, from which hang dripping festering moisture. Oh, help—help !"

" Is not this horrible ?" whispered Mr. Silversides.

The coachman said nothing, and, after a very short respite indeed, the wretched man spoke again.

" Oh, no, no—I did not do it ! Why do you come here with your convulsed features and a rope about your neck ? I know you, O God, yes ! I know you too well. You are Charles Ormond, but I did not kill you. Away, away ! It was the law took your life, not I. Why do you come to terrify me ? Oh, no—no ! do not touch me !"

He shouted aloud in his dismay, and the nurse merely popped her head into the room saying,—

"Oh! he's at his old tricks, I see."

"Look, look!" he murmered. "Is that a madhouse? Who is there, is she not dead? What! not dead yet, not dead yet. No! no! I have no child. God! what is that? Some one moves along in black. I do not know her—what is she to me?

Hush! hush! Oh, what unheard-of agony! No, no, no!—anything but death—anything but death! Hush! there again—the skeleton comes nearer. Help! help! keep him off—keep him off, I say! I will not be held in that fleshless grasp, stand round triple deep, and save me. Oh! is there no mercy on earth or heaven? Help! O God, help!

"I say, Mr. What's-your-name," whispered the coachman, "if it's all the same to you, I'd just as soon go away now, for I don't want to know any more of this sort of thing I can tell you : I don't want to dream about nothing."

"Hush! stay, you are innocent of wrong, and have no cause to fear bad dreams."

"True enough; but it aint pleasant for all that."

Godfrey was silent now, and Mr. Silversides spoke to him.

"Surely, Godfrey, you would be glad of any means which should deprive you of the companionship of all those horrors that oppress your brain. You may depend that no man can be so thoroughly bad but that, if he invoke the mercy of Heaven, and show that his repentance is sincere, by endeavouring to make all the reparations in his power, he may have hope."

"Very good, very good," said Mr. Jones, "say that again, sir."

Godfrey, however, spared them the trouble of addressing any further such remarks to him, or at all events he wished to do so; for, raising one of his arms and clenching his fist he cried,—

"I defy you all, I defy everything, I defy alike Heaven and—"

"Hush! for your own sake, hush!" said Mr. Silversides. "Do not let your impious spirit go further; and since I find you so obdurate,—so dead to all feelings of remorse, I feel that while I tell you that your daughter lives, I am justified in adding to that information, that you shall never behold her."

"My daughter?"

"Yes, your own child! but she shall not have her pure and innocent spirit tortured by a remembrance that there was such a man in existence as yourself. She is wealthy, and has friends around her. If you had proved penitent, instead of as you now show yourself, hardened in iniquity—"

"What—what then?"

"Why, then the greatest kindness that could have been shown to you, would have been to have allowed you for a few minutes to look upon the face of your child."

A bitter imprecation came from Godfrey's lips, and then the attorney, taking the arm of Mr. Jones, said, "if that don't move him, nothing will, so I pray you come away at once, for I am disgusted with the scene here."

Mr. Jones made no remark, but followed the attorney from the room. The nurse threw herself in the way again with a dim hope that another half-crown might be forthcoming, but in this she was disappointed, for neither Mr. Jones nor Mr. Silversides put their hands again in their pockets.

"Shocking!" said the lady, "however, one half-crown is something. I'm getting rather tired of old Godfrey; I only wish he'd make a quiet exit of it, and spare everybody further trouble."

*   *   *   *   *   *

It is scarcely necessary to say that both Mr. Jones and the attorney left the bedside of that guilty man, horrified at the scene they had been witnesses to, and at the horrid villany of Godfrey.

It was quite a relief to get out again into the open air, and to feel the breath of heaven fanning their cheeks once more. Mr. Jones drew a long breath, as he said,—"I say, Mr. Lawyer, that fellow's a greater rascal than even I thought him, by ever so much; I really thought once or twice as I should have been right down choked."

"Ah, you will not easily find his equal."

————

CHAPTER XCVIII.

RETURNS TO THE BLACK LADY AND HER FORTUNES.

WE feel that Marian Whitehead, and those events which immediately concern her, have been now for too long a space of time made to give way to other portions of our tale.

But in a narrative like the present, composed of several distinct actions, as it becomes absolutely necessary to take up the thread of events, in such a manner that all shall conduce to one end; and, therefore, in order that Godfrey should be placed in his real position before the reader, it was a matter of duty, if not of inclination, to introduce upon the stage the young girl, towards whom we cannot but say we feel a large amount of affection and sympathy.

It will be doubtless in the recollection of the reader, that the last time we heard of Marian Whitehead, she was attacked by the rascally emissaries of Godfrey, for the purpose of getting her signature to an exculpatory paper that, in the event of Neville actually becoming an informer against him, should have the effect of invalidating his evidence.

The firm refusal of Marian, although the fear of actual death was before her eyes, to put her name to any such document had reduced the men, who made their way into her bed room, to the necessity of going away with all the bitterness of disappointment. But that bitterness did not last long, inasmuch as to satisfy Godfrey, and to get the reward he had promised them, they signed the paper for Marian Whitehead, and then took it to him.

It is after these events that we now again revert to the unhappy Black Lady.

The events of that night were quite calculated to exercise an injurious influence upon the mind of any one unaccustomed to scenes of violence ; but when we come to consider poor Marian's intellectual condition, we shall not be surprised that the alarm she had been subjected to, naturally altered her for the worse.

In the morning, when the alarm and tumult were over, and her landlord and his wife had had time to consider the matter, and to come to mutual explanations, the latter went to the little room occupied by the Black Lady.

Marian Whitehead was up and dressed, and sitting in a chair placed very nearly in the centre of the apartment. In her hand she held the same paper upon which she appeared to have been writing.

" Well, Miss Whitehead," said the landlady to her, " I really hope you are none the worse for last night. Oh, the wretches! if my husband had been half a man, he would have taken them into custody."

" Hush!" said Marian, " what's o'clock ?"

" Well, I don't know exactly."

" A coach! A coach! Quick! oh, quick! 'Tis not eight yet, by old St. Sepulchre's church clock. Oh, no! They will not take your life, Charles, 'till eight, and there may yet be time to get into the vaults' of St. Paul's."

" Well, I never ! she's wandering worse than ever," ejaculated the landlady.

" There are the evidences of his innocence," said Marian, as she arranged the various papers on her knee. " Yes, there are the evidences : on this, it says that Godfrey is a villain, and on this, that Charles Ormond could not stoop to falsehood. Will not that suffice ? Surely! oh, surely yes, and he must be saved!"

" I declare I'm alarmed," said the landlady. " Miss Whitehead, won't you come down and take a cup of tea, if you please ? You will find yourself the better for it."

" Do not speak to me of aught but the preservation of him who must and shall be saved."

" Whom, my dear ?"

" Oh, Heaven! do you not know they have doomed him to death? and he so innocent too; can you ask me whom, when you know they would fain take the life of Charles Ormond ? His life ? O God, pity them, that they should strive to part that soul and body which Heaven has, in such a wondrous fashion, united."

" Well, I declare, it's as good as a book."

" I must go! I must go!" said Marian, hurriedly; " yes, I must go, or it will be too late ; much too late ; and I do not want to suffer an age of agony, in the shape of repentance. It is not eight yet! Oh, no, it is not eight yet !"

" If you mean eight o'clock, Miss Whitehead, it won't be eight again till evening, for eight it is and past, I can tell you, Miss Whitehead. And as for anybody going to be hung, it is not to happen this morning at all events, or I should have heard of it; for my husband goes to all the executions, though as I often say he is not half a man."

This speech, if one might judge from Marian's manner, did not seem but half intelligible to her; but she sighed deeply, and after a brief pause, tried to walk towards the door of the room : she staggered as she did so, and it appeared as if some sudden giddiness of the brain had come across her; for she placed her thin hand upon her brow, and rested herself, saying in a voice of most angelic calmness and beauty, —

"Is this death ?"

These words, as well as the manner in which they were uttered, much alarmed the landlady, who ran down stairs, to fetch her husband—"the half man," for she really believed that Marian was dying.

When they reached the room again, they found the Black Lady in the same attitude in which she had been left; but there was a death-like pallor upon her face, such as they had not noticed before, so that the suspicion, that something really serious was about to happen, was rather strengthened than diminished by the second observation of her.

The "half man" suggested the propriety of at once sending for a doctor, which, after of course objecting to in words, because it was not her own idea, was done by the wife; and a medical practitioner of the neighbourhood was called in, who, the moment he cast his eyes upon the countenance of the Black Lady, showed, by the seriousness of his physiognomy, that he thought her in a critical position.

"What has happened to her ?" he said; "she seems as if suffering from the reaction of some powerful excitement."

He was duly informed of the proceedings of the previous night, and then he advised that Marian Whitehead should be persuaded, if possible, to go to bed; and that was attempted by the landlady, but unsuccessfully; for all that they could get from the Black Lady were the words—

"Is it eight? Is it eight? Oh, Heaven! is it eight yet ?"

"What does she mean ?" said the medical man. "What makes her so very anxious to know if it is eight ?"

"Well, sir, really we don't exactly know; but she will have it that somebody is to be hung at eight, and that's what appears to make her so very uneasy. I only wish, poor thing, she could be persuaded to send for her friends, if she has any."

These last words seemed to be heard by Marian, and to awaken her to a new train of thought, for she made signs that she wished to write; and when accommodation for so doing was offered to her, she wrote upon a slip of paper the name of the Athertons, with their address; and when the landlady asked her if she wished them sent to, she replied by an inclination of the head; and almost immediately afterwards she fell back in the chair in which she had been sitting, and seemed to have swooned away.

"I expected that," said the medical man.

"Did you?" cried the landlady; "then why didn't you say so ? and we would have sent for the vinegar cruet at once."

"You need not trouble yourself, that will not restore her. I don't think she is long for this world, although she will no doubt recover from the swoon she is in. I think you had better send at once for those whom she has named as her friends."

The people with whom the Black Lady lodged were now thoroughly alarmed, and a messenger was at once dispatched to Atherton, who, when he heard the message that the Black Lady was thought to be dying, and wanted to see him, turned round to Jem, who was with him, and said,—

"There, didn't I tell you so, Jem, that a long time would not elapse before something of the kind would occur ?"

"Yes, master, you did," said Jem. "Poor thing !"

"Well, Jem, you mind the shop, and take all the money you can, while I go and see her. It shan't be said that I didn't answer her summons, poor thing! whenever she chose to send for me. Indeed, I always told her to send for me, if she felt even poorly; but you know she would not, and even made a mystery of her address; so that makes me think she is bad indeed, now that she has sent."

Atherton made the best of his way to the address which the messenger gave him, and was soon at Marian's house, when he was told that she was still in a state of insensibility, but that the medical man had told her he expected that she would shortly recover, although he was of opinion that she would not live beyond a day or two at the utmost.

It was with unfeigned grief that the good-tempered cheesemonger heard this account of Marian, for although, God knows, that in her sad case death might be considered a blessing, Atherton was scarcely a deep thinker enough to come to that conclusion; and all he felt was that one towards whom he felt a deep and lively interest and friendship, was about to go to

"That bourne from whence no traveller returns;"

and he was full of grief accordingly.

"Alas! poor thing," he said, "she has had serious trials, and no wonder she is cut off in this way. I dare say it's all for the best, but I did hope that some day her reason might come back to her, and she would know a little happiness, but as I say, perhaps it's a great deal better as it is, for all I know."

The landlady was very much pleased with Mr. Atherton. He was just the sort of person she liked, and his mode of conversation, too, suited her amazingly, so she gave him the full and complete history, as far as she knew, of the night attack upon the house, which no doubt, by the fright it had given her, had been the direct cause of Marian being thrown into her present state of great physical and mental prostration.

"Oh," said Atherton, "I can guess where those rascals came from."

"Indeed, sir! Can you?"

"Yes. But it's of no use saying anything about it now, till we see if poor Miss Whitehead recovers or not. Alas! I wonder what that wretch, Godfrey, now wants with her? Surely he might let her be in peace with one foot in the grave too, as one may say."

The landlady's curiosity was most alarmingly stimulated by what had been uttered by Atherton, and she eagerly questioned him, but he declined just then to enter into particulars, saying,—

If poor Miss Whitehead dies, you will know all, and so will all the world know all; for I shall be at liberty to publish her papers in 1835, but not before; until then I am bound to keep secret many things that I would otherwise be very glad to tell to everybody, for I don't think they ought to be so kept."

"If you please, mum," said a girl, who had been promised a reward for staying with Marian Whitehead, "if you please, mum, I have just run down to tell you I think she's a coming to herself."

"Then I'll go up and see her," said Atherton; "perhaps the sight of some one she knows may have some good effect upon her; poor thing! who knows; at all events, I can say a few kind words to her, that may calm her mind, if I cannot do her any more good by speaking to her."

CHAPTER XCIX.

THE DEATH AND CONFESSION OF NEVILLE.

WE may now at length fairly conclude that the villain Neville is thoroughly departed, and that any further hopes he may please to entertain of escape from the fate that awaits him must be quite chimerical.

But we shall see that even he had sense enough left him, in the midst of all his violent and bad passions, to feel that he had taken his last throw in the game of existence; for, after the failure of his desperate attempt to escape from

Newgate, it was not at all likely that the authorities would give him the opportunity of trying again.

Behold him then in a cell, to which he was conveyed, laying on his back, and guarded by two turnkeys, while he cursed and roared, in a manner that made even those men, accustomed as they were to the most depraved portion of society, hold up their hands with positive horror.

It seemed now as if the whole object of the scoundrel was to aggravate his position as much as possible, since he had been so completely foiled in the efforts he had made to alleviate it, and he alike launched his invictives at heaven and earth, and all that might be supposed to inherit both.

The chaplain was sent for to him, but the fearful imprecations that came from Neville's lips so alarmed that functionary, that his hair nearly stood on end, and he was glad, in a very few moments, to get out of the cell again, which he did, with a firm conviction, that no amount of preaching would suffice to awaken that most desperate man to better thoughts.

And there he lay for some hours raving in that hideous manner until he was fairly exhausted and could not utter a word, which was a great relief to the men who were placed upon the disagreeable duty of watching him, and who had looked first at him and then at each other in silent wonder at the horrible ingenuity of the oaths that came from his lips.

A deep sleep then came over the wretched man, and for nearly two hours he did not stir hand nor foot. At the expiration of about that period of time, however, it became evident that if in his waking moments he knew not what remorse was, or, at all events, managed to seem to defy it, he could not do so, while under the thaldrom of sleep.

At first he commenced groaning in the most hideous manner imaginable, now and then varying the sound by the utterance of a shriek, while his whole frame seemed convulsively to be attempting to shrink from some horrible and loathsome object.

" Had we not better awaken him ?" said one of the men.

" Oh, no, for God's sake, no ! " said the other, " he will only begin his horrible swearing again, and anything is better than that."

" Well," added the first, " you are right, man, as far as that goes, and so let him sleep on."

" Yes ! and if he fancies the devil has got hold of htm, so much the better ; it's only a little before his proper time."

" True enough ! I should say there was not much difficulty in saying where he should go to."

" No! I wouldn't have his share for a trifle."

" Nor I ! but hark! he's a saying something. Let's listen, who knows but he may let out some secret about his crimes—it does happen sometimes, and what a man won't confess when he's awake he says in his sleep, whether he likes it or not, and you may depend that such a customer as this is, has goue through some rather rummy scenes. Only listen to him, why who in the name of all that's odd is he talking about!"

It was indeed evident that the slumbering of Neville was disturbed by past events, a d now he spoke sufficiently plain, that by exercising a considerable amount of attention, the two turnkeys could make out, with something like clearness, the strange words he uttered.

Thus he spoke :—

" Quick Godfrey, quick ; put the cheques in the letter. Hang Charles Ormond ! Oh yes, of course it's easy enough for two men, if they set about it ingeniously, to hang anybody for forgery. Quick—oh God ! what's that ? a dead man—go—go—go away from me ; I did not do it—oh horror ! don't twist that rope about my neck. I choke, I choke, help ! help ! Godfrey, I am sliding down a precipice, and at the bottom, far down, I see a world of flames, save me. Save me !"

At this point he shook so violently, and grasped at the floor, that It wa wonderful he did not awake; but so it was, this bad man continued under the dominion of that fearful dream.

In a few moments he spoke again:—

"I'm going, O God! I'm going. Will no one lend a hand to save me? will no one raise a finger? Oh, I feel the hot blast of the roaring flames upon my face already, my blood boils in my veins, and my scorched eyes start from their sockets, feeling like balls of molten lead; O God, save me!"

"I say," remarked one of the men, with a shudder, to his companion, "I say, Bennett, I can't stand this, it is dreadful—horrible; and do you know, it puts one all of a shake."

"Hush, hush! recollect all he says."

"I'll be hanged if I can recollect anything, except that I'm all of a tremble and my hair is sticking to my head, all in consequence of the perspiration he's thrown me into; come, do let's wake him up."

"No, no, I say, no! who knows what good effect upon the fellow such a frightful kind of nightmare as he is now suffering from, may not have; perhaps, when he does wake of his own accord, he may be quite a different being, and we should be sorry to spoil that, I'm sure, by awaiking him before his proper time."

"I don't want to spoil anything, but you must confess it's terrible."

"That's true enough; but I suppose it's our business to be horrified, so there's no help for it."

"Hush! he's going to begin again."

"So he is: listen to him, and don't say anything. He don't seem so furious as he was."

This was true; for when Neville spoke again there was a something in his tones which bespoke more the presence of deep dejection, than the wild despair which before had evidently oppressed him. Besides, his talking was more connected, and had fewer extravagances of the imagination.

"There they come," he said, "there they come; what a ghostly train! Yes, I will tell all; I will make a clean breast. Do not press around me in that way. I am going to tell, and then justice may be done on Godfrey. Oh, yes; I will swear that the signature is not yours, I know it is not. The two cheques is the deep move that will be his destruction. He cannot get over that; oh, no, no. He must hang; but, mark me, Godfrey, I will have half; yes, I will have half of everything, even to the money that chances to be in your purse; and Marian Whitehead must die, or I must go mad; for, I tell you, I cannot bear her look, a she bends upon me those sad eyes."

"What a pretty rascal, Bennet, eh?" said one of the men.

"Ay, ay! give him rope enough, as they say, and he will hang himself."

"Of course he will—of course he will. But how quiet he is to what he has been! I feel all the better for that, for I don't mind telling you I was getting in a precious fright. Why, what that fellow said, to my mind, was enough to bring old Nick himself into the cell."

"Oh, stuff!"

"Ah, you may say stuff as long as you like. I know you don't believe in a certain elderly gentleman, but I do."

The congratulations upon the quietness of the prisoner, were rather premature, for just as the other turnkey was about to say something in reply to this last remark, Neville uttered such a terrific yell, that they both jumped again; and then he called so loudly for help, and to be saved from the precipice, and the flames that were at the bottom of it, that, if the walls of the cell had not been of solid stone and of great thickness, he must have alarmed the whole prison.

As it was, the pent-up sounds made a most horrible disturbance in the small space to which they were confined.

"Look, look," he cried. "Here is the woman with blood upon her throat, walking hand-in-hand with Charles Ormond, and they are both dead—yes, both dead. Yet there they walk, talking together about me; oh, horror of horrors! why should they talk about me?   No, no; keep off, will you—keep off. Don't push me over the brink.   Help, help, help!"

Then came another of the frightful yells, and the two turnkeys involuntarily put their hands over their ears, to endeavour, at all events, to shut out some portion of the frighful sounds which echoed around them, filling the two with so much terror, that it was a wonder they did not leave him to himself, and all the additional horrors of loneliness.

The one, however, who had been so urgent before to have him awakened, apparently could stand the terror of the scene no longer, for with his feet he gave Neville so violent a shaking, that, in the course of another minute, he opened his eyes, and looked with a wild and haggard stare about him.

*   *   *   *   *

It was an immense relief to the turnkeys to find that he was awake; and one of them, stooping down to him, said, with more of pity in his tone than one could have supposed he could have felt for one of such a sort as Neville,—

"How do you feel now, eh?"

"Oh, help me—hold me, and I will tell all," said the wretch, faintly. "Don't let me slip over the edge of the precipice into the fire. Oh, don't—oh, don't. Hold me tight, and I will tell all. I will tell how Charles Ormond was hung, though he was innocent. I will tell how Godfrey and I did it all; but hold me, hold me tight."

"If we fetch the governor, will you make a confession?" said one of the men.

"Yes, yes," replied Neville, in a dry, husky tone; "hold me, and I will then tell all. I am dying."

Upon this one of them, as it was indeed his duty to do, went with a report of the state of the prisoner to the governor, while the other found that the only plan by which Neville could be at all kept quiet, was by kneeling down by him, and apparently holding him tight by the arm, lest he should fall down the imaginary precipice, which he fancied was yawning at his feet, and at the bottom of which superstition pictured to him a sea of fire.

The prison officials were not long in obeying the summons to the cell of the murderer.

And now assembled in the cell, where that wretched criminal seemed doomed to die, were the governor of the prison, the chaplain, and one of the sheriffs, who, happening to be in the building at the time, was asked to come and make one of the official witnesses of the confession of iniquity which the terrified Neville had promised to utter.

There was something awful and solemn in a number of men that thus surrounded a fellow creature for the purpose of listening to his own recital of his own frightful crimes. And as for Neville himself, the dreadfully terrified and wild expression of his countenance was a sight never to be forgotten by any there present.

———

CHAPTER C.

NEVILLE'S STATEMENT CRIMINATING GODFREY.

It was some moments before Neville spoke, and, when he did, it was with much more strength and firmness than any one could have given him credit for, considering the desperation of his circumstances.

"I will tell all," he said, "I will tell all; but first, you shall know why I do so."

"Oh!" said the clergyman, "we will assume that the reason why you do so is, that now the close of your life is at hand you wish to do justice to the innocent, and by so doing make what atonement you can for the evil that you have committed."

"You think so, do you?" said Neville; and then slightly raising himself on one arm, bruised and wounded as he was, he shook his clenched fist above his head, and said,—

"No, I tell you all; but it is not for the sake of the innocent nor for the sake of justice, it is for the sake of revenge; yes, for the gratification of that passion of revenge which has ever shared with me my very life. I will denounce Godfrey."

The clergyman was about to say something of a deprecatory character to the dying wretch, but the governor stopped him, remarking to him in a confidential whisper,—

"Really, sir, I don't think you will do any good with such a man as this; and from whatever motive he makes his confession, it is highly necessary for the ends of justice that he should make it; so I think, if you let him alone u___l he has done so, it will be not only as well but much better."

The chaplain of Newgate at that time was not a bigot, so he adopted this good advice, merely replying,—

"Very well; let him say what he likes, and I will try what can be done afterwards."

Neville had remained silent during this brief consultation, if it may be so called, and when it was concluded, he looked at the governor as much as to say,—

"Well, what now have you been talking about me, or what is it you have got to propose?"

"Go on," said the governor; "we are ready and willing to hear all that you have to say."

"Very well, you shall hear it; and you will find it to be necessary to go and arrest a man—Godfrey I of course mean; you must go and arrest him, and place him here in Newgate, in one of its worst cells. Oh! that I had him by the throat—but the hangman will. Yes, surely the hangman will, unless he takes his own life, and that would answer my purpose as well, for I have myself at times thought of that mode of escaping from evils, but could not bring my mind to embrace it. No, no, I could not; and the amount of suffering that the very thought engendered ought surely to be enough almost for my revenge."

No reply was made to this strange comment; and, after a pause, Neville repeated the one word,—

"Drink."

Some wine-and-water was handed to him, which appeared to give him fresh energy; and, after a short time, during which his thoughts seemed to be uncommonly busy, he spoke:—

"It was a number of years ago when I first knew Godfrey. He was better off then, and he wanted some one who could do things in the way of what he called his business that he did not exactly like to appear in himself, so he employed me. It is needless to say how many transactions that will not bear the light we were engaged in together. Let me come to some of the principal ones, and perhaps the one in which you are most interested is that which concerns a young man, named Charles Ormond."

"Yes," said the governor, "we would certainly be glad to hear of that unhappy young man. He was executed for forgery, but there have been various rumours about, that he was innocent."

"He was innocent!" said Neville, in a deep, sepulchral sort of voice, "and I will tell you 'twas being innocent he was made to seem guilty. I will tell you all. It was well managed; if the devil himself had so arranged it, it could not have been better done. You will arrest Godfrey when you know all, and then I shall be quite content."

The persons present listened with the most profound attention to what Neville related to them, but as it simply consisted of what is already known to the readers as regards the atrocious plot which had been concocted, for the purpose of bringing poor Charles Ormond to the scaffold, we need not report it. Suffice it to say, that Neville was perfectly candid, and concealed nothing, and the persons who heard him listened with a shuddering horror to the recital.

"Good God!" said the governor; "then that young man was judicially murdered?"

"He was," said Neville, "and you know now on whom the blame lies. Is it not on me and upon Godfrey? I am here in your power, and am dying. But where is Godfrey? Pray, where is Godfrey?"

"He shall be sent for," said the sheriff; "you need be under no sort of apprehension that your companion in guilt will escape. He shall be promptly enough waited upon. Gentlemen, you are all witnesses of this man's frightful confession, as I cannot help calling it. He is a dreadful subject of contemplation."

"Dreadful!" said Neville; "why do you call it dreadful? or if it be dreadful to you, what do you suppose it is to me? Coin some new word to express what it is to me, since you take dreadful to yourselves. I think now that I see her looking upon me, off—off. I did not kill you, although I tried to do so. Off—off, I say! Do not drag me down with that look of stone."

" What does he mean?" whispered the chaplain.

" I can guess," replied the governor. "He can see in his mind's eye the poor unhappy creature commonly called the Black Lady, who went mad on account of Charles Ormond being hung. Alas! poor thing, how strange and how humiliating to human intelligence is it to think, that for years past, she who was looked upon with pitying commiseration should be right in what she stated regarding Charles Ormond, and we, with all our boasted intelligence and the full possession of our reason, should be wrong."

" It is the will of Heaven," said the chaplain.

" Yes, yes," half screamed Neville, " and are you Marian Whitehead? Do not come nearer to me ; oh, do not! Why do you fix that gaze upon me? Why do you not go to Godfrey? He is more guilty. Go to him—oh, go to him, and spare me, if it be but for a few brief moments!"

" Will you pray?" said the chaplain.

" Who—I—I pray? I pray? Oh! no, no, no! I—I dare not! what should I pray for? Am I fit for heaven? Oh, no, no! No prayers for me. All is over. O God! that the last forty years could but be obliterated from the record of my life!"

" That record may be washed away."

" You mock me—you mock me, I say. How can that dreadful record be washed away? Oh, you come to mock a man who is dying, and who already feels what it is to slip from the world into that abyss from whence there is no return."

" Unhappy man! I do not mock you. That record, were it ten times blacker than it really is, may be washed away by one tear of genuine repentance. Oh! could I but induce you to think that there was a hope of mercy now for such as you, I should think to bring you to prayer; and tell you that the mercy of Heaven is infinite, and surpasses all human understanding."

" No more—no more! Do not speak to me in that strain ; it is useless, I know what I am."

" But you know not what you may be."

" Yes—O God! yes, I do well; I know I am lost—quite lost. Why do you stand around me thus, when there is something yet to do? Have you no hearts, you, who thank your stars that you are virtuous."

" What do you mean?" said the governor. " Explain yourself."

" Why do you not go to Marian Whitehead, and tell her that Charles Ormond's innocence is discovered. Why do you not do that?"

" It is not a bad thought," said the governor. " It was the shock of his execution for forgery that unsettled her brain. Who knows but the sudden announcement that his innocence is known, and fully acknowledged, may restore her to her senses ; although, alas! it cannot drag him from the silence of the tomb."

" It is a happy thought," said the chaplain. " Is there any one here who knows where she is to be found, poor thing! I have seen her only in the streets."

" I can get her address, I think, sir," said one of the men who was present, "or at all events a clue to it. There is a cheesemonger, of the name of Atherton, who has some sort of acquaintance with her, and he may know."

" Then I will go, if you like to accompany me, at once," said the chaplain. " It is a fitting errand for me."

" Hush!" said the governor. " Look at this man."

All eyes were bent upon Neville, whose countenance was most horribly contorted. He uttered a frightful yell, which made every one start back who heard it, and then in a wild shrieking voice, he cried,—

"They come! they come! Legions of them! They seize me! Oh, help! help! help!"

He tossed his head from side to side, and strove to rise from the couch on which he lay; but the turnkeys, in obedience to a signal from the governor, held him down. He struggled with them for a few seconds, and then all was still. The guilty spirit of Neville had winged its flight to the judgment-seat of God. Let us hope that even he has found justice tempered by mercy!

" He is dead, sir," said one of the turnkeys to the governor

" Cover him up, and leave him where he is, for the present," was the reply. " I should not like to be present at many scenes like this—it is too horrible. Come away, come away, and lock the cell.'

CHAPTER CI.

THE VISIT OF ATHERTON TO THE BLACK LADY.

THE reader may well suppose that Miles Atherton was not long in reaching Marian Whitehead's lodging, for he was really much interested in the poor creature, and had acquired that kind of affection for her which results from having protected her. It seems to be a fixed principle of human nature, that we love that which has been, or is, dependent upon us.

No change had taken place in the Black Lady by the time Atherton arrived, except that she was quite silent, and had been so for some time previously, so that those about her had begun to think that she could not speak. The presence of the kind-hearted cheesemonger soon, however, dispelled that idea.

At the first sound of his voice, as he said—" Well, Miss Whitehead, I am come to see how you are," she looked up ; and fixing her eyes upon him with a mournful expression, she beckoned to him to come nearer ; and when he was quite close to her, she clutched his arm, and said,—

" Have you got the key?"

" Got—the—the key—what key? God bless me! Miss Whitehead, you really alarm me!"

" The key of St. Paul's. You know what I mean. The key to the vaults ! Surely you may let him out, now you know how innocent he is? I wish to see him. Oh! where is he? You will not let him starve in those old abodes of the dead ? You surely will not do that, Mr. Atherton, when you have, as you know, saved me?"

" I would do anything in the world," said Atherton, who really seemed at a loss to know what reply to make to her,—" I would do anything in the world, Miss Whitehead, that would give you pleasure ; you may depend upon that, you know."

" Yes, oh, yes! I know that Neville—the villain Neville—would have murdered me, but for you ! What strange noise is that ?"

" I don't hear any noise," said Atherton. " What is it like ?"

" It is like the ringing of bells ; as if some great rejoicing was taking place. Do you not hear how the sounds swell in the air? and to me they seem such a mockery !"

" I hear nothing."

" That's strange, when I hear them so plainly : it's very strange indeed. Hark ! there again ! But answer me one question."

" Of course I will if I can, you may depend."

" Has St. Sepulchre's struck eight yet? Why do I ask? What have I to do with St. Sepulchre's striking eight? And yet how strange it is I tremble like a faded leaf in autumn, lest any one should say Yes."

" What is it, sir," said the landlady to Miles Atherton, " that makes her in such a fever about eight o'clock by St. Sepulchre's church ?"

" Alas!" said Atherton, " I am sorry to say I know too well ; but I cannot explain that to you now ; at some other time I will."

The landlady looked as if she would much rather have had her curiosity satisfied at once, but she did not urge it; and after a few more minutes all her attention, as well as that of Atherton, was engaged in listening to what Marian Whitehead said, as she spoke in low, fearful accents,—

" Mr. Atherton, I think that my pilgrimage is near to its close, and before the shadow of death closes over me for ever, I would fain get you to promise me some things."

"I will not only promise," said Atherton, "but may I be —— never mind, if I don't do them too."

"There are several persons in this world who I think have done me much injury."

"You are not far wrong there, Miss Whitehead, and great scoundrels they are too, but never mind; you may be sure the time will come, sooner or later, when they will wish they had burnt their fingers off first."

"I wish, when I'm no more," said Marian, "that you would call upon those persons, Mr. Atherton; and first and foremost, upon the man Godfrey—do; I wish you to call with a message from me."

"Oh, to be sure, and I hope he will feel it too."

"I hope to Heaven he may! I wish you to go him and say, that at my last moments, I forgave him, and prayed that Heaven would do so likewise."

"What?"

"Have you not heard me plainly?"

"Oh yes! I heard you, but it's monstrous. I call upon such a rascal as Godfrey, after you are no more, should it please God to take you, which I am not at all sure of, and to tell him you forgive him, instead of telling him something that ought to wring his heart, always supposing that he has got such an article?"

"I understand your scruples; but do you suppose that that will not wring his heart?"

Atherton was silent for a few moments, during which he was revolving the matter in his mind, and then he said in a doubtful tone,—

"Well, Miss Whitehead, I will say that there is something in that, and if you wish me to do so, go I will, although I little thought I should ever cross a threshold of Godfrey's; for if there was no other man in the world but him to say good-morning to, I'd rather let my tongue grow rusty than say it."

"I can understand your aversion. Do you not hear the bells now?"

"In faith I do not."

At this juncture the medical man called, and Atherton walked up to the window, while he sat for a few moments by the bedside of his patient. Then he came up to the cheesemonger, and said, in by far too low a tone for Marian to hear him,—

"I presume, sir, by your being here, that you are some friend or relation of Miss Whitehead."

"A friend, certainly," said Atherton, "and one who would do anything in the world for her, poor thing! She has known much trouble, and that's a hard case as concerns her, for a better hearted creature never breathed."

"I have heard," said the surgeon, "that she had severe trials; but what I have now to inform you, sir, is, that they are very nearly over."

"You think, sir, she cannot recover?"

"Not without a miracle; a very short time indeed must close her mortal career. Indeed, I feel that my coming here again was useless, but still it was a satisfaction so to do."

"Of course it was, sir, of course; and as for her, I don't know whether I ought to be sorry or not, for her life, God knows! was not one which ought to be considered as the happiest in the world; it's perhaps a mercy she is going."

"It always is when the mind is in any degree affected. Her best friends must wish her at peace, and there can be no peace for such an one but the peace of the grave."

After these very just remarks, the surgeon left the room and the house. He felt that his art could not stand in the way of the march of the mighty destroyer, Death, when it was determined that he should touch his victim.

As for Atherton, he was sick at heart at the idea of the decease of Marian, notwithstanding his judgment told him he ought not to be so, but rather for her sake to rejoice that there would at length be an end of those sorrows which had destroyed one of the most beautiful mental fabrics ever fashioned by Divinity.

"Do you think of staying till the last, Mr. What's-your-name?" said the landlady to Atherton.

"I should like to do so, if I am not intruding."

"Oh, not at all! Of course it aint agreeable to have a death in the house, but it can't be helped. I pity her, poor thing! and shall always say to my own dying day that it was the fright the thieves gave her last night that did it, and if my husband had been anything but just half a man it would have been different!"

Atherton certainly thought it rather singular that half a man should be anybody's husband; but he made no remark about it, for his time was too much occupied in thinking of poor Marian, who seemed now to have sunk into a kind of stupor. It could not be called exactly sleep, for when she was spoken to, she answered; but then the answer was of a wandering nature, and betrayed the fact that the small remnant of consecutive thought that was left to her was quickly going.

It is a sad thing to set by the bed-side of the dying, and to know that without any great exercise of patience, it would be easy to count the number of respirations which the human being before us will make before death closes the scene of this world upon the senses of one of its actors.

Atherton was neither an educated, nor a very imaginative man, but yet he felt acutely the situation in which he was placed, and some tears dimmed his eyes as he bent over Marian, and said,—

"Are you quite easy and comfortable, Miss Whitehead?"

    *   *   *   *

There was at this moment a slight bustle below, and apparently in the passage of the house. Marian started, and looked earnestly at Miles Atherton, as she said,—

"What is that?—What is that?—Who comes?"

"I don't know. But I dare say it is of no consequence. You are not the only person residing here, Miss Whitehead, and it's probable enough some other resident who don't know that you are unwell has just come in, and banged the door to."

This answer was far from soothing Marian, for she listened like a frightened child; and Atherton, as he heard some footsteps approaching, was rather curious to know what they could mean.

He spoke in a whisper to the landlady who was in the room, asking her what she thought it all meant; but she could give him no idea, and all she could do was to offer to go and see, which she did, and returning in a few moments with a very important-looking face, she observed,—

"Some gentleman wants to see Miss Whitehead: I think he is a clergyman. Oh, here he is. Pray, sir, walk in, if you please, sir. This is Miss Whitehead, if you please sir. She aint very well, and you'll excuse us being rather in a muddle."

The chaplain of Newgate, for it was indeed he, advanced to the bedside, and said, gently—"Miss Whitehead, the entire innocence of Charles Ormond is fully and completely established."

Marian clasped her hands, and a smile of ineffable delight pervaded her countenance. "My God, I thank thee!" she said, and those were nearly the last words that came from her lips in this world.

CHAPTER CII.

TWO DEATHS.

THE landlady would send for the medical man again, and when he came, he said that life still lingered with Marian Whitehead, and he remarked upon the singularly happy expression of her face.

" Did you ever see such an expression ?" he said.

" Never—never before," replied Atherton, " except now and then upon he face, when she seemed to be thinking of other things than those that happen e to be present to her ; then I have seen such an expression cross her face, poor thing !"

" We may conclude, then," said the surgeon, " that in happier times before this blight, as we may term it, came upon her, she always wore that gentle and beautiful look. Alas ! poor thing, she must have suffered much."

" No doubt of it, sir,—no doubt of it. But, sir.—"

" Yes, I am quite willing to answer you any question you may wish to ask."

" Do you think she will linger long in the state she is in ?"

" Certainly not ; it is quite impossible she should linger long in such a state ; but though the pang of death, if it be a pang, has already come and gone, she will feel no more now ; but her last breath will be gently drawn, and you will not know whether she is sleeping or dead."

" Thank Heaven for that much," said Atherton.

" Ah !" said the landlady, as she lifted up her hands, and assumed an extremely sympathetic look, " my first husband went off just like a lamb. ' Sarah,' says he, ' Sarah.'—' Yes,' says I. ' Whatever you do,' says he, ' lead a moral life,' says he, ' sublime morality,' says he, ' for if you don't, you will be covered with odium and contempt.' ' Yes,' says I, and then saying something about pork chops, he went off like a small baby."

" Very affecting," said the surgeon.

" It's very, sir : don't you think Miss Whitehead moved a little just now, sir ?"

" She did."

The surgeon approached the bed, and at the instant he did so Marian opened her half-closed eyes, and clasping her hands together, she said, in tones of such silvery sweetness that they lingered long upon the ears of those who heard them,—

" Charles, I come."

Her eyes closed again, there was a slight shudder throughout the frame, and the earthly troubles of that most estimable and unfortunate being were over.

Atherton walked to the window to conceal his emotions. There was a little workbox there which had belonged to Marian ; it was open, and the scissors caught the eye of Atherton ; he took them in his hand, and approached the bed—in another moment he had severed a lock of hair from the brow of the dead.

As he placed the relic in his bosom, he left the house, ruminating in a low tone f much genuine feeling, and far more pathos than any one would have expected from him,—

" I will keep this, Marian, for your sake, and one of the happiest remembrances I shall have, if I live to be an old man, will be that I was able, in some measure, to smoothe the declining years of the Black Lady."

Atherton did not forget the injunction of Marian to call upon the villain, Godfrey, and he felt, when he left the house that now contained her remains, that he was in a better mood to obey that injunction than he was ever again likely to be, if he should put off doing so till the morrow.

" No," he said, " I am just in the humour to go, so go I will ; and, if his heart is not altogether a bit of flint, he must feel a pang in consequence of the message I bring him, such as no other words could possibly bring to him."

There could be very little doubt of this, always provided Godfrey had the heart to feel at all, but then, from what the reader already knows of that individual, he may well doubt his possession of that article.

Atherton walked hastily, so that he soon reached Godfrey's house.

It had a gloomy look, that large mansion—a far gloomier look than the house in which lay the insensible remains of poor Marian Whitehead ; and Atherton was rather astonished to find the street door swinging open.

This, however, he did not think gave him a right to enter unannounced, so he knocked and rung repeatedly, but without receiving any answer ; until, at last, quite tired of waiting, and conscious of the integrity of his motives, he walked in, and closed the street door behind him.

He looked into every room he came to, but found no one, until opening the door of a chamber on the second floor, which was partially darkened, he heard some one breathing heavily; and then, strange as such a state of things was, he could not but think that he was in the chamber of Godfrey, and that, owing to some circumstance, the villain had been completely deserted by his servants.

Yes, Atherton stood by the bed-side of the man, probably, whom he most hated and despised upon earth—Godfrey, the destroyer of both Marian Whitehead and Charles Ormond.

The glare of astonishment with which Godfrey regarded him had something positively appalling in it; and Atherton recoiled a step or two without speaking, although he had fully intended to perform his errand as quickly as possible.

"What is this?"" cried Godfrey, in a strange, hoarse voice. "What is this? Why am I left alone?"

"I don't know whether you are left alone or not, Mr. Godfrey," said Atherton. "I came to say something to you, and, finding your street door swinging open, and that nobody answered my knocks, I came up to you."

"Thieves, thieves!" cried Godfrey. "Thieves, murderer!"

"I beg your pardon; I aint one of your sort," said Atherton, "and so I am neither a thief nor a murderer; and you shall hear what I have to say."

"What do you want here? You have come to murder me."

"No, I haven't; I wouldn't take so much trouble about you, for though I look upon your life as of no more consequence than that of some wild beast, I'm sure I wouldn't be your executioner."

"Executioner?"

"Ah. You don't like that word, Master Godfrey—I thought you wouldn't, and to tell you my candid opinion, without knowing whether you are very bad or not, or having the least idea whether you will recover or not, I'm quite sure you will never be drowned."

"Never be drowned? What do you mean?"

"Why, if you are born to be hanged, you know, you can't be drowned, very well. That's what I mean, Mr. Godfrey, but that was not exactly what I came to tell you."

"You come to rob the house, that's what you came for; my servants have deserted me, and you are in league with them, and now that I am unable to rise and defend my property, you have come here to plunder me."

"You may say what you like and think what you like," replied Atherton, "but your sayings and your thoughts shall not prevent me from delivering the message I came with. My name is Atherton."

"Atherton—Atherton," repeated Godfrey, as if he were trying to remember the name.

"It's not of the least consequence," added the cheesemonger, "whether you remember having ever seen me before, or hearing my name or not; what I say, anybody might say."

"This is, after all, only some cunning device to rob me—I know it is."

"You know no such thing."

"Then what is your message?"

"Ah, now you are more reasonable, I will tell you. You know what a thundering rascal you have been all your life; you know how you robbed Mrs. Whitehead and her daughter Marian of all they had in the world; and you know how, by an infamous plot, you, with the assistance of Neville, who, thank God, will be hung soon, brought an honest, noble-minded, upright young man, named Charles Ormond, to the scaffold."

"Be off!" cried Godfrey, "be off! what do you mean by all this? It is false."

"It is true."

"No; false as h—."

"Hush! I will not hear you make use of such words; I say it is as true as Heaven."

Godfrey was silent. There was a solemnity about the manner of Atherton that awed Godfrey, and he looked up with a feeling approaching to dismay; for he wondered what would happen next, or what Atherton could possibly have to say to him to induce him to come at such a time to his house, and so persevere in ad-

dressing him, notwithstanding all the discouragement he met with from him, Godfrey.

"I have no liking to stay here," said Atherton, "so you shall soon know what I have to say."

"Quick, quick, quick," muttered Godfrey.

"Marian Whitehead is dead!"

Something between a groan and a shriek came from Godfrey's lips, as Atherton gave him this piece of intelligence, in a tone of voice that did not permit any doubt of its truth.

"Yes, she is dead; and my commission here," added Atherton, "is to bring you her dying——"

"Curses—her dying curses!" shouted Godfrey.

"No, her dying forgivenness," said Atherton.

As he spoke, he turned round and walked from the bedside of the man whom of all created beings, excepting Neville, he held in abhorrence. Atherton had delivered his message, and delivered it effectively too, so he had no wish to linger another moment in that house.

"Stop! stop!" cried Godfrey, "oh, stop! I am alone; my nurse has left me, and I am full of horrible thoughts. Stop! I charge you; stop, even if it be to curse me."

"No," said Atherton, "I have neither curses nor blessings for you. I have performed my errand, and that is all I have to say. If you are alone in this house, which really seems to be the case, you have, I dare say, yourself to thank for it."

Atherton left the chamber, and as he descended the staircase, he fancied there was a good deal of smoke in the air, but he did not think much of it; for, to tell the truth, his mind was too much engrossed with other matters to spend a thought upon what appeared a triviality; so he banged the street door to after him, and walked home to inform Mrs. Atherton of the particulars of his interview with Godfrey.

———

CHAPTER CIII.

THE CONCLUSION.

SLOWLY but surely the room was filling with smoke; and as Godfrey lay, he tried in vain to see the objects around him with their accustomed distinctness. All had a strange, foggy aspect; and, after shivering for a few minutes longer, he fancied that there was an unusual heat in the atmosphere; and then, for the first time, the horrible thought struck him that the house was really on fire, and he incapable of moving, even if the long-tongued flames should be wantoning over his very face.

This frightful thought only drove him on the instant mad, and happy would it indeed have been for him if Heaven had vouchsafed to deprive him of his reason, instead of leaving him fully conscious of the events which now followed each other in rapid and most horrible succession to him.

That the house was in flames, and that those flames had been kindled by his own servants, not, probably, for the purpose of allowing him to be burnt to death, but in order to cover their own peculations, he could now have no doubt; but it was of very little consequence to him whether they anticipated such a catasthrophe or not as his destruction in the fire, provided it came to that.

And yet he could not imagine that no succour should come to him; he had not yet awakened to any such horrible idea fully as that he should be, as it were, roasted alive in his own house.

He knew that the fire, if it were really such, must be soon discovered, and then that he should be rescued, he surely thought, was beyond the possibility of a doubt.

He was quite right as regarded the fire being discovered, for the nurse who had attended upon him, and who was in the immediate neighbourhood, gave the first alarm, but she took care to add that there was no one in the house; for, as she possessed herself of Godfrey's watch, rings, and whatever portable valuables he had in his bed-rooms, she really thought it highly expedient he should perish in the ruins.

"If you please, sir," she said to the active Mr. Somebody, who always attends fires, "if you please, sir, there's a house on fire, but it's quite empty, except some heavy things, and nobody is living in it."

Acting upon this information, those who had the care of the fire engines thought that the best thing they could possibly do, would be to pump away without at all troubling themselves to go into the interior of the building.

Godfrey had his confidence in escape gradually diminish, as minute after minute passed, and no one came to his rescue ; moreover the room was fast filling with so dense a smoke, that he could hardly breathe, much less make himself effectively heard, should he call for assistance.

His situation was becoming each moment more full of horrors.

"Help ! help !" he cried ; but no help came.

And now, when he would have called louder still—when he would have shrieked, so that the earth would have echoed the frightful sound to heaven, he found that he could not do so, and that his voice, once so full and sonorous, had dwindled down to a small whisper.

Oh, what a state for such a man as Godfrey.

He made a frantic effort to move, despite the injuries he had received, and which had confined him to his bed; but the moment he set in action the muscles of his limbs and body to do so, he found that he suffered such frightful torture, from the ends of the broken ribs he had, digging, as it were, into his lungs; so that he was compelled to desist, and await the fate that was accumulating round him.

And now came the hour of retribution—that hour of retribution which had been foretold to Godfrey, and which he had always laughed the very idea of to scorn. He felt that a dreadful death was before him ; and his stern, wicked spirit quailed at last.

"Mercy ! mercy !" he shouted.

It was the first time such a word in such a tone had passed his lips.

"O God ! have mercy upon me !"

The flames roared and crackled ; he could hear the shouts of the people in the street ; he could hear the tramp of horses' feet ; he could hear the loud hurrah ! as every fresh fire-engine arrived upon the scene ; and he could hear the regular beat-beat of the pumps that were at work ;—but no one heard him, his voice was choked by smoke, and no one heard him.

Oh, what must have been the sufferings of that bold, bad man at such a time ! And now the room suddenly appeared to be more free from smoke than it had been since the commencement of the fire, and a thrilling hope came through Godfrey's mind, that after all the flames might be subdued, and he should be saved.

This hope, however, was doomed to be of the most evanescent and fleeting character ; for he soon, alas, for him, wretched man, too soon, found out why it was that there was not so much smoke,—it was simply because there was more flame.

He felt a hot glow upon his face, as if he were in the immediate vicinity of some furnace, and suddenly one of the bed curtains caught fire, and with a hissing sound, was suddenly shrivelled up, scorching him as it went, and giving him a foretaste of what he might have to suffer.

His reason at this moment almost gave way. Happy would it have been for him, if it had completely done so ; but it did not quite, and he was still alive to what was going on.

The other curtains of his bed were caught now by the flames, and he was in the midst of a great body of light. He was frightfully scorched, but after a moment or so, saved himself, by covering the bed-clothes completely over his face. Just before he did so, Godfrey might be said to have taken his last look at the world.

The whole bedstead shook with the violent emotions of the wretched man, an now and then such a hideous yelling sound came from beneath the clothes, that any one who had heard, might have imagined that some wild animal was being burnt to death

But a catastrophe is at hand !

*   *   *   *

With a loud crash the roof fell in.   There was one hideous shriek, which for the first time, made the firemen aware that anything was within the house, and then all was still.

*   *   *   *   *

The charred remains of a human form were got out of the ruins in about a week. They were not at all recognisable, but they were all that remained of Godfrey.

*   *   *   *

Miles Atherton saw that all things respectful and needful were done at the funeral of the Black Lady. She was placed by her mother's side. He likewise made a point of paying all the little debts that she owed, so that no one made any objection to his taking possession of all the little relics of her history which she left behind her.

As regards Atherton's future career, we can only say that he is living now, but we are compelled by a solemn promise, given at the time of editing these papers not to divulge the place of his residence.

He has retired from business, having fallen into a little property, which he did not expect, and which thereforecame all the sweeter to him.

"You know," he said, when he handed to us the Black Lady's MSS,—"you know it would never do to publish my real name, or else I should be found out, notwithstanding all I could do to the contrary."

"Certainly," said we.

"You can then call me Mile Atherton," he said.

From this the readers will perceive that Miles Atherton is not the real name of the kind-hearted cheesemonger, and we are forbidden to say exactly what is.

We should be loath, indeed, to close these pages, without saying something of our old friend, Jem; and we are the more inclined to do so, because that something will be of a very peculiar character. Jem is married, and doing very well, for when the little property we have hinted at came to Atherton, he gave up all his business to his old friend, and a more thriving young man there is not to be found in the city of London ; and we are quite certain, that, although there may be many who deserve as much to thrive as he, there are none who deserve better to do so.

Godfrey's house was completely burnt to the ground, and his daughter, who really was mercifully spared further association with such a father, came into possession of all his money.

She, commissioned her friend, the lawyer in Thavies' Inn, to find out anybody to whom Godfrey had behaved in any way with harshness as regarded money matters, and to make to them ample restitution.

Was it possible that a little use could have been made of the ill-gotten wealth of that bad man who came to so dreadful an end.

*   *   *   *   *

Our tale is over, and those in whose circumstances of joy and sorrow we have for so long a period sympathised with, we shall meet no more. The grave has closed over some, and others live but to remember on the long winter evenings, when all is cold and sterile without, and when the winter's wind makes melancholy music, the sad events which despoiled the world of one of its fairest treasures, in hurrying to a too early tomb Marian Whitehead, the much-wronged, gentle and forgiving BLACK LADY !

THE END.

www.ingramcontent.com/pod-product-compliance
Lightning Source LLC
Chambersburg PA
CBHW080330040726
47505CB00022B/2120